MOLL FLANDERS

broadview editions
series editor: L.W. Conolly

PORTRAIT *of the Celebrated* MOLL FLANDERS
Taken from Life in Newgate

The famous Moll Flanders, *of beauty the boast,*
Belov'd and distinguish'd, long flourish'd the toast,
But beauty is frail and soon comes to decay,
When shift and contrivance must enter in play;
Her arts of intrigue, as this book shall unfold,
Will keep you awake while her story is told.

Pub.d by C. Johnson.

(Courtesy of the Beinecke Library, Yale University.)

MOLL FLANDERS

Daniel Defoe

edited by Paul A. Scanlon

broadview editions

Library and Archives Canada Cataloguing in Publication

Defoe, Daniel, 1661?–1731.
    Moll Flanders / Daniel Defoe ; edited by Paul A. Scanlon.

(Broadview editions)
Includes bibliographical references.
ISBN 1-55111-451-8

    I. Scanlon, Paul A.   II. Title.   III. Series.

PR3404.M6 2005   823'.5   C2004-906515-7

Broadview Editions
The Broadview Editions series represents the ever-changing canon of literature in English by bringing together texts long regarded as classics with valuable lesser-known works.

Advisory editor for this volume: Professor Eugene Benson

Broadview Press Ltd. is an independent, international publishing house, incorporated in 1985. Broadview believes in shared ownership, both with its employees and with the general public; since the year 2000 Broadview shares have traded publicly on the Toronto Venture Exchange under the symbol BDP.

We welcome comments and suggestions regarding any aspect of our publications — please feel free to contact us at the addresses below or at broadview@broadviewpress.com.

North America
Post Office Box 1243, Peterborough, Ontario, Canada K9J 7H5
3576 California Road, Orchard Park, NY, USA 14127
Tel: (705) 743-8990; Fax: (705) 743-8353;
e-mail: customerservice@broadviewpress.com

UK, Ireland, and continental Europe
NBN Plymbridge, Estover Road, Plymouth PL6 7PY UK
Tel: 44 (0) 1752 202301   Fax: 44 (0) 1752 202331
Fax Order Line: 44 (0) 1752 202333
Customer Service: cservs@nbnplymbridge.com Orders: orders@nbnplymbridge.com

Australia and New Zealand
UNIREPS, University of New South Wales
Sydney, NSW, 2052 Australia
Tel: 61 2 9664 0999; Fax: 61 2 9664 5420
email: info.press@unsw.edu.au

www.broadviewpress.com

Broadview Press Ltd. gratefully acknowledges the financial support of the Government of Canada through the Book Publishing Industry Development Program for our publishing activities.

Typesetting and assembly: True to Type Inc., Mississauga, Canada.

PRINTED IN CANADA

Contents

Acknowledgements

I owe a debt of gratitude, in the preparation of the present volume, to a number of people in several countries. Among them are colleagues and friends at Sultan Qaboos University, Oman, including Adrian Roscoe, Andrew Littlejohn, Christopher Gray, Abdulla Al Harrasi and Adel Radwan, who have offered helpful advice and their time. Also Eugene Benson, formerly of the University of Guelph, Canada, has given guidance to the project and provided useful material. And, in quite another important way, Dermot and Kay Mullane, Ireland, have left their mark on the work.

In addition, library staff at Sultan Qaboos University, Ireland's Trinity College, and Canada's Queen's University and McMaster University have been unstinting in their service.

Lastly, as always, I wish to thank my wife Marit, whose contribution has been of a material nature and yet much more.

Introduction

As is well known, Daniel Defoe was greatly interested in the social, political and economic issues of his times. In his pamphlets, periodicals and novels, he writes tirelessly about such matters as the plight of children and the homeless, debtors and prostitution, manufacture and trade, colonization and empire, the legal status of women and proper laws governing marriage. "Between 1715 and 1727 alone," affirms David Blewett, "he produced six books dealing with various aspects of family relationships—courtship, marriage, the bringing up of children, and the treatment of servants ... "[1] A close connection, moreover, can be seen between Defoe's journalistic subjects and his works of fiction. Undoubtedly, a considerable amount of material from his assorted papers found its way into his novels.

Towards the end of the second decade of the eighteenth century, around the time when he first turned to novel writing, Defoe became preoccupied with the interrelated issues of crime and punishment. He and his contemporaries, both in England and on the Continent, were alarmed by the dramatic increase in various sorts of crime, especially those of a violent nature. Housebreakings, muggings and highway robbery, it was believed, had never been so common. And in London there was general complaint that the streets were not safe, day or night, for fear of attacks from footpads.

Growing concern about crime inevitably led to greater interest in criminals, to which the press responded by producing an extraordinary range of criminal literature. As well as the weekly journals and pamphlet lives, there were the sessions papers, ballads and broadsides, the Ordinary of Newgate's *Accounts*, and various collections such as Alexander Smith's *The History of the Lives, of the Most Noted Highway-Men, Foot-Pads, House-Breakers, Shop-Lifts, and Cheats, of Both Sexes, in and About London* (1714). In his periodicals, Defoe also carried innumerable reports of crimes and trials. *Applebee's Journal*, for example, apparently intended more for the entertainment of his readers than for their edification, specialized in accounts of criminals. And in several pamphlets, such as *Some Considerations upon Street-Walkers* (1726), he proposed ways to control crime. Defoe also wrote the lives of some of the famous

---

1 David Blewett, "Changing Attitudes toward Marriage in the Time of Defoe: The Case of Moll Flanders," *Huntington Library Quarterly* 44 (1981): 82-83.

criminals of the 1720s, the two most notorious being John Sheppard and Jonathan Wild, thief-catcher.

Along with pirates and highwaymen, female criminals held a special fascination for contemporary society. With the depressed state of the woollen trade and the return of men in large numbers from continental wars, young women were increasingly driven from their jobs to London and into prostitution and robbery. Many ended up in Newgate prison, and some were celebrated on stage and by the press. "More unusual criminals like Moll King, Sally Salisbury, and Betsy Careless," notes Paula Backscheider, "captured London's imagination, and convicted females on the scaffold and the carts headed for ships to the colonies were familiar sights."[1]

★ ★ ★

It has been said that there were only two full-length biographies of female criminals in English before *Moll Flanders*, Francis Kirkman's *The Counterfeit Lady Unveiled* (1673) and the anonymous *Life and Death of Mrs. Mary Frith* (1662), alias Mal Cutpurse.[2] In any event, there were many other real and fictional female figures of the past and present from whom Defoe could have drawn. Various models for Moll Flanders have been suggested since Gerald Howson's article appeared in 1968,[3] including one Mary Raby. However, as Howson reasoned, Defoe was visiting his friend Nathaniel Mist (of *Mist's Weekly Journal*) at Newgate when Moll King was there and "had plenty of opportunities to talk with her at length." Thus he concludes that Moll Flanders was an imaginative composite of Moll King, her friend Callico Sarah and perhaps other female criminals. What is known for certain is that on 16 July 1720, *Applebee's Journal* printed a letter purportedly from a transported thief. While boasting of her preeminence as a pickpocket, she describes how she "was nab'd by a plaguy Hawks-Ey'd Journey-Man *Mercer*, and so ... got into the Hands of the Law." All the

---

1 Paula R. Backscheider, *Daniel Defoe: His Life* (Baltimore: Johns Hopkins UP, 1989) 482.

2 See John Rietz, "Criminal Ms-Representation: *Moll Flanders* and Female Criminal Biography," *Studies in the Novel* 23 (1991): 184.

3 Gerald Howson, "Who Was Moll Flanders?" *The Times Literary Supplement* 18 Jan. 1968: 63-64. Rev. rept. as "The Fortunes of Moll Flanders," in *Thief-Taker General: The Rise and Fall of Jonathan Wild* (New York: St. Martin's P, 1970) 156-70.

adventures she met with abroad, following her time at Newgate; "I say, are too long for a Letter; *But here I am.*" As such letters, seeking advice or raising problems, were a standard form used by Defoe in *Applebee's Journal*, it is commonly assumed that he not only wrote the letter himself but also hints at the following "history" of *Moll Flanders*.

Whatever its sources, finally, Defoe's conception of this novel was definitely shaped by the conventions of criminal biography. Many such works return to the ancestry and upbringing of the central figure, sometimes recounting youthful incidents involving bad company; and the crimes themselves usually follow, ranging from clever tricks to brutal murders. Invariably, however, the offender is captured and incarcerated, with the case then proceeding to court and the sentence (usually execution) carried out, traditionally presented in graphic detail. Confession and repentance are generally an integral part of the ritual pattern, serving both important social and spiritual functions.

Moll Flanders, of course, is clearly much more than simply another popular example of formulaic criminal lives. Defoe also drew on different familiar literary traditions and his own exceptionally rich and varied background to create a work of originality and genius.

Features of the conduct book are much in evidence, as Moll schools young women in courtship and its pitfalls, as are tales of roguery, guides to etiquette, jest-books and projects (or schemes for improvement). Besides the criminal biography, however, probably the two most profound literary influences on *Moll Flanders* were the spiritual autobiography and the romance pattern, essentially transforming its moral vision and bringing to it a psychological depth unique at the time.

The novel is Moll's story of her life, supposedly "Written in the Year 1683" when she was almost seventy years old. It is of an episodic nature, fitting her experience and style of storytelling, full of action and domestic intrigue. Douglas Brooks divides the narrative into two parts, "the first containing Moll's sexual adventures, the second being her life as a thief, her imprisonment and her transportation to America."[1] But a further division is perhaps warranted, one which separates her childhood and Colchester experience from her years in London and afterwards. The daugh-

---

1 Douglas Brooks, "*Moll Flanders*: An Interpretation," *Essays in Criticism* 19 (1969): 46.

ter of a Newgate felon, Moll was raised for a time by gypsies before becoming a charge of the Colchester parish; the local magistrates then gave her to an old nurse until she could go into service; but with the nurse's death, she was taken in by a well-to-do family, seduced by the elder brother and married to the younger one. Cast from the beginning as an outsider, these various early incidents in Moll's life—as she herself recounts—go far in determining her later behaviour. In fact, maintains Carl Lovitt, "From the standpoint of its impact on shaping Moll's goals, her first love affair is the single most influential experience in her narrative."[1]

What should be recognized from the outset, nevertheless, is that Moll's adventures take the form of a quest, conscious or not on her part, for a better life than the one into which she was born. From her time with the old nurse and tutor Moll seeks independence from drudgery, which from the earliest visits of the mayor's family she equates with gentility. Although she is mistaken in her notion of the term, to become a gentlewoman remains one of her greatest ambitions. While pursuing this end in the home of her prosperous benefactors, Moll falls passionately in love with the elder son, whose frequent pledges of affection and loyalty and regular gifts of money bedazzle her and soon overcome any remaining scruples or resistance.

> ... BUT WHAT my dear? *says he*, I guess what you mean; what if you should be with child, is not that it? Why then, *says he*, I'll take care of you, and provide for you, and the child too, and that you may see I am not in jest, *says he*, here's an earnest for you; and with that he pulls out a silk purse, with an hundred guineas in it, and gave it me; and I'll give you such another, *says he*, every year till I marry you.
>
> My colour came, and went, at the sight of the purse, and with the fire of his proposal together; so that I could not say a word, and he easily perceiv'd it; so putting the purse into my bosom, I made no more resistance to him, but let him do just what he pleas'd; and as often as he pleas'd ... (63-64)[2]

The situation eventually changes, however, as the lover's ardour cools, the daughters of the family grow increasingly envious and

---

1 Carl R. Lovitt, "Defoe's 'Almost Invisible Hand': Narrative Logic as a Structuring Principle in *Moll Flanders*," *Eighteenth-Century Fiction* 6 (1993): 12.

2 All quotations from *Moll Flanders* are from the present text.

suspicious, and the younger brother professes more openly his affection for Moll. In the end, it is the elder brother who, in the starkest of terms, presents her with two options: either to marry his brother, a gentleman, and live in comfort and security, or be cast out into the world with little money and no friends. In deep fear and bitter disappointment, Moll sacrifices love for security in marriage. "It is the momentous realization," notes Blewett, "that there may be love without matrimony as there may be matrimony without love that shapes the whole course of Moll's life."[1]

*　*　*

Following the death in London of the younger brother, after five years of marriage and two children, Moll is once again "left loose to the world" (89). Her Colchester experience, however, has made her more cynical and determined, and has adequately provided for her debut into a predatory society in which money rules and marriage is little more than a market. "I had been trick'd once by *that cheat call'd* LOVE," she reflects, "but the game was over; I was resolv'd now to be married, or nothing, and to be well married, or not at all." It has been said that Moll, in marrying the gentleman-tradesman, ignores her goals. But surely she felt, however mistakenly, that by doing so she had met at least two of them. The couple's grand tour of Oxford in a coach-and-six, addressed as "my lord" and "*her honour,* the Countess," with footmen and a mounted page wearing a feather in his hat, must have convinced Moll that, at least temporarily, she had become a gentlewoman. She has rejected love, if only for a while; and money and security have proved a chimera. Thus relying largely on her wit, beauty and cunning, and her indomitable sense of survival, Moll's education in a patriarchal and rapacious society proceeds apace.

With the departure of the linen-draper husband into debtor's exile in France, leaving Moll with "a husband and no husband," her situation is further complicated by her subsequent marriages and affairs. For not only does she inadvertently marry her brother, but (as George Starr notes) more than once becomes "involved ... with men who have 'a wife and no wife,' so that the ambiguities of her own situation ... [are] compounded by those of the people she

---

1　David Blewett, *Defoe's Art of Fiction*: Robinson Crusoe, Moll Flanders, Colonel Jack *and* Roxana (Toronto: U of Toronto P, 1979) 63.

moves among."[1] In the process, too, a hardening of character takes place, as Moll resorts to tricks and increasingly serious deception in her ceaseless questing. After outsmarting a sea captain and gaining him as a husband for her widowed friend, she cynically sets about the business of securing such a one for herself.

I pick'd out my man without much difficulty, by the judgement I made of his way of courting me; I had let him run on with his protestations and oaths that he lov'd me above all the world; that if I would make him happy, that was enough; all which I knew was upon supposition, nay, it was upon a full satisfaction, that I was very rich, tho' I never told him a word of it myself.

This was my man, but I was to try him to the bottom, and indeed in that consisted my safety; for if he baulk'd, I knew I was undone, as surely as he was undone if he took me ... (106)

Just as Moll rejected love for gentility in her second marriage, she now sacrifices gentility for money and security in this one. As her various goals are redefined and realigned, therefore, it becomes abundantly clear that her early desire to be a gentlewoman no longer adequately reflects her present ambitions or situation.

★ ★ ★

Moll's third marriage takes her to the New World and a plantation in Virginia. Although the voyage is passed over in a few lines, and little is given of conditions in the colony itself, her mother-in-law presents it as a land of great opportunity, where "many a *Newgate* bird becomes a great man" (113). It is a subject to which, under quite different circumstances, Moll will return later in her memoirs. Her life on the plantation is particularly agreeable for a number of years, with little reason for change, until she learns by accident of her true situation: her mother-in-law is actually her mother, the Newgate felon, and her husband her brother. Despite Moll's rogueries, incest is an abomination to her and depicted in terms of utter loathing.

... every thing added to make cohabiting with him the most nauseous thing to me in the world; and I think verily it was come to such a height, that I could almost as willingly have

---

1 G.A. Starr, *Defoe and Casuistry* (Princeton: Princeton UP, 1971) 126.

embrac'd a dog, as have let him offer any thing of that kind to me, for which reason I could not bear the thoughts of coming between the sheets with him ... (123)

Although only dimly aware of it, Moll operates here on a level of natural law. "Time and circumstance sometimes demand that nature be violated," explains Robert Columbus. Yet "Her morality is a vision of society by which decent limits to her behavior are set, and are expressed by her as what is 'natural' and what 'unnatural.'"[1]

Forced under these unnatural marital conditions to leave America, Moll returns to England and resumes her old ways, becoming mistress to a Bath gentleman and even juggling two affairs at the same time. One is with a banker, whom she refers to as "a safe card" (161); the other is with Jemy, a highwayman posing as a wealthy Irish landlord. She marries both of them, but not exactly for the same reasons. Both would seem to offer, in varying degrees, money, security and gentility. But in the case of the banker, it is only temporary, and Jemy deceives her as she deceives him. Yet there is mutual attraction between Moll and the highwayman, and she truly falls in love with him. This is made clear by the strange episode of mental telepathy, a unique supernatural happening in the narrative which guarantees the later return of Jemy after years of separation.

I told him how I had pass'd my time, and how loud I had call'd him to *come back* again; he told me he heard me very plain upon *Delamere Forest*, at a place about 12 miles off: *I smil'd; Nay says he*, do not think I am in jest, for if ever I heard your voice in my life, I heard you call me aloud, and sometimes I thought I saw you running after me; Why said I, what did I say? for I had not nam'd the words to him, You call'd aloud, says he, and said, *O Jemy! O Jemy! come back, come back.* (171)

"For that one brief moment," insists Lovitt, "Moll and Jemy unambiguously inhabit a universe in which supernatural forces influence human lives."[2]

* * *

---

1 Robert R. Columbus, "Conscious Artistry in *Moll Flanders*," *Studies in English Literature, 1500-1900* 3 (1963): 426-28.
2 Lovitt 3.

After the death of her banker husband, Moll finds herself too old, at forty-eight, to compete in the marriage market. Nor was she left a rich widow, due to the ruinous financial losses incurred by her late husband. Consequently, she is forced to follow the same route taken by many women in London, both young and old, who find themselves without friends and with their meagre savings dwindling away—she gives in to the temptation to steal. At first it is a terrifying experience, so irresistible in nature that it can only be explained as the promptings of the Devil. In time, however, necessity gives way to avarice, and fear and guilt lessen their hold as confidence and boldness grow and the name Moll Flanders (given to her by the trade) is known among the inmates of Newgate and beyond. Not only does she become the most accomplished of thieves, taking both pride in her criminal dexterity and pleasure in duping society, but she also grows rich—the richest, her governess tells her, of the trade in England. It has been said that *Moll Flanders* is not essentially of the picaresque tradition, where the hero "delight[s] in his rogueries for their own sake" and engages "in a variety of cheating practices in order to obtain money, but ... never solely in order to obtain money."[1] Nevertheless, Moll certainly shares in this sense of adventure with the picaro and views the game as an opportunity for the exercise of her art and ingenuity.

In fact, similar to the confessions of a number of contemporary female criminals, Moll is unable to give up her illegal activities despite her financial independence or the great risks involved. Warned time and again by her governess, she "could not forbear going abroad again, *as I call'd it now,* any more than I could when my extremity really drove me out for bread" (257). Moll's criminal exploits, as she haunts the streets of London or travels about the countryside, sometimes in disguise and always with an eye to the main chance, are undoubtedly the most episodic part of the novel. Indeed, as Lovitt notes, "The change is dramatic in several respects: not only are Moll's activities qualitatively different, both she and her narrative undergo a thorough metamorphosis."[2] Previously obsessed with achieving security through marriage, she now turns to a solitary life of crime, rapidly developing into "a compleat thief, harden'd to a pitch above all the reflections of con-

---

1 Robert Alter, *Rogue's Progress: Studies in the Picaresque Novel* (Cambridge: Harvard UP, 1964) 46.
2 Lovitt 21.

science or modesty, and to a degree which I must acknowledge I never thought possible in me" (213). Likewise, the narrative consists here essentially of a series of discrete and loosely connected episodes, largely held together by the common theme of criminality. Yet, as Starr points out, *Moll Flanders* embodies a fairly traditional pattern of the sinner's progress.[1] Particularly in this criminal part, marked by foreshadowings and forebodings, there is a definite sense of Moll moving inexorably towards her fate. Newgate casts its long shadow over the entire history, serving as the work's dominant metaphor, with references to it becoming more insistent as Moll's criminal career advances towards its abrupt conclusion. It is "the place," she says mournfully, "that had so long expected me, and which with so much art and success I had so long avoided" (275). It is where she was born; it is where, with her arrest, she will be taken and punished; and it is where she will struggle for redemption.

* * *

Moll describes Newgate as "an emblem of Hell itself, and a kind of entrance into it." Yet like her fellow inmates, she soon becomes totally inured to the life around her, degenerating (as she says herself) into a stone: "I turn'd first stupid and senseless, then brutish and thoughtless, and at last raving mad as any of them were; and in short, I became as naturally pleas'd and easie with the place, as if indeed I had been born there." At the same time, she realizes the justice of it, neither expecting nor deserving any hope. At the blackest moment of her life, therefore, she accepts her doom. But the novel does not end in prison or on the gallows at Tyburn, as would most criminal biographies. Instead, she meets Jemy again, who has been taken with other members of his gang and also imprisoned at Newgate. Her heart is moved and her conscience stirred, as she blames herself for his ruin. She also receives a visit from a young minister (not the Ordinary of Newgate), who "broke into my very soul" (288). This leads to confession and Moll is joyful "at the prospect of being a true penitent." In the meantime, her trial takes place and the death sentence is passed—only to be followed by a reprieve, granted at the last moment through the intercession of the minister. As the six con-

---

1 See G.A. Starr, *Defoe and Spiritual Autobiography* (Princeton: Princeton UP, 1965) 161.

victs sentenced with her are led to their execution, Moll is completely overcome,

> seized with a fit of trembling, as much as I cou'd have been, if I had been in the same condition, as to be sure the day before I expected to be; I was so violently agitated by this surprising fit, that I shook as if it had been in the cold fit of an ague ...
> This fit of crying held me near two hours and as I believe held me till they were all out of the world, and then a most humble penitent serious kind of joy succeeded; a real transport it was, or passion of joy, and thankfulness, but still unable to give vent to it by words, and in this I continued most part of the day. (291-92)

"Her confession ... like those of common criminals," concludes Backscheider, "serve[s] to reunite her with the community and its mores; her repentance associates her with the saints invoked in the spiritual autobiographies."[1]

Moll's sentence of death is commuted to transportation to the colonies, and she soon succeeds in convincing Jemy (although a gentleman) to petition for the same. Defoe, it should be noted, was a proponent of aggressive colonization and strongly supported the new Transportation Act of 1718. Consequently, in setting the destructiveness of imprisonment against the benefits of transportation, the novel can be seen as powerful propaganda for the colonies. Maryland and Virginia were primary destinations for both settlement and transportation during these years and Defoe is careful to present them in an especially favourable light.

In terms of the narrative, however, following Moll's moral regeneration in Newgate and reunion with Jemy, the New World provides a fitting finale to her memoirs. After a pleasant voyage to Virginia, the couple purchase their freedom and immediately set about clearing land (in Maryland) and developing a plantation. Moll is reunited with her son, who has kept land and chattels for her from her mother; confessions follow (though not always fully on Moll's part), which in turn lead to various reconciliations; and of course to prosperity. In rare homespun humour, Jemy sums up the situation upon the arrival of a shipment of goods from England.

---

1   Paula R. Backscheider, *Moll Flanders: The Making of a Criminal Mind* (Boston: Twayne, 1990) 27.

He was amaz'd, and stood a while telling upon his fingers, but said nothing, at last he began thus, Hold lets see, *says he, telling upon his fingers still*; and first on his thumb, there's 246 *l*. in money at first, then two gold watches, diamond rings, and plate, *says he*, upon the fore finger … Well, *says I*, what do you make of all that? Make of it, *says he*, why who says I was deceiv'd, when I married a wife in *Lancashire*? I think I have married a fortune, and a very good fortune too, *says he*. (333)

Finally, in old age, Moll and her husband return to England, to live there in peace and contentment. The quest is over: she has achieved her goals. Rather than an outcome determined by society, therefore, it is one dictated by romance, albeit of a mercantile nature.

* * *

Not long after returning to England, Moll apparently begins her memoirs, a self-declared penitent. The question repeatedly asked, however, is: How sincere is she? In coming to terms with this issue, one must remember that it is the autobiography of an elderly woman who returns to the young girl she once was and to the woman she became. While reflecting on her former actions and experiences, therefore, Moll must attempt to represent both her initial responses and her later judgments at the same time. This creates, in an important way, a double vision—or two Molls, as Robert Donovan[1] and others have called it. There is Moll the character, both victim and predator, who has been thrust into the world of experience and is determined to survive in it at all cost. There is also Moll the narrator, somewhat distanced from the story and bound to present her life in the form of an exemplum. Yet she is able to recall, in particularly tender terms, the sadness of her youth; and while issuing stern warnings to men against debauchery and advising young women on the dangers of marriage, the story is told with considerable sympathy and even a certain bravado. In fact, as Maximillian Novak remarks, "Moll appears to be somewhat confused about the nature and purpose of her story; she *thinks* she is telling a spiritual biography while actually doing something very different."[2]

---

1   See Robert Alan Donovan, *The Shaping Vision: Imagination in the English Novel from Defoe to Dickens* (Ithaca: Cornell UP, 1966) 21-46.

2   Maximillian E. Novak, *Daniel Defoe: Master of Fictions* (Oxford: Oxford UP, 2001) 600.

The complexity of Moll's character and the contradictions and incongruities resulting from the double vision thus pose further problems concerning the question of irony in the novel. The preface, moreover, written by a fictional editor, adds yet another dimension. In the opening passages he informs the reader

> that the original of this story is put into new words, and the stile of the famous lady we here speak of is a little alter'd, particularly she is made to tell her own tale in modester words than she told it at first; the copy which came first to hand, having been written in language, more like one still in *Newgate*, than one grown penitent and humble, as she afterwards pretends to be.
>
> The pen employ'd in finishing her story, and making it what you now see it to be, has had no little difficulty to put it into a dress fit to be seen, and to make it speak language fit to be read ... (39)

The editor is at pains throughout the preface to assure the reader that it "is a story fruitful of instruction." Nevertheless he concludes that Moll, after leading a "sober life" of "industrious management" in the colonies, upon returning to England "was not so extraordinary a penitent, as she was at first." The authenticity of the vocabulary is clearly called into question in these passages, as is the sincerity of Moll's repentance. It is difficult, in light of this, to dismiss the preface as simply an eighteenth-century literary convention, particularly when compared to those of other novels by Defoe. At the same time, to treat the repentant Moll as "an editorial creation"[1] seems also to miss the mark. Perhaps a more helpful approach, therefore, would be to recognize that there is a third voice at work, at least to some extent, adding a further layer to the text's already existing ironies.

It is tempting of course to identify this voice as Defoe's, which is a critical commonplace, but this is to ignore the complexities of the author's relationship with the novel. While Moll often fails to recognize her mistakes, it can be assumed that the respectable contemporary reader would have no such confusion. Yet Moll is represented in such a way as to elicit considerable sympathy as well as abhorrence: we are invited from the preface onwards to abjure the crime but not the criminal. In the *Review* (8 February 1709),

---

1 Larry L. Langford, "Retelling Moll's Story: The Editor's Preface to *Moll Flanders*," *The Journal of Narrative Technique* 22 (1992): 168.

Defoe points out that "the Scripture bids us not despise such a Thief, who steals to satisfie his Hunger; not that the Man is less a Thief, but despise him not, you that know not what Hunger is." This plea is echoed by Moll herself, after a year or so of impoverished living, having reluctantly turned to theft.

... O let none read this part without seriously reflecting on the circumstances of a desolate state, and how they would grapple with meer want of friends and want of bread; it will certainly make them think not of sparing what they have only, but of looking up to Heaven for support, and of the wise man's prayer, *Give me not poverty least I steal.* (203)

"Sympathy keeps breaking in," concludes Starr, "and our ironic detachment—along with Defoe's—is tempered by imaginative identification."[1]

It is quite apparent, furthermore, that this mixture of irony and sympathy is part of a complex and questioning world constructed of language. Genteel euphemisms and circumlocutions, a familiar convention in female criminal biographies, are regularly used by Moll, particularly in relation to sex. "I by little and little yielded to every thing, so that in a word, he did what he pleas'd with me; I need say no more" (233). Moll is also capable of very direct language, however, indeed of a brutal frankness, when for example she brands herself ("in plain English") a whore. According to Robert Alter, Moll's candour derives from a totally different source, Defoe's Dissent, which deeply imbues every aspect of the novel.

This moralist's impulse in Defoe partly explains why his lady of fame is made to call herself bluntly by the name her actions earn her. Moll, a Puritan in all but virtue, generally shies away from words that evoke the physical actuality of her polygamies and prostitutions, but she shows no hesitancy in branding herself a whore because it is a word that is used not so much to describe as to denounce, not to call forth an image but to affirm a stern moral judgment.[2]

It is this moral outlook which cuts across the ironies and contra-

---

1 Starr, *Defoe and Casuistry* 114.
2 Alter 38-39.

dictions of *Moll Flanders*, giving greater coherence to the narrative and further uniting it with Defoe's other writings.

★ ★ ★

When *Moll Flanders* was first published on 27 January 1722, prose fiction was not only popular among a wide readership but also took many different forms, including letters, journals, lives, histories, romances, autobiographies and even ships' logs. Claims of authenticity were common among those works of a more serious nature, partly to avoid charges of dishonesty and partly to distance themselves from the distinctly frivolous kinds of writing that lacked proper entertainment or instruction. Consequently, Defoe (through his editor) begins his preface by distinguishing this "private history" from the "novels and romances" of which "The world is so taken up of late." He emphasizes that the "levity, and looseness" in the narrative are there for "vertuous and religious uses" and that it is up to the reader to approach the story in an appropriate way.

> But as this work is chiefly recommended to those who know how to read it, and how to make the good uses of it, which the story all along recommends to them; so it is to be hop'd that such readers will be much more pleas'd with the moral, than the fable; with the application, than with the relation, and with the end of the writer, than with the life of the person written of. (40)

With such warnings and advice, Defoe felt able to justify the book's publication and to recommend it sufficiently to the world.

Indeed, *The History and Misfortunes of the Famous Moll Flanders* was an immediate success, running through five editions and reprints within the first year. Although not as popular as *Robinson Crusoe* (1719), various pirated abridgements and chapbooks published over the next few years were a measure of its initial reception. The exact nature of its readership is not known for certain, but there is no question about its appeal to the rising middle classes, and especially to female readers. While a contemporary, according to John Bender, claims that Defoe's crime narratives were read by people of "the better Sort,"[1] the *Flying Post* (1 March 1729) portrays a less cultivated following:

---

1 John Bender, *Imagining the Penitentiary: Fiction and the Architecture of Mind in Eighteenth-Century England* (Chicago: U of Chicago P, 1987) 44.

Down in the Kitchen, honest Dick and Doll
Are Studying Col. Jack and Flanders Moll.

No matter. It is clear that the newly-emerging novel was crucial to
the development of a new reading public; but even more, as Ian
Watt suggests, it incited a new kind of reading—one that "makes
us feel that we are in contact not with literature but with the raw
materials of life itself as they are momentarily reflected in the
minds of the protagonists."[1]

If this is so, then *Moll Flanders* marks a beginning of this new
kind of prose fiction, presenting what is generally regarded as the
great theme of the novel: the individual's effort to define herself
against the conflicting demands of society.

---

1 Ian Watt, *The Rise of the Novel: Studies in Defoe, Richardson and Fielding*
   (Berkeley: U of California P, 1967) 193.

Daniel Defoe: A Brief Chronology

1660	Born Daniel Foe, probably in the London parish of St. Giles, Cripplegate, the son of a merchant.
1662	The Foes follow Dr. Samuel Annesley, their family pastor, out of St. Giles Anglican Church and worship henceforth as Dissenters.
1674-79?	Attends the Dissenting Academy of the Rev. Charles Morton, Newington Green, in preparation for the Presbyterian ministry.
1681	Writes a series of poetic meditations (unpublished). About this time decides not to become a Presbyterian minister.
1682	Compiles an anthology entitled "Historical Collections" (unpublished).
c. 1683	Sets up business as a wholesale hosier in Cornhill, near the Royal Exchange.
1684	Marries Mary Tuffley, daughter of a wealthy cooper, who brings a dowry of £3,700. (Mary has eight children between 1687 and 1701.)
1685	Bears arms in support of the Duke of Monmouth's rebellion, but escapes capture following Monmouth's defeat. Receives a general pardon.
1685-92	Active as a merchant and tradesman dealing in hosiery, wine, tobacco and other goods.
1688	First extant publication appears, *A Letter to a Dissenter from his Friend at the Hague*, in support of the "Glorious Revolution" of 1688.
1691	Contributes occasionally to John Dunton's *Athenian Mercury* (1691-97). Publishes *A New Discovery of an Old Intreague*, a satirical poem about City politics.
1692	First bankruptcy, purportedly for £17,000. Imprisoned for debt in the Fleet prison.
1693	Imprisoned for debt in the King's Bench prison. Negotiates terms with creditors. Begins to work for Thomas Neale as a manager-trustee for Neale's private lotteries.
c. 1694	Sets up a brick and tile works at Tilbury.
1695	Adds "De" to his name, thereafter known as "De Foe." Becomes an accountant to one of the commissioners in the Glass Office (retains post until about 1699).

1697	An Essay upon Projects, a lengthy socio-economic treatise written in prison.
1697-1701	Serves as an agent for William III in England and Scotland.
1698	An Enquiry into the Occasional Conformity of Dissenters, the first of many pamphlets on this subject.
1699	An Encomium upon a Parliament, a satirical ballad attacking Parliament for recent follies.
1700	The Pacificator, a long verse essay on literary issues.
1701	The True-Born Englishman, a verse satire ridiculing those who resented King William for being Dutch. It became one of the most popular poems of the century.
1702	The Shortest-Way with the Dissenters, an ironic attack on High-Church extremism. A warrant is issued for his arrest. Reformation of Manners, a formal satire influenced by Juvenal's Satire I.
1703	Confined to Newgate prison for The Shortest-Way, and is made to stand in the pillory three times. Publishes A Hymn to the Pillory. Imprisonment leads to the failure of his brick and tile works, which is followed by a second bankruptcy. Released from Newgate through the intercession of Robert Harley.
1703-14	Serves as a confidential agent and political journalist for Harley (1703-08), then Godolphin (1708-10), then Harley again (1710-14), travelling widely about Britain in this role. Actively promotes the Union of England and Scotland (1707).
1704	The Storm, his first full-length experiment in narrative technique. A Hymn to Victory, a poem celebrating the battle of Blenheim.
1704-13	Review, a periodical dealing with a variety of topical issues, largely in support of Harley's Tory government.
1705	The Consolidator, an allegorical lunar fantasy.
1706	A True Relation of the Apparition of One Mrs. Veal, and Jure Divino, a poem attacking the "divine right" theory. Makes a settlement with his creditors.
1707	Publishes several pamphlets on Scottish affairs. Seeks a government position in Scotland.
1709	The History of the Union of Great Britain. Acts as a spokesman for the Royal Africa Company.

1710	Forms a partnership to manufacture linen table-cloths in Scotland.
1711	Publishes nearly twenty pamphlets on political and economic issues of the day. Acts as a spokesman for the wine wholesalers Brooks and Hellier.
1712	*The Present State of the Parties in Great Britain*, a lengthy account of political and religious developments in England and Scotland.
1713	*Memoirs of Count Tariff*. Arrested and imprisoned twice for debt and alleged treasonable writings.
1713-14	*Mercator*, a periodical advocating trade with France.
1714	Indicted for seditious libel for implying that one of the king's regents was a Jacobite.
1714-15	*The Secret History of the White Staff*, a three-part pamphlet defending Harley's shattered reputation.
1715	*The Family Instructor*, the first of Defoe's conduct books. *An Appeal to Honour and Justice*, an apologia for his own life. Defoe comes to terms with the new Whig government, serving successive Whig ministries until 1730, sometimes by writing for Tory periodicals.
1716-20	*Mercurius Politicus*.
1717	*Memoirs of the Church of Scotland*.
1717-24	Contributes to Mist's *Weekly-Journal*, diluting its radical Tory voice.
1718	*A Continuation of Letters Written by a Turkish Spy*, satirical reflections on divisions in Europe.
1719	*The Life and Strange Surprizing Adventures of Robinson Crusoe*, *The Farther Adventures of Robinson Crusoe*, *The Anatomy of Exchange Alley* and other substantial pamphlets on trade and finance.
1719-21	*Manufacturer*, a periodical in defence of the weavers' trade.
1720	*Commentator*, a miscellaneous journal (January-September), followed by the *Director* (October 1720-January 1721), a periodical about the South Sea affair. *The King of Pirates, Memoirs of a Cavalier, Captain Singleton, Serious Reflections ... of Robinson Crusoe*.
1720-26	Contributes to the *Original Weekly Journal* (later called *Applebee's Original Weekly Journal*), designed primarily for entertainment, specializing in the lives and trials of pirates and felons.

1721	Well-established as a prosperous and prominent citizen of Stoke Newington. His son Benjamin is arrested for his essay in the *London Journal*.
1722	*Moll Flanders, Religious Courtship, A Journal of the Plague Year, Colonel Jack*. Invests in land in Essex, begins farming and tries to start a new brick and tile factory.
1724	*Roxana, The Great Law of Subordination Consider'd, A Tour thro' the Whole Island of Great Britain* (completed 1726), *The History of the Remarkable Life of John Sheppard, A New Voyage Round the World*. Court action taken against him for outstanding debts.
1725	*Every-body's Business, Is No-body's Business, The True and Genuine Account of the Life and Actions of the Late Jonathan Wild, The Complete English Tradesman* (second volume 1727).
1726	*An Essay upon Literature, Some Considerations upon Street-Walkers, The Political History of the Devil*, satirizing the idea of a physical Devil and hell. *A System of Magick*, a history of magic and exposé of contemporary heresy and humbug.
1727	*Conjugal Lewdness, Parochial Tyranny, An Essay on the History and Reality of Apparitions*.
1728	*A Plan of the English Commerce, Second Thoughts Are Best: Or, a Further Improvement of a Late Scheme to Prevent Street Robberies, Street-Robberies, Consider'd*. A suit is begun against him over an old debt.
1729	*The Compleat English Gentleman* (first published 1890). His daughter Sophia marries Henry Baker.
1730	*A Brief State of the Inland or Home Trade*, a diatribe against hawkers and peddlars. Goes into hiding from his creditors.
1731	*An Effectual Scheme for the Immediate Preventing of Street Robberies*. Dies in lodgings in Ropemaker's Alley, London, and is buried in Bunhill Fields, the great Dissenting cemetery.
1732	Mary Defoe dies and is buried in Bunhill Fields beside her husband.

Defoe's Times: A Brief Chronology

1660   Charles II restored to the throne. D'Avenant and Killi-
         grew are granted two royal patents to stage theatrical
         performances in London.
1662   Butler, *Hudibras* (completed 1678). Anon., *The Life and
         Death of Mrs. Mary Frith.*
1662-72 The "Clarendon Code," a series of acts introducing
         severe penalties for religious nonconformity. Presbyteri-
         ans, Independents, Baptists and other sects who are
         unable to conform to the Church of England rules
         become known as Dissenters.
1665-66 Anglo-Dutch War begins. The Great Plague kills more
         than 70,000 people in London.
1666   The Great Fire of London burns for four days and
         nights. Bunyan, *Grace Abounding.*
1667   Treaty of Breda ends Anglo-Dutch War. Milton, *Par-
         adise Lost* (enlarged to twelve books in 1674). Sprat,
         History of the Royal Society.
1668   Dryden becomes Poet Laureate.
1672   Charles II issues Declaration of Indulgence suspending
         laws against Dissenters. Marvell, *The Rehearsal Trans-
         pos'd* (second part 1673).
1673   Charles II is forced by Parliament to withdraw the
         Declaration of Indulgence. The Test Act compels all
         holders of office—civil, military, or crown—to take the
         Oath of Allegiance and communion in the Church of
         England. Kirkman, *The Counterfeit Lady Unveiled.*
1678   The Popish Plot scare. The Second Test Act excludes
         Roman Catholics from Parliament. Bunyan, *The Pil-
         grim's Progress* (second part 1684). Dryden, *All for Love.*
1679   Whigs begin attempt to exclude James, Duke of York,
         from succession to the throne.
1680   Bunyan, *The Life and Death of Mr. Badman.* Rochester,
         Poems (posthumous).
1681   Dryden, *Absalom and Achitophel.* Marvell, *Miscellaneous
         Poems* (posthumous).
1682   Bunyan, *The Holy War.* Dryden, *Religio Laici.* Otway,
         Venice Preserv'd.
1683   Rye House Plot. Execution of Algernon Sidney and
         Lord Russell. Anon., *The Whore's Rhetorick.*

1685	Charles II dies; accession of James II. Monmouth, the illegitimate son of Charles II, rebels and is defeated several weeks later.
1686	James II issues a general pardon, releasing many Dissenters from prison.
1687	James II issues Declaration of Indulgence granting freedom of worship to Dissenters and Roman Catholics. Halifax, *Letter to a Dissenter*. Newton, *Principia Mathematica*.
1688	James II reissues Declaration of Indulgence. William, Prince of Orange, lands at Torbay (the "Glorious Revolution" begins). James II flees the country. Halifax, *The Lady's New-Year's Gift*.
1689	William and Mary crowned. Bill of Rights enacted. Toleration Act allows freedom of worship to Protestant Dissenters (but not to Catholics). William forms Grand Alliance, and war with France begins. Locke, *First Letter on Toleration*. Marvell, *Poems on Affairs of State* (posthumous).
1690	William III defeats James II at the Battle of the Boyne. Locke, *Treatises of Government*.
1691	Walsh, *A Dialogue concerning Women*.
1692	Massacre at Glencoe. L'Estrange, *Fables of Esop and other Mythologists*. Tate, *A Present for the Ladies*.
1694	Bank of England established.
1695	William III captures Namur from the French. The Press Licensing Act lapses.
1696	Navigation Act forbids American colonists to export directly to Scotland or Ireland. A recoinage takes place. Toland, *Christianity Not Mysterious*. Dunton, *The Night-Walker* (published in monthly instalments until 1697).
1697	Treaty of Ryswick ends war with France. Vanbrugh, *The Provok'd Wife*.
1698	British merchant vessels begin carrying slaves to West Indies. London Stock Exchange founded. Behn, *Histories and Novels* (posthumous). Ward, *The London-Spy* (published in monthly instalments until 1702).
1699	William III drafts second Partition Treaty.
1700	Congreve, *The Way of the World*. Astell, *Some Reflections upon Marriage*.
1701	James II dies. Louis XIV recognizes James Stuart the Pretender as king of England. War of the Spanish Succession begins in Europe.

1702	William III dies; accession of Queen Anne. England declares war on France. Tories win majority in general election. A bill to outlaw Occasional Conformity is introduced before Parliament.
1703	Anon., *Hell upon Earth*.
1704	The Duke of Marlborough defeats French at Blenheim. Swift, *Tale of a Tub*.
1705	Blenheim Palace is begun, built for the Duke of Marlborough as a monument to his victories over the French (completed 1725). A general election strengthens the Whig position. Dunton, *The Life and Errors of John Dunton*. Anon., *The London-Bawd*.
1707	The Act of Union is passed, formally uniting the governments of Scotland and England. The British capture Gibraltar. Farquhar, *The Beaux' Stratagem*; Farquhar dies. Fielding is born.
1708	Whigs gain majority in new British Parliament. French attempt a Jacobite invasion in Scotland.
1709	Charles XII is defeated by the Russians at Pultowa and takes refuge in Turkey. Battle of Malplaquet, with loss of 20,000 lives. Swift, *Project for the Advancement of Religion*. Manley, *The New Atalantis*. Ward, *Marriage Dialogues*. Steele begins *The Tatler*.
1710	Parliament is dissolved; subsequent election gives Tories a majority. Berkeley, *Principles of Human Knowledge*.
1711	Peace preliminaries signed between Britain and France. Queen Anne dismisses Duke of Marlborough. Occasional Conformity Bill passed. South Sea Company launched. St. Paul's Cathedral completed. Pope, *Essay on Criticism*. Steele and Addison begin *The Spectator*.
1712	Peace conference opens at Utrecht. Stamp Act imposes duty on periodicals. Pope, *The Rape of the Lock* (completed 1714). Arbuthnot, *The History of John Bull*.
1713	Treaty of Utrecht ends War of Spanish Succession. Whigs are heavily defeated at the general election. Formation of Scriblerus Club. Steele launches the *Guardian* and the *Englishman*. Addison, *Cato*.
1714	Queen Anne dies; accession of George I. Mandeville, *Fable of the Bees (*completed 1728*)*. Smith, *The History of the Lives, of the Most Noted Highway-Men … in and about London*, 2 vols.
1715	First Jacobite Rebellion, led by James Stuart the

Pretender. Harley and Bolingbroke are impeached. Walpole becomes Chancellor of the Exchequer. Death of Louis XIV. Pope, *Iliad* (trans., completed 1720). Le Sage, *Gil Blas* (completed 1735).

1716   Execution of Jacobite leaders captured at Preston the previous year. Gay, *Trivia*.

1717   Walpole resigns as Chancellor of the Exchequer. Harley acquitted of high treason. Anon., *The History of the Press-Yard*.

1718   Quadruple Alliance formed against Spain. Transportation Act passed.

1719   Schism Act and Occasional Conformity Act repealed. Haywood, *Love in Excess*. Addison dies.

1720   South Sea Bubble scandal. Clarendon, *History of the Rebellion of Ireland*.

1721   Walpole becomes Lord of the Treasury and Chancellor of the Exchequer, and is shortly known as "prime minister."

1722   Discovery of the Atterbury Plot. Steele, *The Conscious Lovers*. Swift, *The Last Speech and Dying Words of Ebenezor Elliston*.

1723   Wren dies.

1724   Jack Sheppard, highwayman and popular hero, is hanged at Tyburn. Swift, *Drapier's Letters*. Mandeville, *A Modest Defence of Public Stews*.

1725   Jonathan Wild, the most notorious of the thief-catchers, is hanged at Tyburn. Pope, *Odyssey* (trans., completed 1726). Mandeville, *Enquiry into the Causes of the Frequent Executions at Tyburn*. Anon., *Venus in the Cloister* (trans.).

1726   John Wesley becomes a Fellow of Lincoln College, Oxford, and joins a group known as the Oxford Methodists. Rob Roy imprisoned in Newgate. Swift, *Gulliver's Travels*. Thomson, *The Seasons* (completed 1730).

1727   George I dies; accession of George II. Spain attacks Gibraltar. Haywood, *Philodore and Placentia*.

1728   Cibber, *The Provoked Husband*. Pope, *The Dunciad* (completed 1742). Gay, *The Beggar's Opera*.

1729   An act is passed for the better regulation of attorneys and solicitors. Swift, *A Modest Proposal*. Thomson, *Britannia*. Steele and Congreve die.

1730	Cibber becomes Poet Laureate. Fielding, *The Author's Farce* and *Tom Thumb*. Goldsmith is born.
1731	Treaty of Vienna ends Anglo-French alliance. Marivaux, *Marianne* (final part 1741). Lillo, *The London Merchant*. Hogarth, *A Harlot's Progress* (completed 1732).
1732	Whigs reimpose salt tax.
1733	Pope, *Essay on Man* (completed 1734). Voltaire, *Letters Concerning the English Nation* (trans.).
1734	Marivaux, *Le Paysan parvenu* (final part 1736). Swift, *A Beautiful Young Nymph Going to Bed*.
1735	Pope, *An Epistle to Dr. Arbuthnot*.
1737	Theatrical Licensing Act passed.

A Note on the Text

Although the date on the title page of the first edition of *Moll Flanders* reads MDDCXXI [sic] for 1721, following the Julian calendar, the text was actually published by W. Chetwood and T. Edling (for Edlin) on 27 January 1722. Two further editions, each with separate issues, appeared before the end of the same year, "The Third Edition, Corrected" being considered until fairly recently as the authoritative text and hence taken as the basis for most reprints.

Modern textual scholarship, however, has shown that this "third edition" was only a reissue of "The Second Edition, Corrected" with a new title page. Moreover, there is evidence to suggest that the "corrections" were not made by Defoe himself but by a printer-editor whose primary aim, while correcting obvious errors, was to abridge the first edition. Although in many cases these changes are helpful, they can at times lead to confusion and even alter the meaning of a passage. As well, they risk robbing the original of Moll's vivid and distinctive idiom.

Consequently, most modern texts—including the present one—are based on the first edition of *Moll Flanders*. Second-edition readings, nevertheless, are sometimes adopted, and spelling, punctuation and other accidentals regularized in order to gain greater clarity. In the present edition, only capitalization has been normalized in the interest of the modern reader, and a small number of alterations silently made when misunderstanding might arise from typographical or spelling errors. All else remains as it appears in the original text.

Defoe's original notes have been retained in the text and are identified by asterisks. Where necessary, editorial explanations of Defoe's notes are included in square brackets immediately following the note.

THE
FORTUNES
AND
MISFORTUNES
Of the FAMOUS
Moll Flanders, &c.

Who was Born in NEWGATE, and during a
Life of continu'd Variety for Threescore Years,
besides her Childhood, was Twelve Year a
Whore, five times a *Wife* (whereof once to her
own Brother) Twelve Year a *Thief,* Eight Year a
Transported *Felon* in *Virginia,* at last grew *Rich,*
liv'd *Honest,* and died a *Penitent.*

Written from her own MEMORANDUMS.

LONDON: Printed for, and Sold by W.
CHETWOOD, at *Cato's-Head,* in *Russel-
street, Covent-Garden;* and T. EDLING, at
the *Prince's-Arms,* over-against *Exerter-Change*
in the *Strand.* MDDCXXI.

THE PREFACE

The world is so taken up of late with novels and romances, that it will be hard for a private history[1] to be taken for genuine, where the names and other circumstances of the person are concealed, and on this account we must be content to leave the reader to pass his own opinion upon the ensuing sheets, and take it just as he pleases.

The author is here suppos'd to be writing her own history, and in the very beginning of her account, she gives the reasons why she thinks fit to conceal her true name, after which there is no occasion to say any more about that.

It is true, that the original of this story is put into new words, and the stile of the famous lady we here speak of is a little alter'd, particularly she is made to tell her own tale in modester words than she told it at first; the copy which came first to hand, having been written in language, more like one still in *Newgate*,[2] than one grown penitent and humble, as she afterwards pretends[3] to be.

The pen employ'd in finishing her story, and making it what you now see it to be, has had no little difficulty to put it into a dress fit to be seen, and to make it speak language fit to be read: when a woman debauch'd from her youth, nay, even being the off-spring of debauchery and vice, comes to give an account of her vicious practises, and even to descend to the particular occasions and circumstances, by which she first became wicked, and of all the progression of crime which she run through in three-score year, an author must be hard put to it to wrap it up so clean, as not to give room, especially for vitious readers to turn it to his disadvantage.

All possible care however has been taken to give no leud ideas, no immodest turns in the new dressing up this story, no not to the worst parts of her expressions; to this purpose some of the vicious part of her life, which cou'd not be modestly told, is quite left out, and several other parts, are very much shortn'd; what is left 'tis hop'd will not offend the chastest reader, or the modestest hearer; and as the best use is made even of the worst story, the

---

1 A careful distinction is being made here between authentic autobiography and the highly popular fictitious novels and romances of the times.

2 The main prison of London in the seventeenth and eighteenth centuries. See Appendix B.1.

3 Professes, aspires (not necessarily in the sense of a pretence).

moral 'tis hop'd will keep the reader serious, even where the story might incline him to be otherwise: to give the history of a wicked life repented of, necessarily requires that the wick'd part should be made as wicked, as the real history of it will bear; to illustrate and give a beauty to the penitent part, which is certainly the best and brightest, if related with equal spirit and life.

It is suggested there cannot be the same life, the same brightness and beauty, in relateing the penitent part, as in the criminal part: if there is any truth in that suggestion, I must be allow'd to say, 'tis because there is not the same taste and relish in the reading, and indeed it is too true that the difference lyes not in the real worth of the subject so much as in the gust[1] and palate of the reader.

But as this work is chiefly recommended to those who know how to read it, and how to make the good uses of it, which the story all along recommends to them; so it is to be hop'd that such readers will be much more pleas'd with the moral, than the fable;[2] with the application, than with the relation, and with the end of the writer, than with the life of the person written of.

There is in this story abundance of delightful incidents, and all of them usefully apply'd. There is an agreeable turn artfully given them in the relating, that naturally instructs the reader, either one way, or other. The first part of her leud life with the young gentleman at *Colchester*, has so many happy turns given it to expose the crime, and warn all whose circumstances are adapted to it, of the ruinous end of such things, and the foolish thoughtless and abhorr'd conduct of both the parties, that it abundantly attones for all the lively discription she gives of her folly and wickedness.

The repentance of her lover at the *Bath*, and how brought by the just alarm of his fit of sickness to abandon her; the just caution given there against even the lawful intimacies of the dearest friends, and how unable they are to preserve the most solemn resolutions of vertue without divine assistance; these are parts, which to a just discernment will appear to have more real beauty in them, than all the amorous chain of story, which introduces it.

In a word, as the whole relation is carefully garbl'd[3] of all the levity, and looseness that was in it: so it is all applied, and with the utmost care to vertuous and religious uses. None can without being guilty of manifest injustice, cast any reproach upon it, or upon our design in publishing it.

---

1 Taste, inclination.
2 The story itself.
3 Sifted, cleansed.

The advocates for the stage, have in all ages made this the great argument to persuade people that their plays are useful, and that they ought to be allow'd in the most civiliz'd, and in the most religious government; namely, that they are applyed to vertuous purposes, and that by the most lively representations, they fail not to recommend vertue, and generous principles, and to discourage and expose all sorts of vice and corruption of manners; and were it true that they did so, and that they constantly adhered to that rule, as the test of their acting on the *theatre*, much might be said in their favour.

Throughout the infinite variety of this book, this fundamental is most strictly adhered to; there is not a wicked action in any part of it, but is first or last rendered unhappy and unfortunate: there is not a superlative villain brought upon the stage, but either he is brought to an unhappy end, or brought to be a penitent: there is not an ill thing mention'd, but it is condemn'd, even in the relation, nor a vertuous just thing, but it carries its praise along with it: what can more exactly answer the rule laid down, to recommend, even those representations of things which have so many other just objections lying against them? namely, of example, of bad company, obscene language, and the like.

Upon this foundation this book is recommended to the reader, as a work from every part of which something may be learned, and some just and religious inference is drawn, by which the reader will have something of instruction, if he pleases to make use of it.

All the exploits of this lady of fame, in her depredations upon mankind stand as so many warnings to honest people to beware of them, intimating to them by what methods innocent people are drawn in, plunder'd and robb'd, and by consequence how to avoid them. Her robbing a little innocent child, dress'd fine by the vanity of the mother, to go to the dancing-school, is a good memento[1] to such people hereafter; as is likewise her picking the gold-watch from the young ladies side in the *park*.

Her getting a parcel from a hair-brained wench at the coaches in St. *John-Street*; her booty made at the fire, and again at *Harwich*;[2] all give us excellent warnings in such cases to be more present to ourselves in sudden surprizes of every sort.

Her application to a sober life, and industrious management at last in *Virginia*, with her transported spouse, is a story fruitful of

---

1 Reminder, warning. See below, pp. 205-07.
2 See below, pp. 244-45, 215-17, and 266-68 respectively.

instruction, to all the unfortunate creatures who are oblig'd to seek their re-establishment abroad; whether by the misery of transportation, or other disaster; letting them know, that diligence and application have their due encouragement, even in the remotest parts of the world, and that no case can be so low, so despicable, or so empty of prospect, but that an unwearied industry will go a great way to deliver us from it, will in time raise the meanest creature to appear again in the world, and give him a new cast[1] for his life.

These are a few of the serious inferences which we are led by the hand to in this book, and these are fully sufficient to justifie any man in recommending it to the world, and much more to justifie the publication of it.

There are two of the most beautiful parts still behind,[2] which this story gives some idea of, and lets us into the parts of them, but they are either of them too long to be brought into the same volume; and indeed are, *as I may call them* whole volumes of themselves, (*viz.*) I. The life of her governess, as she calls her, who had run thro', it seems in a few years all the eminent degrees of a gentlewoman, a whore, and a bawd; a midwife, and a midwife-keeper,[3] as *they are call'd*, a pawn-broker, a child-taker,[4] a receiver of thieves, and of thieves purchase, that is to say, of stolen goods; and in a word, her self a thief, a breeder up of thieves, and the like, and yet at last a penitent.

The second is the life of her transported husband, a highwayman; who it seems liv'd a twelve years life of successful villany upon the road, and even at last came off so well, as to be a voluntier transport, not a convict; and in whose life there is an incredible variety.

But as I have said, these are things too long to bring in here, so neither can I make a promise of their coming out by themselves.[5]

We cannot say indeed, that this history is carried on quite to the end of the life of this famous *Moll Flanders*, as she calls herself, for

---

1   Chance (literally, a throw of the dice).
2   Remaining, yet to come.
3   A mistress of an establishment frequently linking prostitution and midwifery. See "Mother Midnight," p. 177 below.
4   A foster-mother who rears deserted children for payment, usually by parish authorities. The role of "Mother Midnight" here, however, seems to be largely concerned with the placing of children (pp. 183 and 187-91 below).
5   There is a hint here, as well as elsewhere in the story, of possible sequels to *Moll Flanders*.

no body can write their own life to the full end of it, unless they can write it after they are dead; but her husband's life being written by a third hand, gives a full account of them both, how long they liv'd together in that country, and how they came both to *England* again, after about eight year, in which time they were grown very rich, and where she liv'd it seems, to be very old; but was not so extraordinary a penitent, as she was at first; it seems only that indeed she always spoke with abhorence of her former life, and of every part of it.

In her last scene, at *Maryland*, and *Virginia*, many pleasant things happen'd, which makes that part of her life very agreeable, but they are not told with the same elegancy as those accounted for by herself; so it is still to the more advantage that we break off here.

THE
HISTORY
AND
MISFORTUNES
Of the FAMOUS
Moll Flanders, &c.

My true name is so well known in the records, or registers at *Newgate*, and in the *Old-Baily*,[1] and there are some things of such consequence still depending there, relating to my particular conduct, that it is not to be expected I should set my name, or the account of my family to this work; perhaps, after my death it may be better known, at present it would not be proper, no, not tho' a general pardon should be issued, even without exceptions and reserve of persons or crimes.

It is enough to tell you, that as some of my worst comrades, who are out of the way of doing me harm, having gone out of the world by the steps and the string,[2] as I often expected to go, knew me by the name of *Moll Flanders*; so you may give me leave to speak of myself, under that name till I dare own who I have been, as well as who I am.

I have been told, that in one of our neighbour nations, whether it be in *France*,[3] or where else, I know not; they have an order from the king, that when any criminal is condemn'd, either to die, or to the gallies,[4] or to be transported,[5] if they leave any children, as such are generally unprovided for, by the poverty or forfeiture of their parents; so they are immediately taken into the care of the government, and put into an hospital call'd the *House of Orphans*, where they are bred up, cloath'd, fed, taught, and when fit to go out, are plac'd out to trades, or to services, so as to be well able to provide for themselves by an honest industrious behaviour.

Had this been the custom in our country, I had not been left a

---

1 The central criminal court, adjoining Newgate prison (obsolete form of *Old Bailey*).
2 That is, the ladder and rope of the gallows.
3 St. Vincent de Paul (1581-1660) established two foundling hospitals in Paris in the first half of the seventeenth century, whereas it was not until the early 1740s that the first one was founded in London.
4 Down through the ages, slaves and convicted criminals were sometimes condemned to man ships called *galleys*.
5 Deportation of convicts to the American colonies, as an alternative to capital punishment, was on the increase during these years and was of particular interest to Defoe. See Appendices A.3 and B.9.

poor desolate girl without friends, without cloaths, without help or helper in the world, as was my fate; and by which, I was not only expos'd to very great distresses, even before I was capable, either of understanding my case, or how to amend it, nor brought into a course of life, which was not only scandalous in itself, but which in its ordinary course, tended to the swift destruction both of soul and body.

But the case was otherwise here, my mother was convicted of felony for a certain petty theft, scarce worth naming, (*viz.*) having an opportunity of borrowing three pieces of fine *Holland*,[1] of a certain draper[2] in *Cheapside*:[3] the circumstances are too long to repeat, and I have heard them related so many ways, that I can scarce be certain, which is the right account.

However it was, this they all agree in, that my mother pleaded her belly,[4] and being found quick with child, she was respited for about seven months, in which time having brought me into the world, and being about again, she was call'd down, as they term it, to her former judgment, but obtain'd the favour of being transported to the plantations, and left me about half a year old; and in bad hands you may be sure.

This is too near the first hours of my life, for me to relate any thing of myself, but by hear say, 'tis enough to mention, that as I was born in such an unhappy place, I had no parish[5] to have recourse to for my nourishment in my infancy, nor can I give the least account how I was kept alive; other, than that as I have been told, some relation of my mothers took me away for a while as a nurse, but at whose expence, or by whose direction I know nothing at all of it.

The first account that I can recollect, or could ever learn of myself, was, that I had wandred among a crew of those people they call *gypsies*, or *Egyptians*; but I believe it was but a very little while that I had been among them, for I had not had my skin dis-

---

1 Expensive linen cloth from that country. For a somewhat similar account, see Appendix A.9.
2 A dealer in fabrics, etc.
3 A stately and spacious street (as described at the time) in the City of London, well inhabited by prosperous merchants.
4 A plea, due to pregnancy, to postpone the execution until after the birth of the child. See below, pp. 276-77.
5 Under the terms of the Act of Settlement of the Poor (1662), poor relief was the responsibility of the church wardens and overseers of each parish. Born in Newgate prison, however, Moll was in effect beyond such support.

colour'd, or blacken'd, as they do very young to all the children they carry about with them,[1] nor can I tell how I came among them, or how I got from them.

It was at *Colchester* in *Essex*, that those people left me; and I have a notion in my head, that I left them there, (that is, that I hid myself and wou'd not go any farther with them) but I am not able to be particular in that account; only this I remember, that being taken up by some of the parish officers of *Colchester*, I gave an account, that I came into the town with the *gypsies*, but that I would not go any farther with them, and that so they had left me, but whither they were gone that I knew not, nor could they expect it of me; for tho' they sent round the country to enquire after them, it seems they could not be found.

I was now in a way to be provided for; for tho' I was not a parish charge upon this, or that part of the town by law; yet as my case came to be known, and that I was too young to do any work, being not above three years old, compassion mov'd the magistrates of the town to order some care to be taken of me, and I became one of their own, as much as if I had been born in the place.

In the provision they made for me, it was my good hap to be put to nurse, as they call it, to a woman who was indeed poor, but had been in better circumstances, and who got a little livelihood by taking such as I was suppos'd to be; and keeping them with all necessaries, till they were at a certain age, in which it might be suppos'd they might go to service, or get their own bread.

This woman had also had a little school, which she kept to teach children to read and to work; and having, as I have said, liv'd before that in good fashion, she bred up the children she took with a great deal of art as well as with a great deal of care.

But that which was worth all the rest, she bred them up very religiously, being herself a very sober pious woman, (2.) very housewifly and clean, and, (3.) very mannerly, and with good behaviour: so that in a word, excepting a plain diet, coarse lodging, and mean cloths, we were brought up as mannerly and as genteely, as if we had been at the dancing school.

I was continu'd here till I was eight years old, when I was terrified with news, that the magistrates, as I think they call'd them, had order'd that I should go to service; I was able to do but very little service where ever I was to go, except it was to run of

---

1 It was widely held that gypsies had originally come from Egypt and dyed the skin of stolen children in order to conceal the theft.

errands, and be a druge to some cook-maid, and this they told me of often, which put me into a great fright; for I had a thorough aversion to going to service, as they call'd it, that is to be a servant, tho' I was so young; and I told my nurse, as we call'd her, that I believ'd I could get my living without going to service if she pleas'd to let me; for she had taught me to work with my needle, and spin worsted, which is the chief trade of that city, and I told her that if she wou'd keep me, I wou'd work for her, and I would work very hard.

I talk'd to her almost every day of working hard; and in short, I did nothing but work and cry all day, which griev'd the good kind woman so much, that at last she began to be concern'd for me, for she lov'd me very well.

One day after this, as she came into the room, where all we poor children were at work, she sat down just over against[1] me, not in her usual place as mistress, but as if she set herself on purpose to observe me, and see me work: I was doing something she had set me to, as I remember, it was marking some shirts, which she had taken to make, and after a while she began to talk to me: Thou foolish child, says she, thou art always crying; (for I was crying then) prethee, what doest cry for? Because they will take me away, *says I*, and put me to service, and I can't work house-work; Well child, says she, but tho' you can't work house-work, as you call it, you will learn it in time, and they won't put you to hard things at first; Yes they will, says I, and if I can't do it, they will beat me, and the maids will beat me to make me do great work, and I am but a little girl, and I can't do it, and then I cry'd again, till I could not speak any more to her.

This mov'd my good motherly nurse, so that she from that time resolv'd I should not go to service yet, so she bid me not cry, and she wou'd speak to Mr. *Mayor*, and I should not go to service till I was bigger.

Well, this did not satisfie me, for to think of going to service, was such a frightful thing to me, that if she had assur'd me I should not have gone till I was 20 years old, it wou'd have been the same to me, I shou'd have cry'd, I believe all the time, with the very apprehension of its being to be so at last.

When she saw that I was not pacify'd yet, she began to be angry with me, And what wou'd you have? *says she*, don't I tell you that you shall not go to service till you are bigger? Ay, says I, but then

---

1 Facing, in full view of.

I must go at last, Why, what? said she, is the girl mad? What, would you be a gentlewoman? Yes *says I*, and cry'd heartily, till I roar'd out again.

This set the old gentlewoman a laughing at me, as you may be sure it would: Well, madam forsooth, says she, *gibing at me*, you would be a gentlewoman, and pray how will you come to be a gentlewoman? What, will you do it by your fingers ends?

Yes, *says I again*, very innocently.

Why, what can you earn, *says she*, what can you get at your work?

Three-pence, *said I*, when I spin, and 4 *d.* when I work plain work.[1]

Alas! poor gentlewoman, *said she again*, laughing, what will that do for thee?

It will keep me, *says I*, if you will let me live with you; and this *I said*, in such a poor petitioning tone, that it made the poor womans heart yearn to me, as she told me afterwards.

But, *says she*, that will not keep you, and buy you cloths too; and who must buy the little gentlewoman cloths, *says she*, and smil'd all the while at me.

I will work harder then, *says I*, and you shall have it all.

Poor child! It won't keep you, *says she*, it will hardly keep you in victuals.

Then I will have no victuals, *says I*, again very innocently, let me but live with you.

Why, can you live without victuals? *says she*, Yes, *again says I*, very much like a child, you may be sure, and still I cry'd heartily.

I had no policy in all this, you may easily see it was all nature, but it was joyn'd with so much innocence, and so much passion, that in short, it set the good motherly creature a weeping too, and she cry'd at last as fast as I did, and then took me, and led me out of the teaching room; Come *says she*, you shan't go to service, you shall live with me, and this pacify'd me for the present.

Sometime after this, she going to wait on the *Mayor*, and talking of such things as belong'd to her business, at last my story came up, and my good nurse told Mr. *Mayor* the whole tale: he was so pleas'd with it, that he would call his lady, and his two daughters to hear it, and it made mirth enough among them, you may be sure.

However, not a week had pass'd over, but on a suddain comes

---

1 Plain sewing as opposed to elaborate needlework.

Mrs. *Mayoress*, and her two daughters to the house to see my old nurse, and to see her school and the children: when they had look'd about them a little: Well, Mrs. ——— says the *Mayoress* to my nurse; and pray which is the little lass that intends to be a gentlewoman? I heard her, and I was terrible frighted at first, tho' I did not know why neither; but Mrs. *Mayoress* comes up to me, Well miss says she, and what are you at work upon? The word miss[1] was a language that had hardly been heard of in our school, and I wondred what sad[2] name it was she call'd me; however, I stood up, made a curtsy, and she took my work out of my hand, look'd on it, and said it was very well; then she took up one of my hands, Nay, says she, the child may come to be a gentlewoman for ought any body knows, she has a gentlewoman's hand, says she; this pleas'd me mightily you may be sure, but Mrs. *Mayoress* did not stop there, but giving me my work again, she put her hand in her pocket, gave me a shilling, and bid me mind my work, and learn to work well, and I might be a gentlewoman for ought she knew.

Now all this while, my good old nurse, Mrs. *Mayoress*, and all the rest of them did not understand me at all, for they meant one sort of thing, by the word gentlewoman, and I meant quite another; for alas, all I understood by being a gentlewoman, was to be able to work for myself, and get enough to keep me without that terrible bug-bear *going to service*, whereas they meant to live great, rich, and high, and I know not what.

Well, after Mrs. *Mayoress* was gone, her two daughters came in, and they call'd for the gentlewoman too, and they talk'd a long while to me, and I answer'd them in my innocent way; but always if they ask'd me whether I resolv'd to be a gentlewoman, I answer'd YES: at last one of them ask'd me, what a gentlewoman was? That puzzel'd me much; but however, I explain'd myself negatively, that it was one that did not go to service, to do house-work; they were pleas'd to be familiar with me, and lik'd my little prattle to them, which it seems was agreeable enough to them, and they gave me money too.

As for my money I gave it all to my mistress nurse, as I call'd her, and told her she should have all I got for myself when I was a gentlewoman, as well as now; by this and some other of my talk, my old tutress began to understand me, about what I meant by

---

1 As the term would only be appropriate under such circumstances when addressing a girl or young woman of some station, there is mild irony intended here.
2 Grave, solemn.

being a gentlewoman; and that I understood by it no more, than to be able to get my bread by my own work, and at last, she ask'd me whether it was not so.

I told her *yes*, and insisted on it, that to do so, was to be a gentlewoman; for says I, there is such a one, naming a woman that mended lace, and wash'd the ladies lac'd-heads,[1] She, *says I*, is a gentlewoman, and they call her madam.

Poor child, says my good old nurse, you may soon be such a gentlewoman as that, for she is a person of ill fame, and has had two or three bastards.

I did not understand any thing of that; but I answer'd, I am sure they call her madam, and she does not go to service, nor do housework, and therefore I insisted that she was a gentlewoman, and I would be such a gentlewoman as that.

The ladies were told all this again to be sure, and they made themselves merry with it, and every now and then the young ladies, Mr. *Mayor's* daughters would come and see me, and ask where the little gentlewoman was, which made me not a little proud of myself.

This held a great while, and I was often visited by these young ladies, and sometimes they brought others with them; so that I was known by it, almost all over the town.

I was now about ten years old, and began to look a little womanish, for I was mighty grave and humble; very mannerly, and as I had often heard the ladies say I was pretty, and would be a very handsome woman, so you may be sure, that hearing them say so, made me not a little proud; however, that pride had no ill effect upon me yet, only as they often gave me money, and I gave it my old nurse, she *honest woman*, was so just to me, as to lay it all out again for me, and gave me head-dresses, and linnen, and gloves and ribbons, and I went very neat, and always clean; for that I would do, and if I had rags on, I would always be clean, or else I would dabble them in water myself; but *I say*, my good nurse, when I had money given me, very honestly laid it out for me, and would always tell the ladies, this, or that, was brought with their money; and this made them oftentimes give me more; till at last, I was indeed call'd upon by the magistrates as I understood it, to go out to service; but then I was come to be so good a workwoman myself, and the ladies were so kind to me, that it was plain I could

---

1 "Head" was the general term for a head-dress, but here it refers specifically to an indoor cap decorated with ribbons and lace.

maintain myself, that is to say, I could earn as much for my nurse as she was able by it to keep me; so she told them, that if they would give her leave, she would keep the gentlewoman as she call'd me, to be her assistant, and teach the children, which I was very well able to do; for I was very nimble at my work, and had a good hand with my needle, though I was yet very young.

But the kindness of the ladies of the town did not end here, for when they came to understand that I was no more maintain'd by the publick allowance, as before, they gave me money oftner than formerly; and as I grew up, they brought me work to do for them; such as linnen to make, and laces to mend, and heads to dress up, and not only paid me for doing them, but even taught me how to do them; so that now I was a gentlewoman indeed, as I understood that word, and as I desir'd to be, for by that time, I was twelve years old, I not only found myself cloaths, and paid my nurse for my keeping, but got money in my pocket too before-hand.

The ladies also gave me cloaths frequently of their own, or their childrens, some stockings, some petticoats, some gowns, some one thing, some another, and these my old woman managed for me like a meer[1] mother, and kept them for me, oblig'd me to mend them, and turn them and twist them to the best advantage, for she was a rare house-wife.

At last one of the ladies took so much fancy to me, that she would have me home to her house, for a month she said, to be among her daughters.

Now tho' this was exceeding kind in her, yet as my old good woman said to her, unless she resolv'd to keep me for good and all, she would do the little gentlewoman more harm than good: Well, says the lady, that's true, and therefore I'll only take her home for a week then, that I may see how my daughters and she agree together, and how I like her temper, and then I'll tell you more; and in the mean time, if any body comes to see her as they us'd to do, you may only tell them, you have sent her out to my house.

This was prudently manag'd enough, and I went to the ladies house, but I was so pleas'd there with the young ladies, and they so pleas'd with me, that I had enough to do to come away, and they were as unwilling to part with me.

However, I did come away, and liv'd almost a year more with my honest old woman, and began now to be very helpful to her;

---

1 Complete, absolute (obsolete form of *mere*). It is this spelling and meaning of the word which is used throughout the narrative.

for I was almost fourteen years old, was tall of my age, and look'd a little womanish; but I had such a tast of genteel living at the ladies house, that I was not so easie in my old quarters as I us'd to be, and I thought it was fine to be a gentlewoman indeed, for I had quite other notions of a gentlewoman now, than I had before; and as I thought, I say, that it was fine to be a gentlewoman, so I lov'd to be among gentlewomen, and therefore I long'd to be there again.

About the time that I was fourteen years and a quarter old, my good old nurse, mother I ought rather to call her, fell sick and dyed; I was then in a sad condition indeed, for as there is no great bustle in putting an end to a poor bodies family, when once they are carried to the grave; so the poor good woman being buried, the parish children she kept were immediately remov'd by the church-wardens; the school was at an end, and the children of it had no more to do but just stay at home, till they were sent some where else; and as for what she left, her daughter a married woman with six or seven children, came and swept it all away at once, and removing the goods, they had no more to say to me, than to jest with me, and tell me, that the little gentlewoman might set up for her self if she pleas'd.

I was frighted out of my wits almost, and knew not what to do, for I was, as it were, turn'd out of doors to the wide world, and that which was still worse, the old honest woman had two and twenty shillings of mine in her hand,[1] which was all the estate the little gentlewoman had in the world; and when I ask'd the daughter for it, she huft[2] me and laught at me, and told me, she had nothing to do with it.

It was true, the good poor woman had told her daughter of it, and that it lay in such a place, that it was the child's money, and had call'd once or twice for me, to give it me, but I was unhappily out of the way, some where or other; and when I came back she was past being in a condition to speak of it: however, the daughter was so honest afterward as to give it me, tho' at first she us'd me cruelly about it.

Now was I a poor gentlewoman indeed, and I was just that very night to be turn'd into the wide world; for the daughter remov'd all the goods, and I had not so much as a lodging to go to, or a bit of bread to eat: but it seems some of the neighbours who had

1 In her possession.
2 Chided, blustered at.

known my circumstances, took so much compassion of me, as to acquaint the lady in whose family I had been a week, as I mention'd above; and immediately she sent her maid to fetch me away, and two of her daughters came with the maid tho' unsent; so I went with them bag and baggage, and with a glad heart you may be sure: the fright of my condition had made such an impression upon me, that I did not want now to be a gentlewoman, but was very willing to be a servant, and that any kind of servant they thought fit to have me be.

But my new generous mistress, for she exceeded the good woman I was with before, in every thing, as well as in the matter of estate; I say in every thing except honesty; and for that, tho' this was a lady most exactly just, yet I must not forget to say on all occasions, that the first tho' poor, was as uprightly honest as it was possible for any one to be.

I was no sooner carried away as I have said by this good gentlewoman, but the first lady, *that is to say*, the *Mayoress* that was, sent her two daughters to take care of me; and another family which had taken notice of me, when I was the little gentlewoman, and had given me work to do, sent for me after her, so that I was mightily made of, as we say; nay, and they were not a little angry, especially, madam the *Mayoress*, that her friend had taken me away from her as she call'd it; for as she said, I was hers by right, she having been the first that took any notice of me; but they that had me, wou'd not part with me; and as for me, tho' I shou'd have been very well treated with any of the others, yet I could not be better than where I was.

Here I continu'd till I was between 17 and 18 years old, and here I had all the advantages for my education that could be imagin'd; the lady had masters home to the house to teach her daughters to dance, and to speak *French*, and to write, and others to teach them musick; and as I was always with them, I learn'd as fast as they; and tho' the masters were not appointed to teach me, yet I learn'd by imitation and enquiry, all that they learn'd by instruction and direction. So that in short, I learn'd to dance, and speak *French* as well as any of them, and to sing much better, for I had a better voice than any of them; I could not so readily come at playing on the harpsicord or spinnet, because I had no instrument of my own to practice on, and could only come at theirs in the intervals, when they left it, which was uncertain, but yet I learn'd tollerably well too, and the young ladies at length got two instruments, that is to say, a harpsicord, and a spinnet too, and then they taught me themselves; but as to dancing they could hardly help my learning country dances, because they always wanted me to make up even number; and on the other hand, they were as heartily willing to learn me every thing that they had been taught themselves, as I could be to take the learning.

By this means I had, as I have said above, all the advantages of education that I could have had, if I had been as much a gentle-woman as they were, with whom I liv'd, and in some things, I had the advantage of my ladies, tho' they were my superiors; but they were all the gifts of nature, and which all their fortunes could not furnish. First, I was apparently[1] handsomer than any of them. Sec-ondly, I was better shap'd, and thirdly, I sung better, by which I mean, I had a better voice; in all which you will I hope allow me to say, I do not speak my own conceit of myself but the opinion of all that knew the family.

I had with all these the common vanity of my sex (*viz.*) that being really taken for very handsome, or if you please for a great beauty, I very well knew it, and had as good an opinion of myself, as any body else could have of me; and particularly I lov'd to hear any body speak of it, which could not but happen to me some-times, and was a great satisfaction to me.

Thus far I have had a smooth story to tell of myself, and in all this part of my life, I not only had the reputation of living in a very good family, and a family noted and respected every where, for vertue and sobriety, and for every valluable thing; but I had the character too of a very sober, modest, and vertuous young woman, and such I had always been; neither had I yet any occasion to think of any thing else, or to know what a temptation to wickedness meant.

But that which I was too vain of, was my ruin, or rather my van-ity was the cause of it. The lady in the house where I was, had two sons, young gentlemen of very promising parts,[2] and of extraordi-nary behaviour; and it was my misfortune to be very well with them both, but they manag'd themselves with me in a quite dif-ferent manner.

The eldest a gay[3] gentleman that knew the town, as well as the country, and tho' he had levity enough to do an ill natur'd thing, yet had too much judgment of things to pay too dear for his pleasures; he began with that unhappy snare to all women, (*viz.*)

---

1 Plainly, obviously.
2 Qualities, attributes.
3 Merry, light-hearted, but also with the suggestion of one given to social pleasures and dissipation.

taking notice upon all occasions how pretty I was, as he call'd it; how agreeable, how well carriaged, and the like; and this he contriv'd so subtilly, as if he had known as well, how to catch a woman in his net, as a patridge when he went a setting; for he wou'd contrive to be talking this to his sisters when tho' I was not by, yet when he knew I was not so far off, but that I should be sure to hear him: his sisters would return softly to him, Hush brother, she will hear you, she is but in the next room; then he would put it off, and talk softlier, as if he had not known it, and begun to acknowledge he was wrong; and then as if he had forgot himself, he would speak aloud again, and I that was so well pleas'd to hear it, was sure to lissen for it upon all occasions.

After he had thus baited his hook, and found easily enough the method how to lay it in my way, he play'd an opener game; and one day going by his sister's chamber when I was there, doing something about dressing her, he comes in with an air of gayty, O! Mrs. *Betty*,[1] said he to me, how do you do Mrs. *Betty*? Don't your cheeks burn, Mrs. *Betty*? I made a curtsy, and blush'd, but said nothing; What makes you talk so brother, *says the lady*; Why, says he, we have been talking of her below stairs this half hour; *Well says his sister*, you can say no harm of her, that I am sure, so 'tis no matter what you have been talking about; Nay, *says he*, 'tis so far from talking harm of her, that we have been talking a great deal of good, and a great many fine things have been said of Mrs. *Betty*, I assure you; and particularly, that she is the handsomest young woman in *Colchester*; and, in short, they begin to toast her health in the town.

I wonder at you brother, *says the sister*; *Betty* wants but one thing, but she had as good want every thing, for the market is against our sex just now; and if a young woman have beauty, birth, breeding, wit, sense, manners, modesty, and all these to an extream; yet if she have not money, she's no body, she had as good want them all, for nothing but money now recommends a woman; the men play the game all into their own hands.

Her younger brother, who was by, cry'd *Hold sister*, you run too fast, I am an exception to your rule I assure you, if I find a woman so accomplish'd as you talk of, *I say*, I assure you, I would not trouble myself about the money.

---

1   "Betty" was a generic name for chambermaids, which perhaps gives greater significance to the brother's playful greeting here. "Mrs." (the abbreviation of *Mistress*) was a polite form of address for both married and unmarried women.

O, *says the sister,* but you will take care not to fancy one then, without the money.

You don't know that neither, *says the brother.*

But why sister, (*says the elder brother*) why do you exclaim so at the men, for aiming so much at the fortune? You are none of them that want a fortune, what ever else you want.

I understand you brother, (*replies the lady very smartly,*) you suppose I have the money, and want the beauty; but as times go now, the first will do without the last, so I have the better of my neighbours.

Well, *says the younger brother,* but your neighbours, as you call them may be even with you; for beauty will steal a husband sometimes in spight of money; and when the maid chances to be handsomer than the mistress, she oftentimes makes as good a market, and rides in a coach before her.

I thought it was time for me to withdraw, and leave them, and I did so; but not so far, but that I heard all their discourse, in which I heard abundance of fine things said of myself, which serv'd to prompt my vanity; but as I soon found, was not the way to encrease my interest in the family; for the sister, and the younger brother fell grieviously out about it; and as he said some very disobliging things to her, upon my account, so I could easily see that she resented them, by her future conduct to me; which indeed was very unjust to me, for I had never had the least thought of what she suspected, as to her younger brother: indeed the elder brother in his distant remote way, had said a great many things, as in jest, which I had the folly to believe were in earnest, or to flatter myself, with the hopes of what I ought to have suppos'd he never intended, and perhaps never thought of.

It happen'd one day that he came running up stairs, towards the room where his sisters us'd to sit and work, as he often us'd to do; and calling to them before he came in, as was his way too, I being there alone, step'd to the door, and said, Sir, the ladies are not here, they are walk'd down the garden; as I step'd forward, to say this towards the door, he was just got to the door, and clasping me in his arms, as if it had been by chance, O! Mrs. *Betty, says he,* are you here? That's better still; I want to speak with you, more than I do with them, and then having me in his arms he kiss'd me three or four times.

I struggl'd to get away, and yet did it but faintly neither, and he held me fast, and still kiss'd me, till he was almost out of breath, and then sitting down, says, *Dear Betty* I am in love with you.

His words I must confess fir'd my blood; all my spirits flew about my heart, and put me into disorder enough, which he might easily have seen in my face: he repeated it afterwards several times, that he was in love with me, and my heart spoke as plain as a voice, that I lik'd it; nay, when ever he said, I am in love with you, my blushes plainly reply'd, *Wou'd you were* sir.

However nothing else pass'd at that time; it was but a surprise, and when he was gone, I soon recover'd myself again. He had stay'd longer with me, but he happen'd to look out at the window, and see his sisters coming up the garden, so he took his leave, kiss'd me again, told me he was very serious, and I should hear more of him very quickly, and away he went leaving me infinitely pleas'd tho' surpris'd, and had there not been one misfortune in it, I had been in the right, but the mistake lay here, that Mrs. *Betty* was in earnest, and the gentleman was not.

From this time my head run upon strange things, and I may truly say, I was not myself; to have such a gentleman talk to me of being in love with me, and of my being such a charming creature, as he told me I was, these were things I knew not how to bear, my vanity was elevated to the last degree: it is true, I had my head full of pride, but knowing nothing of the wickedness of the times, I had not one thought of my own safety, or of my vertue about me; and had my young master offer'd it at first sight, he might have taken any liberty he thought fit with me; but he did not see his advantage, which was my happiness for that time.

After this attack, it was not long, but he found an opportunity to catch me again, and almost in the same posture, indeed it had more of design in it on his part, tho' not on my part; *it was thus*; the young ladies were all gone a visiting with their mother; his brother was out of town; and as for his father, he had been at *London* for a week before; he had so well watched me, that he knew where I was, tho' I did not so much as know that he was in the house; and he briskly comes up the stairs, and seeing me at work comes into the room to me directly, and began just as he did before with taking me in his arms, and kissing me for almost a quarter of an hour together.

It was his younger sisters chamber, that I was in, and as there was no body in the house, but the maids below stairs, he was it may be the ruder: in short, he began to be in earnest with me indeed; perhaps he found me a little too easie, for God knows I made no resistance to him while he only held me in his arms and kiss'd me, indeed I was too well pleas'd with it, to resist him much.

However as it were, tir'd with that kind of work, we sat down, and there he talk'd with me a great while; *he said*, he was charm'd with me, and that he could not rest night, or day till he had told me how he was in love with me; and if I was able to love him again, and would make him happy, I should be the saving of his life; and many such fine things. I said little to him again, but easily discover'd[1] that I was a fool, and that I did not in the least perceive what he meant.

Then he walk'd about the room, and taking me by the hand, I walk'd with him; and by and by, taking his advantage, he threw me down upon the bed, and kiss'd me there most violently; but to give him his due, offer'd no manner of rudeness to me, only kiss'd me a great while; after this he thought he had heard some body come up stairs, so he got off from the bed, lifted me up, professing a great deal of love for me, but told me it was all an honest affection, and that he meant no ill to me; and with that he put five guineas into my hand, and went away down stairs.

I was more confounded with the money than I was before with the love; and began to be so elevated, that I scarse knew the ground I stood on: I am the more particular in this part, that if my story comes to be read by any innocent young body, they may learn from it to guard themselves against the mischiefs which attend an early knowledge of their own beauty; if a young woman once thinks herself handsome, she never doubts the truth of any man, that tells her he is in love with her; for if she believes herself charming enough to captivate him, tis natural to expect the effects of it.

This young gentleman had fir'd his inclination, as much as he had my vanity, and as if he had found that he had an opportunity, and was sorry he did not take hold of it, he comes up again in half an hour, or thereabouts, and falls to work with me again as before, only with a little less introduction.

And, first, when he enter'd the room, he turn'd about, and shut the door. Mrs. *Betty*, said he, I fancy'd before, some body was coming up stairs, but it was not so; however, *adds he*, if they find me in the room with you, they shan't catch me a kissing of you; I told him I did not know who should be coming up stairs, for I believ'd there was no body in the house, but the cook, and the other maid, and they never came up those stairs; Well my dear, *says he*, 'tis good to be sure however, and so he sits down and we began

---

1 Revealed, showed.

to talk; and now, tho' I was still all on fire with his first visit, and said little, he did as it were put words in my mouth, telling me how passionately he lov'd me, and that tho' he could not mention such a thing, till he came to his estate, yet he was resolv'd to make me happy then, and himself too; *that is to say, to marry me,* and abundance of such fine things, which I poor fool did not understand the drift of, but acted as if there was no such thing as any kind of love, but that which tended to matrimony; and if he had spoke of that, I had no room, as well as no power to have said No; but we were not come that length yet.

We had not sat long, but he got up, and stoping my very breath with kisses, threw me upon the bed again, but then being both well warm'd, he went farther with me than decency permits me to mention, nor had it been in my power to have deny'd him at that moment, had he offer'd much more than he did.

However, tho' he took these freedoms with me, it did not go to that, which they call the last favour, which, to do him justice, he did not attempt; and he made that self denial of his a plea for all his freedoms with me upon other occasions after this: when this was over, he stay'd but a little while, but he put almost a handful of gold in my hand, and left me; making a thousand protestations of his passion for me, and of his loving me above all the women in the world.

It will not be strange, if I now began to think, but alas! it was but with very little solid reflection: I had a most unbounded stock of vanity and pride, and but a very little stock of vertue; I did indeed cast[1] sometimes with myself what my young master aim'd at, but thought of nothing, but the fine words, and the gold; whether he intended to marry me, or not to marry me, seem'd a matter of no great consequence to me; nor did my thoughts so much as suggest to me the necessity of making any capitulation[2] for myself, till he came to make a kind of formal proposal to me, as you shall hear presently.

Thus I gave up myself to a readiness of being ruined without the least concern, and am a fair *memento* to all young women, whose vanity prevails over their vertue: nothing was ever so stupid on both sides, had I acted as became me, and resisted as vertue and honour requir'd, this gentleman had either desisted his attacks, finding no room to expect the accomplishment of his

---

1 Deliberate, ponder.
2 Terms or conditions (of agreement).

design, or had made fair, and honourable proposals of marriage; in which case, whoever had blam'd him, no body could have blam'd me. In short, if he had known me, and how easy the trifle he aim'd at, was to be had, he would have troubled his head no farther, but have given me four or five guineas, and have lain with me the next time he had come at me; and if I had known his thoughts, and how hard he thought I would be to be gain'd, I might have made my own terms with him; and if I had not capitulated for an immediate marriage, I might for a maintenance till marriage, and might have had what I would; for he was already rich to excess, besides what he had in expectation; but I seem'd wholly to have abandoned all such thoughts as these, and was taken up onely with the pride of my beauty, and of being belov'd by such a gentleman; as for the gold I spent whole hours in looking upon it; I told[1] the guineas over and over a thousand times a day: never poor vain creature was so wrapt up with every part of the story, as I was, not considering what was before me, and how near my ruin was at the door; indeed I think, I rather wish'd for that ruin, than studyed to avoid it.

In the mean time however, I was cunning enough, not to give the least room to any in the family to suspect me, or to imagine that I had the least correspondence[2] with this young gentleman; I scarce ever look'd towards him in publick, or answer'd if he spoke to me, if any body was near us; but for all that, we had every now and then a little encounter, where we had room for a word or two, and now and then a kiss; but no fair opportunity for the mischief intended; and especially considering that he made more circumlocution, than if he had known my thoughts he had occasion for, and the work appearing difficult to him, he really made it so.

But as the Devil is an unwearied tempter, so he never fails to find opportunity for that wickedness he invites to: it was one evening that I was in the garden, with his two younger sisters, and himself, and all very innocently merry, when he found means to convey a note into my hand, by which he directed me to understand, that he would to morrow desire me publickly to go of an errand for him into the town, and that I should see him somewhere by the way.

Accordingly after dinner, he very gravely says to me, his sisters being all by, Mrs. *Betty*, I must ask a favour of you: What's that?

---

1 Counted.
2 Relationship.

says his second sister; Nay, sister *says he*, very gravely, if you can't spare Mrs. *Betty* to day any other time will do; *yes they said*, they could spare her well enough, and the sister beg'd pardon for asking; which she did but of meer course, without any meaning; Well, but brother, says the eldest sister, you must tell Mrs. *Betty* what it is; if it be any private business, that we must not hear, you may call her out,[1] there she is: Why sister, says the gentleman, very gravely, what do you mean? *I* only desire her to go into the *High-Street*, (and then he pulls out a turn-over[2]) to such a shop, and then he tells them a long story of two fine neckcloths he had bid money for, and he wanted to have me go and make an errand to buy a neck to the turn-over that he showed, to see if they would take my money[3] for the neckcloths; to bid a shilling more, and haggle with them; and then he made more errands, and so continued to have such petty business to do, that *I* should be sure to stay a good while.

When he had given me my errands, he told them a long story of a visit he was going to make to a family they all knew, and where was to be such and such gentlemen, and how merry they were to be; and very formally asks his sisters to go with him, and they as formally excus'd themselves, because of company that they had notice was to come and visit them that afternoon, which by the way he had contriv'd on purpose.

He had scarce done speaking to them, and giving me my errand, but his man came up to tell him that Sir *W———— H———— —s*[4] coach stop'd at the door; so he runs down, and comes up again immediately, Alas! *says he*, aloud, there's all my mirth spoil'd at once; Sir *W————* has sent his coach for me, and desires to speak with me upon some earnest business: it seems this Sir *W———— ————* was a gentleman, who liv'd about three miles out of town, to whom he had spoken on purpose the day before, to lend him his charriot[5] for a particular occasion; and had appointed it to call for him, as it did about three a clock.

Immediately he calls for his best wig,[6] hat and sword, and

---

1 Call her aside.
2 A turn-down collar.
3 That is, if they would now take the amount he had previously offered.
4 The hinting at names throughout in this manner, as though to conceal the identity of real, distinguished people, is a further way of lending authenticity to this "private history."
5 A light, four-wheeled carriage (obsolete form of *chariot*).
6 Towards the end of the seventeenth century the wearing of periwigs (or *wigs*) by gentlemen had become common practice.

ordering his man to go to the other place to make his excuse, that was to say, he made an excuse to send his man away; he prepares to go into the coach: as he was going, he stop'd a while, and speaks mighty earnestly to me about his business, and finds an opportunity to say very softly to me, *Come away my dear as soon as ever you can.* I said nothing, but made a curtsy, as if I had done so to what he said in publick; in about a quarter of an hour I went out too, I had no dress, other than before, except that I had a hood, a mask,[1] a fan and a pair of gloves in my pocket; so that there was not the least suspicion in the house: he waited for me in the coach in a back *lane,* which he knew *I* must pass by; and had directed the coachman whither to go, which was to a certain place, call'd *Mile-End,*[2] where lived a confident of his, where we went in, and where was all the convenience in the world to be as wicked as we pleas'd.

When we were together, he began to talk very gravely to me; and to tell me, he did not bring me there to betray me; that his passion for me, would not suffer him to abuse me; that he resolv'd to marry me as soon as he came to his estate, that in the mean time, if *I* would grant his request, he would maintain me very honourably, and made me a thousand protestations of his sincerity, and of his affection to me; and that he would never abandon me, and as *I* may say, made a thousand more preambles than he need to have done.

However as he press'd me to speak, I told him, I had no reason to question the sincerity of his love to me, after so many protestations, but —— and there I stopp'd, as if I left him to guess the rest; BUT WHAT my dear? *says he,* I guess what you mean; what if you should be with child, is not that it? Why then, *says he,* I'll take care of you, and provide for you, and the child too, and that you may see I am not in jest, *says he,* here's an earnest[3] for you; and with that he pulls out a silk purse, with an hundred guineas in it, and gave it me; and I'll give you such another, *says he,* every year till I marry you.

My colour came, and went, at the sight of the purse, and with the fire of his proposal together; so that I could not say a word, and he easily perceiv'd it; so putting the purse into my bosom, I made no more resistance to him, but let him do just what he

---

1 A fashionable item of female apparel, used not only for protection against the elements but also as a means of disguise.
2 In the 1720s, Defoe held a lease on an estate in the parish of St. Michael, Mile End, a mile or so north of Colchester.
3 Money given in part payment and pledge to bind a contract or bargain.

pleas'd; and as often as he pleas'd; and thus I finish'd my own destruction at once, for from this day, being forsaken of my vertue, and my modesty, I had nothing of value left to recommend me, either to God's blessing, or man's assistance.

But things did not end here, I went back to the town, did the business he publickly directed me to, and was at home before any body thought me long; as for my gentleman, he staid out as he told me he would, till late at night, and there was not the least suspicion in the family, either on his account or on mine.

We had after this, frequent opportunities to repeat our crime; chiefly by his contrivance; especially at home; when his mother and the young ladies went abroad a visiting, which he watch'd so narrowly, as never to miss; knowing always before-hand when they went out; and then fail'd not to catch me all alone, and securely enough; so that we took our fill of our wicked pleasure for near half a year; and yet, which was the most to my satisfaction, I was not with child.

But before this half year was expir'd, his younger brother, of whom I have made some mention in the beginning of the story, falls to work with me; and he finding me alone in the garden one evening, begins a story of the same kind to me, made good honest professions of being in love with me; and in short, proposes fairly and honourably to marry me, and that before he made any other offer to me at all.

I was now confounded and driven to such an extremity, as the like was never known; at least not to me; I resisted the proposal with obstinancy; and now I began to arm my self with arguments: I laid before him the inequallity of the match, the treatment I should meet with in the family; the ingratitude it wou'd be to his good father and mother, who had taken me into their house upon such generous principles, and when I was in such a low condition; and in short, I said every thing to dissuade him from his design that I could imagine, except telling him the truth, which wou'd indeed have put an end to it all, but that I durst not think of mentioning.

But here happen'd a circumstance that I did not expect indeed, which put me to my shifts;[1] for this young gentleman as he was plain and honest, so he pretended to nothing with me, but what was so too; and knowing his own innocence, he was not so careful to make his having a kindness for Mrs. *Betty*, a secret in the house,

---

1 Stratagems.

as his brother was; and tho' he did not let them know that he had talk'd to me about it, yet he said enough to let his sisters perceive he lov'd me, and his mother saw it too, which tho' they took no notice of it to me, yet they did to him, and immediately I found their carriage[1] to me alter'd, more than ever before.

I saw the cloud, tho' I did not foresee the storm; it was easie, *I say*, to see that their carriage to me was alter'd, and that it grew worse and worse every day; till at last I got information among the servants, that I shou'd, in a very little while, be desir'd to remove.

I was not alarm'd at the news, having a full satisfaction that I should be otherwise provided for; and especially, considering that I had reason every day to expect I should be with child, and that then I should be oblig'd to remove without any pretences for it.

After some time, the younger gentleman took an opportunity to tell me, that the kindness he had for me, had got vent[2] in the family; he did not charge me with it, *he said*, for he knew well enough which way it came out; he told me his plain way of talking had been the occasion of it, for that he did not make his respect for me so much a secret as he might have done, and the reason was, that he was at a point;[3] that if I would consent to have him, he would tell them all openly that he lov'd me, and that he intended to marry me: that it was true his father and mother might resent it, and be unkind, but that he was now in a way to live, being bred to the law,[4] and he did not fear maintaining me, agreeable to what I should expect; and that in short, as he believed I would not be asham'd of him, so he was resolv'd not to be asham'd of me, and that he scorn'd to be afraid to own me now, who he resolv'd to own after I was his wife, and therefore I had nothing to do but to give him my hand, and he would answer for all the rest.

I was now in a dreadful condition indeed, and now I repented heartily my easiness with the eldest brother, not from any reflection of conscience, but from a view of the happiness I might have enjoy'd, and had now made impossible; for tho' I had no great scruples of conscience *as I have said* to struggle with, yet I could not think of being a whore to one brother, and a wife to the other; but then it came into my thoughts, that the first brother had promis'd to make me his wife, when he came to his estate; but I presently remember'd what I had often thought of, that he had

---

1 Behaviour, bearing.
2 Had become known.
3 Had decided, resolved.
4 Trained as a lawyer.

never spoken a word of having me for a wife, after he had conquer'd me for a mistress; and indeed till now, tho' I said I thought of it often, yet it gave me no disturbance at all, for as he did not seem in the least to lessen his affection to me, so neither did he lessen his bounty, tho' he had the discretion himself to desire me not to lay out a penny of what he gave me in cloaths, or to make the least show extraordinary, because it would necessarily give jealousie[1] in the family, since every body knew I could come at such things no manner of ordinary way; but by some private friendship, which they would presently have suspected.

But I was now in a great strait, and really knew not what to do; the main difficulty was this, the younger brother not only laid close siege to me, but suffered it to be seen; he would come into his sisters room, and his mothers room, and sit down, and talk a thousand kind things of me, and to me, even before their faces, and when they were all there: this grew so publick, that the whole house talk'd of it, and his mother reprov'd him for it, and their carriage to me appear'd quite altered: in short, his mother had let fall some speeches, as if she intended to put me out of the family, that is in *English*, to turn me out of doors. Now, I was sure this could not be a secret to his brother, only that he might not think as indeed no body else yet did, that the youngest brother had made any proposal to me about it; but as I easily cou'd see that it would go farther, so I saw likewise there was an absolute necessity to speak of it to him, or that he would speak of it to me, and which to do first I knew not; that is, whether I should break it to him, or let it alone till he should break it to me.

Upon serious consideration, for indeed now I began to consider things very seriously, and never till now: I say, upon serious consideration, I resolv'd to tell him of it first, and it was not long before I had an opportunity, for the very next day his brother went to *London* upon some business, and the family being out a visiting, just as it had happen'd before, and as indeed was often the case, he came according to his custom to spend an hour or two with Mrs. *Betty*.

When he came and had sate down a while, he easily perceiv'd there was an alteration in my countenance, that I was not so free and pleasant with him, as I us'd to be, and particularly, that I had been a crying; he was not long before he took notice of it, and ask'd me in very kind terms what was the matter, and if any thing

---

1 Arouse resentful suspicions.

troubl'd me: I wou'd have put it off if I could, but it was not to be conceal'd; so after suffering many importunities to draw that out of me, which I long'd as much as possible to disclose; I told him that it was true, something did trouble me, and something of such a nature, that I could not conceal from him, and yet, that I could not tell how to tell him of it neither; that it was a thing that not only surpriz'd me, but greatly perplex'd me, and that I knew not what course to take, unless he would direct me: he told me with great tenderness, that let it be what it wou'd, I should not let it trouble me, for he would protect me from all the world.

I then begun at a distance, and told him I was afraid the ladies had got some secret information of our correspondence; for that it was easie to see, that their conduct was very much chang'd towards me for a great while, and that now it was come to that pass, that they frequently found fault with me, and sometimes fell quite out with me, tho' I never gave them the least occasion: that whereas, I us'd always to lye with the eldest sister, I was lately put to lye by my self, or with one of the maids; and that I had over-heard them several times talking very unkindly about me; but that which confirm'd it all, was, that one of the servants had told me, that she had heard I was to be turn'd out, and that it was not safe for the family, that I should be any longer in the house.

He smil'd when he heard all this, and I ask'd him, how he could make so light of it, when he must needs know, that if there was any discovery, I was undone for ever? and that even it would hurt him, tho' not ruin him, as it would me: I upbraided him, that he was like all the rest of the sex, that when they had the character and honour of a woman at their mercy, often times made it their jest, and at least look'd upon it as a trifle, and counted the ruin of those, they had had their will of, as a thing of no value.

He saw me warm and serious, and he chang'd his stile immediately; *he told me*, he was sorry I should have such a thought of him; that he had never given me the least occasion for it, but had been as tender of my reputation, as he could be of his own; that he was sure our correspondence had been manag'd with so much address, that not one creature in the family had so much as a suspicion of it; that if he smil'd when I told him my thoughts, it was at the assurance he lately receiv'd, that our understanding one another, was not so much as known or guess'd at; and that when he had told me, how much reason he had to be easie, I should smile as he did, for he was very certain, it would give me a full satisfaction.

This is a mystery I cannot understand, *says I*, or how it should be to my satisfaction, that I am to be turn'd out of doors; for if our correspondence is not discover'd, I know not what else I have done to change the countenances of the whole family to me, or to have them treat me as they do now, who formerly used me with so much tenderness, as if I had been one of their own children.

Why look you child, *says he*, that they are uneasie about you, that is true; but that they have the least suspicion of the case as it is, and as it respects you and I, is so far from being true, that they suspect my brother *Robin*;[1] and in short, they are fully persuaded he makes love to you: nay, the fool has put it into their heads too himself, for he is continually bantring them about it, and making a jest of himself; I confess, I think he is wrong to do so, because he can not but see it vexes them, and makes them unkind to you; but 'tis a satisfaction to me, because of the assurance it gives me, that they do not suspect me in the least, and I hope this will be to your satisfaction too.

So it is, *says I*, one way, but this does not reach my case at all, nor is this the chief thing that troubles me, tho' I have been concern'd about that too: What is it then, *says he*? with which, I fell into tears, and could say nothing to him at all: he strove to pacifie me all he could, but began at last to be very pressing upon me, to tell what it was; at last *I answer'd*, that I thought I ought to tell him too, and that he had some right to know it, besides, that I wanted his direction in the case, for I was in such perplexity, that I knew not what course to take, and then I related the whole affair to him: *I told him*, how imprudently his brother had manag'd himself, in making himself so publick; for that if he had kept it a secret, as such a thing ought to have been, I could but have denied him positively, without giving any reason for it, and he would in time have ceas'd his sollicitations; but that he had the vanity, first, to depend upon it that I would not deny him, and then had taken the freedom to tell his resolution of having me, to the whole house.

I *told him* how far I had resisted him, and *told him* how sincere and honourable his offers were, but *says I*, my case will be doubly hard; for as they carry it ill to me now, because he desires to have me, they'll carry it worse when they shall find I have deny'd him; and they will presently say, there's something else in it, and then out it comes, that I am marry'd already to somebody else, or else that I would never refuse a match so much above me as this was.

This discourse surpriz'd him indeed very much: he *told me*, that

---

1 "Robin" (diminutive of *Robert*), a name traditionally associated with the mischievous sprite Puck (sometimes called Robin Goodfellow).

it was a critical point indeed for me to manage, and he did not see which way I should get out of it; but he would consider of it, and let me know next time we met, what resolution he was come to about it; and in the mean time, desir'd I would not give my consent to his brother, nor yet give him a flat denial, but that I would hold him in suspence a while.

I seem'd to start at his saying, I should not give him my consent; I *told him*, he knew very well, I had no consent to give; that he had engag'd himself to marry me, and that my consent was at the same time engag'd to him; that he had all along told me, I was his wife, and I look'd upon my self as effectually so, as if the ceremony had pass'd; and that it was from his own mouth that I did so, he having all along persuaded me to call myself his wife.[1]

Well, my dear *says he*, don't be concern'd at that now, if I am not your husband, I'll be as good as a husband to you, and do not let those things trouble you now, but let me look a little farther into this affair, and I shall be able to say more next time we meet.

He pacify'd me as well as he could with this, but I found he was very thoughtful, and that tho' he was very kind to me, and kiss'd me a thousand times, and more I believe, and gave me money too, yet he offer'd no more all the while we were together, which was above two hours, and which I much wonder'd at, indeed at that time, considering how it us'd to be, and what opportunity we had.

His brother did not come from *London*, for five or six days, and it was two days more, before he got an opportunity to talk with him; but then getting him by himself, he began to talk very close to him about it; and the same evening got an opportunity, (for we had a long conference together) to repeat all their discourse to me, which as near as I can remember, was to the purpose following. He *told him* he heard strange news of him since he went, (*viz.*) that he made love to Mrs. *Betty*: Well, *says his* brother, a little angrily, and so *I do*, and what then? What has any body to do with that? Nay, *says his* brother, don't be angry *Robin*, I don't pretend to have any thing to do with it; nor do I pretend to be angry with you about it: but I find they do concern themselves about it, and that they have used the poor girl ill about it, which I should take as done to my self; Who do you mean by THEY? *says* Robin, I mean my mother, and the girls, *says the* elder brother.

---

1 Until the passage of the Marriage Act in 1753, despite legal and ecclesiastical penalties, the promise (given freely) of a couple to marry one another was considered binding. See Appendix A.7.

But hark ye, *says his* brother, are you in earnest, do you really love the girl, you may be free with me you know? Why then *says* Robin, I will be free with you, I do love her above all the women in the world, and I will have her, let *them say*, and do what they will, I believe the girl will not deny me.

It stuck me to the heart when he *told me* this, for tho' it was most rational to think I would not deny him, yet I knew in my own conscience, I must deny him, and I saw my ruin in my being oblig'd to do so; but I knew it was my business to talk otherwise then, so I interrupted him in his story thus.

Ay! *said I*, does he think I can not deny him? But he shall find I can deny him, for all that.

Well my dear *says he*, but let me give you the whole story as it went on between us, and then say what you will.

Then he went on and *told me*, that he reply'd thus: But brother, you know she has nothing, and you may have several ladies with good fortunes: 'Tis no matter for that, *said* Robin, I love the girl; and I will never please my pocket in marrying, and not please my fancy; And so my dear *adds he*, there is no opposing him.

Yes, yes, *says I*, you shall see I can oppose him, I have learnt to say No now, tho' I had not learnt it before; if the best lord in the land offer'd me marriage now, I could very chearfully say No to him.

Well, but my dear *says he*, what can you say to him? You know, as you said when we talk'd of it before, he will ask you many questions about it, and all the house will wonder what the meaning of it should be.

Why *says I* smiling, I can stop all their mouths at one clap, by telling him and them too, that I am married already to his elder brother.

He smil'd a little too at the word, but I could see it startled him, and he could not hide the disorder it put him into; however, he return'd, Why tho' that may be true in some sense, yet I suppose you are but in jest, when you talk of giving such an answer as that, it may not be convenient on many accounts.

No, no, *says I* pleasantly, I am not so fond of letting that secret come out, without your consent.

But what then can you say to him, or to them, *says he*, when they find you positive against a match, which would be apparently so much to your advantage?

Why, *says I*, should I be at a loss? First of all, I am not oblig'd to give them any reason at all, on the other hand, I may tell them, I am married already, and stop there, and that will be a full stop too to him, for he can have no reason to ask one question after it.

Ay, *says he*, but the whole house will teize you about that, even to father and mother, and if you deny them positively, they will be disoblig'd at you, and suspicious besides.

Why, *says I*, what can I do? What would you have me do? I was in strait[1] enough before, and as I *told you*, I was in perplexity before, and acquainted you with the circumstances, that I might have your advice.

My dear *says he*, I have been considering very much upon it, you may be sure, and tho' it is a piece of advice, that has a great many mortifications in it to me, and may at first seem strange to you, yet all things consider'd, I see no better way for you, than to let him go on; and if you find him hearty and in earnest, marry him.

I gave him a look full of horror at those words, and turning pale as death, was at the very point of sinking down out of the chair I sat in: when giving a start, My dear, *says he* aloud, what's the matter with you? Where are you a going? and a great many such things; and with joging and calling to me, fetch'd me a little to my self, tho' it was a good while before I fully recover'd my senses, and was not able to speak for several minutes more.

When I was fully recover'd he began again; My dear *says he*, what made you so surpriz'd at what I said, I would have you consider seriously of it? You may see plainly how the family stand in this case, and they would be stark mad if it was my case, as it is my brothers, and for ought I see, it would be my ruin and yours too.

Ay! *says I*, still speaking angrily; are all your protestations and vows to be shaken by the dislike of the family? Did I not always object that to you, and you made a light thing of it, as what you were above, and would not value; and is it come to this now? *said I*, is this your faith and honour, your love, and the solidity of your promises?

He continued perfectly calm, notwithstanding all my reproaches, and I was not sparing of them at all; but *he reply'd* at last, My dear, I have not broken one promise with you yet; I did tell you I would marry you when I was come to my estate; but you see my father is a hail healthy man, and may live these thirty years still, and not be older than several are round us in the town; and you never propos'd my marrying you sooner, because you know it

---

1 Difficulty, distress (obsolete form of *straits*).

might be my ruin; and as to all the rest, I have not fail'd you in any thing, you have wanted for nothing.

I could not deny a word of this, and had nothing to say to it in general; But why then, *says I*, can you perswade me to such a horrid stop,[1] as leaving you, since you have not left me? Will you allow no affection, no love on my side, where there has been so much on your side? Have I made you no returns? Have I given no testimony of my sincerity, and of my passion? Are the sacrifices I have made of honour and modesty to you, no proof of my being ty'd to you in bonds too strong to be broken?

But here my dear, *says he*, you may come into a safe station, and appear with honour, and with splendor at once, and the remembrance of what we have done, may be wrapt up in an eternal silence, as if it had never happen'd; you shall always have my respect, and my sincere affection, only then it shall be honest, and perfectly just to my brother, you shall be my dear sister, as now you are my dear ———— and there he stop'd.

Your dear whore, *says I*, you would have said, if you had gone on; and you might as well have said it; but I understand you: however, I desire you to remember the long discourses you have had with me, and the many hours pains you have taken to perswade me to believe myself an honest woman; that I was your wife intentionally, tho' not in the eye of the world; and that it was as effectual a marriage that had pass'd between us, as if we had been publickly wedded by the parson of the parish; you know and cannot but remember, that these have been your own words to me.

I found this was a little too close upon him, but I made it up in what follows; he stood stock still for a while, and said nothing, and I went on thus; You cannot, *says I*, without the highest injustice believe that I yielded upon all these perswasions without a love not to be questioned, not to be shaken again by any thing that could happen afterward: if you have such dishonourable thoughts of me, I must ask you what foundation in any of my behaviour have I given for such a suggestion.

If then I have yielded to the importunities of my affection; and if I have been perswaded to believe that I am really, and in the essence of the thing your wife, shall I now give the lye to all those arguments, and call myself your whore, or mistress, which is the same thing? And will you transfer me to your brother? Can you transfer my affection? Can you bid me cease loving you, and bid

---

1 Ending, conclusion.

me love him? Is it in my power think you to make such a change at demand? No sir, *said I*, depend upon it 'tis impossible, and whatever the change of your side may be, I will ever be true; and I had much rather, since it is come that unhappy length, be your whore than your brothers wife.

He appear'd pleas'd, and touch'd with the impression of this last discourse, and told me that he stood where he did before; that he had not been unfaithful to me in any one promise he had ever made yet, but that there were so many terrible things presented themselves to his view in the affair before me, and that on my account in particular, that he had thought of the other as a remedy so effectual, as nothing could come up to it: that he thought this would not be an entire parting us, but we might love as friends all our days, and perhaps with more satisfaction, than we should in the station we were now in, as things might happen: that he durst say, I could not apprehend any thing from him, as to betraying a secret, which could not but be the destruction of us both, if it came out: that he had but one question to ask of me, that could lye in the way of it, and if that question was answer'd in the negative, he could not but think still it was the only step I could take.

I guess'd at his question presently, namely, whether I was sure I was not with child? As to that, *I told him*, he need not be concern'd about it, for I was not with child; Why then my dear, *says he*, we have no time to talk farther now; consider of it, and think closely about it, I cannot but be of the opinion still, that it will be the best course you can take; and with this, he took his leave, and the more hastily too, his mother and sisters ringing at the gate, just at the moment that he had risen up to go.

He left me in the utmost confusion of thought; and he easily perceiv'd it the next day, and all the rest of the week, for it was but *Tuesday* evening when we talked; but he had no opportunity to come at me all that week, till the *Sunday* after, when I being indispos'd did not go to church, and he making some excuse for the like, stay'd at home.

And now he had me an hour and a half again by myself, and we fell into the same arguments all over again or at least so near the same, as it would be to no purpose to repeat them; at last, *I ask'd him* warmly what opinion he must have of my modesty, that he could suppose, I should so much as entertain a thought of lying with two brothers? and assur'd him it could never be: *I added* if he was to tell me that he would never see me more, than which nothing but death could be more terrible, yet I could never entertain a thought so dishonourable to my self, and so base to him; and therefore, I entreated him if he had one grain of respect or affection left for me, that he would speak no more of it to me, or that he would pull his sword out and kill me. He appear'd surpriz'd at my obstinancy as he call'd it, *told me.* I was unkind to my self, and unkind to him in it; that it was a crisis unlook'd for upon us both, and impossible for either of us to foresee; but that he did not see any other way to save us both from ruin, and therefore he thought it the more unkind; but that if he must say no more of it to me, he added with an unusual coldness, that he did not know any thing else we had to talk of; and so he rose up to take his leave; I rose up too, as if with the same indifference, but when he came to give me as it were a parting kiss, I burst out into such a passion of crying, that tho' I would have spoke, I could not, and only pressing his hand, seem'd to give him the adieu, but cry'd vehemently.

He was sensibly mov'd with this; so he sat down again, and said a great many kind things to me, to abate the excess of my passion; but still urg'd the necessity of what he had proposed; all the while insisting, that if I did refuse, he would notwithstanding provide for me; but letting me plainly see, that he would decline me in the main point; nay, even as a mistress; making it a point of honour not to lye with the woman, that for ought he knew, might come to be his brothers wife.

The bare loss of him as a gallant was not so much my affliction, as the loss of his person, whom indeed I lov'd to distraction; and the loss of all the expectations I had, and which I always had built my hopes upon, of having him one day for my husband: these things oppress'd my mind so much, that in short, I fell very ill, the agonies of my mind, in a word, threw me into a high feaver, and long it was, that none in the family expected my life.

I was reduc'd very low indeed, and was often delirious and light headed; but nothing lay so near me, as the fear, that when I was light headed, I should say something or other to his prejudice; I was distress'd in my mind also to see him, and so he was to see me, for he really lov'd me most passionately; but it could not be; there was not the least room to desire it, on one side, or other, or so much as to make it decent.

It was near five weeks that I kept my bed, and tho' the violence of my feaver abated in three weeks, yet it several times return'd; and the physicians said two or three times, they could do no more for me, but that they must leave nature and the distemper to fight it out; only strengthening the first with cordials to maintain the strugle: after the end of five weeks I grew better, but was so weak, so alter'd, so melancholly, and recover'd so slowly, that the physicians apprehended I should go into a consumption; and which vex'd me most, they gave it as their opinion, that my mind was oppress'd, that something troubl'd me, and in short, that I was IN LOVE; upon this, the whole house was set upon me to examine me, and to press me to tell, whether I was in love or not, and with who? But as I well might, I deny'd my being in love at all.

They had on this occasion a squable one day about me at table, that had like to have put the whole family in an uproar, and for sometime did so; they happen'd to be all at table, but the father; as for me I was ill, and in my chamber: at the beginning of the talk, which was just as they had finish'd their dinner, the old gentlewoman who had sent me somewhat to eat, call'd her maid to go up, and ask me if I would have any more; but the maid brought down word, I had not eaten half what she had sent me already.

Alas, *says the* old lady, that poor girl; I am afraid she will never be well.

Well, *says the* elder brother, how should Mrs. *Betty* be well, *they say* she is in love?

I believe nothing of it *says the* old gentlewoman.

I don't know *says the* eldest sister, what to say to it, they have made such a rout[1] about her being so handsome, and so charming, and I know not what, and that in her hearing too, that has turn'd the creatures head I believe, and who knows what possessions[2] may follow such doings? For my part I don't know what to make of it.

Why sister, you must acknowledge she is very handsome, *says the* elder brother.

Ay, and a great deal handsomer than you sister, *says* Robin, and that's your mortification.

Well, well, that is not the question, *says his* sister, the girl is well enough,[3] and she knows it well enough; she need not be told of it to make her vain.

We are not a talking of her being vain, *says the* elder brother, but of her being in love; it may be she is in love with herself, it seems my sisters think so.

I would she was in love with me, *says* Robin, I'd quickly put her out of her pain.

---

1 Fuss, clamour.
2 Strong impulses.
3 Fairly attractive.

What d' ye mean by that son, *says the* old lady, how can you talk so?

Why madam, *says* Robin again, very honestly, do you think I'd let the poor girl die for love, and of one that is near at hand to be had too.

Fye brother, *says the* second sister, how can you talk so? Would you take a creature that has not a groat[1] in the world?

Prethee child *says* Robin, beauties a portion,[2] and good humour with it, is a double portion; I wish thou hadst half her stock of both for thy portion: so there was her mouth stopp'd.

I find, *says the* eldest sister, if *Betty* is not in love, my brother is; I wonder he has not broke his mind to *Betty*, I warrant she won't say No.

They that yield when they're ask'd *says* Robin, are one step before them that were never ask'd to yield, sister, and two steps before them that yield before they are ask'd: and that's an answer to you sister.

This fir'd the sister, and she flew into a passion, and said, things were come to that pass, that it was time the wench, *meaning me*, was out of the family; and but that she was not fit[3] to be turn'd out, she hop'd her father and mother would consider of it, as soon as she could be remov'd.

Robin reply'd, that was business for the master and mistress of the family, who were not to be taught by one, that had so little judgment as his eldest sister.

It run up a great deal farther; the sister scolded, *Robin* rally'd[4] and banter'd, but poor *Betty* loss'd ground by it extreamly in the family: I heard of it, and I cry'd heartily, and the old lady came up to me, some body having told her that I was so much concern'd about it: I complain'd to her, that it was very hard the doctors should pass such a censure[5] upon me, for which they had no ground; and that it was still harder, considering the circumstances I was under in the family; that I hop'd I had done nothing to lessen her esteem for me, or given any occasion for the bickering between her sons and daughters; and I had more need to think of a coffin, than of being in love, and beg'd she would not let me suffer in her opinion for any bodies mistakes, but my own.

---

1 An English coin, obsolete by this time, proverbially used to signify a trifling amount of money.
2 Marriage portion, dowry.
3 Well enough.
4 Made fun of, teased.
5 Unfavourable, injurious diagnosis.

She was sensible of the justice of what I said, but *told me*, since there had been such a clamour among them, and that her younger son talk'd after such a rattling way[1] as he did; she desir'd I would be so faithful to her, as to answer her but one question sincerely; I told her I would with all my heart, and with the utmost plainess and sincerity: why then the question was, whether there was any thing between her son *Robert* and me? I told her with all the protestations of sincerity that I was able to make, and as I might well do, that there was not, nor ever had been; I *told her*, that Mr. *Robert* had rattled and jested, as she knew it was his way, and that I took it always as I suppos'd he meant it, to be a wild airy way of discourse that had no signification in it: and again assured her, that there was not the least tittle of what she understood by it between us; and that those who had suggested it, had done me a great deal of wrong, and Mr. *Robert* no service at all.

The old lady was fully satisfy'd, and kiss'd me, spoke chearfully to me, and bid me take care of my health, and want for nothing, and so took her leave: but when she came down, she found the brother and all his sisters together by the ears;[2] they were angry even to passion, at his upbraiding them with their being homely, and having never had any sweet-heart, never having been ask'd the question, and their being so forward as almost to ask first: he rallied them upon the subject of Mrs. *Betty*; how pretty, how good humour'd, how she sung better than they did, and danc'd better, and how much handsomer she was; and in doing this, he omitted no ill-natur'd thing that could vex them, and indeed, push'd too hard upon them: the old lady came down in the height of it, and to put a stop to it, told them all the discourse she had had with me, and how I answer'd, that there was nothing between Mr. *Robert* and I.

She's wrong there, *says* Robin, for if there was not a great deal between us, we should be closer together than we are: I told her I lov'd her hugely, *says he*, but I could never make the jade believe I was in earnest; I do not know how you should *says his* mother, no body in their senses could believe you were in earnest, to talk so to a poor girl, whose circumstances you know so well.

But prethee son *adds she*, since you tell me that you could not make her believe you were in earnest, what must we believe about it? for you ramble so in your discourse, that no body knows

---

1 That is, he talked rapidly in a thoughtless and noisy manner.
2 Arguing loudly.

whether you are in earnest or in jest: but as I find the girl by your own confession has answer'd truely, I wish you would do so too, and tell me seriously, so that I may depend upon it; is there any thing in it or no? Are you in earnest or no? Are you distracted indeed, or are you not? 'Tis a weighty question, and I wish you would make us easie about it.

By my faith madam, *says* Robin, 'tis in vain to mince the matter, or tell any more lyes about it, I am in earnest, as much as a man is, that's going to be hang'd. If Mrs. *Betty* would say she lov'd me, and that she would marry me, I'd have her to morrow morning fasting; and say, *To have, and to hold,* instead of eating my breakfast.

Well, *says the mother,* then there's one son lost; and she said it in a very mournful tone, as one greatly concern'd at it.

I hope not madam, *says* Robin, no man is lost, when a good wife has found him.

Why but child, *says the* old lady, she is a beggar.

Why then madam, she has the more need of charity *says* Robin; I'll take her off of the hands of the parish, and she and I'll beg together.

Its bad jesting with such things, *says the mother.*

I don't jest madam, *says* Robin: we'll come and beg your pardon madam; and your blessing madam, and my fathers.

This is all out of the way son, *says the mother,* if you are in earnest you are undone.

I am afraid not *says he,* for I am really afraid she won't have me, after all my sisters huffing and blustring; I believe I shall never be able to persuade her to it.

That's a fine tale indeed, she is not so far out of her senses neither; Mrs. *Betty* is no fool, *says the youngest sister,* do you think she has learnt to say No, any more than other people?

No Mrs. *Mirth-wit*[1] says Robin, Mrs. *Betty's* no fool; but Mrs. *Betty* may be engag'd some other way, and what then?

Nay, *says the eldest sister,* we can say nothing to that, who must it be to then? She is never out of the doors, it must be between you.

I have nothing to say to that *says* Robin, I have been examin'd enough; there's my brother, if it must be *between us,* go to work with him.

---

1 Probably an allusion to such comic type characters as Gossip Mirth in Ben Jonson's *The Staple of News* (1625).

This stung *the elder brother* to the quick, and he concluded that *Robin* had discover'd something: however, he kept himself from appearing disturb'd; Prethee *says he*, don't go to sham your stories off upon me,[1] I tell you, I deal in no such ware; I have nothing to say to Mrs. *Betty*, nor to any of the *Miss Betty's* in the parish; and with that he rose up and brush'd off.[2]

No, *says the eldest sister*, I dare answer for my brother, he knows the world better.

Thus the discourse ended; but it left *the elder brother* quite confounded: he concluded his brother had made a full discovery, and he began to doubt, whether I had been concern'd in it, or not; but with all his management, he could not bring it about to get at me; at last, he was so perplex'd, that he was quite desperate, and resolv'd he wou'd come into my chamber and see me, whatever came of it: in order to this, he contriv'd it so; that one day after dinner, watching *his eldest sister*, till he could see her go up stairs, he runs after her, *Hark ye sister, says he*, where is this sick woman? May not a body see her? YES, *says the sister*, I believe you may, but let me go first a little, and I'll tell you; so she run up to the door, and gave me notice; and presently call'd to him again: BROTHER, *says she*, you may come if you please; so in he came, just in the same kind of rant: Well, *says he*, at the door *as he came in*, where is this sick body that's in love? How do ye do Mrs. *Betty*? I would have got up out of my chair, but was so weak I could not for a good while; and he saw it and his sister too, and she said, *Come do not strive to stand up*, my brother desires no ceremony, especially, now you are so weak. NO, NO, Mrs. *Betty*, pray sit still *says he*, and so sits himself down in a chair over-against me, and appear'd as if he was mighty merry.

He talk'd a deal of rambling stuff to his sister, and to me; sometimes of one thing, sometimes of another, on purpose to amuse[3] his sister; and every now and then, would turn it upon the old story, directing it to me: Poor Mrs. *Betty, says he*, it is a sad thing to be in love, why it has reduced you sadly; at last I spoke a little, I am glad to see you so merry, sir, *says I*, but I think the doctor might have found some thing better to do, than to make his game at his patients: if I had been ill of no other distemper, I know the proverb too well to have let him come to me: What proverb *says he*? O! I remember it now: what,

---

1 That is, do not attempt to pass off your stories upon me by deceit.
2 Departed hastily.
3 Delude, deceive.

Where love is the case,
The doctor's an ass.[1]

Is not that it Mrs. *Betty?* I smil'd, and said nothing: Nay, *says he,* I think the effect has prov'd it to be love; for it seems the doctor has been able to do you but little service, you mend very slowly they say, I doubt there's somewhat in it Mrs. *Betty,* I doubt[2] you are sick of the incureables, and that is love; I smil'd and said, No, *indeed sir,* that's none of my distemper.

We had a deal of such discourse, and sometimes others that signify'd as little; by and by he ask'd me to sing them a song; at which I smil'd, and said, my singing days were over: at last he ask'd me, if he should play upon his flute to me; his sister said, she believ'd it wou'd hurt me, and that my head could not bear it; I bow'd and said, No, it would not hurt me: And pray madam, *said I,* do not hinder it, I love the musick of the flute very much; then his sister said, Well do then brother; with that he pull'd out the key of his closet, Dear sister, *says he,* I am very lazy, do step to my closet and fetch my flute, it lies in *such a drawer,* naming a place where he was sure it was not, that she might be a little while a looking for it.

As soon as she was gone, he related the whole story to me, of the discourse his brother had about me, and of his pushing it at him, and his concern about it, which was the reason of his contriving this visit to me: I assur'd him, I had never open'd my mouth either to his brother, or to any body else: I told him the dreadful exigence I was in; that my love to him, and his offering to have me forget that affection, and remove it to another, had thrown me down; and that I had a thousand times wish'd I might die, rather than recover, and to have the same circumstances to strugle with as I had before; and that this backwardness to life, had been the great reason of the slowness of my recovering: I added, that I foresaw, that as soon as I was well, I must quit the family; and that as for marrying his *brother,* I abhor'd the thoughts of it, after what had been my case with him, and that he might depend upon it, I would never see his brother again upon that subject: that if he would break all his vows and oaths, and engagements with me, be that between his conscience and his honour, and himself: but he should never be able to say, that I who he had persuaded to call

---

1 Among other sources, this saying is contained in Francisco de Quevedo y Villegas' *Vision* (trans. 1667) and John Ray's *A Collection of English Proverbs* (1678), both listed in Defoe's library.

2 Suspect, fear.

my self his wife, and who had given him the liberty to use me as a wife, was not as faithful to him as a wife ought to be, what ever he might be to me.

He was going to reply, and had said, that he was sorry I could not be persuaded, and was a going to say more, but he heard his sister a coming, and so did I; and yet I forc'd out these few words as a reply, that I could never be persuaded to love one brother, and marry another: he shook his head and said, *Then I am ruin'd*, meaning himself; and that moment his sister enter'd the room, and told him she could not find the flute; Well, *says he* merrily, this laziness won't do, so he gets up, and goes himself to go to look for it, but comes back without it too; not but that he could have found it, but because his mind was a little disturb'd, and he had no mind to play; and besides, the errand he sent his sister of, was answer'd another way; for he only wanted an opportunity to speak to me, which he gain'd, tho' not much to his satisfaction.

I had however, a great deal of satisfaction in having spoken my mind to him with freedom, and with such an honest plainess, as I have related; and tho' it did not at all work that way, I desir'd, *that is to say*, to oblige the person to me the more; yet it took from him all possibility of quiting me, but by a down right breach of honour, and giving up all the faith of a gentleman to me, which he had so often engaged by, never to abandon me, but to make me his wife as soon as he came to his estate.

It was not many weeks after this, before I was about the house again, and began to grow well; but I continu'd melancholly, silent, dull, and retir'd, which amaz'd the whole family, except he that knew the reason of it; yet it was a great while before he took any notice of it, and I *as backward to speak, as he*, carried[1] respectfully to him, but never offer'd to speak a word to him, that was particular of any kind whatsoever; and this continu'd for sixteen or seventeen weeks, so that as I expected every day to be dismiss'd the family, on account of what distaste they had taken another way, in which I had no guilt; so I expected to hear no more of this gentleman, after all his solemn vows, and protestations, but to be ruin'd and abandon'd.

At last I broke[2] the way myself in the family, for my removing; for being talking seriously with the old lady one day, about my own circumstances in the world, and how my distemper had left a

1 Behaved.
2 Opened.

heaviness upon my spirits, that I was not the same thing I was before: the old lady said, I am afraid *Betty*, what I have said to you, about my son, has had some influence upon you, and that you are melancholly on his account; pray will you let me know how the matter stands with you both? if it may not be improper, for as for *Robin*, he does nothing but rally and banter when I speak of it to him: Why truly madam, *said I*, that matter stands as I wish it did not, and I shall be very sincere with you in it, what ever befalls me for it, Mr. *Robert* has several times propos'd marriage to me, which is what I had no reason to expect, my poor circumstances consider'd; but I have always resisted him, and that perhaps in terms more positive than became me, considering the regard that I ought to have for every branch of your family: but *said I*, madam, I could never so far forget my obligations to you, and all your house, to offer to consent to a thing, which I know must needs be disobliging to you, and this I have made my argument to him, and have possitively told him, that I would never entertain a thought of that kind, unless I had your consent, and his fathers also, to whom I was bound by so many invincible obligations.

And is this possible Mrs. *Betty*, says the old lady? Then you have been much juster to us, than we have been to you; for we have all look'd upon you as a kind of a snare to my son; and I had a proposal to make to you, for your removing, for fear of it; but I had not yet mention'd it to you, because I thought you were not thorough well, and I was afraid of grieving you too much, lest it should thro' you down again, for we have all a respect for you still, tho' not so much, as to have it be the ruin of my son; but if it be as you say, we have all wrong'd you very much.

As to the truth of what I say, madam, *said I*, I refer you to your son himself, if he will do me any justice, he must tell you the story just as I have told it.

Away goes the old lady to her daughters, and tells them the whole story, just as I had told it her, and they were surpris'd at it, you may be sure, as I believ'd they would be; one *said*, she could never have thought it; another said, *Robin* was a fool, a *third* said, she would not believe a word of it, and she would warrant that *Robin* would tell the story another way; but the old gentlewoman, who was resolv'd to go to the bottom of it, before I could have the least opportunity of acquainting her son, with what had pass'd, resolv'd too, that she would talk with her son immediately, and to that purpose sent for him, for he was gone but to a lawyers house in the town, upon some petty business of his own, and upon her sending, he return'd immediately.

Upon his coming up to them, for they were all still together; Sit down *Robin, says the old lady,* I must have some talk with you; With all my heart, madam, *says Robin, looking very merry;* I hope it is about a good wife, for I am at a great loss in that affair: How can that be *says his mother,* did not you say, you resolved to have Mrs. *Betty?* Ay madam, says *Robin;* but there is one has *forbid the banns:*[1] Forbid the banns! *says his mother,* who can that be? Even Mrs. *Betty* herself, says *Robin.* How so, *says his mother,* have you ask'd her the question then? *Yes, indeed madam, says* Robin; I have attack'd her in form,[2] five times since she was sick, and am beaten off; the jade is so stout, she won't capitulate, nor yield upon any terms, except such as I cannot effectually grant: Explain your self, *says the mother,* for I am surpris'd, I do not understand you, I hope you are not in earnest.

Why, madam, *says he,* the case is plain enough upon me, it explains itself; she wont have me, *she says;* is not that plain enough? I think 'tis plain, and pretty rough too; Well but *says the mother,* you talk of conditions, that you cannot grant, what, does she want a settlement?[3] Her jointure ought to be according to her portion;[4] but what fortune does she bring you? Nay, as to fortune, *says* Robin, she is rich enough; I am satisfy'd in that point; but 'tis *I* that am not able to come up to her terms, and she is positive she will not have me without.

Here the sisters put in, Madam, *says the second sister,* 'tis impossible to be serious with him; he will never give a direct answer to any thing; you had better let him alone, and talk no more of it to him; you know how to dispose of her out of his way, if you thought there was any thing in it; *Robin* was a little warm'd with his sisters rudeness, but he was even with her; and yet with good manners too: There are two sorts of people, madam, *says he, turning to his mother,* that there is no contending with, that is a wise body and a fool, 'tis a little hard I should engage with both of them together.

The younger sister then put in, We must be fools indeed, *says she,* in my brother's opinion, that he should think we can believe,

---

1 Public notice given in church of an intended marriage, in order that those who know of any impediment thereto may lodge objections.
2 Proposed to her properly.
3 Marriage settlement (by which money or property is fixed between the couple).
4 That is, the annual income settled on a wife by her husband in case he predeceases her ("jointure") should be relative to the size of the dowry ("portion").

he has seriously ask'd Mrs. *Betty* to marry him, and that she has refus'd him.

Answer, and *answer not*, says *Solomon*,[1] *replyed her brother*: when your brother had said to your mother, that he had ask'd her no less than five times, and that it was so, that she positively denied him; methinks a younger sister need not question the truth of it, when her mother did not: My mother you see did not understand it, *says the second sister*: There's some difference *says* Robin, between desiring me to explain it, and telling me she did not believe it.

Well but son, *says the old lady*, if you are dispos'd to let us into the mystery of it, what were these hard conditions? Yes madam *says* Robin, I had done it before now, if the teazers here had not worried me by way of interruption: the conditions are, that I bring my father and you to consent to it, and without that, she protests she will never see me more upon that head; and these conditions *as I said*, I suppose I shall never be able to grant; I hope my warm sisters will be answer'd now, and blush a little; if not, I have no more to say till I hear farther.

This answer was surprizing to them all, tho' less to the mother, because of what I had said to her; as to the daughters they stood mute a great while; but the mother said with some passion, WELL, I had heard this before, *but I cou'd not believe it*; but if it is so, then we have all done BETTY wrong, and she has behav'd better than I ever expected: Nay, *says the eldest sister*, if it is so, she has acted handsomely indeed: I confess *says the mother*, it was none of her fault, if he was fool enough to take a fancy to her; but to give such an answer to him, shews more respect to your father and me, than I can tell how to express; I shall value the girl the better for it, as long as I know her. But I shall not *says* Robin, unless you will give your consent: I'll consider of that a while *says the mother*; I assure you, if there were not some other objections in the way, this conduct of hers would go a great way to bring me to consent: I wish it would go quite thro' with it, *says* Robin; if you had as much thought about making me easie,[2] as you have about making me rich, you would soon consent to it.

Why *Robin, says the mother again*, are you really in earnest? Would you so fain[3] have her as you pretend? Really madam *says*

---

1 Proverbs 26:4-5: "Answer not a fool according to his folly, lest you be like him yourself" and "Answer a fool according to his folly, lest he be wise in his own eyes."

2 Comfortable and without worry.

3 Gladly, willingly.

Robin, I think 'tis hard you should question me upon that head, after all I have said: I won't say that I will have her, how can I resolve that point, when you see I cannot have her without your consent? Besides I am not bound to marry at all: but this I will say, I am in earnest in, that I will never have any body else, if I can help it; so you may determine for me, *Betty*, or no body, is the word; and the question which of the two shall be in your breast to decide madam; provided only, that *my good humour'd sisters here, may have no vote in it.*

All this was dreadful to me, for the mother began to yield, and *Robin* press'd her home in it: on the other hand, she advised with the eldest son, and he used all the arguments in the world to persuade her to consent; alledging his brothers passionate love for me, and my generous regard to the family, in refusing my own advantages, upon such a nice point of honour, and a thousand such things: and as to the father, he was a man in a hurry of publick affairs, and getting money, seldom at home, thoughtful of the main chance;[1] but left all those things to his wife.

You may easily believe, that when the plot was thus, as *they thought* broke out,[2] and that every one thought they knew how things were carried: it was not so difficult, or so dangerous, for the elder brother, who no body suspected of any thing, to have a freer access to me than before: nay the mother, *which was just as he wish'd*, propos'd it to him to talk with Mrs. *Betty*; For it may be son *said she*, you may see farther into the thing than I; and see if you think she has been so positive as *Robin* says she has been, or no. This was as well as he could wish, and he as it were yielding to talk with me at his mother's request, she brought me to him into her own chamber; told me her son had some business with me at her request, and desir'd me to be very sincere with him; and then she left us together, and he went and shut the door after her.

He came back to me, and took me in his arms and kiss'd me very tenderly; but told me, he had a long discourse to hold with me, and it was now come to that crisis, that I should make my self happy or miserable, as long as I liv'd: that the thing was now gone so far, that if I could not comply with his desire, we should be both ruin'd: then he told me the whole story between *Robin*, as he call'd him, and his mother, and sisters, and himself; as it is above: And now dear child, *says he*, consider what it will be to marry a

---

1 That is, preoccupied with one's own interests (usually in regard to making money, etc.).
2 Revealed.

gentleman of a good family, in good circumstances, and with the consent of the whole house, and to enjoy all that the world can give you: and what on the other hand, to be sunk into the dark circumstances of a woman that has lost her reputation; and that tho' I shall be a private friend to you while I live, yet as I shall be suspected always; so you will be afraid to see me, and I shall be afraid to own you.

He gave me no time to reply, but went on with me thus: What has happen'd between us child, so long as we both agree to do so, may be buried and forgotten: I shall always be your sincere friend, without any inclination to nearer intimacy, when you become my sister; and we shall have all the honest part of conversation[1] without any reproaches between us, of having done amiss: I beg of you to consider it, and do not stand in the way of your own safety and prosperity; and to satisfie you that I am sincere, *added he,* I here offer you 500 *l.* in money, to make you some amends for the freedoms I have taken with you, which we shall look upon as some of the follies of our lives, which 'tis hop'd we may repent of.

He spoke this in so much more moving terms than it is possible for me to express, and with so much greater force of argument than I can repeat, that I only recommend it to those who read the story, to suppose, that as he held me above an hour and half in that discourse, so he answer'd all my objections, and fortified his discourse with all the arguments, that humane wit and art could devise.

I cannot say, however, that any thing he said, made impression enough upon me, so as to give me any thought of the matter; till he told me at last very plainly, that if I refus'd, he was sorry to add, that he could never go on with me in that station as we stood before; that tho' he lov'd me as well as ever, and that I was as agreeable to him, as ever; yet, sense of vertue had not so far forsaken him, as to suffer him to lye with a woman, that his brother courted to make his wife; and if he took his leave of me, with a denial in this affair; whatever he might do for me in the point of support, grounded on his first engagement of maintaining me, yet he would not have me be surpriz'd, that he was oblig'd to tell me, he could not allow himself to see me any more; and that indeed I could not expect it of him.

I receiv'd this last part with some tokens of surprize and disorder, and had much a do, to avoid sinking down, for indeed I lov'd

---

1   Close association, intimacy.

him to an extravagance, not easie to imagine; but he perceiv'd my disorder, he entreated me to consider seriously of it, assur'd me that it was the only way to preserve our mutual affection, that in this station we might love as friends, with the utmost passion, and with a love of relation untainted, free from our just reproaches, and free from other peoples suspicions; that he should ever acknowledge his happiness owing to me; that he would be debtor to me as long as he liv'd, and would be paying that debt as long as he had breath; thus he wrought me up, in short, to a kind of hesitation in the matter; having the dangers on one side represented in lively figures, and indeed heightn'd by my imagination of being turn'd out to the wide world, a meer cast off whore, *for it was no less*, and perhaps expos'd as such; with little to provide for myself; with no friend, no acquaintance in the whole world, *out of*[1] *that town*, and there I could not pretend to stay; all this terrify'd me to the last degree, and he took care upon all occasions to lay it home to me, in the worst colours that it could be possible to be drawn in; on the other hand, he fail'd not to set forth the easy prosperous life, which I was going to live.

He answer'd all that I could object from affection, and from former engagements, with telling me the necessity that was before us of taking other measures now; and as to his promises of marriage, the nature of things *he said*, had put an end to that, by the probability of my being his brothers wife, before the time to which his promises all referr'd.

Thus in a word, I may say, he reason'd me out of my reason; he conquer'd all my arguments, and I began to see a danger that I was in, which I had not consider'd of before, and that was of being drop'd by both of them, and left alone in the world to shift for myself.

This, and his perswasion, at length prevail'd with me to consent, tho' with so much reluctance, that it was easie to see I should go to church, like a bear to the stake;[2] I had some little apprehensions about me too, lest my new spouse, who by the way, I had not the least affection for, should be skilful enough to challenge me on another account, upon our first coming to bed together; but whether he did it with design, or not, I know not; but his elder brother took care to make him very much fuddled before he went

---

1 Outside.
2 With great reluctance (a common proverb drawn from the popular sport of bear-baiting).

to bed; so that I had the satisfaction of a drunken bedfellow the first night: how he did it I know not, but I concluded that he certainly contriv'd it, that his brother might be able to make no judgment of the difference between a maid and a married woman; nor did he ever entertain any notions of it, or disturb his thoughts about it.

I should go back a little here, to where I left off; the elder brother, having thus manag'd me, his next business was to manage his mother, and he never left till he had brought her to acquiesce, and be passive in the thing; even without acquainting the father, other than by post letters: so that she consented to our marrying privately, and leaving her to manage the father afterwards.

Then he cajol'd with his brother, and perswaded him what service he had done him, and how he had brought his mother to consent, which *tho' true*, was not indeed done to serve him, but to serve himself; but thus diligently did he cheat him, and had the thanks of a faithful friend for shifting off his whore into his brothers arms for a wife. So certainly does interest banish all manner of affection, and so naturally do men give up honour and justice, humanity, and even Christianity, to secure themselves.

I must now come back to brother *Robin*, as we always call'd him; who having got his mother's consent *as above*, came big[1] with the news to me, and told me the whole story of it, with a sincerity so visible, that I must confess it griev'd me, that I must be the instrument to abuse so honest a gentleman; but there was no remedy, he would have me, and I was not oblig'd to tell him, that I was his brother's whore, tho' I had no other way to put him off; so I came gradually into it, to his satisfaction, and behold, we were married.

Modesty forbids me to reveal the secrets of the marriage bed, but nothing could have happen'd more suitable to my circumstances than that, *as above*, my husband was so fuddled when he came to bed, that he could not remember in the morning, whether he had had any conversation[2] with me or no, and I was oblig'd to tell him *he had*, tho' in reallity *he had not*, that I might be sure he could make no enquiry about any thing else.

It concerns the story in hand very little, to enter into the farther particulars of the family, or of myself, for the five years that I liv'd with this husband; only to observe that I had two children by him,

1 Full of (literally, pregnant).
2 Sexual intercourse.

and that at the end of five year he died: he had been really a very good husband to me, and we liv'd very agreeably together; but as he had not receiv'd much from them, and had in the little time he liv'd acquir'd no great matters, so my circumstances were not great; nor was I much mended[1] by the match: indeed I had preserv'd the elder brother's bonds to me, to pay me 500 *l.* which he offer'd me for my consent to marry his brother; and this with what I had saved of the money he formerly gave me, and about as much more by my husband, left me a widow with about 1200 *l.* in my pocket.

My two children were indeed taken happily off of my hands, by my husband's father and mother, and that by the way was all they got by Mrs. *Betty.*

I confess I was not suitably affected with the loss of my husband; nor indeed can I say, that I ever lov'd him as I ought to have done, or as was proportionable to the good usage I had from him, for he was a tender, kind, good humour'd man as any woman could desire; but his brother being so always in my sight, *at least,* while we were in the country, was a continual snare to me; and I never was in bed with my husband, but I wish'd my self in the arms of his brother; and tho' his brother never offer'd me the least kindness that way, after our marriage, but carried it just as a brother ought to do; yet, it was impossible for me to do so to him: in short, I committed adultery and incest with him every day in my desires, which without doubt, was as effectually criminal in the nature of the guilt, as if I had actually done it.[2]

Before my husband died, his elder brother was married, and we being then remov'd to *London,* were written to by the old lady to come, and be at the wedding; my husband went, but I pretended indisposition, and that I could not possibly travel, so I staid behind; for in short, I could not bear the sight of his being given to another woman, tho' I knew I was never to have him my self.

I was now *as above,* left loose to the world, and being still young and handsome, as every body said of me, *and I assure you, I thought my self so,* and with a tollerable fortune in my pocket, I put no small value upon my self: I was courted by several very considerable tradesmen; and particularly, very warmly by one, a *linnen-*

---

1 Financially improved.
2 Elsewhere in his writings Defoe refers to this form of adultery, such as in *An Essay on the History and Reality of Apparitions* (1727): a woman is told that by loving a married man she "had intentionally committed Whoredom with him ... " (chap. 10). Also see Appendix A.7.

draper, at whose house after my husband's death I took a lodging, his sister being my acquaintance; here I had all the liberty, and all the opportunity to be gay, and appear in company that I could desire; my landlord's sister being one of the madest, gayest things alive, and not so much mistress of her vertue, as I thought at first she had been: she brought me into a world of wild company, and even brought home several persons, *such as she lik'd well enough to gratifie*, to see her pretty widow, *so she was pleas'd to call me*, and that name I got in a little time in publick; now as fame and fools make an assembly, I was here wonderfully caress'd;[1] had abundance of admirers, and such as call'd themselves *lovers*; but I found not one fair proposal among them all; as for their common design, that I understood too well to be drawn into any more snares of that kind: the case was alter'd with me, I had money in my pocket, and had nothing to say to them: I had been trick'd once by *that cheat call'd* LOVE, but the game was over; I was resolv'd now to be married, or nothing, and to be well married, or not at all.

I lov'd the company indeed of men of mirth and wit, men of gallantry and figure, and was often entertain'd with such, as I was also with others; but I found by just observation, that the brightest men came upon the dullest errand, *that is to say*, the dullest, as to what I aim'd at; on the other hand, those who came with the best proposals, were the dullest and most disagreeable part of the world: I was not averse to a tradesman, but then I would have a tradesman forsooth, that was something of a gentleman too; that when my husband had a mind to carry me to the court, or to the play, he might become a sword,[2] and look as like a gentleman, as another man; and not be one that had the mark of his apron-strings upon his coat, or the mark of his hat upon his perriwig; that should look as if he was set on to his sword, when his sword was put on to him, and that carried his trade in his countenance.

Well, at last I found this amphibious creature, this *land-water-thing*, call'd, *a gentleman-tradesman*; and as a just plague upon my folly, I was catch'd in the very snare, which *as I might say*, I laid for my self; *I say laid for my self*, for I was not trepan'd[3] I confess, but I betray'd my self.

This was a *draper* too, for tho' my comrade would have brought me to a bargain with her brother; yet when it came to the point, it

---

1 Flattered, sought after.
2 That is, wear a sword well.
3 Tricked, ensnared.

was it seems for a mistress, not a wife, and I kept true to this notion, that a woman should never be kept for a mistress, that had money to keep her self.

Thus my pride, not my principle, my money, not my vertue, kept me honest; tho' as it prov'd, I found I had much better have been sold by my *she comrade* to her brother, than have sold my self as I did to a tradesman, that was rake, gentleman, shop keeper, and beggar all together.

But I was hurried on (by my fancy to a gentleman) to ruin my self in the grossest manner that ever woman did; for my new husband coming to a lump of money at once, fell into such a profusion of expence, that all I had, and all he had before, if he had any thing worth mentioning, would not have held it out above one year.

He was very fond of me for about a quarter of a year, and what I got by that, was, that I had the pleasure of seeing a great deal of my money spent upon my self, and as I may say, had some of the spending it too: Come, my dear, *says he to me one day*, shall we go and take a turn into the country for about a week? Ay, my dear, *says I*, whither would you go? I care not whither *says he*, but I have a mind to look like quality for a week; we'll go to OXFORD *says he*: How *says I*, shall we go, I am no horse woman, and 'tis too far for a coach; Too far *says he*, no place is too far for a coach and six: if I carry you out, you shall travel like a dutchess; Hum *says I*, my dear 'tis a frolick, but if you have a mind to it I don't care. Well the time was appointed, we had a rich coach, very good horses, a coachman, postilion,[1] and two footmen in very good liveries;[2] a gentleman on horseback, and a page with a feather in his hat upon another horse; the servants all call'd him my lord, and the innkeepers you may be sure did the like, and I was *her honour*, the Countess; and thus we travel'd to OXFORD, and a very pleasant journey we had; for, give him his due, not a beggar alive knew better how to be a lord than my husband: we saw all the rareties at OXFORD,[3] talk'd with two or three fellows of colleges, about putting out a young nephew, that was left to his lordship's care to the university, and of their being his tutors; we diverted our selves

---

1 One who rides the near horse of the leaders to guide the horses drawing a coach. (Also *postillion*.)
2 The distinctive dress worn by a person's servants, etc.
3 Among these rareties Defoe was probably thinking of the Ashmolean Museum, which opened in 1682 (well after Moll's visit but years before the composition of the novel).

with bantering several other poor scholars, with hopes of being at least his lordship's chaplains and putting on a scarf;[1] and thus having liv'd like quality indeed, as to expence; we went away for *Northampton*, and in a word, in about twelve days ramble came home again, to the tune of about 93 *l.* expence.

Vanity is the perfection of a fop;[2] my husband had this excellence, that he valued nothing of expence, and as his history you may be sure, has very little weight[3] in it; 'tis enough to tell you, that in about two years and a quarter he broke,[4] and was not so happy to get over into the *Mint*,[5] but got into a *spunging-house*,[6] being arrested in an action too heavy for him to give bail to, so he sent for me to come to him.

It was no surprize to me, for I had foreseen *sometime*, that all was going to wreck, and had been taking care to reserve something if I could, *tho' it was not much* for myself: but when he sent for me, he behav'd much better than I expected, and told me plainly, he had plaid the fool and suffer'd himself to be surpriz'd which he might have prevented; that now he foresaw he could not stand it, and therefore he would have me go home, and in the night take away every thing I had in the house of any value and secure it; and after that, he told me, that if I could get away 100 *l.* or 200 *l.* in goods out of the shop, I should do it, Only *says he,* let me know nothing of it, neither what you take, or whither you carry it; for as for me *says he,* I am resolv'd to get out of this house and be gone; and if you never hear of me more, my dear, *says he,* I wish you well; I am only sorry for the injury I have done you: he said some very handsome things to me indeed at parting; for *I told you* he was a *gentleman,* and that was all the benefit I had of his being so; that he used me very handsomely, and with good manners upon all occasions, even to the last, only spent all I had, and left me to rob the creditors for something to subsist on.

However, I did as he bad me, *that you may be sure,* and having thus taken my leave of him, I never saw him more; for he found

1 Part of the clerical costume worn by a nobleman's chaplain.
2 A vain, affected man who is preoccupied with his clothes, manners, etc.
3 Substance, value.
4 Became bankrupt.
5 An area in Southwark, across the River Thames from London, which provided sanctuary for debtors. Its status as such was the subject of much contemporary concern, leading to parliamentary action in 1723.
6 A place, traditionally near a prison, kept by a bailiff or sheriff's officer in which newly-arrested debtors were confined. (Also *sponging-house.*)

means to break out of the bailiff's house that night, or the next, and got over into *France*;[1] and for the rest, the creditors scrambl'd for it as well as they could: how I knew not, for I could come at no knowledge of any thing, more than this; that he came home about three a clock in the morning, caus'd the rest of his goods to be remov'd into the *Mint*, and the shop to be shut up; and having rais'd what money he could get together, he got over as I said to *France*, from whence I had one or two letters from him, and no more.

I did not see him when he came home, for he having given me such instructions as above, and I having made the best of my time; I had no more business back again at the house, not knowing but I might have been stop'd there by the creditors; for a *Commission of Bankrupt*,[2] being soon after issued, they might have stop'd me by orders from the commissioners: but my husband having so dextrously got out of the bailiff's house by letting himself down in a most desperate manner, from almost the top of the house, to the top of another building, and leaping from thence which was almost two stories, and which was enough indeed to have broken his neck: he came home and got away his goods, before the creditors could come to seize, *that is to say*, before they could get out the commission, and be ready to send their officers to take possession.

My husband was so civil to me, *for still I say, he was much of a gentleman*, that in the first letter he wrote me from *France*, he let me know where he had pawn'd 20 pieces of fine *Holland* for 30 *l.* which were really worth above 90 *l.* and enclos'd me the token, and an order for the taking them up, paying the money, which I did, and made in time above 100 *l.* of them, having leisure to cut them and sell them, some and some,[3] to private families, as opportunity offer'd.

However with all this, and all that I had secur'd before, I found upon casting things up, my case was very much alter'd, and my fortune much lessen'd, for including the Hollands, and a parcel of fine muslins, which I carry'd off before, and some plate, and other

---

1 In the *Review* (1 March 1709), Defoe deplores the fact that over 5,000 debtors, "who being made desperate by the Cruelty of Creditors," were forced to flee the country.

2 The legal authorization, received by the creditors from the appointed commissioners, to seize and distribute (through officers) the goods of the bankrupt.

3 Bit by bit.

things; I found I could hardly muster up 500 *l.* and my condition was very odd, for tho' I had no child, (*I had had one by my gentleman draper, but it was buried,*) yet I was a widow bewitch'd, I had a husband, and no husband, and I could not pretend[1] to marry again, tho' I knew well enough my husband would never see *England* any more, if he liv'd fifty years: *thus I say*, I was limitted from marriage,[2] what offer soever might be made me: and I had not one friend to advise with, in the condition I was in, at least not one I durst trust the secret of my circumstances to, for if the commissioners were to have been inform'd where I was, I should have been fetch'd up, and examin'd upon oath, and all I had sav'd be taken away from me.

Upon these apprehensions the first thing I did, was to go quite out of my knowledge,[3] and go by another name: this I did effectually, for I went into the *Mint* too, took lodgings in a very private place, drest me up in the habit of a widow, and call'd myself Mrs. *Flanders.*

Here, however I conceal'd myself, and tho' my new acquaintances knew nothing of me, yet I soon got a great deal of company about me; and whether it be that women are scarce among the sorts of people that generally are to be found there; or that some consolation in the miseries of the place, are more requisite than on other occasions; I soon found an agreeable woman was exceedingly valuable among the sons of affliction[4] there; and that those that wanted money to pay half a crown in the pound to their creditors, and that run in debt at the sign of the *Bull*[5] for their dinners, would yet find money for a supper, if they lik'd the woman.

However, I kept myself safe yet, tho' I began like my Lord *Rochester's* mistress,[6] that lov'd his company, but would not admit him farther, to have the scandal of a whore, without the joy; and upon this score tir'd with the place and indeed with the company too, I began to think of removing.

---

1 Venture, attempt.
2 Although the Church of England forbade remarriage after separation or divorce, many Puritan (and some Anglican) divines argued that it ought to be allowed under certain conditions.
3 That is, beyond where she was known.
4 See Proverbs 31:5-9.
5 This inn, with its identifying sign, is probably the one described in William Rendle and Philip Norman, *The Inns of Old Southwark and their Associations* (London, 1888) 262-67.
6 Moll is recalling lines from "Song," a lyric by John Wilmot, second Earl of Rochester (1647-80), in which he urges Phyllis not to "Dye with the scandal of a Whore, And never know the joy."

It was indeed a subject of strange reflection to me, to see men who were overwhelm'd in perplex'd circumstances; who were reduc'd some degrees below being ruin'd; whose families were objects of their own terror and other peoples charity; yet while a penny lasted, nay, even beyond it, endeavouring to drown their sorrow in their wickedness; heaping up more guilt upon themselves, labouring to forget former things, which now it was the proper time to remember, making more work for repentance, and sinning on, as a remedy for sin past.

But it is none of my talent to preach; these men were too wicked, even for me; there was something horrid and absurd in their way of sinning, for it was all a force even upon themselves; they did not only act against conscience, but against nature; they put a rape upon their temper to drown the reflections, which their circumstances continually gave them; and nothing was more easie than to see how sighs would interrupt their songs, and paleness, and anguish sit upon their brows, in spight of the forc'd smiles they put on; nay, sometimes it would break out at their very mouths, when they had parted with their money for a lewd treat, or a wicked embrace; I have heard them, turning about, fetch a deep sigh, and cry *What a dog am I!* Well *Betty*, my dear, I'll drink thy health tho', *meaning the honest wife,* that perhaps had not a half a crown for herself, and three or four children: the next morning they are at their penitentials again, and perhaps the poor weeping wife comes over to him, either brings him some account of what his creditors are doing, and how she and the children are turn'd out of doors, or some other dreadful news; and this adds to his self reproaches; but when he has thought and por'd on it till he is almost mad, having no principles to support him, nothing within him, or above him, to comfort him; but finding it all darkness on every side, he flyes to the same relief again, (*viz.*) to drink it away, debauch it away, and falling into company of men in just the same condition with himself, he repeats the crime, and thus he goes every day one step onward of his way to destruction.

I was not wicked enough for such fellows as these *yet;* on the contrary, I began to consider here *very seriously* what I had to do; how things stood with me, and what course I ought to take: I knew I had no friends, no not one friend, or relation in the world; and that little I had left apparently wasted, which when it was gone, I saw nothing but misery and starving was before me: upon these considerations, I say, and fill'd with horror at the place I was in, and the dreadful objects, which I had always before me, *I resolv'd to be gone.*

I had made an acquaintance with a very sober good sort of a woman, who was a widow too like me, but in better circumstances; her husband had been a captain of a merchant ship, and having had the misfortune to be cast away coming home on a voyage from the *West-Indies*, which would have been very profitable, if he had come safe; was so reduc'd by the loss, that tho' he had saved his life then, it broke his heart, and kill'd him afterwards, and his widow being persued by the creditors was forc'd to take shelter in the *Mint*: she soon made things up with the help of friends, and was at liberty again; and finding that I rather was there to be conceal'd, than by any particular prosecutions, and finding also that I agreed with her, *or rather she with me* in a just abhorrence of the place, and of the company; she invited me to go home with her, till I could put myself in some posture of settling in the world to my mind; withal telling me, that it was ten to one, but some good captain of a ship might take a fancy to me, and court me, in that part of the town where she liv'd.

I accepted her offer, and was with her half a year, and should have been longer; but in that interval what she propos'd to me happen'd to herself, and she marry'd very much to her advantage; but whose fortune soever was upon the encrease, mine seem'd to be upon the wane, and I found nothing present, except two or three boatswains,[1] or such fellows, but as for the commanders they were generally of two sorts. I. Such as having good business, *that is to say*, a good ship, resolved not to marry, but with advantage, that is, with a good fortune. 2. Such as being out of employ, wanted a wife to help them to a ship, I mean. (I.) a wife, who having some money could enable them to hold, as they call it, a good part of a ship themselves, so to encourage owners to come in; or. (2.) a wife who if she had not money, had friends who were concern'd in shipping, and so could help to put the young man into a good ship, which to them is as good as a portion, and neither of these was my case; so I look'd like one that was to *lye on hand*.[2]

This knowledge I soon learnt by experience, (*viz.*) that the state of things was altered, as to matrimony, and that I was not to expect at *London*, what I had found in the country; that marriages were here the consequences of politick schemes, for forming interests, and carrying on business, and that LOVE had no share, or but very little in the matter.

---

1 A ship's officer who has charge of the deck crew, sails, rigging, etc.
2 Be disposed of.

That, as my sister in law, at *Colchester* had said; beauty, wit, manners, sence, good humour, good behaviour, education, vertue, piety, or any other qualification, whether of body or mind, had no power to recomend: that money only made a woman agreeable: that men chose mistresses indeed by the gust of their affection, and it was requisite to a whore to be handsome, well shap'd, have a good mein,[1] and a graceful behaviour; but that for a wife, no deformity would shock the fancy, no ill qualities, the judgement; the money was the thing; the portion was neither crooked, or monstrous, but the money was always agreeable, whatever the wife was.

On the other hand, as the market run very unhappily on the mens side, I found the women had lost the privilege of saying NO, that it was a favour now for a woman to have THE QUESTION ask'd, and if any young lady had so much arrogance as to counterfeit a negative, she never had the opportunity given her of denying twice; much less of recovering that false step, and accepting what she had but seem'd to decline: the men had such choice every where, that the case of the women was very unhapy; for they seem'd to plie at every door, and if the man was by great chance refus'd at one house, he was sure to be receiv'd at the next.

Besides this, I observ'd that the men made no scruple to set themselves out, and to go a fortune hunting, *as they call it*, when they had really no fortune themselves to demand it, or merit to deserve it; and that they carry'd it so high,[2] that a woman was scarce allow'd to enquire after the character, or estate of the person that pretended to her. This, I had an example of, in a young lady at the next house to me, and with whom I had contracted an intimacy; she was courted by a young captain, and though she had near 2000 *l.* to her fortune, she did but enquire of some of his neighbours about his character, his morals, or substance; and he took occasion at the next visit to let her know, truly, that he took it very ill, and that he should not give her the trouble of his visits any more: I heard of it, and as I had begun my acquaintance with her, I went to see her upon it: she enter'd into a close conversation with me about it, and unbosom'd herself very freely; I perceiv'd presently that tho' she thought herself very ill us'd, yet she had no power to resent it, and was exceedingly piqu'd that she had lost him, and particularly that another of less fortune had gain'd him.

---

1 Bearing, manner (spelled *mien*).
2 That is, they behaved with such arrogance.

I fortify'd her mind against such a meanness, *as I call'd it*; I told her, that as low as I was in the world, I would have despis'd a man that should think I ought to take him upon his own recommendation only, without having the liberty to inform myself of his fortune, and of his character; also *I told her*, that as she had a good fortune, she had no need to stoop to the dissaster of the times; that it was enough that the men could insult us that had but little money to recommend us; but if she suffer'd such an affront to pass upon her without resenting it, she would be render'd low-priz'd upon all occasions, and would be the contempt of all the women in that part of the town; that a woman can never want an opportunity to be reveng'd of a man that has us'd her ill and that there were ways enough to humble such a fellow as that, or else certainly women were the most unhappy creatures in the world.

I found she was very well pleas'd with the discourse, and she told me seriously that she would be very glad to make him sensible of her just resentment, and either to bring him on again, or have the satisfaction of her revenge being as publick as possible.

I told her, that if she would take my advice, I would tell her how she should obtain her wishes in both those things; and that I would engage I would bring the man to her door again, and make him beg to be let in: *she smil'd at that*, and soon let me see, that if he came to her door, her resentment was not so great as to give her leave to let him stand long there.

However, she lissened very willingly to my offer of advice; so *I told her*, that the first thing she ought to do, was a piece of justice to herself; namely, that whereas she had been told by several people, that he had reported among the ladies, that he had left her, and pretended to give the advantage of the negative to himself; she should take care to have it well spread among the women, which she could not fail of an opportunity to do in a neighbourhood, so addicted to family news, as that she liv'd in was; that she had enquired into his circumstances, and found he was not the man as to estate he pretended to be: let them be told madam, *said I*, that you had been well inform'd that he was not the man that you expected, and that you thought it was not safe to meddle with him, that you heard he was of an ill temper, and that he boasted how he had us'd the women ill upon many occasions, and that particularly he was debauch'd in his morals, *&c.* The last of which indeed had some truth in it; but at the same time, I did not find that she seem'd to like him much the worse for that part.

As I had put this into her head, she came most readily into it; immediately she went to work to find instruments, and she had very little difficulty in the search; for telling her story in general to a couple of gossips in the neighbourhood, it was the chat of the tea table all over that part of the town, and I met with it where ever I visited: also, as it was known that I was acquainted with the young lady herself, my opinion was ask'd very often, and I confirm'd it with all the necessary aggravations, and set out his character in the blackest colours; but then as a piece of secret intelligence, I added, as what the other gossips knew nothing of (*viz.*) that I had heard he was in very bad circumstances; that he was under a necessity of a fortune to support his interest with the owners of the ship he commanded: that his own part was not paid for, and if it was not paid quickly his owners would put him out of the ship, and his chief mate was likely to command it, who offer'd to buy that part which the captain had promis'd to take.

I added, for I confess I was heartily piqu'd at the rogue, *as I call'd him*, that I had heard a rumour too, that he had a wife alive at *Plymouth*, and another in the *West Indies*, a thing which they all knew was not very uncommon for such kind of gentlemen.

This work'd as we both desir'd it, for presently the young lady at next door, *who had a father and mother that govern'd, both her, and her fortune*, was shut up, and her father forbid him the house: also in one place more where he went, the woman had the courage, *however strange it was*, to say No, and he could try no where but he was reproached with his pride, and that he pretended not to give the women leave to enquire into his character, *and the like.*

Well, by this time he began to be sensible of his mistake, and having allarm'd[1] all the women on that side the water, he went over to *Ratcliff*[2] and got access to some of the ladies there; but tho' the young women there too, were according to the fate of the day, pretty willing to be ask'd, yet such was his ill luck, that his character follow'd him over the water, and his good name was much the same there, as it was on our side; so that tho' he might have had wives enough, yet it did not happen among the women that had good fortunes, which was what he wanted.

But this was not all, she very ingeniously manag'd another thing her self, for she got a young gentleman, who was a relation, and was indeed a marry'd man, to come and visit her two or three times a week in a very fine chariot and good liveries, and her two agents and I also, presently spread a report all over, that this

---

1 Aroused to a sense of danger (through his behaviour, etc.).
2 A village in the parish of Stepney on the north bank of the Thames.

gentleman came to court her; that he was a gentleman of a thousand pounds a year, and that he was fallen in love with her, and that she was going to her aunt's in the city, because it was inconvenient for the gentleman to come to her with his coach in *Redriff*[1] the streets being so narrow and difficult.

This took immediately, the captain was laugh'd at in all companies, and was ready to hang himself; he tryed all the ways possible to come at her again, and wrote the most passionate letters to her in the world, excusing his former rashness, and in short, by great application, obtained leave to wait on her again, *as he said*, to clear his reputation.

At this meeting she had her full revenge of him; for *she told him* she wondred what he took her to be, that she should admit any man to a treaty of so much consequence, as that of marriage, without enquiring very well into his circumstances; that if he thought she was to be huff'd[2] into wedlock, and that she was in the same circumstances which her neighbours might be in, (*viz.*) to take up with the first good Christian that came, he was mistaken; that in a word his character was really bad, or he was very ill beholding to his neighbours; and that unless he could clear up some points, in which she had justly been prejudiced, she had no more to say to him, but to do herself justice, and give him the satisfaction of knowing, that she was not afraid to say No, either to him, or any man else.

With that she told him what she had heard, *or rather rais'd*[3] *herself by my means, of his character*; his not having paid for the part he pretended to own of the ship he commanded; of the resolution of his owners to put him out of the command, and to put his mate in his stead; and of the scandal rais'd on his morals; his having been reproach'd with such and such women; and his having a wife at *Plymouth* and in the *West-Indies, and the like*; and she ask'd him, whether he could deny that she had good reason, if these things were not clear'd up, to refuse him, and in the mean time to insist upon having satisfaction in points so significant as they were?

He was so confounded at her discourse that he could not answer a word, and she almost began to believe that all was true, by his disorder, tho' at the same time she knew that she had been the raiser of all those reports herself.

---

1 An area on the south bank of the River Thames, commonly inhabited (like Ratcliff) by seamen.
2 Bullied, hectored.
3 Stirred up (damaging reports).

After some time he recover'd himself a little, and from that time became the most humble, the most modest, and the most importunate man alive in his courtship.

She carried her jest on a great way, she ask'd him, if he thought she was so at her last shift,[1] that she could or ought to bear such treatment, and if he did not see that she did not want[2] those who thought it worth their while to come farther to her than he did, meaning the gentleman who she had brought to visit her by way of sham.

She brought him by these tricks to submit to all possible measures to satisfie her, as well of his circumstances, as of his behaviour. He brought her undeniable evidence of his having paid for his part of the ship; he brought her certificates from his owners, that the report of their intending to remove him from the command of the ship, and put his chief mate in, was false and groundless; in short, he was quite the reverse of what he was before.

Thus I convinc'd her, that if the men made their advantage of our sex in the affair of marriage, upon the supposition of there being such choice to be had, and of the women being so easie; it was only owing to this, that the women wanted courage to maintain their ground, and to play their part; and that according to my Lord *Rochester*,

A woman's ne'er so ruin'd but she can
Revenge herself on her undoer, man.[3]

After these things, this young lady plaid her part so well, that tho' she resolved to have him, and that indeed having him was the main bent of her design, yet she made his obtaining her be TO HIM the most difficult thing in the world; and this she did, not by a haughty reserv'd carriage,[4] but by a just policy, turning the tables upon him, and playing back upon him his own game; for as he pretended by a kind of lofty carriage, to place himself above the occasion of a character,[5] and to make enquiring into his character a kind of an affront to him; she broke with him upon that subject; and at the same time that she made him submit to all possible

---

1 Resort, expedient.
2 Lack.
3 Rochester, "A Letter from Artemisia in the Town to Chloe in the Country" (somewhat misquoted). See above, p. 94, n. 6.
4 Behaviour, deportment.
5 That is, the need of a report on his character.

enquiry after his affairs, she apparently shut the door against his looking into her own.

It was enough to him to obtain her for a wife, as to what she had, she told him plainly, that as he knew her circumstances, it was but just she should know his; and tho' at the same time he had only known her circumstances by common fame, yet he had made so many protestations of his passion for her, that he could ask no more but her hand to his grand request, *and the like ramble*[1] *according to the custom of lovers*: in short, he left himself no room to ask any more questions about her estate, and she took the advantage of it like a prudent woman, for she plac'd part of her fortune so in trustees, without letting him know any thing of it, that it was quite out of his reach, and made him be very well content with the rest.

It is true she was pretty well besides, that is to say, she had about 1400 *l.* in money, which she gave him, and the other, after some time, she brought to light, as a perquisite to her self; which he was to accept as a mighty favour, seeing though it was not to be his, it might ease him in the article[2] of her particular expences; and I must add, that by this conduct the gentleman himself became not only the more humble in his applications to her to obtain her, but also was much the more an obliging husband to her when he had her: I cannot but remind the ladies here how much they place themselves below the common station of a wife, which if I may be allow'd not to be partial is low enough already; *I say* they place themselves below their common station, and prepare their own mortifications, by their submitting so to be insulted by the men before-hand, which I confess I see no necessity of.

This relation may serve therefore to let the ladies see, that the advantage is not so much on the other side, as the men think it is; and tho' it may be true, that the men have but too much choice among us; and that some women may be found, who will dishonour themselves, be cheap, and easy to come at, and will scarce wait to be ask'd; yet if they will have women, *as I may say*, worth having, they may find them as uncomatable[3] as ever; and that those that are otherwise, are a sort of people that have such defficiencies, *when had*, as rather recommend the ladies that are difficult than encourage the men to go on with their easie courtship, and expect wives equally valluable that will come at first call.

---

1 Empty, clichéd speech.
2 Terms (of agreement).
3 Unattainable, inaccessible. (Also *uncomeatable*, as in second edition.)

Nothing is more certain, than that the ladies always gain of the men, by keeping their ground, and letting their pretended lovers see they can resent being slighted, and that they are not affraid of saying No. They, I observe insult us mightily, with telling us of the number of women; that the wars and the sea, and trade, and other incidents have carried the men so much away, that there is no proportion between the numbers of the sexes; and therefore the women have the disadvantage; but I am far from granting that the number of the women is so great, or the number of the men so small; but if they will have me tell the truth, the disadvantage of the women, is a terrible scandal upon the men, and it lyes here, and here only; *namely*, that the age is so wicked, and the sex so debauch'd, that in short the number of such men, as an honest woman ought to meddle with, is small indeed, and it is but here and there that a man is to be found who is fit for a woman to venture upon.

But the consequence even of that too amounts to no more than this; that women ought to be the more nice;[1] for how do we know the just[2] character of the man that makes the offer? To say, that the woman should be the more easie on this occasion, is to say, we should be the forwarder to venture, because of the greatness of the danger; which in my way of reasoning is very absurd.

On the contrary, the women have ten thousand times the more reason to be wary, and backward, by how much the hazard of being betray'd is the greater; and would the ladies consider this, and act the wary part, they would discover every cheat that offer'd; for, *in short*, the lives of very few men now a-days will bear a character; and if the ladies do but make a little enquiry, they will soon be able to distinguish the men, and deliver[3] themselves: as for women that do not think their own safety worth their thought, that impatient of their present state, resolve *as they call it* to take the first good Christian that comes; that runs into matrimony, as a horse rushes into the battle; I can say nothing to them, but this, that they are a sort of ladies that are to be pray'd for among the rest of distemper'd people; and to me they look like people that venture their whole estates in a lottery[4] where there is a hundred thousand blanks to one prize.

---

1 Difficult to please, fastidious.
2 Exact, precise.
3 Save.
4 From 1694 to 1826 state lotteries were held at intervals to raise money for public works. This system encouraged gambling even among the poor and led to profiteering by unscrupulous ticket-mongers.

No man of common sense will value a woman the less, for not giving up herself at the first attack, or for not accepting his proposal without enquiring into his person or character; on the contrary, he must think her the weakest of all creatures in the world, as the rate of men now goes; in short, he must have a very contemptible opinion of her capacities, nay, even of her understanding, that having but one cast for her life, shall cast that life away at once, and make matrimony like death, be *a leap in the dark.*

I would fain have the conduct of my sex a little regulated in this particular, which is the thing, in which of all the parts of life, I think at this time we suffer most in: 'tis nothing but lack of courage, the fear of not being marry'd at all, and of that frightful state of life, call'd *an old maid*; of which I have a story to tell by itself: this I say, is the woman's snare; but would the ladies once but get above that fear, and manage rightly, they would more certainly avoid it by standing their ground, in a case so absolutely necessary to their felicity, than by exposing themselves as they do; and if they did not marry so soon as they may do otherwise, they would make themselves amends by marrying safer; she is always married too soon, who gets a bad husband, and she is never married too late, who gets a good one: in a word, there is no woman, *deformity, or lost reputation excepted*, but if she manages well, may be marry'd safely one time or other; but if she precipitates herself, it is ten thousand to one but she is undone.

But I come now to my own case, in which there was at this time no little nicety. The circumstances I was in, made the offer of a good husband, the most necessary thing in the world to me; but I found soon that to be made cheap, and easy, was not the way: it soon began to be found that the widow had no fortune, and to say this, was to say all that was ill of me; for I began to be dropt in all the discourses of matrimony: being well bred, handsome, witty, modest and agreeable; all which I had allowed to my character, whether justly, or no, is not to the purpose; I say, all these would not do without the dross,[1] which was now become more valuable than virtue itself. In short, *the widow*, they said, *had no money.*

I resolv'd therefore, as to the state of my present circumstances; that it was absolutely necessary to change my station, and make a new appearance in some other place where I was not known, and even to pass by another name if I found occasion.

I communicated my thoughts to my intimate friend the captain's lady; who I had so faithfully serv'd in her case with the cap-

---

1 Money (informal usage).

tain; and who was as ready to serve me in the same kind as I could desire: I made no scruple to lay my circumstances open to her, my stock was but low, for I had made but about 540 *l.* at the close of my last affair, and I had wasted some of that; however, I had about 460 *l.* left, a great many very rich cloaths, a gold watch, and some jewels, tho' of no extraordinary value, and about 30 or 40 *l.* left in linnen not dispos'd of.

My dear and faithful friend, the captain's wife was so sensible of the service I had done her in the affair above, that she was not only a steddy friend to me, but knowing my circumstances, she frequently made me presents as money came into her hands; such as fully amounted to a maintenance; so that I spent none of my own; and at last she made this unhappy proposal to me (*viz.*) that as we had observ'd, *as above*, how the men made no scruple to set themselves out as persons meriting a woman of fortune, when they had really no fortune of their own; it was but just to deal with them in their own way, and if it was possible, to deceive the deceiver.[1]

The captain's lady, in short put this project into my head, and told me if I would be rul'd by her I should certainly get a husband of fortune, without leaving him any room to reproach me with want of my own; I told her as I had reason to do, that I would give up myself wholly to her directions, and that I would have neither tongue to speak, or feet to step, in that affair, but as she should direct me; depending that she would extricate one out of every difficulty that she brought me into, which she said she would answer for.

The first step she put me upon, was to call her cousin, and go to a relations house of hers in the country, where she directed me; and where she brought her husband to visit me, and calling me cousin, she work'd matters so about, that her husband and she together invited me most passionately to come to town and be with them, for they now liv'd in a quite different place from where they were before. In the next place she tells her husband, that I had at least 1500 *l.* fortune, and that after some of my relations I was like to have a great deal more.

It was enough to tell her husband this, there needed nothing on my side; I was but to sit still and wait the event, for it presently went all over the neighbourhood that the young widow at Captain ——s was a fortune, that she had at least 1500 *l.* and perhaps a great deal more, and *that the captain said so*; and if the captain was

---

1 The first part of a popular proverb, originally in Latin: "To deceive the deceiver is no deceit" (*Fallere fallentem non est fraus*).

ask'd at any time about me, he made no scruple to affirm it, tho' he knew not one word of the matter, other than that his wife had told him so; and in this he thought no harm, for he really believ'd it to be so, because he had it from his wife; so slender a foundation will those fellows build upon, if they do but think there is a fortune in the game: with the reputation of this fortune, I presently found myself bless'd with admirers enough, and that I had my choice of men, as scarce as they said they were, *which by the way confirms what I was saying before*: this being my case, I who had a subtile game to play, had nothing now to do but to single out from them all, the properest man that might be for my purpose; *that is to say*, the man who was most likely to depend upon the *hear say* of a fortune, and not enquire too far into the particulars; and unless I did this, *I did nothing*, for my case would not bare much enquiry.

I pick'd out my man without much difficulty, by the judgement I made of his way of courting me; I had let him run on with his protestations and oaths that he lov'd me above all the world; that if I would make him happy, that was enough; all which I knew was upon supposition, nay, it was upon a full satisfaction,[1] that I was very rich, tho' I never told him a word of it myself.

This was my man, but I was to try him to the bottom, and indeed in that consisted my safety; for if he baulk'd, I knew I was undone, as surely as he was undone if he took me; and if I did not make some scruple about his fortune, it was the way to lead him to raise some about mine; and first therefore, I pretended on all occasions to doubt his sincerity, and told him, perhaps he only courted me for my fortune; he stop'd my mouth in that part, with the thunder of his protestations, *as above*, but still I pretended to doubt.

One morning he pulls off his diamond ring, and writes upon the glass[2] of the sash[3] in my chamber this line,
You I love, and you alone.
I read it, and ask'd him to lend me his ring, with which I wrote under it thus,
And so in love says every one.
He takes his ring again, and writes another line thus,
Virtue alone is an estate.
I borrow'd it again, and I wrote under it,

---

1 Conviction.
2 Writing upon windowpanes, especially of inns, was a custom of the period. The stones in jewellery were frequently used to inscribe sayings, verses, the "scribbling" of lovers, etc.
3 Window frame (here used in the sense of the window itself).

But money's vertue; gold is fate.

He colour'd as red as fire to see me turn so quick upon him, and in a kind of a rage told me he would conquer me, and writes again *thus,*

I scorn your gold, and yet I love.

I ventur'd all upon the last cast of poetry, as you'll see, for I wrote boldly under his last,

I'm poor: let's see how kind you'll prove.

This was a sad truth to me, whether he believ'd me or no I cou'd not tell; I supposed then that he did not. However he flew to me, took me in his arms, and kissing me very eagerly, and with the greatest passion imaginable he held me fast till he call'd for a pen and ink, and then *told me* he could not wait the tedious writing on the glass, but pulling out a piece of paper, he began and wrote again,

Be mine, with all your poverty.

I took his pen and follow'd him immediately thus,

Yet secretly you hope I lie.

He told me that was unkind, because it was not just, and that I put him upon contradicting me, which did not consist with good manners, any more than with his affection; and therefore since I had insensibly drawn him into this poetical scribble, he beg'd I would not oblige him to break it off, so he writes again,

Let love alone be our debate.

I wrote again,

She loves enough, that does not hate.

This he took for a favour, and so laid down the cudgels,[1] that is to say the pen; I say he took it for a favour, and a mighty one it was, if he had known all: however he took it as I meant it, that is, to let him think I was inclin'd to go on with him, as indeed I had all the reason in the world to do, for he was the best humoured merry sort of a fellow that I ever met with; and I often reflected on my self, how doubly criminal it was to deceive such a man; but that necessity, which press'd me to a settlement suitable to my condition, was my authority for it, and certainly his affection to me, and the goodness of his temper, however they might argue against using him ill, yet they strongly argued to me, that he would better take the disappointment, than some fiery tempered wretch, who might have nothing to recommend him but those passions which would serve only to make a woman miserable all her days.

Besides, tho' I had jested with him, as he suppos'd it, so often about my poverty, yet, when he found it to be true, he had fore-

---

1 Ended the dispute.

closed all manner of objection, seeing[1] whether he was in jest or in earnest, he had declar'd he took me without any regard to my portion, and whether I was in jest or in earnest, I had declar'd my self to be very poor, so that *in a word*, I had him fast both ways; and tho' he might say afterwards he was cheated, yet he could never say that I had cheated him.

He persued me close after this, and as I saw there was no need to fear losing him, I play'd the indifferent part with him longer than prudence might otherwise have dictated to me: but I considered how much this caution and indifference would give me the advantage over him, when I should come to be under the necessity of owning my own circumstances to him; and I manag'd it the more warily, because I found he inferr'd from thence, as indeed he ought to do, that I either had the more money, or the more judgment, and would not venture at all.

I took the freedom one day, after we had talk'd pretty close to the subject, to tell him, that it was true I had receiv'd the compliment of a lover from him; namely, that he would take me without enquiring into my fortune, and I would make him a suitable return in this, (*viz.*) that I would make as little enquiry into his as consisted with reason, but I hoped he would allow me to ask a few questions, which he should answer or not as he thought fit; and that I would not be offended if he did not answer me at all; one of these questions related to our manner of living, and the place where, because I had heard he had a great plantation in *Virginia*, and that he had talk'd of going to live there, and I told him I did not care to be transported.

He began from this discourse to let me voluntarily into all his affairs, and to tell me in a frank open way, all his circumstances, by which I found he was very well to pass in the world; but that great part of his estate consisted of three plantations, which he had in *Virginia*, which brought him in a very good income, generally speaking, to the tune of 300 *l.* a year; but that if he was to live upon them, would bring him in four times as much; very well, thought I, you shall carry me thither as soon as you please, tho' I won't tell you so before-hand.

I jested with him extremely about the figure he would make in *Virginia*; but I found he would do any thing I desired, tho' he did not seem glad to have me undervalue his plantations, so I turn'd my tale; I told him I had good reason not to desire to go there to

---

1 Since, because.

live, because if his plantations were worth so much there, I had not a fortune suitable to a gentleman of 1200 *l.* a year, as he said his estate would be.

He reply'd generously, he did not ask what my fortune was, he had told me from the beginning he would not, and he would be as good as his word; but whatever it was, he assur'd me he would never desire me to go to *Virginia* with him, or go thither himself without me, unless I was perfectly willing, and made it my choice.

All this, you may be sure, was as I wish'd, and indeed nothing could have happen'd more perfectly agreeable; I carried it on as far as this with a sort of indifferency, that he often wondred at, more than at first, but which was the only support of his courtship;[1] and I mention it the rather to intimate again to the ladies, that nothing but want of courage for such an indifferency, makes our sex so cheap, and prepares them to be ill us'd as they are; would they venture the loss of a pretending fop now and then, who carries it high upon the point of his own merit, they would certainly be slighted less, and courted more; had I discovered really and truly what my great fortune was, and that in all I had not full 500 *l.* when he expected 1500 *l.* yet I had hook'd him so fast, and play'd him so long, that I was satisfied he would have had me in my worst circumstances; and indeed it was less a surprize to him when he learnt the truth, than it would have been, because having not the least blame to lay on me, who had carried it with an air of indifference to the last, he could not say one word, except that indeed he thought it had been more, but that if it had been less he did not repent his bargain; only that he should not be able to maintain me so well as he intended.

In short, we were married, and very happily married on my side I assure you, *as to the man*; for he was the best humour'd man that ever woman had, but his circumstances were not so good as I imagined, as on the other hand he had not bettered himself by marrying so much as he expected.

When we were married I was shrewdly put to it[2] to bring him that little stock I had, and to let him see it was no more; but there was a necessity for it, so I took my opportunity one day when we were alone, to enter into a short dialogue with him about it; MY DEAR, *said I*, we have been married a fortnight, is it not time to let

---

1 That is, her indifference in itself was reason enough for him to continue his courtship of her.
2 That is, she was placed in a position which demanded much skill and cunning.

you know whether you have got a wife with something, or with nothing? Your own time for that, my dear, *says he*, I am satisfied that I have got the wife I love, I have not troubled you much, *says he*, with my enquiry after it.

That's true, *said I*, but I have a great difficulty upon me about it, which I scarce know how to manage.

What's that, my dear, *says he*?

Why, *says I*, 'tis a little hard upon me, and 'tis harder upon you; I am told that Captain ——— (meaning my friend's husband) has told you I had a great deal more money than I ever pretended to have, and I am sure I never employ'd him to do so.

Well, *says he*, Captain ——— may have told me so, but what then, if you have not so much that may lye at his door, but you never told me what you had, so I have no reason to blame you if you have nothing at all.

That is so just, *said I*, and so generous, that it makes my having but a little a double affliction to me.

The less you have, my dear, *says he*, the worse for us both; but I hope your affliction you speak of, is not caus'd for fear I should be unkind to you, for want of a portion, No No, if you have nothing tell me plainly, and at once; I may perhaps tell the captain he has cheated me, but I can never say you have cheated me, for did you not give it under your hand that you were poor, and so I ought to expect you to be.

Well, said I, *my dear*, I am glad I have not been concern'd in deceiving you before marriage, if I deceive you since, 'tis ne'er the worse; *that I am poor* is too true, but not so poor as to have nothing neither; so I pull'd out some bank bills, and gave him about a hundred and sixty pounds, There's something, my dear, *says I*, and not quite all neither.

I had brought him so near to expecting nothing, by what I had said before, that the money, tho' the sum was small in it self, was doubly welcome to him; he own'd it was more than he look'd for, and that he did not question by my discourse to him, but that my fine cloths, gold watch, and a diamond ring or two had been all my fortune.

I let him please himself with that 160 *l.* two or three days, and then having been abroad that day, and as if I had been to fetch it, I brought him a hundred pounds more home in gold, and told him there was a little more portion for him; and in short, in about a week more I brought him 180 *l.* more, and about 60 *l.* in linnen, which I made him believe I had been oblig'd to take with the 100 *l.* which I gave him in gold, as a composition for a debt[1] of 600 *l.* being little more than five shilling in the pound, and overvalued too.

And now, MY DEAR, *says I to him,* I am very sorry to tell you, that there is all, and that I have given you my whole fortune; I added, that if the person who had my 600 *l.* had not abus'd me, I had been worth a thousand pound to him, but that as it was, I had been faithful to him, and reserv'd nothing to my self, but if it had been more he should have had it.

He was so oblig'd by the manner, and so pleas'd with the sum, for he had been in a terrible fright lest it had been nothing at all, that he accepted it very thankfully: and thus I got over the fraud of *passing for a fortune without money,* and cheating a man into marrying me on pretence of a fortune; which, *by the way,* I take to be one of the most dangerous steps a woman can take, and in which she runs the most hazard of being ill us'd afterwards.

My husband, *to give him his due,* was a man of infinite good nature, but he was no fool; and finding his income not suited to the manner of living which he had intended, if I had brought him what he expected, and being under a disappointment in his return of [2] his plantations in *Virginia,* he discover'd many times his inclination of going over to *Virginia* to live upon his own; and often would be magnifying the way of living there, how cheap, how plentiful, how pleasant, *and the like.*

I began presently to understand his meaning, and I took him up very plainly one morning, and told him that I did so; that I found his estate turn'd to to no account at this distance, compar'd to what it would do if he liv'd upon the spot, and that I found he had a mind to go and live there; and I added, that I was sensible he had been disappointed in a wife, and that finding his expectations not answer'd that way, I could do no less to make him amends than tell him, that I was very willing to go over to *Virginia* with him and live there.

He said a thousand kind things to me upon the subject of my making such a proposal to him: he told me, that however he was disappointed in his expectations of a fortune, he was not disappointed in a wife; and that I was all to him that a wife could be, and he was more than satisfied in the whole when the particulars were put together; but that this offer was so kind, that it was more than he could express.

---

1 An agreement that a partial amount of a debt be paid in lieu of the whole.
2 Profit from.

To bring the story short, we agreed to go; *he told me*, that he had a very good house there, that it was well furnish'd, that his mother was alive and liv'd in it, and one sister, which was all the relations he had; that as soon as he came there, his mother would remove to another house which was her own for life, and his after her decease; so that I should have all the house to my self; and I found all this to be exactly as he had said.

To make this part of the story short, we put on board the ship *which we went in*, a large quantity of good furniture for our house, with stores of linnen and other necessaries, and a good cargoe for sale, and away we went.

To give an account of the manner of our voyage, which was long and full of dangers, is out of my way, I kept no journal, neither did my husband; all that I can say is, that after a terrible passage, frighted twice with dreadful storms, and once with what was still more terrible, I mean a pyrate, who came on board and took away almost all our provisions; and which would have been beyond all to me, they had once taken my husband to go along with them but by entreaties were prevail'd with to leave him: I say, after all these terrible things, we arriv'd in *York River* in *Virginia*, and coming to our plantation, we were receiv'd with all the demonstrations of tenderness and affection (by my husband's mother) that were possible to be express'd.

We liv'd here all together, my mother-in-law, *at my entreaty*, continuing in the house, for she was too kind a mother to be parted with; my husband likewise continued the same as at first, and I thought my self the happiest creature alive; when an odd and surprizing event put an end to all that felicity in a moment, and rendered my condition the most uncomfortable, if not the most miserable, in the world.

My mother was a mighty chearful good humour'd old woman, I may call her old woman, for her son was above thirty; I say she was very pleasant, good company, and us'd to entertain *me, in particular*, with abundance of stories to divert me, as well of the country we were in, as of the people.

Among the rest, she often told me how the greatest part of the inhabitants of the colony came thither in very indifferent circumstances from *England*; that, generally speaking, they were of two sorts, either (1.) such as were brought over by masters of ships to be sold as servants, *such we call them*, my dear, *says she*, but they are more properly call'd *slaves*. Or, (2.) such as are transported from *Newgate* and other prisons, after having been found guilty of felony and other crimes punishable with death.[1]

When they come here, says she, we make no difference, the planters buy them, and they work together in the field till their time is out; when 'tis expir'd, *said she*, they have encouragement given them to plant for themselves; for they have a certain number of acres of land allotted them by the country, and they go to work to clear and cure the land,[2] and then to plant it with tobacco and corn[3] for their own use; and as the tradesmen and merchants will trust them with tools, and cloaths, and other necessaries, upon the credit of their crop before it is grown, so they again plant every year a little more than the year before, and so buy whatever they want with the crop that is before them.

Hence child, *says she*, many a *Newgate* bird becomes a great man, and we have, *continued she*, several justices of the peace, officers of the train bands,[4] and magistrates of the towns they live in, that have been burnt in the hand.[5]

She was going on with that part of the story, when her own part in it interrupted her, and with a great deal of good-humour'd confidence she told me, she was one of the second sort of inhabitants herself; that she came away openly, having ventur'd too far in a particular case, so that she was become a criminal, And here's the mark of it, CHILD, *says she*, and pulling off her glove, look ye here, *says she*, turning up the palm of her hand, and shewed me a very fine white arm and hand, but branded in the inside of the hand, as in such cases it must be.

This story was very moving to me, but my mother (smiling) said, You need not think such a thing strange, *daughter*, for as I told you, some of the best men in this country are burnt in the hand, and they are not asham'd to own it; there's Major ——— *says she*, he was an eminent pickpocket; there's Justice *Ba———r* was a

---

1 Even at the time there was some controversy not only concerning the interchangeability of these terms (*servant* and *slave*) but also the extent to which the actual treatment differed between these two forms of servitude. There was also of course a third category, the black slave, who was sold as a servant for life. See Appendices A.3 and B.9.

2 That is, to remove the timber from the land and prepare it for planting.

3 Grain.

4 Bands of citizens trained to bear arms in order to help keep the peace or for purposes of defence.

5 Branded as convicted felons. As well as serving as a form of punishment, this practice was also a means of showing mercy to first offenders.

shoplifter, and both of them were burnt in the hand, and I could name you several, such as they are.

We had frequent discourses of this kind, and abundance of instances she gave me of the like; after some time, as she was telling some stories of one that was transported but a few weeks ago, I began in an intimate kind of way to ask her to tell me something of her own story, which she did with the utmost plainness and sincerity; how she had fallen into very ill company in *London* in her young days, occasion'd by her mother sending her frequently to carry victuals and other relief to a kinswoman of hers who was a prisoner in *Newgate*, and who lay in a miserable starving condition, was afterwards condemned to be hang'd, but having got respite by pleading her belly, dyed afterwards in the prison.

Here my mother-in-law ran out in a long account of the wicked practices in that dreadful place, and how it ruin'd more young people than all the town besides; And child, *says my mother*, perhaps you may know little of it, or it may be have heard nothing about it, but depend upon it, *says she*, we all know here, that there are more thieves and rogues made by that one prison of *Newgate*, than by all the clubs and societies of villains in the nation; 'tis that cursed place, *says my mother*, that half peoples this colony.[1]

Here she went on with her own story so long, and in so particular a manner, that I began to be very uneasy, but coming to one particular that requir'd telling her name, I thought I should have sunk down in the place; she perceived I was out of order, and asked me if I was not well, and what ail'd me? I told her I was so affected with the melancholy story she had told, and the terrible things she had gone thro', that it had overcome me; and I beg'd of her to talk no more of it: *Why*, my dear, *says she, very kindly*, what need these things trouble you? These passages were long before your time, and they give me no trouble at all now, nay I look back on them with a particular satisfaction, as they have been a means to bring me to this place. Then she went on to tell me how she very luckily fell into a good family, where behaving herself well, and her mistress dying, her master married her, by whom she had my husband and his sister, and that by her diligence and good management after her husband's death, she had improv'd the plantations to such a degree as they then were, so that most of the estate was of her getting, not her husband's, for she had been a widow upwards of sixteen year.

---

1 See Appendix B.1.

I heard this part of the story with very little attention, because I wanted much to retire and give vent to my passions, which I did soon after; and let any one judge what must be the anguish of my mind, when I came to reflect, that this was certainly no more or less *than my own mother*, and I had now had two children, and was big with another by my own brother, and lay with him still every night.

I was now the most unhappy of all women in the world: O had the story never been told me, all had been well; it had been no crime to have lain with my husband, since as to his being my relation, I had known nothing of it.

I had now such a load on my mind that it kept me perpetually waking; to reveal it, *which would have been some ease to me*, I cou'd not find wou'd be to any purpose, and yet to conceal it wou'd be next to impossible; nay, I did not doubt but I should talk of it in my sleep, and tell my husband of it whether I would or no: if I discover'd it, the least thing I could expect was to lose my husband, for he was too nice and too honest a man to have continued my husband after he had known I had been his sister, so that I was perplex'd to the last degree.

I leave it to any man to judge what difficulties presented to my view, I was away from my native country at a distance prodigious, and the return to me unpassable; I liv'd very well, but in a circumstance unsufferable in it self; if I had discover'd my self to my mother, it might be difficult to convince her of the particulars, and I had no way to prove them: *on the other hand*, if she had question'd or doubted me, I had been undone, for the bare suggestion would have immediately separated me from my husband, without gaining[1] my mother or him, who would have been neither a husband or a brother; so that between the surprise on one hand, and the uncertainty on the other, I had been sure to be undone.

In the mean time, as I was but too sure of the fact, I liv'd therefore in open avowed incest and whoredom, and all under the appearance of an honest wife; and tho' I was not much touched with the crime of it, yet the action had something in it shocking to nature, and made my husband, *as he thought himself*, even nauseous to me.

However, upon the most sedate consideration, I resolv'd, that it was absolutely necessary to conceal it all, and not make the least discovery of it either to mother or husband; and thus I liv'd with

---

1 Helping, serving.

the greatest pressure imaginable for three year more, but had no more children.

During this time my mother used to be frequently telling me old stories of her former adventures, which however were no ways pleasant to me; for by it, tho' she did not tell it me in plain terms, yet I could easily understand joyn'd with what I had heard my self, of my first tutors, that in her younger days she had been both WHORE and THIEF; but I verily believe she had lived to repent sincerely of both, and that she was then a very pious sober and religious woman.

Well, let her life have been what it would then, it was certain that my life was very uneasie to me; for I liv'd, as I have said, but in the worst sort of whoredom, and as I cou'd expect no good of it, so really no good issue came of it, and all my seeming prosperity wore off and ended in misery and destruction; it was some time indeed before it came to this, for, but I know not by what ill fate guided, every thing went wrong with us afterwards, and that which was worse, my husband grew strangely alter'd; froward,[1] jealous, and unkind, and I was as impatient of bearing his carriage, as the carriage was unreasonable and unjust: these things proceeded so far, that we came at last to be in such ill terms with one another, that I claim'd a promise of him which he entered willingly into with me, when I consented to come from *England* with him (*viz.*) that if I found the country not to agree with me, or that I did not like to live there, I should come away to *England* again when I pleas'd, giving him a year's warning to settle his affairs.

I say *I now claim'd this promise of him*, and I must confess I did it not in the most obliging terms that could be in the world neither; but I insisted that he treated me ill, that I was remote from my friends, and could do my self no justice, and that he was jealous without cause, my conversation[2] having been unblameable, and he having no pretence[3] for it, and that to remove to *England*, would take away all occasion from him.

I insisted so peremptorily upon it, that he could not avoid coming to a point, either to keep his word with me or to break it; and this notwithstanding he used all the skill he was master of, and employ'd his mother and other agents to prevail with me to alter my resolutions; indeed the bottom of the thing lay at my heart,

---

1 Unreasonable, perverse.
2 Conduct, behaviour.
3 Cause, grounds.

and that made all his endeavours fruitless, for my heart was alienated from him, *as a husband*; I loathed the thoughts of bedding with him, and used a thousand pretences of illness and humour[1] to prevent his touching me, fearing nothing more than to be with child again by him, which to be sure would have prevented, or at least delay'd my going over to *England*.

However, at last I put him so out of humour, that he took up a rash and fatal resolution. In short I should not go to *England*; and tho' he had promis'd me, yet it was an unreasonable thing for me to desire it, that it would be ruinous to his affairs, would unhinge his whole family, and be next to an undoing him in the world; that therefore I ought not to desire it of him, and that no wife in the world that valu'd her family and her husbands prosperity would insist upon such a thing.

This plung'd[2] me again, for when I considered the thing calmly, and took my husband as he really was, a diligent careful man in the main work of laying up an estate for his children, and that he knew nothing of the dreadful circumstances that he was in; I could not but confess to myself that my proposal was very unreasonable, and what no wife that had the good of her family at heart wou'd have desir'd.

But my discontents were of another nature; I look'd upon him no longer as a husband, but as a near relation the son of my own mother, and I resolv'd some how or other to be clear of him, but which way I did not know, nor did it seem possible.

It is said *by the ill-natured world* of our sex, that if we are set on a thing, it is impossible to turn us from our resolutions: *in short*, I never ceas'd poreing upon the means to bring to pass my voyage, and came that length with my husband at last, as to propose going without him. This provok'd him to the last degree, and he call'd me not only an unkind wife, but an unnatural mother, and ask'd me how I could entertain such a thought without horror as that of leaving my two children (for one was dead) without a mother, and to be brought up by strangers, and never to see them more? *It was true*, had things been right, I should not have done it, but now, *it was* my real desire never to see them, or him either any more; and as to the charge of unnatural I could easily answer it to myself, while I knew that the whole relation was unnatural in the highest degree in the world.

---

1 Mood, temper.
2 Depressed, overwhelmed.

However, it was plain there was no bringing my husband to any thing; he would neither go with me, or let me go without him, and it was quite out of my power to stir without his consent,[1] as any one that knows the constitution of the country I was in, knows very well.

We had many family quarrels about it, and they began (in time) to grow up to a dangerous height, for as I was quite estrang'd from my husband (*as he was call'd*) in affection, so I took no heed to my words, but sometimes gave him language that was provoking: and, *in short*, strove all I could to bring him to a parting with me, which was what above all things in the world I desir'd most.

He took my carriage very ill, and indeed he might well do so, for at last I refus'd to bed with him, and carrying on the breach upon all occasions to extremity he told me once he thought I was mad, and if I did not alter my conduct, he would put me under cure; that is to say, into a *mad-house*:[2] I told him he should find I was far enough from mad, and that it was not in his power, or any other villians to murther[3] me; I confess at the same time I was heartily frighted at his thoughts of putting me into a *mad-house*, which would at once have destroy'd all the possibility of breaking the truth out, whatever the occasion might be; for that then, no one would have given credit to a word of it.

This therefore brought me to a resolution, *whatever came of it* to lay open my whole case; but which way to do it, or to whom, was an inextricable difficulty, and took me up many months to resolve; *in the mean time*, another quarrel with my husband happen'd, which came up to such a mad extream as almost push'd me on to tell it him all to his face; but tho' I kept it in so as not to come to the particulars, I spoke so much as put him into the utmost confusion, and in the end brought out the whole story.

He began with a calm expostulation upon my being so resolute to go to *England*; I defended it; and one hard word bringing on another as is usual in all family strife, *he told me*, I did not treat him as if he was my husband, or talk of my children, as if I was a mother; and *in short*, that I did not deserve to be us'd as a wife: that he

---

1 According to English law (which had legal force in the plantations other than on strictly local matters), the will of the wife was subject to the will of the husband.

2 Defoe spoke out on numerous occasions against the confinement of sane people in "private mad-houses" under the direction of friends or family. See Appendix A.2.

3 Destroy (obsolete form of *murder*).

had us'd all the fair means possible with me; that he had argu'd with all the kindness and calmness, that a husband or a Christian ought to do, and that I made him such a vile return, that I treated him rather like a dog than a man, and rather like the most contemptible stranger than a husband: that he was very loth to use violence with me, but that *in short*, he saw a necessity of it now, and that for the future he should be oblig'd to take such measures as should reduce me to my duty.

My blood was now fir'd to the utmost, *tho' I knew what he had said was very true*, and nothing could appear more provok'd; I told him for his fair means and his foul they were equally contemn'd[1] by me; that for my going to *England*, I was resolv'd on it, come what would; and that as to treating him not like a husband, and not showing my self a mother to my children, there might be something more in it than he understood at present; but, for his farther consideration, I thought fit to tell him thus much, that he neither was my lawful husband, nor they lawful children, and that I had reason to regard neither of them more than I did.

I confess I was mov'd to pity him when I spoke it, for he turn'd pale as death, and stood mute as one thunder struck, and once or twice I thought he would have fainted; *in short*, it put him in a fit something like an apoplex;[2] he trembl'd, a sweat or dew ran off his face, and yet he was cold as a clod, so that I was forced to run and fetch something[3] for him to keep life in him; when he recover'd of that, he grew sick and vomited, and in a little after was put to bed, and in the next morning was, as he had been indeed all night, in a violent fever.

However it went off again, and he recovered tho' but slowly, and when he came to be a little better, he told me, I had given him a mortal wound with my tongue, and he had only one thing to ask before he desir'd an explanation; I interrupted him, and told him I was sorry I had gone so far, since I saw what disorder it put him into, but I desir'd him not to talk to me of explanations, for that would but make things worse.

This heighten'd his impatience, and indeed perplex'd him beyond all bearing; for now he began to suspect that there was some mystery yet unfolded, but could not make the least guess at

---

1 Despised, scorned.
2 A stroke (obsolete form of *apoplexy*). This would seem to be a symptom of what later develops into a case of melancholy. See below, p. 128, n. 1.
3 That is, some kind of alcoholic stimulant.

the real particulars of it; all that run in his brain was, that I had another husband alive, which I could not say in fact might not be true; but I assur'd him however, there was not the least of that in it; and indeed as to my other husband he was effectually dead in law to me, and had told me I should look on him as such, so I had not the least uneasiness on that score.

But now I found the thing too far gone to conceal it much longer, and my husband himself gave me an opportunity to ease my self of the secret much to my satisfaction; he had laboured with me three or four weeks, *but to no purpose*, only to tell him, whether I had spoken those words only as the effect of my passion, to put him in a passion? or whether there was anything of truth in the bottom of them? But I continued inflexible, and would explain nothing, unless he would first consent to my going to *England*, which he would never do, *he said*, while he liv'd; on the other hand I said it was in my power to make him willing when I pleas'd, NAY to make him entreat me to go; and this increased his curiosity, and made him importunate to the highest degree, *but it was all to no purpose.*

At length he tells all this story to his mother, and sets her upon me to get the main secret out of me, and she us'd her utmost skill with me indeed; but I put her to a full stop at once, *by telling her* that the reason and mystery of the whole matter lay in herself; and that it was my respect to her that had made me conceal it, and that in short I could go no farther, and therefore conjur'd[1] her not to insist upon it.

She was struck dumb at this suggestion, and could not tell what to say or to think; but laying aside the supposition as a policy[2] of mine, continued her importunity on account of her son, and if possible to make up the breach between us two; as to that, *I told her*, that it was indeed a good design in her, but that it was impossible to be done; and that if I should reveal to her the truth of what she desir'd, she would grant it to be impossible, and cease to desire it: at last I seem'd to be prevail'd on by her importunity, and told her I dar'd trust her with a secret of the greatest importance, and she would soon see that this was so, and that I would consent to lodge it in her breast, if she would engage solemnly not to acquaint her son with it without my consent.

She was long in promising this part, but rather than not come at the main secret she agreed to that too, and after a great many

---

1 Appealed to, implored.
2 Cunning scheme, trick.

other preliminaries, I began and told her the whole story: first I told her how much she was concern'd in all the unhappy breach which had happen'd between her son and me, by telling me her own story, and her *London* name; and that the surprize she see I was in, was upon that occasion: then I told her my own story and my name, and assur'd her by such other tokens as she could not deny that I was no other, nor more or less than her own child, *her daughter* born of her body in *Newgate*; the same that had sav'd her from the gallows by being in her belly, and the same that she left in such and such hands when she was transported.

It is impossible to express the astonishment she was in; she was not inclin'd to believe the story, or to remember the particulars; for she immediately foresaw the confusions that must follow in the family upon it; but every thing concurr'd so exactly with the stories she had told me of her self, and which if she had not told me, she would perhaps have been content to have denied, that she had stop'd her own mouth, and she had nothing to do but to take me about the neck and kiss me, and cry most vehemently over me, without speaking one word for a long time together; at last she broke out, *Unhappy child!* says she, what miserable chance could bring thee hither? and in the arms of my own son too! *Dreadful girl!* says she, *why we are all undone!* Married to thy own brother! Three children, and two alive, all of the same flesh and blood! My son and my daughter lying together as husband and wife! All confusion and destraction for ever! *Miserable family!* What will become of us? What is to be said? What is to be done? And thus she run on for a great while, nor had I any power to speak, or if I had, did I know what to say, for every word wounded me to the soul: with this kind of amasement[1] on our thoughts we parted for the first time, tho' my mother was more surpriz'd than I was, because it was more news to her than to me: however, she promis'd again to me at parting, that she would say nothing of it to her son, till we had talk'd of it again.

It was not long, you may be sure, before we had a second conference upon the same subject; when, as if she had been willing to forget the story she had told me of herself, or to suppose that I had forgot some of the particulars, she began to tell them with alterations and omissions; but I refresh'd her memory, and set her to rights in many things which I supposed she had forgot, and then came in so opportunely with the whole history, that it was impos-

---

1 Extreme consternation, frenzy.

sible for her to go from it; and then she fell into her rhapsodies[1] again, and exclamations at the severity of her misfortunes: when these things were a little over with her we fell into a close debate about what should be first done before we gave an account of the matter to my husband, but to what purpose could be all our consultations? We could neither of us see our way thro' it, nor see how it could be safe to open such a scene to him; it was impossible to make any judgment, or give any guess at what temper he would receive it in, or what measures he would take upon it; and if he should have so little government of himself, as to make it publick, we easily foresaw that it would be the ruin of the whole family, and expose my mother and me to the last degree; and if at last he should take the advantage the law would give him, he might put me away with disdain, and leave me to sue for the little portion that I had, and perhaps wast it all in the suit, and then be a beggar; the children would be ruin'd too, having no legal claim to any of his effects;[2] and thus I should see him perhaps in the arms of another wife in a few months and be my self the most miserable creature alive.

My mother was as sensible of this as I; and upon the whole, we knew not what to do; after some time, we came to more sober resolutions, but then it was with this misfortune too, that my mother's opinion and mine were quite different from one another, and indeed inconsistent with one another; for my mother's opinion was, that I should bury the whole thing entirely, and continue to live with him as my husband, till some other event should make the discovery of it more convenient; and that in the mean time she would endeavour to reconcile us together again, and restore our mutual comfort and family peace, that we might lie as we us'd to do together, and so let the whole matter remain a secret as close as death, for child, *says she*, we are both undone if it comes out.

To encourage me to this, she promis'd to make me easy in my circumstances as far as she was able, and to leave me what she could at her death, secur'd for me separately from my husband; so that if it should come out afterwards, I should not be left destitute, but be able to stand on my own feet, and procure justice from him.

---

1 Extravagant and disconnected expressions of emotion.
2 Once a divorce is obtained on grounds of consanguinity (or blood relationship), the children become illegitimate and have no claim to the father's property. The wife, at most, would be entitled to the unspent portion of her dowry.

This proposal did not agree at all with my judgment of the thing, tho' it was very fair and kind in my mother, but my thoughts run quite another way.

As to keeping the thing in our own breasts, and letting it all remain as it was, I told her it was impossible; and I ask'd her how she cou'd think I cou'd bear the thoughts of lying with my own brother? In the next place I told her that her being alive was the only support of the discovery, and that while she own'd me for her child, and saw reason to be satisfyed that I was so, no body else would doubt it; but that if she should die before the discovery, I should be taken for an impudent creature that had forg'd such a thing to go away from my husband, or should be counted craz'd and distracted: then I told her how he had threaten'd already to put me into a mad-house, and what concern I had been in about it, and how that was the thing that drove me to the necessity of discovering it to her as I had done.

From all which I told her, that I had on the most serious reflections I was able to make in the case, come to this resolution, which I hop'd she would like, as a medium between both, (*viz.*) that she should use her endeavours with her son to give me leave to go for *England*, as I had desired, and to furnish me with a sufficient sum of money, either in goods along with me, or in bills for my support there, all along suggesting, that he might one time or other think it proper to come over to me.

That when I was gone she should then in cold blood, and after first obliging him in the solemnest manner possible to secresie, discover the case to him; doing it gradually, and as her own discretion should guide her, so that he might not be surpriz'd with it, and fly out into any passions and excesses on my account, or on hers; and that she should concern herself to prevent his slighting the children, or marrying again, unless he had a certain account of my being dead.

This was my scheme, and my reasons were good; I was really alienated from him in the consequence of these things; indeed I mortally hated him as a husband, and it was impossible to remove that riveted aversion I had to him; *at the same time* it being an unlawful incestuous living added to that aversion; and tho' I had no great concern about it in point of conscience, yet every thing added to make cohabiting with him the most nauseous thing to me in the world; and I think verily it was come to such a height, that I could almost as willingly have embrac'd a dog, as have let him offer any thing of that kind to me, for which reason I could not bear the thoughts of coming between the sheets with him; I cannot say that I was right in point of policy in carrying it such a length, while at the same time I did not resolve to discover the thing to him; but I am giving an account of what was, not of what ought or ought not to be.

In this directly opposite opinion to one another my mother and I continued a long time, and it was impossible to reconcile our judgments; many disputes we had about it, but we could never either of us yield our own, or bring over the other.

I insisted on my aversion to lying with my own brother; and she insisted upon its being impossible to bring him to consent to my going from him to *England*; and in this uncertainty we continued, not differing so as to quarrel, or any thing like it; but so as not to be able to resolve what we should do to make up that terrible breach that was before us.

At last I resolv'd on a desperate course, and *told my mother* my resolution, (*viz.*) that in short, I would tell him of it my self; my mother was frighted to the last degree at the very thoughts of it; but *I bid her be easie*, told her I would do it gradually and softly, and with all the art and good humour I was mistress of, and time it also as well as I could, taking him in good humour too: *I told her* I did not question but if I cou'd be hypocrite enough to feign more affection to him than I really had, I should succeed in all my design, and we might part by consent, and with a good agreement, for I might love him well enough for a brother, tho' I could not for a husband.

All this while he lay at[1] my mother to find out, if possible, what was the meaning of that dreadful expression of mine, as he call'd it, which I mention'd before; namely, *that I was not his lawful wife, nor my children his legal children*: my mother put him off, told him she could bring me to no explanations, but found there was something that disturb'd me very much, and she hop'd she should get it out of me in time, and in the mean time recommended to him earnestly to use me more tenderly, and win me with his usual good carriage; *told him* of his terrifying and affrighting me with his threats of sending me to a madhouse, and the like, and advis'd him not to make a woman desperate on any account whatever.

He promis'd her to soften his behaviour, and bid her assure me that he lov'd me as well as ever, and that he had no such design as that of sending me to a madhouse, whatever he might say in his passion; also he desir'd my mother to use the same perswasions to

---

1 Persistently questioned.

me too, that our affections might be renew'd, and we might live together in a good understanding as we us'd to do.

I found the effects of this treaty presently; my husband's conduct was immediately alter'd, and he was quite another man to me; nothing could be kinder and more obliging than he was to me upon all occasions; and I could do no less than make some return to it, *which I did as well as I cou'd*; but it was but in an awkward manner at best, for nothing was more frightful to me than his caresses, and the apprehensions of being with child again by him, was ready to throw me into fits; and this made me see that there was an absolute necessity of breaking the case to him without any more delay, which however I did with all the caution and reserve imaginable.

He had continued his alter'd carriage to me near a month, and we began to live a new kind of life with one another; and could I have satisfied my self to have gone on with it, I believe it might have continued as long as we had continued alive together. One evening as we were sitting and talking very friendly together under a little auning, which serv'd as an arbour at the entrance from our house into the garden, he was in a very pleasant agreeable humour, and said abundance of kind things to me, relating to the pleasure of our present good agreement, and the disorders of our past breach, and what a satisfaction it was to him, that we had room to hope we should never have any more of it.

I fetch'd a deep sigh, and told him there was no body in the world could be more delighted than I was, in the good agreement we had always kept up, or more afflicted with the breach of it, and should be so still, but I was sorry to tell him that there was an unhappy circumstance in our case, which lay too close to my heart, and which I knew not how to break to him, that rendred my part of it very miserable, and took from me all the comfort of the rest.

He importun'd me to tell him what it was; I told him I could not tell how to do it, that while it was conceal'd from him, I alone was unhappy; but if he knew it also, we should be both so, and that therefore to keep him in the dark about it was the kindest thing that I could do, and it was on that account alone that I kept a secret from him, the very keeping of which I thought would first or last be my destruction.

It is impossible to express his surprize at this relation, and the double importunity which he used with me to discover it to him: he told me I could not be call'd kind to him, nay, I could not be faithful to him if I conceal'd it from him; I told him I thought so too, and yet I could not do it. He went back to what I had said before to him, and told me he hoped it did not relate to what I had said in my passion; and that he had resolv'd to forget all that, as the effect of a rash provok'd spirit; I told him I wish'd I could forget it all too, but that it was not to be done, the impression was too deep, and I cou'd not do it, it was impossible.

He then told me he was resolved not to differ with me in any thing, and that therefore he would importune me no more about it, resolving to acquiesce in whatever I did or said; only begg'd I would then agree, that whatever it was, it should no more interrupt our quiet and our mutual kindness.

This was the most provoking thing he could have said to me, for I really wanted his farther importunities, that I might be prevail'd with to bring out that which indeed it was like death to me to conceal; so I answer'd him plainly, that I could not say I was glad not to be importuned, tho' I could not tell how to comply; But come, *my dear, said I,* what conditions will you make with me upon the opening this affair to you?

Any conditions in the world, *said he,* that you can in reason desire of me; Well, *said I,* come, give it me under your hand,[1] that if you do not find I am in any fault, or that I am willingly concern'd in the causes of the misfortune that is to follow, you will not blame me, use me the worse, do me any injury, or make me be the sufferer for that which is not my fault.

That, *says he,* is the most reasonable demand in the world; not to blame you for that which is not your fault; give me a pen and ink, *says he,* so I ran in and fetch'd a pen, ink, and paper, and he wrote the condition down in the very words I had proposed it, and sign'd it with his name; Well, says he, *what is next,* my dear?

Why, *says I,* the next is, that you will not blame me for not discovering the secret of it to you before I knew it.

Very just again, *says he,* with all my heart; so he wrote down that also and sign'd it.

Well, *my dear,* says I, then I have but one condition more to make with you, and that is, that as there is no body concern'd in it but you and I, you shall not discover it to any person in the world, except your own mother; and that in all the measures you shall take upon the discovery, as I am equally concern'd in it with you, *tho' as innocent as your self,* you shall do nothing in a passion, nothing to my prejudice, or to your mother's prejudice, without my knowledge and consent.

---

1 That is, give me your written agreement.

This a little amaz'd him, and he wrote down the words distinctly, but read them over and over before he sign'd them, hesitating at them several times, and repeating them; *My mother's* prejudice! *and your prejudice!* What mysterious thing can this be? However, at last he sign'd it.

Well, *says I*, my dear, I'll ask you no more under your hand, but as you are to bear the most unexpected and surprizing thing that perhaps ever befel any family in the world, I beg you to promise me you will receive it with composure and a presence of mind suitable to a man of sense.

I'll do my utmost, *says he*, upon condition you will keep me no longer in suspence, for you terrify me with all these preliminaries.

Well then, *says I*, it is this, as I told you before in a heat, that I was not your lawful wife, and that our children were not legal children; so I must let you know now in calmness, and in kindness, but with affliction enough that *I am* your own sister, *and you* my own brother, and that we are both the children of our mother now alive, and in the house, who is convinc'd of the truth of it, in a manner not to be denied or contradicted.

I saw him turn pale, and look wild, and I said, Now remember your promise, and receive it with presence of mind; for who cou'd have said more to prepare you for it, than I have done? However I call'd a servant, and got him a little glass of rum, which is the usual dram[1] of the country, for he was just fainting away.

When he was a little recover'd, *I said to him,* This story you may be sure requires a long explanation, and therefore have patience and compose your mind to hear it out, and I'll make it as short as I can, and with this, I told him what I thought was needful of the fact, and particularly how my mother came to discover it to me, as above; And now my dear, *says I*, you will see reason for my capitulations, and that I neither have been the cause of this matter, nor could be so, and that I could know nothing of it before now.

I am fully satisfy'd of that, *says he*, but 'tis a dreadful surprize to me; however, I know a remedy for it all, and a remedy that shall put an end to all your difficulties, without your going to *England*; That would be strange, *said I*, as all the rest; No, No, *says he*, I'll make it easie, there's nobody in the way of it all, but myself: he look'd a little disorder'd, when he said this, but I did not apprehend any thing from it at that time, believing as it us'd to be said,

---

1 Alcoholic drink (small draught). As well as rum, cider and wine were also popular.

that they who do those things never talk of them; or that they who talk of such things never do them.

But things were not come their height with him, and I observ'd he became pensive and melancholly; and in a word, as I thought a little distemper'd in his head;[1] I endeavour'd to talk him into temper, and to reason him into a kind of scheme for our government in the affair, and sometimes he would be well, and talk with some courage about it; but the weight of it lay too heavy upon his thoughts, and in short, it went so far that he made two attempts upon himself, and in one of them had actually strangled himself, and had not his mother come into the room in the very moment, he had died; but with the help of a *negro* servant, she cut him down and recover'd him.

Things were now come to a lamentable height in the family: my pity for him now began to revive that affection, which at first I really had for him, and I endeavour'd sincerely by all the kind carriage I could to make up the breach; but in short, it had gotten too great a head,[2] it prey'd upon his spirits, and it threw him into a long ling'ring consumption, tho' it happen'd not to be mortal. In this distress I did not know what to do, as his life was apparently declining, and I might perhaps have marry'd again there, very much to my advantage, it had been certainly my business to have staid in the country; but my mind was restless too, and uneasie; I hanker'd after coming to *England*, and nothing would satisfie me without it.

In short, by an unwearied importunity my husband who was apparently decaying, as I observ'd, was at last prevail'd with, and so *my own fate pushing me on*, the way was made clear for me, and *my mother concurring*, I obtain'd a very good cargo for my coming to *England*.

When I parted with my brother, for such I am now to call him; we agreed that after I arriv'd he should pretend to have an account that I was dead in *England*, and so might marry again when he would; he promis'd, and engag'd to me to correspond with me as a sister, and to assist and support me as long as I liv'd; and that if

1 According to the doctrine of the Greek physician Hippocrates (c.460-c.357 BC), complete health could prevail only if the four humours (or "tempers")—blood, yellow bile, black bile and phlegm—were in balance. Melancholy resulted from a malignancy of the black bile, which in this case ascends to the head and leads to attempted suicide. By Defoe's time, however, this theory had been somewhat discredited.
2 Advanced too far.

he dy'd before me, he would leave sufficient to his mother to take care of me still, in the name of a sister, and he was in some respect careful[1] of me, when he heard of me; but it was so oddly mannag'd that I felt the disappointments very sensibly afterwards, as you shall hear in its time.

I came away for *England* in the month of *August*, after I had been eight years in that country, and now a new scene of misfortunes attended me, which perhaps few women have gone thro' the like of.

We had an indifferent good voyage, till we came just upon the coast of *England*, and where we arriv'd in two and thirty days, but were then ruffled with two or three storms, one of which drove us away to the coast of *Ireland*, and we put in at *Kinsale*: we remain'd there about thirteen days, got some refreshment on shore, and put to sea again, tho' we met with very bad weather again in which the ship sprung[2] her main-mast, *as they call'd it, for I knew not what they meant*: but we got at last into *Milford Haven* in *Wales*, where tho' it was remote from our port; yet having my foot safe upon the firm ground of my native country the isle of *Britain*, I resolv'd to venture it no more upon the waters, which had been so terrible to me; so getting my cloths, and money on shore with my bills of loading, and other papers, I resolv'd to come for *London*, and leave the ship to get to her port as she could; the port whither she was bound, was to *Bristol*, where my brothers chief correspondent liv'd.

I got to *London*, in about three weeks, where I heard a little while after that the ship was arriv'd in *Bristol*; but at the same time had the misfortune to know that by the violent weather she had been in, and the breaking of her mainmast; she had great damage on board, and that a great part of her cargo was spoil'd.

I had now a new scene of life upon my hands, and a dreadful appearance it had; I was come away with a kind of final farewel; what I brought with me, was indeed considerable, had it come safe, and by the help of it I might have married again tollerably well; but as it was, I was reduc'd to between two or three hundred pounds in the whole, and this without any hope of recruit:[3] I was entirely without friends, nay, even so much as without acquaintance, for I found it was absolutely necessary not to revive former acquaintances; and as for my subtle friend that set me up former-

---

1 Considerate.
2 Split, cracked.
3 A fresh supply, replenishment.

ly for a fortune she was dead, and her husband also; as I was inform'd upon sending a person unknown to enquire.

The looking after my cargo of goods soon after oblig'd me to take a journey to *Bristol,* and during my attendance upon that affair, I took the diversion of going to the *Bath,* for as I was still far from being old, so my humour, which was always gay, continu'd so to an extream; and being now, *as it were,* a woman of fortune, tho' I was a woman without a fortune, I expected something, or other might happen in my way, that might mend my circumstances as had been my case before.

The *Bath*[1] is a place of gallantry enough; expensive, and full of snares; I went thither indeed in the view of taking any thing that might offer; but I must do myself that justice, as to protest I knew nothing amiss, I meant nothing but in an honest way; nor had I any thoughts about me at first that look'd the way, which afterwards I suffered them to be guided.

Here I stay'd the whole latter season,[2] *as it is call'd there,* and contracted some unhappy acquaintance, which rather prompted the follies, I fell afterwards into, than fortify'd me against them: I liv'd pleasantly enough, kept good company, *that is to say,* gay fine company; but had the discouragement to find this way of living sunk me exceedingly, and that as I had no settl'd income, so spending upon the main stock was but a certain kind of *bleeding to death*; and this gave me many sad reflections in the intervals of my other thoughts: however I shook them off, and still flatter'd myself that something or other might offer for my advantage.

But I was in the wrong place for it; I was not now at *Redriff* where if I had set myself tollerably up, some honest sea captain or other might have talk'd with me upon the honourable terms of matrimony; but I was at the *Bath* where men find a mistress sometimes, but very rarely look for a wife; and consequently all the particular acquaintances a woman can expect to make there, must have some tendency that way.

I had spent the first season well enough, for tho' I had contracted some acquaintance with a gentleman, who came to the *Bath* for his diversion, yet I had enter'd into no *felonious treaty,* as it might be call'd: I had resisted some casual offers of gallantry, and had manag'd that way well enough; I was not wicked enough

---

1 Situated on the Avon in southwestern England, Bath received royal patronage in the early seventeenth century and became one of the most fashionable spas in England. See Appendix A.6.

2 That is, the period following the high summer season.

to come into the crime for the meer vice of it, and I had no extraordinary offers made me that tempted me with the main thing which I wanted.

However I went this length the first season, (*viz.*) I contracted an acquaintance with a woman in whose house I lodg'd, who tho' she did not keep an ill house,[1] *as we call it,* yet had none of the best principles in herself: I had on all occasions behav'd myself so well as not to get the least slur upon my reputation on any account whatever, and all the men that I had convers'd with, were of so good reputation that I had not given the least reflection[2] by conversing with them; nor did any of them seem to think there was room for a wicked correspondence,[3] if they had any of them offered it; yet there was one gentleman, *as above,* who always singl'd me out for the diversion of my company, as he call'd it, which *as he was pleas'd to say* was very agreeable to him, but at that time there was no more in it.

I had many melancholly hours at the *Bath* after all the company was gone, for tho' I went to *Bristol* sometimes for the disposing my effects, and for recruits of money, yet I chose to come back to *Bath* for my residence, because being on good terms with the woman in whose house I lodg'd in the summer, I found that during the winter I liv'd rather cheaper there than I could do any where else; here, *I say,* I pass'd the winter as heavily as I had pass'd the autumn chearfully; but having contracted a nearer intimacy with the said woman, in whose house I lodg'd, I could not avoid communicating to her something of what lay hardest upon my mind, and particularly the narrowness of my circumstances, and the loss of my fortune by the damage of my goods by sea: I told her also that I had a mother and a brother in *Virginia* in good circumstances, and as I had really written back to my mother in particular to represent my condition, and the great loss I had receiv'd, which indeed came to almost 500 *l.* so I did not fail to let my new friend know, that I expected a supply from thence, and so indeed I did; and as the ships went from *Bristol* to *York* River in *Virginia,* and back again generally in less time than from *London,* and that my brother corresponded chiefly at *Bristol,* I thought it was much better for me to wait here for my returns, than to go to *London,* where also I had not the least acquaintance.

---

1 Bawdy house.
2 That is, I had not given rise to censure, reproach or abuse.
3 Relationship.

My new friend appear'd sensibly affected with my condition, and indeed was so very kind, as to reduce the rate of my living with her to so low a price during the winter, that she convinced me she got nothing by me; and as for lodging during the winter, I paid nothing at all.

When the spring season came on, she continu'd to be as kind to me as she could, and I lodg'd with her for a time, till it was found necessary to do otherwise; she had some persons of character that frequently lodg'd in her house, and in particular the gentleman who, as I said, singl'd me out for his companion the winter before; and he came down again with another gentleman in his company and two servants, and lodg'd in the same house: I suspected that my landlady had invited him thither, letting him know that I was still with her, but she deny'd it, and protested to me that she did not, and he said the same.

In a word, this gentleman came down and continu'd to single me out for his peculiar confidence as well as conversation; he was a compleat[1] gentleman, *that must be confess'd*, and his company was very agreeable to me, as mine, *if I might believe him*, was to him; he made no professions to me but of an extraordinary respect, and he had such an opinion of my virtue, that *as he often profess'd*, he believ'd if he should offer any thing else, I should reject him with contempt; he soon understood from me that I was a widow, that I had arriv'd at *Bristol* from *Virginia* by the last ships; and that I waited at *Bath* till the next *Virginia fleet* should arrive, by which I expected considerable effects; I understood by him, and by others of him, that he had a wife, but that the lady was distemper'd in her head, and was under the conduct of her own relations, which he consented to, to avoid any reflections that might, *as was not unusual in such cases*, be cast on him for mismanaging her cure; and in the mean time he came to the *Bath* to divert his thoughts from the disturbance of such a melancholy circumstance as that was.

My landlady, who of her own accord encourag'd the correspondence on all occasions, gave me an advantageous character of him, as of a man of honour and of virtue, as well as of a great estate; and indeed I had a great deal of reason to say so of him too; for tho' we lodg'd both on a floor, and he had frequently come into my chamber, even when I was in bed; and I also into his when he

---

1 Perfect, consummate.

was in bed,[1] yet he never offered any thing to me farther than a kiss, or so much as solicited me to any thing till long after, as you shall hear.

I frequently took notice to my landlady of his exceeding modesty, and she again used to tell me, she believ'd it was so from the beginning; however she used to tell me that she thought I ought to expect some gratification from him for my company, for indeed he did, as it were, engross me,[2] and I was seldom from him; *I told her* I had not given him the least occasion to think I wanted it, or that I would accept of it from him; *she told me* she would take that part upon her, and she did so, and manag'd it so dextrously, that the first time we were together alone, after she had talk'd with him, he began to enquire a little into my circumstances, as how I had subsisted my self since I came on shore? and whether I did not want money? I stood off very boldly, I told him that tho' my cargo of tobacco was damag'd, yet that it was not quite lost; that the merchant I had been consign'd to, had so honestly manag'd for me that I had not wanted; and that I hop'd, with frugal management, I should make it hold out till more would come, which I expected by the next fleet; that in the mean time I had retrench'd my expences, and whereas I kept a maid last season, now I liv'd without; and whereas I had a chamber and a dining-room then on the first floor, *as he knew*, I now had but one room two pair of stairs,[3] *and the like*; But I live *said I*, as well satisfy'd now as I did then; *adding*, that his company had been a means to make me live much more chearfully than otherwise I should have done, for which I was much oblig'd to him; and so I put off all room for any offer for the present: however, it was not long before he attack'd me again, and told me he found that I was backward to trust him with the secret of my circumstances, *which he was sorry for*; assuring me that he enquir'd into it with no design to satisfie his own curiosity, but meerly to assist me, if there was any occasion; but since I would not own my self to stand in need of any assistance, he had but one thing more to desire of me, and that was, that I would promise him that when I was any way streighten'd,[4] or like to be so, I would

---

1 Such visits in polite society among friends of both sexes were not uncommon at this time. Indeed, the practice (known as "bundling") of unmarried couples sleeping together, usually fully dressed, was tolerated throughout the eighteenth century. See below, pp. 137-38.

2 Occupy my attention completely.

3 Up two flights of stairs.

4 In financial distress (obsolete form of *straitened*).

frankly tell him of it, and that I would make use of him with the same freedom that he made the offer, *adding*, that I should always find I had a true friend, tho' perhaps I was afraid to trust him.

I omitted nothing *that was fit to be said by one infinitely oblig'd*, to let him know, that I had a due sense of his kindness; and indeed from that time, I did not appear so much reserv'd to him as I had done before, tho' still within the bounds of the strictest virtue on both sides; but how free soever our conversation was, I cou'd not arrive to that sort of freedom which he desir'd, (*viz.*) to tell him I wanted money, tho' I was secretly very glad of his offer.

Some weeks pass'd after this, and still I never ask'd him for money; when my landlady, a cunning creature, who had often press'd me to it, but found that I cou'd not do it, makes a story of her own inventing, and comes in bluntly to me when we were together, O widow, *says she*, I have bad news to tell you this morning; What is that, said I, are the *Virginia* ships taken by the *French? for that was my fear*. No, no, *says she*, but the man you sent to *Bristol* yesterday for money is come back, and says he has brought none.

Now I could by no means like her project; I thought it look'd too much like prompting him, which indeed he did not want, and I saw clearly that I should lose nothing by being backward to ask, so I took her up short; I can't imagine why he should say so to you, *said I*, for I assure you he brought me all the money I sent him for, and here it is *said I*, (pulling out my purse with about 12 guineas in it) and added, I intend you shall have most of it by and by.

He seem'd distasted[1] a little at her talking as she did at first, as well as I, taking it as I fancied he would as something forward of her; but when he saw me give such an answer, he came immediately to himself again: the next morning we talk'd of it again, when I found he was fully satisfy'd; and smiling said, he hop'd I would not want money and not tell him of it, and that I had promis'd him otherwise: I told him I had been very much dissatisfy'd at my landladies talking so publickly the day before of what she had nothing to do with; but I suppos'd she wanted what I ow'd her, which was about eight guineas, which I had resolv'd to give her, and had accordingly given it her the same night she talk'd so foolishly.

He was in a mighty good humour, when he heard me say, *I had paid her*, and it went off into some other discourse at that time; but the next morning he having heard me up about my room before

---

1 Displeased.

him, he call'd to me, *and I answering*, he ask'd me to come into his chamber; he was in bed when I came in, and he made me come and sit down on his bed side, *for he said*, he had something to say to me, which was of some moment: after some very kind expressions he ask'd me, if I would be very honest to him, and give a sincere answer to one thing he would desire of me? After some little cavil with him at the word *sincere*, and asking him if I had ever given him any answers which were not sincere, I promis'd him I would; why then his request was, *he said*, to let him see my purse; I immediately put my hand into my pocket, *and laughing at him*, pull'd it out, and there was in it three guineas and a half; *then he ask'd me*, if there was all the money I had? I told him no, *laughing again*, not by a great deal.

Well then, *he said*, he would have me promise to go and fetch him all the money I had every farthing: *I told him I would*, and I went into my chamber, and fetch'd him a little private drawer, where I had about six guineas more, and some silver, and threw it all down upon the bed, and told him there was all my wealth, honestly to a shilling: he look'd a little at it, but did not tell[1] it, and huddled it all into the drawer again, and then reaching his pocket, pull'd out a key, and bad then me open a little walnuttree box, he had upon the table, and bring him such a drawer, which I did, in which drawer, there was a great deal of money in gold, I believe near 200 guineas, but I knew not how much: he took the drawer, and taking my hand, made me put it in, and take a whole handful; I was backward at that, but he held my hand hard in his hand, and put it into the drawer, and made me take out as many guineas almost as I could well take up at once.

When I had done so, he made me put them into my lap, and took my little drawer, and pour'd out all my own money among his, and bad me get me gone, and carry it all home into my own chamber.

I relate this story the more particularly because of the good humour there was in it, and to show the temper with which we convers'd: it was not long after this, but he began every day to find fault with my cloths, with my laces, and head-dresses; and in a word, press'd me to buy better, which by the way I was willing enough to do, tho' I did not seem to be so; for I lov'd nothing in the world better than fine clothes, I told him I must housewife[2] the

---

1 Count.
2 Manage with skill and thrift.

money he had lent me, or else I should not be able to pay him again. He then told me in a few words, that as he had a sincere respect for me, and knew my circumstances, he had not lent me that money, but given it me, and that he thought I had merited it from him, by giving him my company so intirely as I had done: after this, he made me take a maid, and keep house, and his friend that came with him to *Bath*, being gone, he oblig'd me to dyet him,[1] which I did very willingly, believeing *as it appear'd*, that I should lose nothing by it, nor did the woman of the house fail to find her account in it too.

We had liv'd thus near three months, when the company beginning to wear away at the *Bath*, he talk'd of going away, and fain he would have me to go to *London* with him: I was not very easie in that proposal, not knowing what posture[2] I was to live in there, or how he might use me: but while this was in debate he fell very sick; he had gone out to a place in *Somersetshire* called *Shepton*, where he had some business, and was there taken very ill, and so ill that he could not travel, so he sent his man back to *Bath* to beg me that I would hire a coach and come over to him. Before he went, he had left all his money and other things of value with me, and what to do with them I did not know, but I secur'd them as well as I could, and lock'd up the lodgings and went to him, where I found him very ill indeed; however, I perswaded him to be carry'd in a litter[3] to the *Bath*, where there was more help and better advice to be had.

He consented, and I brought him to the *Bath*, which was about fifteen miles, *as I remember*: here he continued very ill of a fever, and kept his bed five weeks, all which time I nurs'd him and tended him my self, as much and as carefully as if I had been his wife; indeed if I had been his wife I could not have done more; I sat up with him so much and so often, that at last indeed he would not let me sit up any longer, and then I got a pallate bed[4] into his room, and lay in it just at his bed's feet.

I was indeed sensibly affected with his condition, and with the apprehension of losing such a friend as he was, and was like to be to me, and I us'd to sit and cry by him many hours together: however at last he grew better, and gave hopes that he would recover, as indeed he did, tho' very slowly.

---

1 Board (obsolete form of *diet*).
2 Position, situation.
3 A vehicle containing a couch shut in by curtains (in this case probably drawn by horses).
4 A small, straw bed or couch (obsolete form of *pallet*).

Were it otherwise than what I am going to say, I should not be backward to disclose it, as it is apparent I have done in other cases in this account; but I affirm, that thro' all this conversation, abating the freedom of coming into the chamber when I or he was in bed, and abating the necessary offices of attending him night and day when he was sick, there had not pass'd the least immodest word or action between us. O! that it had been so to the last.

After some time he gathered strength, and grew well apace, and I would have remov'd my palate bed, but he would not let me till he was able to venture himself without any body to sit up with him, and then I remov'd to my own chamber.

He took many occasions to express his sense of my tenderness and concern for him; and when he grew quite well, he made me a present of fifty guineas for my care, and, as he call'd it, for hazarding my life to save his.

And now he made deep protestations of a sincere inviolable affection for me, but all along attested it to be with the utmost reserve for my virtue, and his own: I told him I was fully satisfyed of it; he carried it that length that he protested to me, that if he was naked in bed with me, he would as sacredly preserve my virtue, as he would defend it if I was assaulted by a ravisher; I believ'd him, and told him I did so; but this did not satisfie him, he would, *he said*, wait for some opportunity to give me an undoubted testimony of it.

It was a great while after this that I had occasion, on my own business, to go to *Bristol*, upon which he hir'd me a coach, and would go with me, and did so; and now indeed our intimacy increas'd: from *Bristol* he carry'd me to *Gloucester*, which was meerly a journey of pleasure to take the air; and here it was our hap to have no lodging in the inn but in one large chamber with two beds in it: the master of the house going up with us to show his rooms, and coming into that room, said very frankly to him, Sir, *it is none of my business to enquire whether the lady be your spouse or no, but if not, you may lie as honestly in these two beds as if you were in two chambers*, and with that he pulls a great curtain which drew quite cross the room, and effectually divided the beds; Well, *says my friend*, very readily, these beds will do, and as for the rest, we are too near a kin to lye together, tho' we may lodge near one another; and this put an honest face on the thing too. When we came to go to bed he decently went out of the room till I was in bed, and then went to bed in the bed on his own side of the room, but lay there talking to me a great while.

At last repeating his usual saying, that he could lye in the naked bed with me and not offer me the least injury, he starts out of his bed, and now, my dear, *says he,* you shall see how just I will be to you, and that I can keep my word, and away he comes to my bed.

I resisted a little, but I must confess I should not have resisted him much, if he had not made those promises at all; so after a little struggle, *as I said,* I lay still and let him come to bed; when he was there he took me in his arms, and so I lay all night with him, but he had no more to do with me, or offer'd any thing to me other than embracing me, as I say, in his arms, no not the whole night, but rose up and dress'd him in the morning, and left me as innocent for[1] him as I was the day I was born,

This was a surprizing thing to me, and perhaps may be so to others who know how the laws of nature work; for he was a strong vigorous brisk person; nor did he act thus on a principle of religion at all, *but of meer affection;* insisting on it, that tho' I was to him the most agreeable woman in the world, yet because he lov'd me he cou'd not injure me.

I own it was a noble principle, but as it was what I never understood before, so it was to me perfectly amazing. We travel'd the rest of the journey as we did before, and came back to the *Bath,* where, as he had opportunity to come to me when he would, he often repeated the moderation, and I frequently lay with him, and he with me, and altho' all the familiarities between man and wife were common to us, yet he never once offered to go any farther, and he valued himself much upon it; I do not say that I was so wholly pleas'd with it as he thought I was: for I own I was much wickeder than he, *as you shall hear presently.*

We liv'd thus near two year, only with this exception, that he went three times to *London* in that time, and once he continued there four months, but, to do him justice, he always supply'd me with money to subsist me very handsomly.

Had we continued thus, I confess we had had much to boast of; but as wise men say, it is ill venturing too near the brink of a command,[2] so we found it; and here again I must do him the justice to own, that the first breach was not on his part: it was one night that we were in bed together warm and merry, and having drank, I think, a little more wine that night, both of us, than usual, tho' not in the least to disorder either of us, when after some other fol-

1 In spite of.
2 Commandment.

lies which I cannot name, and being clasp'd close in his arms, *I told him, (I repeat it with shame and horror of soul)* that I cou'd find in my heart to discharge him of his engagement[1] for one night and no more.

He took me at my word immediately, and after that, there was no resisting him; neither indeed had I any mind to resist him any more, let what would come of it.

Thus the government of our virtue was broken, and I exchang'd the place of friend, for that unmusical harsh-sounding title of WHORE. In the morning we were both at our penitentials, I cried very heartily, he express'd himself very sorry; but that was all either of us could do at that time; and the way being thus clear'd, and the bars of virtue and conscience thus removed, we had the less difficulty afterwards to struggle with.

It was but a dull kind of conversation that we had together for all the rest of that week, I look'd on him with blushes; and every now and then started that melancholy objection, *What if I should be with child now? What will become of me then?* He encourag'd me by telling me, that as long as I was true to him he would be so to me; and since it was gone such a length, (which indeed he never intended) yet if I was with child, he would take care of that, and of me too: this harden'd us both; I assur'd him if I was with child, I would die for want of a midwife rather than name him as the father of it; and he assur'd me I should never want if I should be with child: these mutual assurances harden'd us in the thing; and after this we repeated the crime as often as we pleas'd, till at length, as I had fear'd, so it came to pass, and I was indeed with child.

After I was sure it was so, and I had satisfied him of it too, we began to think of taking measures for the managing it, and I pro-pos'd trusting the secret to my landlady, and asking her advice, which he agreed to: my landlady, a woman (as I found) us'd to such things, made light of it; she said she knew it would come to that at last, and made us very merry about it: as I said above, we found her an experienc'd old lady at such work; she undertook every thing, engag'd to procure a midwife and a nurse, to satisfie all enquiries, and bring us off with reputation, and she did so very dexterously indeed.

When I grew near my time, she desir'd my gentleman to go away to *London,* or make as if he did so; when he was gone, she

1 Promise.

acquainted the parish officers[1] that there was a lady ready to lye in at her house, but that she knew her husband very well, and gave them, as she pretended, an account of his name, which she called Sir *Walter Cleave*;[2] telling them, he was a very worthy gentleman, and that she would answer for all enquiries, and the like: this satisfied the parish officers presently, and I lay INN with as much credit as I could have done if I had really been my Lady *Cleave*; and was assisted in my travel[3] by three or four of the best citizens wives of *Bath*, who liv'd in the neighbourhood, which however made me a little the more expensive to him, I often expressed my concern to him about it, but he bid me not be concern'd at it.

As he had furnish'd me very sufficiently with money for the extraordinary expences of my lying inn, I had every thing very handsome about me; but did not affect to be gay or extravagant neither; besides, knowing my own circumstances, and knowing the world as I had done, and that such kind of things do not often last long, I took care to lay up as much money as I could for a wet day, as I call'd it; making him believe it was all spent upon the extraordinary appearance of things in my lying inn.

By this means, and including what he had given me as above, I had at the end of my lying inn about 200 guineas by me, including also what was left of my own.

I was brought to bed of a fine boy indeed, and a charming child it was; and when he heard of it he wrote me a very kind obliging letter about it, and then told me, he thought it would look better for me to come away for *London* as soon as I was up and well, that he had provided appartments for me at *Hammersmith*[4] as if I came thither only from *London*, and that after a little while I should go back to the *Bath*, and he would go with me.

---

1 As illegitimate and abandoned children were the responsibility of the parish in which they were born, the financial and marital status of pregnant women newly arrived in the parish was generally of concern to the parish officers. Under the terms of the Law of Settlement and Removal (1662), an unmarried pregnant woman without sufficient support could be returned to the parish in which she was deemed to have a "settlement."

2 Perhaps an allusion to a well-known goldsmith named Edward Cleave, who was in partnership with John Cox in Cornhill between 1715 and 1720. Or Defoe may have been punning on the word "cleave," which in contemporary slang meant a wanton woman.

3 The labour and pain of childbirth (obsolete form of *travail*).

4 A village in Middlesex, west of London.

I lik'd this offer very well, and accordingly hir'd a coach on purpose, and taking my child and a wet-nurse to tend and suckle it, and a maid servant with me, away I went for *London*.

He met me at *Reading* in his own chariot, and taking me into that, left the servant and the child in the hir'd coach, and so he brought me to my new lodgings at *Hammersmith*; with which I had abundance of reason to be very well pleas'd, for they were very handsome rooms, and I was very well accommodated.

And now I was indeed in the height of what I might call my prosperity, and I wanted nothing but to be a wife, which however could not be in this case, there was no room for it; and therefore on all occasions I study'd to save what I could, as I have said above, against a time of scarcity; knowing well enough that such things as these do not always continue, that men that keep mistresses often change them, grow weary of them, or jealous of them, or something or other happens to make them withdraw their bounty; and sometimes the ladies that are thus well us'd, are not careful by a prudent conduct to preserve the esteem of their persons, or the nice article of their fidelity, and then they are justly cast off with contempt.

But I was secur'd in this point, for as I had no inclination to change, so I had no manner of acquaintance in the whole house, and so no temptation to look any farther; I kept no company but in the family where I lodg'd, and with a clergyman's lady at next door; so that when he was absent I visited no body, nor did he ever find me out of my chamber or parlor whenever he came down, if I went any where to take the air it was always with him.

The living in this manner with him, and his with me, was certainly the most undesigned thing in the world; he often protested to me, that when he became first acquainted with me, and even to the very night when we first broke in upon our rules, he never had the least design of lying with me; that he always had a sincere affection for me, but not the least real inclination to do what he had done; I assur'd him I never suspected him, that if I had, I should not so easily have yielded to the freedoms which brought it on, but that it was all a surprize, and was owing to the accident of our having yielded too far to our mutual inclinations that night; and indeed I have often observ'd since, and leave it as a caution to the readers of this story; that we ought to be cautious of gratifying our inclinations in loose and lewd freedoms, lest we find our resolutions of virtue fail us in the juncture when their assistance should be most necessary.

It is true, *and I have confess'd it before*, that from the first hour I began to converse with him, I resolv'd to let him lye with me, if he offer'd it; but it was because I wanted his help and assistance, and I knew no other way of securing him than that: but when we were that night together, and, as I have said, had gone such a length, I found my weakness, the inclination was not to be resisted, but I was oblig'd to yield up all even before he ask'd it.

However he was so just to me that he never upbraided me with that; nor did he ever express the least dislike of my conduct on any other occasion, but always protested he was as much delighted with my company as he was the first hour we came together, I mean came together as bedfellows.

It is true that he had no wife, that is to say, she was as no wife to him, and so I was in no danger that way, but the just reflections of conscience oftentimes snatch a man, especially a man of sense, from the arms of a mistress, as it did him at last, tho' on another occasion.

On the other hand, tho' I was not without secret reproaches of my own conscience for the life I led, and that even in the greatest height of the satisfaction I ever took, yet I had the terrible prospect of poverty and starving which lay on me as a frightful spectre, so that there was no looking behind me: but as poverty brought me into it, so fear of poverty kept me in it, and I frequently resolv'd to leave it quite off, if I could but come to lay up money enough to maintain me: but these were thoughts of no weight, and whenever he came to me they vanish'd; for his company was so delightful, that there was no being melancholly when he was there, the reflections were all the subject of those hours when I was alone.

I liv'd six year in this happy but unhappy condition, in which time I brought him three children, but only the first of them liv'd; and tho' I remov'd twice in those six years, yet I came back the sixth year to my first lodgings at *Hammersmith*: here it was that I was one morning surpriz'd with a kind, but melancholy letter from my gentleman; intimating, that he was very ill, and was afraid he should have another fit of sickness, but that his wife's relations being in the house with him, it would not be practicable to have me with him, which however he express'd his great dissatisfaction in, and that he wish'd I cou'd be allowed to tend and nurse him as I did before.

I was very much concern'd at this account, and was very impatient to know how it was with him; I waited a fortnight or thereabouts, and heard nothing, which surpriz'd me, and I began to be very uneasy indeed; I think I may say, that for the next fortnight I was near to distracted: it was my particular difficulty, that I did not know directly where he was; for I understood at first he was in the lodgings of his wife's mother; but having remov'd my self to *London*, I soon found by the help of the direction I had for writing my letters to him, how to enquire after him, and there I found that he was at a house in *Bloomsbury*, whither he had, a little before he fell sick, remov'd his whole family; and that his wife and wife's mother were in the same house, tho' the wife was not suffered to know that she was in the same house with her husband.

Here I also soon understood that he was at the last extremity, which made me almost at the last extremity too, to have a true account: one night I had the curiosity to disguise my self like a servant maid in a round cap and straw hat, and went to the door, as sent[1] by a lady of his neighbourhood, where he liv'd before, and giving master and mistresses service, I said I was sent to know how Mr. ⸺ did, and how he had rested that night; in delivering this message I got the opportunity I desir'd, for speaking with one of the maids, I held a long gossips tale with her, and had all the particulars of his illness, which I found was a pleurisie attended with a cough and a fever; she told me also who was in the house, and how his wife was, who, by her relation,[2] they were in some hopes might recover her understanding; but as to the gentleman himself, *in short* she told me the doctors said there was very little hopes of him, that in the morning they thought he had been dying, and that he was but little better then, for they did not expect that he could live over the next night.

This was heavy news for me, and I began now to see an end of my prosperity, and to see also that it was very well I had play'd the good housewife, and secur'd or saved something while he was alive, for that now I had no view of *my own living* before me.

It lay very heavy upon my mind too, that I had a son, a fine lovely boy, above five years old, and no provision made for it, at least that I knew of; with these considerations, and a sad heart, I went home that evening, and began to cast with my self how I should live, and in what manner to bestow my self, for the residue of my life.

You may be sure I could not rest without enquiring again very quickly what was become of him; and not venturing to go my self, I sent several sham messengers, till after a fortnights waiting

---

1 As if sent.
2 That is, according to the maid's account.

longer, I found that there was hopes of his life, tho' he was still very ill; then I abated my sending any more to the house, and in some time after I learnt in the neighbourhood that he was about house, and then that he was abroad[1] again.

I made no doubt then but that I shou'd soon hear of him, and began to comfort my self with my circumstances being, as I thought, recovered; I waited a week, and two weeks, and with much surprize and amazement I waited near two months and heard nothing, but that being recover'd he was gone into the country for the air, and for the better recovery after his distemper; after this it was yet two months more, and then I understood he was come to his city-house again, but still I heard nothing from him.

I had written several letters for[2] him, and directed them as usual, and found two or three of them had been call'd for, *but not the rest*: I wrote again in a more pressing manner than ever, and in one of them let him know, that I must be forc'd to wait on him myself, representing my circumstances, the rent of lodgings to pay, and the provision for the child wanting, and my own deplorable condition, destitute of subsistence after his most solemn engagement, to take care of, and provide for me; I took a copy of this letter, and finding it lay at the house, near a month, and was not call'd for, I found means to have the copy of it, put into his own hands at a coffee-house, where I had by enquiry found he us'd to go.

This letter forc'd an answer from him, by which, tho' I found I was to be abandon'd, yet I found he had sent a letter to me sometime before, desiring me to go down *to the Bath again*, its contents I shall come to presently.

It is true that sick beds are the times, when such correspondences as this are look'd on with different countenance, and seen with other eyes than we saw them with, or than they appear'd with before: my lover had been at the gates of death, and at the very brink of eternity; and it seems had been strook with a due remorse, and with sad reflections upon his past life of gallantry, and levity; and among the rest, this criminal correspondence with me, which was neither more or less, than a long continu'd life of adultery had represented it self, as it really was, not as it had been formerly thought by him to be, and he look'd upon it now with a just, and a religious aborrence.

---

1 Able to get out of the house.
2 To.

I cannot but observe also, and leave it for the direction of my sex in such cases of pleasure, that when ever sincere repentance succeeds such a crime as this, there never fails to attend a hatred of the object; and the more the affection might seem to be before, the hatred will be the more in proportion: it will always be so, indeed it can be no otherwise; for there cannot be a true and sincere abhorrence of the offence, and the love to the cause of it remain, there will with an abhorrence of the sin be found a detestation of the fellow sinner; you can expect no other.

I found it so here, tho' good manners, and justice in this gentleman, kept him from carrying it on to any extream; but the short history of his part in this affair, was thus; he perceiv'd by my last letter, and by all the rest, which he went for after,[1] that I was not gone to the *Bath*, that his first letter had not come to my hand, upon which he writes me this following,

Madam,

I am surpriz'd that my letter dated the 8th of last month did not come to your hand, I give you my word it was deliver'd at your lodgings, and to the hands of your maid.

I need not acquaint you with what has been my condition for sometime past; and how having been at the edge of the grave, I am by the unexpected and undeserv'd mercy of Heaven restor'd again: in the condition I have been in, it cannot be strange to you that our unhappy correspondence has not been the least of the burthens which lay upon my conscience; I need say no more, those things that must be repented of, must be also reform'd.

I wish you would think of going back to the Bath, *I enclose you here a bill for 50 l. for clearing your self at your lodgings, and carrying you down, and hope it will be no surprize to you to add, that on this account only, and not for any offence given me on your side, I can* SEE YOU NO MORE; *I will take due care of the child, leave him where he is, or take him with you, as you please; I wish you the like reflections, and that they may be to your advantage. I am,* &c.

I was struck with this letter as with a thousand wounds, such as I cannot describe; the reproaches of my own conscience were such as I cannot express, for I was not blind to my own crime: and I reflected that I might with less offence have continued with my

---

1 Called for afterwards.

brother, and liv'd with him as a wife, since there was no crime in our marriage on that score, neither of us knowing it.

But I never once reflected that I was all this while a marry'd woman, a wife to Mr. —— the linnen draper, who tho' he had left me by the necessity of his circumstances, had no power to discharge me from the marriage contract which was between us, or to give me a legal liberty to marry again; so that I had been no less than a whore and an adultress all this while: I then reproach'd my self with the liberties I had taken, and how I had been a snare to this gentleman, and that indeed I was principal in the crime; that now he was mercifully snatch'd out of the gulph[1] by a convincing work[2] upon his mind, but that I was left as if I was forsaken of God's grace, and abandon'd by Heaven to a continuing in my wickedness.

Under these reflections I continu'd very pensive and sad for near a month, and did not go down to the *Bath*, having no inclination to be with the woman who I was with before; lest, as I thought, she should prompt me to some wicked course of life again, as she had done; and besides, I was very loth she should know I was cast off as above.

And now I was greatly perplex'd about my little boy; it was death to me to part with the child, and yet when I consider'd the danger of being one time or other left with him to keep without a maintenance to support him, I then resolv'd to leave him where he was; but then I concluded also to be near him my self too, that I might have the satisfaction of seeing him, without the care of providing for him.

I sent my gentleman a short letter therefore, that I had obey'd his orders in all things, but that of going back to the *Bath*, which I cou'd not think of for many reasons; that however parting from him was a wound to me that I could never recover, yet that I was fully satisfied his reflections were just, and would be very far from desiring to obstruct his reformation or repentance.

Then I represented my own circumstances to him in the most moving terms that I was able: I told him that those unhappy distresses which first mov'd him to a generous and an honest friendship for me, would, I hope, move him to a little concern for me now; tho' the criminal part of our correspondence, which I

1 Abyss (obsolete form of *gulf*).
2 This is the first stage of repentance in theological terms, by which a penitent is convinced of the evil nature of the sin and of his or her own guilt.

believed neither of us intended to fall into at that time, was broken off; that I desir'd to repent as sincerely as he had done, but entreated him to put me in some condition, that I might not be expos'd to the temptations which the Devil never fails to excite us to from the frightful prospect of poverty and distress; and if he had the least apprehensions of my being troublesome to him, I beg'd he would put me in a posture to go back to my mother in *Virginia*, from whence he knew I came, and that would put an end to all his fears on that account; I concluded, that if he would send me 50 *l.* more to facilitate my going away, I would send him back a general release, and would promise never to disturb him more with any importunities; unless it was to hear of the well-doing of the child, who if I found my mother living, and my circumstances able, I would send for to come over to me, and take him also effectually off of his hands.

This was indeed all a cheat thus far, *viz.* that I had no intention to go to *Virginia*, as the account of my former affairs there may convince any body of; but the business was to get this last fifty pounds of him, if possible, knowing well enough it would be the last penny I was ever to expect.

However, the argument I us'd, namely, of giving him a general release, and never troubling him any more, prevail'd effectually with him, and he sent me a bill for the money by a person who brought with him a general release for me to sign, and which I frankly[1] sign'd, and receiv'd the money; and thus, tho' full sore against my will, a final end was put to this affair.

And here I cannot but reflect upon the unhappy consequence of too great freedoms between persons stated[2] as we were, upon the pretence of innocent intentions, love of friendship, *and the like*; for the flesh has generally so great a share in those friendships, that it is great odds but inclination prevails at last over the most solemn resolutions; and that vice breaks in at the breaches of decency, which really innocent friendship ought to preserve with the greatest strictness; but I leave the readers of these things to their own just reflections, which they will be more able to make effectual than I, who so soon forgot my self, and am therefore but a very indifferent monitor.[3]

I was now a single person again, *as I may call my self*, I was loos'd from all the obligations either of wedlock or mistressship in

---

1 Freely, unreservedly.
2 Situated, placed.
3 One who counsels or warns.

the world; except my husband the linnen draper, who I having not now heard from in almost fifteen year, no body could blame me for thinking my self entirely freed from; seeing also he had at his going away told me, that if I did not hear frequently from him, I should conclude he was dead, and I might freely marry again to whom I pleas'd.

I now began to cast up[1] my accounts; I had by many letters, and much importunity, and with the intercession of my mother too, had a second return[2] of some goods from my brother, *as I now call him*, in *Virginia*, to make up the damage of the cargo I brought away with me, and this too was upon the condition of my sealing a general release to him, and to send it him by his correspondent at *Bristol*, which though I thought hard of, yet I was oblig'd to promise to do: however, I manag'd so well in this case, that I got my goods away before the release was sign'd, and then I always found something or other to say to evade the thing, and to put off the signing it at all; till *at length* I pretended I must write to my brother, and have his answer, before I could do it.

Including this recruit, and before I got the last 50 *l.* I found my strength to amount, put all together, to about 400 *l.* so that with that I had above 450 *l.* I had sav'd above 100 *l.* more, but I met with a disaster with that, which was this; that a goldsmith in whose hands I had trusted it, broke,[3] so I lost 70 *l.* of my money, the man's composition not making above 30 *l.* out of his 100 *l.* I had a little plate,[4] but not much, and was well enough stock'd with cloaths and linnen.

With this stock I had the world to begin again; but you are to consider, that I was not now the same woman as when I liv'd at *Redriff*; for first of all I was near 20 years older, and did not look the better for my age, nor for my rambles to *Virginia* and back again; and tho' I omitted nothing that might set me out to advantage, except painting,[5] for that I never stoop'd to, and had pride enough to think I did not want it, yet there would always be some difference seen between five and twenty, and two and forty.

I cast about innumerable ways for my future state of life and began to consider very seriously what I should do, *but nothing offer'd*;

---

1 Add up, calculate.
2 Consignment.
3 Went bankrupt. Although the Bank of England was founded in 1694, goldsmiths continued to be the nation's bankers during this period.
4 Such things as coins and household articles made of valuable metals.
5 Cosmetics.

I took care to make the world take me for something more than I was, and had it given out that I was a fortune, and that my estate was in my own hands, the last of which was very true, the first of it was as above: I had no acquaintance, which was one of my worst misfortunes, and the consequence of that was, I had no adviser, at least who cou'd advise and assist together; and above all, I had no body to whom I could in confidence commit the secret of my circumstances to, and could depend upon for their secresie and fidelity; and I found by experience, that to be friendless is the worst condition, next to being in want, that a woman can be reduc'd to: *I say a woman*, because 'tis evident men can be their own advisers, and their own directors, and know how to work themselves out of difficulties and into business better than women; but if a woman has no friend to communicate her affairs to, and to advise and assist her, 'tis ten to one but she is undone; nay, and the more money she has, the more danger she is in of being wrong'd and deceiv'd; and this was my case in the affair of the hundred pound which I left in the hand of the goldsmith, *as above*, whose credit, it seems, was upon the ebb before, but I that had no knowledge of things, and no body to consult with, knew nothing of it, and so lost my money.

In the next place, when a woman is thus left desolate and void of council, she is just like a bag of money, or a jewel dropt on the highway, which is a prey to the next comer; if a man of virtue and upright principles happens to find it, he will have it cried,[1] and the owner may come to hear of it again; but how many times shall such a thing fall into hands that will make no scruple of siezing it for their own, to once that it shall come into good hands.

This was evidently my case, for I was now a loose unguided creature, and had no help, no assistance, no guide for my conduct: I knew what I aim'd at, and what I wanted, but knew nothing how to pursue the end by direct means; I wanted to be plac'd in a settled state of living, and had I happen'd to meet with a sober good husband, I should have been as faithful and true a wife to him as virtue it self could have form'd: if I had been otherwise, the vice came in always at the door of necessity, not at the door of inclination; and I understood too well, by the want of it, what the value of a settl'd life was, to do any thing to forfeit the felicity of it; nay, I should have made the better wife for all the difficulties I had pass'd thro', by a great deal; nor did I in any of the times that I had

---

1 Give public notice that it is found.

been a wife, give my husbands the least uneasiness on account of my behaviour.

But all this was nothing; I found no encouraging prospect; I waited, I liv'd regularly, and with as much frugality as became my circumstances, but nothing offer'd; nothing presented, and the main stock wasted apace; what to do I knew not, the terror of approaching poverty lay hard upon my spirits: I had some money, but where to place it I knew not, nor would the interest of it maintain me, at least not in *London*.

At length a new scene open'd: there was in the house, where I lodg'd, a north country woman that went for a gentlewoman, and nothing was more frequent in her discourse, than her account of the cheapness of provisions, and the easie way of living in her county; how plentiful and how cheap every thing was, what good company they kept, and the like; till at last I told her she almost tempted me to go and live in her county; for I that was a widow, tho' I had sufficient to live on, yet had no way of encreasing it, and that *London* was an expensive and extravagant place; that I found I could not live here under a hundred pound a year, unless I kept no company, no servant, made no appearance, and buried my self in privacy, as if I was oblig'd to it by necessity.

I should have observ'd, that she was always made to believe, as every body else was, that I was a great fortune, or at least that I had three or four thousand pounds, if not more, and all in my own hands; and she was mighty sweet upon me when she thought me inclin'd in the least to go into her country; she said she had a sister liv'd near *Liverpool*, that her brother was a considerable gentleman there, and had a great estate also in *Ireland*; that she would go down there in about two months, and if I would give her my company thither, I should be as welcome as her self for a month or more as I pleas'd, till I should see how I lik'd the country; and if I thought fit to live there, she would undertake they would take care, tho' they did not entertain lodgers themselves, they would recommend me to some agreeable family, where I shou'd be plac'd to my content.

If this woman had known my real circumstances, she would never have laid so many snares, and taken so many weary steps to catch a poor desolate creature that was good for little when it was caught; and indeed I, whose case was almost desperate, and thought I cou'd not be much worse, was not very anxious about what might befall me, provided they did me no personal injury; so I suffered my self, tho' not without a great deal of invitation, and great professions of sincere friendship and real kindness, *I say* I suffer'd my self to be prevail'd upon to go with her, and accordingly I pack'd up my baggage, and put my self in a posture for a journey, tho' I did not absolutely know whither I was to go.

And now I found my self in great distress; what little I had in the world was all in money, except as before, a little plate, some linnen, and my cloaths; as for houshold stuff I had little or none, for I had liv'd always in lodgings; but I had not one friend in the world with whom to trust that little I had, or to direct me how to dispose of it, and this perplex'd me night and day; I thought of the bank, and of the other companies in *London*,[1] but I had no friend to commit the management of it to, and to keep and carry about with me bank bills, talleys,[2] orders, and such things, I look'd upon it as unsafe; that if they were lost my money was lost, and then I was undone; and on the other hand I might be robb'd, and perhaps murder'd in a strange place for them; this perplex'd me strangely, and what to do I knew not.

It came in my thoughts one morning that I would go to the *bank* my self, where I had often been to receive the interest of some bills I had, which had interest payable on them, and where I had found the clark, to whom I applyed my self, very honest and just to me, and particularly so fair one time, that when I had misstold[3] my money, and taken less than my due, and was coming away, he set me to rights and gave me the rest, which he might have put into his own pocket.

I went to him, and represented my case very plainly, *and ask'd if he would trouble himself to be my adviser, who was a poor friendless widow, and knew not what to do: he told me,* if I desir'd his opinion of any thing within the reach of his business, he would do his endeavour that I should not be wrong'd, but that he would also help me to a good sober person who was a grave man of his acquaintance, who was a clark in such business too, tho' not in their house, whose judgment was good, and whose honesty I might depend upon, *for,* added he, *I will answer for him, and for every step he takes; if he wrongs you,* madam, *of one farthing,*[4] *it shall lye at my door, I will make it good;* and he delights to assist people in such cases, he does it as an act of charity.

---

1 That is, the Bank of England and the shops of goldsmiths. See above, p. 148, n. 3.
2 Sticks with notches which represent the amount of a debt or payment.
3 Miscounted.
4 A British coin worth one-fourth of a penny, used proverbially to signify a very small amount of money.

I was a little at a stand at this discourse, but after some pause I told him, I had rather have depended upon him because I had found him honest, but if that cou'd not be, I would take his recommendation sooner than any ones else; *I dare say*, madam, says he, *that you will be as well satisfied with my friend as with me, and he is thoroughly able to assist you, which I am not*; it seems he had his hands full of the business of the bank, and had engag'd to meddle with no other business than that of his office, which I heard afterwards, but did not understand then: he added, that his friend should take nothing of me for his advice or assistance, and this indeed encourag'd me very much.

He appointed the same evening after the bank was shut, and business over, for me to meet him and his friend; and indeed as soon as I saw his friend, and he began but to talk of the affair, I was fully satisfied that I had a very honest man to deal with, his countenance spoke it, and his character, as I heard afterwards, was every where so good, that I had no room for any more doubts upon me.

After the first meeting, in which I only said what I had said before, we parted, and he appointed me to come the next day to him, *telling me*, I might in the mean time satisfie my self of him by enquiry, which however I knew not how well to do, having no acquaintance my self.

Accordingly I met him the next day, when I entered more freely with him into my case, *I told him* my circumstances at large,[1] that *I was a widow* come over from *America*, perfectly desolate and friendless; that I had a little money, and but a little, and was almost distracted for fear of losing it, having no friend in the world to trust with the management of it; that I was going into the north of *England* to live cheap, that my stock might not waste; that I would willingly lodge my money in the bank, but that I durst not carry the bills about me, and the like, as above; and how to correspond about it, or with who, I knew not.

He told me I might lodge the money in the bank as an account, and its being entred in the books would entitle me to the money at any time, and if I was in the north I might draw bills on the cashire and receive it when I would; but that then it would be esteem'd as running cash, and the bank would give no interest for it; that I might buy stock with it, and so it would lye in store for me, but that then if I wanted to dispose of it, I must come up to

---

1 At length, fully.

town on purpose to transfer it, and even it would be with some difficulty I should receive the half yearly dividend, unless I was here in person, or had some friend I could trust with having the stock in his name to do it for me, and that would have the same difficulty in it as before; and with that he look'd hard at me *and smil'd a little*; at last, *says he*, Why do you not get a head steward,[1] madam, that may take you and your money together into keeping, and then you would have the trouble taken off of your hands? Ay, sir, and the money too it may be, *said I*, for truly *I find the hazard that way is as much as 'tis t'other way*; but I remember, *I said*, secretly to my self, I wish you would ask me the question fairly, I would consider very seriously on it before I said No.

He went on a good way with me, and I thought once or twice he was in earnest, but to my real affliction, I found at last he had a wife; but when he own'd he had a wife he shook his head, and said with some concern, that indeed he had *a wife*, and *no wife*: I began to think he had been in the condition of my late lover, and that his wife had been distemper'd or lunatick, or some such thing: however, we had not much more discourse at that time, but he told me he was in too much hurry of business then, but that if I would come home to his house after their business was over, he would by that time consider what might be done for me, to put my affairs in a posture of security: I told him I would come, and desir'd to know where he liv'd: he gave me a direction in writing, and when he gave it me he read it to me, and said, There 'tis, madam, if you dare trust your self with me: Yes, sir, *said I*, I believe I may venture to trust you with my self, for you have a wife you say, and I don't want a husband; besides, I dare trust you with my money, which is all I have in the world, and if that were gone, I may trust my self any where.

He said some things in jest that were very handsome and mannerly, and would have pleas'd me very well if they had been in earnest; *but that pass'd over*, I took the directions, and appointed to attend him at his house at seven a clock the same evening.

When I came he made several proposals for my placing my money in the bank, in order to my having interest for it; but still some difficulty or other came in the way, which he objected as not safe; and I found such a sincere disinterested honesty in him, that I began to muse with my self, that I had certainly found the honest man I wanted; and that I could never put my self into better

---

1 That is, a husband.

hands; so I told him with a great deal of frankness that I had never met with man or woman yet that I could trust, or in whom I cou'd think my self safe, but that I saw he was so disinterestedly concern'd for my safety, that *I said* I would freely trust him with the management of that little I had, if he would accept to be steward for a poor widow that could give him no salary.

He smil'd, and standing up with great respect saluted me; he told me he could not but take it very kindly that I had so good an opinion of him; that he would not deceive me, that he would do any thing in his power to serve me and expect no sallary; but that he cou'd not by any means accept of a trust, that it might bring him to be suspected of self-interest, and that if I should die he might have disputes with my executors, which he should be very loth to encumber himself with.

I told him if those were all his objections I would soon remove them, and convince him, that there was not the least room for any difficulty; for that *first* as for suspecting him, if ever I should do it now was the time to suspect him, and not put the trust into his hands, and whenever I did suspect him, he could but throw it up then and refuse to go any farther; *then* as to executors, I assur'd him I had no heirs, nor any relations in *England*, and I would have neither heirs or executors but himself, unless I should alter my condition before I died, and then his trust and trouble should cease together, which however I had no prospect of yet; but I told him if I died as I was, it should be all his own, and he would deserve it by being so faithful to me as I was satisfied he would be.

He chang'd his countenance at this discourse, and ask'd me, how I came to have so much good will for him? and looking very much pleas'd, said, he might very lawfully wish he was a single man for my sake; I smil'd and told him, that as he was not, my offer could have no design upon him in it, and to wish, as he did, was not to be allow'd 'twas criminal to his wife.

He told me I was wrong; for, *says he*, madam, as I said before, I have a wife and no wife, and 'twould be no sin to me to wish her hang'd, if that were all; I know nothing of your circumstances that way, sir, *said I*; but it cannot be innocent to wish your wife dead; I tell you, *says he again*, she is a wife and no wife; you don't know what I am, or what she is.

That's true, *said I*, sir, I do not know what you are, but I believe you to be an honest man, and that's the cause of all my confidence in you.

Well, well, *says he*, and so I am, *I hope*, too, but I am something else too, madam; for, *says he*, to be plain with you, I am a *cuckold*, and she is a *whore*; he spoke it in a kind of jest, but it was with such an awkward smile, that I perceiv'd it was what stuck very close to him, and he look'd dismally when he said it.

That alters the case indeed, sir, *said I*, as to that part you were speaking of; but *a cuckold* you know may be an honest man, it does not alter that case at all; besides I think, *said I*, since your wife is so dishonest to you, you are too honest to her, to own her for your wife; but that, *said I*, is what I have nothing to do with.

Nay, *says he*, I do think to clear my hands of her, for to be plain with you, madam, *added he*, I am no contented cuckold neither: *on the other hand*, I assure you it provokes me to the highest degree, but I can't help my self, she that will be *a whore*, will be a *whore*.

I wav'd[1] the discourse, and began to talk of my business, but I found he could not have done with it, so I let him alone, and he went on to tell me all the circumstances of his case, too long to relate here, particularly, that having been out of *England* some time before he came to the post he was in, she had had two children in the mean time by an officer of the army; and that when he came to *England*, and, upon her submission,[2] took her again, and maintain'd her very well, yet she run away from him with a linnen-draper's apprentice; robb'd him of what she could come at, and continued to live from him still; So that, madam, *says he*, she is a whore not by necessity, which is the common bait of your sex, but by inclination, and for the sake of the vice.

Well, I pitied him and wish'd him well rid of her, and still would have talk'd of my business, but it would not do; at last he looks steadily at me, *Look you*, madam, *says he*, you came to ask advice of me, and I will serve you as faithfully as if you were my own sister; but I must turn the tables,[3] since you oblige me to do it, and are so friendly to me, and I think I must ask advice of you; *tell me what must a poor abus'd fellow do with* a whore? *What can I do* to do my self justice *upon her?*

Alas, *sir, says I*, 'tis a case too nice[4] for me to advise in, but it seems she has run away from you, so you are rid of her fairly; what can you desire more? Ay she is gone indeed, *said he*, but I am not clear of her for all that.

That's true, *says I*, she may indeed run you into debt, but the

---

1 Put aside (confused with *waived*).
2 Demonstrations of submissiveness.
3 Reverse the situation and thereby gain the advantage.
4 Too subtle, requiring too fine a discernment.

law has furnish'd you with methods to prevent that also, you may cry her down,[1] *as they call it.*

No, no, *says he,* that is not the case neither, I have taken care of all that; 'tis not that part that I speak of, but I would be rid of her so that I might marry again.

Well, sir, *says I,* then you must divorce her; if you can prove what you say, you may certainly get that done, and then, I suppose, you are free.[2]

That's very tedious and expensive, *says he.*

Why, *says I,* if you can get any woman you like to take your word, I suppose your wife would not dispute the liberty with you that she takes herself.

Ay, *says he,* but 'twou'd be hard to bring an honest woman to do that; and for the other sort, *says he,* I have had enough of her to meddle with any more whores.

It occurr'd to me presently, I would have taken your word with all my heart, if you had but ask'd me the question, but that was to my self; *to him I reply'd,* Why you shut the door against any honest woman accepting you, for you condemn all that should venture upon you at once, and conclude, that really a woman that takes you now, can't be honest.

Why, *says he,* I wish you would satisfie me that an honest woman would take me, I'd venture it, and then turns short upon me, *Will you take me,* madam?

That's not a fair question, *says I,* after what you have said; however, lest you should think I wait only for a recantation of it, I shall answer you plainly No *not I;* my business is of another kind with you, and I did not expect you would have turn'd my serious application to you in my own distracted case, into a comedy.

Why, madam, *says he,* my case is as distracted as yours can be, and I stand in as much need of advice as you do, for I think if I have not relief some where, I shall be mad my self, and I know not what course to take, I protest to you.

Why, sir, *says I,* 'tis easie to give advice in your case, much easier than it is in mine; Speak then, *says he,* I beg of you, for now you encourage me.

Why, *says I,* if your case is so plain as you say it is, you may be legally divorc'd, and then you may find honest women enough to

---

1 That is, proclaim publicly that you are no longer responsible for her debts.
2 For further information, see Appendix A.2.

ask the question of fairly, the sex is not so scarce that you can want a wife.

Well then, *said he*, I am in earnest, I'll take your advice, but shall I ask you one question seriously before hand?

Any question, *said I*, but that you did before.

No, that answer will not do, *said he*, for, in short, that is the question I shall ask.

You may ask what questions you please, but you have my answer to that already, *said I*; besides sir, *said I*, can you think so ill of me as that I would give any answer to such a question beforehand? Can any woman alive believe you in earnest, or think you design any thing but to banter her?

Well, well, *says he*, I do not banter you, I am in earnest, consider of it.

But, sir, *says I, a little gravely*, I came to you about my own business, I beg of you let me know, what you will advise me to do?

I will be prepar'd, *says he*, against you come again.

Nay, *says I*, you have forbid my coming any more.

Why so, *said he*, and look'd a little surpriz'd?

Because, *said I*, you can't expect I should visit you on the account you talk of.

Well, *says he*, you shall promise me to come again however, and I will not say any more of it till I have gotten the divorce, but I desire you will prepare to be better condition'd[1] when that's done, for you shall be the woman, or I will not be divorc'd at all: why I owe it to your unlooked for kindness, if it were to nothing else, but I have other reasons too.

He could not have said any thing in the world that pleas'd me better; however, I knew that the way to secure him was to stand off while the thing was so remote, as it appear'd to be, and that it was time enough to accept of it when he was able to perform it; so I said very respectfully to him, it was time enough to consider of these things, when he was in a condition to talk of them; in the mean time I told him, I was going a great way from him, and he would find objects enough to please him better: we broke off here for the present, and he made me promise him to come again the next day, for his resolutions upon my own business, which after some pressing I did; tho' had he seen farther into me, I wanted no pressing on that account.

I came the next evening accordingly, and brought my maid with

---

1 Disposed.

me, *to let him see* that I kept a maid, but I sent her away, as soon as I was gone in: he would have had me let the maid have staid, but I would not, but order'd her aloud to come for me again about nine a-clock, but he forbid that, and told me he would see me safe home, which by the way I was not very well pleas'd with, supposing he might do that to know where I liv'd, and enquire into my character, and circumstances: however, I ventur'd that, for all that the people there, or thereabout knew of me, was to my advantage; and all the character he had of me, after he had enquir'd, was, *that I was a woman of fortune*, and that I was a very modest sober body; which whether true or not in the main, yet you may see how necessary it is, for all women who expect any thing in the world, to preserve the character of their virtue, even when perhaps they may have sacrific'd the thing itself.

I found, *and was not a little pleas'd with it*, that he had provided a supper for me: I found also he liv'd very handsomely, and had a house very handsomely furnish'd, all which I was rejoyc'd at indeed, for I look'd upon it as all my own.

We had now a second conference upon the subject matter of the last conference: he laid his business very home indeed; he protested his affection to me, and indeed I had no room to doubt it; he declar'd that it began from the first moment I talk'd with him, and long before I had mention'd leaving my effects with him; 'Tis no matter when it begun, *thought I*, if it will but hold, 'twill be well enough: *he then told me*, how much the offer I had made of trusting him with my effects, and leaving them to him, had engag'd him; So I intended it should, *thought I*, but then I thought you had been a single man too: after we had supp'd, I observ'd he press'd me very hard to drink two or three glasses of wine, which however I declin'd; but drank one glass or two: he then told he had a proposal to make to me, which I should promise him I would not take ill, if I should not grant it: I told him I hop'd he would make no dishonourable proposal to me, especially in his own house, and that if it was such, I desir'd he would not propose it, that I might not be oblig'd to offer any resentment to him, that did not become the respect I profess'd for him, and the trust I had plac'd in him, in coming to his house; and beg'd of him he would give me leave to go away, and accordingly began to put on my gloves, and prepare to be gone, tho' at the same time I no more intended it, than he intended to let me.

Well, he importun'd me not to talk of going, he assur'd me he had no dishonourable thing in his thoughts about me, and was very far from offering any thing to me that was dishonourable and if I thought so, he would chuse to say no more of it.

That part I did not relish at all; I told him, I was ready to hear any thing that he had to say, depending that he would say nothing unworthy of himself, or unfit for me to hear; upon this, he told me his proposal was this, that I would marry him, tho' he had not yet obtain'd the divorce from the whore his wife; and to satisfie me that he meant honourably, he would promise not to desire me to live with him, or go to bed to him till the divorce was obtain'd: my heart said yes to this offer at first word, but it was necessary to play the hypocrite a little more with him; so I seem'd to decline the motion with some warmth, and besides a little condemning the thing as unfair, told him, that such a proposal could be of no signification,[1] but to entangle us both in great difficulties; for if he should not at last obtain the divorce, yet we could not dissolve the marriage, neither could we proceed in it; so that if he was disappointed in the divorce, I left him to consider what a condition we should both be in.

In short, I carried on the argument against this so far, that I convinc'd him, it was not a proposal that had any sense in it: WELL then he went from it to another, and that was, that I would sign and seal a contract with him, conditioning to marry him as soon as the divorce was obtain'd, and to be void if he could not obtain it.

I told him such a thing was more rational than the other; but as this was the first time that ever I could imagine him weak enough to be in earnest in this affair, I did not use to say YES at first asking, I would consider of it.

I play'd with this lover, as an angler does with a trout: I found I had him fast on the hook, so I jested with his new proposal; and put him off: I told him he knew little of me, and bad him enquire about me; I let him also go home with me to my lodging, tho' I would not ask him to go in, for I told him it was not decent.

In short, I ventur'd to avoid signing a contract of marriage, and the reason why I did it, was because the lady that had invited me so earnestly to go with her into *Lancashire* insisted so possitively upon it, and promised me such great fortunes, and such fine things there, that I was tempted to go and try; Perhaps, *said I*, I may mend myself[2] very much, and then I made no scruple in my thoughts, of quitting my honest citizen, who I was not so much in love with, as not to leave him for a richer.

---

1 Consequence, significance.
2 Improve my position.

In a word I avoided a contract; but told him I would go into the *north*, that he should know where to write to me by the consequence of the business I had entrusted with him, that I would give him a sufficient pledge of my respect for him; for I would leave almost all I had in the world in his hands; and I would thus far give him my word, that as soon as he had su'd out a divorce from his first wife, if he would send me an account of it, I would come up to *London*, and that then we would talk seriously of the matter.

It was a base design I went with, *that I must confess*, tho' I was invited thither with a design much worse than mine was, as the sequel will discover; well I went with my friend, *as I call'd her*, into *Lancashire*; all the way we went she caressed me with the utmost appearance of a sincere undissembled affection; treated me, except my coach hire all the way; and her brother brought a gentleman's coach to *Warrington*, to receive us, and we were carried from thence to *Liverpool* with as much ceremony as I could desire: we were also entertain'd at a merchant's house in *Liverpool* three or four days very handsomely: I forbear to tell his name, because of what follow'd; then she told me she would carry me to an uncles house of hers, where we should be nobly entertain'd; she did so, her uncle as she call'd him, sent a coach and four horses for us, and we were carried near forty miles, I know not whither.

We came however to a gentleman's seat,[1] where was a numerous family, a large park, extraordinary company indeed, and where she was call'd cousin; I told her if she had resolv'd to bring me into such company as this, she should have let me have prepar'd my self, and have furnish'd my self with better cloths; the ladies took notice of that, and told me very genteely, they did not value people in their country so much by their cloths, as they did in *London*; that their cousin had fully inform'd them of my quality, and that I did not want cloths to set me off; in short, they entertain'd me not like what I was, but like what they thought I had been, namely, a widow lady of a great fortune.

The first discovery I made here was, that the family were all *Roman Catholicks*,[2] and the cousin too, who I call'd my friend; however, *I must say*, that nothing in the world could behave better to me; and I had all the civility shown me that I could have had, if

---

1 Estate.

2 A large population of Roman Catholics lived at this time in the county of Lancashire. Their Jacobite sympathies, particularly during and after the rising of 1715, made them the objects of official concern and considerable public hostility.

I had been of their opinion: the truth is, I had not so much principle of any kind, as to be nice[1] in point of religion; and I presently learn'd to speak favourably of the *Romish Church*; particularly I told them I saw little, but the prejudice of education in all the differences that were among Christians about religion, and if it had so happen'd that my father had been a *Roman Catholick*, I doubted not but I should have been as well pleas'd with their religion as my own.

This oblig'd them in the highest degree, and as I was besieg'd day and night with good company, and pleasant discourse, so I had two or three old ladies that lay at me upon the subject of religion too; I was so complaisant that tho' I would not compleatly engage, yet I made no scruple to be present at their mass, and to conform to all their gestures as they shew'd me the pattern, but I would not come too cheap; so that I only in the main encourag'd them to expect that I would turn *Roman Catholick*, if I was instructed in the *Catholick doctrine* as they call'd it, and so the matter rested.

I stay'd here about six weeks; and then my conducter led me back to a country village, about six miles from *Liverpool*, where her brother, (as she call'd him) came to visit me in his own chariot, and in a very good figure, with two footmen in a good livery; and the next thing was to make love to me:[2] as it had happen'd to me, one would think I could not have been cheated, and indeed I thought so myself, having a safe card[3] at home, which I resolv'd not to quit, unless I could mend myself very much: however in all appearance this brother was a match worth my lissening to, and the least his estate was valued at, was a 1000 *l.* a year, but the sister said it was worth 1500 *l.* a year, and lay most of it in *Ireland*.

I that was a great fortune, and pass'd for such, was above being ask'd how much my estate was; and my false friend taking it upon a foolish hearsay had rais'd it from 500 *l.* to 5000 *l.* and by the time she came into the country she call'd it 15000 *l.* The *Irishman*,[4] for such I understood him to be, was stark mad at this bait: in short, he courted me, made me presents, and run in debt like a mad man for the expences of his equipage, and of his courtship: he had to give him his due, the appearance of an extraordinary fine gentle-

---

1 Fastidiously careful, punctilious.
2 Court me.
3 Reliable expedient.
4 The Irish fortune-hunter is a familiar figure in literature of the period, though generally appearing as a comic type.

man; he was tall, well shap'd, and had an extraordinary address; talk'd as naturally of his park, and his stables; of his horses, his game-keepers, his woods, his tenants, and his servants, as if we had been in the mansion-house,[1] and I had seen them all about me.

He never so much as ask'd me about my fortune, or estate; but assur'd me that when we came to *Dublin* he would joynture me in 600 *l.* a year good land; and that he would enter into a deed of settlement, or contract here, for the performance of it.[2]

This was such language indeed as I had not been us'd to, and I was here beaten out of all my measures;[3] I had a she devil in my bosom, every hour telling me how great her brother liv'd: one time she would come for my orders, how I would have my coaches painted, and how lin'd; and another time what cloths my page should wear: in short, my eyes were dazl'd, I had now lost my power of saying no, and to cut the story short, I consented to be married; but to be the more private we were carried farther into the country, and married by a Romish clergyman, which I was assur'd would marry us as effectually as a Church of *England* parson.[4]

I cannot say, but I had some reflections in this affair, upon the dishonourable forsaking my faithful citizen; who lov'd me sincerely, and who was endeavouring to quit himself of a scandalous whore, by whom he had been indeed barbarously us'd, and promis'd himself infinite happiness in his new choice; which choice was now giving up her self to another in a manner almost as scandalous as hers could be.

But the glittering show of a great estate, and of fine things, which the deceived creature that was now my deceiver represented every hour to my imagination, hurried me away, and gave me no time to think of *London*, or of any thing there, much less of the obligation I had to a person of infinitely more real merit than what was now before me.

But the thing was done, I was now in the arms of my new

---

1 Manor house.

2 That is, he would agree to a marriage settlement in which land yielding 600 pounds per year would be set aside to support Moll after his death (a *jointure*). See above, p. 83 , nn. 3-4.

3 Standards of judgment.

4 Although valid, marriages performed by Roman Catholic clergy during this period were regarded as irregular and treated with some suspicion. See Appendix A.2.

spouse, who appear'd still the same as before; great even to magnificence, and nothing less than a thousand pound a year could support the ordinary equipage he appear'd in.

After we had been marry'd about a month, he began to talk of my going to *West-Chester* in order to embark for *Ireland*. However, he did not hurry me, for we staid near three weeks longer, and then he sent to *Chester* for a coach to meet us at the *Black Rock*, as they call it, over-against[1] *Liverpool*: thither we went in a fine boat they call a pinnace with six oars, his servants, and horses, and baggage going in the ferry boat. He made his excuse to me, that he had no acquaintance at *Chester*, but he would go before and get some handsome apartment for me at a private house; I ask'd him how long we should stay at *Chester*? He said not at all, any longer than one night or two, but he would immediately hire a coach to go to *Holyhead*; then I told him he should by no means give himself the trouble to get private lodgings for one night or two, for that *Chester* being a great place, I made no doubt but there would be very good inns and accommodation enough; so we lodg'd at an inn in the West Street, not far from the cathedral, I forget what sign it was at.[2]

Here my spouse talking of my going to *Ireland*, ask'd me if I had no affairs to settle at *London* before we went off; I told him no not of any great consequence, but what might be done as well by letter from *Dublin*: Madam, says he very respectfully, I suppose the greatest part of your estate, which my sister tells me is most of it in money in the Bank of *England*, lies secure enough, but in case it requir'd transferring, or any way altering its property, it might be necessary to go up to *London*, and settle those things before we went over.

I seemed to look strange at it, and told him I knew not what he meant; that I had no effects in the Bank of *England* that I knew of; and I hoped he could not say that I had ever told him I had: no, he said, I had not told him so, but his sister had said the greatest part of my estate lay there, and *I only mention'd it my dear*, said he, *that if there was any occasion to settle it, or order any thing about it, we might not be oblig'd to the hazard and trouble of another voyage back again*, for he added, that he did not care to venture me too much upon the sea.

---

1 Across (the River Mersey) from.
2 Although Moll is probably referring to the Yacht Inn on Watergate Street (not "West Street"), Defoe was familiar with the region and later gives an account of Chester in *A Tour thro' the Whole Island of Great Britain* (1724-27). See Appendix A.6.

I was surpriz'd at this talk, and began to consider very serious-ly, what the meaning of it must be? And it presently occurr'd to me that my friend, who call'd him brother, had represented me in colours which were not my due; and I thought, since it was come to that pitch, that I would know the bottom of it before I went out of *England*, and before I should put my self into I knew not whose hands, in a strange country.

Upon this I call'd his sister into my chamber the next morning, and letting her know the discourse her brother and I had been upon, the evening before, I conjur'd her to tell me, what she had said to him, and upon what foot[1] it was that she had made this marriage? She own'd that she had told him that I was a great for-tune, and said, that she was told so at *London: Told so*, says I warm-ly, *did I ever tell you so?* No, she said, it was true I did not tell her so, but I had said several times, that what I had, was in my own disposal: I did so, *return'd I very quickly and hastily*, but I never told you I had any thing call'd a fortune; no not that I had one hundred pounds, or the value of an hundred pounds in the world; and how did it consist with my being a fortune, *said I*, that I should come here into the north of *England* with you, only upon the account of living cheap? At these words which I spoke warm and high, my husband, and her brother as she call'd him, came into the room; and I desir'd him to come and sit down, for I had something of moment to say before them both, which it was absolutely neces-sary he should hear.

He look'd a little disturb'd at the assurance with which I seem'd to speak it, and came and sat down by me, having first shut the door; upon which I began, for I was very much provok'd, and turning my self to him, I am afraid, says I, *my dear*, for I spoke with kindness on his side, that you have a very great abuse put upon you, and an injury done you never to be repair'd in your marrying me, which however as I have had no hand in it, I desire I may be fairly acquitted of it; and that the blame may lie where it ought to lie, and no where else, for I wash my hands of every part of it.

What injury can be done me, *my dear*, says he, in marrying you? I hope it is to my honour and advantage every way; I will soon explain it to you, says I, and I fear you will have no reason to think your self well us'd, but I will convince you, *my dear, says I again*, that I have had no hand in it, and there I stop'd a while.

---

1 Footing, basis.

He look'd now scar'd and wild, and began, I believ'd, to suspect what follow'd; however, looking towards me, and saying only *Go on*, he sat silent, as if to hear what I had more to say; so I went on; I ask'd you last night, said I, speaking to him, if ever I made any boast to you of my estate, or ever told you I had any estate in the Bank of *England*, or any where else, and you own'd I had not, as is most true; and I desire you will tell me here, before your sister, if ever I gave you any reason from me to think so, or that ever we had any discourse about it, and he own'd again I had not; *but said*, I had appeared always as a woman of fortune, and he depended on it that I was so, and hoped he was not deceived. I am not enquiring yet whether you have been deceived or not, *said I*, I fear you have, *and I too*; but I am clearing my self from the unjust charge of being concern'd in deceiving you.

I have been now asking your sister if ever I told her of any fortune or estate I had, or gave her any particulars of it; and she owns I never did: And pray, madam, *said I, turning my self to her*, be so just to me, before your brother, to charge me, if you can, if ever I pretended to you that I had an estate; and why, if I had, should I come down into this country with you on purpose to spare *that little I had*, and live cheap? She could not deny one word, but said she had been told in *London* that I had a very great fortune, and that it lay in the Bank of *England*.

And now, *dear sir*, said I, *turning my self to my new spouse again*, be so just to me as to tell me who has abus'd both you and me so much, as to make you believe I was a fortune, and prompt you to court me to this marriage? He cou'd not speak a word, but pointed to her; and after some more pause, flew out in the most furious passion that ever I saw a man in my life; cursing her, and calling her all the whores and hard names he could think of; and that she had ruin'd him, declaring that she had told him I had fifteen thousand pounds, and that she was to have five hundred pounds of him for procuring this match for him: he then added, directing his speech to me, that she was none of his sister, but had been his whore for two years before, that she had had one hundred pound of him in part of this bargain, and that he was utterly undone if things were as I said; and in his raving *he swore* he would let her heart's blood out immediately, which frighted her and me too; *she cried*, said she had been told so in the house where I lodg'd; but this aggravated him more than before, that she should put so far upon him, and run things such a length upon no other authority than *a hear-say*; and then turning to me again, said very honestly, he was afraid we were both undone; for to be plain, *my dear*, I have no estate, *says he,* what little I had, this devil has made me run out in waiting on you, and putting me into this equipage; she took the opportunity of his being earnest in talking with me, and got out of the room, and I never saw her more.

I was confounded now as much as he, and knew not what to say: I thought many ways that I had the worst of it, but his saying he was undone, and that he had no estate neither, put me into a meer distraction; Why, *says I to him,* this has been a hellish juggle, for we are married here upon the foot of a double fraud, you are undone by the disappointment it seems, and if I had had a fortune I had been cheated too, for you say you have nothing.

You would indeed have been cheated, my dear, *says he,* but you would not have been undone, for fifteen thousand pound would have maintain'd us both very handsomly in this country; and I assure you, *added he,* I had resolv'd to have dedicated every groat[1] of it to you; I would not have wrong'd you of a shilling, and the rest I would have made up in my affection to you, and tenderness of you as long as I liv'd.

This was very honest indeed, and I really believe he spoke as he intended, and that he was a man that was as well qualified to make me happy, as to his temper and behaviour, as any man ever was; but his having no estate, and being run into debt on this ridiculous account in the country, made all the prospect dismal and dreadful, and I knew not what to say, or what to think of my self.

I told him it was very unhappy, that so much love, and so much good-nature, as I discovered in him, should be thus precipitated into misery; that I saw nothing before us but ruin, for as to me, it was my unhappiness, that what little I had was not able to relieve us a week, and with that I pull'd out a bank bill of 20 *l.* and eleven guineas, which I told him I had saved out of my little income; and that by the account that creature had given me of the way of living in that country, I expected it would maintain me three or four year; that if it was taken from me I was left destitute, and he knew what the condition of a woman among strangers must be, if she had no money in her pocket; however, I told him if he would take it, there it was.

He told me with a great concern, and I thought I saw tears stand in his eyes, that he would not touch it, that he abhorr'd the thoughts of stripping me, and making me miserable; that on the

1 An English silver coin which was obsolete by this time, regarded as a trifling amount.

contrary, he had fifty guineas left, which was all he had in the world, and he pull'd it out and threw it down on the table, bidding me take it, tho' he were to starve for want of it.

I return'd, with the same concern for him, that I could not bear to hear him talk so; that on the contrary, if he could propose any probable method of living, I would do any thing that became me on my part, and that I would live as close and as narrow as he cou'd desire.

He beg'd of me to talk no more at that rate, for it would make him distracted; he said he was bred a gentleman, tho' he was reduced to a low fortune; and that there was but one way left which he cou'd think of, and that would not do, unless I cou'd answer him one question, which however he said he would not press me to; I told him I would answer it honestly, whether it would be to his satisfaction or no, that I could not tell.

Why then, my dear, tell me plainly, *says he* will the little you have keep us together in any figure, or in any station or place, or will it not?

It was my happiness hitherto that I had not discovered myself, or my circumstances at all; no not so much as my name; and seeing there was nothing to be expected from him, however good humoured, and however honest he seem'd to be, but to live on what I knew would soon be wasted, I resolv'd to conceal everything, but the *bank bill*, and the eleven guineas, which I had own'd; and I would have been very glad to have lost that, and have been set down where he took me up; I had indeed another *bank bill* about me of 30 *l.* which was the whole of what I brought with me, as well to subsist on in the country, as not knowing what might offer; because this creature, the *go-between* that had thus betray'd us both, had made me believe strange things of my marrying to my advantage in the country, and I was not willing to be without money whatever might happen. This bill I concealed, and that made me the freer of the rest, in consideration of his circumstances, for I really pittied him heartily.

But to return to his question, I told him I never willingly deceiv'd him, and I never would: I was very sorry to tell him that the little I had would not subsist us; that it was not sufficient to subsist me alone in the *south* country; and that this was the reason that made me put my self into the hands of that woman, who call'd him brother, she having assur'd me that I might board very handsomely at a town call'd *Manchester*,[1] where I had not yet

1 See Appendix A.6.

been, for about six pound a year, and my whole income not being above 15 *l.* a year, I thought I might live easie upon it, and wait for better things.

He shook his head, and remain'd silent, and a very melancholly evening we had; however we supped together, and lay together that night, and when we had almost supp'd he look'd a little better and more chearful, and call'd for a bottle of wine; Come my dear, *says he,* tho' the case is bad, it is to no purpose to be dejected, come be as easie as you can, I will endeavour, to find out some way or other to live; if you can but subsist your self, that is better than nothing, I must try the world again; a man ought to think like a man: to be discourag'd, is to yield to the misfortune; with this he fill'd a glass, and drank to me, holding my hand, and pressing it hard in his hand all the while the wine went down, and protesting afterward his main concern was for me.

It was really a truly gallant spirit he was of, and it was the more grievous to me: 'tis something of relief even to be undone by a man of honour, rather than by a scoundrel; but here the greatest disappointment was on his side, for he had really spent a great deal of money, deluded by this madam the procuress; and it was very remarkable on what poor terms she proceeded; first the baseness of the creature herself is to be observ'd, who for the getting one hundred pound herself, could be content to let him spend three or four more, tho' perhaps it was all he had in the world, and more than all; when she had not the least ground, more than a little tea-table chat, to say that I had any estate, or was a fortune, *or the like*: it is true the design of deluding a woman of a fortune, if I had been so, was base enough; the putting the face of great things upon poor circumstances was a fraud, and bad enough; but the case a little differ'd too, and that in his favour, for he was not a rake that made a trade to delude women, and as some have done get six or seven fortunes after one another, and then riffle[1] and run away from them; but he was really a gentleman, unfortunate and low, but had liv'd well; and tho' if I had had a fortune I should have been enrag'd at the slut for betraying me; yet really for the man, a fortune would not have been ill bestow'd on him, for he was a lovely person indeed; of generous principles, good sense, and of abundance of good humour.

We had a great deal of close conversation that night, for we neither of us slept much; he was as penitent, for having put all those

---

1 Rob.

cheats upon me as if it had been felony, and that he was going to execution; he offer'd me again every shilling of the money he had about him, and said, he would go into the army and seek the world for more.

I ask'd him, why he would be so unkind to carry me into *Ireland*, when I might suppose he cou'd not have subsisted me there? He took me in his arms, My dear, *said he*, depend upon it, I never design'd to go to *Ireland* at all, much less to have carried you thither; but came hither to be out of the observation of the people, who had heard what I pretended to, and withal, that no body might ask me for money before I was furnish'd to supply them.

But where then, *said I*, were we to have gone next?

Why my dear, *said he*, I'll confess the whole scheme to you as I had laid it; I purpos'd here to ask you something about your estate, as you see I did, and when you, as I expected you would had enter'd into some account with me of the particular, I would have made an excuse to you, to have put off our voyage to *Ireland* for some time, and to have gone first towards *London*.

Then my dear, *said he*, I resolv'd to have confess'd all the circumstances of my own affairs to you, and let you know I had indeed made use of these artifices to obtain your consent to marry me, but had now nothing to do but to ask you pardon, and to tell you how abundantly, *as I have said above*,[1] I would endeavour to make you forget what was past, by the felicity of the days to come.

Truly, *said I to him*, I find you would soon have conquer'd me; and it is my affliction now, that I am not in a condition to let you see how easily I should have been reconcil'd to you; and have pass'd by all the tricks you had put upon me, in recompence of so much good humour; but my dear, *said I*, what can we do now? We are both undone, and what better are we for our being reconcil'd together, seeing we have nothing to live on.

We propos'd a great many things, but nothing could offer, where there was nothing to begin with: he beg'd me at last to talk no more of it, for *he said*, I would break his heart; so we talk'd of other things a little, till at last he took a husbands leave of me,[2] and so we went to sleep.

He rise[3] before me in the morning, and indeed having lain

---

1 This phrase was deleted from the second edition, the editor probably recognizing the breach in narrative technique in having it spoken by the husband.
2 That is, they had sexual intercourse.
3 Rose. (*Rise* was a past tense commonly used in the eighteenth century.)

awake almost all night, I was very sleepy, and lay till near eleven a-clock, in this time he took his horses, and three servants, and all his linnen and bagage, and away he went, leaving a short, but moving letter for me on the table, as follows.

My Dear,

   I am a dog; I have abus'd you; but I have been drawn in to do it by a base creature, contrary to my principle, and the general practice of my life: forgive me, my dear! *I ask you pardon with the greatest sincerity; I am the most miserable of men, in having deluded you: I have been so happy to possess you, and am now so wretch'd as to be forc'd to fly from you: forgive me,* my dear; *once more I say forgive* me! *I am not able to see you ruin'd by me, and myself unable to support you; our marriage is nothing, I shall never be able to see you again: I here discharge you from it; if you can marry to your advantage do not decline it on my account; I here swear to you on my faith, and on the word of a man of honour, I will never disturb your repose if I should know of it, which however is not likely: on the other hand, if you should not marry, and if good fortune should befall me, it shall be all yours where ever you are.*

   I have put some of the stock of money I have left, into your pocket; take places for your self and your maid in the stage-coach, and go for London; *I hope it will bear your charges thither, without breaking into your own: again I sincerely ask your pardon, and will do so, as often as I shall ever think of you.*

Adieu my dear for ever,

I am yours most affectionatly,

A. E.[1]

Nothing that ever befel me in my life, sunk so deep into my heart as this farewel: I reproach'd him a thousand times in my thoughts for leaving me, for I would have gone with him thro' the world, if I had beg'd my bread. I felt in my pocket, and there I found ten guineas, his gold watch, and two little rings, one a small diamond ring, worth only about six pound, and the other a plain gold ring.

   I sat me down and look'd upon these things two hours together, and scarce spoke a word, till my maid interrupted me, by telling me my dinner was ready: I eat[2] but little, and after dinner I fell

---

1   "J.E." in the second edition.
2   Ate. (*Eat* was another acceptable past tense at this time.)

into a vehement fit of crying, every now and then, calling him by his name, which was *James, O Jemy!* said I, *come back, come back,* I'll give you all I have; I'll beg, I'll starve with you, and thus I run raving about the room several times, and then sat down between whiles, and then walking about again, call'd upon him to *come back,* and then cry'd again; and thus I pass'd the afternoon; till about seven a-clock when it was near dusk in the evening, being *August,* when to my unspeakable surprize he comes back into the inn, but without a servant, and comes directly up into my chamber.

I was in the greatest confusion imaginable, and so was he too: I could not imagine what should be the occasion of it; and began to be at odds with myself whether to be glad or sorry; but my affection byass'd all the rest, and it was impossible to conceal my joy, which was too great for smiles, for it burst out into tears. He was no sooner entered the room, but he run to me and took me in his arms, holding me fast and almost stopping my breath with his kisses, but spoke not a word; at length I began, My dear, *said I,* how could you go away from me? to which he gave no answer, for it was impossible for him to speak.

When our extasies were a little over, he told me he was gone about 15 mile, but it was not in his power to go any farther, without coming back to see me again, and to take his leave of me once more.

I told him how I had pass'd my time, and how loud I had call'd him to *come back* again; he told me he heard me very plain upon *Delamere Forest,*[1] at a place about 12 miles off: *I smil'd; Nay says he,* do not think I am in jest, for if ever I heard your voice in my life, I heard you call me aloud, and sometimes I thought I saw you running after me; Why said I, what did I say? for I had not nam'd the words to him, You call'd aloud, says he, and said *O Jemy! O Jemy! come back, come back.*

I laught at him; *My dear says he,* do not laugh, for depend upon it, I heard your voice as plain as you hear mine now; if you please, I'll go before a magistrate and make oath of it; I then began to be amaz'd and surpriz'd, and indeed frighted, and told him what I had really done, and how I had call'd after him, as above.[2]

When we had amus'd[3] ourselves a while about this, I said to him, Well, you shall go away from me no more, I'll go all over the

---

1 In north-eastern Cheshire.
2 For information on Defoe and the supernatural, see Appendix A.8.
3 Perplexed, astonished.

world with you rather: *he told me*, it would be a very difficult thing for him to leave me, but since it must be, he hoped I would make it as easie to me as I could; but as for him, it would be his destruction, that he foresaw.

However he told me, that he consider'd he had left me to travel to *London* alone, which was too long a journey; and that as he might as well go that way, as any way else, he was resolv'd to see me safe thither, or near it; and if he did go away then without taking his leave, I should not take it ill of him, and this he made me promise.

He told me how he had dismiss'd his three servants, sold their horses, and sent the fellows away to seek their fortunes, and all in a little time, at a town on the road, I know not where; And *says he*, it cost me some tears all alone by myself, to think how much happier they were than their master, for they could go to the next gentleman's house to see for a service, whereas, *said he*, I knew not whither to go, or what to do with myself.

I told him, I was so compleatly miserable in parting with him, that I could not be worse; and that now he was come again, I would not go from him, if he would take me with him, let him go whither he would, or do what he would; and in the mean time I agreed that we would go together to *London*; but I could not be brought to consent he should go away at last, and not take his leave of me, as he propos'd to do; but told him jesting, that if he did, I would call him back again as loud as I did before; then I pull'd out his watch and gave it him back, and his two rings, and his ten guineas; but he would not take them, which made me very much suspect that he resolv'd to go off upon the road, and leave me.

The truth is, the circumstances he was in, the passionate expressions of his letter, the kind gentlemanly treatment I had from him in all the affair, with the concern he show'd for me in it, his manner of parting with that large share which he gave me of his little stock left; all these had joyn'd to make such impressions on me, that I really lov'd him most tenderly, and could not bear the thoughts of parting with him.

Two days after this we quitted *Chester*, I in the stage coach, and he on horseback; I dismiss'd my maid at *Chester*; he was very much against my being without a maid, but she being a servant hired in the country, and I resolving to keep no servant at *London*, I told him it would have been barbarous to have taken the poor wench, and have turn'd her away as soon as I came to town; and it would also have been a needless charge on the road, so I satisfy'd him, and he was easie enough on that score.

He came with me as far as *Dunstable*, within 30 miles of *London*, and then he told me fate and his own misfortunes oblig'd him to leave me, and that it was not convenient for him to go to *London* for reasons, which it was of no value to me to know, and I saw him preparing to go. The stage coach we were in, did not usually stop at *Dunstable*, but I desiring it but for a quarter of an hour, they were content to stand at an inn-door a while, and we went into the house.

Being in the inn, I told him I had but one favour more to ask of him, and that was, that since he could not go any farther, he would give me leave to stay a week or two in the town with him, that we might in that time think of something to prevent such a ruinous thing to us both, as a final separation would be; and that I had something of moment to offer to him, that I had never said yet, and which perhaps he might find practicable to our mutual advantage.

This was too reasonable a proposal to be denied, so he call'd the landlady of the house *and told her*, his wife was taken ill, and so ill that she cou'd not think of going any farther in the stage coach, which had tyr'd her almost to death, and ask'd if she cou'd not get us a lodging for two or three days in a private house, where I might rest me a little, for the journey had been too much for me? The landlady, a good sort of woman, well bred, and very obliging, came immediately to see me; *told me*, she had two or three very good rooms in a part of the house quite out of the noise, and if I saw them, she did not doubt but I would like them, and I should have one of her maids, that should do nothing else but be appointed to wait on me; this was so very kind, that I could not but accept of it and thank her; so I went to look on the rooms, and lik'd them very well, and indeed they were extraordinarily furnish'd, and very pleasant lodgings; so we paid the stage coach, took out our baggage, and resolv'd to stay here a while.

Here *I told him* I would live with him now till all my money was spent, but would not let him spend a shilling of his own: we had some kind squabble about that, but *I told him* it was the last time I was like to enjoy his company, and I desir'd he would let me be master in that thing only, and he should govern in every thing else, so he acquiesc'd.

Here one evening taking a walk into the fields, *I told him* I would now make the proposal to him I had told him of; accordingly I related to him how I had liv'd in *Virginia*, that I had a mother, I believ'd, was alive there still, tho' my husband was dead some years; *I told him*, that had not my effects miscarry'd, which by the way I magnify'd pretty much, I might have been fortune good enough to him to have kept us from being parted in this manner: then I entered into the manner of peoples going over to those countries to settle, how they had a quantity of land given them by the constitution of the place; and if not, that it might be purchased at so easie a rate that it was not worth naming.

I then gave him a full and distinct account of the nature of planting, how with carrying over but two or three hundred pounds value in *English* goods, with some servants and tools, a man of application would presently lay a foundation for a family, and in a very few years be certain to raise an estate.

I let him into the nature of the product of the earth, how the ground was cur'd and prepared, and what the usual encrease of it was; and demonstrated to him, that in a very few years, with such a beginning, we should be as certain of being rich, as we were now certain of being poor.

He was surpriz'd at my discourse; for we made it the whole subject of our conversation for near a week together, in which time I laid it down in black and white, *as we say*, that it was morally impossible, with a supposition of any reasonable good conduct,[1] but that we must thrive there and do very well.

Then I told him what measures I would take to raise such a sum as 300 *l.* or thereabouts; and I argued with him how good a method it would be to put an end to our misfortunes, and restore our circumstances in the world, to what we had both expected, and I added, that after seven years, if we liv'd, we might be in a posture to leave our plantation in good hands, and come over again and receive the income of it, and live here and enjoy it; and I gave him examples of some that had done so, and liv'd now in very good circumstances in *London*.

In short, I press'd him so to it, that he almost agreed to it, but still something or other broke it off again; till at last he turn'd the tables, and he began to talk almost to the same purpose of *Ireland*.

He told me that a man that could confine himself to a country life, and that cou'd but find stock to enter upon any land, should have farms there for 50 *l.* a year, as good as were here let for 200 *l.* a year; that the produce was such, and so rich the land, that if much was not laid up, we were sure to live as handsomely upon it as a gentleman of 3000 *l.* a year could do in *England*; and that he

---

1 Management.

had laid a scheme to leave me in *London*, and go over and try; and if he found he could lay a handsome foundation of living suitable to the respect he had for me, as he doubted not he should do, he would come over and fetch me.

I was dreadfully afraid that upon such a proposal he would have taken me at my word, (*viz.*) to sell my little income, as I call'd it, and turn it into money, and let him carry it over into *Ireland* and try his experiment with it; but he was too just to desire it, or to have accepted it if I had offered it; and he anticipated me in that, for he added, that he would go and try his fortune that way, and if he found he cou'd do any thing at it to live, then, by adding mine to it when I went over, we should live like our selves; but that he would not hazard a shilling of mine till he had made the experiment with a little, and he assur'd me that if he found nothing to be done in *Ireland*, he would then come to me and join in my project for *Virginia*.

He was so earnest upon his project being to be try'd first, that I cou'd not withstand him; how ever, he promis'd to let me hear from him in a very little time after his arriving there, to let me know whether his prospect answer'd his design, that if there was not a probability of success, I might take the occasion to prepare for our other voyage, and then, he assur'd me, he would go with me to *America* with all his heart.

I could bring him to nothing farther than this: however, those consultations entertain'd us near a month, during which I enjoy'd his company, which indeed was the most entertaining that ever I met with in my life before. In this time he let me into the whole story of his own life, which was indeed surprizing, and full of an infinite variety sufficient to fill up a much brighter history for its adventures and incidents, that any I ever saw in print: but I shall have occasion to say more of him hereafter.

We parted at last, tho' with the utmost reluctance on my side, and indeed he took his leave very unwillingly too, but necessity oblig'd him, for his reasons were very good why he would not come to *London*, as I understood more fully some time afterwards.

I gave him a direction how to write to me, tho' still I reserv'd the grand secret, and never broke my resolution, which was not to let him ever know my true name, who I was, or where to be found; he likewise let me know how to write a letter to him, so that he said he wou'd be sure to receive it.

I came to *London* the next day after we parted, but did not go directly to my old lodgings; but for another nameless reason took a private lodging in St. *John's-Street*, or as it is vulgarly call'd St.

Jones's near *Clarkenwell*;[1] and here being perfectly alone, I had leisure to sit down and reflect seriously upon the last seven months ramble I had made, for I had been abroad no less; the pleasant hours I had with my last husband I look'd back on with an infinite deal of pleasure; but that pleasure was very much lessen'd, when I found some time after that I was really with child.

This was a perplexing thing because of the difficulty which was before me, where I should get leave to lye inn; it being one of the nicest[2] things in the world at that time of day, for a woman that was a stranger, and had no friends, to be entertain'd in that circumstance without security,[3] which by the way I had not, neither could I procure any.

I had taken care all this while to preserve a correspondence with my honest friend at the bank, or rather he took care to correspond with me, for he wrote to me once a week; and tho' I had not spent my money so fast as to want any from him, yet I often wrote also to let him know I was alive; I had left directions in *Lancashire*, so that I had these letters, which he sent, convey'd to me; and during my recess at St. *Jones's* I receiv'd a very obliging letter from him, assuring me that his process for a divorce from his wife went on with success, tho' he met with some difficulties in it that he did not expect.

I was not displeas'd with the news, that his process was more tedious than he expected; for tho' I was in no condition to have had him yet, not being so foolish to marry him when I knew my self to be with child by another man, as some I know have ventur'd to do; yet I was not willing to lose him, and in a word, resolv'd to have him if he continu'd in the same mind, as soon as I was up again; for I saw apparently I should hear no more from my other husband; and as he had all along press'd me to marry, and had assur'd me he would not be at all disgusted[4] at it, or ever offer to claim me again, so I made no scruple to resolve to do it if I could, and if my other friend stood to his bargain; and I had a great deal of reason to be assur'd that he would stand to it, by the letters he wrote to me, which were the kindest and most obliging that could be.

---

1 Immediately north of the City of London, the bustling district of
   Clerkenwell was particularly known at this time not only for its inns and
   brothels but as a stagecoach stop for all parts of the kingdom.
2 Most delicate.
3 Proof of marital and financial status, demanded by the parish officers, in
   order to "secure" the parish. See above, p. 140, n. 1.
4 Displeased.

I now grew big, and the people where I lodg'd perceiv'd it, and began to take notice of it to me, and as far as civility would allow, intimated that I must think of removing; this put me to extreme perplexity, and I grew very melancholy, for indeed I knew not what course to take, I had money, but no friends, and was like now to have a child upon my hands to keep, which was a difficulty I had never had upon me yet, as the particulars of my story hitherto makes appear.

In the course of this affair I fell very ill, and my melancholy really encreas'd my distemper; my illness prov'd at length to be only an ague, but my apprehensions were really that I should miscarry; I should not say apprehensions, for indeed I would have been glad to miscarry, but I cou'd never be brought to entertain so much as a thought of endeavouring to miscarry, or of taking any thing to make me miscarry, I abhorr'd, I say so much as the thought of it.

However, speaking of it in the house, the gentlewoman who kept the house propos'd to me to send for a midwife; I scrupled it at first, but after some time consented to it, but told her I had no particular acquaintance with any midwife, and so left it to her.

It seems the mistress of the house was not so great a stranger to such cases as mine was, as I thought at first she had been, as will appear presently, and she sent for a midwife of the right sort, that is to say, the right sort for me.

The woman appear'd to be an experienc'd woman in her business, I mean as a midwife, but she had another calling too, in which she was as expert as most women, if not more: my landlady had told her I was very melancholy, and that she believ'd that had done me harm; and once, *before me*, said to her, Mrs. B——— *meaning the midwife*, I believe this lady's trouble is of a kind that is prety much in your way, and therefore if you can do any thing for her, pray do, for she is a very civil gentlewoman, and so she went out of the room.

I really did not understand her, but my Mother Midnight[1] began very seriously to explain what she meant, as soon as she was gone: Madam, *says she*, you seem not to understand what your landlady means, and when you do understand it, you need not let her know at all that you do so.

She means that you are under some circumstances that may render your lying-inn difficult to you, and that you are not willing to be expos'd; I need say no more, but to tell you, that if you think fit to communicate so much of your case to me, *if it be so*, as is nec-

---

1 Slang for a midwife (who was often also a bawd).

essary; for I do not desire to pry into those things, I perhaps may be in a condition to assist you, and to make you perfectly easie, and remove all your dull thoughts upon that subject.

Every word this creature said was a cordial to me, and put new life and new spirit into my very heart; my blood began to circulate immediately, and I was quite another body; I eat my victuals again, and grew better presently after it: she said a great deal more to the same purpose, and then having press'd me to be free with her, and promis'd in the solemnest manner to be secret, she stop'd a little, as if waiting to see what impression it made on me, and what I would say.

I was too sensible of the want I was in of such a woman, not to accept her offer; *I told her* my case was partly as she guess'd, and partly not, for I was really married, and had a husband, tho' he was in such circumstances, and so remote at that time, as that he cou'd not appear publickly.

She took me short, *and told me*, that was none of her business, all the ladies that came under her care were married women to her; every woman, *says she*, that is with child has a father for it, and whether that father was a husband or no husband, was no business of hers; her business was to assist me in my present circumstances, whether I had a husband or no; for, *madam, says she*, to have a husband that cannot appear, is to have no husband in the sense of the case, and therefore whether you are a wife or a mistress is all one to me.

I found presently, that whether I was a whore or a wife, I was to pass for a whore here, so I let that go; *I told her*, it was true as she said, but that however, if I must tell her my case, I must tell it her as it was: so I related it to her as short as I could, and I concluded it to her thus, *I trouble you with all this*, madam, said I, *not that, as you said before, it is much to the purpose* in your affair, but this is to the purpose, *namely, that I am not in any pain about being seen, or being publick or conceal'd, for 'tis perfectly indifferent to me; but my difficulty is, that I have no acquaintance in this part of the nation.*

I understand you, madam, *says she*, you have no security to bring to prevent the parish impertinences usual in such cases; and perhaps, *says she*, do not know very well how to dispose of the child when it comes;[1] The last, *says I*, is not so much my concern

---

1 In *Parochial Tyranny* (1727), Defoe attacks the "hellish Commerce" of "those Church-Wardens and Vestries who lump it with Harlots and Whore-mongers, and take Bastards from off their Hands at so much *per* Head" at "from two Guineas to five, according to the Circumstances."

as the first: Well, madam, *answers the midwife*, dare you put your self into my hands, I live in such a place, tho' I do not enquire after you, you may enquire after me, my name is *B——* I live in such a street, naming the street, at the sign of the *Cradle*,[1] my profession is a midwife, and I have many ladies that come to my house to lye-inn; I have given security to the parish in general terms to secure them from any charge, from whatsoever shall come into the world under my roof; I have but one question to ask in the whole affair, madam, *says she*, and if that be answer'd, you shall be entirely easie for all the rest.

I presently understood what she meant, and told her, Madam, *I believe I understand you*; I thank God, *tho' I want friends in this part of the world, I do not want money, so far as may be necessary, tho' I do not abound in that neither:* this I added, because I would not make her expect great things; Well madam, *says she*, that is the thing indeed, without which nothing can be done in these cases, and yet, *says she*, you shall see that I will not impose upon you, or offer any thing that is unkind to you, and if you desire it, you shall know every thing before hand, that you may suit your self to the occasion, and be either costly or sparing as you see fit.

I told her, she seem'd to be so perfectly sensible of my condition, that I had nothing to ask of her but this, that as I had told her that I had money sufficient, but not a great quantity, she would order it so, that I might be at as little superfluous charge as possible.

She replyed, that she would bring in an account of the expences of it, in two or three shapes, and like a *bill of fare*, I should chuse as I pleas'd, and I desir'd her to do so.

The next day she brought it, and the copy of her three bills was as follows.

	l.	*s.*	*d.*
1. For three months lodging in her house, including my dyet at 10*s.* a week	06	00	0
2. For a nurse for the month, and use of child-bed linen	01	10	0
3. For a minister to christen the child, and to the godfathers and clark	01	10	01
4. For a supper at the christening if I had five friends at it	01	00	0

---

1 This inn, it has been suggested, is located in Cradle Court, near St. John's Street.

For her fees as a midwife, and the taking off the
trouble of the parish   03   03   0
To her maid-servant attending   00   10   0
     13   13   0

This was the first bill, the second was in the same terms.

	l.	*s.*	*d.*
1. For three months lodging and diet, *&c.* at 20*s.* per week	13	00	0
2. For a nurse for the month, and the use of linnen and lace	02	10	0
3. For the minister to christen the child, *&c.* as above	02	00	0
4. For a supper, and for sweetmeats	03	03	0
For her fees, as above	05	05	0
For a servant-maid	01	00	0
	26	18	0

This was the second rate bill, the third, *she said*, was for a degree
higher, and when the father, or friends appeared.

1. For three months lodging and diet, having two rooms and a garret for a servant	30	00	0
2. For a nurse for the month, and the finest suit of child-bed linen	04	04	0
3. For the minister to christen the child, *&c.*	02	10	0
4. For a supper, the gentlemen to send in the wine	06	00	0
For my fees, *&c.*	10	10	0
The maid, besides their own maid only	00	10	0
	53	14	0

I look'd upon all the three bills, and smil'd, *and told her* I did not
see but that she was very reasonable in her demands, all things
consider'd, and for that I did not doubt but her accommodations
were good.

She told me, I should be judge of that, when I saw them: *I told
her*, I was sorry to tell her that I fear'd I must be her lowest rated
customer, and *perhaps madam*, said I, *you will make me the less welcome upon that account*. No not at all, *said she*, for where I have one
of the third sort, I have two of the second, and four to one of the
first, and I get as much by them in proportion, as by any; but if

you doubt my care of you, I will allow any friend you have to over-look, and see if you are well waited on, or no.

Then she explain'd the particulars of her bill; In the first place, madam, *said she*, I would have you observe, that here is three months keeping, you are but 10 *s*. a week, I undertake to say you will not complain of my table: I suppose, *says she*, you do not live cheaper where you are now; No indeed, *said I*, nor so cheap, for I give six shillings *per* week for my chamber, and find my own diet as well as I can, which costs me a great deal more.

Then madam, *says she*, if the child should not live, or should be dead born, as you know sometime happens, then there is the min-ister's article saved; and if you have no friends to come to you, you may save the expence of a supper; so that take those articles out madam, *says she*, your lying-in will not cost you above 5 *l*. 3 *s*. in all, more than your ordinary charge of living.

This was the most reasonable thing that I ever heard of; so I smil'd, and told her I would come and be her customer; but *I told her also*, that as I had two months, and more to go, I might perhaps be oblig'd to stay longer with her than three months, and desir'd to know if she would not be oblig'd to remove me before it was proper; No, *she said*, her house was large, and besides, she never put any body to remove, that had lain inn, till they were willing to go; and if she had more ladies offer'd, she was not so ill belov'd among her neighbours, but she could provide accommodation for twenty, if there was occasion.

I found she was an eminent lady in her way, and *in short*, I agreed to put myself into her hands, and promis'd her: she then talk'd of other things, look'd about into my accommodations, where was found fault with my wanting attendance, and conve-niencies, and that I should not be us'd so at her house: *I told her*, I was shy of speaking, for the woman of the house look'd stranger, or at least I thought so since I had been ill, because I was with child; and I was afraid she would put some affront or other upon me, supposing that I had been able to give but a slight account of myself.

O dear, *said she*, her ladyship is no stranger to these things; she has try'd to entertain ladies in your condition several times, but could not secure the parish; and besides, she is not such a nice lady as you take her to be; however, since you are agoing you shall not meddle[1] with her, but I'll see you are a little better look'd after

---

1 Mix, mingle.

while you are here, than I think you are, and it shall not cost you the more neither.

I did not understand her at all; however I thank'd her, and so we parted; the next morning she sent me a chicken roasted and hot, and a pint bottle of sherry, and order'd the maid to tell me that she was to wait on me every day as long as I stay'd there.

This was surprisingly good and kind, and I accepted it very willingly: at night she sent to me again, to know if I wanted any thing, and how I did, and to order the maid to come to her in the morning for my dinner; the maid had order to make me some chocolat in the morning before she came away, and did so, and at noon she brought me the sweetbread of a breast of veal whole, and a dish of soup for my dinner, and after this manner she nurs'd me up at a distance, so that I was mightily well pleas'd, and quickly well, for indeed my dejections before were the principal part of my illness.

I expected as usually is the case among such people, that the servant she sent me would have been some impudent brazen wench of *Drury-Lane*[1] breeding and I was very uneasie at having her with me, upon that account, so I would not let her lie in that house, the first night by any means, but had my eyes about me as narrowly as if she had been a publick thief.

My gentlewoman guess'd presently what was the matter, and sent her back with a short note, that I might depend upon the honesty of her maid; that she would be answerable for her upon all accounts; and that she took no servants into her house, without very good security for their fidelity: I was then perfectly easie, and indeed the maids behaviour spoke for its self, for a modester, quieter, soberer girl never came into any bodies family, and I found her so afterwards.

As soon as I was well enough to go abroad, I went with the maid to see the house, and to see the apartment I was to have; and every thing was so handsome and so clean, and well; that in short, I had nothing to say, but was wonderfully pleas'd, and satisfy'd with what I had met with, which considering the melancholy circumstances I was in, was far beyond what I look'd for.

It might be expected that I should give some account of the nature of the wicked practice of this woman, in whose hands I was now fallen; but it would be but too much encouragement to the vice, to let the world see, what easie measures were here taken to

---

1 A district in London notorious for its brothels and general low life.

rid the women's unwelcome burthen of a child clandestinely gotten:[1] this grave matron had several sorts of practise, and this was one particular, that if a child was born, tho' not in her house, for she had the occasion to be call'd to many private labours, she had people at hand, who for a peice of money would take the child off their hands, and off from the hands of the parish too; and those children, as she said were honestly provided for, and taken care of: what should become of them all, considering so many, as by her account she was concern'd with, I cannot conceive.

I had many times discourses upon that subject with her; but she was full of this argument, that she sav'd the life of many an innocent lamb, as she call'd them, which would otherwise perhaps have been murder'd; and of many a woman, who made desperate by the misfortune, would otherwise be tempted to destroy their children, and bring themselves to the gallows: I granted her that this was true, and a very commendable thing, provided the poor children fell into good hands afterwards, and were not abus'd, starv'd, and neglected by the nurses that bred them up; she answer'd, that she always took care of that, and had no nurses in her business, but what were very good honest people, and such as might be depended upon.

I cou'd say nothing to the contrary, and so was oblig'd to say, Madam I do not question you do your part honestly, but what those people do afterwards, is the main question, and she stop'd my mouth again with saying, that she took the utmost care about it.

The only thing I found in all her conversation on these subjects, that gave me any distaste, was, that one time in discoursing about my being so far gone with child, and the time I expected to come, she said something that look'd as if she could help me off with my burthen sooner, if I was willing; or in *English*, that she could give me something to make me miscarry, if I had a desire to put an end to my troubles that way; but I soon let her see that I abhorr'd the thoughts of it; and to do her justice, she put it off so cleverly, that I cou'd not say she really intended it, or whether she only mentioned the practise as a horrible thing; for she couch'd her words so well, and took my meaning so quickly, that she gave her negative before I could explain my self.

To bring this part into as narrow a compass as possible, I quitted my lodging at St. *Jones's* and went to my new governess, for so

---

1 Begotten.

they call'd her in the house, and there I was indeed treated with so much courtesy, so carefully look'd to, so handsomely provided, and every thing so well, that I was surpris'd at it, and cou'd not at first see what advantage my governess made of it; but I found afterwards that she profess'd to make no profit of the lodgers diet, nor indeed cou'd she get much by it, but that her profit lay in the other articles of her management, and she made enough that way, I assure you; for 'tis scarce credible what practice she had, as well abroad as at home, and yet all upon the private account, or in plain *English*, the whoring account.

While I was in her house, which was near four months, she had no less than twelve ladies of pleasure brought to bed within doors, and I think she had two and thirty, or thereabouts, under her conduct without doors, whereof one, as nice as she was with me, was lodg'd with my old landlady at St. *Jones's.*

This was a strange testimony of the growing vice of the age, and such a one, that as bad as I had been my self, it shock'd my very senses, I began to nauceate the place I was in, and above all, the wicked practice; and yet I must say that I never saw, or do I believe there was to be seen, the least indecency in the house the whole time I was there.

Not a man was ever seen to come up stairs, except to visit the lying-inn ladies within their month, nor then without the old lady with them, who made it a piece of the honour of her management, that no man should touch a woman, no not his own wife, within the month; nor would she permit any man to lye in the house upon any pretence whatever, no not tho' she was sure it was with his own wife, and her general saying for it was, that she car'd not how many children was born in her house, but she would have none got[1] there if she could help it.

It might perhaps be carried farther than was needful, but it was an error of the right hand[2] if it was an error, for by this she kept up the reputation, such as it was, of her business, and obtain'd this character, that tho' she did take care of the women when they were debauch'd, yet she was not instrumental to their being debauch'd at all, and yet it was a wicked trade she drove too.

While I was here, and before I was brought to bed, I receiv'd a letter from my trustee at the bank full of kind obliging things, and earnestly pressing me to return to *London*: it was near a fortnight

---

1 Begotten.
2 Of the proper kind.

old when it came to me, because it had been first sent into *Lancashire*, and then return'd to me; he concludes with telling me that he had obtain'd a decree,[1] I think he call'd it, against his wife, and that he would be ready to make good his engagement to me, if I would accept of him, adding a great many protestations of kindness and affection, such as he would have been far from offering if he had known the circumstances I had been in, and which as it was I had been very far from deserving.

I returned an answer to this letter, and dated it at *Leverpool*, but sent it by a messenger, alledging that it came in cover to a friend in town; I gave him joy of his deliverance, but rais'd some scruples at the lawfulness of his marrying again, and told him, I suppos'd he would consider very seriously upon that point before he resolv'd on it, the consequence being too great for a man of his judgment to venture rashly upon a thing of that nature; so concluded, wishing him very well in whatever he resolv'd, without letting him into any thing of my own mind, or giving any answer to his proposal of my coming to *London* to him, but mention'd at a distance my intention to return the latter end of the year, this being dated in *April*.

I was brought to bed about the middle of *May*, and had another brave[2] boy, and my self in as good condition as usual on such occasions: my governess did her part as a midwife with the greatest art and dexterity imaginable, and far beyond all that ever I had had any experience of before.

Her care of me in my travail, and after in my lying-inn, was such, that if she had been my own mother it cou'd not have been better; let none be encourag'd in their loose practises from this dexterous lady's management; for she is gone to her place, and I dare say has left nothing behind her that can or will come up to it.

I think I had been brought to bed about twenty two days when I receiv'd another letter from my friend at the bank, with the surprizing news that he had obtain'd a final sentence of divorce against his wife, and had serv'd her with it on such a day, and that he had such an answer to give to all my scruples about his marrying again, as I could not expect, and as he had no desire of; for that his wife, who had been under some remorse before for her usage of him, as soon as she had the account that he had gain'd his point, had very unhappily destroy'd her self that same evening.

He express'd himself very handsomly as to his being concern'd

---

1 A preliminary (rather than final) judgment of the ecclesiastical court in divorce proceedings.
2 Fine.

at her disaster, but clear'd himself of having any hand in it, and that he had only done himself justice in a case in which he was notoriously injur'd and abus'd: however, he said that he was extremely afflicted at it, and had no view of any satisfaction left in this world, but only in the hope that I wou'd come and relieve him by my company; and then he press'd me violently indeed to give him some hopes, that I would at least come up to town and let him see me, when he would farther enter into discourse about it.

I was exceedingly surpriz'd at the news, and began now serious-ly to reflect on my present circumstances, and the inexpressible misfortune it was to me to have a child upon my hands, and what to do in it I knew not; at last I open'd my case at a distance to my governess, I appear'd melancholy and uneasie for several days, and she lay at me continually to know what troubl'd me; I could not for my life tell her that I had an offer of marriage, after I had so often told her that I had a husband, so that I really knew not what to say to her; I own'd I had something which very much troubl'd me, but at the same time told her I cou'd not speak of it to any one alive.

She continued importuning me several days, but it was impos-sible, *I told her*, for me to commit the secret to any body; this, instead of being an answer to her, encreas'd her importunities; she urg'd her having been trusted with the greatest secrets of this nature, that it was her business to conceal every thing, and that to discover things of that nature would be her ruin; she ask'd me if ever I had found her tatling to her of other people's affairs, and how could I suspect her? *She told me* to unfold my self to her, was telling it to no body; that she was silent as death; that it must be a very strange case indeed, that she could not help me out of; but to conceal it, was to deprive myself of all possible help, or means of help, and to deprive her of the opportunity of serving me. *In short*, she had such a bewitching eloquence, and so great a power of per-swasion, that there was no concealing any thing from her.

So I resolv'd to unbosome myself to her, I told her the history of my *Lancashire* marriage, and how both of us had been disap-pointed; how we came together, and how we parted: how he absolutely discharg'd me, as far as lay in him, and gave me free lib-erty to marry again,[1] protesting that if he knew it he would never

---

1 As legal separation or annulment of a marriage was difficult to obtain, sep-aration (or "divorce") by mutual consent was commonly practised. The issue of divorce and remarriage was the subject of much controversy at this time, both from a moral and legal standpoint. Defoe takes up the matter on a number of occasions, for example in *Applebee's Journal* (16 January and 24 April 1725) and *Conjugal Lewdness* (1727). See Appendix A.7.

claim me, or disturb, or expose me; that I thought I was free, but was dreadfully afraid to venture, for fear of the consequences that might follow in case of a discovery.

Then I told her what a good offer I had; show'd her my friends two last letters, inviting me to come to *London*, and let her see with what affection and earnestness they were written, but blotted out the name, and also the story about the dissaster of his wife, only that she was dead.

She fell a laughing at my scruples about marrying, and told me the other was no marriage, but a cheat on both sides; and that as we were parted by mutual consent, the nature of the contract was destroy'd, and the obligation was mutually discharg'd: she had arguments for this at the tip of her tongue; and *in short*, reason'd me out of my reason; not but that it was too by the help of my own inclination.

But then came the great and main difficulty, and that was the child; this she told me in so many words must be remov'd, and that so, as that it should never be possible for any one to discover it: I knew there was no marrying without entirely concealing that I had had a child, for he would soon have discover'd by the age of it, that it was born, nay and gotten too, since my parly[1] with him, and that would have destroy'd all the affair.

But it touch'd my heart so forcibly to think of parting entirely with the child, and for ought I knew, of having it murther'd, or starv'd by neglect and ill-usuage,[2] (which was much the same) that I could not think of it, without horror; I wish all those women who consent to the disposing their children out of the way, *as it is call'd* for decency sake, would consider that 'tis only a contriv'd method for murther; that is to say, a killing their children with safety.

It is manifest to all that understand any thing of children, that we are born into the world helpless and uncapable, either to supply our own wants, or so much as make them known; and that without help, we must perish; and this help requires not only an assisting hand, whether of the mother, or some body else; but there are two things necessary in that assisting hand, that is, care

---

1 Talk (spelled *parley*).
2 In the *House of Commons Journals* (8 March 1716), a parliamentary committee reported that "a great many parish Infants, and exposed Bastard Children, are inhumanly suffered to die by the Barbarity of Nurses, especially Parish Nurses, who are a sort of People void of Commiseration or Religion, hired by the Chuchwardens to take off a Burden from the Parish at the cheapest and easiest Rates they can ... "

and skill, without both which, half the children that are born would die; nay, tho' they were not to be deny'd food; and one half more of those that remain'd would be cripples or fools, lose their limbs, and perhaps their sense: I question not, but that these are partly the reasons why affection was plac'd by nature in the hearts of mothers to their children; without which they would never be able to give themselves up, as 'tis necessary they should, to the care and waking pains needful to the support of their children.

Since this care is needful to the life of children, to neglect them is to murther them; again to give them up to be manag'd by those people, who have none of that needful affection, plac'd by nature in them, is to neglect them in the highest degree; nay, in some it goes farther, and is a neglect in order to their being lost; so that 'tis even an intentional murther, whether the child lives or dies.

All those things represented themselves to my view, and that in the blackest and most frightful form; and as I was very free with my governness, who I had now learn'd to call mother; I represented to her all the dark thoughts which I had upon me about it, and told her what distress I was in: she seem'd graver by much at this part than at the other; but as she was harden'd in these things beyond all possibility of being touch'd with the religious part, and the scruples about the murther; so she was equally impenetrable in that part, which related to affection: she ask'd me if she had not been careful, and tender of me in my lying-inn, as if I had been her own child? I told her I own'd she had. Well my dear, *says she*, and when you are gone, what are you to me? And what would it be to me if you were to be hang'd? Do you think there are not women, who as it is their trade, and they get their bread by it, value themselves upon their being as careful of children, as their own mothers can be, and understand it rather better? Yes, yes, child, *says she*, fear it not, how were we nurs'd ourselves? Are you sure, you was nurs'd up by your own mother? And yet you look fat, and fair child, says the old beldam,[1] and with that she stroak'd me over the face; Never be concern'd child, s*ays she*, going on in her drolling way; I have no murtherers about me; I employ the best, and the honestest nurses that can be had; and have as few children miscarry under their hands, as there would, if they were all nurs'd by mothers; we want neither care nor skill.

She touch'd me to the quick, when she ask'd if I was sure that

---

1 An aged woman, more particularly a term used in addressing nurses; but well before this time it also meant hag or witch.

I was nurs'd by my own mother; on the contrary I was sure I was not; and I trembled, and look'd pale at the very expression; Sure said I, to myself, this creature cannot be a witch, or have any conversation with a spirit that can inform her what was done with me before I was able to know it myself; and I look'd at her as if I had been frighted; but reflecting that it cou'd not be possible for her to know any thing about me, that disorder went off, and I began to be easie, but it was not presently.

She perceiv'd the disorder I was in, but did not know the meaning of it; so she run on in her wild talk upon the weakness of my supposing, that children were murther'd, because they were not all nurs'd by the mother; and to perswade me that the children she dispos'd of, were as well us'd as if the mothers had the nursing of them themselves.

It may be true mother, *says I,* for ought I know, but my doubts are very strongly grounded, Indeed; come then, *says she,* lets hear some of them: Why first, *says I,* you give a piece of money to these people to take the child off the parents hands, and to take care of it as long as it lives; now we know mother, *said I,* that those are poor people, and their gain consists in being quit of the charge as soon as they can; how can I doubt but that, as it is best for them to have the child die, they are not over solicitous about its life.

This is all vapours[1] and fancy, *says the old woman,* I tell you their credit depends upon the child's life, and they are as careful as any mother of you all.

O mother, *says I,* if I was but sure my little baby would be carefully look'd to, and have justice done it, I should be happy indeed; but it is impossible I can be satisfy'd in that point, unless I saw it, and to see it, would be ruin and destruction to me, as now my case stands, so what to do I know not.

A fine story! *says the governess,* you would see the child, and you would not see the child; you would be conceal'd and discover'd both together; these are things impossible my dear, so you must e'n do as other conscientious mothers have done before you; and be contented with things as they must be, tho' they are not as you wish them to be.

I understood what she meant by conscientious mothers, she would have said conscientious whores; but she was not willing to

---

1 Depression of spirits, melancholy (supposedly caused by the corruption of black bile, which produced exhalations in the lower organs of the body that rose to the head). See above, p. 128, n. 1.

disoblige me, for really in this case I was not a whore, because legally married, the force of my former marriage excepted.

However let me be what I would, I was not come up to that pitch of hardness, common to the profession; I mean to be unnatural, and regardless of the safety of my child, and I preserv'd this honest affection so long, that I was upon the point of giving up my friend at the *bank*, who lay so hard at me to come to him, and marry him, that *in short*, there was hardly any room to deny him.

At last my old governness came to me, with her usual assurance. Come my dear, *says she*, I have found out a way how you shall be at a certainty, that your child shall be used well, and yet the people that take care of it shall never know you, or who the mother of the child is.

O mother, *says I*, if you can do so, you will engage me to you[1] for ever: Well, *says she*, are you willing to be at some small annual expence, more than what we usually give to the people we contract with? Ay, *says I*, with all my heart, provided I may be conceal'd; As to that, says *the governness*, you shall be secure, for the nurse shall never so much as dare to enquire about you, and you shall once or twice a year go with me and see your child, and see how 'tis used, and be satisfy'd that it is in good hands, no body knowing who you are.

Why, *said I*, do you think mother, that when I come to see my child, I shall be able to conceal my being the mother of it, do you think that possible?

Well, well, *says my governess*, if you discover it, the nurse shall be never the wiser; for she shall be forbid to ask any questions about you, or to take any notice; if she offers it she shall lose the money which you are to be suppos'd to give her, and the child be taken from her too.

I was very well pleas'd with this; so the next week a country woman was brought from *Hertford*, or thereabouts,[2] who was to take the child off our hands entirely, for 10 *l*. in money; but if I would allow 5 *l*. a year more to her, she would be obliged to bring the child to my governesses house as often as we desired, or we should come down and look at it, and see how well she us'd it.

The woman was a very wholesome look'd likely woman, a cottager's wife, but she had very good cloaths and linnen, and every

---

1 That is, I will be indebted to you.
2 According to Ned Ward's satire, *The Parish Gutt'lers: Or, The Humours of a Select Vestry* (1722), parish officers disposed of unwanted children by sending them off to Hereford and nearby country towns north of London.

thing well about her, and with a heavy heart and many a tear I let her have my child: I had been down at *Hertford* and look'd at her and at her dwelling, which I lik'd well enough; and I promis'd her great things if she would be kind to the child, so she knew at first word that I was the child's mother; but she seem'd to be so much out of the way, and to have no room to enquire after me, that I thought I was safe enough, so in short I consented to let her have the child, and I gave her ten pound, that is to say I gave it to my governess, who gave it the poor woman before my face, she agreeing never to return the child back to me, or to claim any thing more for its keeping or bringing up; only that I promised, if she took a great deal of care of it, I would give her something more as often as I came to see it; so that I was not bound to pay the five pound, only that I promised my governess I would do it: and thus my great care was over, after a manner, which tho' it did not at all satisfie my mind, yet was the most convenient for me, as my affairs then stood, of any that cou'd be thought of at that time.

I then began to write to my friend at the bank in a more kindly style, and particularly about the beginning of *July* I sent him a letter, that I purpos'd to be in town sometime in *August*; he return'd me an answer in the most passionate terms imaginable, and desir'd me to let him have timely notice, and he would come and meet me two days journey: this puzzl'd me scurvily,[1] and I did not know what answer to make to it; once I was resolv'd to take the stage coach to *West-Chester* on purpose only, to have the satisfaction of coming back, that he might see me really come in the same coach; for I had a jealous[2] thought, though I had no ground for it at all, lest he should think I was not really in the country, and it was no ill-grounded thought, as you shall hear presently.

I endeavour'd to reason my self out of it, but it was in vain, the impression lay so strong on my mind, that it was not to be resisted; at last it came as an addition to my new design of going in the country, that it would be an excellent blind to my old governess, and would cover entirely all my other affairs, for she did not know in the least whether my new lover liv'd in *London* or in *Lancashire*, and when I told her my resolution, she was fully perswaded it was in *Lancashire*.

Having taken my measures[3] for this journey, I let her know it,

---

1 Sorely.
2 Apprehensive, fearful.
3 Plans or course of action.

and sent the maid that tended me from the beginning, to take a place for me in the coach; she would have had me let the maid have waited on me down to the last stage, and come up again in the waggon, but I convinc'd her it wou'd not be convenient;[1] when I went away she told me, she would enter into no measures for correspondence, for she saw evidently that my affection to my child would cause me to write to her, and to visit her too when I came to town again; I assur'd her it would, and so took my leave, well satisfied to have been freed from such a house, however good my accommodations there had been, as I have related above.

I took the place in the coach not to its full extent, but to a place call'd *Stone* in *Cheshire*,[2] I think it is, where I not only had no manner of business, but not so much as the least acquaintance with any person in the town or near it: but I knew that with money in the pocket one is at home any where, so I lodg'd there two or three days, till watching my opportunity, I found room in another stage coach, and took passage back again for *London*, sending a letter to my gentleman, that I should be such a certain day at *Stony-Stratford*, where the coachman told me he was to lodge.

It happen'd to be a chance coach that I had taken up, which having been hired on purpose to carry some gentlemen to *West-Chester* who were going for *Ireland*, was now returning, and did not tye it self up to exact times or places as the stages did, so that having been oblig'd to lye still a *Sunday*[3] he had time to get himself ready to come out, which otherwise he cou'd not have done.

However, his warning was so short, that he could not reach to *Stony-Stratford* time enough to be with me at night, but he met me at a place call'd *Brickill* the next morning, as we were just coming into the town.

I confess I was very glad to see him, for I had thought my self a little disappointed over night, seeing I had gone so far to contrive my coming on purpose: he pleas'd me doubly too by the figure he came in, for he brought a very handsome (gentleman's) coach and four horses with a servant to attend him.

---

1 Coaches went "down" from London to the country and "up" from the country to London. The governess proposes a less expensive journey for the maid, and would have her travel down with Moll to the last stage-coach stop but then up by herself on a cheaper stage wagon.

2 Actually in Staffordshire, but perhaps an error purposely made to lend support to Moll's acknowledged lack of familiarity with the place.

3 Under the Sunday Observance Act (1677), stagecoaches were prohibited from operating on Sunday. Although not regularly enforced, travellers were obliged to obtain warrants signed by a justice of the peace.

He took me out of the stage coach immediately, which stop'd at an inn in *Brickill*,[1] and putting in to the same inn he set up his own coach, and bespoke[2] his dinner; I ask'd him what he meant by that, for I was for going forward with the journey; he said no, I had need of a little rest upon the road, and that was a very good sort of a house, tho' it was but a little town; so we would go no farther that night, whatever came of it.

I did not press him much, for since he had come so far to meet me, and put himself to so much expence, it was but reasonable I should oblige him a little too, so I was easy as to that point.

After dinner we walk'd to see the town, to see the church, and to view the fields, and the country as is usual for strangers to do, and our landlord was our guide in going to see the church; I observ'd my gentleman enquir'd pretty much about the parson, and I took the hint immediately, that he certainly would propose to be married; and tho' it was a sudden thought, it follow'd presently, that in short I would not refuse him; for to be plain with my circumstances, I was in no condition now to say No, I had no reason now to run any more such hazards.

But while these thoughts run round in my head, which was the work but of a few moments, I observ'd my landlord took him aside and whisper'd to him, tho' not very softly neither, for so much I over-heard, *Sir, if you shall have occasion* —the rest I cou'd not hear, but it seems it was to this purpose, *Sir, if you shall have occasion for a minister, I have a friend a little way off that will serve you, and be as private as you please*; my gentleman answer'd loud enough for me to hear, *Very well, I believe I shall.*

I was no sooner come back to the inn, but he fell upon me with irresistable words, that since he had had the good fortune to meet me, and every thing concurr'd, it wou'd be hastening his felicity if I would put an end to the matter just there; What do you mean, *says I*, colouring a little, what in an inn, and upon the road! Bless us all, *said I*, as if I had been surpriz'd, how can you talk so! O I can talk so very well, *says he*, I came a purpose to talk so, and I'll show you that I did, and with that he pulls out a great bundle of papers; You fright me, *said I*, what are all these; Don't be frighted, my dear, *said he*, and kiss'd me, *this was the first time that he had been so free to call me my dear*; then he repeated it, Don't be fright-

---

1   Little Brickhill in Buckinghamshire lies on the great post road from
    London to Chester.
2   Ordered.

ed, you shall see what it is all, then he laid them all abroad;[1] there was first the deed or sentence of divorce from his wife, and the full evidence of her playing the whore; then there was the certificates of the minister and church-wardens of the parish where she liv'd, proving that she was buried, and intimating the manner of her death; the copy of the coroner's warrant for a jury to sit upon her, and the verdict of the jury, who brought it in *Non compos mentis*;[2] all this was indeed to the purpose, and to give me satisfaction, tho', by the way, I was not so scrupulous, had he known all, but that I might have taken him without it: however, I look'd them all over as well as I cou'd, and told him, that this was all very clear indeed, but that he need not have given himself the trouble to have brought them out with him, for it was time enough: Well *he said*, it might be time enough for me, but no time but the present time was time enough for him.

There were other papers roll'd up, and I ask'd him, what they were? Why, ay, *says he*, that's the question I wanted to have you ask me; so he unrolls them, and takes out a little chagreen[3] case, and gives me out of it a very fine diamond ring; I could not refuse it, if I had a mind to do so, for he put it upon my finger; so I made him a curtsy, and accepted it; then he takes out another ring, And this, *says he*, is for another occasion, so he puts that in his pocket. Well, but let me see it tho', *says I*, and smil'd, I guess what it is, I think you are mad: I should have been mad if I had done less, *says he*, and still he did not show it me, and I had a great mind to see it; so I says, Well but let me see it; Hold, *says he*, first look here, then he took up the roll again, and read it, and behold! it was a license for us to be married: Why, *says I*, are you distracted? Why you were fully satisfy'd that I would comply, and yield at first word, or resolv'd to take no denial; The last is certainly the case, *said he*; But you may be mistaken, *said I*, No, no, *says he*, how can you think so? I must not be denied, I can't be denied, and with that he fell to kissing me so violently, I could not get rid of him.

There was a bed in the room, and we were walking to and again,[4] eager in the discourse, at last he takes me by surprize in his arms, and threw me on the bed and himself with me, and holding me fast in his arms, but without the least offer of any undecency,

---

1 Out.

2 "Not having control of the mind" (Latin). That is, she was found to be insane in the eyes of the law.

3 A rough-grained, untanned leather, frequently dyed green. (Also *sha-green*.)

4 Back and forth.

courted me to consent with such repeated entreaties and arguments; protesting his affection and vowing he would not let me go, till I had promised him, that at last I said, Why you resolve not to be deny'd indeed, I think: No, no, *says he*, I must not be denyed, I won't be deny'd, I can't be deny'd: Well, well, *said I*, and giving him a slight kiss, then you shan't be deny'd, *said I*, let me get up.

He was so transported with my consent, and the kind manner of it, that I began to think once, he took it for a marriage, and would not stay for the form, but I wrong'd him, for he gave over kissing me, took me by the hand, pull'd me up again, and then giving me two or three kisses again, thank'd me for my kind yielding to him; and was so overcome with the satisfaction and joy of it, that I saw tears stand in his eyes.

I turn'd from him, for it fill'd my eyes with tears too; and I ask'd him leave to retire a little to my chamber: if ever I had a grain of true repentance for a vitious and abominable life for 24 years past, it was then. O! what a felicity is it to mankind, *said I*, to myself, that they cannot see into the hearts of one another! How happy had it been for me, if I had been wife to a man of so much honesty, and so much affection from the beginning?

Then it occour'd to me what an abominable creature am I! and how is this innocent gentleman going to be abus'd by me! How little does he think, that having divorc'd a whore, he is throwing himself into the arms of another! that he is going to marry one that has lain with two brothers, and has had three children by her own brother! one that was born in *Newgate*, whose mother was a whore, and is now a transported thief; one that has lain with thirteen men, and has had a child since he saw me! Poor gentleman! *said I*, what is he going to do? After this reproaching my self was over, it followed thus: Well, if I must be his wife, if it please God to give me grace, I'll be a true wife to him, and love him suitably to the strange excess of his passion for me; I will make him amends, if possible, by what he shall see, for the cheats and abuses I put upon him, which he does not see.

He was impatient for my coming out of my chamber, but finding me long, he went down stairs, and talk'd with my landlord about the parson.

My landlord, an officious, tho' well-meaning fellow, had sent away for the neighbouring clergy man; and when my gentleman began to speak of it to him, and talk of sending for him, Sir, says he to him, my friend is in the house; so without any more words he brought them together: when he came to the minister, he ask'd him if he would venture to marry a couple of strangers that were both willing? The parson said that Mr. —— had said something to him of it; that he hop'd it was no clandestine business;[1] that he seem'd to be a grave gentleman, and he suppos'd madam was not a girl, so that the consent of friends[2] should be wanted; To put you out of doubt of that, says my gentleman, read this paper, and out he pulls the license; I am satisfied, says the minister, where is the lady? You shall see her presently, says my gentleman.

When he had said thus, he comes up stairs, and I was by that time come out of my room, so he tells me the minister was below, and that he had talk'd with him, and that upon showing him the license, he was free to marry us with all his heart, but he asks to see you, so he ask'd if I would let him come up.

'Tis time enough, *said I*, in the morning, is it not? Why, *said he*, my dear, he seem'd to scruple whether it was not some young girl stolen from her parents, and I assur'd him we were both of age to command our own consent; and that made him ask to see you; Well, *said I*, do as you please; so up they brings the parson, and a merry good sort of gentleman he was; he had been told, it seems, that we had met there by accident, that I came in the *Chester* coach, and my gentleman in his own coach to meet me; that we were to have met last night at *Stony-Stratford*, but that he could not reach so far: Well, sir, *says the parson*, every ill turn has some good in it; the disappointment, sir, *says he to my gentleman*, was yours, and the good turn is mine, for if you had met at *Stony-Stratford* I had not had the honour to marry you: LANDLORD *have you a Common-Prayer Book*.[3]

I started as if I had been frighted, Lord, sir, *says I*, what do you mean, what to marry in an inn, and at night too: Madam, *says the minister*, if you will have it be in the church you shall; but I assure you your marriage will be as firm here as in the church; we are not tyed by the canons to marry no where but in the church; and if you will have it in the church it will be as publick as a country fair; and as for the time of day it does not at all weigh in this case, our princes are married in their chambers, and at eight or ten a clock at night.[4]

---

1 Due to the virtual abduction of young women for their fortunes, Parliament had passed severe laws against clandestine marriages, making it a felony to marry a minor without the consent of her father. See Appendix A.2 and 7.

2 Kinsmen or near relations.

3 The book of services and prayers used in the Church of England.

4 Although exceptions were made for the upper classes, both times and places were carefully prescribed in the canons of the Church of England. Unbeneficed clergymen, however, were often willing to perform illegal, private marriages, as is the case here.

I was a great while before I could be perswaded, and pretended not to be willing at all to be married but in the church; but it was all grimace;[1] so I seem'd at last to be prevail'd on, and my landlord, and his wife, and daughter, were call'd up: my landlord was father and clark[2] and all together, and we were married, and very merry we were; tho' I confess the self-reproaches which I had upon me before, lay close to me, and extorted every now and then a deep sigh from me, which my bridegroom took notice of, and endeavour'd to encourage me, thinking, poor man, that I had some little hesitations at the step I had taken so hastily.

We enjoy'd our selves that evening compleatly, and yet all was kept so private in the inn, that not a servant in the house knew of it, for my landlady and her daughter waited on me, and would not let any of the maids come up stairs, except while we were at supper: my landlady's daughter I call'd my bride-maid, and sending for a shop-keeper the next morning, I gave the young woman a good suit of knots,[3] as good as the town would afford, and finding it was a lace-making town, I gave her mother a piece of bone-lace for a head.[4]

One reason that my landlord was so close[5] was, that he was unwilling the minister of the parish should hear of it;[6] but for all that somebody heard of it, so as that we had the bells set a ringing the next morning early, and the musick, such as the town would afford, under our window;[7] but my landlord brazen'd it out, that we were marry'd before we came thither, only that being his former guess,[8] we would have our wedding supper at his house.

We cou'd not find in our hearts to stir the next day; for in short having been disturb'd by the bells in the morning, and having per-

---

1 Sham, hypocrisy.
2 Assistant to the clergyman.
3 A set of decorative ribbon bows.
4 Lace for trimming head-dresses was often made by knitting with bobbins made from bone. This was probably the main lacemaking region of England at this time.
5 Close-mouthed, secretive in manner.
6 The parish priest would of course object to an uncanonical marriage. Instead he would require the publishing of the banns and that the wedding be performed in church in daylight.
7 A traditional serenade of raucous and sometimes obscene music (shortly later known as *charivari*), played outside the window of a newly-wedded couple.
8 Obsolete form of *guests*.

haps not slept over much before, we were so sleepy afterwards that we lay in bed till almost twelve a clock.

I beg'd my landlady that we might not have any more musick in the town, nor ringing of bells, and she manag'd it so well that we were very quiet: but an odd passage interrupted all my mirth for a good while; the great room of the house look'd into the street, and my new spouse being below stairs, I had walk'd to the end of the room, and it being a pleasant warm day, I had opened the window, and was standing at it for some air, when I saw three gentlemen come by on horseback and go into an inn just against[1] us.

It was not to be conceal'd, nor was it so doubtful as to leave me any room to question it, but the second of the three was my *Lancashire* husband: I was frighted to death, I never was in such a consternation in my life, I thought I should have sunk into the ground, my blood run chill in my veins, and I trembl'd as if I had been in a cold fit of an ague: I say there was no room to question the truth of it, I knew his cloaths, I knew his horse, and I knew his face.

The first sensible reflection I made was, that my husband was not by to see my disorder, and that I was very glad of: the gentlemen had not been long in the house but they came to the window of their room, as is usual; but my window was shut you may be sure: however, I cou'd not keep from peeping at them, and there I saw him again, heard him call out to one of the servants of the house for something he wanted, and receiv'd all the terryfying confirmations of its being the same person, that were possible to be had.

My next concern was to know, if possible, what was his business there; but that was impossible; sometimes my imagination form'd an idea of one frightful thing, sometimes of another; sometimes I thought he had discover'd me, and was come to upbraid me with ingratitude and breach of honour; and every moment I fancied he was coming up the stairs to insult me; and innumerable fancies came into my head of what was never in his head, nor ever could be, unless the Devil had reveal'd it to him.

I remain'd in this fright near two hours, and scarce ever kept my eye from the window or door of the inn, where they were: at last hearing a great clutter[2] in the passage of their inn, I run to the window, and, to my great satisfaction, see them all three go out again

---

1 Opposite.
2 Bustle, hubbub.

and travel on westward; had they gone towards *London*, I should have been still in a fright, lest I should meet him on the road again, and that he should know me; but he went the contrary way, and so I was eas'd of that disorder.

We resolv'd to be going the next day, but about six a clock at night we were alarm'd with a great uproar in the street, and people riding as if they had been out of their wits, and what was it but a hue and cry[1] after three highway men, that had rob'd two coaches, and some other travellers near *Dunstable* Hill, and notice had, it seems, been given, that they had been seen at *Brickill* at such a house, meaning the house where those gentlemen had been.

The house was immediately beset and search'd, but there were witnesses enough that the gentlemen had been gone above three hours; the crowd having gathered about, we had the news presently; and I was heartily concern'd now another way: I presently told the people of the house, that I durst to say those were not the persons, for that I knew one of the gentlemen to be a very honest person, and of a good estate in *Lancashire*.

The constable,[2] who came with the hue and cry, was immediately inform'd of this, and came over to me to be satisfy'd from my own mouth, and I assur'd him that I saw the three gentlemen as I was at the window, that I saw them afterwards at the windows of the room they din'd in; that I saw them afterwards take horse, and I could assure him I knew one of them to be such a man, that he was a gentleman of a very good estate, and an undoubted character in *Lancashire*, from whence I was just now upon my journey.

The assurance with which I deliver'd this, gave the mob gentry[3] a check, and gave the constable such satisfaction, that he immediately sounded a retreat, told his people these were not the men, but that he had an account they were very honest gentlemen, and so they went all back again; what the truth of the matter was I knew not, but certain it was that the coaches were rob'd at *Dunstable* Hill, and 560 *l.* in money taken, besides some of the lace merchants that always travel that way had been visited too; as to the three gentlemen, that remains to be explain'd hereafter.

---

1 The pursuit of a felon by a constable and local people, usually announced by loud shouts.
2 Constables were, at this time, local citizens chosen annually by the parish. See below, p. 250, n. 1.
3 That is, the simple, uncultivated country people who made up the hue and cry (but with both words probably being used as well to convey a sense of Moll's derision).

Well, this alarm stop'd us another day, tho' my spouse was for travelling, and told me that it was always safest travelling after a robbery, for that the thieves were sure to be gone far enough off when they had allarm'd the country; but I was afraid and uneasy, and indeed principally lest my old acquaintance should be upon the road still, and should chance to see me.

I never liv'd four pleasanter days together in my life, I was a meer bride[1] all this while, and my new spouse strove to make me entirely easie in every thing; O could this state of life have continued! how had all my past troubles been forgot, and my future sorrows been avoided? But I had a past life of a most wretched kind to account for, some of it in this world as well as in another.

We came away the fifth day; and my landlord, because he saw me uneasie, mounted himself, his son, and three honest country fellows with good fire-arms, and, without telling us of it, follow'd the coach, and would see us safe into *Dunstable*; we could do no less than treat them very handsomely at *Dunstable*, which cost my spouse about ten or twelve shillings, and something he gave the men for their time too, but my landlord would take nothing for himself.

This was the most happy contrivance for me that could have fallen out, for had I come to *London* unmarried, I must either have come to him for the first night's entertainment, or have discovered to him that I had not one acquaintance in the whole city of *London* that could receive a poor bride for the first night's lodging with her spouse: but now being an old married woman, I made no scruple of going directly home with him, and there I took possession at once of a house well furnish'd, and a husband in very good circumstances, so that I had a prospect of a very happy life, if I knew how to manage it; and I had leisure to consider of the real value of the life I was likely to live; how different it was to be from the loose ungovern'd part I had acted before, and how much happier a life of virtue and sobriety is, than that which we call a life of pleasure.

O had this particular scene of life lasted, or had I learnt from that time I enjoy'd it, to have tasted the true sweetness of it, and had I not fallen into the poverty which is the sure bane of virtue, how happy had I been, not only here, but perhaps for ever? for while I liv'd thus, I was really a penitent for all my life pass'd, I look'd back on it with abhorrence, and might truly be said to hate my self for it; I often reflected how my lover at the *Bath*, strook by

---

1 A bride in the full sense of the term (obsolete form of *mere*).

the hand of God, repented and abandon'd me, and refus'd to see me any more, tho' he lov'd me to an extreme; but I, prompted by that worst of devils, poverty, return'd to the vile practice, and made the advantage of what they call a handsome face, be the relief to my necessities, and beauty be a pimp to vice.

Now I seem'd landed in a safe harbour, after the stormy voyage of life past was at an end; and I began to be thankful for my deliverance; I sat many an hour by my self, and wept over the remembrance of past follies, and the dreadful extravagances of a wicked life, and sometimes I flatter'd my self that I had sincerely repented.

But there are temptations which it is not in the power of human nature to resist,[1] and few know what would be their case, if driven to the same exigences: as covetousness is the root of all evil,[2] so poverty is, I believe, the worst of all snares: but I wave that discourse till I come to the experiment.[3]

I liv'd with this husband in the utmost tranquility; he was a quiet, sensible, sober man, virtuous, modest, sincere, and in his business diligent and just: his business was in a narrow compass, and his income sufficient to a plentiful way of living in the ordinary way; I do not say to keep an equipage,[4] and make a figure as the world calls it, nor did I expect it, or desire it; for as I abhorr'd the levity and extravagance of my former life, so I chose now to live retir'd, frugal, and within our selves; I kept no company, made no visits; minded my family, and oblig'd my husband; and this kind of life became a pleasure to me.

We liv'd in an uninterrupted course of ease and content for five years, when a sudden blow from an almost invisible hand, blasted all my happiness, and turn'd me out into the world in a condition the reverse of all that had been before it.

My husband having trusted one of his fellow clarks with a sum of money too much for our fortunes to bear the loss of, the clark fail'd, and the loss fell very heavy on my husband, yet it was not so great neither, but that if he had had spirit and courage to have look'd his misfortunes in the face, his credit was so good, that as I told him, he would easily recover it; for to sink under

---

1   This is a common theme in Defoe's writing, exemplified by the following remark in *Review* (8 February 1709): "The honestest Man in the World will eat his Neighbours Loaf if it be in his Cupboard, rather than perish."
2   I Timothy 6:10.
3   Practical proof.
4   Coach, horses and attendant servants.

trouble is to double the weight,[1] and he that will die in it shall die in it.

It was in vain to speak comfortably to him, the wound had sunk too deep, it was a stab that touch'd the vitals, he grew melancholy and disconsolate, and from thence lethargick,[2] and died; I foresaw the blow, and was extremely oppress'd in my mind, for I saw evidently that if he died I was undone.

I had had two children by him and no more, for to tell the truth, it began to be time for me to leave bearing children, for I was now eight and forty, and I suppose if he had liv'd I should have had no more.

I was now left in a dismal and disconsolate case indeed, and in several things worse than ever: first it was past the flourishing time with me when I might expect to be courted for a mistress; that agreeable part had declin'd some time, and the ruins only appear'd of what had been; and that which was worse than all was this, that I was the most dejected, disconsolate creature alive; I that had encourag'd my husband, and endeavour'd to support his spirits under his trouble, could not support my own; I wanted that spirit in trouble which I told him was so necessary to him for bearing the burthen.

But my case was indeed deplorable, for I was left perfectly friendless and helpless, and the loss my husband had sustain'd had reduc'd his circumstances so low, that tho' indeed I was not in debt, yet I could easily foresee that what was left would not support me long; that while it wasted daily for subsistence, I had no way to encrease it one shilling, so that it would be soon all spent, and then I saw nothing before me but the utmost distress, and this represented it self so lively to my thoughts, that it seem'd as if it was come, before it was really very near; also my very apprehensions doubl'd the misery, for I fancied every sixpence that I paid but for a loaf of bread, was the last that I had in the world, and that to-morrow I was to fast, and be starv'd to death.

In this distress I had no assistant, no friend to comfort or advise me, I sat and cried and tormented my self night and day; wring-

---

1 A favourite saying of Defoe, which Moll's governess uses again in slightly altered form shortly after Moll's arrival at Newgate prison (p. 277 below).
2 A morbid drowsiness and apathy, essentially similar in character to the medical condition of Moll's brother-husband (see above, p. 119, n. 2). Defoe expresses his attitude towards such people in the *Review* (17 May 1712): "I have not more Contemptible Thoughts of a Dog, a Bear, or any Brute, than I have of a Man, whom I see ... soon *dejected* ... "

ing my hands, and sometimes raving like a distracted woman; and indeed I have often wonder'd it had not affected my reason, for I had the vapours[1] to such a degree, that my understanding was sometimes quite lost in fancies and imaginations.

I liv'd two years in this dismal condition wasting that little I had, weeping continually over my dismal circumstances, and as it were only bleeding to death, without the least hope or prospect of help from God or man; and now I had cried so long, and so often, that tears were, as I might say, exhausted, and I began to be desperate, for I grew poor apace.

For a little relief I had put off my house and took lodgings, and as I was reducing my living so I sold off most of my goods, which put a little money in my pocket, and I liv'd near a year upon that, spending very sparingly, and eeking things out to the utmost; but still when I look'd before me, my very heart would sink within me at the inevitable approach of misery and want: O let none read this part without seriously reflecting on the circumstances of a desolate state, and how they would grapple with meer want of friends and want of bread; it will certainly make them think not of sparing what they have only, but of looking up to Heaven for support, and of the wise man's prayer, *Give me not poverty least I steal.*[2]

Let 'em remember that a time of distress is a time of dreadful temptation, and all the strength to resist is taken away; poverty presses, the soul is made desperate by distress, and what can be done? It was one evening, when being brought, as I may say, to the last gasp, I think I may truly say I was distracted and raving, when prompted by I know not what spirit,[3] and as it were, doing I did not know what, or why; I dress'd me, for I had still pretty good cloaths, and went out: I am very sure I had no manner of design in my head, when I went out, I neither knew or considered where to go, or on what business; but as the Devil carried me out and laid his bait for me, so he brought me to be sure to the place, for I knew not whither I was going or what I did.

Wandring thus about I knew not whither, I pass'd by an apothecary's shop in *Leadenhall-Street,*[4] where I saw lye on a stool just before the counter a little bundle wrapt in a white cloth;

---

1   Depression of spirits.
2   Proverbs 30:8-9 (paraphrased). The *Review* (15 September 1711) is devoted to the "wise man's prayer." Also see Appendix A.4.
3   For further information on Defoe and the supernatural, see Appendix A.8.
4   Near Leadenhall Market in the City of London, Leadenhall Street was an important place of trade and a busy thoroughfare.

beyond it, stood a maid servant with her back to it, looking up towards the top of the shop, where the apothecary's apprentice, as I suppose, was standing up on the counter, with his back also to the door, and a candle in his hand, looking and reaching up to the upper shelf for something he wanted, so that both were engag'd mighty earnestly, and no body else in the shop.

This was the bait; and the Devil who I said laid the snare, as readily prompted me, as if he had spoke, for I remember, and shall never forget it, 'twas like a voice spoken to me over my shoulder, Take the bundle; be quick; do it this moment; it was no sooner said but I step'd into the shop, and with my back to the wench, as if I had stood up for a cart that was going by,[1] I put my hand behind me and took the bundle, and went off with it, the maid or the fellow not perceiving me, or any one else.

It is impossible to express the horror of my soul all the while I did it: when I went away I had no heart to run, or scarce to mend my pace; I cross'd the street indeed, and went down the first turning I came to, and I think it was a street that went thro' into *Fenchurch-Street*,[2] from thence I cross'd and turn'd thro' so many ways and turnings that I could never tell which way it was, nor where I went, for I felt not the ground, I stept on, and the farther I was out of danger, the faster I went, till tyr'd and out of breath, I was forc'd to sit down on a little bench at a door, and then I began to recover, and found I was got into *Thames-Street* near *Billinsgate*: I rested me a little and went on, my blood was all in a fire, my heart beat as if I was in a sudden fright: in short, I was under such a surprize that I still knew not whither I was a going, or what to do.

After I had tyr'd my self thus with walking a long way about, and so eagerly, I began to consider and make home to my lodging, where I came about nine a clock at night.

What the bundle was made up for, or on what occasion laid where I found it, I knew not, but when I came to open it I found there was a suit of child-bed linnen in it, very good and almost new, the lace very fine; there was a silver porringer[3] of a pint, a small silver mug and six spoons, some other linnen, a good smock, and three silk handkerchiefs, and in the mug wrap'd up in a paper eighteen shillings and six-pence in money.

---

1 That is, as if she had got out of the way of a passing cart by stepping into the shop entrance.
2 The distance from Fenchurch Street to Billingsgate, on the River Thames below London Bridge, is roughly half a mile.
3 A small bowl for soup, porridge, etc., especially used by children.

All the while I was opening these things I was under such dreadful impressions of fear, and in such terror of mind, tho' I was perfectly safe, that I cannot express the manner of it; I sat me down and cried most vehemently; Lord, *said I*, what am I now? A thief! Why I shall be taken next time and be carry'd to *Newgate* and be try'd for my life![1] And with that I cry'd again a long time, and I am sure, as poor as I was, if I had durst for fear, I would certainly have carried the things back again; but that went off after a while: well, I went to bed for that night, but slept little, the horror of the fact was upon my mind, and I knew not what I said or did all night, and all the next day: then I was impatient to hear some news of the loss; and would fain know how it was, whether they were a poor bodies goods, or a rich; Perhaps, *said I*, it may be some poor widow like me, that had pack'd up these goods to go and sell them for a little bread for herself and a poor child, and are now starving and breaking their hearts, for want of that little they would have fetch'd, and this thought tormented me worse than all the rest, for three or four days time.

But my own distresses silenc'd all these reflections, and the prospect of my own starving, which grew every day more frightful to me, harden'd my heart by degrees; it was then particularly heavy upon my mind, that I had been reform'd, and had, as I hop'd, repented of all my pass'd wickednesses; that I had liv'd a sober, grave, retir'd life for several years, but now I should be driven by the dreadful necessity of my circumstances to the gates of destruction, soul and body; and two or three times I fell upon my knees, praying to God, as well as I could, for deliverance; but I cannot but say my prayers had no hope in them; I knew not what to do, it was all fear without, and dark within; and I reflected on my pass'd life as not sincerely repented of, that Heaven was now beginning to punish me on this side the grave, and would make me as miserable as I had been wicked.

Had I gone on here I had perhaps been a true penitent; but I had an evil counsellor within, and he was continually prompting me to relieve my self by the worst means; so one evening he tempted me again by the same wicked impulse that had said, *Take that bundle*, to go out again and seek for what might happen.

I went out now by day-light, and wandred about I knew not whither, and in search of I knew not what, when the Devil put a

---

1 According to the Shoplifting Act (1699), any theft from a shop, warehouse, coach-house or stable to the value of five shillings was a capital offence.

snare in my way of a dreadful nature indeed, and such a one as I have never had before or since; going thro' *Aldersgate-Street* there was a pretty little child had been at a dancing-school, and was going home, all alone, and my prompter, like a true devil, set me upon this innocent creature; I talk'd to it, and it prattl'd to me again, and I took it by the hand and led it a long till I came to a pav'd alley that goes into *Bartholomew Close*, and I led it in there; the child said that was not its way home; I said, Yes, my dear it is, I'll show you the way home; the child had a little necklace on of gold beads, and I had my eye upon that, and in the dark of the alley I stoop'd, pretending to mend the child's clog that was loose, and took off her necklace and the child never felt it, and so led the child on again: here, I say, the Devil put me upon killing the child in the dark alley, that it might not cry; but the very thought frighted me so that I was ready to drop down, but I turn'd the child about and bad it go back again, for that was not its way home; the child said so she would, and I went thro' into *Bartholomew Close*, and then turn'd round to another passage that goes into *Long-Lane*, so away into *Charterhouse-Yard* and out into *St. John's-Street*, then crossing into *Smithfield*, went down *Chick-Lane* and into *Field-Lane* to *Holbourn-Bridge*,[1] when mixing with the crowd of people usually passing there, it was not possible to have been found out; and thus I enterpriz'd my second sally into the world.[2]

The thoughts of this booty put out all the thoughts of the first, and the reflections I had made wore quickly off; poverty, as I have said, harden'd my heart, and my own necessities made me regardless of any thing: the last affair left no great concern upon me, for as I did the poor child no harm, I only said to my self, I had given the parents a just reproof for their negligence in leaving the poor little lamb to come home by it self, and it would teach them to take more care of it another time.

This string of beads was worth about twelve or fourteen pounds, I suppose it might have been formerly the mother's, for it was too big for the child's wear, but that, perhaps, the vanity of the mother to have her child look fine at the dancing school, had made her let the child wear it, and no doubt the child had a maid sent to take care of it, but she, like a careless jade, was taken up per-

---

1 This was one of the most disreputable districts of London during these years, a familiar haunt of the underworld.

2 That is, the world of crime. For a similar account elsewhere in Defoe's writings, see Appendix A.9.

haps with some fellow that had met her by the way, and so the poor baby wandred till it fell into my hands.

However, I did the child no harm, I did not so much as fright it, for I had a great many tender thoughts about me yet, and did nothing but what, as I may say, meer necessity drove me to.

I had a great many adventures after this, but I was young in the business, and did not know how to manage, otherwise than as the Devil put things into my head; and indeed he was seldom backward to me: one adventure I had which was very lucky to me; I was going thro' *Lombard-Street*[1] in the dusk of the evening, just by the end of *Three King Court*, when on a sudden comes a fellow running by me as swift as lightning, and throws a bundle that was in his hand just behind me, as I stood up against the corner of the house at the turning into the alley; just as he threw it in he said, God bless you mistress let it lie there a little, and away he runs swift as the wind: after him comes two more, and immediately a young fellow without his hat, crying Stop thief, and after him two or three more, they pursued the two last fellows so close, that they were forced to drop what they had got, and one of them was taken into the bargain, the other got off free.

I stood stock still all this while till they came back, dragging the poor fellow they had taken, and luging the things they had found, extremely well satisfied that they had recovered the booty, and taken the thief; and thus they pass'd by me, for I look'd only like one who stood up while the crowd was gone.

Once or twice I ask'd what was the matter, but the people neglected answering me, and I was not very importunate; but after the crowd was wholly pass'd, I took my opportunity to turn about and take up what was behind me and walk away: this indeed I did with less disturbance than I had done formerly, for these things I did not steal, but they were stolen to my hand: I got safe to my lodgings with this cargo, which was a peice of fine black lustring silk,[2] and a peice of velvet; the latter was but part of a peice of about a 11 yards; the former was a whole peice of near 50 yards; it seems it was a *mercer's*[3] shop that they had rifled, I say rifled, because the goods were so considerable that they had lost; for the goods that they recover'd were pretty many, and I believe came to

---

1 Famous for its impressive buildings, Lombard Street was largely inhabited at this time by goldsmiths, bankers and eminent tradesmen.
2 A glossy silk fabric.
3 A dealer in textiles, especially silks and other costly materials.

about six or seven several[1] peices of silk: how they came to get so many I could not tell; but as I had only robb'd the thief I made no scruple at taking these goods, and being very glad of them too.

I had pretty good luck thus far, and I made several adventures more, tho' with but small purchase,[2] yet with good success, but I went in daily dread that some mischief would befal me, and that I should certainly come to be hang'd at last: the impression this made on me was too strong to be slighted, and it kept me from making attempts that for ought I know might have been very safely perform'd; but one thing I cannot omit, which was a bait to me many a day. I walk'd frequently out into the villages round the town to see if nothing would fall in my way there; and going by a house near *Stepney*, I saw on the window-board two rings, one a small diamond ring, and the other a plain gold ring, to be sure laid there by some thoughtless lady, that had more money than forecast,[3] perhaps only till she wash'd her hands.

I walk'd several times by the window to observe if I could see whether there was any body in the room or no, and I could see no body, but still I was not sure; it came presently into my thoughts to rap at the glass, as if I wanted to speak with some body, and if any body was there they would be sure to come to the window, and then I would tell them to remove those rings, for that I had seen two suspicious fellows take notice of them: this was a ready thought, I rapt once or twice and no body came, when seeing the coast clear, I thrust hard against the square of glass, and broke it with very little noise, and took out the two rings, and walk'd away with them very safe, the diamond ring was worth about 3 *l.* and the other about 9 *s.*

I was now at a loss for a market for my goods, and especially for my two peices of silk, I was very loth to dispose of them for a trifle; as the poor unhappy theives in general do, who after they have ventured their lives for perhaps a thing of value, are fain[4] to sell it for a song when they have done; but I was resolv'd I would not do thus whatever shift I made, unless I was driven to the last extremity; however I did not well know what course to take: at last I resolv'd to go to my old governness, and acquaint myself with her again: I had punctually supply'd the 5 *l.* a year to her for my little boy as long as I was able; but at last was oblig'd to put a stop to it:

---

1 Separate, different.
2 Gain, booty.
3 Foresight.
4 Glad.

however I had written a letter to her, wherein I had told her that my circumstances were reduc'd very low; that I had lost my husband, and that I was not able to do it any longer, and so beg'd that the poor child might not suffer too much for its mother's misfortunes.

I now made her a visit, and I found that she drove something of the old trade still, but that she was not in such flourishing circumstances as before; for she had been sued by a certain gentleman, who had had his daughter stolen from him; and who it seems she had helped to convey away; and it was very narrowly that she escap'd the gallows; the expence also had ravag'd her, and she was become very poor; her house was but meanly furnished, and she was not in such repute for her practice as before; however she stood upon her legs, as they say, and as she was a stirring bustling woman, and had some stock left, she was turn'd *pawn broker, and liv'd pretty well.*

She receiv'd me very civilly, and with her usual obliging manner told me, she would not have the less respect for me, for my being reduc'd; that she had taken care my boy was very well look'd after, tho' I could not pay for him, and that the woman that had him was easie,[1] so that I needed not to trouble myself about him, till I might be better able to do it effectually.

I told her I had not much money left, but that I had some things that were monies worth, if she could tell me how I might turn them into money; she ask'd me what it was I had, I pull'd out the string of gold beads, and told her it was one of my husbands presents to me; then I show'd her the two parcels of silk which I told her I had from *Ireland,* and brought up to town with me; and the little diamond ring; as to the small parcel of plate and spoons, I had found means to dispose of them myself before; and as for the childbed linnen I had, she offer'd me to take it herself, believing it to have been my own; she told me that she was turn'd *pawnbroker,* and that she would sell those things for me as pawn'd to her, and so she sent presently for proper agents that bought them, being in her hands, without any scruple, and gave good prizes[2] too.

I now began to think this necessary[3] woman might help me a little in my low condition to some business; for I would gladly have turn'd my hand to any honest employment if I could have got it;

---

1 Comfortably off (obsolete form of *easy*).
2 Obsolete form of *prices*.
3 Useful.

but here she was defficient; honest business did not come within her reach; if I had been younger, perhaps she might have helped me to a spark,[1] but my thoughts were off of that kind of livelihood, as being quite out of the way after 50, which was my case, and so I told her.

She invited me at last to come, and be at her house till I could find something to do, and it should cost me very little, and this I gladly accepted of, and now living a little easier, I enter'd into some measures to have my little son by my last husband taken off;[2] and this she made easie too, reserving a payment only of 50 *l.* a year, if I could pay it. This was such a help to me, that for a good while I left off the wicked trade that I had so newly taken up; and gladly I would have got my bread by the help of my needle if I cou'd have got work, but that was very hard to do for one that had no manner of acquaintance in the world.

However at last I got some quilting-work for ladies beds, peticoats, and the like; and this I lik'd very well and work'd very hard, and with this I began to live; but the diligent Devil who resolv'd I should continue in his service, continually prompted me to go out and take a walk, that is to say, to see if any thing would offer in the old way.

One evening I blindly obeyed his summons, and fetch'd a long circuit thro' the streets, but met with no purchase and came home very weary, and empty; but not content with that, I went out the next evening too, when going by an alehouse I saw the door of a little room open, next the very street, and on the table a silver tankard, things much in use in publick houses at that time; it seems some company had been drinking there, and the careless boys had forgot to take it away.

I went into the box frankly,[3] and setting the silver tankard on the corner of the bench, I sat down before it, and knock'd with my foot, a boy came presently, and I bad him fetch me a pint of warm ale, for it was cold weather; the boy run, and I heard him go down the sellar to draw the ale; while the boy was gone, another boy come into the room, and cried, *D' ye call*, I spoke with a melancholly air, and said, No child, the boy is gone for a pint of ale for me.

While I sat here, I heard the woman in the bar say Are they all gone in the five, which was the box I sat in, and the boy said *Yes*;

---

1 Suitor, lover.
2 That is, taken off her hands.
3 Openly.

Who fetch'd the tankard away? *says the woman,* I did, *says another boy,* that's it, pointing it seems to another tankard, which he had fetch'd from another box by mistake; or else it must be, that the rogue forgot that he had not brought it in, which certainly he had not.

I heard all this, much to my satisfaction, for I found plainly that the tankard was not mist, and yet they concluded it was fetch'd away; so I drank my ale, call'd to pay, and as I went away, *I said,* Take care of your plate child, meaning a silver pint mug, which he brought me drink in; the boy said, *Yes madam, very welcome,* and away I came.

I came home to my governess, and now I thought it was a time to try her, that if I might be put to the necessity of being expos'd,[1] she might offer me some assistance; when I had been at home some time, and had an opportunity of talking to her, I told her I had a secret of the greatest consequence in the world to commit to her if she had respect enough for me to keep it a secret: she told me she had kept one of my secrets faithfully; why should I doubt her keeping another? I told her the strangest thing in the world had befallen me, and that it had made a thief of me, even without any design; and so told her the whole story of the tankard: And have you brought it away with you my dear, *says she,* To be sure I have, *says I,* and shew'd it her. But what shall I do now, *says I,* must not I carry it[2] again?

Carry it again! *says she,* Ay, if you are minded to be sent to *Newgate* for stealing it; Why, *says I,* they can't be so base to stop me, when I carry it to them again? You don't know those sort of people child, *says she,* they'll not only carry you to *Newgate,* but hang you too without any regard to the honesty of returning it; or bring in an account of all the other tankards they have lost for you to pay for: What must I do then? *says I;* Nay, *says she,* as you have plaid the cunning part and stole it, you must e'n keep it, there's no going back now; besides child, *says she,* don't you want[3] it more than they do? I wish you cou'd light of such a bargain once a week.

This gave me a new notion of my *governess,* and that since she was turn'd *pawn broker,* she had a sort of people about her, that were none of the honest ones that I had met with there before.

I had not been long there, but I discover'd it more plainly than

---

1 That is, of revealing her theft.
2 Carry it back.
3 Need.

before, for every now and then I saw hilts of swords, spoons, forks, tankards, and all such kind of ware brought in, not to be pawn'd, but to be sold down right; and she bought every thing that came without asking any questions, but had very good bargains as I found by her discourse.

I found also that in the following this trade, she always melted down the plate she bought, that it might not be challeng'd; and she came to me and told me one morning that she was going to melt, and if I would, she would put my tankard in, that it might not be seen by any body; I told her with all my heart; so she weigh'd it, and allow'd me the full value in silver again; but I found she did not do the same to the rest of her customers.

Sometime after this, as I was at work, and very melancholly, she begins to ask me what the matter was? as she was us'd to do; I told her my heart was heavy, I had little work, and nothing to live on, and knew not what course to take; she laugh'd and told me I must go out again and try my fortune; it might be that I might meet with another peice of plate. O, mother! *says I*, that is a trade I have no skill in, and if I should be taken I am undone at once; *says she*, I cou'd help you to a school-mistress, that shall make you as dexterous as her self: I trembled at that proposal for hitherto I had had no confederates, nor any acquaintance among that tribe; but she conquer'd all my modesty, and all my fears; and in a little time, by the help of this confederate I grew as impudent a thief, and as dexterous as ever *Moll Cut-purse* was, tho' if fame does not belie her, not half so handsome.[1]

The comrade she helped me to, dealt in three sorts of craft, (*viz.*) shop-lifting, stealing of shop-books, and pocket-books, and taking off gold watches from the ladies sides, and this last she did so dexteriously that no woman ever arriv'd to the perfection of that art, so as to do it like her: I lik'd the first and the last of these things very well, and I attended her some time in the practise, just as a deputy attends a midwife without any pay.

At length she put me to practise, she had shewn me her art, and I had several times unhook'd a watch from her own side with great dexterity; at last she show'd me a prize, and this was a young lady big with child who had a charming watch, the thing was to be

---

1 This was the alias for Mary Frith (1584?-1659), one of the most notorious thieves of the seventeenth century. With regard to her looks, a spinster in *Applebee's Journal* (6 April 1723) says: "I have seen her Picture ... and I can Vouch she was a very comely Jade." For further details, see *The Life and Death of Mrs. Mary Frith* (London, 1662).

done as she came out of church; she goes on one side of the lady, and pretends, just as she came to the steps, to fall, and fell against the lady with so much violence as put her into a great fright, and both cry'd out terribly; in the very moment that she jostl'd the lady, I had hold of the watch, and holding it the right way, the start she gave drew the hook out and she never felt it; I made off immediately, and left my schoolmistress to come out of her pretended fright gradually, and the lady too; and presently the watch was miss'd; Ay, *says my comrade*, then it was those rogues that thrust me down, I warrant ye; I wonder the gentlewoman did not miss her watch before, then we might have taken them.

She humour'd[1] the thing so well that no body suspected her, and I was got home a full hour before her: this was my first adventure in company; the watch was indeed a very fine one, and had a great many trinkets about it, and my governess allow'd us 20 *l.* for it, of which I had half, and thus I was enter'd a compleat thief, harden'd to a pitch above all the reflections of conscience or modesty, and to a degree which I must acknowledge I never thought possible in me.

Thus the Devil who began, by the help of an irresistable poverty, to push me into this wickedness, brought me on to a height beyond the common rate, even when my necessities were not so great, or the prospect of my misery so terrifying; for I had now got into a little vein of work, and as I was not at a loss to handle my needle, it was very probable, as acquaintance came in, I might have got my bread honestly enough.

I must say, that if such a prospect of work had presented it self at first, when I began to feel the approach of my miserable circumstances; I say, had such a prospect of getting my bread by working presented it self then, I had never fallen into this wicked trade, or into such a wicked gang as I was now embark'd with; but practise had hardened me, and I grew audacious to the last degree; and the more so, because I had carried it on so long, and had never been taken; for in a word, my new partner in wickedness *and I* went on together so long, without being ever detected, that we not only grew bold, but we grew rich, and we had at one time one and twenty gold watches in our hands.

I remember that one day being a little more serious than ordinary, and finding I had so good a stock before-hand as I had, for I had near 200 *l.* in money for my share; it came strongly into my

---

1 Managed.

mind, no doubt from some kind spirit, if such there be; that as at first poverty excited me, and my distresses drove me to these dreadful shifts; so seeing those distresses were now relieved, and I could also get something towards a maintenance by working, and had so good a bank to support me, why should I not now leave off, as they say, while I was well; that I could not expect to go always free; and if I was once surpris'd, and miscarry'd, I was undone.

This was doubtless the happy minute, when if I had hearken'd to the blessed hint from whatsoever hand it came I had still a cast for an easie life; but my fate was otherwise determin'd, the busie Devil that so industriously drew me in, had too fast hold of me to let me go back; but as poverty brought me into the mire, so avarice kept me in, till there was no going back; as to the arguments which my reason dictated for perswading me to lay down, avarice stept in and said, Go on, go on; you have had very good luck, go on till you have gotten four or five hundred pound, and then you shall leave off, and then you may live easie without working at all.

Thus I that was once in the Devil's clutches, was held fast there as with a charm, and had no power to go without the circle, till I was ingulph'd in labyrinths of trouble too great to get out at all.

However, these thoughts left some impression upon me, and made me act with some more caution than before, and more than my directors us'd for themselves. My comerade, as I call'd her, but rather she should have been called my teacher, with another of her scholars,[1] was the first in the misfortune, for happening to be upon the hunt for purchase, they made an attempt upon a linnen-draper in *Cheapside*,[2] but were snap'd[3] by a hawks-ey'd journey-man,[4] and seiz'd with two pieces of cambrick,[5] which were taken also upon them.

This was enough to lodge them both in *Newgate*, where they had the misfortune to have some of their former sins brought to remembrance; two other indictments being brought against them, and the facts being prov'd upon them, they were both condemned to die; they both pleaded their bellies, and were both voted quick

---

1 The idea of treating criminals as scholars, who graduate from "Newgate College," was popular during this period. See Appendix B.1.
2 This incident is reminiscent of the one told by Moll of her mother's theft and incarceration. See above, p. 46.
3 Caught.
4 One who has served his apprenticeship in a craft or a trade and is in the employ of another.
5 A finely woven white linen fabric (obsolete form of *cambric*).

with child;[1] tho' my tutress was no more with child than I was.

I went frequently to see them, and condole with them, expecting that it would be my turn next; but the place gave me so much horror, reflecting that it was the place of my unhappy birth, and of my mother's misfortunes, that I could not bear it, so I was forc'd to leave off going to see them.

And O! cou'd I have but taken warning by their disasters, I had been happy still, for I was yet free, and had nothing brought against me; but it could not be, my measure was not yet fill'd up.[2]

My comerade having the brand of an old offender,[3] was executed; the young offender was spar'd, having obtain'd a reprieve; but lay starving a long while in prison, till at last she got her name into what they call a circuit pardon[4] and so came off.

This terrible example of my comerade frighted me heartily, and for a good while I made no excursions; but one night, in the neighbourhood of my governesses house, they cryed Fire; my governess look'd out, for we were all up, and cryed immediately that such a gentlewoman's house was all of a light fire a top, and so indeed it was: here she gives me a jog, Now, child, says she, there is a rare opportunity, the fire being so near that you may go to it before the street is block'd up with the crowd; she presently gave me my cue, Go, child, *says she*, to the house, and run in and tell the lady, or any body you see, that you come to help them, and that you came from such a gentlewoman (that is one of her acquaintance farther up the street); she gave me the like cue to the next house, naming another name that was also an acquaintance of the gentlewoman of the house.

Away I went, and coming to the house I found them all in confusion, you may be sure; I run in, and finding one of the maids, Lord! sweetheart, *said I*, how came this dismal accident? Where is your mistress? And how does she do? Is she safe? And where are the children? I come from Madam ——— to help you; away runs the maid, Madam, madam, *says she*, screaming as loud as she cou'd yell, *here is a gentlewoman come from Madam ——— to help us.* The poor woman half out of her wits, with a bundle under her

---

1 Judged to be pregnant. See above, p. 46, n. 4.
2 Possibly a reworking of Matthew 23:32.
3 A capital sentence could only be reduced once to branding (the burnt hand). See above, p. 113, n. 5.
4 Probably a court (rather than "circuit") pardon was meant, which was one of the general pardons. (Compositor's error?)

arm, and two little children, comes towards me, *Lord, madam, says I*, let me carry the poor children to Madam ———, she desires you to send them; she'll take care of the poor lambs, and immediately I takes one of them out of her hand, and she lifts the tother up into my arms; *Ay, do, for God sake*, says she, *carry them to her; O thank her for her kindness*: Have you *any thing else to secure*, madam? says I, *she will take care of it*: O dear! ay, says she, *God bless her, and thank her, take this bundle of plate and carry it to her too; O she is a good woman; O Lord, we are utterly ruin'd, utterly undone*; and away she runs from me out of her wits, and the maids after her, and away comes I with the two children and the bundle.[1]

I was no sooner got into the street, but I saw another woman come to me, O! *says she*, mistress, in a piteous tone, you will let fall the child; come, this is a sad time, let me help you, and immediately lays hold of my bundle to carry it for me; No, *says I*, if you will help me, take the child by the hand, and lead it for me but to the upper end of the street, I'll go with you and satisfie you for your pains.

She cou'd not avoid going, after what I said, but the creature, in short, was one of the same business with me, and wanted nothing but the bundle; however, she went with me to the door, for she cou'd not help it; when we were come there I whisper'd her, *Go child*, said I, *I understand your trade*, you may meet with purchase enough.

She understood me and walk'd off; I thundered at the door with the children, and as the people were rais'd before by the noise of the fire, I was soon let in, and I said, *Is madam awake, pray tell her* Mrs. ——— *desires the favour of her to take the two children in*; poor lady, *she will be undone, their house is all of a flame*; they took the children in very civily, pitied the family in distress, and away came I with my bundle; one of the maids ask'd me, if I was not to leave the bundle too? I said No, sweetheart, 'tis to go to another place, it does not belong to them.

I was a great way out of the hurry now, and so I went on, clear of any body's enquiry, and brought the bundle of plate, which was very considerable, strait home, and gave it to my old governess; she told me she would not look into it, but bad me go out again to look for more.

She gave me the like cue to the gentlewoman of the next house to that which was on fire, and I did my endeavour to go, but by

---

1 For a similar account by Defoe, see Appendix A.2.

this time the allarm of fire was so great, and so many engines play-ing,[1] and the street so throng'd with people, that I cou'd not get near the house, whatever I cou'd do; so I came back again to my governesses, and taking the bundle up into my chamber, I began to examine it: it is with horror that I tell what a treasure I found there; 'tis enough to say, that besides most of the family plate, which was considerable, I found a gold chain, an old fashion'd thing, the locket of which was broken, so that I suppose it had not been us'd some years, but the gold was not the worse for that; also a little box of burying rings,[2] the lady's wedding-ring, and some broken bits of old lockets of gold, a gold watch, and a purse with about 24 *l.* value in old pieces of gold coin, and several other things of value.

This was the greatest and the worst prize that ever I was con-cern'd in, for indeed, tho' as I have said above, I was harden'd now beyond the power of all reflection in other cases, yet it really touch'd me to the very soul, when I look'd into this treasure, to think of the poor disconsolate gentlewoman who had lost so much by the fire besides; and who would think to be sure that she had sav'd her plate and best things; how she wou'd be surpriz'd and afflicted when she should find that she had been deceiv'd, and should find that the person that took her children and her goods, had not come, as was pretended, from the gentlewoman in the next street, but that the children had been put upon her without her own knowledge.

I say I confess the inhumanity of this action mov'd me very much, and made me relent exceedingly, and tears stood in my eyes upon that subject: but with all my sense of its being cruel and inhuman, I cou'd never find in my heart to make any restitution: the reflection wore off, and I began quickly to forget the circum-stances that attended the taking them.

Nor was this all, for tho' by this jobb I was become consider-ably richer than before, yet the resolution I had formerly taken of leaving off this horrid trade, when I had gotten a little more, did not return; but I must still get farther, and more; and the avarice join'd so with the success, that I had no more thoughts of coming to a timely alteration of life; tho' without it I cou'd expect no safe-ty, no tranquility in the possession of what I had so wickedly gain'd; but a little more, and a little more, was the case still.

---

1 That is, playing streams of water on the fire.
2 Money might be left to close friends to buy funeral rings, or sometimes they were given as mementos to mourners at the funeral itself.

At length yielding to the importunities of my crime, I cast off all remorse and repentance; and all the reflections on that head, turn'd to no more than this, that I might perhaps come to have one booty more that might compleat my desires; but tho' I certainly had that one booty, yet every hit look'd towards another, and was so encouraging to me to go on with the trade, that I had no gust[1] to the thought of laying it down.

In this condition, harden'd by success, and resolving to go on, I fell into the snare in which I was appointed to meet with my last reward for this kind of life: but even this was not yet, for I met with several successful adventures more in this way of being undone.

I remain'd still with my governess, who was for a while really concern'd for the misfortune of my comerade that had been hang'd, and who it seems knew enough of my governess to have sent her the same way, and which made her very uneasy; indeed she was in a very great fright.

It is true, that when she was gone, and had not open'd her mouth to tell what she knew, my governess was easy as to that point, and perhaps glad she was hang'd; for it was in her power to have obtain'd a pardon at the expence of her friends;[2] but on the other hand, the loss of her, and the sense of her kindness in not making her market[3] of what she knew, mov'd my governess to mourn very sincerely for her: I comforted her as well as I cou'd, and she in return harden'd me to merit more compleatly the same fate.

However as I have said it made me the more wary, and particularly I was very shie of shoplifting, especially among the *mercers*, and *drapers* who are a set of fellows, that have their eyes very much about them: I made a venture or two among the lace folks, and the mileners,[4] and particularly at one shop, where I got notice of two young women who were newly set up, and had not been bred to the trade: there, I think I carried off a peice of bonelace, worth six or seven pound, and a paper[5] of thread; but this was but once, it was a trick that would not serve again.

It was always reckon'd a safe job when we heard of a new shop,

---

1 Inclination, liking.
2 A pardon could be obtained by a convicted burglar by giving information which would lead to the conviction or two or more thieves.
3 Marketing, making a deal.
4 Vendors of women's dress ware (e.g., hats, ribbons, gloves), especially those originally made in Milan (obsolete form of *milliners*).
5 Packet, paperful.

and especially when the people were such as were not bred to shops; such may depend upon it, that they will be visited once or twice at their beginning, and they must be very sharp indeed if they can prevent it.

I made another adventure or two, but they were but trifles too, tho' sufficient to live on; after this nothing considerable offering for a good while, I began to think that I must give over the trade in earnest; but my governess, who was not willing to lose me, and expected great things of me, brought me one day into company with a young woman and a fellow that went for her husband, tho' as it appear'd afterwards she was not his wife, but they were partners it seems in the trade they carried on; and partners in something else too. *In short*, they robb'd together, lay together, were taken together, and at last were hang'd together.

I came into a kind of league with these two, by the help of my governess, and they carried me out into three or four adventures, where I rather saw them commit some coarse and unhandy robberies, in which nothing but a great stock of impudence on their side, and gross negligence on the peoples side who were robb'd, could have made them successful; so I resolv'd from that time forward to be very cautious how I adventur'd upon any thing with them; and indeed when two or three unlucky projects were propos'd by them, I declin'd the offer, and perswaded them against it: one time they particularly propos'd robbing a watchmaker of 3 gold watches, which they had ey'd in the day time, and found the place where he laid them; one of them had so many keys of all kinds, that he made no question to open the place, where the watchmaker had laid them; and so we made a kind of an appointment; but when I came to look narrowly into the thing, I found they propos'd breaking open the house; and this as a thing out of my way, I would not embark in; so they went without me: they did get into the house by main force, and broke up the lock'd place where the watches were, but found but one of the gold watches, and a silver one, which they took, and got out of the house again very clear, but the family being alarm'd cried out Thieves, and the man was pursued and taken, the young woman had got off too, but unhappily was stop'd at a distance, and the watches found upon her; and thus I had a second escape, for they were convicted, and both hang'd, being old offenders, tho' but young people; as *I said before*, that they robbed together, and lay together, so now they hang'd together, and there ended my new partnership.

I began now to be very wary, having so narrowly escap'd a

scouring,[1] and having such an example before me; but I had a new tempter, who prompted me every day, I mean my governess; and now a prize presented, which as it came by her management, so she expected a good share of the booty; there was a good quantity of flanders-lace lodg'd in a private house, where she had gotten intelligence of it; and Flanders-lace, being then prohibited,[2] it was a good booty to any custom-house officer that could come at it: I had a full account from my governess, as well of the quantity as of the very place where it was conceal'd, and I went to a custom-house officer, and told him I had such a discovery to make to him, of such a quantity of lace, if he would assure me that I should have my due share of the reward: this was so just an offer, that nothing could be fairer; so he agreed, and taking a constable, and me with him, we beset the house; as I told him, I could go directly to the place, he left it to me, and the hole being very dark, I squeez'd myself into it with a candle in my hand, and so reach'd the peices out to him, taking care as I gave him some, so to secure as much about myself as I could conveniently dispose of: there was near 300 *l.* worth of lace in the whole; and I secur'd about 50 *l.* worth of it to myself: the people of the house were not owners of the lace, but a merchant who had entrusted them with it; so that they were not so surpriz'd as I thought they would be.

I left the officer overjoy'd with his prize, and fully satisfy'd with what he had got; and appointed to meet him at a house of his own directing, where I came after I had dispos'd of the cargo I had about me, of which he had not the least suspicion; when I came to him, he began to capitulate[3] with me, believing I did not understand the right I had to a share in the prize, and would fain have put me off with twenty pound, but I let him know that I was not so ignorant as he suppos'd I was; and yet I was glad too, that he offer'd to bring me to a certainty;[4] I ask'd 100 *l.* and he rise up to 30 *l.* I fell to 80 *l.* and he rise again to 40 *l.* in a word, he offer'd 50 *l.* and I consented, only demanding a peice of lace, which I thought came to about 8 or 9 pound, as if it had been for my own wear, and he agreed to it, so I got 50 *l.* in money paid me that same

---

1 Beating, drubbing.
2 Acts protecting the home industry against the importation of foreign lace had been passed since the reign of Charles II. As Flanders lace was much in fashion, however, it was smuggled into the country and sold under the counter in shops.
3 Bargain, make terms.
4 A definite figure.

night, and made an end of the bargain; nor did he ever know who I was, or where to enquire for me; so that if it had been discover'd, that part of the goods were embezzel'd; he could have made no challenge upon me for it.

I very punctually[1] divided this spoil with my governess, and I pass'd with her from this time for a very dexterous manager in the nicest cases; I found that this last was the best, and easiest sort of work that was in my way, and I made it my business to enquire out prohibited goods; and after buying some usually betray'd them, but none of these discoveries amounted to any thing considerable; not like that I related just now; but I was willing to act safe, and was still cautious of running the great risques which I found others did, and in which they miscarried every day.

The next thing of moment, was an attempt at a gentlewoman's gold watch, it happen'd in a crowd, at a meeting-house, where I was in very great danger of being taken; I had full hold of her watch, but giving a great jostle, as if some body had thrust me against her, and in the juncture giving the watch a fair pull, I found it would not come, so I let it go that moment, and cried out as if I had been kill'd, that some body had trod upon my foot, and that there was certainly *pick-pockets* there; for some body or other had given a pull at my watch, for you are to observe, that on these adventures we always went very well dress'd, and I had very good cloaths on, and a gold watch by my side, as like a lady as other folks.

I had no sooner said so, but the tother gentlewoman cried out *A pick-pocket* too, for some body, *she said*, had try'd to pull her watch away.

When I touch'd her watch, I was close to her, but when I cry'd out, I stop'd as it were short, and the crowd bearing her forward a little, she made a noise too, but it was at some distance from me, so that she did not in the least suspect me; but when she cried out *A pick-pocket*, some body cried Ay, and here has been another, this gentlewoman has been attempted too.

At that very instant, a little farther in the crowd, and very luckily too, they cried out *A pick-pocket* again, and really seiz'd a young fellow in the very fact. This, tho' unhappy for the wretch was very opportunely for my case, tho' I had carried it off handsomely enough before, but now it was out of doubt, and all the loose part of the crowd run that way, and the poor boy was deliver'd up to

---

1 Precisely, exactly.

the rage of the street, which is a cruelty I need not describe, and which however they are always glad of, rather than to be sent to *Newgate*, where they lie often a long time, till they are almost perish'd, and sometimes they are hang'd, and the best they can look for, if they are convicted, is to be transported.

This was a narrow escape to me, and I was so frighted, that I ventur'd no more at gold watches a great while; there was indeed a great many concurring circumstances in this adventure, which assisted to my escape; but the chief was, that the woman whose watch I had pull'd at was a fool; that is to say, she was ignorant of the nature of the attempt, which one would have thought she should not have been, seeing she was wise enough to fasten her watch, so, that it could not be slipt up; but she was in such a fright, that she had no thought about her proper for the discovery; for she, when she felt the pull scream'd out, and push'd herself forward, and put all the people about her into disorder, but said not a word of her watch, or of a *pick-pocket*, for at least two minutes time; which was time enough for me, and to spare; for as I had cried out behind her, *as I have said*, and bore myself back in the crowd as she bore forward; there were several people, at least seven or eight, the throng being still moving on, that were got between me and her in that time, and then I crying out *A pick-pocket*, rather sooner than she, or at least as soon, she might as well be the person suspected as I, and the people were confus'd in their enquiry; whereas, had she with a presence of mind needful on such an occasion, as soon as she felt the pull, not skream'd out as she did, but turn'd immediately round, and seiz'd the next body that was behind her, she had infallibly taken me.

This is a direction not of the kindest sort to the fraternity; but 'tis certainly a key to the clue[1] of *a pick-pockets* motions, and whoever can follow it, will as certainly catch the thief as he will be sure to miss if he does not.

I had another adventure, which puts this matter out of doubt, and which may be an instruction for posterity in the case of *a pick-pocket*, my good old governess to give a short touch at her history, tho' she had left off the trade, was as I may say, born *a pick-pocket*, and as I understood afterward had run thro' all the several degrees of that art, and yet had never been taken but once; when she was so grossly detected, that she was convicted and orderd to be transported; but being a woman of a rare tongue, and withal

---

1 Tangle (or *clew*).

having money in her pocket; she found means, the ship putting into *Ireland* for provisions, to get on shore there, where she liv'd and practis'd her old trade for some years; when falling into another sort of bad company, she turn'd midwife and procuress, and play'd a hundred pranks there, which she gave me a little history of in confidence between us as we grew more intimate; and it was to this wicked creature that I ow'd all the art and dexterity I arriv'd to, in which there were few that ever went beyond me, or that practis'd so long without any misfortune.

It was after those adventures in *Ireland*, and when she was pretty well known in that country, that she left *Dublin*, and came over to *England*, where the time of her transportation being not expir'd, she left her former trade, for fear of falling into bad hands again, for then she was sure to have gone to wreck: here she set up the same trade she had followed in *Ireland*, in which she soon by her admirable management, and a good tongue, arriv'd to the height, which I have already describ'd, and indeed began to be rich tho' her trade fell off again afterwards; as I have hinted before.

I mention thus much of the history of this woman here, the better to account for the concern she had in the wicked life I was now leading; into all the particulars of which she led me as it were by the hand, and gave me such directions, and I so well follow'd them, that I grew the greatest artist of my time, and work'd myself out of every danger with such dexterity, that when several more of my comrades run themselves into *Newgate* presently, and by that time they had been half a year at the trade, I had now practis'd upwards of five year, and the people at *Newgate*, did not so much as know me; they had heard much of me indeed, and often expected me there; but I always got off, tho' many times in the extreamest danger.

One of the greatest dangers I was now in, was that I was too well known among the trade, and some of them whose hatred was owing rather to envy, than any injury I had done them began to be angry, that I should always escape when they were always catch'd and hurried to *Newgate*. These were they that gave me the name of *Moll Flanders*: for it was no more of affinity with my real name, or with any of the names I had ever gone by, than black is of kin to white, except that once, as before I call'd my self Mrs. *Flanders*, when I sheltered myself in the *Mint*; but that these rogues never knew, nor could I ever learn how they came to give me the name, or what the occasion of it was.

I was soon inform'd that some of these who were gotten fast

into *Newgate*, had vowed to impeach[1] me; and as I knew that two or three of them were but too able to do it, I was under a great concern about it, and kept within doors for a good while; but my governess who I always made partner in my success, and who now plaid a sure[2] game with me, for that she had a share of the gain, and no share in the hazard, *I say*, my governess was something impatient of my leading such a useless unprofitable life, as she call'd it; and she laid a new contrivance for my going abroad, and this was to dress me up in mens cloths,[3] and so put me into a new kind of practise.

I was tall and personable, but a little too smooth fac'd for a man; however as I seldom went abroad but in the night, it did well enough; but it was a long time before I could behave in my new cloths: I mean, as to my craft; it was impossible to be so nimble, so ready, so dexterous at these things, in a dress so contrary to nature; and as I did every thing clumsily, so I had neither the success, or the easiness of escape that I had before, and I resolv'd to leave it off; but that resolution was confirm'd soon after by the following accident.

As my governess had disguis'd me like a man, so she joyn'd me with a man, a young fellow that was nimble enough at his business, and for about three weeks we did very well together. Our principal trade was watching shop-keepers compters,[4] and slipping off any kind of goods we could see carelesly laid any where, and we made several very good bargains as we call'd them at this work: and as we kept always together, so we grew very intimate, yet he never knew that I was not a man; nay, tho' I several times went home with him to his lodgings, according as our business directed, and four or five times lay with him all night: but our design lay another way, and it was absolutely necessary to me to conceal my sex from him, as appear'd afterwards: the circumstances of our living, coming in late, and having such and such business to do as requir'd that no body should be trusted with coming into our lodgings, were such as made it impossible to me to refuse lying with him, unless I would have own'd my sex, and as it was I effectually conceal'd my self.

But his ill, and my good fortune, soon put an end to this life,

---

1 Testify against, charge another as guilty.
2 Safe, secure.
3 One of the disguises used as well by Moll Cut-Purse (see above, p. 212, n. 1).
4 Obsolete form of *counters.*

which I must own I was sick of too, on several other accounts: we had made several prizes in this new way of business, but the last would have been extraordinary; there was a shop in a certain street which had a warehouse behind it that look'd into another street, the house making the corner of the turning.

Through the window of the warehouse we saw lying on the counter or show-board which was just before it, five pieces of silks, besides other stuffs; and tho' it was almost dark, yet the people being busie in the fore shop with customers, had not had time to shut up those windows, or else had forgot it.

This the young fellow was so overjoy'd with, that he could not restrain himself, it lay all within his reach he said, and he swore violently to me that he would have it, if he broke down the house for it; I disswaded him a little, but saw there was no remedy, so he run rashly upon it, slipt out a square out of the sash window dexterously enough, and without noise, and got out four pieces of the silks, and came with them towards me, but was immediately pursued with a terrible clutter and noise; we were standing together indeed, but I had not taken any of the goods out of his hand, when I said to him hastily, You are undone, fly for God sake; he run like lightning, and I too, but the pursuit was hotter after him because he had the goods, than after me; he dropt two of the pieces which stop'd them a little, but the crowd encreas'd and pursued us both; they took him soon after with the other two pieces upon him, and then the rest followed me; I run for it and got into my governesses house, whither some quick-eyed people follow'd me so warmly as to fix me there;[1] they did not immediately knock at the door, by which I got time to throw off my disguise, and dress me in my own cloths; besides, when they came there, my governess, who had her tale ready, kept her door shut, and call'd out to them and told them there was no man came in there; the people affirm'd there did a man come in there, and swore they would break open the door.

My governess, not at all surpriz'd, spoke calmly to them, told them they should very freely come and search her house, if they would bring a constable, and let in none but such as the constable would admit, for it was unreasonable to let in a whole crowd; this they could not refuse, tho' they were a crowd; so a constable was fetch'd immediately, and she very freely open'd the door, and the constable kept the door, and the men he appointed search'd the

---

1 That is, to place her presence there with certainty.

house, my governess going with them from room to room; when she came to my room she call'd to me, and said aloud; Cousin, pray open the door, here's some gentlemen that must come and look into your room.

I had a little girl with me, which was my governesses grand-child, as she call'd her; and I bad her open the door, and there sat I at work with a great litter of things about me, as if I had been at work all day, being my self quite undress'd, with only night-cloaths on my head, and a loose morning gown wrapt about me: my governess made a kind of excuse for their disturbing me, telling me partly the occasion of it, and that she had no remedy but to open the doors to them, and let them satisfie themselves, for all she could say to them would not satisfie them: I sat still, and bid them search the room if they pleas'd, for if there was any body in the house, I was sure they was not in my room; and as for the rest of the house I had nothing to say to that, I did not understand what they look'd for.

Every thing look'd so innocent and so honest about me, that they treated me civiller than I expected, but it was not till they had search'd the room to a nicety, even under the bed, in the bed, and every where else, where it was possible any thing cou'd be hid; when they had done this, and cou'd find nothing, they ask'd my pardon for troubling me, and went down.

When they had thus searched the house from bottom to top, and then from top to bottom, and cou'd find nothing, they appeas'd the mob pretty well; but they carried my governess before the justice: two men swore that they see the man, who they pursued, go into her house: my governess rattled and made a great noise that her house should be insulted, and that she should be used thus for nothing; that if a man did come in, he might go out again presently for ought she knew, for she was ready to make oath that no man had been within her doors all that day as she knew of, and that was very true indeed; that it might be indeed that as she was above stairs, any fellow in a fright might find the door open, and run in for shelter when he was pursued, but that she knew nothing of it; and if it had been so, he certainly went out again, perhaps at the other door, for she had another door into an alley, and so had made his escape and cheated them all.

This was indeed probable enough, and the justice satisfied him-self with giving her an oath, that she had not receiv'd or admitted any man into her house to conceal him, or protect or hide him from justice: this oath she might justly take, and did so, and so she was dismiss'd.

It is easie to judge what a fright I was in upon this occasion, and it was impossible for my governess ever to bring me to dress in that disguise again; for, as I told her, I should certainly betray my self.

My poor partner in this mischief was now in a bad case, for he was carried away before my Lord Mayor, and by his worship committed to *Newgate*, and the people that took him were so willing, as well as able, to prosecute him, that they offer'd themselves to enter into recognisances[1] to appear at the sessions, and persue the charge against him.

However, he got his indictment deferr'd, upon promise to discover his accomplices, and particularly, the man that was concern'd with him in this robbery, and he fail'd not to do his endeavour, for he gave in my name who he call'd *Gabriel Spencer*, which was the name I went by to him, and here appear'd the wisdom of my concealing my name and sex from him, which if he had ever known I had been undone.

He did all he cou'd to discover this *Gabriel Spencer*; he describ'd me, he discover'd the place where he said I lodg'd, and in a word, all the particulars that he cou'd of my dwelling; but having conceal'd the main circumstances of my sex from him, I had a vast advantage, and he never cou'd hear of me; he brought two or three families into trouble by his endeavouring to find me out, but they knew nothing of me, any more than that he had a fellow with him that they had seen, but knew nothing of; and as for my governess, tho' she was the means of his coming to me, yet it was done at second hand, and he knew nothing of her.

This turn'd to his disadvantage, for having promis'd discoveries, but not being able to make it good, it was look'd upon as a trifling with the justice of the city, and he was the more fiercely persued by the shopkeepers who took him.

I was however terribly uneasie all this while, and that I might be quite out of the way, I went away from my governesses for a while; but not knowing whither to wander, I took a maid servant with me, and took the stage coach to *Dunstable* to my old landlord and landlady, where I had liv'd so handsomly with my *Lancashire* husband: here I told her a formal[2] story, that I expected my husband every day from *Ireland*, and that I had sent a letter to him that I would meet him at *Dunstable* at her house, and that he

---

1 The posting of bonds and pledges of money as surety to appear in court in order to testify against the accused.
2 Circumstantial, elaborate.

would certainly land, if the wind was fair, in a few days, so that I was come to spend a few days with them till he should come, for he would either come post,[1] or in the *West-Chester* coach I knew not which, but which soever it was, he would be sure to come to that house to meet me.

My landlady was mighty glad to see me, and my landlord made such a stir with me, that if I had been a princess I cou'd not have been better used, and here I might have been welcome a month or two if I had thought fit.

But my business was of another nature, I was very uneasie (tho' so well disguis'd that it was scarce possible to detect me) lest this fellow should some how or other find me out; and tho' he cou'd not charge me with this robbery, having perswaded him not to venture, and having also done nothing in it my self but run away, yet he might have charg'd me with other things, and have bought his own life at the expence of mine.

This fill'd me with horrible apprehensions: I had no recourse, no friend, no confident but my old governess, and I knew no remedy but to put my life in her hands, and so I did, for I let her know where to send to me, and had several letters from her while I stayed here, some of them almost scar'd me out of my wits; but at last she sent me the joyful news that he was hang'd, which was the best news to me that I had heard a great while.

I had stay'd here five weeks, and liv'd very comfortably indeed, (the secret anxiety of my mind excepted) but when I receiv'd this letter I look'd pleasantly again, and told my landlady that I had receiv'd a letter from my spouse in *Ireland*, that I had the good news of his being very well, but had the bad news that his business would not permit him to come away so soon as he expected, and so I was like to go back again without him.

My landlady complemented me upon the good news however, that I had heard he was well, For I have observ'd, madam, *says she*, you han't been so pleasant[2] as you us'd to be; you have been over head and ears in care for him, I dare say, *says the good woman*; 'tis easie to be seen there's an alteration in you for the better, *says she*: Well, I am sorry the esquire can't come yet, *says my landlord*, I should have been heartily glad to have seen him, but I hope, when you have certain news of his coming, you'll take a step hither again, madam; *says he*, you shall be very welcome whenever you please to come.

---

1 On horseback, hiring horses from post-houses en route.
2 Merry, gay.

With all these fine complements we parted, and I came merry enough to *London*, and found my governess as well pleas'd as I was; and now she told me she would never recommend any partner to me again, for she always found, *she said*, that I had the best luck when I ventur'd by my self; and so indeed I had, for I was seldom in any danger when I was by my self, or if I was, I got out of it with more dexterity than when I was entangled with the dull measures of other people, who had perhaps less forecast, and were more rash and impatient than I; for tho' I had as much courage to venture as any of them, yet I used more caution before I undertook a thing, and had more presence of mind when I was to bring my self off.

I have often wondered even at my own hardiness another way, that when all my companions were surpriz'd, and fell so suddainly into the hand of justice, and that I so narrowly escap'd, yet I could not all that while enter into one serious resolution to leave off this trade; and especially considering that I was now very far from being poor, that the temptation of necessity, which is generally the introduction of all such wickedness was now remov'd; for I had near 500 *l.* by me in ready money, on which I might have liv'd very well, if I had thought fit to have retir'd; but *I say*, I had not so much as the least inclination to leave off; no not so much as I had before when I had but 200 *l.* before-hand, and when I had no such frightful examples before my eyes as these were; from hence 'tis evident to me, that when once we are harden'd in crime, no fear can affect us, no example give us any warning.[1]

I had indeed one comrade, whose fate went very near me[2] for a good while, tho' I wore it off too in time, that case was indeed very unhappy; I had made a prize of a piece of very good damask[3] in a *mercers* shop, and went clear off myself;[4] but had convey'd the peice to this companion of mine, when we went out of the shop; and she went one way, and I went another: we had not been long out of the shop, but the *mercer* mist his peice of stuff, and sent his messengers, one, one way, and one another, and they presently seiz'd her that had the peice, with the damask upon her; as for me, I had very luckily step'd into a house where there was a lace chamber, up one pair of stairs, and had the satisfaction, or the terror

---

1 For a somewhat similar remark by Betty Blewskin, a fellow pickpocket and shoplifter, see Appendix A.3.
2 Considerably moved me.
3 A rich patterned fabric, usually of silk or linen.
4 Left undetected.

indeed of looking out of the window upon the noise they made, and seeing the poor creature drag'd away in triumph to the justice, who immediately committed her to *Newgate*.

I was careful to attempt nothing in the lace-chamber, but tumbl'd their goods pretty much to spend time; then bought a few yards of edging, and paid for it, and came away very sad hearted indeed; for the poor woman, who was in tribulation for what I only had stolen.

Here again my old caution stood me in good stead; namely, that tho' I often robb'd with these people, yet I never let them know who I was, or where I lodg'd; nor could they ever find out my lodging, tho' they often endeavour'd to watch me to it. They all knew me by the name of *Moll Flanders*, tho' even some of them rather believ'd I was she, than knew me to be so; my name was publick among them indeed; but how to find me out they knew not, nor so much as how to guess at my quarters, whether they were at the east-end of the town, or the west; and this wariness was my safety upon all these occasions.

I kept close a great while upon the occasion of this womans disaster; I knew that if I should do any thing that should miscarry, and should be carried to prison she would be there, and ready to witness against me, and perhaps save her life at my expence; I consider'd that I began to be very well known by name at the *Old Baily*, tho' they did not know my face; and that if I should fall into their hands, I should be treated as an old offender; and for this reason, I was resolv'd to see what this poor creatures fate should be before I stirr'd abroad, tho' several times in her distress I convey'd money to her for her relief.

At length she came to her tryal, she pleaded she did not steal the things; but that one Mrs. *Flanders*, as she heard her call'd, (for she did not know her) gave the bundle to her after they came out of the shop, and bad her carry it home to her lodging. They ask'd her where this Mrs. *Flanders* was? but she could not produce her, neither could she give the least account of me; and the *mercers* men swearing positively that she was in the shop when the goods were stolen; that they immediately miss'd them, and pursu'd her, and found them upon her; thereupon the jury brought her in guilty; but the court considering that she really was not the person that stole the goods, an inferiour assistant, and that it was very possible she could not find out this Mrs. *Flanders*, *meaning me*, tho' it would save her life, which indeed was true; I say considering all this, they allow'd her to be transported, which was the utmost favour she could obtain, only that the court told her, that if she could in the mean time produce the said Mrs. *Flanders*, they would intercede for her pardon, that is to say, if she could find me out, and hang me, she should not be transported: this I took care to make impossible to her, and so she was shipp'd off in pursuance of her sentence a little while after.

I must repeat it again, that the fate of this poor woman troubl'd me exceedingly; and I began to be very pensive, knowing that I was really the instrument of her disaster; but the preservation of my own life, which was so evidently in danger, took off all my tenderness; and seeing she was not put to death, I was very easie at her transportation, because she was then out of the way of doing me any mischief whatever should happen.

The disaster of this woman was some months before that of the last recited story, and was indeed partly the occasion of my governess proposing to dress me up in mens cloths, that I might go about unobserv'd, as indeed I did; but I was soon tir'd of that disguise, *as I have said*, for indeed it expos'd me to too many difficulties.

I was now easie, as to all fear of witnesses aganst me, for all those, that had either been concern'd with me, or that knew me by the name of *Moll Flanders*, were either hang'd or transported; and if I should have had the misfortune to be taken, I might call myself any thing else, as well as *Moll Flanders*, and no old sins could be plac'd to my account; so I began to run a tick[1] again, with the more freedom, and several successful adventures I made, tho' not such as I had made before.

We had at that time another fire happen'd not a great way off from the place where my governess liv'd, and I made an attempt there, as before, but as I was not soon enough before the crowd of people came in, and could not get to the house I aim'd at; instead of a prize, I got a mischief,[2] which had almost put a period to my life, and all my wicked doings together; for the fire being very furious, and the people in a great fright in removing their goods, and throwing them out of window; a wench from out of a window threw a featherbed just upon me; it is true, the bed being soft it broke no bones; but as the weight was great, and made greater by the fall, it beat me down, and laid me dead for a while; nor did the people concern themselves much to deliver me from it, or to recover me at all; but I lay like one dead and neglected a good while; till some body going to remove the bed out of the way,

---

1 A tally or score (of debts). That is, Moll takes up her life of crime again.
2 An injury, especially one done by a person.

helped me up; it was indeed a wonder the people in the house had not thrown other goods out after it, and which might have fallen upon it, and then I had been inevitably kill'd; but I was reserved for further afflictions.

This accident however spoil'd my market for that time, and I came home to my governess very much hurt, and bruised, and frighted to the last degree, and it was a good while before she could set me upon my feet again.

It was now a merry time of the year, and *Bartholomew* Fair[1] was begun; I had never made any walks that way, nor was the common part of the fair of much advantage to me; but I took a turn this year into the cloisters,[2] and among the rest, I fell into one of the raffling shops:[3] it was a thing of no great consequence to me, nor did I expect to make much of it; but there came a gentleman extreamly well dress'd, and very rich, and as 'tis frequent to talk to every body in those shops he singl'd me out, and was very particular with me; first told he me he would put in for me to raffle, and did so; and some small matter coming to his lot, he presented it to me,[4] I think it was a feather muff: then he continu'd to keep talking to me with a more than common appearance of respect; but still very civil and much like a gentleman.

He held me in talk so long till at last he drew me out of the raffling place to the shop-door, and then to take a walk in the cloister, still talking of a thousand things cursorily without any thing to the purpose; at last he told me that without complement he was charm'd with my company, and ask'd me if I durst trust myself in a coach with him; he told me he was a man of honour, and would not offer any thing to me unbecoming him as such: I seem'd to decline it a while, but suffer'd myself to be importun'd a little, and then yielded.

I was at a loss in my thoughts to conclude at first what this gentleman design'd; but I found afterward he had had some drink

---

1 Held annually in West Smithfield in late August, and dating back to the twelfth century, Bartholomew Fair had once been an important trade fair. But by Defoe's time it had become infamous for its rowdiness and unsavoury forms of entertainment.
2 A bustling arcade adjacent to Bartholomew Fair, notorious for its gambling and prostitution, which attracted people from all levels of society.
3 Shops (and booths) offering games of chance, especially one involving the casting of three dice.
4 If a gentleman won, it was the custom for him to present the prize to the lady next to him, whether he knew her or not.

in his head; and that he was not very unwilling to have some more: he carried me in the coach to the *Spring-Garden*, at *Knight's-Bridge*,[1] where we walk'd in the gardens, and he treated me very handsomely; but I found he drank very freely, he press'd me also to drink, but I declin'd it.

Hitherto he kept his word with me, and offer'd me nothing amiss; we came away in the coach again, and he brought me into the streets and by this time it was near ten a-clock at night, and he stop'd the coach at a house, where it seems he was acquainted, and where they made no scruple to show us up stairs into a room with a bed in it; at first I seem'd to be unwilling to go up, but after a few words, I yielded to that too, being indeed willing to see the end of it, and in hopes to make something of it at last; as for the bed, &c. I was not much concern'd about that part.

Here he began to be a little freer with me than he had promis'd; and I by little and little yielded to every thing, so that in a word, he did what he pleas'd with me; I need say no more; all this while he drank freely too, and about one in the morning we went into the coach again; the air, and the shaking of the coach made the drink he had get more up in his head than it was before, and he grew uneasy in the coach, and was for acting over again, what he had been doing before; but as I thought my game now secure, I resisted him, and brought him to be a little still, which had not lasted five minutes, but he fell fast asleep.

I took this opportunity to search him to a nicety; I took a gold watch, with a silk purse of gold, his fine full bottom perrewig, and silver fring'd gloves, his sword, and fine snuff-box, and gently opening the coach-door, stood ready to jump out while the coach was going on; but the coach stopping in the narrow street beyond *Temple-Bar*[2] to let another coach pass, I got softly out, fasten'd the door again, and gave my gentleman and the coach the slip both together, and never heard more of them.[3]

This was an adventure indeed unlook'd for, and perfectly undesign'd by me; tho' I was not so past the merry part of life, as to

1 Of the five "Spring Gardens" at this time, the one in Knightsbridge (on the western outskirts of London) was among the most disreputable.

2 This street is at the junction of the Strand and Fleet Street, where a gate (designed by Sir Christopher Wren) marked the boundary between the City of London and the City of Westminster.

3 This phrase is omitted in the second edition. Perhaps it is meant to give emphasis to the fact that Moll got clean away; more likely, as she does hear a good deal more of the gentleman, Defoe had probably not yet planned the complete episode.

forget how to behave, when a fop so blinded by his appetite should not know an old woman from a young: I did not indeed look so old as I was by ten or twelve year; yet I was not a young wench of seventeen, and it was easie enough to be distinguish'd: there is nothing so absurd, so surfeiting,[1] so ridiculous as a man heated by wine in his head, and a wicked gust in his inclination together; he is in the possession of two devils at once, and can no more govern himself by his reason than a mill can grind without water; his vice tramples upon all that was in him that had any good in it, if any such thing there was; nay, his very sense is blinded by its own rage, and he acts absurdities even in his view; such is drinking more, when he is drunk already; picking up a common woman, without regard to what she is, or who she is; whether sound or rotten, clean or unclean; whether ugly or handsome, whether old or young, and so blinded, as not really to distinguish; such a man is worse than lunatick; prompted by his vicious corrupted head he no more knows what he is doing, than this wretch of mine knew when I pick'd his pocket of his watch and his purse of gold.

These are the men of whom *Solomon* says, *They go like an ox to the slaughter, till a dart strikes through their liver;*[2] an admirable description, *by the way*, of the foul disease,[3] which is a poisonous deadly contagion mingling with the blood, whose center or fountain is in the liver; from whence, by the swift circulation of the whole mass, that dreadful nauceous plague strikes immediately thro' his liver, and his spirits are infected, his vitals stab'd thro' as with a dart.

It is true this poor unguarded wretch was in no danger from me, tho' I was greatly apprehensive at first, of what danger I might be in from him; but he was really to be pitied in one respect, that he seem'd to be a good sort of a man in himself; a gentleman that had no harm in his design; a man of sense, and of a fine behaviour; a comely handsome person, a sober solid countenance, a charming beautiful face, and everything that cou'd be agreeable; only had unhappily had some drink the night before, had not been in bed, as he told me when we were together, was hot, and his blood fir'd with wine, and in that condition his reason *as it were* asleep, had given him up.

As for me, my business was his money, and what I could make

---

1 Disgusting, nauseating.
2 Proverbs 7:22-23. The liver was supposedly the seat of love and violent passion.
3 Syphilis.

of him, and after that if I could have found out any way to have done it, I would have sent him safe home to his house, and to his family, for 'twas ten to one but he had an honest virtuous wife, and innocent children, that were anxious for his safety, and would have been glad to have gotten him home, and have taken care of him, till he was restor'd to himself; and then with what shame and regret would he look back upon himself? How would he reproach himself with associating himself with a whore? pick'd up in the worst of all holes, the cloister, among the dirt and filth of all the town? How would he be trembling for fear he had got the pox, for fear a dart had struck through his liver, and hate himself every time he look'd back upon the madness and brutality of his debauch? How would he, if he had any principles of honour, as I verily believe he had, I say how would he abhor the thought of giving any ill distemper, if he had it, as for ought he knew he might, to his modest and virtuous wife, and thereby sowing the contagion in the life-blood of his posterity?

Would such gentlemen but consider the contemptible thoughts which the very women they are concern'd with, in such cases as these, have of them, it wou'd be a surfeit to them: as I said above, they value not the pleasure, they are rais'd by no inclination to the man, the passive jade thinks of no pleasure but the money; and when he is as it were drunk in the extasies of his wicked pleasure, her hands are in his pockets searching for what she can find there; and of which he can no more be sensible in the moment of his folly, than he can fore-think of it when he goes about it.

I knew a woman that was so dexterous with a fellow, who indeed deserv'd no better usage, that while he was busie with her another way, convey'd his purse with twenty guineas in it out of his fob pocket, where he had put it for fear of her, and put another purse with guilded counters[1] in it into the room of it: after he had done, he says to her, Now han't you pick'd my pocket? She jested with him, and told him she suppos'd he had not much to lose; he put his hand to his fob, and with his fingers felt that his purse was there, which fully satisfy'd him, and so she brought off his money; and this was a trade with her, she kept a sham gold watch, that is a watch of silver guilt, and a purse of counters in her pocket to be ready on all such occasions; and I doubt not practis'd it with success.

I came home with this last booty to my governess, and really

---

1 Imitation coins.

when I told her the story it so affected her, that she was hardly able to forbear tears, to think how such a gentleman run a daily risque of being undone, every time a glass of wine got into his head.

But as to the purchase I got, and how entirely I stript him, she told me it pleas'd her wonderfully; Nay, child, *says she*, the usage may, for ought I know, do more to reform him, than all the sermons that ever he will hear in his life, and if the remainder of the story be true, so it did.

I found the next day she was wonderful inquisitive about this gentleman; the description I had given her of him, his dress, his person, his face, every thing concur'd to make her think of a gentleman whose character she knew, and family too; she mus'd a while, and I going still on with the particulars, she starts up, *says she*, I'll lay a hundred pound I know the gentleman.

I am sorry you do, *says I*, for I would not have him expos'd on any account in the world; he has had injury enough already by me, and I would not be instrumental to do him any more: No, no *says she*, I will do him no injury, I assure you, but you may let me satisfie my curiosity a little, for if it is he, I warrant you I find it out: I was a little startled at that, and told her with an apparent concern in my face, that by the same rule he might find me out, and then I was undone: *she return'd warmly*, Why, do you think I will betray you, child? No, no, *says she*, not for all he is worth in the world; I have kept your counsel in worse things than these, sure you may trust me in this: so I said no more at that time.

She laid her scheme another way, and without acquainting me of it, but she was resolv'd to find it out, if possible; so she goes to a certain friend of hers who was acquainted in the family, that she guess'd at, and told her friend she had some extraordinary business with such a gentleman (who by the way was no less than a baronet, and of a very good family) and that she knew not how to come at him without somebody to introduce her: her friend promis'd her very readily to do it, and accordingly goes to the house to see if the gentleman was in town.

The next day she comes to my governess and tells her, that Sir ——— was at home, but that he had met with a disaster and was very ill, and there was no speaking with him; What disaster, *says my governess hastily*, as if she was surpriz'd at it? Why, *says her friend*, he had been at *Hampstead*[1] to visit a gentleman of his acquaintance, and as he came back again he was set upon and rob-

---

1 A village north of London, fashionable during this period for its spa.

b'd; and having got a little drink too, as they suppose, the rogues abus'd him, and he is very ill: Robb'd, *says my governess*, and what did they take from him; Why, *says her friend*, they took his gold watch, and his gold snuff-box, his fine perriwig, and what money he had in his pocket, which was considerable to be sure, for Sir ———— never goes without a purse of guineas about him.

Pshaw! says my old governess jeering, I warrant you he has got drunk now and got a whore, and she has pick'd his pocket, and so he comes home to his wife and tells her he has been robb'd; that's an old sham, a thousand such tricks are put upon the poor women every day.

Fye, *says her friend*, I find you don't know Sir ————, why he is as civil a gentleman, there is not a finer man, nor a soberer grave modester person in the whole city; he abhors such things, there's no body that knows him will think such a thing of him: Well, well, *says my governess*, that's none of my business, if it was, I warrant I should find there was something of that kind in it; your modest men in common opinion are sometimes no better than other people, only they keep a better character, or if you please, are the better hypocrites.

No, no, *says her friend*, I can assure you Sir ———— is no hypocrite, he is really an honest sober gentleman, and he has certainly been robb'd: Nay, *says my governess*, it may be he has, it is no business of mine I tell you; I only want to speak with him, my business is of another nature; But, *says her friend*, let your business be of what nature it will, you cannot see him yet, for he is not fit to be seen, for he is very ill, and bruis'd very much: Ay, *says my governess*, nay then he has fallen into bad hands to be sure; and then she ask'd gravely, Pray where is he bruised? Why in his head, *says her friend*, and one of his hands, and his face, for they us'd him barbarously. Poor gentleman, *says my governess*, I must wait then till he recovers, and adds, I hope it will not be long, for I want very much to speak with him.

Away she comes to me and tells me this story, I have found out your fine gentleman, and a fine gentleman he was, *says she*, but mercy on him, he is in a sad pickle now, I wonder what the D————l you have done to him; why you have almost kill'd him: I look'd at her with disorder enough; I kill'd him! *says I*, you must mistake the person, I am sure I did nothing to him, he was very well when I left him, *said I*, only drunk and fast asleep; I know nothing of that, *says she*, but he is in a sad pickle now, and so she told me all that her friend had said to her: Well then, *says I*, he fell into bad hands after I left him, for I am sure I left him safe enough.

About ten days after, or a little more, my governess goes again to her friend, to introduce her to this gentleman; she had enquir'd other ways in the mean time, and found that he was about again, if not abroad again, so she got leave to speak with him.

She was a woman of an admirable address, and wanted no body to introduce her; she told her tale much better than I shall be able to tell it for her, for she was a mistress of her tongue, as I have said already: she told him that she came, tho' a stranger, with a single design of doing him a service, and he should find she had no other end in it; that as she came purely on so friendly an account, she beg'd a promise from him, that if he did not accept what she should officiously[1] propose, he would not take ill, that she meddl'd with what was not her business; she assur'd him that as what she had to say was a secret that belong'd to him only, so whether he accepted her offer or not, it should remain a secret to all the world, unless he expos'd it himself; nor should his refusing her service in it, make her so little show her respect, as to do him the least injury, so that he should be entirely at liberty to act as he thought fit.

He look'd very shy at first, and said he knew nothing that related to him that requir'd much secresie; that he had never done any man any wrong, and car'd not what any body might say of him; that it was no part of his character to be unjust to any body, nor could he imagine in what any man cou'd render him any service; but that if it was so disinterested a service as she said, he could not take it ill from any one that they should endeavour to serve him; and so, as it were, left her at liberty either to tell him, or not to tell him, as she thought fit.

She found him so perfectly indifferent, that she was almost afraid to enter into the point with him; but however, after some other circumlocutions, she told him, that by a strange and unaccountable accident she came to have a particular knowledge of the late unhappy adventure he had fallen into; and that in such a manner, that there was no body in the world but herself and him that were acquainted with it, no not the very person that was with him.

He look'd a little angrily at first, What adventure? *said he*; Why, sir, *said she*, of your being robb'd coming from *Knightsbr———*, *Hampstead*, sir, I should say, *says she*; be not surpris'd, sir, *says she*, that I am able to tell you every step you took that day from the *cloyster* in *Smithfield*, to the *Spring-Garden* at *Knightsbridge*, and

1 Kindly, obligingly.

thence to the ———— in the *Strand*, and how you were left asleep in the coach afterwards; I say let not this surprize you, for sir I do not come to make a booty of you, I ask nothing of you, and I assure you the woman that was with you knows nothing who you are, and never shall; and yet perhaps I may serve you farther still, for I did not come barely to let you know, that I was inform'd of these things, as if I wanted a bribe to conceal them; assure your self, sir, *said she*, that whatever you think fit to do or say to me, it shall be all a secret as it is, as much as if I were in my grave.

He was astonish'd at her discourse, and said gravely to her, Madam, you are a stranger to me, but it is very unfortunate, that you should be let into the secret of the worst action of my life, and a thing that I am so justly asham'd of, that the only satisfaction of it to me was, that I thought it was known only to God and my own conscience: Pray, sir, *says she*, do not reckon the discovery of it to me, to be any part of your misfortune; it was a thing, I believe, you were surprised into, and perhaps the woman us'd some art to prompt you to it; however, you will never find any just cause, *said she*, to repent that I came to hear of it; nor can your own mouth be more silent in it than I have been, and ever shall be.

Well, *says he*, but let me do some justice to the woman too, whoever she is, I do assure you she prompted me to nothing, she rather declin'd me, it was my own folly and madness that brought me into it all, ay and brought her into it too; I must give her her due so far: as to what she took from me, I cou'd expect no less from her in the condition I was in, and to this hour I know not whether she robb'd me or the coachman; if she did it I forgive her, and I think all gentlemen that do so, should be us'd in the same manner; but I am more concern'd for some other things than I am for all that she took from me.

My governess now began to come into the whole matter, and he open'd himself freely to her; First, she said to him, in answer to what he had said about me, I am glad sir you are so just to the person that you were with; I assure you she is a gentlewoman, and no woman of the town; and however you prevail'd with her so far as you did, I am sure 'tis not her practise; you run a great venture[1] indeed, sir, but if that be any part of your care, I am perswaded you may be perfectly easie, for I dare assure you no man has touch'd her, before you, since her husband, and he has been dead now almost eight year.

---

1 Risk (of venereal disease).

It appear'd that this was his grievance,[1] and that he was in a very great fright about it; however, when my governess said this to him he appeared very well pleased; and said, Well, madam, to be plain with you, if I was satisfy'd of that, I should not so much value what I lost; for as to that, the temptation was great, and perhaps she was poor and wanted it: If she had not been poor Sir ———, *says my governess*, I assure you she would never have yielded to you; and as her poverty first prevailed with her to let you do as you did, so the same poverty prevail'd with her to pay her self at last, when she saw you was in such a condition, that if she had not done it, perhaps the next coach-man or chair-man[2] might have done it.

Well, *says he*, much good may it do her; I say again, all the gentlemen that do so, ought to be us'd in the same manner, and then they would be cautious of themselves; I have no more concern about it, but on the score which you hinted at before, madam: here he entered into some freedoms with her on the subject of what pass'd between us, which are not so proper for a woman to write, and the great terror that was upon his mind with relation to his wife, for fear he should have receiv'd any injury from me, and should communicate it farther; and ask'd her at last if she cou'd not procure him an opportunity to speak with me; my governess gave him farther assurances of my being a woman clear from any such thing, and that he was as entirely safe in that respect, as he was with his own lady; but as for seeing me, she said it might be of dangerous consequence; but however, that she would talk with me, and let him know my answer; using at the same time some arguments to perswade him not to desire it, and that it cou'd be of no service to him; seeing she hop'd he had no desire to renew a correspondence with me, and that on my account it was a kind of putting my life in his hands.

He told her, he had a great desire to see me, that he would give her any assurances that were in his power, not to take any advantages of me, and that in the first place he would give me a general release from all demands of any kind; she insisted how it might tend to a farther divulging the secret, and might in the end be injurious to him, entreating him not to press for it, so at length he desisted.

---

1 Distress, worry.
2 A bearer of a sedan chair (a closed vehicle seating one person which was carried between poles by two men). Convenient for short distances in crowded streets, "chairs" first became popular in Queen Anne's reign.

They had some discourse upon the subject of the things he had lost, and he seem'd to be very desirous of his gold watch, and told her if she cou'd procure that for him, he would willingly give as much for it as it was worth, she told him she would endeavour to procure it for him and leave the valuing it to himself.

Accordingly the next day she carried the watch, and he gave her 30 guineas for it, which was more than I should have been able to make of it, tho' it seems it cost much more; he spoke something of his perriwig, which it seems cost him threescore guineas, and his snuff-box, and in a few days more, she carried them too; which oblig'd him very much, and he gave her thirty more, the next day I sent him his fine sword, and cane *gratis*, and demanded nothing of him, but I had no mind to see him, unless it had been so, that he might be satisfy'd I knew who he was, which he was not willing to.

Then he entered into a long tale with her of the manner how she came to know all this matter; she form'd a long talk of that part; how she had it from one, that I had told the whole story to, and that was to help me dispose of the goods, and this confident brought the things to her, she being by profession a *pawn-broker*; and she hearing of his worship's dissaster, guess'd at the thing in general; that having gotten the things into her hands, she had resolv'd to come and try as she had done: she then gave him repeated assurances that it should never go out of her mouth, and tho' she knew the woman very well, yet she had not let her know, *meaning me*, any thing of it; *that is to say*, who the person was, which by the way was false; but however it was not to his damage, for I never open'd my mouth of it to any body.

I had a great many thoughts in my head about my seeing him again, and was often sorry that I had refus'd it; I was perswaded that if I had seen him, and let him know that I knew him, I should have made some advantage of him, and perhaps have had some maintenance from him; and tho' it was a life wicked enough, yet it was not so full of danger as this I was engag'd in. However those thoughts wore off, and I declin'd seeing him again, for that time; but my governess saw him often, and he was very kind to her, giving her something almost every time he saw her; one time in particular she found him very merry, and as she thought he had some wine in his head, and he press'd her again very earnestly to let him see that woman, that *as he said*, had bewitch'd him so that night; my governess, who was from the beginning for my seeing him, told him, he was so desirous of it, that she could almost yield to it, if she cou'd prevail upon me; adding that if he would please to come to her house in the evening she would endeavour it, upon his repeated assurances of forgetting what was pass'd.

Accordingly she came to me and told me all the discourse; *in short*, she soon byass'd me to consent, in a case which I had some regret in my mind for declining before: so I prepar'd to see him: I dress'd me to all the advantage possible I assure you, and for the first time us'd a little art; I say for the first time, for I had never yielded to the baseness of paint before, having always had vanity enough to believe I had no need of it.

At the hour appointed he came; and as she observ'd before, so it was plain still, that he had been drinking, tho' very far from what we call being in drink: he appear'd exceeding pleas'd to see me, and enter'd into a long discourse with me, upon the old affair, I beg'd his pardon very often, for my share of it; protested I had not any such design when first I met him; that I had not gone out with him, but that I took him for a very civil gentleman; and that he made me so many promises of offering no uncivility to me.

He alledg'd[1] the wine he drank, and that he scarce knew what he did, and that if it had not been so, I should never have let him take the freedom with me that he had done: he protested to me that he never touch'd any woman but me since he was married to his wife, and it was a surprise upon him; complimented me upon being so particularly agreeable to him, and the like, and talk'd so much of that kind, till I found he had talk'd himself almost into a temper to do the same thing over again: but I took him up short, I protested I had never suffer'd any man to touch me since my husband died, which was near eight year; he said he believed it to be so truly; and added that madam, had intimated as much to him, and that it was his opinion of that part which made him desire to see me again; and that since he had once broke in upon his vertue with me, and found no ill consequences, he cou'd be safe in venturing there again; and so in short it went on to what I expected, and to what will not bear relating.

My old governess had foreseen it, as well as I, and therefore led him into a room which had not a bed in it, and yet had a chamber within it, which had a bed, whither we withdrew for the rest of the night, and in short, after some time being together, he went to bed, and lay there all night, I withdrew, but came again undress'd in the morning before it was day, and lay with him the rest of the time.

---

1 Gave as an excuse, blamed.

Thus you see having committed a crime once, is a sad handle to the committing of it again; whereas all the regret, and reflections wear off when the temptation renews it self; had I not yielded to see him again, the corrupt desire in him had worn off, and 'tis very probable he had never fallen into it, with any body else, as I really believe he had not done before.

When he went away, I told him I hop'd he was satisfy'd he had not been robb'd again; he told me he was satisfy'd in that point, and cou'd trust me again; and putting his hand in his pocket gave me five guineas, which was the first money I had gain'd that way for many years.

I had several visits of the like kind from him, but he never came into a settled way of maintenance, which was what I would have been best pleas'd with: once indeed he ask'd me how I did to live, I answer'd him pretty quick, that I assur'd him I had never taken that course that I took with him; but that indeed I work'd at my needle, and could just maintain myself, that sometimes it was as much as I was able to do, and I shifted[1] hard enough.

He seem'd to reflect upon himself, that he should be the first person to lead me into that, which he assur'd me he never intended to do himself; and it touch'd him a little, *he said*, that he should be the cause of his own sin, and mine too: he would often make just reflections also upon the crime itself, and upon the particular circumstances of it, with respect to himself; how wine introduc'd the inclinations, how the Devil led him to the place, and found out an object to tempt him, and he made the moral always himself.

When these thoughts were upon him he would go away, and perhaps not come again in a months time or longer; but then as the serious part wore off, the lewd part would wear in, and then he came prepar'd for the wick'd part; thus we liv'd for some time; tho' he did not KEEP,[2] as they call it, yet he never fail'd doing things that were handsome, and sufficient to maintain me without working, and which was better, without following my old trade.

But this affair had its end too; for after about a year, I found that he did not come so often as usual, and at last he left it off altogether without any dislike,[3] or bidding adieu; and so there was an end of that short scene of life, which added no great store to me, only to make more work for repentance.

---

1 Got on.
2 That is, keep Moll as his mistress.
3 Disagreement, antipathy.

However during this interval, I confin'd my self pretty much at home; at least being thus provided for, I made no adventures, no not for a quarter of a year after he left me; but then finding the fund[1] fail, and being loth to spend upon the main stock, I began to think of my old trade, and to look abroad into the street again; and my first step was lucky enough.

I had dress'd myself up in a very mean habit, for as I had several shapes[2] to appear in I was now in an ordinary stuff-gown, a blue apron and a straw-hat;[3] and I plac'd myself at the door of the Three Cups Inn in St. *John Street*: there were several carriers[4] us'd the inn, and the stage coaches for *Barnet*, for *Toteridge*, and other towns that way,[5] stood always in the street, in the evening, when they prepar'd to set out; so that I was ready for any thing that offer'd for either one or other: the meaning was this, people come frequently with bundles and small parcels to those inns, and call for such carriers, or coaches as they want, to carry them into the country; and there generally attends women, porters wives, or daughters, ready to take in[6] such things for their respective people that employ them.

It happen'd very oddly that I was standing at the inn-gate, and a woman that had stood there before, and which was the porter's wife belonging to the *Barnet* stage coach, having observ'd me, ask'd if I waited for any of the coaches; I told her yes, I waited for my mistress, that was coming to go to *Barnet*; she ask'd me who was my mistress, and I told her any madam's name that came next me;[7] but as it seem'd I happen'd upon a name, a family of which name liv'd at *Hadly* just beyond *Barnet*.

I said no more to her, or she to me a good while, but by and by, some body calling her at a door a little way off, she desir'd me that if any body call'd for the *Barnet* coach, I would step and call her at the house, which it seems was an ale-house; I said yes very readily, and away she went.

She was no sooner gone; but comes a wench and a child, puffing and sweating, and asks for the *Barnet* coach, I answer'd presently *Here*, Do you belong to the *Barnet* coach, *says she?* Yes

1 Income, revenue.
2 Disguises.
3 That is, in typical servant's dress.
4 Coaches and wagons.
5 Coaching towns on the Great North Road (to Scotland).
6 Look after.
7 That is, the first name that came to mind.

sweetheart, *said I,* what do ye want? I want room, for two passengers *says she,* Where are they sweetheart, *said I?* Here's this girl, pray let her go into the coach, *says she,* and I'll go and fetch my mistress, Make hast then sweetheart, *says I,* for we may be full else; the maid had a great bundle under arm; so she put the child into the coach, *and I said,* You had best put your bundle into the coach too; No, *says she,* I am afraid some body should slip it away from the child, Give it me then, *said I,* and I'll take care of it; Do then, *says she,* and be sure you take care of it, I'll answer for it, *said I,* if it were for twenty pound value. There take it then, *says she,* and away she goes.

As soon as I had got the bundle, and the maid was out of sight, I goes on towards the ale-house, where the porter's wife was, so that if I had met her, I had then only been going to give her the bundle, and to call her to her business, as if I was going away, and cou'd stay no longer; but as I did not meet her I walk'd away, and turning into *Charter-House-Lane,* made off thro' *Charter-House-Yard,* into *Long-Lane,* then cross'd into *Bartholomew-Close,* so into *Little-Britain,* and thro' the *Blue-Coat-Hospital* into *Newgate-Street.*[1]

To prevent my being known, I pull'd off my blue apron, and wrapt the bundle in it, which before was made up in a piece of painted callico, and very remarkble;[2] I also wrapt up my straw-hat in it, and so put the bundle upon my head; and it was very well, that I did thus, for coming thro' the *Blue-Coat-Hospital,* who should I meet but the wench, that had given me the bundle to hold; it seems she was going with her mistress, who she had been gone to fetch to the *Barnet* coaches.

I saw she was in hast, and I had no business to stop her: so away she went, and I brought my bundle safe home to my governess; there was no money, nor plate, or jewels in the bundle; but a very good suit of *Indian* damask, a gown and petticoat, a lac'd head and ruffles of very good Flanders-lace, and some linnen, and other things, such as I knew very well the value of.

This was not indeed my own invention, but was given me by one that had practis'd it with success, and my governess lik'd it extreamly; and indeed I try'd it again several times, tho' never twice near the same place; for the next time I try'd it in *White-*

---

1 The area was a maze of alleys, lanes and courts, apparently quite familiar to Moll. The Blue Coat Hospital on Newgate Street was another name for Christ's Hospital, a famous charitable school for the young.
2 Noticeable, conspicuous.

Chappel just by the corner of *Petty-Coat-Lane,* where the coaches stand that go out to *Stratford* and *Bow* and that side of the country,[1] and another time at the *Flying-Horse,* without *Bishops-Gate,* where the *Chester*[2] coaches then lay,[3] and I had always the good luck to come off with some booty.

Another time I plac'd myself at a warehouse by the waterside, where the coasting vessels from the *north* come, such as from *New-Castle* upon *Tyne, Sunderland,* and other places; here the warehouse, being shut, comes a young fellow with a letter; and he wanted a box, and a hamper[4] that was come from *New-Castle* upon *Tyne,* I ask'd him if he had the marks[5] of it, so he shows me the letter, by vertue of which he was to ask for it, and which gave an account of the contents, the box being full of linnen, and the hamper full of glass-ware; I read the letter, and took care to see the name, and the marks, the name of the person that sent the goods, the name of the person that they were sent to, then I bad the messenger come in the morning, for that the warehouse keeper, would not be there any more that night.

Away went I, and getting materials in a publick house, I wrote a letter from Mr. *John Richardson* of *New-Castle* to his dear cousin *Jemey Cole,* in *London,* with an account that he had sent by such a vessel, (for I remember'd all the particulars to a tittle,) so many pieces of huckaback linnen,[6] so many ells[7] of *Dutch* Holland and the like, in a box, and a hamper of flint glasses from Mr. *Henzill's* glass-house[8] and that the box was mark'd I C. No I.[9] and the hamper was directed by a label on the cording.

About an hour after I came to the warehouse, found the ware-

---

1 Stagecoaches departed from the junction of Whitechapel Street and Petticoat Lane for such places east of London as Stratford and Bow, on the River Lea.

2 "Cheston" in both the first and second editions, which is almost certainly a mistake for "Chester."

3 The Flying Horse Inn, just outside (or "without") Bishops Gate, was one of the coaching inns mainly for northward travel.

4 A large covered basket, usually made of wicker, used as a packing case.

5 The identifying device on an object indicating ownership, here being "IC. No. I" (below).

6 A coarse linen used for towelling, etc.

7 The English ell, formerly used in measuring cloth, was equal to 45 inches.

8 Defoe knew Newcastle upon Tyne and was familiar with the glass-house there owned by the Henzells. Flint glass was a pure, lustrous glass made orginally from ground flint.

9 Probably meaning "Box No. I, sent to Jeremy Cole."

house-keeper, and had the goods deliver'd me without any scruple; the value of the linnen being about 22 pound.

I could fill up this whole discourse with the variety of such adventures which daily invention directed to, and which I manag'd with the utmost dexterity, and always with success.

At length, as when does the pitcher come safe home that goes so very often to the well,[1] I fell into some small broils,[2] which tho' they cou'd not affect me fatally, yet made me known, which was the worst thing next to being found guilty, that cou'd befall me.

I had taken up the disguise of a widow's dress; it was without any real design in view, but only waiting for any thing that might offer, as I often did: it happen'd that while I was going along the street in *Covent Garden*, there was a great cry of Stop thief, stop thief; some artists had it seems put a trick upon a shop-keeper, and being pursued, some of them fled one way, and some another; and one of them was, they said, dress'd up in widow's weeds, upon which the mob gathered about me, and some said I was the person, others said no, immediately came the mercer's journeyman, and he swore aloud I was the person, and so seiz'd on me; however, when I was brought back by the mob to the mercer's shop, the master of the house said freely that I was not the woman that was in his shop, and would have let me go immediately; but another fellow said gravely, Pray stay till Mr. ————, *meaning the journeyman*, comes back for he knows her; so they kept me by force near half an hour; they had call'd a constable, and he stood in the shop as my jayler; and in talking with the constable I enquir'd where he liv'd, and what trade he was; the man not apprehending in the least what happened afterwards, readily told me his name, and trade, and where he liv'd; and told me as a jest, that I might be sure to hear of his name when I came to the *Old Bayley*.

Some of the servants likewise us'd me saucily, and had much ado to keep their hands off of me, the master indeed was civiler to me than they; but he would not yet let me go tho' he owned he could not say I was in his shop before.

I began to be a little surly with him, and told him I hop'd he would not take it ill, if I made my self amends upon him in a more legal way another time; and desir'd I might send for friends to see me have right done me: No, *he said*, he could give no such liberty, I might ask it when I came before the justice of peace, and seeing

1 A common proverb of the period, perhaps with its origins in Ecclesiastes 12:6.
2 Quarrels, noisy arguments.

I threaten'd him, he would take care of me in the mean time, and would lodge me safe in *Newgate*: I told him it was his time now, but it would be mine by and by, and govern'd my passion as well as I was able; however, I spoke to the constable to call me a porter, which he did, and then I call'd for pen, ink, and paper, but they would let me have none; I ask'd the porter his name, and where he liv'd, and the poor man told it me very willingly; I bad him observe and remember how I was treated there; that he saw I was detain'd there by force; I told him I should want his evidence in another place, and it should not be the worse for him to speak; the porter said he would serve me with all his heart; But, madam, *says he*, let me hear them refuse to let you go, then I may be able to speak the plainer.

With that I spoke aloud to the master of the shop, and said, Sir, you know in your own conscience that I am not the person you look for, and that I was not in your shop before, therefore I demand that you detain me here no longer, or tell me the reason of your stopping me; the fellow grew surlier upon this than before, and said he would do neither till he thought fit; Very well, said I to the constable and to the porter, you will be pleas'd to remember this, gentlemen, another time; the porter said, *Yes, madam,* and the constable began not to like it, and would have perswaded the mercer to dismiss him, and let me go, since, as he said, he own'd I was not the person; Good sir, *says the mercer to him tauntingly,* are you a justice of peace, or a constable? I charg'd you with her, pray do you do your duty: the constable told him a little mov'd, but very handsomely, *I know my duty, and what I am, sir, I doubt you hardly know what you are doing;* they had some other hard words, and in the mean time the journey-men,[1] impudent and unmanly to the last degree, used me barbarously, and one of them, the same that first seized upon me, pretended he would search me, and began to lay hands on me: I spit in his face, call'd out to the constable, and bad him take notice of my usage; And pray, Mr. Constable, *said I,* ask that villain's name, pointing to the man; the constable reprov'd him decently, told him that he did not know what he did, for he knew that his master acknowledg'd I was not the person that was in his shop; And, says the constable, I am afraid your master is bringing himself and me too into trouble, if this gentlewoman comes to prove who she is, and where she was, and it appears that

---

1 It was not uncommon for shopkeepers to employ more journeymen and apprentices than their businesses warranted as a safeguard against theft.

she is not the woman you pretend to; *Dam her, says the fellow again*, with an impudent harden'd face, she is the lady you may depend upon it, I'll swear she is the same body that was in the shop, and that I gave the pieces of satin that is lost into her own hand, you shall hear more of it when Mr. *William* and *Anthony, those were other journeymen*, come back, they will know her again as well as I.

Just as the insolent rogue was talking thus to the constable, comes back Mr. *William* and Mr. *Anthony*, as he call'd them, and a great rabble with them, bringing along with them the true widow that I was pretended to be; and they came sweating and blowing into the shop, and with a great deal of triumph dragging the poor creature in a most butcherly manner up towards their master, who was in the back shop, and cryed out aloud, Here's the widow, sir, we have catch'd her at last; What do ye mean by that, *says the master*, why we have her already, there she sits, *says he*, and Mr. —— *says he*, can swear this is she: the other man who they call'd Mr. *Anthony* replyed, Mr. —— may say what he will, and swear what he will, but this is the woman, and there's the remnant of sattin she stole, I took it out of her cloaths with my own hand.

I sat still now, and began to take a better heart but smil'd and said nothing; the master look'd pale; the constable turn'd about and look'd at me; *Let 'em alone Mr. Constable*, said I, *let 'em go on*; the case was plain and could not be denied, so the constable was charg'd with the right thief, and the mercer told me very civily he was sorry for the mistake, and hoped I would not take it ill; that they had so many things of this nature put upon them every day, that they cou'd not be blam'd for being very sharp in doing themselves justice; Not take it ill, sir! *said I*, How can I take it well? If you had dismiss'd me when your insolent fellow seiz'd on me in the street, and brought me to you; and when you your self acknowledg'd I was not the person, I would have put it by, and not taken it ill, because of the many ill things I believe you have put upon you daily; but your treatment of me since has been unsufferable, and especially that of your servant, I must and will have reparation for that.

Then he began to parly with me, said he would make me any reasonable satisfaction, and would fain have had me told him what it was I expected; I told him I should not be my own judge, the law should decide it for me, and as I was to be carried before a magistrate, I should let him hear there what I had to say; he told me there was no occasion to go before the justice now, I was at liberty to go where I pleased, and so calling to the constable told him, he might let me go, for I was discharg'd; the constable said

calmly to him, Sir, you ask'd me just now, if I knew whether I was
a constable or a justice, and bad me do my duty, and charg'd me
with this gentlewoman as a prisoner; now, sir, I find you do not
understand what is my duty, for you would make me a justice
indeed; but I must tell you it is not in my power: I may keep a prisoner when I am charg'd with him, but 'tis the law and the magistrate alone that can discharge that prisoner; therefore 'tis a mistake, sir, I must carry her before a justice now, whether you think
well of it or not: the mercer was very high with the constable at
first; but the constable happening to be not a hir'd officer,[1] but a
good substantial kind of man, I think he was a corn-chandler, and
a man of good sense, stood to his business, would not discharge
me without going to a justice of the peace; and I insisted upon it
too: when the mercer see that, Well, *says he to the constable*, you may
carry her where you please, I have nothing to say to her; But sir,
says the constable, you will go with us, I hope, for 'tis you that
charg'd me with her; No not I, *says the mercer*, I tell you I have
nothing to say to her: But pray sir do, *says the constable*, I desire it
of you for your own sake, for the justice can do nothing without
you: Prithee fellow, *says the mercer*, go about your business, I tell
you I have nothing to say to the gentlewoman, I charge you in the
king's name to dismiss her: Sir, *says the constable*, I find you don't
know what it is to be a constable, I beg of you don't oblige me to
be rude to you; I think I need not, you are rude enough already,
says the mercer: No, sir, *says the constable*, I am not rude, you have
broken the peace in bringing an honest woman out of the street,
when she was about her lawful occasion, confining her in your
shop, and ill using her here by your servants; and now can you say
I am rude to you? I think I am civil to you in not commanding or
charging you in the king's name to go with me, and charging every
man I see, that passes your door, to aid and assist me in carrying
you by force, this you cannot but know I have power to do, and yet
I forbear it, and once more entreat you to go with me: well, he
would not for all this, and gave the constable ill language: however, the constable kept his temper, and would not be provoked; and

---

1   Before the establishment of a regular police force, local citizens were
    chosen annually by the parish to serve as constables. But it was an
    unpopular office, both troublesome and unsalaried, and many parish-
    ioners (including Defoe) paid fines rather than serve. The task gradually
    shifted to hired deputies, resulting in even greater inefficiency and cor-
    ruption. Defoe sets forth here an ideal constable, one knowledgeable of
    the law, prepared to enforce it, and honest.

then I put in and said, Come, Mr. Constable, let him alone, I shall find ways enough to fetch him before a magistrate, I don't fear that; but there's the fellow, *says I*, he was the man that seized on me, as I was innocently going along the street, and you are a witness of his violence with me since, give me leave to charge you with him, and carry him before the justice; Yes, madam, *says the constable*, and turning to the fellow, Come young gentleman, *says he to the journey-man*, you must go along with us, I hope you are not above the constable's power, tho' your master is.

The fellow look'd like a condemn'd thief, and hung back, then look'd at his master, as if he cou'd help him; and he, like a fool, encourag'd the fellow to be rude, and he truly resisted the constable, and push'd him back with a good force when he went to lay hold on him, at which the constable knock'd him down, and call'd out for help, and immediately the shop was fill'd with people, and the constable seiz'd the master and man, and all his servants.

The first ill consequence of this fray was, that the woman they had taken, who was really the thief, made off, and got clear away in the crowd; and two others that they had stop'd also, whether they were really guilty or not, that I can say nothing to.

By this time some of his neighbours having come in, and, upon inquiry, seeing how things went, had endeavour'd to bring the hot-brain'd mercer to his senses; and he began to be convinc'd that he was in the wrong; and so at length we went all very quietly before the justice, with a mob of about 500 people at our heels; and all the way I went I could hear the people ask what was the matter? and others reply and say, a mercer had stop'd a gentlewoman instead of a thief, and had afterwards taken the thief, and now the gentlewoman had taken the mercer, and was carrying him before the justice; this pleas'd the people strangely[1] and made the crowd encrease, and they cry'd out as they went, Which is the rogue? Which is the mercer? and especially the women, then when they saw him they cryed out, *That's he, that's he*; and every now and then came a good dab of dirt at him; and thus we march'd a good while, till the mercer thought fit to desire the constable to call a coach to protect himself from the rabble; so we rode the rest of the way, the constable and I, and the mercer and his man.

When we came to the justice, which was an ancient gentleman in *Bloomsbury*, the constable giving first a summary account of the matter the justice bad me speak, and tell what I had to say; and

---

1 Greatly, extremely.

first he asked my name, which I was very loath to give, but there was no remedy, so I told him my name was *Mary Flanders*, that I was a widow, my husband being a sea captain, dyed on a voyage to *Virginia*; and some other circumstances I told, which he cou'd never contradict, and that I lodg'd at present in town with such a person, naming my governess; but that I was preparing to go over to *America*, where my husband's effects lay, and that I was going that day to buy some cloaths to put my self into second mourning,[1] but had not yet been in any shop, when that fellow, pointing to the mercer's journeyman came rushing upon me with such fury, as very much frighted me, and carried me back to his masters shop; where tho' his master acknowledg'd I was not the person; yet he would not dismiss me, but charg'd a constable with me.

Then I proceeded to tell how the journeyman treated me; how they would not suffer me to send for any of my friends; how afterwards they found the real thief, and took the very goods they had lost upon her, and all the particulars as before.

Then the constable related his case; his dialogue with the *mercer* about discharging me, and at last his servants refusing to go with him, when he had charg'd him with him,[2] and his master encouraging him to do so; and at last his striking the constable, and the like, all as I have told it already.

The justice then heard, the *mercer* and his man; the *mercer* indeed made a long harangue of the great loss they have daily by lifters and thieves; that it was easy for them to mistake, and that when he found it, he would have dismiss'd me, *&c.* as above, as to the journeyman he had very little to say, but that he pretended other of the servants told him, that I was really the person.

Upon the whole, the justice first of all told me very courteously I was discharg'd; that he was very sorry that the *mercers* man should in his eager pursuit have so little discretion, as to take up an innocent person for a guilty person; that if he had not been so unjust as to detain me afterward, he believ'd I would have forgiven the first affront; that however it was not in his power to award me any reparation for any thing, other, than by openly reproving them, which he should do; but he suppos'd I would apply to such

---

1 During the first year of mourning a widow traditionally wore unrelieved black garments. After that period, however, a form of dress somewhat less severe could be adopted. See Moll's attire below, p. 255.

2 That is, the mercer's servant refuses to go with the constable after Moll had charged the constable to take him. In the second edition, "he" was correctly changed to "I."

methods as the law directed; in the mean time he would bind him over.

But as to the breach of the peace committed by the journeyman, he told me he should give me some satisfaction for that, for he should commit him to *Newgate* for assaulting the constable, and for assaulting of me also.

Accordingly he sent the fellow to *Newgate*, for that assault, and his master gave bail, and so we came away; but I had the satisfaction of seeing the mob wait upon them both as they came out, holooing, and throwing stones and dirt at the coaches they rode in, and so I came home to my governess.

After this hustle,[1] coming home, and telling my governess the story, she falls a laughing at me; Why are you merry, *says I?* The story has not so much laughing room in it, as you imagine; I am sure I have had a great deal of hurry and fright too, with a pack of ugly rogues. *Laugh,* says my governess, I laugh child to see what a lucky creature you are; why this jobb will be the best bargain to you, that ever you made in your life, if you manage it well: I warrant you, *says she,* you shall make the *mercer* pay you 500 *l.* for damages, besides what you shall get of the journeyman.

I had other thoughts of the matter than she had; and especially, because I had given in my name to the justice of peace; and I knew that my name was so well known among the people at *Hicks's Hall,*[2] the *Old Baily,* and such places, that if this cause came to be tryed openly, and my name came to be enquir'd into, no court would give much damages, for the reputation of a person of such a character; however, I was oblig'd to begin a prosecution in form, and accordingly my governess found me out a very creditable sort of a man to manage it, being an attorney of very good business, and of good reputation, and she was certainly in the right of this; for had she employ'd a petty fogging hedge soliciter,[3] or a man not known, and not in good reputation, I should have brought it to but little.

I met this attorney, and gave him all the particulars at large, as they are recited above; and he assur'd me, it was a case, *as he said,* that would very well support itself, and that he did not question, but that a jury would give very considerable damages on such an occasion; so taking his full instructions, he began the prosecution,

---

1 Rough treatment.
2 The sessions court for the county of Middlesex, located on St. John's Street.
3 A petty, unscrupulous lawyer (who plies his trade under hedges).

and the *mercer* being arrested, gave bail; a few days after his giving bail, he comes with his attorney to my attorney, to let him know, that he desir'd to accommodate the matter;[1] that it was all carried on in the heat of an unhappy passion; that his client, *meaning me,* had a sharp provoking tongue, that I us'd them ill, gibbing at them, and jeering them, even while they believed me to be the very person, and that I had provok'd them, and the like.

My attorney manag'd as well on my side; made them believe I was a widow of fortune, that I was able to do myself justice, and had great friends to stand by me too, who had all made me promise to sue to the utmost, and that if it cost me a thousand pound, I would be sure to have satisfaction, for that the affronts I had receiv'd were unsufferable.

However they brought my attorney to this, that he promis'd he would not blow the coals, that if I enclin'd to an accommodation, he would not hinder me, and that he would rather perswade me to peace than to war; for which they told him he should be no loser, all which he told me very honestly, and told me that if they offer'd him any bribe, I should certainly know it; but upon the whole he told me very honestly that if I would take his opinion, he would advise me to make it up with them; for that as they were in a great fright, and were desirous above all things to make it up, and knew that let it be what it would, they would be alotted to bear all the costs of the suit; he believ'd they would give me freely more than any jury or court of justice would give upon a trial: I ask'd him what he thought they would be brought to; he told me he could not tell, as to that; but he would tell me more when I saw him again.

Some time after this, they came again to know if he had talk'd with me: he told them he had, that he found me not so averse to an accommodation as some of my friends were, who resented the disgrace offer'd me, and set me on; that they blow'd the coals in secret, prompting me to revenge, or to do myself justice, as they call'd it; so that he could not tell what to say to it; he told them he would do his endeavour to persuade me, but he ought to be able to tell me what proposal they made: they pretended they could not make any proposal, because it might be made use of against them; and he told them, that by the same rule he could not make any offers, for that might be pleaded in abatement of what damages a jury might be inclin'd to give: however after some discourse and

---

1 To reach a settlement (out of court).

mutual promises that no advantage should be taken on either side, by what was transacted then, or at any other of those meetings, they came to a kind of a treaty; but so remote, and so wide from one another, that nothing could be expected from it; for my attorney demanded 500 *l.* and charges, and they offer'd 50 *l.* without charges; so they broke off, and the *mercer* propos'd to have a meeting with me myself; and my attorney agreed to that very readily.

My attorney gave me notice to come to this meeting in good cloaths, and with some state,[1] that the *mercer* might see I was something more than I seem'd to be that time they had me: accordingly I came in a new suit of second mourning, according to what I had said at the justices; I set myself out too, as well as a widows dress in second mourning would admit; my governess, also furnish'd me with a good pearl neck-lace, that shut in behind with a locket of diamonds, which she had in pawn; and I had a very good gold watch by my side; so that in a word, I made a very good figure, and as I stay'd,[2] till I was sure they were come, I came in a coach to the door with my maid with me.

When I came into the room, the *mercer* was surpriz'd, he stood up and made his bow, which I took a little notice of, and but a little, and went and sat down, where my own attorney had pointed to me to sit, for it was his house; after a little while, the *mercer* said, he did not know me again, and began to make some compliments his way;[3] I told him, I believe he did not know me at first, and that if he had, I believ'd he would not have treated me as he did.

He told me he was very sorry for what had happen'd, and that it was to testifie the willingness he had to make all possible reparation, that he had appointed this meeting; that he hop'd I would not carry things to extremity, which might be not only too great a loss to him, but might be the ruin of his business and shop, in which case I might have the satisfaction of repaying an injury with an injury ten times greater; but that I would then get nothing, whereas he was willing to do me any justice that was in his power, without putting himself, or me to the trouble or charge of a suit at law.

I told him I was glad to hear him talk so much more like a man of sense than he did before; that it was true, acknowledgement in most cases of affronts was counted reparation sufficient; but this had gone too far to be made up so; that I was not revengeful, nor did I seek his ruin, or any mans else, but that all my friends were

1 Display of wealth and social position.
2 Waited.
3 In his own way.

unanimous not to let me so far neglect my character, as to adjust a thing of this kind without a sufficient reparation of honour: that to be taken up for a thief was such an indignity as could not be put up, that my character was above being treated so by any that knew me; but because in my condition of a widow, I had been for sometime careless of myself, and negligent of myself, I might be taken for such a creature, but that for the particular usage I had from him afterward, and then I repeated all as before, it was so provoking I had scarce patience to repeat it.

Well he acknowledg'd all, and was mighty humble indeed; he made proposals very handsome; he came up to a hundred pounds, and to pay all the law charges, and added that he would make me a present of a very good suit of cloths; I came down to three hundred pounds, and I demanded that I should publish an advertisement of the particulars in the common news papers.

This was a clause he never could comply with; however at last he came up by good management of my attorney to 150 *l.* and a suit of black silk coaths, and there I agreed and as it were at my attornies request complied with it; he paying my attornies bill and charges, and gave us a good supper into the bargain.

When I came to receive the money, I brought my governess with me, dress'd like an old dutchess, and a gentleman very well dress'd, who we pretended courted me, but I call'd him cousin, and the lawyer was only to hint privately to him, that this gentleman courted the widow.

He treated us handsomely indeed, and paid the money chearfully enough; so that it cost him 200 *l.* in all, or rather more: at our last meeting when all was agreed, the case of the journeyman came up, and the *mercer* beg'd very hard for him, told me he was a man that had kept a shop of his own, and been in good business, had a wife and several children, and was very poor, that he had nothing to make satisfaction with, but he should come to beg my pardon on his knees, if I desir'd it as openly as I pleas'd: I had no spleen[1] at the sawcy rogue, nor were his submissions any thing to me, since there was nothing to be got by him; so I thought it was as good to throw that in generously as not, so I told him I did not desire the ruin of any man, and therefore at his request I would forgive the wretch, it was below me to seek any revenge.

When we were at supper he brought the poor fellow in to make acknowledgement, which he would have done with as much mean

---

1 Grudge.

humility, as his offence was with insulting haughtiness and pride, in which he was an instance of a campleat baseness of spirit, impious, cruelter, and relentless when uppermost, and in prosperity; abject and low spirited when down in affliction: however I abated his cringes, told him I forgave him, and desir'd he might withdraw, as if I did not care for the sight of him, tho' I had forgiven him.

I was now in good circumstances indeed, if I could have known my time for leaving off, and my governess often said I was the richest of the trade in *England*, and so I believe I was; for I had 700 *l.* by me in money, besides cloaths, rings, some plate, and two gold watches, and all of them stol'n, for I had innumerable jobbs, besides these I have mention'd; O! had I even now had the grace of repentance, I had still leisure to have look'd back upon my follies, and have made some reparation; but the satisfaction I was to make for the publick mischiefs I had done, was yet left behind; and I could not forbear going abroad again, *as I call'd it now*, any more than I could when my extremity really drove me out for bread.

It was not long after the affair with the *mercer* was made up, that I went out in an equipage[1] quite different from any I had ever appear'd in before; I dress'd myself like a beggar woman, in the coursest and most despicable rags I could get, and I walk'd about peering, and peeping into every door and window I came near; and indeed I was in such a plight[2] now, that I knew as ill how to behave in as ever I did in any; I naturally abhorr'd dirt and rags; I had been bred up tite[3] and cleanly, and could be no other, whatever condition I was in; so that this was the most uneasie disguise to me that ever I put on: I said presently to myself that this would not do, for this was a dress that every body was shy, and afraid of; and I thought every body look'd at me, as if they were afraid I should come near them, lest I should take something from them, or afraid to come near me, lest they should get something from me: I wandered about all the evening the first time I went out, and made nothing of it, but came home again wet, draggl'd and tired; however I went out again, the next night, and then I met with a little adventure, which had like to have cost me dear; as I was standing near a tavern door, there comes a gentleman on horse back, and lights at the door, and wanting to go into the tavern, he calls one of the drawers[4] to hold his horse; he stay'd pretty long in the

1 Outfit, dress.
2 Attire.
3 Tidy.
4 A tapster, bartender.

tavern, and the drawer heard his master call, and thought he would be angry with him; seeing me stand by him, when he call'd to me, Here woman, *says he*, hold this horse a while, till I go in, if the gentleman comes, he'll give you something; *Yes says I*, and takes the horse, and walks off with him very soberly, and carri'd him to my governess.

This had been a booty to those that had understood it; but never was poor thief more at a loss to know what to do with any thing that was stolen; for when I came home, my governess was quite confounded, and what to do with the creature, we neither of us knew; to send him to a stable was doing nothing, for it was certain that publick notice would be given in the *Gazette*,[1] and the horse describ'd, so that we durst not go to fetch it again.

All the remedy we had for this unlucky adventure was to go and set up the horse at an inn, and send a note by a porter to the tavern, that the gentleman's horse that was lost such a time, was left at such an inn, and that he might be had there; that the poor woman that held him, having led him about the street, not being able to lead him back again, had left him there; we might have waited till the owner had publish'd, and offer'd a reward, but we did not care to venture the receiving the reward.

So this was a robbery and no robbery, for little was lost by it, and nothing was got by it, and I was quite sick of going out in a beggar's dress, it did not answer at all, and besides I thought it was ominous and threatning.

While I was in this disguise, I fell in with a parcel of folks of a worse kind than any I ever sorted[2] with, and I saw a little into their ways too, these were coiners of money,[3] and they made some very good offers to me, as to profit; but the part they would have had me have embark'd in, was the most dangerous part; I mean that of the very working the dye,[4] as they call it, which had I been taken, had been certain death, and that at a stake,[5] *I say*, to be burnt to death at a stake; so that tho' I was to appearance, but a beggar; and

---

1 *The London Gazette*, issued by authority twice a week, contained legal and government notices.
2 Consorted, associated.
3 Counterfeiters.
4 The engraving stamp, for impressing a design upon blank coins (obsolete form of *die*).
5 Coining, regarded as high treason, was punishable by burning at the stake. On 5 July 1721, Barbara Spencer was burnt at the stake at Tyburn, the place of public execution for the county of Middlesex.

they promis'd mountains of gold and silver to me, to engage; yet it would not do; it is true if I had been really a beggar, or had been desperate as when I began, I might perhaps have clos'd with it, for what care they to die, that can't tell how to live? But at present this was not my condition, at least I was for no such terrible risques as those; besides the very thoughts of being burnt at a stake, struck terror into my very soul, chill'd my blood, and gave me the vapours to such a degree as I could not think of it without trembling.

This put an end to my disguise too, for as I did not like the proposal, so I did not tell them so; but seem'd to relish it, and promis'd to meet again; but I durst see them no more, for if I had seen them, and not complied, tho' I had declin'd it with the greatest assurances of secrecy in the world, they would have gone near to have murther'd me to make sure work, and make themselves easy,[1] *as they call it*; what kind of easiness that is, they may best judge that understand how easy men are, that can murther people to prevent danger.

This and horse stealing were things quite out of my way, and I might easily resolve I would have no more to say to them; my business seem'd to lye another way, and tho' it had hazard enough in it too, yet it was more suitable to me, and what had more of art in it, more room to escape, and more chances for a coming off, if a surprize should happen.

I had several proposals made also to me about that time, to come into a gang of house-breakers; but that was a thing I had no mind to venture at neither, any more than I had at the coining trade; I offer'd to go along with two men, and a woman, that made it their business to get into houses by stratagem, and with them I was willing enough to venture; but there was three of them already, and they did not care to part,[2] nor I to have too many in a gang, so I did not close with them, but declin'd them, and they paid dear for their next attempt.

But at length I met with a woman that had ofen told me what adventures she had made, and with success at the water-side, and I clos'd with her, and we drove on our business pretty well: one day we came among some *Dutch* people at St. *Catherines*,[3] where we went on pretence to buy goods that were privately got on shore: I was two or three times in a house, where we saw a good

---

1 Free from care or apprehension.
2 That is, to separate into couples.
3 Since the mid-sixteenth century there had been a colony of Dutch and Flemings in this area on the River Thames, east of the Tower of London.

quantity of prohibited goods, and my companion once brought away three peices of *Dutch* black silk that turn'd to good account, and I had my share of it; but in all the journeys I made by myself, I could not get an opportunity to do any thing, so I laid it aside; for I had been so often, that they began to suspect something, and were so shy, that I saw nothing was to be done.

This baulk'd[1] me a little, and I resolv'd to push at something or other, for I was not us'd to come back so often without purchase; so the next day I dress'd myself up fine, and took a walk to the other end of the town, I pass'd thro' the *Exchange* in the *Strand*,[2] but had no notion of finding any thing to do there, when on a sudden I saw a great clutter in the place, and all the people, shopkeepers as well as others, standing up, and staring, and what should it be? but some great dutchess come into the *Exchange*; and they said the queen was coming; I set myself close up to a shopside with my back to the compter,[3] as if to let the crowd pass by, when keeping my eye upon a parcel of lace, which the shop-keeper was showing to some ladies that stood by me; the shop-keeper and her maid were so taken up with looking to see who was a coming, and what shop they would go to, that I found means to slip a paper[4] of lace into my pocket, and come clear off with it, so the lady millener paid dear enough for her gaping after the queen.

I went off from the shop, as if driven along by the throng, and mingling myself with the crowd, went out at the other door of the *Exchange*, and so got away before they miss'd their lace; and because I would not be follow'd, I call'd a coach and shut myself up in it; I had scarse shut the coach doors up, but I saw the milleners maid, and five or six more come running out into the street, and crying out as if they were frighted; they did not cry Stop thief, because no body ran away, but I cou'd hear the word robb'd, and lace, two or three times, and saw the wench wringing her hands, and run staring, to, and again, like one scar'd; the coachman that had taken me up, was getting up into the box, but was not quite up, so that the horses had not begun to move, so that I was terrible uneasy; and I took the packet of lace and laid it ready to have dropt it out at the flap of the coach, which opens before just behind the coachman; but to my great satisfaction in less than a

---

1 Disappointed, frustrated (or *balked*).
2 The New Exchange (as distinct from the Royal Exchange), a fahionable arcade on the south side of the Strand.
3 Obsolete form of *counter*.
4 Packet, parcel.

minute, the coach began to move, that is to say, as soon as the coachman had got up, and spoken to his horses; so he drove away without any interruption, and I brought off my purchase, which was worth near twenty pound.

The next day I dress'd me up again, but in quite different cloths, and walk'd the same way again; but nothing offer'd till I came into St. *James's Park*, where I saw abundance of fine ladies in the *park*, walking in the *Mall*,[1] and among the rest, there was a little miss, a young lady of about 12 or 13 years old, and she had a sister, as I suppose it was, with her, that might be about nine year old: I observ'd the biggest had a fine gold watch on, and a good necklace of pearl, and they had a footman in livery with them; but as it is not usual for the footmen to go behind[2] the ladies in the *Mall*; so I observ'd the footman stop'd at their going into the *Mall*, and the biggest of the sisters spoke to him, which I perceiv'd was to bid him be just there when they came back.

When I heard her dismiss the footman, I step'd up to him, and ask'd him, what little lady that was? and held a little chat with him, about what a pretty child it was with her, and how genteel, and well carriag'd the lady, the eldest would be; how womanish, and how grave; and the fool of a fellow told me presently who she was, that she was Sir *Thomas* ———'s eldest daughter of *Essex*, and that she was a great fortune, that her mother was not come to town yet; but she was with Sir *William* ———'s lady of *Suffolk*, at her lodgings in *Suffolk-Street*, and a great deal more; that they had a maid and a woman to wait on them, besides, Sir *Thomas's* coach, the coachman and himself, and that young lady was governess to the whole family as well here, as at home too; and in short, told me abundance of things enough for my business.

I was very well dress'd, and had my gold watch, as well as she; so I left the footman, and I puts myself in a rank with[3] this young lady, having stay'd till she had taken one double turn in the *Mall*, and was going forward again, by and by, I saluted her by her name, with the title of Lady *Betty*: I ask'd her when she heard from her father? when my lady her mother would be in town and how she did?

I talk'd so familiarly to her of her whole family that she cou'd not suspect, but that I knew them all intimately: I ask'd her why

1   The Mall in St. James's Park, adjacent to St. James's Palace, was the most fashionable promenade in London.
2   To walk behind.
3   That is, she began walking alongside.

she would come abroad without Mrs. *Chime* with her (that was the name of her woman) to take care of Mrs. *Judith* that was her sister. Then I enter'd into a long chat with her about her sister, what a fine little lady she was, and ask'd her if she had learn'd *French*, and a thousand such little things to entertain her, when on a sudden we see the guards[1] come, and the crowd run to see the king go by to the Parliament-House.

The ladies run all to the side of the *Mall*, and I help'd my lady to stand upon the edge of the boards on the side of the *Mall*, that she might be high enough to see; and took the little one and lifted her quite up; during which, I took care to convey the gold watch so clean away from the Lady *Betty*, that she never felt it, nor miss'd it, till all the crowd was gone, and she was gotten into the middle of the *Mall* among the other ladies.

I took my leave of her in the very crowd, and said to her, as if in hast, Dear Lady *Betty* take care of your little sister, and so the crowd did, as it were thrust me away from her, and that I was oblig'd unwillingly to take my leave.

The hurry in such cases is immediately over, and the place clear as soon as the king is gone by; but as there is always a great running and clutter just as the king passes; so having drop'd the two little ladies, and done my business with them, without any miscarriage, I kept hurring on among the crowd, as if I run to see the king, and so I got before the crowd and kept so, till I came to the end of the *Mall*, when the king going on toward the Horse-Guards;[2] I went forward to the passage, which went then thro' against the lower end of the *Hay-Market*, and there I bestow'd a coach upon myself, and made off; and I confess I have not yet been so good as my word (*viz.*) to go and visit my Lady *Betty*.

I was once of the mind to venture staying with Lady *Betty*, till she mist the watch, and so have made a great out-cry about it with her, and have got her into her coach, and put my self in the coach with her, and have gone home with her; for she appear'd so fond of me, and so perfectly deceiv'd by my so readily talking to her of all her relations and family, that I thought it was very easy to push the thing farther, and to have got at least the neck-lace of pearl; but when I consider'd that tho' the child would not perhaps have suspected me, other people might, and that if I was search'd I should be discover'd; I thought it was best to go off with what I had got, and be satisfy'd.

---

1 The Horse Guards (the cavalry brigade of the royal household).
2 That is, the parade grounds for the Horse Guards.

I came accidentally afterwards to hear, that when the young lady miss'd her watch, she made a great out-cry in the *park*, and sent her footman up and down, to see if he could find me out, she having describ'd me so perfectly, that he knew presently that it was the same person that had stood and talked so long with him, and ask'd him so many questions about them; but I was gone far enough out of their reach before she could come at her footman to tell him the story.

I made another adventure after this, of a nature different from all I had been concern'd in yet, and this was at a gaming-house near *Covent-Garden*.

I saw several people go in and out; and I stood in the passage a good while with another woman with me, and seeing a gentleman go up that seem'd to be of more than ordinary fashion, I said to him, Sir, pray don't they give women leave to go up? *Yes madam, says he*, and to play too if they please; I mean so sir, *said I*; and with that, he said he would introduce me if I had a mind; so I follow'd him to the door, and he looking in, There, madam, *says he*, are the gamesters, if you have a mind to venture; I look'd in and said to my comrade, aloud, Here's nothing but men, I won't venture among them; at which one of the gentlemen cry'd out, You need not be afraid madam, here's none but fair gamesters, you are very welcome to come and set[1] what you please; so I went a little nearer and look'd on, and some of them brought me a chair, and I sat down and see the box[2] and dice go round a pace; then I said to my comrade, The gentlemen play too high for us, come let us go.

The people were all very civil, and one gentleman in particular encourag'd me, and said, Come madam, if you please to venture, if you dare trust me I'll answer for it; you shall have nothing put upon you here; No sir, *said I*, smiling, I hope the gentlemen wou'd not cheat a woman; but still I declin'd venturing, tho' I pull'd out a purse with money in it, that they might see I did not want money.

After I had sat a while, one gentleman said to me jeering, Come madam, I see you are afraid to venture for yourself; I always had good luck with the ladies, you shall set for me, if you won't set for yourself; I told him, Sir I should be very loth to lose your money, tho' I added, I am pretty lucky too; but the gentlemen play so high, that I dare not indeed venture my own.

---

1 Set down, wager.
2 A leather cup containing the dice. This is a game called Hazard, in which the chances are complicated by a number of arbitrary rules.

Well, well, *says he*, there's ten guineas madam, set them for me; so I took his money and set, himself looking on; I run out nine of the guineas by one and two at a time, and then the box coming to the next man to me, my gentleman gave me ten guineas more, and made me set five of them at once, and the gentleman who had the box threw out,[1] so there was five guineas of his money again; he was encourag'd at this, and made me take the box, which was a bold venture: however, I held the box so long that I had gain'd him his whole money, and had a good handful of guineas in my lap, and which was the better luck, when I threw out, I threw but at one or two of those that had set me, and so went off easie.

When I was come this length, I offer'd the gentleman all the gold, for it was his own; and so would have had him play for himself, pretending I did not understand the game well enough: he laugh'd, and said if I had but good luck, it was no matter whether I understood the game or no; but I should not leave off: however he took out the 15 guineas that he had put in at first, and bad me play with the rest: I would have told[2] them to see how much I had got, but he said No, no, don't tell them, I believe you are very honest, and 'tis bad luck to tell them, so I play'd on.

I understood the game well enough, tho' I pretended I did not, and play'd cautiously; it was to keep a good stock in my lap, out of which I every now and then convey'd some into my pocket; but in such a manner, and at such convenient times, as I was sure he cou'd not see it.

I play'd a great while, and had very good luck for him, but the last time I held the box, they set me high, and I threw boldly at all; I held the box till I gain'd near fourscore guineas, but lost above half of it back at the last throw; so I got up, for I was afraid I should lose it all back again, and said to him, Pray come sir now and take it and play for your self, I think I have done pretty well for you; he would have had me play'd on, but it grew late, and I desir'd to be excus'd. When I gave it up to him, I told him I hop'd he would give me leave to tell it now, that I might see what I had gain'd, and how lucky I had been for him; when I told them, there was threescore, and three guineas. Ay, *says I*, if it had not been for that unlucky throw I had got you a hundred guineas; so I gave him all the money, but he would not take it till I had put my hand into it, and taken some for myself, and bid me please myself; I refus'd it, and

---

1 Lost his throw.
2 Counted.

was positive I would not take it myself, if he had a mind to any thing of that kind it should be all his own doings.

The rest of the gentlemen seeing us striving, cry'd give it her all; but I absolutely refus'd that; then one of them said, D———n ye *Jack*, half it with her, don't you know you should be always upon even terms with the ladies; so in short, he divided it with me, and I brought away 30 guineas, besides about 43, which I had stole privately, which I was sorry for afterwards, because he was so generous.

Thus I brought home 73 guineas, and let my old governess see what good luck I had at play: however, it was her advice that I should not venture again, and I took her council, for I never went there any more; for I knew as well as she, if the itch of play came in, I might soon lose that, and all the rest of what I had got.

Fortune had smil'd upon me to that degree, and I had thriven so much, and my governess too, for she always had a share with me, that really the old gentlewoman began to talk of leaving off while we were well, and being satisfy'd with what we had got; but, I know not what fate guided me, I was as backward to it now as she was when I propos'd it to her before, and so in an ill hour we gave over the thoughts of it for the present, and in a word, I grew more hardn'd and audacious than ever, and the success I had, made my name as famous as any thief of my sort ever had been at *Newgate*, and in the *Old-Bayly*.

I had sometimes taken the liberty to play the same game over again, which is not according to practice, which however succeeded not amiss; but generally I took up new figures, and contriv'd to appear in new shapes every time I went abroad.

It was now a rumbling[1] time of the year, and the gentlemen being most of them gone out of town, *Tunbridge*, and *Epsom*,[2] and such places were full of people, but the city was thin, and I thought our trade felt it a little, as well as others; so that at the latter end of the year I joyn'd myself with a gang, who usually go every year to *Sturbridge* Fair, and from thence to *Bury* Fair,[3] in *Suffolk*: we

---

1 Possibly "rambling," as in the second edition. During the early part of the summer, the court, the nobility and seemingly much of London moved into the country.

2 Both were fashionable spas, the latter already known for its horse-racing on the downs.

3 Like Bartholomew Fair, both were popular annual events held in the late summer. They were familiar to Defoe, who makes several references to them in *A Tour thro' the Whole Island of Great Britain* (1724-27).

promis'd our selves great things here, but when I came to see how things were, I was weary of it presently; for except meer picking of pockets, there was little worth meddling with; neither if a booty had been made, was it so easy carrying it off, nor was there such a variety of occasion for business in our way, as in *London*; all that I made of the whole journey, was a gold watch at *Bury* Fair, and a small parcel of linnen at *Cambridge*, which gave me an occasion to take leave of the place: it was an old bite,[1] and I thought might do with a country shop keeper, tho' in *London* it would not.

I bought at a linnen draper's shop, not in the fair, but in the town of *Cambridge*, as much fine Holland and other things as came to about seven pound; when I had done, I bad them be sent to such an inn, where I had purposely taken up my being[2] the same morning, as if I was to lodge there that night.

I order'd the draper to send them home to me, about such an hour to the inn where I lay, and I would pay him his money; at the time appointed the draper sends the goods, and I plac'd one of our gang at the chamber door, and when the innkeeper's maid brought the messenger to the door, who was a young fellow, an apprentice, almost a man; she tells him her mistress was a sleep, but if he would leave the things, and call in about an hour, I should be awake, and he might have the money; he left the parcel very readily, and goes his way, and in about half an hour my maid and I walk'd off, and that very evening I hired a horse, and a man to ride before me, and went to *Newmarket*, and from thence got my passage in a coach that was not quite full to St. *Edmund's Bury*; where as I told you I could make but little of my trade, only at a little country *opera*-house,[3] made a shift to carry off a gold watch from a ladies side, who was not only intollerably merry, but as I thought a little fuddled,[4] which made my work much easier.

I made off with this little booty to *Ipswich*, and from thence to *Harwich*; where I went into an inn, as if I had newly arriv'd from *Holland*, not doubting but I should make some purchase among the foreigners that came on shore there; but I found them generally empty of things of value, except what was in their portman-

---

1 Deception, trick.
2 Residence.
3 Although there is no evidence of permanent theatre at Bury until 1734, an advertisement appeared in the *Suffolk Mercury* (25 September 1721) announcing three concerts "for the Diversion of the Quality and Gentry, in the time of Bury-Fair ... "
4 Drunk.

teuas,[1] and *Dutch* hampers, which were generally guarded by footmen; however, I fairly[2] got one of their portmanteuas one evening out of the chamber where the gentleman lay, the footman being fast a sleep on the bed, and I suppose very drunk.

The room in which I lodg'd, lay next to the *Dutchman's*, and having dragg'd the heavy thing with much a-do out of the chamber into mine; I went out into the street, to see if I could find any possibility of carrying it off; I walk'd about a great while but could see no probability, either of getting out the thing, or of conveying away the goods that was in it if I had open'd it, the town being so small, and I a perfect stranger in it; so I was returning with a resolution to carry it back again, and leave it where I found it: just in that very moment I heard a man make a noise to some people to make hast, for the boat was going to put off, and the tide would be spent; I call'd to the fellow, What boat is it friend, *says I*, that you belong to? The *Ipswich* wherry, madam, *says he*: When do you go off, *says I?* This moment madam, *says he*, do you want to go thither? Yes, *said I*, if you can stay till I fetch my things: Where are your things madam, *says he?* At such an inn, *said I*: Well I'll go with you madam, *says he*, very civilly, and bring them for you; Come away then, *says I*, and takes him with me.

The people of the inn were in great hurry, the packet-boat[3] from *Holland*, being just come in, and two coaches just come also with passengers from *London*, for another packet-boat that was going off for *Holland*, which coaches were to go back next day with the passengers that were just landed: in this hurry it was not much minded,[4] that I came to the bar,[5] and paid my reckoning, telling my landlady I had gotten my passage by sea in a wherry.

These wherries are large vessels, with good accommodation for carrying passengers from *Harwich* to *London*; and tho' they are call'd wherries, which is a word us'd in the *Thames* for a small boat, row'd with one or two men; yet these are vessels able to carry twenty passengers, and ten or fifteen ton of goods, and fitted to bear the sea; all this I had found out by enquiring the night before into the several ways of going to *London*.

---

1 Cases, valises (spelled *portmanteaus*). However, Moll describes it later as a "trunk, or portmanteua, for it was like a trunk ... " For a somewhat similar experience, see Appendix A.9.
2 Actually (but possiby either *quietly* or *cleanly*).
3 A vessel travelling at regular intervals between two ports carrying freight, passengers and mail.
4 Noticed.
5 Counter.

My landlady was very courteous, took my money for my reckoning, but was call'd away, all the house being in a hurry; so I left her, took the fellow up to my chamber, gave him the trunk, or portmanteua, for it was like a trunk, and wrapt it about with an old apron, and he went directly to his boat with it, and I after him, no body asking us the least question about it; as for the drunken *Dutch* footman he was still a sleep, and his master with other foreign gentlemen at supper, and very merry below; so I went clean off with it to *Ipswich*, and going in the night, the people of the house knew nothing, but that I was gone to *London*, by the *Harwich* wherry as I had told my landlady.

I was plagu'd at *Ipswich* with the custom-house officers, who stopt my trunk, *as I call'd it*, and would open, and search it; I was willing I told them, they should search it, but my husband had the key, and he was not yet come from *Harwich*; this I said, that if upon searching it, they should find all the things be such, as properly belong'd to a man rather than a woman, it should not seem strange to them; however, they being possitive to open the trunk, I consented to have it be broken open, that is to say, to have the lock taken off, which was not difficult.

They found nothing for their turn, for the trunk had been search'd before, but they discover'd several things very much to my satisfaction, as particularly a parcel of money in *French* pistoles, and some *Dutch* ducatoons, or *rix* dollars,[1] and the rest was chiefly two perriwigs, wearing linnen, and razors, wash-balls,[2] perfumes and other useful things, necessaries for a gentleman; which all pass'd for my husband's, and so I was quit of them.

It was now very early in the morning, and not light, and I knew not well what course to take; for I made no doubt but I should be pursued in the morning, and perhaps be taken with the things about me; so I resolv'd upon taking new measures; I went publickly to an inn in the town with my trunk, *as I call'd it*, and having taken the substance out, I did not think the lumber[3] of it worth my concern; however, I gave it the landlady of the house with a charge to take great care of it, and lay it up safe till I should come again, and away I walk'd into the street.

---

1 Pistoles, ducatoons, and rix-dollars were coins current at this time in various European countries, the pistole made of gold and the other two of silver.
2 Balls of soap, often coloured and scented, for washing the hands and face, and for shaving.
3 Useless items.

When I was got into the town a great way from the inn, I met with an antient woman who had just open'd her door, and I fell into chat with her, and ask'd her a great many wild questions of things all remote to my purpose and design, but in my discourse I found by her how the town was situated, that I was in a street which went out towards *Hadly*; but that such a street went towards the water-side, such a street went into the heart of the town; and at last such a street went towards *Colchester*, and so the *London* road lay there.

I had soon my ends[1] of this old woman; for I only wanted to know which was *London* road, and away I walk'd as fast as I could; not that I intended to go on foot, either to *London* or to *Colchester*, but I wanted to get quietly away from *Ipswich*.

I walk'd about two or three mile, and then I met a plain countryman, who was busy about some husbandry work I did not know what; and I ask'd him a great many questions first, not much to the purpose; but at last told him I was going for *London*, and the coach was full, and I cou'd not get a passage, and ask'd him if he cou'd not tell me where to hire a horse that would carry double, and an honest man to ride before me to *Colchester*, so that I might get a place there in the coaches; the honest clown[2] look'd earnestly at me, and said nothing for above half a minute; when scratching his pole,[3] A horse say you, and to *Colchester* to carry double; why yes mistress, alack-a-day, you may have horses enough for money; Well friend, *says I*, that I take for granted, I don't expect it without money: Why but mistress, *says he*, how much are you willing to give; Nay, says I again, friend, I don't know what your rates are in the country here, for I am a stranger; but if you can get one for me, get it as cheap as you can, and I'll give you somewhat for your pains.

Why that's honestly said too, says the countryman; *Not so honest neither*, said I, to myself, *if thou knewest all*; Why mistress, *says he*, I have a horse that will carry double, and I don't much care if I go my self with you; *and the like*:[4] Will you, *says I?* Well I believe you are an honest man, if you will, I shall be glad of it, I'll pay you in reason; Why look ye mistress, *says he*, I won't be out of reason with you then, if I carry you to *Colechester*, it will be worth five shillings for myself and my horse, for I shall hardly come back to night.

---

1 That is, she had soon got what she was after.
2 Rustic, boor, bumpkin.
3 The top of the head (obsolete form of *poll*).
4 And so forth.

In short, I hir'd the honest man and his horse; but when we came to a town upon the road, I do not remember the name of it, but it stands upon a river,[1] I pretended myself very ill, and I could go no farther that night, but if he would stay there with me, because I was a stranger I would pay him for himself and his horse with all my heart.

This I did because I knew the *Dutch* gentlemen and their servants would be upon the road that day, either in the stage coaches, or riding post, and I did not know but the drunken fellow, or some body else that might have seen me at *Harwich*, might see me again, and so I thought that in one days stop they would be all gone by.

We lay all that night there, and the next morning it was not very early when I set out, so that it was near ten a-clock by that time I got to *Colechester*: it was no little pleasure that I saw the town, where I had so many pleasant days, and I made many enquiries after the good old friends, I had once had there, but could make little out, they were all dead or remov'd; the young ladies had been all married or gone to *London*; the old gentleman, and the old lady that had been my early benefactress all dead; and which troubled me most the young gentleman my first lover, and afterwards my brother-in-law was dead; but two sons men grown, were left of him, but they too were transplanted to *London*.

I dismiss'd my old man here, and stay'd incognito for three or four days in *Colechester*, and then took a passage in a waggon, because I would not venture being seen in the *Harwich* coaches; but I needed not have used so much caution, for there was no body in *Harwich* but the woman of the house, could have known me; nor was it rational to think that she, considering the hurry she was in, and that she never saw me but once, and that by candle light, should have ever discover'd me.

I was now return'd to *London*, and tho' by the accident of the last adventure, I got something considerable, yet I was not fond of any more country rambles, nor should I have ventur'd abroad again if I had carried the trade on to the end of my days; I gave my governess a history of my travels, she lik'd the *Harwich* journey well enough, and in discoursing of these things between our selves she observ'd, that a thief being a creature that watches the advantages of other peoples mistakes, 'tis impossible but that to one that is vigilant and industrious many opportunities must happen, and

---

1   Probably Stratford St. Mary, Suffolk, on the River Stour.

therefore she thought that one so exquisitely keen in the trade as I was, would scarce fail of something extraordinary where ever I went.

On the other hand, every branch of my story, if duly consider'd, may be useful to honest people, and afford a due caution to people of some sort, or other to guard against the like surprizes, and to have their eyes about them when they have to do with strangers of any kind, for 'tis very seldom that some snare or other is not in their way. The moral indeed of all my history is left to be gather'd by the senses and judgment of the reader; I am not qualified to preach to them, let the experience of one creature compleatly wicked, and compleatly miserable be a storehouse of useful warning to those that read.

I am drawing now towards a new variety of the scenes of life: upon my return, being hardened by a long race of crime, and success unparalell'd, at least in the reach of my own knowledge, I had, as I have said, no thoughts of laying down a trade, which if I was to judge by the example of others, must however end at last in misery and sorrow.

It was on the *Christmas-day* following in the evening, that to finish a long train of wickedness, I went abroad to see what might offer in my way; when going by a working silver-smiths in *Foster-Lane*,[1] I saw a tempting bait indeed, and not to be resisted by one of my occupation; for the shop had no body in it, as I could see, and a great deal of loose plate lay in the window, and at the seat of the man, who usually as I suppose work'd at one side of the shop.

I went boldly in and was just going to lay my hand upon a peice of plate, and might have done it, and carried it clear off, for any care that the men who belong'd to the shop had taken of it; but an officious fellow in a house, not a shop, on the other side of the way, seeing me go in, and observing that there was no body in the shop, comes running over the street, and into the shop, and without asking me what I was, or who, seizes upon me, and cries out for the people of the house.

I had not as I said above, touch'd any thing in the shop, and seeing a glimpse of some body running over to the shop, I had so much presence of mind, as to knock very hard with my foot on the floor of the house, and was just calling out too, when the fellow laid hands on me.

---

1 Located in Aldersgate Ward, Foster Lane was known for its silversmiths. Evidently this shop forged and worked plate as well as selling it.

However as I had always most courage, when I was in most danger; so when the fellow laid hands on me, I stood very high upon it, that I came in, to buy half a dozen of silver spoons, and to my good fortune, it was a silversmith's that sold plate, as well as work'd plate, for other shops: the fellow laugh'd at that part, and put such a value upon the service that he had done his neighbour, that he would have it be that I came not to buy, but to steal, and raising a great crowd, I said to the master of the shop, who by this time was fetch'd home from some neighbouring place, that it was in vain to make noise, and enter into talk there of the case; the fellow had insisted, that I came to steal, and he must prove it, and I desir'd we might go before a magistrate without any more words; for I began to see I should be too hard for the man that had seiz'd me.

The master and mistress of the shop were really not so violent, as the man from tother side of the way, and the man said, Mistress you might come into the shop with a good design for ought I know, but it seem'd a dangerous thing for you to come into such a shop as mine is, when you see no body there, and I cannot do so little justice to my neighbour, who was so kind to me, as not to acknowledge he had reason on his side; tho' upon the whole I do not find you attempt'd to take any thing, and I really know not what to do in it: I press'd him to go before a magistrate with me, and if any thing cou'd be prov'd on me, that was like a design of robbery, I should willingly submit, but if not I expected reparation.

Just while we were in this debate, and a crowd of people gather'd about the door came by Sir *T. B.* an alderman of the city, and justice of the peace, and the goldsmith[1] hearing of it goes out, and entreated his worship to come in and decide the case.

Give the goldsmith his due, he told his story with a great deal of justice and moderation, and the fellow that had come over, and seiz'd upon me, told his with as much heat, and foolish passion, which did me good still, rather than harm: it came then to my turn to speak, and I told his worship that I was a stranger in *London*, being newly come out of the *north*, that I lodg'd in such a place, that I was passing this street, and went into the goldsmiths shop to buy half a dozen of spoons, by great good luck I had an old silver spoon in my pocket, which I pull'd out, and told him I had carried that spoon to match it with half a dozen of new ones, that it might match some I had in the country.

---

1 Previously referred to as a silversmith's shop.

That seeing no body in the shop, I knock'd with my foot very hard to make the people hear, and had also call'd aloud with my voice: tis true, there was loose plate in the shop, but that no body cou'd say I had touch'd any of it, or gone near it; that a fellow came running into the shop out of the street, and laid hands on me in a furious manner, in the very moments, while I was calling, for the people of the house; that if he had really had a mind to have done his neighbour any service, he should have stood at a distance, and silently watch'd to see whether I had touch'd any thing, or no, and then have clap'd in[1] upon me, and taken me in the fact: That is very true, *says Mr. Alderman,* and turning to the fellow that stopt me, he ask'd him if it was true that I knock'd with my foot, he said yes I had knock'd, but that might be because of his coming; Nay, says *the alderman,* taking him short, now you contradict yourself, for just now you said, she was in the shop with her back to you, and did not see you till you came upon her; now it was true, that my back was partly to the street, but yet as my business was of a kind that requir'd me to have my eyes every way, so I really had a glance of him running over, as I said before, tho' he did not perceive it.

After a full hearing, the alderman gave it as his opinion, that his neighbour was under a mistake, and that I was innocent, and the goldsmith acquisc'd in it too, and his wife, and so I was dismiss'd; but as I was going to depart, Mr. *Alderman* said, But *hold madam,* if you were designing to buy spoons I hope you will not let my friend here lose his customer by the mistake: I readily answer'd, No sir, I'll buy the spoons still if he can match my odd spoon, which I brought for a pattern, and the goldsmith shew'd me some of the very same fashion; so he weigh'd the spoons, and they came to five and thirty shillings, so I pulls out my purse to pay him, in which I had near 20 guineas, for I never went without such a sum about me, what ever might happen, and I found it of use at other times as well as now.

When Mr. *Alderman* saw my money, *he said,* Well madam, now I am satisfy'd you were wrong'd, and it was for this reason, that I mov'd you should buy the spoons, and staid till you had bought them, for if you had not had money to pay for them, I should have suspected that you did not come into the shop with an intent to buy, for indeed the sort of people who come upon those designs that you have been charg'd with, are seldom troubl'd with much gold in their pockets, as I see you are.

---

1 Burst in.

I smil'd, and told his worship, that then I ow'd something of his favour to my money, but I hop'd he saw reason also in the justice he had done me before; he said, Yes he had, but this had confirm'd his opinion, and he was fully satisfy'd now of my having been injur'd; so I came off with flying colours, tho' from an affair, in which I was at the very brink of destruction.

It was but three days after this, that not at all made cautious by my former danger as I us'd to be, and still pursuing the art which I had so long been employ'd in, I ventur'd into a house where I saw the doors open, and furnish'd myself as I thought verily without being perceiv'd, with two peices of flower'd silks, such as they call brocaded silk, very rich; it was not a mercers shop, nor a warehouse of a mercer, but look'd like a private dwelling-house, and was it seems inhabited by a man that sold goods for the weavers to the mercers, like a broker or factor.[1]

That I may make short of this black part of this story, I was attack'd by two wenches that came open mouth'd at me just as I was going out at the door, and one of them pull'd me back into the room, while the other shut the door upon me; I would have given them good words, but there was no room for it; two firery dragons cou'd not have been more furious than they were; they tore my cloths, bully'd and roar'd as if they would have murther'd me; the mistress of the house came next, and then the master, and all outrageous, for a while especially.

I gave the master very good words, told him the door was open, and things were a temptation to me, that I was poor, and distress'd, and poverty was what many could not resist, and beg'd him with tears to have pity on me; the mistress of the house was mov'd with compassion, and enclin'd to have let me go, and had almost perswaded her husband to it also, but the sawcy wenches were run even before they were sent, and had fetch'd a constable, and then the master said, he could not go back, I must go before a justice, and answer'd his wife that he might come into trouble himself if he should let me go.

The sight of the constable indeed struck me with terror, and I thought I should have sunk into the ground; I fell into faintings, and indeed the people themselves thought I would have died, when the woman argued again for me, and entreated her husband, seeing they had lost nothing to let me go: I offer'd him to pay for the two peices whatever the value was, tho' I had not got them,

---

1 Agent.

and argued that as he had his goods, and had really lost nothing, it would be cruel to pursue me to death, and have my blood for the bare attempt of taking them; I put the constable in mind that I had broke no doors, nor carried any thing away; and when I came to the justice, and pleaded there that I had neither broken any thing to get in, nor carried any thing out, the justice was enclin'd to have releas'd me; but the first sawcy jade that stop'd me, affirming that I was going out with the goods, but that she stop'd me and pull'd me back as I was upon the threshold, the justice upon that point committed me, and I was carried to *Newgate*; that horrid place! My very blood chills at the mention of its name; the place, where so many of my comrades had been lock'd up, and from whence they went to the fatal tree;[1] the place where my mother suffered so deeply, where I was brought into the world, and from whence I expected no redemption, but by an infamous death: to conclude, the place that had so long expected me, and which with so much art and success I had so long avoided.

I was now fix'd indeed; 'tis impossible to describe the terror of my mind, when I was first brought in, and when I look'd round upon all the horrors of that dismal place: I look'd on myself as lost, and that I had nothing to think of, but of going out of the world, and that with the utmost infamy; the hellish noise, the roaring, swearing and clamour, the stench and nastiness, and all the dreadful croud of afflicting things that I saw there; joyn'd together to make the place seem an emblem of Hell itself, and a kind of an entrance into it.

Now I reproach'd myself with the many hints I had had, *as I have mentioned above*, from my own reason, from the sense of my good circumstances, and of the many dangers I had escap'd to leave off while I was well, and how I had withstood them all, and hardened my thoughts against all fear; it seem'd to me that I was hurried on by an inevitable and unseen fate to this day of misery, and that now I was to expiate all my offences at the gallows, that I was now to give satisfaction to justice with my blood, and that I was come to the last hour of my life, and of my wickedness together: these things pour'd themselves in upon my thoughts in a confus'd manner, and left me overwhelm'd with melancholly and despair.

---

1 The gallows. As public executions generally took place at Tyburn (the site of the present Marble Arch), the gallows there became known as Tyburn tree. But there were also other nicknames, such as the deadly nevergreen, the three-legged mare and the triple tree.

Then I repented heartily of all my life past, but that repentance yielded me no satisfaction, no peace, no not in the least, because, *as I said to myself*, it was repenting after the power of farther sinning was taken away: I seem'd not to mourn that I had committed such crimes, and for the fact, as it was an offence against God and my neighbour; but I mourn'd that I was to be punish'd for it; I was a penitent as I thought, not that I had sinn'd, but that I was to suffer, and this took away all the comfort, and even the hope of my repentance in my own thoughts.

I got no sleep for several nights or days after I came into that wretch'd place, and glad I wou'd have been for some time to have died there, tho' I did not consider dying as it ought to be consider'd neither, indeed nothing could be fill'd with more horror to my imagination than the very place, nothing was more odious to me than the company that was there: O! if I had but been sent to any place in the world, and not to *Newgate*, I should have thought myself happy.

In the next place, how did the harden'd wretches that were there before me triumph over me? What! Mrs. *Flanders* come to *Newgate* at last? What Mrs. *Mary*, Mrs. *Molly*, and after that plain *Moll Flanders*? They thought the Devil had help'd me they said, that I had reign'd so long, they expected me there many years ago, and was I come at last? Then they flouted me with my dejections, welcom'd me to the place, wish'd me joy, bid me have a good heart, not to be cast down, things might not be so bad as I fear'd, and the like; then call'd for brandy, and drank to me; but put it all up to my score,[1] for they told me I was but just come to the college,[2] *as they call'd it*, and sure I had money in my pocket, tho' they had none.

I ask'd one of this crew how long she had been there? She said four months; I ask'd her, how the place look'd to her when she first came into it? Just as it did now to me, *says she*, dreadful and frightful, that she thought she was in Hell, and I believe so still, *adds she, but it is natural to me now, I don't disturb myself about it*: I suppose says I, you are in no danger of what is to follow: Nay, *says she*, for you are mistaken there I assure you, for I am under sentence,[3] only I pleaded my belly, but I am no more with child, than the

---

1 That is, charged the brandy to Moll's account. It was the custom that all new prisoners pay for a round of drinks for the other inmates, readily purchased from the keepers. See Appendix B.1.
2 Traditional slang term for Newgate. See above, p. 214, n. 1.
3 That is, sentence of death.

judge that try'd me, and I expect to be call'd down next sessions; *this* CALLING DOWN, *is calling down to their former judgement, when a woman has been respited for her belly, but proves not to be with child, or if she has been with child, and has been brought to bed.* Well says I, and are you thus easy? Ay, *says she,* I can't help myself, what signifyes being sad? If I am hang'd there's an end of me, *says she,* and away she turns dancing, and sings as she goes the following peice of *Newgate* wit,

> *If I swing by the string,*
> *I shall hear the *bell ring.*
>   And then there's an end of poor Jenny.*

I mention this, because it would be worth the observation of any prisoner, who shall hereafter fall into the same misfortune and come to that dreadful place of *Newgate*; how time, necessity, and conversing with the wretches that are there familiarizes the place to them; how at last they become reconcil'd to that which at first was the greatest dread upon their spirits in the world, and are as impudently chearful and merry in their misery, as they were when out of it.

I can not say, as some do, this devil is not so black, as he is painted; for indeed no colours can represent the place to the life; nor any soul conceive aright of it, but those who have been sufferers there: but how Hell should become by degrees so natural, and not only tollerable, but even agreeable, is a thing unintelligible, but by those who have experienc'd it, as I have.

The same night that I was sent to *Newgate,* I sent the news of it to my old governess, who was surpriz'd at it you may be sure, and spent the night almost as ill out of *Newgate,* as I did in it.

The next morning, she came to see me, she did what she cou'd to comfort me, but she saw that was to no purpose; however, as she said, to sink under the weight, was but to encrease the weight, she immediately applied her self to all the proper methods to prevent the effects of it, which we fear'd; and first she found out the two fiery jades that had surpriz'd me; she tamper'd with them, persuad'd them, offer'd them money, and in a word, try'd all

---

* The bell at St. *Sepulcher's* which tolls upon execution day. [It was said that the big bell at St. Sepulchre's church, across from Newgate, was rung on the night preceding an execution and during the next morning as the procession made its way to Tyburn, stopping off for prayers at the church. However, Moll refers later only to the ringing of the bell (p. 291 below) as it "usher'd in the day" of execution. See Appendix B.1.]

imaginable ways to prevent a prosecution; she offer'd one of the wenches 100 *l.* to go away from her mistress, and not to appear against me; but she was so resolute, that tho' she was but a servant-maid, at 3 *l.* a year wages or thereabouts, she refus'd it, and would have refus'd it, as my governess said she believ'd, if she had offer'd her 500 *l.* Then she attack'd the tother maid, she was not so hard hearted in appearance as the other; and sometimes seem'd inclin'd to be merciful; but the first wench kept her up, and chang'd her mind, and would not so much as let my governess talk with her, but threatn'd to have her up for tampering with the evidence.

Then she apply'd to the master, that is to say, the man whose goods had been stol'n, and particularly to his wife, who as I told you was enclin'd at first to have some compassion for me; she found the woman the same still, but the man alledg'd he was bound by the justice that committed me, to prosecute, and that he should forfeit his recognizance.[1]

My governess offer'd to find friends that should get his recognizances off of the file, as they call it, and that he should not suffer; but it was not possible to convince him, that could be done, or that he could be safe any way in the world, but by appearing against me; so I was to have three witnesses of fact against me, the master and his two maids, that is to say, I was as certain to be cast for my life,[2] as I was certain that I was alive, and I had nothing to do, but to think of dying, and prepare for it: I had but a sad foundation to build upon, as I said before, for all my repentance appear'd to me to be only the effect of my fear of death, not a sincere regret for the wicked life that I had liv'd, and which had brought this misery upon me, or for the offending my Creator, who was now suddenly to be my judge.

I liv'd many days here under the utmost horror of soul; I had death as it were in view, and thought of nothing night and day, but of gibbets and halters, evil spirits and devils; it is not to be express'd by words how I was harrass'd, between the dreadful apprehensions of death, and the terror of my conscience reproaching me with my past horrible life.

---

1 That is, he posted a bond engaging himself to continue the prosecution and appear in court in order to testify against Moll, the usual penalty for not doing so being 40 pounds.
2 Sentenced to hang.

The Ordinary of *Newgate*[1] came to me, and talk'd a little in his way, but all his divinity run upon confessing my crime, as he call'd it, (tho' he knew not what I was in for) making a full discovery, and the like, without which he told me God would never forgive me; and he said so little to the purpose, that I had no manner of consolation from him; and then to observe the poor creature preaching confession and repentance to me in the morning, and find him drunk with brandy and spirits by noon; this had something in it so shocking, that I began to nauseate the man more, than his work, and his work too by degrees for the sake of [2] the man; so that I desir'd him to trouble me no more.

I know not how it was, but by the indefatigable application of my diligent governess I had no bill[3] preferr'd against me the first sessions, I mean to the grand jury, at *Guild-Hall*;[4] so I had another month, or five weeks before me, and without doubt this ought to have been accepted by me, as so much time given me for reflection upon what was past, and preparation for what was to come, or in a word, I ought to have esteem'd it, as a space given me for repentance, and have employ'd it as such; but it was not in me, I was sorry (*as before*) for being in *Newgate*, but had very few signs of repentance about me.

On the contrary, like the waters in the caveties, and hollows of mountains, which petrifies and turns into stone whatever they are suffer'd to drop upon; so the continual conversing with such a crew of hell-hounds as I was with had the same common operation upon me, as upon other people, I degenerated into stone; I turn'd first stupid and senseless, then brutish and thoughtless, and at last raving mad as any of them were; and in short, I became as naturally pleas'd and easie with the place, as if indeed I had been born there.

It is scarce possible to imagine that our natures should be capable of so much degeneracy, as to make that pleasant and agreeable that in it self is the most compleat misery. Here was a circum-

---

1   The chaplain of the prison, whose main duty was to prepare condemned prisoners for death. Although at least five men held this office during Defoe's life, there is evidence to suggest that the depiction here was inspired particularly by two contemporary Ordinaries of Newgate, Paul Lorrain and Samuel Smith. For two somewhat different accounts, see Appendix B.2 and 10.
2   Because of.
3   Indictment, formal charge. See below, p. 283, n. 1.
4   The meeting hall of the Corporation of the City of London.

stance, that I think it is scarce possible to mention a worse; I was as exquisitely miserable as speaking of common cases, it was possible for any one to be that had life and health, and money to help them as I had.

I had a weight of guilt upon me enough to sink any creature who had the least power of reflection left, and had any sense upon them of the happiness of this life, or the misery of another; then I had at first remorse indeed, but no repentance; I had now neither remorse or repentance: I had a crime charg'd on me, the punishment of which was death by our law; the proof so evident, that there was no room for me so much as to plead not guilty; I had the name of old offender, so that I had nothing to expect but death in a few weeks time, neither had I myself any thoughts of escaping, and yet a certain strange lethargy of soul possess'd me, I had no trouble, no apprehensions, no sorrow about me, the first surprize was gone; I was, I may well say I know not how; my senses, my reason, nay, my conscience were all a-sleep; my course of life for forty years had been a horrid complication of wickedness, whoredom, adultery, incest, lying, theft, and in a word, every thing but murther and treason had been my practice from the age of eighteen, or thereabouts to threescore; and now I was in-gulph'd in the misery of punishment, and had an infamous death just at the door, and yet I had no sense of my condition, no thought of Heaven or Hell at least, that went any farther than a bare flying touch, like the stich or pain that gives a hint and goes off; I neither had a heart to ask God's mercy, or indeed to think of it, and in this I think I have given a brief description of the compleatest misery on earth.

All my terrifying thoughts were past, the horrors of the place, were become familiar, and I felt no more uneasinesses at the noise and clamours of the prison, than they did who made that noise; in a word, I was become a meer *Newgate-bird*, as wicked and as outragious as any of them; nay, I scarce retain'd the habit and custom of good breeding, and manners, which all along till now run thro' my conversation; so thoro' a degeneracy had possess'd me, that I was no more the same thing that I had been, than if I had never been otherwise than what I was now.

In the middle of this harden'd part of my life, I had another sudden surprize, which call'd me back a little to that thing call'd sorrow, which indeed I began to be past the sense of before: they told me one night, that there was brought into the prison late the night before three highway-men, who had committed a robbery somewhere on the road to *Windsor, Hounslow-Heath,* I think it was, and were pursu'd to *Uxbridge* by the country,[1] and were taken there after a gallant resistance, in which I know not how many of the country people were wounded, and some kill'd.

It is not to be wonder'd that we prisoners, were all desirous enough to see these brave topping[2] gentlemen that were talk'd up to be such, as their fellows had not been known, and especially because it was said they would in the morning be remov'd into the press-yard,[3] having given money to the head-master of the prison, to be allow'd the liberty of that better part of the prison: so we that were women plac'd ourselves in the way that we would be sure to see them; but nothing cou'd express the amazement and surprize I was in, when the very first man that came out I knew to be my *Lancashire* husband, the same with whom I liv'd so well at *Dunstable*, and the same who I afterwards saw at *Brickill*, when I was married to my last husband, as has been related.

I was struck dumb at the sight, and knew neither what to say, or what to do, he did not know me, and that was all the present relief I had, I quitted my company, and retir'd as much as that dreadful place suffers any body to retire, and I cry'd vehemently for a great while; Dreadful creature, that I am, *said I*, how many poor people have I made miserable? How many desperate wretches have I sent to the Devil; this gentleman's misfortunes I plac'd all to my own account: he had told me at *Chester*, he was ruin'd by that match, and that his fortunes were made desperate on my account; for that thinking I had been a fortune he was run into debt more than he was able to pay, and that he knew not what course to take; that he would go into the army, and carry a musquet, or buy a horse and take a tour,[4] as he call'd it; and tho' I never told him that I was a fortune, and so did not actually deceive him myself, yet I did encourage the having it thought that I was so, and by that means I was the occasion originally of his mischief.

The surprize of this thing only, struck deeper into my thoughts, and gave me stronger reflections than all that had befallen me before; I griev'd day and night for him, and the more, for that they told me, he was the captain of the gang, and that he had committed so many robberies, that *Hind*, or *Whitney*, or the *Golden*

---

1 Local people.
2 Eminent, noted.
3 An area of Newgate with apartments belonging to the keeper's house, which were let to prisoners who could afford the high fees and other charges. See Appendix B.1.
4 Criminal jargon for "become a highwayman."

Farmer[1] were fools to him; that he would surely be hang'd if there were no more men left in the country he was born in; and that there would abundance of people come in against him.

I was overwhelm'd with grief for him; my own case gave me no disturbance compar'd to this, and I loaded my self with reproaches on his account; I bewail'd his misfortunes, and the ruin he was now come to, at such a rate, that I relish'd nothing now, as I did before, and the first reflections I made upon the horrid detestable life I had liv'd, began to return upon me, and as these things return'd my abhorrance of the place I was in, and of the way of living in it, return'd also; in a word, I was perfectly chang'd, and become another body.

While I was under these influences of sorrow for him, came notice to me that the next sessions approaching, there would be a bill preferr'd to the grand jury against me, and that I should be certainly try'd for my life at the *Old-Baily*: my temper was touch'd before,[2] the harden'd wretch'd boldness of spirit, which I had acquir'd in the prison abated, and conscious guilt began to flow in upon my mind: in short, I began to think, and to think is one real advance from Hell to Heaven; all that hellish harden'd state and temper of soul, which I have said so much of before, is but a deprivation of thought; he that is restor'd to his power of thinking, is restor'd to himself.

As soon as I began, I say to think, the first thing that occurr'd to me broke out thus; Lord! what will become of me, I shall certainly die! I shall be cast to be sure, and there is nothing beyond that but death! I have no friends, what shall I do? I shall be certainly cast; Lord, have mercy upon me, what will become of me? This was a sad thought, you will say, to be the first after so long time that had started into my soul of that kind, and yet even this was nothing but fright, at what was to come; there was not a word of sincere repentance in it all: however, I was indeed dreadfully dejected, and disconsolate to the last degree; and as I had no friend in the world to communicate my distress'd thoughts to, it lay so heavy upon me, that it threw me into fits, and swoonings

---

1   These three were among the most notorious highwaymen of the seventeenth century, whose lives were recounted in the criminal literature and chapbooks of the day. In the end, all of them were executed, Captain James Hind by being hanged, drawn and quartered. William Davis was known as the "Golden Farmer" because supposedly he paid his debts in gold and concealed his criminal activities by posing as a farmer.

2   My habitual outlook was already affected.

several times a-day: I sent for my old governess, and she, *give her her due*, acted the part of a true friend, she left me no stone unturn'd to prevent the grand jury finding out one or two of the jury men,[1] talk'd with them, and endeavour'd to possess them with favourable dispositions,[2] on account that nothing was taken away, and no house broken, *&c.* but all would not do, they were overruled by the rest, the two wenches swore home to the fact, and the jury found the bill against me for robbery and housebreaking, that is for felony and burglary.

I sunk down when they brought me news of it, and after I came to myself again, I thought I should have died with the weight of it: my governess acted a true mother to me, she pittied me, she cryed with me, and for me; but she cou'd not help me; and to add to the terror of it, 'twas the discourse all over the house, that I should die for it; I cou'd hear them talk it among themselves very often; and see them shake their heads, and say they were sorry for it, and the like, as is usual in the place; but still no body came to tell me their thoughts, till at last one of the keepers came to me privately, and said with a sigh, Well Mrs. *Flanders*, you will be tried a *Friday*, (this was but a *Wednesday*,) what do you intend to do? I turn'd as white as a clout,[3] and said, God knows what I shall do, for my part I know not what to do; Why, *says he*, I won't flatter you,[4] I would have you prepare for death, for I doubt you will be cast, and as they say, you are an old offender, I doubt you will find but little mercy; they say, *added he*, your case is very plain, and that the witnesses swear so home against you, there will be no standing it.

This was a stab into the very vitals of one under such a burthen as I was oppress'd with before, and I cou'd not speak to him a word good or bad, for a great while, but at last I burst out into tears, and said to him, Lord! Mr. —— what must I do? Do, *says he*, send for the Ordinary, send for a minister, and talk with him, for indeed Mrs. *Flanders*, unless you have very good friends, you are no woman for this world.

---

1   The second edition reads: "... she left me no stone unturn'd to prevent the grand jury finding the bill, she went to one or two of the jury men ... "
A bill of indictment was said to be "found" when the grand jury declared the evidence to be probable and worthy of further consideration.
2   That is, she attempted to convince a few members of the grand jury that there was not sufficient evidence to try Moll.
3   Piece of cloth ("as white as a sheet").
4   Raise your hopes.

This was plain dealing indeed, but it was very harsh to me, at least I thought it so: he left me in the greatest confusion imaginable, and all that night I lay awake; and now I began to say my prayers, which I had scarce done before since my last husband's death, or from a little while after; and truly I may well call it, saying my prayers; for I was in such a confusion, and had such horrour upon my mind, that tho' I cry'd, and repeated several times the ordinary expression of, *Lord have mercy upon me*; I never brought my self to any sense of my being a miserable sinner, as indeed I was, and of confessing my sins to God, and begging pardon for the sake of Jesus Christ; I was overwhelm'd with the sense of my condition, being try'd for my life, and being sure to be condemn'd, and then I was as sure to be executed, and on this account, I cry'd out all night, Lord! what will become of me? Lord! what shall I do? Lord! I shall be hang'd, Lord have mercy upon me, and the like.

My poor afflicted governess was now as much concern'd as I, and a great deal more truly penitent; tho' she had no prospect of being brought to tryal and sentence, not but that she deserv'd it as much as I, and so she said herself; but she had not done any thing herself for many years, other than receiving what I, and others stole, and encouraging us to steal it:[1] but she cry'd and took on, like a distracted body, wringing her hands, and crying out that she was undone, that she believ'd there was a curse from Heaven upon her, that she should be damn'd, that she had been the destruction of all her friends, that she had brought such a one, and such a one, and such one to the gallows; and there she reckon'd up ten or eleven people, some of which I have given an account of that came to untimely ends, and that now she was the occasion of my ruin, for she had persuaded me to go on, when I would have left off: I interrupted her there; No mother, no, *said I*, don't speak of that, for you would have had me left off when I got the mercer's money again, and when I came home from *Harwich*, and I would not hearken to you, therefore you have not been to blame, it is I only have ruin'd myself, I have brought myself to this misery, and thus we spent many hours together.

Well there was no remedy, the prosecution went on, and on the *Thursday* I was carried down to the sessions-house, where I was

---

1 If convicted, however, buyers or receivers of stolen goods could be transported to America for fourteen years. See Appendix, B.9.

arraign'd,[1] as they call'd it, and the next day I was appointed to be try'd. At the arraignment I pleaded not guilty, and well I might, for I was indicted for felony and burglary; that is for feloniously stealing two pieces of brocaded silk, value 46 *l.* the goods of *Anthony Johnson,* and for breaking open his doors; whereas I knew very well they could not pretend to prove I had broken up the doors, or so much as lifted up a latch.

On the *Friday* I was brought to my tryal, I had exhausted my spirits with crying for two or three days before, that[2] I slept better the *Thursday* night than I expected, and had more courage for my tryal, than indeed I thought possible for me to have.

When the tryal began, and the indictment was read, I would have spoke, but they told me the witnesses must be heard first, and then I should have time to be heard. The witnesses were the two wenches, a couple of hard mouth'd[3] jades indeed, for tho' the thing was truth in the main, yet they aggravated it to the utmost extremity, and swore I had the goods wholly in my possession, that I had hid them among my cloaths, that I was going off with them, that I had one foot over the threshold when they discovered themselves, and then I put tother over, so that I was quite out of the house in the street with the goods before they took hold of me, and then they seiz'd me, and brought me back again, and they took the goods upon me: the fact in general was all true, but I believe, and insisted upon it, that they stop'd me before I had set my foot clear of the threshold of the house; but that did not argue much, for certain it was, that I had taken the goods, and that I was bringing them away, if I had not been taken.

But I pleaded that I had stole nothing, they had lost nothing, that the door was open, and I went in seeing the goods lye there, and with design to buy, if seeing no body in the house, I had taken any of them up in my hand, it cou'd not be concluded that I intended to steal them, for that I never carried them farther than the door to look on them with the better light.

The court would not allow that by any means, and made a kind of a jest of my intending to buy the goods, that being no shop for the selling of any thing, and as to carrying them to the door to look at them, the maids made their impudent mocks upon that, and spent their wit upon it very much; told the court I had look'd at

1 Called to answer on criminal charges. For somewhat similar accounts, see Appendix B.1.
2 So that.
3 Wilful, obstinate.

them sufficiently, and approv'd them very well, for I had pack'd them up under my cloaths, and was a going with them.

In short, I was found guilty of felony, but acquited of the burglary,[1] which was but small comfort to me, the first bringing me to a sentence of death, and the last would have done no more: the next day, I was carried down to receive the dreadful sentence, and when they came to ask me what I had to say, why sentence should not pass, I stood mute a while, but some body that stood behind me, prompted me aloud to speak to the judges, for that they cou'd represent things favourably for me: this encourag'd me to speak, and I told them I had nothing to say to stop the sentence; but that I had much to say, to bespeak the mercy of the court, that I hop'd they would allow something in such a case, for the circumstances of it, that I had broken no doors, had carried nothing off, that no body had lost any thing; that the person whose goods they were was pleas'd to say, he desir'd mercy might be shown, which indeed he very honestly did, that at the worst it was the first offence, and that I had never been before any court of justice before: and in a word, I spoke with more courage than I thought I cou'd have done, and in such a moving tone, and tho' with tears, yet not so many tears as to obstruct my speech, that I cou'd see it mov'd others to tears that heard me.

The judges sat grave and mute, gave me an easy hearing, and time to say all that I would, but saying neither yes, or no to it, pronounc'd the sentence of death upon me; a sentence that was to me like death itself, which after it was read confounded me; I had no more spirit left in me, I had no tongue to speak, or eyes to look up either to God or man.

My poor governess was utterly disconsolate, and she that was my comforter before, wanted comfort now herself, and sometimes mourning, sometimes raging, was as much out of herself (as to all outward appearance) as any mad woman in *Bedlam*:[2] nor was she only disconsolate as to me, but she was struck with horror at the sense of her own wicked life, and began to look back upon it with a taste quite different from mine; for she was penitent to the highest degree for her sins, as well as sorrowful for the misfortune: she sent for a minister too, a serious pious good man, and apply'd her-

---

1 That is, Moll is found guilty of stealing the goods ("felony") but not of breaking into the shop or of leaving the premises with the stolen goods ("burglary").
2 Properly, Bethlehem Hospital, an institution for the insane in Moorfields.

self with such earnestness by his assistance to the work of a sincere repentance, that I believe, and so did the minister too, that she was a true penitent, and which is still more, she was not only so for the occasion, and at that juncture, but she continu'd so, as I was inform'd to the day of her death.

It is rather to be thought of, than express'd what was now my condition; I had nothing before me but present death; and as I had no friends to assist me, or to stir for me, I expected nothing but to find my name in the dead warrant,[1] which was to come down for the execution the *Friday* afterward, of five more and myself.

In the mean time my poor distress'd governess sent me a minister, who at her request first, and at my own afterwards came to visit me: he exhorted me seriously to repent of all my sins, and to dally no longer with my soul; not flattering myself with hopes of life, which he said, he was inform'd there was no room to expect, but unfeignedly to look up to God with my whole soul, and to cry for pardon in the name of Jesus Christ. He back'd his discourses with proper quotations of Scripture, encouraging the greatest sinner to repent, and turn from their evil way, and when he had done, he kneel'd down and pray'd with me.

It was now, that for the first time I felt any real signs of repentance; I now began to look back upon my past life with abhorrence, and having a kind of view into the other side of time, the things of life, as I believe they do with every body at such a time, began to look with a different aspect, and quite another shape, than they did before; the greatest and best things, the views of felicity, the joy, the griefs of life were quite other things; and I had nothing in my thoughts, but what was so infinitely superior to what I had known in life, that it appear'd to me to be the greatest stupidity in nature to lay any weight upon any thing tho' the most valuable in this world.

The word eternity represented itself with all its incomprehensible additions, and I had such extended notions of it, that I know not how to express them: among the rest, how vile, how gross, how absurd did every pleasant thing look? I mean, that we had counted pleasant before; especially when I reflected that these sordid trifles were the things for which we forfeited eternal felicity.

With these reflections came in, of meer course,[2] severe reproaches of my own mind for my wretched behaviour in my past life; that I had forfeited all hope of any happiness in the eternity that I was

---

1 A writ authorizing the execution of those listed.
2 Inevitably, entirely naturally.

just going to enter into, and on the contrary was entitul'd to all that was miserable, or had been conceiv'd of misery; and all this with the frightful addition of its being also eternal.

I am not capable of reading lectures of instruction to any body, but I relate this in the very manner in which things then appear'd to me, as far as I am able; but infinitely short of the lively impressions which they made on my soul at that time; indeed those impressions are not to be explain'd by words, or if they are, I am not mistress of words enough to express them; it must be the work of every sober reader to make just reflections on them, as their own circumstances may direct; and without question, this is what every one at sometime or other may feel something of; I mean a clearer sight into things to come, than they had here, and a dark view of their own concern in them.

But I go back to my own case; the minister press'd me to tell him, as far as I thought convenient, in what state I found myself as to the sight I had of things beyond life; he told me he did not come as Ordinary of the place, whose business it is to extort confessions from prisoners,[1] for private ends, or for the farther detecting of other offenders; that his business was to move me to such freedom of discourse as might serve to disburthen my own mind, and furnish him to administer comfort to me as far as was in his power; and assur'd me, that whatever I said to him should remain with him, and be as much a secret as if it was known only to God and myself; and that he desir'd to know nothing of me, but as above, to qualifie him to apply proper advice and assistance to me, and to pray to God for me.

This honest friendly way of treating me, unlock'd all the sluces of my passions: he broke into my very soul by it; and I unravell'd all the wickedness of my life to him: in a word, I gave him an abridgement of this whole history; I gave him the picture of my conduct for 50 years in miniature.

I hid nothing from him, and he in return exhorted me to a sincere repentance, explain'd to me what he meant by repentance, and then drew out such a scheme of infinite mercy, proclaim'd from Heaven to sinners of the greatest magnitude, that he left me nothing to say, that look'd like despair or doubting of being accepted, and in this condition he left me the first night.

---

1 "Newgate biographies" were popular in catchpenny form, frequently claiming to be the condemned man's own words as taken down by the Ordinary of Newgate. See Appendix B.2 and 6.

He visited me again the next morning, and went on with his method of explaining the terms of divine mercy, which according to him consisted of nothing more, or more difficult than that of being sincerely desirous of it, and willing to accept it; only a sincere regret for, and hatred of those things I had done, which render'd me so just an object of divine vengeance: I am not able to repeat the excellent discourses of this extraordinary man; 'tis all that I am able to do to say, that he reviv'd my heart, and brought me into such a condition, that I never knew any thing of in my life before: I was cover'd with shame and tears for things past, and yet had at the same time a secret surprizing joy at the prospect of being a true penitent, and obtaining the comfort of a penitent, I mean the hope of being forgiven; and so swift did thoughts circulate, and so high did the impressions they had made upon me run, that I thought I cou'd freely have gone out that minute to execution, without any uneasiness at all, casting my soul entirely into the arms of infinite mercy as a penitent.

The good gentleman was so mov'd also in my behalf, with a view of the influence, which he saw these things had on me, that he blessed God he had come to visit me, and resolv'd not to leave me till the last moment, that is not to leave visiting me.

It was no less than 12 days after our receiving sentence, before any were order'd for execution, and then upon a *Wednesday* the dead warrant, *as they call it*, came down, and I found my name was among them; a terrible blow this was to my new resolutions, indeed my heart sunk within me, and I swoon'd away twice, one after another, but spoke not a word: the good minister was sorely afflicted for me, and did what he could to comfort me with the same arguments, and the same moving eloquence that he did before, and left me not that evening so long as the prison-keepers would suffer him to stay in the prison, unless he wou'd be lock'd up with me all night, which he was not willing to be.

I wonder'd much that I did not see him all the next day, *it being but the day before the time appointed for execution*; and I was greatly discouraged, and dejected in my mind, and indeed almost sunk for want of that comfort, which he had so often, and with such success yeilded me on his former visits; I waited with great impatience, and under the greatest oppressions of spirits imaginable; till about four a-clock he came to my apartment, for I had obtain'd the favour by the help of money, nothing being to be done in that place without it, not to be kept in the condemn'd hole,[1] as they

---

1 Or "hold." See Appendix B.1 and 5.

call it, among the rest of the prisoners, who were to die, but to have a little dirty chamber to my self.

My heart leap'd within me for joy, when I heard his voice at the door even before I saw him; but let any one judge what kind of motion I found in my soul, when after having made a short excuse for his not coming, he shew'd me that his time had been employ'd on my account; that he had obtain'd a favourable report from the Recorder[1] to the Secretary of State in my particular case, and in short that he had brought me a reprieve.

He us'd all the caution that he was able in letting me know a thing, which it would have been a double cruelty to have conceal'd; and yet it was too much for me; for as grief had overset me before, so did joy overset now, and I fell into a much more dangerous swooning than I did at first, and it was not without a great difficulty that I was recover'd at all.

The good man having made a very Christian exhortation to me, not to let the joy of my reprieve, put the remembrance of my past sorrow out of my mind; and having told me that he must leave me, to go and enter the reprieve in the books, and show it to the sheriffs, stood up just before his going away, and in a very earnest manner pray'd to God for me, that my repentance might be made unfeign'd and sincere; and that my coming back as it were into life again, might not be a returning to the follies of life, which I had made such solemn resolutions to forsake, and to repent of them; I joyn'd heartily in the petition, and must needs say, I had deeper impressions upon my mind all that night, of the mercy of God in sparing my life; and a greater detestation of my past sins, from a sense of the goodness which I had tasted in this case, than I had in all my sorrow before.

This may be thought inconsistent in it self, and wide from the business of this book; particularly, I reflect that many of those who may be pleas'd and diverted with the relation of the wild and wicked part of my story, may not relish this, which is really the best part of my life, the most advantageous to myself, and the most instructive to others; such however will I hope allow me the liberty to make my story compleat: it would be a severe satyr on such,[2] to say they do not relish the repentance as much as they do the

---

1 Appointed by the Court of Aldermen of the City of London, the Recorder was a person with wide legal knowledge who, among other duties, acted as a chief judge of the Old Bailey.
2 Satire (formerly associated with *satyr* and so spelled). That is, it would be an unsparing criticism or exposure of such readers.

crime; and that they had rather the history were a compleat tragedy, as it was very likely to have been.

But I go on with my relation, the next morning there was a sad scene indeed in the prison; the first thing I was saluted with in the morning, was the tolling of the great bell at St. *Sepulchres*, as they call it, which usher'd in the day: as soon as it began to toll, a dismal groaning and crying was heard from the condemn'd hole, where there lay six poor souls, who were to be executed that day, some for one crime, some for another, and two of them for murther.

This was follow'd by a confus'd clamour in the house; among the several sorts of prisoners, expressing their awkward sorrows for the poor creatures that were to die, but in a manner extreamly differing one from another; some cried for them; some huzza'd,[1] and wish'd them a good journey; some damn'd and curst those that had brought them to it, that is meaning the evidence, or prosecutors; many pittying them; and some few, but very few praying for them.

There was hardly room for so much composure of mind, as was requir'd for me to bless the merciful Providence that had as it were snatch'd me out of the jaws of this destruction: I remained as it were dumb and silent, overcome with the sense of it, and not able to express what I had in my heart; for the passions on such occasions as these, are certainly so agitated as not to be able presently to regulate their own motions.

All the while the poor condemn'd creatures were preparing to their death, and the Ordinary *as they call him*, was busy with them, disposing them to submit to their sentence: I say all this while I was seiz'd with a fit of trembling, as much as I cou'd have been, if I had been in the same condition, as to be sure the day before I expected to be; I was so violently agitated by this surprising fit, that I shook as if it had been in the cold fit of an ague; so that I could not speak or look, but like one distracted: as soon as they were all put into the carts and gone, which however I had not courage enough to see, *I say*, as soon as they were gone, I fell into a fit of crying involuntarily, and without design, but as a meer distemper,[2] and yet so violent, and it held me so long, that I knew not what course to take, nor could I stop, or put a checque to it, no not with all the strength and courage I had.

---

1 Cheered. (*Huzza* is an earlier form of *hurrah* or *hurray*.)
2 An utter derangement.

This fit of crying held me near two hours and as I believe held me till they were all out of the world, and then a most humble penitent serious kind of joy succeeded; a real transport it was, or passion of joy, and thankfulness, but still unable to give vent to it by words, and in this I continued most part of the day.

In the evening the good minister visited me again, and then fell to his usual good discourses, he congratulated my having a space yet allow'd me for repentance, whereas the state of those six poor creatures was determin'd, and they were now pass'd the offers of salvation; he earnestly press'd me to retain the same sentiments of the things of life, that I had when I had a view of eternity; and at the end of all, told me I should not conclude that all was over, that a reprieve was not a pardon, that he could not yet answer for the effects of it; however, I had this mercy, that I had more time given me, and that it was my business to improve that time.

This discourse, tho' very seasonable, left a kind of sadness on my heart, as if I might expect the affair would have a tragical issue still, which however he had no certainty of, and I did not indeed at that time question him about it, he having said that he would do his utmost to bring it to a good end, and that he hoped he might, but he would not have me secure;[1] and the consequence prov'd that he had reason for what he said.

It was about a fortnight after this, that I had some just apprehensions that I should be included in the next dead warrant at the ensuing sessions; and it was not without great difficulty, and at last an humble petition for transportation,[2] that I avoided it, so ill was I beholding to fame, and so prevailing was the fatal report of being an old offender, tho' in that they did not do me strict justice, for I was not in the sense of the law an old offender, whatever I was in the eye of the judge; for I had never been before them in a judicial way before, so the judges could not charge me with being an old offender, but the Recorder was pleas'd to represent my case as he thought fit.

I had now a certainty of life indeed, but with the hard condi-

---

1 Feeling certain (of a pardon).
2 Until 1718 the penalty of exile or transportation, as ordered by the courts, was illegal. But a convicted felon could be pardoned upon the condition that he transport himself out of the country, the terms being set by the authorities. This was the device used for the transportation of convicts between 1655 and the introduction of a new law in 1718. It is estimated that by 1722 about sixty percent of the convicted male, clergyable felons and forty-six percent of the women were transported.

tions of being order'd for transportation, which indeed was a hard condition in it self, but not when comparatively considered; and therefore I shall make no comments upon the sentence, nor upon the choice I was put to; we shall all choose any thing rather than death, especially when 'tis attended with an uncomfortable prospect beyond it, which was my case.

The good minister whose interest, tho' *a stranger to me*, had obtain'd me the reprieve, mourn'd sincerely for this part; he was in hopes, *he said*, that I should have ended my days under the influence of good instruction, that I might not have forgot my former distresses, and that I should not have been turned loose again among such a wretched a crew as they generally are, who are thus sent abroad where, *as he said*, I must have more than ordinary secret assistance from the grace of God, if I did not turn as wicked again as ever.

I have not for a good while mentioned my governess, who had during most, if not all of this part been dangerously sick, and being in as near a view of death, by her disease, as I was by my sentence, was a very great penitent; I say, I have not mention'd her, nor indeed did I see her in all this time, but being now recovering, and just able to come abroad, she came to see me.

I told her my condition, and what a different flux and reflux of fears, and hopes I had been agitated with; I told her, what I had escap'd, and upon what terms, and she was present, when the minister express'd his fears of my relapsing into wickedness upon my falling into the wretch'd companies, that are generally transported: indeed I had a melancholly reflection upon it in my own mind, for I knew what a dreadful gang was always sent away together, and I said to my governess, that the good minister's fears were not without cause: Well, well, *says she*, but I hope you will not be tempted with such a horrid example as that, and as soon as the minister was gone, she told me, she would not have me discourag'd, for perhaps ways and means might be found out to dispose of me in a particular way, by my self, of which she would talk farther to me afterward.

I look'd earnestly at her, and I thought she look'd more chearful than she usually had done, and I entertain'd immediately a thousand notions of being deliver'd, but could not for my life imagin the methods, or think of one that was in the least feizible; but I was too much concerned in it, to let her go from me without explaining herself, which tho' she was very loth to do, yet my importunity prevail'd, and while I was still pressing, she answer'd me in few words, thus, Why, *you have money, have you not* ? Did you ever know one in your life that was transported, and had a hundred pound in his pocket, I'll warrant you child, *says she*.

I understood her presently, but told her I would leave all that to her, but I saw no room to hope for any thing, but a strict execution of the order, and as it was a severity that was esteem'd a mercy, there was no doubt but it would be strictly observ'd; she said no more, but this, *We will try what can be done*, and so we parted for that night.

I lay in the prison near fifteen weeks after this order for transportation was sign'd; what the reason of it was, I know not, but at the end of this time I was put on board of a ship in the *Thames*, and with me a gang of thirteen, as harden'd vile creatures as ever *Newgate* produc'd in my time; and it would really well take up a history longer than mine to describe the degrees of impudence, and audacious villany that those thirteen were arriv'd to; and the manner of their behaviour in the voyage; of which I have a very diverting account by me, which the captain of the ship, who carried them over gave me the minutes of, and which he caus'd his mate to write down at large.

It may perhaps be thought trifling to enter here into a relation of all the little incidents which attended me in this interval of my circumstances; I mean between the final order for my transportation, and the time of my going on board the ship, and I am too near the end of my story, to allow room for it, but something relating to me, *and my Lancashire husband*, I must not omit.

He had, *as I have observ'd already* been carried from the master's side of the ordinary prison, into the press-yard,[1] with three of his comrades, for they found another to add to them after some time; here for what reason I knew not, they were kept in custody without being brought to tryal almost three months, it seems they found means to bribe or buy off some of those who were expected to come in against them, and they wanted evidence for some time to convict them: after some puzzle on this account at first, they made a shift to get proof enough against two of them, to carry them off;[2] but the other two, of which my *Lancashire* husband was one, lay still in suspence: they had I think one positive evidence against each of them; but the law strictly obliging them to have

---

1 Newgate was divided into three sections, the most desirable for prisoners being the press-yard. For further information, see Appendix B.1.
2 That is, to convict and hang them.

two witnesses,[1] they cou'd make nothing of it; yet it seems they were resolv'd not to part with the men neither, not doubting but a farther evidence would at last come in; and in order to this, I think publication was made, that such prisoners being taken, any one that had been robb'd by them might come to the prison and see them.

I took this opportunity to satisfy my curiosity, pretending that I had been robb'd in the *Dunstable* coach, and that I would go to see the two highway-men; but when I came into the press-yard, I so disguis'd myself, and muffled my face up so, that he cou'd see little of me, and consequently knew nothing of who I was, and when I came back, I said publickly that I knew them very well.

Immediately it was rumour'd all over the prison, that *Moll Flanders* would turn evidence against one of the highway men, and that I was to come off by it from the sentence of transportation.

They heard of it, and immediately my husband desir'd to see this Mrs. *Flanders* that knew him so well, and was to be an evidence against him, and accordingly, I had leave given to go to him. I dress'd myself up as well as the best cloths that I suffer'd myself ever to appear in there, would allow me, and went to the press-yard, but had for some time a hood over my face; he said little to me at first, but ask'd me if I knew him; I told him, Yes, very well; but as I conceal'd my face, so I counterfeited my voice, that he had not the least guess at who I was: he ask'd me where I had seen him, I told him between *Dunstable* and *Brickhill*, but turning to the keeper that stood by, I ask'd if I might not be admitted to talk with him alone, he said, Yes, yes, as much as I pleas'd, and so very civilly withdrew.

As soon as he was gone, and I had shut the door, I threw off my hood, and bursting out into tears, *My dear*, says I, *do you not know me*? He turn'd pale and stood speechless, like one thunder struck, and not able to conquer the surprize, said no more but this, *Let me sit down*; and sitting down by a table, he laid his elbow upon the table, and leaning his head on his hand, fix'd his eyes on the ground as one stupid: I cry'd so vehemently on the other hand, that it was a good while e'er I could speak any more; but after I had given some vent to my passion by tears, I repeated the same

---

1 However, according to Giles Jacob, *A New Law Dictionary* (1729, under "Evidence"), "The Testimony of one single Evidence is sufficient for the King in all Causes, except for Treason; where there must be two Witnesses to the same overt Act ... "

words: MY DEAR, *do you not know me?* at which he answer'd YES, and said no more a good while.

After some time continuing in the surprize, *as above,* he cast up his eyes towards me and said, *How could you be so cruel?* I did not readily understand what he meant; and I answer'd, How can you call me cruel? What have I been cruel to you in? *To come to me,* says he, *in such a place as this, is it not to insult me? I have not robb'd* you, *at least not on* the highway?

I perceiv'd by this, that he knew nothing of the miserable circumstances I was in, and thought that having got some intelligence of his being there, I had come to upbraid him with his leaving me; but I had too much to say to him to be affronted, and told him in few words, that I was far from coming to insult him, but at best I came to condole mutually, that he would be easily satisfy'd, that I had no such view, when I should tell him that *my condition was worse than his, and that many ways*: he look'd a little concern'd at the general expression of my condition being worse than his; but with a kind of a smile, look'd a little wildly, and said, How can that be? When you see me feter'd, and in *Newgate*, and two of my companions executed already; can you say your condition is worse than mine?

Come my dear, *says I,* we have a long peice of work to do, if I should be to relate, or you to hear my unfortunate history; but if you are dispos'd to hear it, you will soon conclude with me that my condition is worse than yours: How is that possible, *says he again,* when I expect to be cast for my life the very next sessions? Yes *says I,* 'tis very possible when I shall tell you that I have been cast for my life three sessions ago, and am under sentence of death, is not my case worse than yours?

Then indeed he stood silent again, like one struck dumb, and after a little while he starts up, Unhappy couple! *says he,* how can this be possible? I took him by the hand, Come MY DEAR, *said I,* sit down, and let us compare our sorrows: I am a prisoner in this very house, and in a much worse circumstance than you, and you will be satisfy'd I do not come to insult you, when I tell you the particulars; and with this we sat down together, and I told him so much of my story as I thought was convenient, bringing it at last to my being reduc'd to great poverty, and representing myself as fallen into some company that led me to relieve my distresses by a way that I had been utterly unacquainted with, and that they making an attempt at a tradesman's house I was seiz'd upon, for having been but just at the door, the maid-servant pulling me in; that I neither had broke any lock, or taken any thing away, and that notwithstanding that I was brought in guilty, and sentenc'd to die; but that the judges having been made sensible of the hardship of my circumstances, had obtain'd leave to remit the sentence upon my consenting to be transported.

I told him I far'd the worse for being taken in the prison for one *Moll Flanders*, who was a famous successful thief, that all of them had heard of, but none of them had ever seen, but that *as he knew well* was none of my name; but I plac'd all to the account of my ill fortune, and that under this name I was dealt with as an old offender, tho' this was the first thing they had ever known of me. I gave him a long particular of things that had befallen me, since I saw him; but I told him that I had seen him since he might think I had, and then gave him an account how I had seen him at *Brickhill*; how furiously he was pursued, and how by giving an account that I knew him, and that he was a very honest gentleman, one Mr. ——— the *heu and cry* was stopp'd, and the high constable went back again.

He listen'd most attentively to all my story, and smil'd at most of the particulars, being all of them petty matters, and infinitely below what he had been at the head of; but when I came to the story of little *Brickill*, he was surpriz'd, *And was it you my dear*, said he, *that gave the check to the mob that was at our heels there, at Brickill*:Yes *said I*, it was I indeed, and then I told him the particulars which I had observ'd of him there. *Why then*, said he, *it was you that sav'd my life at that time*, and I am glad I owe my life to you, for I will pay the debt to you now, and I'll deliver you from the present condition you are in, or I will die in the attempt.

I told him by no means; it was a risque too great, not worth his running the hazard of, and for a life not worth his saving; 'twas no matter for that he said, it was a life worth all the world to him; a life that had given him a new life; for *says he*, I was never in real danger of being taken, but that time; till the last minute when I was taken: indeed *he told* me his danger then lay in his believing he had not been pursued that way; for they had gone off from *Hockly*[1] quite another way, and had come over the enclos'd country into *Brickill*, not by the road and were sure they had not been seen by any body.

Here he gave a long history of his life, which indeed would make a very strange history, and be infinitely diverting. He told me he took to the road about twelve year before he marry'd me; that

---

1 Hockliffe, Bedfordshire, commonly known at this time as Hockley in the Hole.

the woman which call'd him brother, was not really his sister, or any kin to him; but one that belong'd to their gang, and who keeping correspondence with them, liv'd always in town, having good store of acquaintance, that she gave them a perfect intelligence of persons going out of town, and that they had made several good booties by her correspondence; that she thought she had fix'd a fortune for him, when she brought me to him, but happen'd to be disappointed, which he really could not blame her for: that, if it had been his good luck, that I had had the estate, which she was inform'd I had, he had resolv'd to leave off the road, and live a retired sober life, but never to appear in publick till some general pardon had been pass'd, or till he could, for money have got his name into some particular pardon, that so he might have been perfectly easy, but that as it had proved otherwise he was oblig'd to put off his equipage, and take up the old trade again.

He gave me a long account of some of his adventures, and particularly one, when he robb'd the *West Chester* coaches, near *Lichfield*, when he got a very great booty; and after that, how he robb'd five grasiers,[1] in the *west*, going to *Burford* Fair in *Wiltshire*[2] to buy sheep; he told me he got so much money on those two occasions, that if he had known where to have found me, he would certainly have embrac'd my proposal of going with me to *Virginia*; or to have settled in a plantation, on some other parts of the *English* colonies in *America*.

He told me he wrote two or three letters to me, directed according to my order, but heard nothing from me: this I indeed knew to be true, but the letters coming to my hand in the time of my latter husband, I could do nothing in it, and therefore chose to give no answer, that so he might rather believe they had miscarried.

Being thus disappointed, *he said*, he carried on the old trade ever since, tho' when he had gotten so much money, *he said*, he did not run such desperate risques as he did before; then he gave me some account of several hard and desperate encounters which he had with gentlemen on the road, who parted too hardly[3] with their money; and shew'd me some wounds he had receiv'd, and he had one or two very terrible wounds indeed, as particularly one by a pistol bullet which broke his arm; and another with a sword, which ran him quite thro' the body, but that missing his vitals he was

---

1 Raisers of cattle, particularly those who fatten them for the market (obsolete form of *graziers*).
2 Burford is in Oxfordshire, not Wiltshire.
3 Reluctantly, unwillingly.

cur'd again; one of his comrades having kept with him so faithfully, and so friendly, as that he assisted him in riding near 80 miles
before his arm was set, and then got a surgeon in a considerable
city, remote from that place where it was done, pretending they
were gentlemen traveling towards *Carlisle*, and that they had been
attack'd on the road by highway-men, and that one of them had
shot him into the arm, and broke the bone.

This *he said*, his friend manag'd so well, that they were not suspected at all, but lay still till he was perfectly cur'd: he gave me so
many distinct accounts of his adventures, at it is with great reluctance, that I decline the relating them; but I consider that this is
my own story, not his.

I then enquir'd into the circumstances of his present case at
that time, and what it was he expected when he came to be try'd;
he told me that they had no evidence against him, or but very little; for that of three roberries, which they were all charg'd with, it
was his good fortune, that he was but in one of them, and that
there was but one witness to be had for that fact, which was not
sufficient; but that it was expected some others would come in
against him; that he thought indeed, when he first see me, that I
had been one that came of that errand; but that if no body came
in against him, he hop'd he should be clear'd; that he had had
some intimation, that if he would submit to transport himself, he
might be admitted to it without a tryal, but that he could not think
of it with any temper,[1] and thought he could much easier submit
to be hang'd.[2]

I blam'd him for that, and told him I blam'd him on two
accounts; first because, if he was transported, there might be an
hundred ways for him that was a gentleman, and a bold enterprizing man to find his way back again, and perhaps some ways
and means to come back before he went. He smil'd at that part,
and said he should like the last the best of the two, for he had a
kind of horror upon his mind at his being sent over to the plantations as *Romans* sent condemn'd slaves to work in the mines; that
he thought the passage into another state, let it be what it would,
much more tolerable at the gallows, and that this was the general
notion of all the gentlemen, who were driven by the exigence of
their fortunes to take the road; that at the place of execution there

---

1 Calmness, patience.
2 In *Mercurius Politicus* (December 1716), Defoe speaks of a man who
  chose rather to be hanged than transported, claiming "that he was bred
  a Gentleman, and could not Labour."

was at least an end of all the miseries of the present state, and as for what was to follow, a man was in his opinion, as likely to repent sincerely in the last fortnight of his life under the pressures and agonies of a jayl, and the condemn'd hole, as he would ever be in the woods and wildernesses of *America*; that servitude and hard labour were things gentlemen could never stoop to, that it was but the way to force them to be their own executioners afterwards, which was much worse, and that therefore he could not have any patience when he did but think of being transported.

I used the utmost of my endeavour to perswade him, and joyn'd that known womans rhetorick to it, I mean that of tears: I told him the infamy of a publick execution was certainly a greater pressure upon the spirits of a gentleman, than any of the mortifications that he could meet with abroad could be; that he had at least in the other a chance for his life, whereas here he had none at all; that it was the easiest thing in the world for him to manage the captain of the ship, who were generally speaking, men of good humour, and some gallantry; and a small matter of conduct,[1] especially if there was any money to be had, would make way for him to buy himself off, when he came to *Virginia*.

He look'd wishfully at me, and I thought I guess'd at what he meant, *that is to say*, that he had no money, but I was mistaken, his meaning was another way; *You hinted just now*, my dear said he, *that there might be a way of coming back before I went, by which I understood you, that it might be possible to buy it off here; I had rather give 200 l. to prevent going, than 100 l. to be set at liberty when I came there.* That is my dear, said I, *because you do not know the place so well as I do:* That may be, said he, *and yet I believe as well as you know it, you would do the same unless it is because,* as you told me, *you have a mother there.*

I told him, as to my mother, it was next to impossible, but that she must be dead many years before; and as for any other relations that I might have there, I knew them not now: that since the misfortunes I had been under, had reduc'd me to the condition I had been in for some years, I had not kept up any correspondence with them, and that he would easily believe, I should find but a cold reception from them, if I should be put to make my first visit in the condition of a transported felon; that therefore if I went thither, I resolv'd not to see them; but that I had many views in going there, if it should be my fate, which took off all the uneasy part of it; and if he found himself oblig'd to go also, I should easily

---

1 Management.

instruct him how to manage himself, so as never to go a servant at all, especially since I found he was not destitute of money, which was the only friend in such a condition.

He smil'd, and said, he did not tell me he had money; I took him up short, and told him I hop'd he did not understand by my speaking, that I should expect any supply from him if he had money; that on the other hand, tho' I had not a great deal, yet I did not want, and while I had any I would rather add to him, than weaken him in that article, seeing what ever he had, I knew in the case of transportation he would have occasion of it all.

He express'd himself in a most tender manner upon that head: he told me what money he had was not a great deal, but that he would never hide any of it from me if I wanted it; and that he assur'd me he did not speak with any such apprehensions; that he was only intent upon what I had hinted to him before he went; that here he knew what to do with himself, but there he should be the most ignorant helpless wretch alive.

I told him he frighted and terify'd himself with that which had no terror in it; that if he had money, as I was glad to hear he had, he might not only avoid the servitude, suppos'd to be the consequence of transportation; but begin the world upon a new foundation, and that such a one as he cou'd not fail of success in, with but the common application usual in such cases; that he could not but call to mind, that it was what I had recommended to him many years before, and had propos'd it for our mutual subsistence, and restoring our fortunes in the world; and I would tell him now, that to convince him both of the certainty of it, and of my being fully acquainted with the method, and also fully satisfy'd in the probability of success, he should first see me deliver myself from the necessity of going over at all, and then that I would go with him freely, and of my own choice, and perhaps carry enough with me to satisfy him that I did not offer it, for want of being able to live without assistance from him; but that I thought our mutual misfortunes had been such, as were sufficient to reconcile us both to quitting this part of the world, and living where no body could upbraid us with what was past, or we be in any dread of a prison; and without the agonies of a condemn'd hole to drive us to it, where we should look back on all our past disasters with infinite satisfaction, when we should consider that our enemies should entirely forget us, and that we should live as new people in a new world, no body having any thing to say to us, or we to them.

I press'd this home to him with so many arguments, and answer'd all his own passionate objections so effectually, that he embrac'd me, and told me, I treated him with such a sincerity, and affection as overcame him; that he would take my advice, and would strive to submit to his fate, in hope of having the comfort of my assistance, and of so faithful a counsellor, and such a companion in his misery; but still he put me in mind of what I had mention'd before; namely, that there might be some way to get off, before he went, and that it might be possible to avoid going at all, which he said would be much better. I told him he should see, and be fully satisfy'd that I would do my utmost in that part too, and if it did not succeed, yet that I would make good the rest.

We parted after this long conference, with such testimonies of kindness and affection as I thought were equal, if not superior to that at our parting at *Dunstable*; and now I saw more plainly than before, the reason why he declin'd coming at that time any farther with me toward *London* than *Dunstable*; and why when we parted there, he told me it was not convenient for him to come part of the way to *London* to bring me going,[1] as he would otherwise have done: I have observ'd that the account of his life, would have made a much more pleasing history, than this of mine; and indeed nothing in it, was more strange than this part, (*viz.*) that he had carried on that desperate trade full five and twenty year, and had never been taken, the success he had met with, had been so very uncommon, and such, that sometimes he had liv'd handsomely and retir'd, in one place for a year or two at a time, keeping himself and a man-servant to wait on him, and has often sat in the coffee-houses, and heard the very people who he had robb'd give accounts of their being robb'd, and of the places and circumstances, so that he cou'd easily remember that it was the same.

In this manner it seems he liv'd near *Leverpool* at the time, he unluckily married me for a fortune: had I been the fortune he expected, I verily believe, as he said, that he would have taken up[2] and liv'd honestly all his days.

He had with the rest of his misfortunes the good luck not to be actually upon the spot, when the robbery was done, which he was committed for; and so none of the persons robb'd cou'd swear to him, or had any thing to charge upon him; but it seems as he was taken, with the gang, one hard-mouth'd countryman swore home to him; and they were like to have others come in according to the publication they had made, so that they expect-

1 To accompany me.
2 Started afresh, begun again.

ed more evidence against him, and for that reason he was kept in hold.[1]

However, the offer which was made to him of admitting him to transportation was made, as I understood upon the intercession of some great person who press'd him hard to accept of it before a tryal; and indeed as he knew there were several that might come in against him, I thought his friend was in the right, and I lay at him night and day to delay it no longer.

At last, with much difficulty he gave his consent, and as he was not therefore admitted to transportation in court, and on his petition as I was, so he found himself under a difficulty to avoid embarking himself as I had said he might have done; his great friend, who was his intercessor for the favour of that grant, having given security for him that he should transport himself, and not return within the term.[2]

This hardship broke all my measures,[3] for the steps I took afterwards for my own deliverance, were hereby render'd wholly ineffectual, unless I would abandon him, and leave him to go to *America* by himself; than which he protested he would much rather venture,[4] altho' he were certain to go directly to the gallows.

I must now return to my own case, the time of my being transported according to my sentence was near at hand; my governess who continu'd my fast friend, had try'd to obtain a pardon, but it could not be done unless with an expence too heavy for my purse, considering that to be left naked and empty, unless I had resolv'd to return to my old trade again, had been worse than my transportation, because there I knew I could live, here I could not. The good minister stood very hard on another account to prevent my being transported also; but he was answer'd, that indeed my life had been given me at his first solicitations, and therefore he ought to ask no more; he was sensibly griev'd at my going, because, *as he said*, he fear'd I should lose the good impressions, which a prospect of death had at first made on me, and which were since encreas'd by his instructions, and the pious gentleman was exceedingly concern'd about me on that account.

---

1 Custody.
2 Security was often required as surety against the return of a convict until his term of transportation (usually seven years) had expired. The husband's penalty, however, proves to be more severe than this, as is revealed below, pp. 307-09.
3 That is, her plans to escape transportation.
4 That is, he would rather run the risk of a trial or even an escape than be transported.

On the other hand, I really was not so sollicitous about it, as I was before, but I industriously conceal'd my reasons for it from the minister, and to the last he did not know, but that I went with the utmost reluctance and affliction.

It was in the month of *February* that I was with seven other convicts, *as they call'd us*, deliver'd to a merchant that traded to *Virginia*, on board a ship, riding, as they call'd it, in *Deptford* Reach: the officer of the prison deliver'd us on board, and the master of the vessel gave a discharge for us.

We were for that night clapt under hatches, and kept so close, that I thought I should have been suffocated for want of air, and the next morning the ship weigh'd, and fell down the river[1] to a place they call *Bugby's Hole*,[2] which was done, as they told us by the agreement of the merchant, that all opportunity of escape should be taken from us: however when the ship came thither, and cast anchor, we were allow'd more liberty, and particularly were permitted to come upon the deck, but not upon the quarter-deck, that being kept particularly for the captain, and for passengers.

When by the noise of the men over my head, and the motion of the ship, I perceiv'd that they were under sail, I was at first greatly surpriz'd, fearing we should go away directly, and that our friends would not be admitted to see us any more; but I was easy soon after when I found they had come to an anchor again, and soon after that we had notice given by some of the men where we were, that the next morning we should have the liberty to come upon deck, and to have our friends come and see us if we had any.

All that night I lay upon the hard boards of the deck, as the other prisoners did, but we had afterwards the liberty of little cabins for such of us as had any bedding to lay in them; and room to stow any box or trunk for cloths, and linnen, if we had it, (which might well be put in) for some of them had neither shirt or shift, or a rag of linnen or woollen, but what was on their backs, or a farthing of money to help themselves; and yet I did not find but they far'd well enough in the ship, especially the women, who got money of the seamen for washing their cloths sufficient to purchase any common things that they wanted.

When the next morning we had the liberty to come upon the deck, I ask'd one of the officers of the ship, whether I might not have the liberty to send a letter on shore to let my friends know

---

1 Weighed anchor and moved downstream.
2 A place on the Thames between Blackwall and Woolwich, near the mouth of the River Lea.

where the ship lay, and to get some necessary things sent to me. This was it seems the boatswain, a very civil courteous sort of man, who told me I should have that, or any other liberty that I desir'd, that he could allow me with safety; I told him I desir'd no other; and he answer'd that the ships boat would go up to *London* the next tide, and he would order my letter to be carried.

Accordingly when the boat went off, the boatswain came to me, and told me the boat was going off, and that he went in it himself, and ask'd me if my letter was ready, he would take care of it; I had prepared myself you may be sure, pen, ink and paper beforehand, and I had gotten a letter ready directed to my governess, and enclos'd another for my fellow prisoner, which however I did not let her know was my husband, not to the last; in that to my governess, I let her know where the ship lay, and press'd her earnestly to send me what things I knew she had got ready for me, for my voyage.

When I gave the boatswain the letter, I gave him a shilling with it, which I told him was for the charge of a messenger or porter, which I entreated him to send with the letter, as soon as he came on shore, that if possible I might have an answer brought back by the same hand, that I might know what was become of my things, For SIR, *says I*, if the ship should go away before I have them on board I am undone.

I took care when I gave him the shilling, to let him see that I had a little better furniture[1] about me, than the ordinary prisoners, for he saw that I had a purse, and in it a pretty deal of money, and I found that the very sight of it, immediately furnish'd me with very different treatment from what I should otherwise have met with in the ship; for tho' he was very courteous indeed before, in a kind of natural compassion to me, as a woman in distress; yet he was more than ordinarily so, afterwards, and procur'd me to be better treated in the ship, than, *I say*, I might otherwise have been; as shall appear in its place.

He very honestly had my letter deliver'd to my governess own hands, and brought me back an answer from her in writing; and when he gave me the answer, gave me the shilling again, *There*, says he, there's your shilling again too, for I deliver'd the letter my self; I could not tell what to say, I was so surpris'd at the thing; but after some pause, *I said*, Sir you are too kind, it had been but reasonable that you had paid yourself coach hire then.

---

1 Bedclothes, linen, etc.

No, no, *says he*, I am over paid: what is the gentlewoman, your sister?

No, sir, *said I*, she is no relation to me, but she is a dear friend, and all the friends I have in the world: Well, *says he*, there are few such friends in the world: why she cryes after you like a child, Ay, *says I again*, she would give a hundred pound, I believe, to deliver me from this dreadful condition I am in.

Would she so? *says he*, for half the money I believe, I cou'd put you in a way how to deliver yourself, but this he spoke softly that no body cou'd hear.

Alas! sir, *said I*, but then that must be such a deliverance as if I should be taken again, would cost me my life; Nay, *said he*, if you were once out of the ship you must look to yourself afterwards, that I can say nothing to; so we drop'd the discourse for that time.

In the mean time my governess faithful to the last moment, convey'd my letter to the prison to my husband, and got an answer to it, and the next day came down herself to the ship, bringing me in the first place a *sea-bed* as they call it, and all its furniture, such as was convenient, but not to let the people think it was extraordinary; she brought with her a *sea-chest*, that is a chest, such as are made for seamen with all the conveniencies in it, and fill'd with every thing almost that I could want; and in one of the corners of the chest, where there was a private drawer was my bank of money, *that is to say*, so much of it as I had resolv'd to carry with me; for I order'd a part of my stock to be left behind me, to be sent afterwards in such goods as I should want when I came to settle; for money in that country is not of much use where all things are bought for tobacco,[1] much more is it a great loss to carry it from hence.

But my case was particular; it was by no means proper to me to go thither without money or goods, and for a poor convict that was to be sold as soon as I came on shore, to carry with me a cargo of goods would be to have notice taken of it, and perhaps to have them seiz'd by the publick; so I took part of my stock with me thus, and left the other part with my governess.

My governess brought me a great many other things, but it was not proper for me to look too well provided in the ship, at least, till

---

1 While money was used as petty cash in America, tobacco was certainly the main standard for trade. This is borne out by contemporary accounts, for example Robert Beverley's *The History and Present State of Virginia* (1705), ed. Louis B. Wright (Chapel Hill: U of North Carolina P, 1947) 314. Also see Appendix A.4.

I knew what kind of a captain we should have. When she came into the ship, I thought she would have died indeed; her heart sunk at the sight of me, and at the thoughts of parting with me in that condition, and she cry'd so intolerably, I cou'd not for a long time have any talk with her.

I took that time to read my fellow prisoners letter, which however greatly perplex'd me; he told me he was determin'd to go, but found it would be impossible for him to be discharg'd time enough for going in the same ship, and which was more than all, he began to question whether they would give him leave to go in what ship he pleas'd, tho' he did voluntarily transport himself; but that they would see him put on board such a ship as they should direct, and that he would be charg'd upon the captain as other convict prisoners were; so that he began to be in dispair of seeing me till he came to *Virginia*, which made him almost desperate; seeing that on the other hand, if I should not be there, if any accident of the sea, or of mortality should take me away, he should be the most undone creature there in the world.

This was very perplexing, and I knew not what course to take; I told my governess the story of the boatswain, and she was mighty eager with me to treat with him; but I had no mind to it, till I heard whether my husband, or fellow prisoner, *so she call'd him*, cou'd be at liberty to go with me or no; at last I was forc'd to let her into the whole matter, except only, that of his being my husband; I told her I had made a positive bargain or agreement with him to go, if he could get the liberty of going in the same ship, and that I found he had money.

Then I read a long lecture to her of what I propos'd to do when we came there, how we could plant, settle, and in short, grow rich without any more adventures, and as a great secret, I told her that we were to marry as soon as he came on board.

She soon agreed chearfully to my going, when she heard this, and she made it her business from that time to get him out of the prison in time, so that he might go in the same ship with me, which at last was brought to pass tho' with great difficulty, and not without all the forms of a transported prisoner *convict*, which he really was not yet, for he had not been try'd, and which was a great mortification to him. As our fate was now determin'd, and we were both on board, actually bound to *Virginia*, in the despicable quality of transported convicts destin'd to be sold for slaves, I for five year, and he under bonds and security not to return to *England* any more, as long as he liv'd; he was very much dejected and cast down; the mortification of being brought on board as he was, like a prisoner, piqu'd him very much, since it was first told him he should transport himself, and so that he might go as a gentleman at liberty; it is true he was not order'd to be sold when he came there, as we were, and for that reason he was oblig'd to pay for his passage to the captain, which we were not; as to the rest, he was as much at a loss as a child what to do with himself, or with what he had, but by directions.[1]

Our first business was to compare our stock: he was very honest to me, and told me his stock was pretty good when he came into the prison, but the living there as he did in a figure like a gentleman, *and which was ten times as much*, the making of friends, and soliciting his case, had been very expensive; and in a word, all his stock that he had left was an hundred and eight pounds, which he had about him all in gold.

I gave him an account of my stock as faithfully, that is to say of what I had taken to carry with me, for I was resolv'd what ever should happen, to keep what I had left with my governess, in reserve; that in case I should die, what I had with me was enough to give him, and that which was left in my governess hands would be her own, which she had well deserv'd of me indeed.

My stock which I had with me was two hundred forty six pounds, some odd shillings; so that we had three hundred and fifty four pound between us, but a worse gotten estate was scarce ever put together to begin the world with.

Our greatest misfortune as to our stock, was that it was all in money, which every one knows is an unprofitable cargoe to be carryed to the plantations; I believe his was really all he had left in the world, as he told me it was; but I who had between seven and eight hundred pounds in bank when this disaster befel me, and who had one of the faithfulest friends in the world to manage it for me, considering she was a woman of no manner of religious principles, had still three hundred pounds left in her hand, which I reserv'd, as above, besides some very valuable things, as particularly two gold watches, some small peices of plate, and some rings; all stolen goods; the plate, rings and watches were put up in my chest with the money, and with this fortune, and in the sixty first year of my age, I launch'd out into a new world, as I may call it, in the condition (as to what appear'd) only of a poor nak'd convict, order'd to be transported in respite from the gallows; my cloaths were

---

1 At this point the second edition inserts two paragraphs now on the next page, beginning "In this condition … " and ending "… *and I'll always take your advice.*"

poor and mean, but not ragged or dirty, and none knew in the whole ship that I had any thing of value about me.

However, as I had a great many very good cloaths, and linnen in abundance, which I had order'd to be pack'd up in two great boxes, I had them shipp'd on board, not as my goods, but as consign'd to my real name in *Virginia*; and had the bills of loading sign'd by a captain in my pocket; and in these boxes was my plate and watches, and every thing of value except my money, which I kept by itself in a private drawer in my chest, which cou'd not be found, or open'd if found, without splitting the chest to peices.

In this condition I lay for three weeks in the ship, not knowing whether I should have my husband with me or no; and therefore not resolving how, or in what manner to receive the honest boatswain's proposal, which indeed he thought a little strange at first.

At the end of this time, behold my husband came on board; he look'd with a dejected angry countenance, his great heart was swell'd with rage and disdain; to be drag'd along with[1] three keepers of *Newgate*, and put on board like a convict, when he had not so much as been brought to a tryal; he made loud complaints of it by his friends, for it seems he had some interest;[2] but his friends got some checque in their application, and were told he had had *favour enough*, and that they had receiv'd such an account of him since the last grant of his transportation, that he ought to think himself very well treated that he was not prosecuted a new. This answer quieted him at once, for he knew too much what might have happen'd, and what he had room to expect; and now he saw the goodness of the advice to him, which prevail'd with him to accept of the offer of a voluntary transportation, and after his chagrine at these hell hounds, *as he call'd them*, was a little over; he look'd a little compos'd, began to be chearful, and as I was telling him how glad I was to have him once more out of their hands, took me in his arms, and acknowledg'd with great tenderness, that I had given him the best advice possible, *My dear*, says he, *thou hast twice sav'd my life, from hence forward it shall be all employ'd for you, and I'll always take your advice.*

The ship began now to fill, several passengers came on board, who were embark'd on no criminal account, and these had accommodations assign'd them in the great cabbin, and other parts of

---

1 By.
2 Influence due to personal connections.

the ship, whereas we *as convicts* were thrust down below, I know not where; but when my husband came on board, I spoke to the boatswain, who had so early given me hints of his friendship in carrying my letter; I told him he had befriended me in many things, and I had not made any suitable return to him, and with that I put a guinea into his hands; I told him that my husband was now come on board, that tho' we were both under the present misfortunes, yet we had been persons of a differing character from the wretched crew that we came with, and desir'd to know of him, whether the captain might not be mov'd, to admit us to some conveniences in the ship, for which we would make him what satisfaction he pleas'd, and that we would gratifie him for his pains in procuring this for us. He took the guinea as I cou'd see with great satisfaction, and assur'd me of his assistance.

Then he told us, he did not doubt but that the captain who was one of the best humour'd gentlemen in the world, would be easily brought to accommodate us, as well as we cou'd desire, and to make me easie, told me he would go up the next tide on purpose to speak to the captain about it. The next morning happening to sleep a little longer than ordinary, when I got up, and began to look abroad, I saw the boatswain among the men in his ordinary business; I was a little melancholly at seeing him there, and going forwards to speak to him, he saw me, and came towards me, but not giving him time to speak first, I said smiling, *I doubt,*[1] *sir, you have forgot us,* for I see you are very busy; he return'd presently,[2] Come along with me, and you shall see, so he took me into the great cabbin, and there sat a good sort of a gentlemanly man for a seaman writing, and with a great many papers before him.

Here says the boatswain to him that was a writing, is the gentlewoman that the captain spoke to you of, and turning to me, he said, I have been so far from forgetting your business, that I have been up at the captain's house, and have represented faithfully to the captain what you said, relating to your being furnished with better conveniences for your self, and your husband; and the captain has sent this gentleman, who is mate of the ship down with me, on purpose to show you every thing, and to accommodate you fully to your content, and bid me assure you that you shall not be treated like what you were at first expected to be, but with the same respect as other passengers are treated.

---

1 Fear.
2 Replied immediately.

The mate then spoke to me, and not giving me time to thank the boatswain for his kindness confirm'd what the boatswain had said, and added that it was the captain's delight to show himself kind, and charitable, especially, to those that were under any misfortunes, and with that he shew'd me several cabbins built up, some in the great cabbin, and some partition'd off, out of the steerage,[1] but opening into the great cabbin on purpose for the accommodation of passengers, and gave me leave to choose where I would; however I chose a cabbin, which open'd into the steerage, in which was very good conveniencies to set our chest, and boxes, and a table to eat on.

The mate then told me, that the boatswain had given so good a character of me, and of my husband, as to our civil behaviour, that he had orders to tell me, we should eat with him, if we thought fit, during the whole voyage on the common terms of passengers; that we might lay in some fresh provisions, if we pleas'd; or if not, he should lay in his usual store, and we should have share with him: this was very reviving news to me, after so many hardships, and afflictions as I had gone thro' of late; I thank'd him, and told him, the captain should make his own terms with us, and ask'd him leave to go and tell my husband of it who was not very well, and was not yet out of his cabbin: accordingly I went, and my husband whose spirits were still so much sunk with the indignity (as he understood it) offered him, that he was scarce yet himself, was so reviv'd with the account I gave him of the reception we were like to have in the ship, that he was quite another man, and new vigour and courage appear'd in his very countenance; so true is it, that the greatest of spirits, when overwhelm'd by their afflictions, are subject to the greatest dejections, and are the most apt to despair and give themselves up.

After some little pause to recover himself, my husband come up with me, and gave the mate thanks for the kindness, which he had express'd to us, and sent suitable acknowledgement by him to the captain, offering to pay him by advance, what ever he demanded for our passage, and for the conveniences he had help'd us to; the mate told him, that the captain would be on board in the afternoon, and that he would leave all that till he came; accordingly in the afternoon the captain came, and we found him the same cour-

---

1 An area of the after part of a ship which is immediately in front of the main cabin, sometimes referred to as the "second cabin" (not modern usage).

teous obliging man, that the boatswain had represented him to be; and he was so well pleas'd with my husband's conversation, that in short, he would not let us keep the cabbin we had chosen, but gave us one, that as I said before, open'd into the great cabbin.

Nor were his conditions exorbitant, or the man craving and eager to make a prey of us, but for fifteen guineas we had our whole passage and provisions, and cabbin, eat at the captain's table, and were very handsomely entertain'd.

The captain lay himself in the other part of the great cabbin, having let his round house,[1] *as they call it*, to a rich planter, who went over, with his wife, and three children, who eat by themselves; he had some other ordinary passengers, who quarter'd in the steerage, and as for our old fraternity, they were kept under the hatches while the ship lay there, and came very little on the deck.

I could not refrain acquainting my governess with what had happen'd, it was but just that she, who was so really concern'd for me, should have part in my good fortune; besides I wanted her assistance to supply me with several necessaries, which before I was shy of letting any body see me have, that it might not be publick; but now I had a cabbin and room to set things in; I order'd abundance of good things for our comfort in the voyage, as brandy, sugar, lemons, &c. to make punch, and treat our benefactor, the captain; and abundance of things for eating and drinking in the voyage; also a larger bed, and bedding proportion'd to it; so that in a word, we resolv'd to want for nothing in the voyage.

All this while I had provided nothing for our assistance, when we should come to the place, and begin to call ourselves planters; and I was far from being ignorant of what was needful on that occasion; particularly all sorts of tools for the planters-work, and for building; and all kinds of furniture for our dwelling, which if to be bought in the country, must necessarily cost double the price.

So I discours'd that point with my governess, and she went and waited upon the captain, and told him, that she hop'd ways might be found out, for her two unfortunate cousins, *as she call'd us*, to obtain our freedom when we came into the country, and so enter'd into a discourse with him about the means and terms also, of which I shall say more in its place; and after thus sounding the captain, she let him know, tho' we were unhappy in the circumstance that occasion'd our going, yet that we were not unfurnish'd

---

1 A cabin or apartment built on the after part of the quarter-deck, usually reserved for officers.

to set our selves to work in the country; and were resolv'd to settle, and live there as planters, if we might be put in a way how to do it: the captain readily offer'd his assistance, told her the method of entering upon such business, and how easy, nay, how certain it was for industrious people to recover their fortunes in such a manner: Madam, *says he,* 'tis no reproach to any man in that country to have been sent over in worse circumstances than I perceive your cousins are in, provided they do but apply with diligence and good judgment to the business of that place when they come there.

She then enquir'd of him what things it was necessary we should carry over with us, and he like a very honest as well as knowing man, told her thus: Madam, your cousins in the first place must procure some body to buy them as servants, in conformity to the conditions of their transportation, and then in the name of that person, they may go about what they will; they may either purchase some plantations already begun, or they may purchase land of the government of the country, and begin where they please, and both will be done reasonably; she bespoke his favour in the first article, which he promis'd to her to take upon himself, and indeed faithfull perform'd it; and as to the rest, he promis'd to recommend us to such as should give us the best advice, and not to impose upon us, which was as much as could be desir'd.

She then ask'd him, if it would not be necessary to furnish us with a stock of tools and materials for the business of planting, and he said, Yes, by all means, and then she begg'd his assistance in it; she told him she would furnish us with every thing that was convenient whatever it cost her; he accordingly gave her a long particular of things necessary for a planter, which by his account came to about fourscore, or an hundred pounds; and in short, she went about as dexterously to buy them, as if she had been an old *Virginia* merchant; only that she bought by my direction above twice as much of every thing as he had given her a list of.

These she put on board in her own name, took his bills of loading for them, and endorst those bills of loading to my husband, ensuring the cargo afterwards in her own name, by our order; so that we were provided for all events, and for all disasters.

I should have told you that my husband gave her all his whole stock of 180 *l.* which as I have said, he had about him in gold, to lay out thus, and I gave her a good sum besides; so that I did not break into the stock, which I had left in her hands at all, but after we had sorted out our whole cargo, we had yet near 200 *l.* in money, which was more than enough for our purpose.

In this condition very chearful, and indeed joyful at being so happily accommodated as we were; we set sail from *Bugby's-Hole* to *Gravesend*,[1] where the ship lay about ten days more, and where the captain came on board for good and all. Here the captain offer'd us a civility, which indeed we had no reason to expect. Namely, to let us go on shore, and refresh ourselves, upon giving our words in a solemn manner, that we would not go from him, and that we would return peaceably on board again: this was such an evidence of his confidence in us, that it overcome my husband, who in a meer principle of gratitude, told him as he could not be in any capacity to make a suitable return for such a favour, so he could not think of accepting of it; nor could he be easy that the captain should run such a risque: after some mutual civilities, I gave my husband a purse, in which was 80 guineas, and he puts it into the captain's hand: There captain, *says he,* there's part of a pledge for our fidelity, if we deal dishonestly with you on any account, 'tis your own, and on this we went on shore.

Indeed the captain had assurance enough of our resolutions to go, for that having made such provision to settle there, it did not seem rational that we would chuse to remain here at the expence and peril of life, for such it must have been, if we had been taken again. In a word, we went all on shore with the captain, and supp'd together in *Gravesend*; where we were very merry, staid all night, lay at the house where we supp'd, and came all very honestly on board again with him in the morning. Here we bought ten dozen bottles of good beer, some wine, some fowls, and such things as we thought might be acceptable on board.

My governess was with us all this while, and went with us round into the *Downs*,[2] as did also the captain's wife with whom she went back; I was never so sorrowful at parting with my own mother as I was at parting with her, and I never saw her more: we had a fair easterly wind sprung up the third day after we came to the *Downs*, and we sail'd from thence the 10th of *April*; nor did we touch any more at any place, till being driven on the coast of *Ireland* by a very hard gale of wind, the ship came to an anchor in a little *bay*, near the mouth of a river, whose name I remember not, but they said the river came down from *Limerick*, and that it was the largest river in *Ireland*.[3]

---

1 All outward-bound ships on the River Thames dropped anchor at Gravesend for a final customs clearance.
2 A famous rendezvous for ships, off the east coast of Kent.
3 The River Shannon.

Here being detain'd by bad weather for some time, the captain who continu'd the same kind good humour'd man as at first, took us two on shore with him again: he did it now in kindness to my husband indeed, who bore the sea very ill, and was very sick, especially when it blew so hard: here we bought in again, store of fresh provisions, especially beef, pork, mutton and fowls, and the captain stay'd to pickle up five or six barrels of beef to lengthen out the ships store. We were here not above five days, when the weather turning mild, and a fair wind; we set sail again and in two and forty days came safe to the coast of *Virginia*.

When we drew near to the shore, the captain call'd me to him, and told me that he found by my discourse, I had some relations in the place, and that I had been there before, and so he suppos'd I understood the custom, in their disposing the convict prisoners when they arriv'd; I told him I did not, and that as to what relations I had in the place, he might be sure I would make my self known to none of them while I was in the circumstances of a prisoner, and that as to the rest, we left ourselves entirely to him to assist us, as he was pleas'd to promise us he wou'd do. He told me I must get some body in the place to come and buy us as servants, and who must answer for us to the governor of the country, if he demanded us; I told him we should do as he should direct; so he brought a planter to treat with him, as it were for the purchase of these two servants, my husband and me, and there we were formally sold to him, and went a shore with him: the captain went with us, and carried us to a certain house whether it was to be call'd a tavern or not, I know not, but we had a bowl of punch there made of rum, *&c.* and were very merry. After some time the planter gave us a certificate of discharge, and an acknowledgement of having serv'd him faithfully, and we were free from him the next morning, to go whither we would.[1]

For this peice of service the captain demanded of us 6000 weight of tobacco, which he said he was accountable for to his freighter,[2] and which we immediately bought for him, and made him a present of 20 guineas, besides, with which he was abundantly satisfy'd.

1 According to the *American Weekly Mercury* (14 February 1721), announcing the arrival of a number of convicts in Maryland, the term of service (though not the period of transportation) could be avoided by paying the cost of the passage. For a somewhat different account, see Appendix B.9.
2 A contractor who, for a fixed sum, undertook the transportation, etc., of convicts to America.

It is not proper to enter here into the particulars of what part of the colony of *Virginia* we settled in, for divers reasons; it may suffice to mention that we went into the great river of *Potomack*, the ship being bound thither; and there we intended to have settled at first, tho' afterwards we altered our minds.

The first thing I did of moment after having gotten all our goods on shore, and plac'd them in a storehouse, or warehouse, which with a lodging we hir'd at the small place or village, where we landed; I say the first thing was to enquire after my mother, and after my brother, (that fatal person who I married as a husband, as I have related at large;[1]) a little enquiry furnish'd me with information that Mrs. ———, that is my mother was dead; that my brother (or husband) was alive, which I confess I was not very glad to hear; but which was worse, I found he was remov'd from the plantation where he liv'd formerly, and where I liv'd with him, and liv'd with one of his sons in a plantation just by the place where we landed, and where we had hir'd a warehouse.

I was a little surpriz'd at first, but as I ventured, to satisfy my self, that he could not know me, I was not only perfectly easy, but had a great mind to see him, if it was possible to do so without his seeing me; in order to that I found out by enquiry the plantation where he liv'd, and with a woman of that place, who I got to help me, like what we call a *chairwoman*,[2] I rambl'd about towards the place, as if I had only a mind to see the country, and look about me; at last I came so near that I saw the dwelling-house: *I ask'd the woman* whose plantation that was, *she said*, it belong'd to such a man, and looking out a little to our right hands, There says she, is the gentleman that owns the plantation, and his father with him: What are their Christian names? said I, I know not *said she*, what the old gentlemans name is, but his sons name is *Humphry*, and I believe, *says she*, the fathers is so too; you may guess, if you can, what a confus'd mixture of joy and fright possest my thoughts upon this occasion, for I immediately knew that this was no body else, but my own son, by that father she shewed me, who was my own brother: I had no mask, but I ruffled my hoods so about my face, that I depended upon it, that after above 20 years absence, and withal not expecting any thing of me in that part of the world, he would not be able to know any thing of me; but I need not have us'd all that caution, for the old gentleman was grown dim sight-

---

1 At length, fully.
2 A woman hired usually on a daily basis to do basic housework (spelled *charwoman*).

ed, by some distemper, which had fallen upon his eyes, and could but just see well enough to walk about, and not run against a tree, or into a ditch. The woman that was with me, had told me that, by a meer accident, knowing nothing of what importance it was to me: as they drew near to us, *I said,* Does he know you Mrs. *Owen?* so they call'd the woman, Yes, *said she,* if he hears me speak, he will know me; but he can't see well enough to know me, or any body else; and so she told me the story of his sight, as I have related: this made me secure, and so I threw open my hoods again, and let them pass by me: it was a wretched thing for a mother thus to see her own son, a handsome comely young gentleman in flourishing circumstances, and durst not make herself known to him; and durst not take any notice of him; let any mother of children that reads this, consider it, and but think with what anguish of mind I restrain'd myself; what yearnings of soul I had in me to embrace him, and weep over him; and how I thought all my entrails turn'd within me, that my very bowels mov'd,[1] and I knew not what to do; as I now know not how to express those agonies: when he went from me I stood gazing and trembling, and looking after him as long as I could see him; then sitting down on the grass, just at a place I had mark'd, I made as if I lay down to rest me, but turn'd from her, and lying on my face wept, and kiss'd the ground that he had set his foot on.

I cou'd not conceal my disorder so much from the woman, but that she perceiv'd it, and thought I was not well, which I was oblig'd to pretend was true; upon which she press'd me to rise, the ground being damp and dangerous, which I did accordingly, and walk'd away.

As I was going back again, and still talking of this gentleman, and his son, a new occasion of melancholy offer'd itself *thus*: the woman began, as if she would tell me a story to divert me; There goes, *says she*, a very odd tale among the neighbours where this gentleman formerly liv'd: What was that, *said I?* Why, says she, that old gentleman going to *England*, when he was a young man, fell in love with a young lady there, one of the finest women that ever was seen, and married her, and brought her over hither to his mother, who was then living. He liv'd here several years with her, *continu'd she*, and had several children by her, of which the young gentleman that was with him now, was one, but after some time, the old gen-

---

1 That is, she was deeply moved (the bowels being considered the seat of the tender emotions).

tlewoman his mother talking to her, of something relating to herself, when she was in *England*, and of her circumstances in *England*, which were bad enough; the daughter-in-law, began to be very much surpriz'd, and uneasy, and in short, examining further into things it appear'd past all contradiction, that she (the old gentlewoman) was her own mother, and that consequently, that son was his wives own brother, which struck the whole family with horror, and put them into such confusion, that it had almost ruin'd them all; the young woman would not live with him, the son, her brother and husband, for a time went distracted, and at last, the young woman went away for *England*, and has never been heard of since.

It is easy to believe that I was strangely affected with this story; but 'tis impossible to describe the nature of my disturbance: I seem'd astonish'd at the story, and ask'd her a thousand questions about the particulars, which I found she was thoroughly acquainted with; at last I began to enquire into the circumstances of the family, how the old gentlewoman, *I mean, my mother* died, and how she left what she had; for my mother had promis'd me very solemnly, that when she died, she would do something for me, and leave it so, as that, if I was living, I should one way or other come at it, without its being in the power of her son, *my brother and husband* to prevent it: she told me she did not know exactly how it was order'd; but she had been told, that *my mother* had left a sum of money, and had tyed her plantation for the payment of it,[1] to be made good to the daughter, if ever she could be heard of, either in *England*, or else where; and that the trust was left with this son, who was the person that we saw with his father.

This was news too good for me to make light of, and you may be sure fill'd my heart with a thousand thoughts, what course I should take, how, and when, and in what manner I should make myself known, or whether I should ever make myself known, or no.

Here was a perplexity that I had not indeed skill to manage myself in, neither knew I what course to take: it lay heavy upon my mind night, and day, I could neither sleep or converse, so that my husband perceiv'd it, and wonder'd what ail'd me, strove to divert me, but it was all to no purpose; he press'd me to tell him what it was troubled me, but I put it off, till at last importuning me con-

---

1 That is, the payment of the money had been attached ("tied") to the inheritance of the plantation.

tinually, I was forc'd to form a story, which yet had a plain truth to lay it upon too; I told him I was troubled because I found we must shift our quarters, and alter our scheme of settling, for that I found I should be known, if I stay'd in that part of the country, for that my mother being dead, several of my relations were come into that part where we then was, and that I must either discover myself to them, which in our present circumstances was not proper on many accounts, or remove, and which to do I knew not, and that this it was that made me so melancholly, and so thoughtful.

He joyn'd with me in this, that it was by no means proper for me to make myself known to any body in the circumstances, in which we then were; and therefore he told me he would be willing to remove to any other part of the country,[1] or even to any other country if I thought fit; but now I had another difficulty, which was, that if I remov'd to any other colony, I put myself out of the way of ever making a due search after those effects, which my mother had left: again, I could never so much as think of breaking the secret of my former marriage to my new husband; it was not a story, as I thought that would bear telling, nor could I tell what might be the consequences of it; and it was impossible to search into the bottom of the thing without making it publick all over the country, as well who I was, as what I now was also.

In this perplexity I continu'd a great while, and this made my spouse very uneasy; for he found me perplex'd, and yet thought I was not open with him, and did not let him into every part of my grievance; and he would often say, he wondred what he had done, that I would not trust him with what ever it was, especially if it was grievous, and afflicting; the truth is, he ought to have been trusted with every thing; for no man in the world could deserve better of a wife; but this was a thing I knew not how to open to him, and yet having no body to disclose any part of it to, the burthen was too heavy for my mind; for let them say what they please of our sex not being able to keep a secret; my life is a plain conviction to me of the contrary; but be it our sex, or the man's sex, a secret of moment should always have a confident, a bosom friend, to whom we may communicate the joy of it, or the grief of it, be it which it will, or it will be a double weight upon the spirits, and perhaps become even insupportable in itself; and this I appeal to all human testimony for the truth of.

And this is the cause why many times men as well as women, and men of the greatest, and best qualities other ways, yet have

---

1 Region.

found themselves weak in this part, and have not been able to bear the weight of a secret joy, or of a secret sorrow; but have been oblig'd to disclose it, even for the meer giving vent to themselves, and to unbend the mind, opprest with the load and weights which attended it; nor was this any token of folly, or thoughtlessness at all, but a natural consequence of the thing; and such people had they struggl'd longer with the oppression, would certainly have told it in their sleep, and disclos'd the secret, let it have been of what fatal nature soever, without regard to the person to whom it might be expos'd: this necessity of nature, is a thing which works sometimes with such vehemence, in the minds of those who are guilty of any atrocious villany; such as secret murther in particular, that they have been oblig'd to discover it, tho' the consequence would necessarily be their own destruction: now tho' it may be true that the divine justice ought to have the glory of all those discoveries and confessions, yet 'tis as certain that Providence which ordinarily works by the hands of nature, makes use here of the same natural causes to produce those extraordinary effects.[1]

I could give several remarkable instances of this in my long conversation with crime, and with criminals; I knew one fellow, that while I was a prisoner in *Newgate*, was one of those they called then *night-flyers*,[2] I know not what other word they may have understood it by since; but he was one, who by connivance was admitted to go abroad every evening, when he play'd his pranks, and furnish'd those honest people they call thief-catchers[3] with business to find out next day, and restore *for a reward*, what they had stolen the evening before: this fellow was as sure to tell in his sleep all that he had done, and every step he had taken, what he had stole, and where, as sure as if he had engag'd to tell it waking, and that there was no harm or danger in it; and therefore he was

---

1 In *Applebee's Journal* (2 March 1723), Defoe says that "in cases of Treason, Murther, and the like Crimes, how often have we seen, that when the Guilty Persons have apply'd themselves ... to conceal their Guilt, and to make their Escape from Justice; they have ... by a Faltering Tongue ... or by some unconcealable Part of their Conduct, been their own Betrayers ... "

2 A slang term for prisoners who were released at night by their jailors to steal for mutual gain.

3 A disreputable breed of men who hunted thieves for reward, often working hand-in-hand with the criminals themselves. The most notorious of the thief-catchers was Jonathan Wild (1682?-1725), who was eventually imprisoned at Newgate and then hanged at Tyburn. His life was written both by Defoe (1725) and by Fielding (1743).

oblig'd after he had been out to lock himself up, or be lock'd up by some of the keepers that had him in fee,[1] that no body should hear him; but on the other hand, if he had told all the particulars, and given a full account of his rambles and success to any comrade, any brother thief, or to his employers, *as I may justly call them*, then all was well with him, and he slept as quietly as other people.

As the publishing this account of my life, is for the sake of the just moral of every part of it, and for instruction, caution, warning and improvement to every reader, so this will not pass I hope for an unnecessary digression concerning some people, being oblig'd to disclose the greatest secrets either of their own, or other peoples affairs.

Under the certain oppression of this weight upon my mind, I labour'd in the case I have been naming; and the only relief I found for it, was to let my husband into so much of it, as I thought would convince him of the necessity there was, for us to think of settling, in some other part of the world, and the next consideration before us, was, which part of the *English* settlements we should go to; my husband was a perfect stranger to the country, and had not yet so much as a geographical knowledge of the situation of the several places; and I, that till I wrote this, did not know what the word geographical signify'd, had only a general knowledge from long conversation with people that came from, or went to several places; but this I knew, that *Maryland, Pensilvania*, East and West *Jersy, New York*, and *New England*, lay all north of *Virginia*, and that they were consequently all colder climates, to which, for that very reason, I had an aversion; for that as I naturally lov'd warm weather, so now I grew into years, I had a stronger inclination to shun a cold climate; I therefore consider'd of going to *Carolina*, which is the most southern colony of the *English*, on the continent of *America*, and hither I propos'd to go; and the rather, because I might with great ease come from thence at any time, when it might be proper to enquire after my mothers effects, and to make myself known enough to demand them.

With this resolution, I propos'd to my husband our going away from where we was, and carrying all our effects with us to *Carolina*, where we resolv'd to settle, for my husband readily agreed to the first part (*viz.*) that it was not at all proper to stay where we was, since I had assur'd him we should be known there, and the rest I effectually conceal'd from him.

---

1 In their pay.

But now I found a new difficulty upon me: the main affair grew heavy upon my mind still, and I could not think of going out of the country, without *some how or other* making enquiry into the grand affair of what my mother had done for me; nor cou'd I with any patience bear the thought of going away, and not make myself known to my old husband, (*brother*) or to my child, his son, only I would fain have had this done without my new husband having any knowledge of it, or they having any knowledge of him, or that I had such a thing as a husband.

I cast about innumerable ways in my thoughts how this might be done: I would gladly have sent my husband away to *Carolina*, with all our goods, and have come after myself; but this was impracticable, he would never stir without me, being himself per-fectly unacquainted with the country, and with the methods of settling there, or any where else: then I thought we would both go first with part of our goods, and that when we were settled I should come back to *Virginia*, and fetch the remainder; but even then I knew he would never part with me, and be left there to go on alone; the case was plain, he was bred a gentleman, and by consequence was not only unacquainted,[1] but indolent, and when we did settle, would much rather go out into the woods with his gun, which they call there hunting,[2] and which is the ordinary work of the *Indians*, and which they do as servants; I say he would much rather do that, than attend the natural business of his plantation.

These were therefore difficulties unsurmountable, and such as I knew not what to do in, I had such strong impressions on my mind about discovering myself to my *brother*, formerly my *husband*, that I could not withstand them; and the rather, because it run constantly in my thoughts, that if I did not do it, while he liv'd, I might in vain endeavour to convince my son afterward, that I was really the same person, and that I was his mother, and so might both lose the assistance and comfort of the relation, and the benefit of whatever it was my mother had left me; and yet on the other hand, I cou'd never think it proper to discover myself to them in the circumstances I was in; as well relating to the having a husband with me, as to my being brought over by a legal transportation, as a criminal; on both which accounts it was absolutely necessary to

1 That is, not acquainted with work.
2 Moll calls attention here (and again on p. 325) to an Americanism. In England a distinction is customarily made between hunting (animals with dogs) and shooting (game with guns).

me to remove from the place where I was, and come again to him, as from another place, and in another figure.

Upon those considerations, I went on with telling my husband, the absolute necessity there was of our not settling in *Potomack* River, at least that we should be presently made publick there, whereas if we went to any other place in the world, we should come in, with as much reputation, as any family that came to plant: that as it was always agreeable to the inhabitants to have families come among them to plant, who brought substance with them, either to purchase plantations, or begin new ones, so we should be sure of a kind agreeable reception, and that without any possibility of a discovery of our circumstances.

I told him in general too, that as I had several relations in the place where we was, and that I durst not now let myself be known to them, because they would soon come into a knowledge of the occasion and reason of my coming over, which would be to expose myself to the last degree; so I had reason to believe that my mother who died here had left me something, and perhaps considerable, which it might be very well worth my while to enquire after; but that this too could not be done without exposing us publickly, unless we went from hence; and then where ever we settled, I might come as it were to visit and to see my brother and nephews, make myself known to them, claim and enquire after what was my due, be receiv'd with respect, and at the the same time have justice done me with chearfulness and good will; whereas if I did it now, I could expect nothing but with trouble, such as exacting it by force, receiving it with curses and reluctance, and with all kinds of affronts; which he would not perhaps bear to see; that in case of being oblig'd to legal proofs of being really her daughter, I might be at loss, be oblig'd to have recourse to *England*, and it may be to fail at last, and so lose it, whatever it might be: with these arguments, and having thus acquainted my husband with the whole secret so far as was needful to him, we resolv'd to go and seek a settlement in some other colony, and at first thoughts, *Carolina* was the place we pitch'd upon.

In order to this we began to make enquiry for vessels going to *Carolina*, and in a very little while got information, that on the other side the *bay, as they call it*, namely, in *Maryland* there was a ship, which came from *Carolina*, loaden with rice, and other goods, and was going back again thither, and from thence *to Jamaica*, with provisions: on this news we hir'd a sloop[1] to take in

---

1 A small, one-masted vessel.

our goods, and taking as it were a final farewel of *Potowmack* River, we went with all our cargo over to *Maryland*.

This was a long and unpleasant voyage, and my spouse said it was worse to him than all the voyage from *England*, because the weather was but indifferent,[1] the water rough, and the vessel small and inconvenient; in the next place we were full a hundred miles up *Potowmack* River, in a part which they call *Westmoreland* County, and as that river is by far the greatest in *Virginia*, and I have heard say, it is the greatest river in the world that falls into another river, and not directly into the sea; so we had base weather in it, and were frequently in great danger; for tho' they call it but a river, 'tis frequently so broad, that when we were in the middle, we could not see land on either side for many leagues together: then we had the great river, or bay of *Chesapeake* to cross, which is where the river *Potowmack* falls into it, near thirty miles broad, and we entered more great vast waters, whose names I know not, so that our voyage was full two hundred mile, in a poor sorry sloop with all our treasure, and if any accident had happened to us, we might at last have been very miserable; supposing we had lost our goods and saved our lives only, and had then been left naked and destitute, and in a wild strange place, not having one friend or acquaintance in all that part of the world? The very thoughts of it gives me some horror, even since the danger is past.

Well, we came to the place in five days sailing, I think they call it *Philips's Point*,[2] and behold when we came thither, the ship bound to *Carolina*, was loaded and gone away but three days before. This was a disappointment, but however, I that was to be discourag'd with nothing, told my husband that since we could not get passage to *Carolina*, and that the country we was in, was very fertile and good; we would if he lik'd of it, see if we could find out any thing for our turn where we was, and that if he lik'd things we would settle here.

We immediately went on shore, but found no conveniences just at that place, either for our being on shore, or preserving our goods on shore, but was directed by a very honest Quaker, who we found there to go to a place, about sixty miles east; that is to say, nearer the mouth of the *bay*, where he said he liv'd, and where we

---

1 Not particularly good.
2 George E. Gifford suggests that Moll and her husband landed at the present Clay Island, in the mouth of the Nanticoke River, Dorchester County, Maryland ("Daniel Defoe and Maryland," *Maryland Historical Magazine*, 53 [1957]: 308).

should be accommodated, either to plant, or to wait for any other place to plant in, that might be more convenient, and he invited us with so much kindness and simple honesty that we agreed to go, and the Quaker himself went with us.

Here we bought us two servants, (*viz.*) an *English* woman-servant just come on shore from a ship of *Leverpool*, and a *negro* man-servant; things absolutely necessary for all people that pretended[1] to settle in that country: this honest Quaker was very helpful to us, and when we came to the place that he propos'd to us, found us out a convenient storehouse, for our goods, and lodging for ourselves, and our servants; and about two months, or thereabout afterwards, by his direction we took up a large peice of land from the governor[2] of that country, in order to form our plantation, and so we laid the thoughts of going to *Carolina* wholly aside, having been very well receiv'd here, and accommodated with a convenient lodging, till we could prepare things, and have land enough cur'd, and timber and materials provid'd for building us a house, all which we manag'd by the direction of the Quaker; so that in one years time, we had near fifty acres of land clear'd, part of it enclos'd, and some of it planted with tobacco, tho' not much; besides, we had garden ground, and corn sufficient to help supply our servants with roots, and herbs, and bread.

And now I persuaded my husband to let me go over the *bay* again, and enquire after my friends; he was the willinger to consent to it now, because he had business upon his hands sufficient to employ him, besides his gun to divert him, which they call hunting there, and which he greatly delighted in; and indeed we us'd to look at one another, sometimes with a great deal of pleasure, reflecting how much better that was, not than *Newgate* only, but than the most prosperous of our circumstances in the wicked trade that we had been both carrying on.

Our affair was in a very good posture, we purchased of the proprietors of the colony, as much land for 35 pound, paid in ready money, as would make a sufficient plantation to employ between fifty and sixty servants, and which being well improv'd, would be sufficient to us as long as we could either of us live; and as for children I was past the prospect of any thing of that kind.

But our good fortune did not end here, I went, *as I have said*, over the *bay*, to the place, where my brother, once a husband liv'd;

---

1 Intended, proposed.
2 "Government" in second edition.

but I did not go to the same village, where I was before, but went up another great river, on the east side of the river *Potowmack*, call'd *Rapahannock* River, and by this means came on the back of his plantation, which was large, and by the help of a navigable creek, or little river, that run into the *Rapahannock*, I came very near it.

I was now fully resolv'd to go up *point-blank*, to my brother (husband) and to tell him who I was; but not knowing what temper I might find him in, or how much out of temper rather, I might make him by such a rash visit, I resolv'd to write a letter to him first to let him know who I was, and that I was come not to give him any trouble upon the old relation, which I hop'd was entirely forgot; but that I apply'd to him as a sister to a brother, desiring his assistance in the case of that provision, which our mother at her decease had left for my support, and which I did not doubt but he would do me justice in, especially considering that I was come thus far to look after it.

I said some very tender kind things in the letter about his son, which I told him he knew to be my own child, and that as I was guilty of nothing in marrying him any more than he was in marrying me, neither of us having then known our being at all related to one another; so I hop'd he would allow me the most passionate desire of once seeing my one, and only child,[1] and of showing something of the infirmities of a mother in preserving a violent affection for him, who had never been able to retain any thought of me one way or other.

I did believe that having receiv'd this letter, he would immediately give it to his son to read; I having understood his eyes being so dim, that he cou'd not see to read it; but it fell out better than so, for as his sight was dim, so he had allow'd his son to open all letters that came to his hand for him, and the old gentleman being from home, or out of the way when my messenger came, my letter came directly to my sons hand, and he open'd and read it.

He call'd the messenger in, after some little stay, and ask'd him where the person was who gave him the letter, the messenger told him the place, which was about seven miles off, so he bid him stay, and ordering a horse to be got ready, and two servants, away he came to me with the messenger: let any one judge the consternation I was in, when my messenger came back, and told me the old gentleman was not at home, but his son was come along with him, and was just coming up to me: I was perfectly confounded, for I

---

1 That is, the only surviving child Moll bore her brother.

knew not whether it was peace or war, nor cou'd I tell how to behave: however, I had but a very few moments to think, for my son was at the heels of the messenger, and coming up into my lodgings, ask'd the fellow at the door something, I suppose it was, *for I did not hear it, so as to understand it,* which was the gentlewoman that sent him, for the messenger said, *There she is sir,* at which he comes directly up to me, kisses me, took me in his arms, and embrac'd me with so much passion, that he could not speak, but I could feel his breast heave and throb like a child that cries, but sobs, and cannot cry it out.

I can neither express or describe the joy, that touch'd my very soul, when I found, *for it was easy to discover that part,* that he came not as a stranger, but as a son to a mother, and indeed as a son, who had never before known what a mother of his own was; in short, we cryed over one another a considerable while, when at last he broke out first, MY DEAR MOTHER, says he, *are you still alive! I never expected to have seen your face;* as for me, I cou'd say nothing a great while.

After we had both recover'd ourselves a little, and were able to talk, he told me how things stood; as to what I had written to his father, he told me he had not shewed my letter to his father, or told him any thing about it; that what his grandmother left me, was in his hands, and that he would do me justice to my full satisfaction; that as to his father, he was old and infirm both in body and mind, that he was very fretful, and passionate, almost blind, and capable of nothing; and he question'd whether he would know how to act in an affair, which was of so nice a nature as this, and that therefore he had come himself, as well to satisfy himself in seeing me, which he could not restrain himself from, as also to put it into my power, to make a judgement after I had seen how things were, whether I would discover myself to his father, or no.

This was really so prudently, and wisely manag'd, that I found my son was a man of sense, and needed no direction from me; I told him, I did not wonder that his father was, as he had describ'd him, for that his head was a little touch'd before I went away; and principally his disturbance was, because I could not be perswaded to conceal our relation, and to live with him as my husband, after I knew that he was my brother: that as he knew better than I, what his fathers present condition was, I should readily joyn with him in such measures as he would direct: that I was indifferent, as to seeing his father, since I had seen him first, and he cou'd not have told me better news, than to tell me that what his grandmother had left me, was entrusted in his hands, who I doubted not now he knew who I was, would *as he said,* do me justice: I enquir'd then how long my mother had been dead, and where she died, and told so many particulars of the family, that I left him no room to doubt the truth of my being really and truly his mother.

My son then enquir'd where I was, and how I had dispos'd myself; I told him I was on the *Maryland* side of the *bay,* at the plantation of a particular friend, who came from *England* in the same ship with me, that as for that side of the *bay* where he was, I had no habitation; he told me I should go home with him, and live with him, if I pleas'd, as long as I liv'd: that as to his father he knew no body, and would never so much as guess at me; I consider'd of that a little, and told him, that tho' it was really no little concern to me to live at a distance from him; yet I could not say it would be the comfortabless[1] thing in the world to me to live in the house with him; and to have that unhappy object always before me, which had been such a blow to my peace before; that tho' I should be glad to have his company (my son) or to be as near him as possible while I stay'd, yet I could not think of being in the house where I should be also under constant restraint, for fear of betraying myself in my discourse, nor should I be able to refrain some expressions in my conversing with him as my son, that might discover the whole affair, which would by no means be convenient.

He acknowledged that I was right in all this, But then DEAR MOTHER, says he, *you shall be as near me as you can*; so he took me with him on horseback to a plantation, next to his own, and where I was as well entertain'd as I cou'd have been in his own; having left me there he went away home, telling me we would talk of the main business the next day, and having first called me his aunt, and given a charge to the people, who it seems were his tenants, to treat me with all possible respect; about two hours after he was gone, he sent me a maid-servant, and a *negro* boy to wait on me, and provisions ready dress'd for my supper; and thus I was as if I had been in a new world, and began secretly now to wish that I had not brought my *Lancashire* husband from *England* at all.

However, that wish was not hearty neither, for I lov'd my *Lancashire* husband entirely, as indeed I had ever done from the beginning; and he merited from me as much as it was possible for a man to do, but that by the way.

The next morning my son came to visit me again almost as soon as I was up; after a little discourse, he first of all pull'd out a

---

1 Obsolete form of *most comfortable,* which is used in the second edition.

deer skin bag, and gave it me, with five and fifty *Spanish* pistoles[1] in it, and told me that was to supply my expences from *England*, for tho' it was not his business to enquire, yet he ought to think I did not bring a great deal of money out with me; it not being usual to bring much money into that country: then he pull'd out his grandmother's will, and read it over to me, whereby it appear'd, that she had left a small plantation, *as he call'd it*, on *York* River, that is, where my mother liv'd, to me, with the stock of servants and cattle upon it, and given it in trust to this son of mine for my use, when ever he should hear of my being alive, and to my heirs, if I had any children, and in default of heirs, to whomsoever I should by will dispose of it; but gave the income of it, till I should be heard of, or found, to my said son; and if I should not be living, then it was to him, and his heirs.

This plantation, tho' remote from him, he said he did not let out,[2] but manag'd it by a head clerk, steward, as he did another that was his fathers, that lay hard by it, and went over himself three or four times a year to look after it; I ask'd him what he thought the plantation might be worth, *he said*, if I would let it out, he would give me about sixty pounds a year for it; but if I would live on it, then it would be worth much more, and he believ'd would bring me in about 150 *l.* a year; but seeing I was likely either to settle on the other side the *bay*, or might perhaps have a mind to go back to *England* again, if I would let him be my steward he would manage it for me, as he had done for himself, and that he believ'd he should be able to send me as much tobacco to *England* from it, as would yeild me about 100 *l.* a year, sometimes more.

This was all strange news to me, and things I had not been us'd to; and really my heart began to look up more seriously, than I think it ever did before, and to look with great thankfulness to the hand of Providence, which had done such wonders for me, who had been myself the greatest wonder of wickedness, perhaps that had been suffered to live in the world; and I must again observe, that not on this occasion only, but even on all other occasions of thankfulness, my past wicked and abominable life never look'd so monstruous to me, and I never so compleatly abhorr'd it, and reproach'd myself with it, as when I had a sense upon me of Providence doing good to me, while I had been making those vile returns on my part.

---

1 See above, p. 268, n. 1.
2 Lease, rent.

But I leave the reader to improve these thoughts, as no doubt they will see cause, and I go on to the fact; my sons tender carriage, and kind offers fetch'd tears from me, almost all the while he talk'd with me; indeed I could scarce discourse with him, but in the intervals of my passion; however, at length I began, and expressing myself with wonder at my being so happy to have the trust of what I had left, put into the hands of my own child; I told him, that as to the inheritance of it, I had no child but him in the world,[1] and was now past having any, if I should marry, and therefore would desire him to get a writing drawn, which I was ready to execute, by which I would after me give it wholly to him, and to his heirs; and in the mean time smiling, I ask'd him, what made him continue a batchelor so long; his answer was kind, and ready, that *Virginia* did not yield any great plenty of wives, and that since I talk'd of going back to *England*, I should send him a wife from *London*.

This was the substance of our first days conversation, the pleasantest day that ever past over my head in my life, and which gave me the truest satisfaction: he came every day after this, and spent great part of his time with me, and carried me about to several of his friends houses, where I was entertain'd with great respect; also I dined several times at his own house, when he took care always to see his half dead father so out of the way, that I never saw him, or he me: I made him one present, and it was all I had of value, and that was one of the gold watches, of which I mention'd above, that I had two in my chest, and this I happen'd to have with me, and I gave it him at his third visit: I told him, I had nothing of any value to bestow but that, and I desir'd he would now and then kiss it for my sake; *I did not indeed tell him* that I had stole it from a gentlewomans side, at a meeting-house in *London*, that's by the way.

He stood a little while hesitating, as if doubtful whether to take it or no; but I press'd it on him, and made him accept it, and it was not much less worth than his leather-pouch full of *Spanish* gold; no, tho' it were to be reckon'd, as if at *London*, whereas it was worth twice as much there, where I gave it him; at length he took it, kiss'd it, told me the watch should be a debt upon him, that he would be paying, as long as I liv'd.

A few days after he brought the writings of gift,[2] and the scrivener[3] with them, and I sign'd them very freely, and deliver'd

---

1 That is, he will be the sole heir.
2 The legal writs (transferring the property to Moll).
3 A professional clerk, notary.

them to him with a hundr'd kisses; for sure nothing ever pass'd between a mother, and a tender dutiful child, with more affection: the next day he brings me an obligation under his hand and seal, whereby he engag'd himself to manage, and improve the plantation for my account, and with his utmost skill, and to remit the produce to my order where-ever I should be, and withal, to be oblig'd himself to make up the produce a hundred pound a year to me: when he had done so, he told me, that as I came to demand it before the crop was off,[1] I had a right to the produce of the current year, and so he paid me an hundred pound in *Spanish* peices of eight, and desir'd me to give him a receipt for it as in full for that year, ending at *Christmas* following; this being about the latter end of *August*.

I stay'd here above five weeks, and indeed had much a do to get away then. Nay, he would have come over the *bay* with me, but I would by no means allow him to it; however, he would send me over in a sloop of his own, which was built like a yatch,[2] and serv'd him as well for pleasure as business: this I accepted of, and so after the utmost expressions both of duty, and affection, he let me come away, and I arriv'd safe in two days at my friends the Quakers.

I brought over with me for the use of our plantation, three horses with harness, and saddles; some hogs, two cows, and a thousand other things, the gift of the kindest and tenderest child that ever woman had: I related to my husband all the particulars of this voyage, except that I called my son my cousin; and first I told him, that I had lost my watch, which he seem'd to take as a misfortune; but then I told him how kind my cousin had been, that my mother had left me such a plantation, and that he had preserv'd it for me, in hopes some time or other he should hear from me; then I told him that I had left it to his management, that he would render me a faithful account of its produce; and then I pull'd him out the hundred pound in silver, as the first years produce, and then pulling out the deer skin purse, with the pistoles, And here my dear, *says I*, is the gold watch. My husband, *so is Heavens goodness sure to work the same effects, in all sensible minds, where mercies touch the heart*, lifted up both his hands, and with an extasy of joy, *What is God a doing* says he, *for such an ungrateful dog as I am!* Then I let him know, what I had brought over in the sloop, besides all this; I mean the horses, hogs, and cows, and other stores for our planta-

---

1 Harvested.
2 A light, fast-sailing vessel, used especially by the social elite (obsolete form of *yacht*).

tion; all which added to his surprize, and fill'd his heart with thankfulness; and from this time forward I believe he was as sincere a penitent, and as thoroughly a reform'd man, as ever God's goodness brought back from a profligate, a highway-man, and a robber. I could fill a larger history than this, with the evidences of this truth, and but that I doubt that part of the story will not be equally diverting as the wicked part, I have had thoughts of making a volume of it by itself.

As for myself, as this is to be my own story, not my husbands, I return to that part which relates to myself; we went on with our plantation, and manag'd it with the help and diversion of such friends as we got there,[1] by our obliging behaviour, and especially the honest Quaker, who prov'd a faithful generous and steady friend to us; and we had very good success; for having a flourishing stock to begin with, as *I have said*; and this being now encreas'd, by the addition of a hundred and fifty pound *sterling* in money, we enlarg'd our number of servants, built us a very good house, and cur'd every year a great deal of land. The second year I wrote to my old governess, giving her part[2] with us of the joy of our success, and order'd her how to lay out the money I had left with her, which was 250 *l.* as above, and to send it to us in goods, which she perform'd, with her usual kindness and fidelity, and all this arriv'd safe to us.

Here we had a supply of all sorts of cloaths, as well for my husband, as for myself; and I took especial care to buy for him all those things that I knew he delighted to have; as two good long wigs, two silver hilted swords, three or four fine fowling peices, a fine saddle with holsters and pistoles[3] very handsome, with a scarlet cloak; and in a word, every thing I could think of to oblige him; and to make him appear, as he really was, a very fine gentleman: I order'd a good quantity of such houshold-stuff, as we yet wanted with linnen of all sorts for us both; as for my self, I wanted very little of cloths, or linnen, being very well furnished before: the rest of my cargo consisted in iron-work, of all sorts, harness for horses, tools, cloaths for servants, and wollen-cloth, stuffs,[4] serges,[5]

---

1 That is, their friends there turned their attention from their own work in order to help Moll and her husband. (In the second edition "diversion" is replaced by "direction.")
2 Asking her to share.
3 Pistols.
4 Textile material.
5 Garments made of strong, twilled material.

stockings, shoes, hats and the like, such as servants wear, and whole peices[1] also, to make up for servants, all by direction of the Quaker; and all this cargo arriv'd safe, and in good condition, with three women servants, lusty wenches, which my old governess had pick'd up for me, suitable enough to the place, and to the work we had for them to do; one of which happen'd to come double, having been got with child by one of the seamen in the ship, as she own'd afterwards, before the ship got so far as *Gravesend*; so she brought us a stout boy, about 7 months after her landing.

My husband you may suppose was a little surpriz'd at the arriving of all this cargo from *England*, and talking with me after he saw the account of the particular;[2] My dear, *says he*, what is the meaning of all this? I fear you will run us too deep in debt: when shall we be able to make return for it all? I smil'd, and told him that it was all paid for, and then I told him, that not knowing what might befal us in the voyage, and considering what our circumstances might expose us to; I had not taken my whole stock with me, that I had reserv'd so much in my friends hands, which now we were come over safe, and was settled in a way to live, I had sent for as he might see.

He was amaz'd, and stood a while telling upon his fingers, but said nothing, at last he began thus, Hold lets see, *says he, telling upon his fingers still*; and first on his thumb, there's 246 *l.* in money at first, then two gold watches, diamond rings, and plate, *says he*, upon the fore finger, then upon the next finger, here's a plantation on *York* River, a 100 *l.* a year, then 150 in money; then a sloop load of horses, cows, hogs and stores, and so on to the thumb again; and now, *says he*, a cargo cost 250 *l.* in *England*, and worth here twice the money, Well, *says I*, what do you make of all that? Make of it, *says he*, why who says I was deceiv'd, when I married a wife in *Lancashire*? I think I have married a fortune, and a very good fortune too, *says he*.

In a word, we were now in very considerable circumstances, and every year encreasing; for our new plantation grew upon our hands insensibly;[3] and in eight year which we lived upon it, we brought it to such a pitch, that the produce was, at least, 300 *l.* sterling a year; I mean, worth so much in *England*.

After I had been a year at home again, I went over the bay to see my son, and to receive another year's income of my plantation;

---

1 Lengths of material in which other fabric is woven.
2 Details.
3 Imperceptibly.

and I was surpriz'd to hear, just at my landing there, that my old husband was dead, and had not been bury'd above a fortnight. This, I confess, was not disagreeable news, because now I could appear as I was in a marry'd condition; so I told my son before I came from him, that I believed I should marry a gentleman who had a plantation near mine; and tho' I was legally free to marry, as to any obligation that was on me before, yet that I was shye of it, lest the blot should some time or other be reviv'd, and it might make a husband uneasy; my son the same kind dutiful and obliging creature as ever, treated me now at his own house, paid me my hundred pound, and sent me home again loaded with presents.

Some time after this, I let my son know I was marry'd, and invited him over to see us; and my husband wrote a very obliging letter to him also, inviting him to come and see him; and he came accordingly some months after, and happen'd to be there just when my cargo from *England* came in, which I let him believe belong'd all to my husband's estate, not to me.

It must be observ'd, that when the old wretch, my brother (husband) was dead, I then freely gave my husband an account of all that affair, and of this cousin, as I had call'd him before, being my own son by that mistaken unhappy match: he was perfectly easy in the account, and told me he should have been as easy if the old man, as we call'd him, had been alive; For, *said he*, it was no fault of yours, nor of his; it was a mistake impossible to be prevented; he only reproach'd him with desiring me to conceal it, and to live with him as a wife, after I knew that he was my brother, that, he said, was a vile part: thus all these little difficulties were made easy, and we liv'd together with the greatest kindness and comfort imaginable; we are now grown old: I am come back to *England*, being almost seventy years of age, my husband sixty eight, having perform'd much more than the limited terms of my transportation: and now notwithstanding all the fatigues, and all the miseries we have both gone thro', we are both in good heart and health; my husband remain'd there sometime after me to settle our affairs, and at first I had intended to go back to him, but at his desire I alter'd that resolution, and he is come over to *England* also, where we resolve to spend the remainder of our years in sincere penitence, for the wicked lives we have lived.

Written in the Year 1683.

FINIS.

Appendix A: Related Writings by Defoe

[Most of the important themes contained in *Moll Flanders*, as well as certain features of character and various incidents, are found in other writings by Defoe. They appear throughout his long career, particularly in the journals and pamphlets, and in two later novels, *Colonel Jack* and *Roxana*.]

1. From *An Essay upon Projects* (1697)

OF BANKRUPTS

This Chapter has some Right to stand next to that of Fools; for besides the common acceptation of late, which makes *every Unfortunate Man a Fool*, I think no man so much made a Fool of as a *Bankrupt*.

If I may be allow'd so much liberty with our Laws, which are generally good, and above all things are temper'd with Mercy, Lenity, and Freedom, This has something in it of Barbarity; it gives a loose to the Malice and Revenge of the Creditor, as well as a Power to right himself, while it leaves the Debt or no way to show himself honest: It contrives all the ways possible to drive the Debtor to despair, and encourages no new Industry, for it makes him perfectly uncapable of any thing but *starving*.

This Law, especially as it is now frequently executed, tends wholly to the Destruction of the Debtor, and yet very little to the Advantage of the Creditor.

The Severities to the Debtor are unreasonable, and, if I may so say, a little inhuman; for it not only strips him of all in a moment, but renders him for ever incapable of helping himself, or relieving his Family by future Industry. If he 'scapes from Prison, which is hardly done too, if he has nothing left, he must starve, or live on Charity; if he goes to work, no man dare pay him his Wages, but he shall pay it again to the Creditors; if he has any private Stock left for a Subsistence, he can put it no where; every man is bound to be a Thief, and take it from him: If he trusts it in the hands of a Friend, he must receive it again as a great Courtesy, for that Friend is liable to account for it. I have known a poor man prosecuted by a Statute to that degree, that all he had left was a little

Money, which he knew not where to hide; at last, that he might not starve, he gives it to his Brother, who had entertain'd him; the Brother, after he had his Money, quarrels with him to get him out of his House; and when he desires him to let him have the Money lent him, gives him this for Answer, *I cannot pay you safely, for there is a Statute against you*; which run the poor man to such Extremities, that he destroy'd himself. Nothing is more frequent, than for men who are reduc'd by Miscarriage in Trade, to compound and Set up again, and get good Estates; but a *Statute*, as we call it, for ever shuts up all doors to the Debtor's Recovery; as if Breaking were a Crime so Capital, that he ought to be cast out of Human Society, and expos'd to Extremities worse than Death. And, which will further expose the fruitless Severity of this law, 'tis easy to make it appear, That all this Cruelty to the Debtor is so far (generally speaking) from advantaging the Creditors, that it destroys the Estate, consumes it in extravagant Charges, and unless the Debtor be consenting, seldom makes any considerable Dividends. And I am bold to say, There is no Advantage made by the prosecuting of a Statute with Severity, but what might be doubly made by Methods more merciful. And tho' I am not to prescribe to the Legislators of the Nation, yet by way of Essay I take leave to give my Opinion and my Experience in the Methods, Consequences, and Remedies of this Law.

OF ACADEMIES

An Academy for Women

I have often thought of it as one of the most barbarous Customs in the world, considering us as a Civiliz'd and a Christian Countrey, that we deny the advantages of Learning to Women. We reproach the Sex every day with Folly and Impertinence, while I am confident, had they the advantages of Education equal to us, they wou'd be guilty of less than our selves.

One wou'd wonder indeed how it shou'd happen that Women are conversible at all, since they are only beholding to Natural Parts for all their Knowledge. Their Youth is spent to teach them to Stitch and Sow, or make Bawbles: They are taught to Read indeed, and perhaps to Write their Names, or so; and that is the heighth of a Woman's Education. And I wou'd but ask any who slight the Sex for their Understanding, What is a Man (a Gentleman, I mean) good for, that is taught no more?

I need not give Instances, or examine the Character of a Gentleman with a good Estate, and of a good Family, and with tolerable Parts, and examine what Figure he makes for want of Education.

The Soul is plac'd in the Body like a rough Diamond, and must be polish'd, or the Lustre of it will never appear: And 'tis manifest, that as the Rational Soul distinguishes us from Brutes, so Education carries on the distinction, and makes some less brutish than others: This is too evident to need any demonstration. But why then shou'd Women be deni'd the benefit of Instruction? ...

The Capacities of Women are suppos'd to be greater, and their Senses quicker than those of the Men; and what they might be capable of being bred to, is plain from some Instances of Female-Wit, which this Age is not without; which upbraids us with Injustice, and looks as if we deni'd Women the advantages of Education, for fear they shou'd *vye* with the Men in their Improvements.

To remove this Objection, and that Women might have at least a needful Opportunity of Education in all sorts of Useful Learning, I propose the Draught of an Academy for that purpose....

When I talk therefore of an Academy for Women, I mean both the Model, the Teaching, and the Government, different from what is propos'd by that Ingenious Lady,[1] for whose Proposal I have a very great Esteem, and also a great Opinion of her Wit; different too from all sorts of Religious Confinement, and above all, from *Vows of Celibacy*.

Wherefore the Academy I propose should differ but little from Publick Schools, wherein such Ladies as were willing to study, shou'd have all the advantages of Learning suitable to their Genius....

The Persons who Enter, shou'd be taught all sorts of Breeding suitable to both their Genius and their Quality; and in particular, *Musick* and *Dancing*, which it wou'd be cruelty to bar the Sex of, because they are their Darlings: But besides this, they shou'd be taught Languages, as particularly *French* and *Italian*; and I wou'd venture the Injury of giving a Woman more Tongues than one.

They shou'd, as a particular Study, be taught all the Graces of Speech, and all the necessary Air of Conversation; which our common Education is so defective in, that I need not expose it: They shou'd be brought to read Books, and especially History, and so to read as to make them understand the World, and be able to know and judge of things when they hear of them....

---

1 Mary Astell, author of *A Serious Proposal to the Ladies for the Advancement of their True and Great Interest* (1694).

Women, in my observation, have little or no difference in them, but as they are, or are not distinguish'd by Education. Tempers[1] indeed may in some degree influence them, but the main distinguishing part is their Breeding.

The whole Sex are generally Quick and Sharp: I believe I may be allow'd to say generally so; for you rarely see them lumpish and heavy when they are Children, as Boys will often be. If a Woman be well-bred, and taught the proper Management of her Natural Wit, she proves generally very sensible and retentive: And without partiality, a Woman of Sense and Manners is the Finest and most Delicate Part of God's Creation; the Glory of her Maker, and the great Instance of his singular regard to Man, his Darling Creature, to whom he gave the best Gift either God could bestow, or man receive ...

2. From the *Review* (19 February 1704-11 June 1713)[2]

A Supplement to the Advice from the Scandal Club,
no. 5, 1705[3]

Gentlemen,
SOme Days ago I sent you a Note, and earnestly beg'd a Solution to the following Query. Whether I may have any hopes from a Lady who is far beyond me in Fortune, but has given me some Encouragement, but is not willing to marry without the Consent of some Persons who are against her marrying me? She's engag'd till such a Term of Years are expired. Now, I desire to know, what way to use? Whether I may hope? &c. But Gentlemen, you must have receiv'd my former Letter sign'd A.B.C. *I don't question. I impatiently expected an Answer in your* Saturday's Review, *but was disappointed. I hope your next will be satisfactory, and I desire it be. The thing is real. Her Engagement is so, that she cannot in Conscience or Interest do otherwise; and I beg you to insert the Answer to my former Query in my other Letter, and I shall expect it in your next* Review.

---

1 Temperaments, dispositions.
2 More magazine than newspaper, the *Review* was at first published weekly, then bi-weekly, and finally tri-weekly, apparently in response to its growing popularity.
3 When Defoe published the *Review* in the form of a volume at the end of the first year, he added an advertisement in response to one of the most popular features of the journal: "*With an Entertaining Part in every Sheet, Being Advice from the Scandal Club, to the Curious Enquirers; in Answer to Letters sent them for that Purpose.*"

The short Question here amounts but to this, whether you may hope to obtain a Lady that won't marry you without the Consent of somebody who will not Consent?

To this they would have answer'd, That they refer you to time and your own Artifices to work upon the Lady. But, Sir, when you add in the Margin of your Second Letter, she is under such Engagements, that in Conscience, and in Interest she cannot, you foreclose us and your self; for the Society are positively of Opinion, you ought not either to hope or sollicite the Person to act against her Conscience and Interest, but especially the first.

AMong the several Persons who apply to this Society to dissolve at least their Promises of Marriage if not their real Contracts, the following is one of the hardest Cases.

SIR,

THE generous Encouragement which you give to all Persons that desire your Advice, makes me give you this trouble; and I hope you will do me the Favour of a speedy Answer to the following Questions, which shall be gratefully acknowledg'd.

Qu. I. *What Method must a Man pursue here in* England, *to prove a Marriage, (supposing the Woman to deny it) being wedded by a Priest of the Church of* Rome, *in the Presence only of another Person, being also a Priest of the same Religion?*

Qu. 2. *Whether if this Marriage (the Woman refusing to co-habit with the Husband, and taking some extravagant Freedoms) be not invalid before God, and the Man at Liberty to take another Woman to Wife?*

Your Answer will give me unexpressible Satisfaction, and I am satisfied you would not deny my Request, if you knew my deplorable Condition. I hope in God that I shall see my Case in your next Review.

Upon the Honour of a Gentleman, I will return the Favour.

March 10. 1705.

Really, Sir, on your Case the Society seem'd doubtful a long time, and were very unwilling to meddle; but your Importunity, and hoping it may be of Use to you, prevail'd with them.

I. Sir, supposing you were once marryed, and that Marriage consummated, all the Laws in the World, except for natural Imperfection or Adulterous Practices, cannot dissolve it.

As to your being marryed by a Priest of the Church of *Rome*, the Society cannot give you any Encouragement from thence; for the Essence of Matrimony consisting in the mutual Consent of Parties, the publick Sanction, which is the Debt of the Subject to mutual Society in Obedience to the Law, is not at all the less valid for being perform'd by a Priest of the Church of *Rome*; it is requisite to be perform'd by those whose Office it is to perform it; in which Case we allow the Marriages of the Quakers, and several other Sorts of Dissenters, and why not the *Roman* Clergy as well as others?

As to the Proof, 'tis indeed a hard thing to prove a Marriage where the Evidence, for other Reasons, dare not appear; but, Sir, if the Proof of this be worth while, and the Persons who married you, are in, or will go into any Foreign Country, and certifie there your marriage before proper Authorities, no Doubt you may obtain a Commission or Delegation for the taking such Testimony either in *Holland* or *Scotland*, or elsewhere; the Case else would be very hard with all such as marry out of the *English* Dominions, who when they arrive here, may deny their Marriages and abandon their Wives.

If the Marriage you mention was not consummated, and the Woman refuses to Co-habit, or the extravagant Freedoms you mention, amount to enough to sue a Divorce; without doubt you may be free, otherwise they do not see how they can relieve you.

THE Society according to their Promise in *Review* No 15. have inserted the following Madam *Celinda's* Letter, with its Answer.

Gentlemen,
I Own my selfe one of the Admirers of your Works, finding both Mirth and Improvement by them. I ask your Pardon for troubling you with this Story, but Necessity urges me to do it.

I am a young Gentlewoman, of a competent Fortune; I have liv'd the greatest Part of my time in the Country, where I have had a great many profest Admirers; some of them Men of pretty handsome Estates; but such entire Lovers of a Country Life, (to which I have an Aversion) that for that very Reason I dismist them, with a Resolution, with the Consent of my Friends, to come to London, where I have been for some time fatigu'd with the Addresses of several importunate Suitors, viz. Gentlemen of small Estates, having no Business to keep them from Idleness, Lawyers, Physicians, and Linnen-Drapers; 'tis my way to give some Glympse of Encouragement to most, till such time as I discover their Circumstances and Dispositions; some I have approved of better than others, but upon your Advice (as from that of a Parent) I shall rely; my Guardian is Self-interested, and I dare not confide in his Choice. As for

Lawyers, I do not disapprove of them, only for this Reason, they general-
ly make but indifferent Husbands, being from the Inns of Court, as it is
now degenerated, brought up in Lewdness.[1] *As for Physicians, I declare*
to you, I should not like them for Bed-Fellows, after their coming from
Patients troubled with Malignant Distempers, which may be infectious.
Lastly, as for Linnen-Drapers, Tom Pitkin *has frighted me; but tho' I'm*
sure to be well secured from all Dangers, yet my Friends advise me not to
a Trade, because it deprives me of my Gentility. Now Gentlemen, imag-
ine me young and Handsome in the Eye of the World, never having
receiv'd one Blemish upon my Reputation; my Parents deceas'd, wanti-
ng of them, I adopt you as such, and as such. I beg you would pardon
my Prolixity, and give me your Cordial Advice in your next Review;
having taken a Place in the Coach for Fryday *next, where I will con-*
sider upon the tender Advice you give. Gentlemen, this is the first Love-
Letter I ever wrote. Pray don't discourage your real Admirers, Celinda.

Tuesday Evening.

Really, Madam, upon reading your Letter, the Society gave it
as their Opinion, that you are one of those Ladies, whom Heaven,
in Justice to their very extraordinary Nicety, suffers to be puzzled
with their own Curiosities.

Our City Sparks cannot please, because they are Tradesmen,
and you scorn to go to Bed to any thing but a Gentleman; for fear,
they presume, of spoiling the Breed.

Then you cannot marry, a Gentleman, because you have an
Aversion to living in the Country.

Now this is really a puzzling Case, for when a Lady cannot
please her self, who can please her? She that cannot be pleased
either in the Country, or City, who can advise her?

However, Madam, to please you, if possible, The Soci[e]ty having thought of all the Sorts you object against, observe the Church
and the Army, have very fortunately escap'd your Censure.

Now, Madam, the Field is wide, a good honest Parson, with
God's Blessing, and a tollerable Living, in, or near the City, fits
you to a Hair; for there you miss the Lewdness of the Lawyers, the
Bankrup[t]sie of the Merchants, the Mechanism[2] of the Tradesmen; there's the Man of God and the Gentleman both in a Lump,
and his Discretion may assist to regulate your Judgment.

---

1 In an ill-bred, ill-mannered way.
2 Baseness, lowness.

But Madam, if that sort of Life is too Grave for you; a Soldier is a Gentleman by his Profession, and his Sword pares off all the Dirt of a Mechanick Original,[1] and reconciles this Contradiction, that a Lady may be a Beggar, and a Gentlewoman altogether.

Besides, Madam, in this Gentleman's Circumstances, you may live in City, Town, or Country, where you can, *where you please*, we should say; and so it is hop'd your Difficulty is over; if not, they desire to hear farther.

Saturday, June 8, 1706

Mr. *REVIEW*,
YOU have all along profess'd to be impartial in your Censures of things vicious and scandalous; and, that without Respect of Persons you will speak all Sorts of needful Truths, to which you have set your Hand in the Introduction to your Volumes of the Review.

We herewith send you a true History of one of the most villainous and most barbarous Actions, that has ever been heard of in a Protestant Country; and which we doubt not will fill you with Detestation at the Writing, and every honest Christian with like Abhorrence at the Reading.

It is aggravated with unusual Circumstances, and we cannot without some Horrour let you know, that this black Scene has been acted by an own Mother and two Sons, upon her own Daughter and their own Sister; whose unnatural Proceedings we leave to your Censure, and come to the Fact.

A certain Citizen of good Character and Repute, and a long Trader in *London*, dy'd about six Years since,—and being possess'd of a very good Estate; after providing for his Widow and two Sons, about 2800 *l.* in Money came to his youngest Daughter, besides other demands yet undetermin'd.

This young Lady being of Age to take care of her self, and particularly sensible enough to discern, that her Mother and both her Brothers used her unkindly; and not at all backward to provide for her own Quiet, soon after her Fathers Death, took care to remove out of their Family; and that she might not be at all at their Mercy, took Care also to secure her Estate; which she had no small reason to suspect, they at least grudg'd her the Enjoyment of, if they had no ill Design upon the thing it self....

It was not long after these things, when the following Method

---

1 Base or low born.

was taken with this young Gentlewoman; whether to secure her Money, and *take care of her*, as had been promised, the World may judge.

About 3 Months since, the two Brothers of this young Gentlewoman, consulting with a certain known Attorney related to the Person, who had her Money, what Measures to take with her; were advised, as we suppose, to petition the Lord Keeper,[1] for a Commission of Lunacy against her; and that it might be the better obtain'd, they joyn HER OWN MOTHER in the horrid Attempt, and she signs the said Petition.

What the Meaning of such a Petition was, we need not inform you, nor how by this Power, they would not only have her effectually in their own keeping, but her Estate also; allowing her perhaps 10 or 20 *l. per Ann.* to be maintain'd as a Lunatick....

The Design being fully ripe, and compleated by the rash Verdict of the Jury aforesaid, the rest of the Scene is all Violence and Fury, for these People having provided proper Instruments, come up Stairs to this Gentlewoman into her Chamber, on some frivolous Pretences, the Time unusually late, and on a *Saturday* Night; they had to admit them, provided two Women and one Man; the Man, as we are since inform'd, a Door-Keeper in *Bedlam*,[2] and one of the Women, a Nurse in a Mad-house.

These coming into her Chamber, seize upon her in a most barbarous manner, hand-cuff her Hands behind her with Irons; bound her Legs together with Cords, and attempted to thrust a Handkerchief or Cloth into her Mouth; and in this cruel manner carried her away by Force, put her into a Coach, and hurried her to one of our private *Bedlams*, putting her into the Hands of the aforesaid infamous Apothecary; of whom the World will hear more hereafter.

In this House, she continued about 6 or 7 Weeks under the most horrid Treatment that ever was heard of, by his express Command, and often in his Presence, and we want Words to express it to you; but the farther Particulars are preparing for the World, and to which we refer you....

In this horrid Condition, and under this most Villianous Treatment, they kept her about seven Weeks; no body, but whom that Apothecary permitted, being suffer'd to come near her.

---

1 A high officer of state, who had custody of the great seal. The office is now vested in the Lord Chancellor.
2 See above, p. 286, n. 2.

But at last some Neighbours, where she had lodg'd, and who us'd to visit her, missing her at her lodging, and having providentially gain'd some Hints of her Condition, were mov'd in meer Pity and Compassion to enquire into her Circumstances; and having learn'd enough to fill them with Abhorrence of the Matter, in meer Charity, and without any Design, but to redeem her out of such a miserable Condition, they apply'd themselves to us, who give you this Account; who being mov'd with the like Commiseration and Charity, immediately caused a Petition to be deliver'd to my Lord Keeper, for leave to visit the poor Gentlewoman, and enquire into her Circumstances, Health, and Understanding.

Upon this Enquiry made by proper Persons, and such as were no way aw'd by the Threatnings of her Brothers, and their Accomplices, tho' they were very free with their Language and Insults, they found the young Woman of a perfectly sound Mind and Memory, horribly abus'd and deeply afflicted at her Misfortune; but clear in her Judgment, compos'd in her Mind, and of good Understanding.

Whereupon a Petition was immediately drawn in her Name to my Lord Keeper, praying, that she might be brought before his Lordship in order to be examin'd, whether she ought to be treated as a Lunatick, or no?

Upon this Petition, an Order was obtain'd for her to attend, which she accordingly did; and *in short*, my Lord-Keeper was so full satisfied in all the Particulars aforesaid, and of her being no Lunatick, that his Lordship was pleas'd to express him self with the utmost Detestation and Abhorrence of such villainous Proceedings, order'd the Commission of Lunacy to be immediately superseeded, and all Proceedings thereon to be dissolv'd and made void; for it is to be observ'd, that the Brothers and Mother of this young Woman had obtain'd with their Commission of Lunacy, an order to have the Guardianship of the Lunatick committed to them, as also the Possession of her Estate.

Saturday, June 25, 1709

I Am upon examining the Advantages to *England* by the Encrease of People, and particularly as to the Consumption of the Produce of our Land; in order to [do] this, I began to examine in my last, what every single Person, living after the Manner of *England*, may be said to consume in this Nation—I crave leave to repeat so much of the Calculate, as is necessary to state the Fact.

I alledge, that every grown Person living, *as we call it*, plentifully in *England*, according to the common Rate of the middling People of *England*, Citizens, Shop-keepers, Merchants, and Gentlemen; for the two first, I assure you, live as well as the last, and perhaps something better—These, I say, consume one with another; for every single Head,

2 Quarter of Wheat, in Bread, Pies, Pudings.

4 Quarter of Barley, in Drink.

I Quarter of Peas or Beans, green or dry.

I Large fat Bullock.

6 Fat Sheep.

4 Lambs.

2 Calves.

I Hog.

100 Weight of Butter and Cheese, or the Value in Milk; besides Fowl, Fruits, Roots, Garden-Stuff, *&c.* all which employ some Part both of Land and Labour.

But because we must take a Calculate from such a *Medium*, as may be proportion'd to the Conditions of all the People, and the Poor may be set against the Rich—I'll state it again.

The People are divided into;

I. The Great, who live profusely.

2. The Rich, who live very plentifully.

3. The middle Sort, who live well.

4. The working Trades, who labour hard, but feel no Want.

5. The Country People, Farmers, *&c.* who fare indifferently.

6. The Poor, that fare hard.

7. The Miserable, that really pinch and suffer Want.

Take these then at the middle, I allow, that the Luxury of the two first makes up in the Consumption, what the Necessities of the two last abate: Then I say, the middle Sort of People, who in short live the best, and consume the most of any in the Nation, and perhaps in the World, and who are the most numerous also among us, and with whom the general Wealth of this Nation is found; these, I say, as much over do it, as the Farmers, my *5th* Sort, *who by the way all over* England *live very well too*, can be suppos'd to under-do it—Take then the *4th* Sort for the *Medium*—And there I'll make my Calculation—Suppose a Carpenter, a Smith, a Weaver, or any such Workman, what you will, that is industrious, works hard, and feels no Want, let him live in the Country or City, *North* or *South*, where you will; for in this, one Country will answer another.

As I said in my last, if the Gentleman eats more Pies and Puddings, this Man eats more Bread; if the Rich drinks more Wine, this drinks more Ale or Strong-Beer, for it is the Support of his Vigour and Strength—If a rich Man eats more Veal and Lamb, Fowl and Fish; this Man eats more Beef and Bacon, and add to it, has a better Stomach, a Happiness almost as great as to have Food to eat—As to the Milk, if the rich Man eats more Butter, more Cream, mor[e] white Meats, *or as the Song calls them*, Fools, Flawns,[1] and Custards—Our Workman eats more hard Cheese and Salt-Butter, than all the other put together....

Saturday, January 31, 1713

IT is a Remark of my own, but, perhaps, too well to be justified by the Experience of most who shall read this Paper, that tho' the Trade of the Nation, by the Confession of all Men of Sense, was *never* more decayed, Money *never* scarcer, the Number of Bankrupts *never* greater, the Cries of the Poor *never* louder, and the rate of Provisions, for some Years past, one with another, *never* higher; yet the Pride, the Luxury, the Expensive Way of Living, the costly Furniture and Ostentation, both in Equipage, Cloaths, Feeding and Wearing, were never greater in this Nation....

I remember an Accident, which gave me a Scetch of this very Thing, and which I could not avoid taking Notice of: Sometime since, being upon Business, *very late*, in the City, it was my Lot to come along the Street, just as a sudden and terrible Fire broke out in a Citizens House, *in none of the Wealthiest part of the Town neither*; I forbear the Place, for the sake of the Particulars.—I could contribute little to the helping the Good People in their Distress; nor was I very well qualified to Carry Water, or Work an Engin; besides the Street was presently full of People for that Work: But, I plac'd my self in a convenient Corner, near the Fire, to look on, and, indeed, the Consternation of the Poor People was not fruitless of Remarks.

And First, I was, I confess, surprized to hear the Skreeks[2] and Lamentations of the Poor Ladies, as well in the Houses on either side, as opposite to the House that was on Fire; after the first Fright was express'd with a great deal of Noise, terrible Gestures and Distortions, I observ'd all hands at Work, to Remove: The Chamber-Maids were hurried down Stairs, *Betty, Betty*, says a Lady, aloud you may be sure, *have you got the Plate?* Yes, Madam,

---

1 A kind of cheesecake or flan. Also a pancake.
2 Screams, screeches.

says *Betty: Here take the Cabinet,* says Madam, *Run to my Mothers; there's all my Jewels, have a Care of them BETTY:* Away runs *Betty*: This, I think, was about the Degree of a Fish-monger's Lady:—At a House that was in great Danger, they were, like Sea-Men in a Storm, to lighten the Ship, throwing their Goods out at Window; and, *Indeed, I think, they had as good have let them be burnt*: Here I saw, out of a *Shopkeeper's* House, Velvet Hangings, Embroidered Chairs, Damask Curtains, Plumes of Feathers; and, in short, Furniture equal to what, formerly, suffis'd the greatest of our Nobility; thrown into a Street flowing a Foot Deep with Water and Mud, trodden Under-Foot by the Crowd, and then carried off Piece-Meal as well as they could: It was not the Fright the People were in, or the Error of their destroying their Goods in that Hurry, that was so much matter of Observation to me, as to see the Furniture that came out of such Houses, far better than any Removed at the late Fire, at the *French* Ambassadors.

In the House which I stood nearest too, which was opposite to the Fire, and which was in great Danger too, the Wind blowing the Flame, which was very Furious, directly into the Windows; The Woman, or Mistress, or Lady, call her as you will, had several small Children; her Maids, or Nurses, or whatever they were, made great Diligence to bring the Poor Children half naked, and asleep, Down-Stairs in their Arms; and wrapping them up carefully, run out of the House with them; One of these Maids coming again, as if to fetch Another, meets her Mistress, whose Concern, it seems, lay another way, with a Great Bundle, the Mistress screams out to her, *MARY, MARY, Take care of my Cloaths; Carry them away; I'll go fetch the Rest*: The Maid, more concern'd for the Children, than the Mother, *Cries out louder* than her Mistress, *Lord, Madam, Where's Master* Tommy? *The Child will be burnt in the Bed*: Throws down the Cloaths, and runs up Stairs: The Mistress, whose fine Cloaths lay nearer her Heart, than her Child, Cries out, *Oh! There's all my Cloaths*; Snatches up the Great Bundle, and runs out of the House half naked, with it, and leaves the Wench to go fetch her Child; who, Poor Lamb, was almost suffocated with the Smoke and Heat.

3. From *Applebee's Journal* (25 June 1720-14 May 1726)[1]

Saturday, July 16, 1720

To the Author of the Original Journal.

SIR,

I FIND many People send their Cases to *Public Writers* for their Advice, and I suppose receive Satisfaction by the Answers their Eminences give them back again; or that the making their Cases Publick is *in its self* something of Assistance to them in the several Circumstances they are in, otherwise they would never give themselves and the Authors of *Journals* so much Trouble; now my Case being Extraordinary, you will easily see I have at least as much reason to make it Public as other People, and therefore I desire to be heard with Patience.

I am, Sir, an *Elder,* and well known Sister, of the *File,* but lest all the Readers should not understand the Cant of our Profession, you may take it in plain *English,* I was, in the former part of my Life, an eminent *Pick-Pocket,* and you may observe also that while I kept in the Employment I was bred up to, I did very well, and kept out of Harms way, for I was so Wary, so Dexterous, kept so retir'd to my self, and did my Work so well, that I was never detected, *no never,* was never pump'd, never taken, and I may add I began to lay up Money, and be before-hand in the World; not that I had any Thought of leaving off my Trade neither; no, nor ever should have done it, if I had been as rich as the best of my Trade in *Exchange Alley.*[2]

But *Curse of ill Company,* I was unhappily drawn a-side out of my ordinary and lawful Calling into the dangerous Business of *Shop-lifting,* and being not half so clever and nimble at that as I was at my own Trade, I was nab'd by a plaguy Hawks-Ey'd Journey-Man *Mercer,* and so I got into the Hands of the Law. It went

---

1 First called the *Original Weekly Journal* and then *Applebee's Original Weekly Journal,* Defoe was not only a major contributor to it but at times controlled the editorial policy.

2 Exchange Alley in Cornhill was notorious for pickpockets and shoplifters, who were particularly attracted by the increasing number of stockbrokers and their clients in the area. However, in *The Anatomy of Exchange Alley* (1719) Defoe remarks: "Is not the whole doctrine of stock-jobbing a science of fraud? And are not all the dealers meer original thieves and pick-pockets?"

very hard with me upon this Occasion, and to make my Story short, I run thro' all the *several Ways of being Undone*; I mean the *Newgate* Ways, for I was Tryed, Condemn'd, pleaded my Belly, had a Verdict of the *Jades* they call Matrons in my Favour, and at length having obtain'd a suspicion of Hanging, I got to be Transported.

How I was sent over, or whether sent over or no, and of what use the little Money I had laid up *as above*, has been to me in all my Tribulation, is not to the present Purpose, and besides is too long a Story to tell in a Letter; it may suffice to the Case in hand to let you know, *and the World by your Means*, that I am at the present Writing hereof among the Number of the Inhabitants of *Old England*; whether I was Transported, what Adventures I met with abroad, *if I was abroad*, and how I came hither again, I say, are too long for a Letter;[1] *But here I am.*

Now as my being here is a new Tresspass, and may bring me back to the Gallows, from whence it may be *truly* said I came, I am not quite so easie as I was before, tho' I am prudently retir'd to my first Employ, and find I can do pretty well at it; but that which makes me more in Danger is the meeting Yesterday with One of my old Acquaintance; he salutes me publickly in the Street, with a long out-cry, *O brave Moll*, says he, *Why what do you do out of your Grave? Was not you Transported? Hold your Tongue Jack*, says I, for God's Sake, what have you a mind to ruin me? D—— me, says he, *you Jade* give me a Twelver[2] than, *or I'll tell this minute*; I was forc'd to do it, and so the Rogue has a Milch[3] Cow of me, as long as I live.

But this is not all, for it may happen, that I may miscarry in my Business too, and if once I come into the Hands of the unmerciful again, I am gone for ever; pray give your Advice, how such a dexterous Sinner, *as I am*, must go on, for this kind of Life does not do now, so cleverly as it us'd to do:

your Friend and Servant,

Moll.

---

1 Generally assumed to be a hint at the forthcoming "history" of *Moll Flanders*.
2 Twelve pence.
3 Milking.

Saturday, January 26, 1723

To the Author of the Original Journal.

SIR,

I HAVE been often thinking to write a line or two to you about the desperate Temper of our wicked People, *I mean those they call convict Felons* in returning from Transportation, as we see they do daily, at the Peril of their Lives.

How they find ways and means at *Virginia,* and the Places they are carried to, to avoid the Servitude they are Sentenc'd to, and to get Passage back to *England,* is a thing well worth consideration; and I may speak of it by it self; but that is not the present business, no doubt Measures might be taken by the Governments Direction to prevent it, and to make it impossible, so that the poor wretched Creatures should not have it in their Power, to bring themselves to the Gallows as they do every Day, but of that I say hereafter, it is not our present Work.

But what Infatuation is it that possesses the People I am speaking of, that they should at all hazards, nay, almost at a certainty of Death and Shame, push back *as they do* from their Transportation, to a place where, they are as it were, almost sure to be taken, as they are sure to Dye when they are taken.

It can not be the meer Dread and Terror of the Place and Labour they are doom'd to do at *Virginia,* for tho' it be what may be call'd Labour, yet I affirm, it is the best and easiest of its kind, that any Country in the World confines their Criminals to undergo....

In a Word, their Labour is not harder, or their Usage worse than many hired Servants in *England* o[n] Yearly Wages; and tis evident even before their Eyes, the Negro Servants even in the same Plantation, and under the same Masters, are in worse Circumstances (infinitely worse) than they; as they are not only us'd worse, but are without Redemption, without Hope, without any end of their Misery, for them or their Posterity.

But here their time being out, which generally is no more than seven or fourteen Years, they are sure of being Free; and not only so, but have an opportunity of Planting for themselves, and that with such Encouragement, that nothing but a stated Aversion to an honest Life, or to a diligent Application to Business, can prevent their accepting it with the utmost Thankfulness; nor are they without innumerable Instances on the Spot, which way soever they turn, of good substantial Families, rais'd from the same beginnings; namely, where Offenders like themselves, made sensible of the Danger of Death which they had escap'd, and of the benefit of an industrious Life, which was before them, have applyed themselves to the planting of Land, and by their own Labour and Application, with the Assistance of the Country Bounty, have by little and little, rais'd themselves to good Circumstances, and in the end, by a continu'd addition, have prosper'd and grown Rich.

It is certain, that every Servant thus finishing the Time of his Servitude, has an Opportunity put into his Hands (as it may be call'd) to set up for himself: He may have Land assign'd him by the Country, and he may have Credit for Cloaths, Tools and Necessaries for his Support, till what he can prepare and plant may be brought to perfection, and then he pays by the Crop, and gains Credit till the next Crop; so that they cannot say they have no Stock to set up with, no Tools to work with, no Cloaths, and the like.

This is a fair Offer of Heaven to such Creatures to begin, not only a new Condition of Life, but even a new Life itself; and, which is very particulair, here they are sure never to be upbraided with either the Crimes or Misfortunes of their former Life: To be reform'd, is so much real Credit to them, and so valued by all about them in that Place, that it is equal, if not superior, even to not having been guilty at all.

Upon their being thus reform'd, and applying themselves with Honesty and Industry to a due Course of Business, they are as sure of rising in the World, as they are sure of Misery and Death in the contrary.

Who then in their Wits would decline wearing out with Patience the Life of Servitude, which is in it self but short, with so certain a Prospect of Safety and Success; who would choose to come back a thousand Leagues, to seek in the stead of it certain Death, Infamy, and the Gallows: and yet we see every Day Examples of these Creatures, who suffer Death for flying from their own Felicity, and who choose to die with Shame, rather than to live happy and easy, at the small Expense of five or six or seven Years Servitude....

Yours, &c.

Saturday, November 21, 1724

To the Author of the Original Journal.
Mr. App.

I AM a poor unfortunate Creature, as my Story will tell you at large, I was born in *Newgate*, the famous *Moll Flanders* was my Aunt, but she met with good Fortune to set her above all her poor Relations, and I am left under infinite Disappointments.

I have been Transported twice, and have both times found Ways and Means not only to come back again, but to avoid being Taken again till Acts of Indemnity, and length of Time gave me leave to appear Abroad.

I have follow'd the Trade of Pilfering, and stealing some Years, and was got to a tollerable State of Life, that I could now have liv'd without it; but the habit has been so become a Nature to me, that I believe I should have walk'd in my sleep to pick Pockets, if I had deny'd my self the liberty of doing it waking, so I have continu'd the Trade a great many Years with uninterrupted Success, and now what strange Thing do you think has befallen me: Would you think it Mr. *App.* that I should have fall in Love after so much good Education as I have been Mistress of?

But so it is, I have been so deeply in Love with your late Friend *John Sheppard*,[1] that I have been quite distracted. His Escaping with such Dexterity as you have heard out of *Newgate* charm'd me, and if I could have found him during the little time of Liberty he enjoy'd, I had certainly had him.

What tho' I am 20 Year older than he, we should have made a suitable Match in all other things: For as he was the most dexterous House-breaker in *England*; so I pretend to be the cleanest-handed Shoplift, and the nicest[2] Pick-Pocket in *Europe*. I offer Mr. *App* to go into a Mercer's-Shop, and tell him I come to take such a peice of Silk by slight of Hand, and he shall neither miss the peice, or perceive me to touch it, but shall think he sees the peice of Silk lye upon the Compter all the while....

Perhaps you have never heard of me, nor does the Fame of our Profession ever spread to any extraordinary a Degree, till they come to *Newgate*; but I have been so long forgotten there, that the

---

1 Highwayman and popular hero, John Sheppard escaped several times from Newgate prison prior to his execution at Tyburn in 1724. A letter in "the Hand-writing of JOHN SHEPPARD" was published in the *Review* (31 October 1725), sending "my kind Love" to Mr. Applebee.
2 Deftest.

present Incumbents, not Mr. [Pitt]¹ himself knows any thing of me.

Now had *John Sheppard* and I made a Match, what cleaver² Couple should we have made, and what Pockets, what fasten Watches, what Purses of Money could have escaped us by Daylight, and what Bolted Shops, or Barricaded Houses have kept me out by Night? In a Word, Mr. *App.* we would have visited *Lombard-street* itself, no Iron Bars could have kept us out, no Iron Chest have withstood us within; but all is over, poor SHEPPARD is gone, and in him the expertest House-breaker in *England* is gone.

And am I not under a vast Disappointment now, when poor dexterous *Jack* is thus snatch'd from us by his evil Fate, after two of the immitable Escapes, and after having twice had his Liberty, but not been able to preserve himself.

Alas poor SHEPPARD! I have lost my Love, and all the hopes I had cherish'd of an universal Plunder are gone so far that I am left under an inexpressible Grief.

Your Humble Servant,
Betty Blewskin. (Catch me if you can.)

John Sheppard, the famous House-breaker, was on Monday last executed at Tyburn, pursuant to the Rule of Court of the King's-Bench,³ Westminster. He being an enterprizing Fellow, it was thought necessary to put Handcuffs on him in carrying him to the Gallows; which could not be done but by main Force, he struggling against it with all his Might; and being search'd before he was put in the Cart, they found conceal'd about him a Claspe Knife, with which 'tis thought he designed to cut the Cord wherewith he was ty'd, and then to leap among the Mob, as his last Refuge. The Crowd of Spectators all the Way was prodigiously great. An Undertaker with a Hearse follow'd him to Tyburn, in order as we are told, to bring back the Corpse to be interr'd in St. Sepulcher's Church Yard; but the Populace having a Notion that it was design'd to convey him to the Surgeons, carry'd off the Body upon their Shoulders to an Alehouse in Long-Acre, and the Undertaker and his Men got off with great Difficulty.

---

1 William Pitt, Keeper of Newgate prison from 1707 to 1732.
2 Clever (obsolete form), in the sense of dexterous or "sharp to seize."
3 The supreme court of common law in the kingdom.

Saturday, May 29, 1725

On *Monday* about the usual Time *Jonathan Wild*[1] was executed at *Tyburn*. Never was there seen so prodigious a Concourse of People before, not even upon the most popular Occasion of that Nature. The famous *Jack Sheppard*[2] had a tolerable Number to attend his *Exit*, but no more to be compared to the present, than a Regiment to an Army; and which is very remarkable, in all that innumerable Crowd there was not one pitying Eye to be seen, nor one compassionate Word to be heard, but on the contrary, whereever he came, there was nothing but Hollowing and Huzzas[3] as it had been upon a Triumph; nay, so far had he incurr'd the Resentment of the Populace that they pelted him with Stones, &c. in several Places,[4] one of which in *Holbern* broke his Head to that Degree that the Blood ran down plentifully, which Barbarity tho' as unjustifiable as unusual, yet may serve to deterr others from treading in his Steps when they find the Consequence so universally odious. At the Place of Execution the People continu'd very outragious, so that it was impossible either for *Jonathan* or any of the rest to be very compos'd; however he behav'd himself better than could be well expected, considering the perpetual Insults, Peltings, &c. that he suffer'd. All the Indulgence he receiv'd was his not having his Hands ty'd all the Way; and at the Place of Execution, he was admitted to sit in the Cart till the Minister came, the others having been ty'd up a considerable Time. When he was turn'd off, there was an Universal Shout among the Spectators. As the Cart drew away, his Arms being loose, he happen'd to catch hold of the Coiner,[5] but was immediately parted from him. His body was carry'd off in a Coach and four to the Sign of the *Adam and Eve*[6] near *Pancreas* Church, in order to be interr'd in the Church-yard there, where one of his former w[i]ve[s] lies buried, which was done on *Tuesday* Night last. About two of the Clock in the Morning he had taken a Dose of Liquid *Laudanum*,[7] in order to have dispatch'd himself, but swallowing too much, it proved too

---

1 See above, p. 320, n. 3.
2 See above, p. 352, n. 1.
3 Shouting and cheers.
4 That is, en route to Tyburn.
5 Counterfeiter (whose name is given later in the passage).
6 A tavern of this name.
7 Any of various preparations in which opium is the main ingredient, but probably here being a mixture of opium and alcohol.

strong for his Stomach and came up again, however it seem'd to have a stupifying Effect upon him; So desirous he was to avoid the Execution of one Sentence, tho' with the utmost Hazard of suffering another unspeakable more dreadful. At the same Time and Place were executed *Robert Harpham* for High Treason, in counterfeiting the current Coin of the Kingdom, *William Sterry* and *Robert Samford* for the Highway.

4. From *Colonel Jack* (London, 1722)[1]

... I had learn'd from him [Major Jack, his "brother"] in General, that the Business was Picking of Pockets, and I fancy'd that tho' the Ingenuity of the Trade consisted very much in slight of Hand, a good Address,[2] and being very Nimble, yet that it was not at all difficult to learn; and especially I thought the Opportunities were so many, the Country People that come to *London*, so foolish, so gaping, and so engag'd in looking about them, that it was a Trade with no great hazard annex'd to it, and might be easily learn'd, if I did but know in general the Manner of it, and how they went about it.

THE subtile Devil never absent from his Business, but ready at all Occasions to encourage his Servants, remov'd all these Difficulties, and brought me into an Intimacy with one of the most exquisite Divers, or Pick-pockets in the Town; and this our Intimacy was of no less a Kind, than that, as I had an Inclination to be as wicked as any of them, he was for taking Care that I should not be disappointed.

HE was above the little Fellows, who went about stealing Trifles, and Baubles in *Bartholomew-Fair*,[3] and run the Risque of being Mobb'd for three or four Shillings; his aim was at higher things, even at no less than considerable Sums of Money, and Bills[4] for more.

HE solicited me earnestly to go and take a Walk with him ...

---

1   *Colonel Jack* was first published on 20 December 1722, almost eleven months after *Moll Flanders*. Excerpts and page references here are from *The History and Remarkable Life of the Truly Honourable Col. Jacques Commonly Call'd Col. Jack*, ed. Samuel Holt Monk (London: Oxford UP, 1965).

2   Dexterity, skill.

3   See above, p. 232, n.1.

4   A written order for the payment of money, drawn on a person of a business establishment.

adding that after he had shown me my Trade a little, he would let me be as wicked as I would, that is, as he express'd it, that after he had made me capable, I should set up for myself if I pleas'd, and he would only wish me good Luck. (17-18)

* * *

SOON after this, we Walk'd out again, and then we try'd our Fortune in the places, by the *Exchange*[1] a Second time. Here we began to act separately, and I undertook to Walk by my self, and the first thing I did accurately, was a trick I play'd, that argued some Skill, for a new Beginner, for I had never seen any Business of that Kind done before: I saw two Gentlemen mighty Eager in Talk, and one pull'd out a Pocket-book two or three times, and then slipt it into his Coat-pocket again, and then out it came again, and Papers were taken out, and others put in; and then in it went again, and so several times, the Man being still warmly Engag'd with another Man, and two or three others standing hard by them; the last time he put his Pocket-book into his Pocket, he might have been said, to thro' it in, rather than put it in with his Hand, and the Book lay End way, resting upon some other Book, or something else in his Pocket; so that it did not go quite down, but one Corner of it was seen above his Pocket.

THIS Careless way of Men putting their Pocket-books into a Coat-pocket, which is so easily Div'd into, by the least Boy that has been us'd to the Trade, can never be too much blam'd; the Gentlemen are in great Hurries, their Heads and Thoughts entirely taken up, and it is impossible they should be Guarded enough against such little Hawks Eyed Creatures, as we were; and therefore, they ought either never to put their Pocket-books up at all, or to put them up more secure, or to put nothing of Value into them ... (45)

* * *

THEN as to Principle, 'tis true I had no Foundation lay'd in me by Education; and being early led by my fate into Evil, I had the less Sense of its being Evil left upon my Mind: But when I began to grow to an Age of understanding, and to know that I was a Thief,

---

1 Probably the Royal (as distinct from the New) Exchange. Rebuilt after the Great Fire of 1666, it became the hub of London's highly cosmopolitan mercantile life.

growing up in all manner of Villany, and ripening a-pace for the Gallows, it came often into my thoughts that I was going wrong, that I was in the high Road to the Devil, and several times would stop short, and ask my self, if this was the Life of a Gentleman?

BUT these little things wore off again, as often as they came on, and I follow'd the old Trade again; especially when *Will* came to prompt me as I have observ'd, for he was a kind of a Guide to me in all these things, and I had by Custom and Application, together with seeing his way, learnt to be as acute a Workman as my Master.

BUT to go back where I left off, *Will* came to me as I have said, and telling me how much better Business he was fallen into, would have me go along with him, and I should be a Gentleman: *Will* it seems understood that Word in a quite differing manner from me; for his Gentleman was nothing more or less than a Gentleman Thief, a Villain of a higher Degree than a Pick-pocket; and one that might do something more Wicked, and better Entituling him to the Gallows, than could be done in our way: But my Gentleman that I had my Eye upon, was another thing quite, tho' I cou'd not really tell how to describe it neither. (61-62)

* * *

... but I was surpris'd the very next Morning, when going cross *Rosemary-lane*, by the End of the Place, which is call'd *Rag-Fair*, I heard one call *Jack*, he had said something before, which I did not hear, but upon hearing the Name *Jack*, I look'd about me, immediately saw three Men, and after them a Constable coming towards me with great Fury; I was in a great Surprize, and started to run, but one of them clap'd in upon me, and got hold of me, and in a Moment the rest surrounded me, and I was taken, I ask'd them what they wanted, and what I had done; they told me it was no Place to Talk of that there; but show'd me their Warrant, and bad me read it, and I should know the rest when I came before the Justice, so they hurried me away.

I took the Warrant, but to my great Affliction, I could know nothing by that, for I could not read, so I desir'd them to read it, and they read it that they were to Apprehend a known Thief, that went by the Name of one of the three *Jacks* of *Rag-Fair*, for that he was Charg'd upon Oath, with having been a Party in a notorious Robbery, Burglary, and Murther, committed so and so, in such a Place, and on such a Day.

IT was to no purpose for me to deny it, or to say I knew nothing of it, that was none of their Business they said; that must be disputed, they told me, before the Justice, where I would find that it was sworn positively against me, and then perhaps I might be better satisfied.

I HAD no remedy, but Patience, and as my Heart was full of Terror and Guilt, so I was ready to die with the weight of it; as they carried me a long; for as I very well knew that I was Guilty of the first Days work, tho' I was not of the last; so I did not doubt, but I should be sent to *Newgate*, and then I took it for granted I must be hang'd; for to go to *Newgate*, and to be hang'd were to me, as things which necessarily followed one another. (77-78)

★   ★   ★

HERE he [the ship's captain] talk'd calmly to us, that he was really very sorry, for what had befallen us, that he perceiv'd we had been Trappan'd,[1] and that the Fellow, who had brought us on Board was a Rogue that was employ'd by a sort of wicked Merchants, not unlike himself; that he suppos'd he had been represented to us, as Captain of the Ship, and ask'd us if it was not so? we told him yes, and gave him a large Account of ourselves, and how we came to the Woman's House to enquire for some Master of a *Collier*[2] to get a Passage to *London*, and that this Man engag'd to carry us to *London* in his own Ship, and the like ...

HE told us he was very sorry for it, and he had no hand [in] it; but it was out of his Power to help us, and let us know very plainly what our Condition was; namely, that we were put on Board his Ship as Servants to be deliver'd at *Maryland*, to such a Man, who he named to us; but that however if we would be quiet, and orderly in the Ship, he would use us well in the Passage, and take care we should be us'd well when we came there, and that he would do any thing for us that lay in his Power; but if we were unruly and refractory we could not expect but he must take such Measures as to oblige us to be satisfied; and that in short, we must be Handcuffed, carried down between the Decks, and kept as Prisoners, for it was his Business to take care that no Disturbance must be in the Ship....

WE had a very good Voyage, no Storms all the way, and a Northerly Wind almost 20 Days together; so that in a Word, we

1 Entrapped (obsolete form and meaning).
2 A ship for carrying coal.

made the Capes of *Virginia* in two and Thirty Days, from the Day we steer'd West, as I have said which was in the Latitude of 60 Degrees, 30 Minutes; being to the North of the Isle of *Great Britain*, and this they said was a very quick Passage.

NOTHING material happen'd to me, during the Voyage, and indeed when I came there I was oblig'd to act in so narrow a Compass, that nothing very material could Present it self.

WHEN we came a shore, which was in a great River, which they call *Potomack*, the Captain ask'd us, but me more particularly, whether I had any thing to propose to him now? ... I saw no Remedy ... and indeed I was grown indifferent, for I considered all the way on the Voyage, that as I was bred a Vagabond, had been a Pick-pocket, and a Soldier, and was run from my Colours,[1] and that I had no settled Abode in the World, nor any Employ to get any thing by, except that wicked one I was bred to, which had the Gallows at the Heels of it; I did not see, but that this Service might be as well to me as other Business; and this I was particularly satisfied with when they told me, that after I had Served out the five Years Servitude, I should have the Courtisie of the Country, *as they call'd it*; that is a certain Quantity of Land to Cultivate and Plant for myself; so that now I was like to be brought up to something, by which I might live without that wretched thing, call'd stealing; which my very Soul abhorr'd, and which I had given over, as I have said ever since that wicked time, that I robb'd the poor Widow of *Kentish* Town. (112-17)

★ ★ ★

... People, who are either Transported, or otherwise Trappan'd into those Places, are generally thought to be rendered miserable, and undone; whereas, on the contrary, I would encourage them upon my own Experience to depend upon it, that if their own Diligence in the time of Service, gains them but a good Character, which it will certainly do, if they can deserve it, there is not the poorest, and most despicable Felon that ever went over, but may after his time is serv'd, begin for himself, and may in time be sure of raising a good Plantation.

FOR Example, I will now take a Man in the meanest Circumstances of a Servant, who has serv'd out his 5 or 7 Years, (suppose a Transported Wretch for 7 Years.) The custom of

---

1 That is, deserted his army regiment.

the Place was then (what it is since I know not) that on his Master's certifying that he had serv'd his time out faithfully he had 50 Acres of Land allotted him, for Planting, and on this Plan he begins.

SOME had a Horse, a Cow, and three Hogs given, or rather lent them as a Stock for the Land, which they made an allowance for, at a certain Time and Rate.

CUSTOM has made it a Trade, to give Credit to such Beginners as these, for Tools, Cloths, Nails, Iron-work, and other things necessary for their Planting; and which the Persons so giving Credit to them, are to be paid for out of the Crop of *Tobacco* which they shall Plant; nor is it in the Debtors power to Defraud the Creditor of Payment in that manner; and as *Tobacco* is their Coin, as well as their Product; so all things are to be Purchas'd at a certain quantity of *Tobacco*, the Price being so Rated.

THUS the naked Planter has Credit at his Beginning, and immediately goes to Work, to cure the Land, and Plant *Tobacco*; and from this little Beginning, have some of the most considerable Planters in *Virginia* and in *Maryland* also, rais'd themselves, namely, from being without a Hat, or a Shoe, to Estates of 40 or 50000 Pound; and in this Method, I may add, no Diligent Man ever Miscarried, if he had Health to Work, and was a good Husband;[1] for he every Year encreases a little, and every Year adding more Land, and Planting more *Tobacco*, which is real Money, he must Gradually encrease in Substance, till at length he gets enough to Buy *Negroes*, and other Servants, and then never Works himself any more.

IN a Word, every *Newgate* Wretch, every Desperate forlorn Creature; the most Despicable ruin'd Man in the World, has here a fair Opportunity put into his Hands to begin the World again, and that upon a Foot of certain Gain, and in a Method exactly Honest; with a Reputation, that nothing past will have any Effect upon; and innumerable People have thus rais'd themselves from the worst Circumstances in the World; Namely, from the *Condemn'd-Hole*[2] in *Newgate*. (152-53)

* * *

---

1 Husbandman, farmer.
2 See above, p. 289, n. 1.

How much is the Life of a Slave in *Virginia*, to be preferr'd to that of the most prosperous Thief in the World! here I[1] live miserable, but honest; suffer wrong, but do no wrong; my Body is punish'd, but my Conscience is not loaded; and as I us'd to say, that I had no Leisure to look in, but I would begin when I had some Recess, sometime to spare; now God has found me Leisure to Repent; he run on in this manner a great while, giving Thanks, I believe most heartily, for his being deliver'd from the wretch'd Life he had liv'd, tho' his Misery were to be ten Fold, as much as it was.

I WAS sincerely Touch'd with his Discourse on this Subject, I had known so much of the real difference of the Case, that I could not but be affected with it, tho' till now I confess I knew little of the religious Part: I had been an Offender as well as he, tho' not altogether in the same Degree, but I knew nothing of the Penitence; neither had I look'd back upon any thing, as a Crime; but as a Life dishonourable, and not like a Gentleman, which run much in my Thoughts, as I have several times mention'd.

WELL, but now, *says I*, you talk Penitently, and I hope you are sincere, but what would be your Case, if you were deliver'd from the miserable Condition of a Slave sold for Money, which you are now in? should you not, think you, be the same Man?

BLESSED be God, *says he*, that if I thought I should, I would sincerely pray that I might not be Deliver'd, and that I might for ever be a Slave rather than a Sinner.

WELL, but *says I*, suppose you to be under the same necessity, in the same starving Condition, Should you not take the same Course?

HE replied very sharply, that shows us the need we have of the Petition in the Lord's Prayer: *Lead us not into Temptation*; and of *Solomon's* or *Agar's* Prayer: *Give me not Poverty, least I Steal.*[2] I should ever beg of God not to be left to such Snares as Human Nature cannot resist. But I have some hope that I should venture to Starve, rather than to Steal; but I also beg to be deliver'd from the Danger, because I know not my own Strength....

I press'd him no more you may be sure, after an answer so very particular, and affecting as this was; it was easy to see the Man was a sincere Penitent, not sorrowing for the Punishment he was suffering under; for his Condition was no part of his Affection, he was rather thankful for it, as above; but his Concern was a feeling

---

1 A transported felon from Bristol speaks to Colonel Jack of his life as a thief and of his later repentance.

2 See above, p. 203, n. 2.

and affecting Sence of the Wicked and Abominable Life he had led, the abhorr'd Crimes he had Committed, both against God and Man, and the little Sence he had had of the Condition he was in, that even till he came to the Place where he now was.

I ask'd him if he had no Reflections of this kind, after, or before his Sentence, he told me, *Newgate, for the Prison at* Bristol *is call'd, so it seems, as well as that at* London, was a place that seldom made Penitents, but often made Villains worse, till they learn'd to defie God and Devil. But, that however, he cou'd look back with this Satisfaction; that he could say, he was not altogether insensible of it, even then; but nothing that amounted to a thorough Serious looking up to Heaven: That he often indeed look'd in, and reflected upon his past mispent Life, even before he was in Prison, when the Intervals of his wicked Practises gave some time for Reflection, and he would sometimes say to himself, Whether am I going? To what, will all these things bring me at last? And where will they End? Sin and Shame follow one another, and I shall certainly come to the Gallows; *then said he,* I wou'd strike upon my Breast, and say: O wicked Wretch, when wilt thou Repent! And would answer my self as often; Never! Never! Except it be in a Gaol, or at a Gibbet.

THEN *said he,* I would Weep, and Sigh, and look back a little upon my wretched Life, the History of which would make the World amaz'd; but Alas! the prospect was so Dark, and it fill'd me with so much Terror, that I cou'd not bear it; then, I would fly to Wine and Company for relief, that Wine brought on Excess, and that Company being always wicked Company like my self, brought on Temptation; and then all Reflection Vanish'd, and I was the same Devil as before.

HE spoke this with so much Affection, that his Face was ever smiling, when he talk'd of it, and yet his Eyes had Tears standing in them, at the same time, and all the time; for he had a delightful Sorrow, if that be a proper Expression, in speaking of it. (162-65)

★ ★ ★

I mention these things [concerning the transported felon from Bristol] the more at large, that if any unhappy Wretch, who may have the Disaster to fall into such Circumstances as these, may come to see this Account, they may learn the following short Lessons from these Examples.

1. THAT *Virginia,* and a State of Transportation, may be the happiest Place and Condition they were ever in, for this Life,

as by a sincere Repentance, and a diligent Application to the Business they are put to; they are effectually deliver'd from a Life of a flagrant Wickedness, and put in a perfectly new Condition, in which they have no Temptation to the Crimes they formerly committed, and have a prospect of Advantage for the future.

2. THAT in *Virginia*, the meanest, and most despicable Creature after his time of Servitude is expir'd, if he will but apply himself with Diligence and Industry to the Business of the Country, is sure (Life and Health suppos'd) both of living Well and growing Rich.

As this is a foundation, which the most unfortunate Wretch alive is entitul'd to; a Transported Felon, is in my Opinion a much happier Man, than the most prosperous untaken Thief in the Nation; nor are those poor young People so much in the wrong, as some imagine them to be, that go voluntarily over to those Countries, and in order to get themselves carried over, and plac'd there, freely bind themselves there; especially if the Persons into whose Hands they fall, do any thing honestly by them; for as it is to be suppos'd that those poor People knew not what Course to take before, or had miscarried in their Conduct before; here they are sure to be immediately provided for, and after the expiration of their time, to be put into a Condition to provide for themselves ... (173-74)

                               ★ ★ ★

THERE dwelt a Lady, in a House opposite to the House I lodg'd in, who made an extraordinary Figure, indeed she went very well Dress'd, and was a most beautiful Person; she was well Bred, Sung admirably fine, and sometimes I could hear her very distinctly, the Houses being over against one another, in a narrow Court ...

THIS Lady put herself so often in my way, that I could not in good Manners forbear taking Notice of her, and giving her the Ceremony of my Hat, when I saw her at her Window, or at the Door, or when I pass'd her in the Court, so that we became almost acquainted at a distance; sometimes she also visited at the House I lodg'd at, and it was generally contriv'd, that I should be introduced when she came; and thus by degrees we became more intimately acquainted, and often convers'd together in the Family, but always in Publick, at least for a great while.

I WAS a meer Boy in the Affair of Love, and knew the least of what belong'd to a Woman, of any Man in *Europe* of my Age; the thoughts of a Wife, much less of a Mistress, had never so much as taken the least hold of my Head, and I had been till now as perfectly unacquainted with the Sex, and as unconcern'd about them, as I was when I was ten Year old ...

BUT I know not by what Witch-Craft in the Conversation of this Woman, and her singling me out upon several Occasions, I began to be ensnared, I knew not how, or to what End; and was on a sudden so embarrass'd in my Thoughts about her, that like a Charm she had me always in her Circle; if she had not been one of the subtilest Women on Earth, she could never have brought me to have given myself the least Trouble about her, but I [was] drawn in by the Magick of a Genius capable to Deceive a more wary Capacity than mine, and it was impossible to resist her.

SHE attack'd me without ceasing, with the fineness of her Conduct, and with Arts which were impossible to be ineffectual; she was ever, as it were, in my View; often in my Company, and yet kept herself so on the Reserve, so surrounded continually with Obstructions, that for several Months after she could perceive I sought an Opportunity to speak to her, she rendered it impossible, nor could I ever break in upon her, she kept her Guard so well....

ALL this while nothing was more certain then that she intended to have me, if she could catch, and it was indeed a kind of a Catch, for she manag'd all by Art, and drew me in with the most resolute backwardness, that it was almost impossible not to be deceiv'd by it; on the other Hand, she did not appear to be a Woman despicable, neither was she poor, or in a Condition that should require so much Art to draw any Man in, but the Cheat was really on my Side; for she was unhappily told, that I was vastly Rich, a great Merchant, and that she would live like a Queen, which I was not at all Instrumental in putting upon her, neither did I know that she went upon that Motive. (186-88)

*   *   *

BUT I, that was to be the most unhappy Fellow alive in the Article of Matrimony, had at last a Disappointment of the worst sort, even here; I had three fine Children by her, and in her time of her lying inn with the last, she got some Cold, that she did not in a long time get off, and in short she grew very sickly: In being so continually ill, and out of Order, she very unhappily got a Habit of drinking Cordials and hot Liquors; Drink, like the Devil, when it gets hold of any one, tho' but a little, it goes on by little and little to their Destruction; so in my Wife, her Stomach being weak and faint, she first took this Cordial, then that, till in short, she could not live without them, and from a Drop to a Sup, from a Sup to a Dram, from a Dram to a Glass, and so on to Two, till at last, she took in short, to what we call drinking.

As I likened Drink to the Devil, in its gradual Possession of the Habits and Person, so it is yet more like the Devil in its Encroachment on us, where it gets hold of our Sences; in short, my beautiful, good humour'd, modest, well bred Wife, grew a Beast, a Slave to Strong Liquor, and would be drunk at her own Table, nay, in her own Closet by her self; till instead of a well made, fine Shape, she was as Fat as an Hostess;[1] her fine Face bloated and blotch'd, had not so much as the Ruins of the most beautiful Person alive; nothing remain'd but a good Eye, that indeed, she held to the last: In short, she lost her Beauty, her Shape, her Manners, and at last her Virtue; and giving her self up to Drinking, kill'd her self in about a Year and a half, after she first began that cursed Trade ... (240)

5. From *Roxana* (London, 1724)[2]

Well, I know not what to do, *says I*, to Amy [Roxana's maid].

Do! *says Amy,* Your Choice is fair and plain; here you may have a handsome, charming Gentleman, be rich, live pleasantly, and in Plenty; or refuse him, and want a Dinner, go in Rags, live in Tears; in s[h]ort, beg and starve; you know this is the Case, Madam, *says Amy,* I wonder how you can say you know not what to do.

Well, *Amy, says I,* the Case is as you say, and I think verily I must yield to him; but then, *said I, mov'd by Conscience,* don't talk any more of your Cant, of its being Lawful that I ought to Marry again, and that he ought to Marry again, and such Stuff as that; 'tis all Nonsense, *says I, Amy,* there's nothing in it, let me hear no more of that; for if I yield, 'tis in vain to mince the Matter, I am a Whore, *Amy,* neither better nor worse, I assure you.

---

1 The mistress of an inn.

2 *Roxana* was first published on 29 February 1724, the last of Defoe's narratives dealing with the social issues of his times. Excerpts and page references here are from *Roxana: The Fortunate Mistress or, a History of the Life and Vast Variety of Fortunes of Mademoiselle de Beleau, afterwards called the Countess de Wintselsheim in Germany,* ed. Jane Jack (London: Oxford UP, 1964).

I don't think so, Madam, by no means, *says Amy*, I wonder how you can talk so; and then she run on with her Argument of the Unreasonableness that a Woman should be oblig'd to live single, or a Man to live single in such Cases, as before: Well, *Amy, said I*, come let us dispute no more, for the longer I enter into that Part, the greater my Scruples will be; but if I let it alone, the Necessity of my present Circumstances is such, that I believe I shall yield to him, if he should importune me much about it, but I should be glad he would not do it all, but leave me as I am.

As to that, Madam, you may depend, *says Amy*, he expects to have you for his Bedfellow to Night; I saw it plainly in his Management all Day, and at last he told you so too, as plain, I think, as he cou'd: Well, well, *Amy, said I*, I don't know what to say, if he will, he must, I think, I don't know how to resist such a Man, that has done so much for me: I don't know how you shou'd, *says Amy*.

Thus *Amy* and I canvass'd the Business between us; the Jade prompted the Crime, which I had but too much Inclination to commit; that is to say, not as a Crime, for I had nothing of the Vice in my Constitution; my Spirits were far from being high; my Blood had no Fire in it, to kindle the Flame of Desire; but the Kindness and good Humour of the Man, and the Dread of my own Circumstances concurr'd to bring me to the Point, and I even resolv'd, before he ask'd, to give up my Virtue to him, whenever he should put it to the Question. (40-41)

★ ★ ★

We liv'd as merrily, and as happily, after this, as cou'd be expected, considering our Circumstances; I mean as to the pretended Marriage, *&c.* and as to that, my Gentleman had not the least Concern about him for it; but as much as I was harden'd, and that was as much, as I believe, ever any wicked Creature was, yet I could not help it; there was, and would be, Hours of Intervals, and of dark Reflections which came involuntarily in, and thrust in Sighs into the middle of all my Songs; and there would be, sometimes, a heaviness of Heart, which intermingl'd itself with all my Joy, and which would often fetch a Tear from my Eye; and let others pretend what they will, I believe it impossible to be otherwise with anybody; there can be no substantial Satisfaction in a Life of known Wickedness; Conscience will, and does, often break in upon them at particular times, let them do what they can to prevent it.

But I am not to preach, but to relate, and whatever loose Reflections were, and how often soever those dark Intervals came on, I did my utmost to conceal them from him; ay, and to suppress and smother them too in myself, and to outward Appearance we liv'd as chearfully, and as agreeably, as it was possible for any Couple in the World to live.

After I had thus liv'd with him something above two Year, truly, I found my-self with-Child ... my Gentleman was mightily pleas'd at it, and nothing could be kinder than he was in the Preparations he made for me, and for my Lying-in, which was, however, very private, because I car'd for as little Company as possible; nor had I kept up my neighbourly Acquaintance; so that I had no-body to invite upon such an Occasion.

I was brought to-Bed very well ... but the Child died at about six Weeks old, so all that Work was to do over again, that is to say, the Charge, the Expence, the Travel, &c. (48-49)

* * *

... I told him, I did not know what might be the reason, but that I had a strange Terror upon my Mind, about his going, and that, if he did go, I was perswaded some Harm wou'd attend him; he smil'd, and return'd, Well, my Dear, if it should be so, you are now richly provided for; all that I have here, I give to you; and with that, he takes up the Casket, or Case, Here, *says he*, hold your Hand, there is a good Estate for you, in this Case; if any thing happens to me, 'tis all your own, I give it you for yourself; and with that, he put the Casket, the fine Ring, and his Gold Watch, all into my Hands, and the Key of his Scrutore[1] besides, adding, and in my Scrutore there is some Money, 'tis all your own.

I star'd at him, as if I was frighted, for I thought all his Face look'd like a Death's-Head; and then, immediately, I thought I perceiv'd his Head all Bloody; and then his Cloaths look'd Bloody too; and immediately it all went off, and he look'd as he really did; immediately I fell a-crying, and hung about him, My Dear *said I*, I am frighted to Death; you shall not go, depend upon it, some Mischief will befal you; I did not tell him how my vapourish Fancy had represented him to me, that I thought was not proper; besides he wou'd only have laugh'd at me, and wou'd have gone away with a Jest about it: But I press'd him seriously not to go that Day, or if he did, to promise me to come Home to *Paris* again by Daylight: He look'd a little graver then, than he did before; told me, he was not apprehensive of the least Danger; but if there was, he

1 Escritoire, writing desk.

wou'd either take Care to come in the Day, or, as he had said before, wou'd stay all Night.

But all these Promises came to nothing; for he was set upon in the open Day, and robb'd, by three Men on Horseback, mask'd, as he went; and one of them, who, it seems, rifled him, while the rest stood to stop the Coach, stabb'd him into the Body with a Sword, so that he died immediately ... (52-53)

* * *

It wou'd look a little too much like a Romance here, to repeat all the kind things he said to me, on that Occasion; but I can't omit one Passage; as he saw the Tears drop down my Cheek, he pulls out a fine Cambrick Han[d]kerchief, and was going to wipe the Tears off, but check'd his Hand, as if he was afraid to deface something; I say, he check'd his Hand, and toss'd the Handkerchief to me, to do it myself; I took the Hint immediately, and with a kind of pleasant Disdain, *How, my Lord*! said I, *Have you kiss'd me so often, and don't you know whether I am Painted, or not? Pray let your Highness satisfie yourself, that you have no Cheats put upon you; for once let me be vain enough to say, I have not deceiv'd you with false Colours*: With this, I put a Handkerchief into his Hand, and taking his Hand into mine, I made him wipe my Face so hard, that he was unwilling to do it, for fear of hurting me.

He appear'd surpriz'd, more than ever, and swore, which was the first time that I had heard him swear, from my first knowing him, that he cou'd not have believ'd there was any such Skin, without Paint, in the World ... (72)

* * *

All this while I said I knew not what, and said what I was no more able to do, than he [the prince] was able to leave me; which, at that time, he own'd he cou'd not do, no, not for the Princess herself.

But another Turn of Affairs determin'd this Matter; for the Princess was taken very ill, and in the Opinion of all her Physicians,very dangerously so; in her Sickness she desir'd to speak with her Lord, and to take her Leave of him: At this grievous Parting, she said so many passionate kind Things to him; lamented that she had left him no Children; she had had three, but they were dead; hinted to him, that it was one of the chief things which gave her Satisfaction in Death, as to this World; that she should leave him room to have Heirs to his Family, by some Princess that should supply her Place ... and thus with the most moving, and most passionate Expressions of her Affection to him, took her last Leave of him, and died the next Day.

This Discourse from a Princess so valuable in herself, and so dear to him, and the Loss of her following so immediately after, made such deep Impressions on him, that he look'd back with Detestation upon the former Part of his Life; grew melancholly and reserv'd; chang'd his Society, and much of the general Conduct of his Life; resolv'd on a Life regulated most strictly by the Rules of Virtue, and Piety; and in a word, was quite another Man.

The first Part of his Reformation, was a Storm upon me; for, about ten Days after the Princess's Funeral, he sent a Message to me by his Gentleman, intimating, tho' in very civil Terms, and with a short Preamble, or Introduction, that he desir'd I wou'd not take it ill that he was oblig'd to let me know, that *he could see me no more*: His Gentleman told me a long Story of the new Regulation of Life his Lord had taken up, and that he had been so afflicted for the Loss of his Princess, that he thought it would either shorten his Life, or he wou'd retire into some Religious House, to end his Days in Solitude.

I need not direct any-body to suppose how I receiv'd this News; I was indeed, exceedingly surpriz'd at it, and had much a-do to support myself, when the first Part of it was deliver'd; tho' the Gentleman deliver'd his Errand with great Respect, and with all the Regard to me, that he was able, and with a great deal of Ceremony; also telling me how much he was concern'd to bring me such a Message. (108-10)

*   *   *

... I had no Inclination to be a Wife again, I had had such bad Luck with my first Husband, I hated the Thoughts of it; I found, that a Wife is treated with Indifference, a Mistress with a strong Passion; a Wife is look'd upon, as but an Upper-Servant, a Mistress is a Sovereign; a Wife must give up all she has; have every Reserve she makes for herself, be thought hard of, and be upbraided with her very *Pin-Money*; whereas a Mistress makes the Saying true, *that what the Man has*, is hers, and *what she has*, is her own; the Wife bears a thousand Insults, and is forc'd to sit still and bear it, or part and be undone; a Mistress insulted, helps herself immediately, and takes another.

These were my wicked Arguments for Whoring, for I never set against them the Difference another way, I may say, every other way; *how that,* FIRST, A Wife appears boldly and honourably with her Husband; lives at Home, and possesses his House; his Servants, his Equipages, and has a Right to them all, and to call them her own; entertains his Friends, owns his Children, and has the return of Duty and Affection from them, as they are here her own, and claims upon his Estate, by the Custom of *England,* if he dies, and leaves her a Widow.

The Whore sculks about in Lodgings; is visited in the dark; disown'd upon all Occasions, before God and Man; is maintain'd indeed, for a time; but is certainly condemn'd to be abandon'd at last, and left to the Miseries of Fate, and her own just Disaster: If she has any Children, her Endeavour is to get rid of them, and not maintain them; and if she lives, she is certain to see them all hate her, and be asham'd of her; while the Vice rages, and the Man is in the Devil's Hand, *she has him*; and while she has him, she makes *a Prey of him*; but if he happens to fall Sick; if any Disaster befals him, the Cause of all lies upon her; he is sure to lay all his Misfortunes at her Door; and if once he comes to Repentance, or makes but one Step towards a Reformation, he begins with her; leaves her; uses her as she deserves; hates her; abhors her; and *sees her no more*; and that with this never-failing Addition, namely, That the more sincere and unfeign'd his Repentance is, the more earnestly he looks up; and the more effectually he looks in, the more his Aversion to her, encreases; and he curses her from the Bottom of his Soul; nay, it must be from a kind of Excess of Charity, if he so much as wishes God may forgive her. (132-33)

* * *

For now I began not to be sick of his Lordship only, but really I began to be sick of the Vice [of prostitution]; and as I had good Leisure now to divert and enjoy myself in the World, as much as it was possible for any Woman to do, that ever liv'd in it; so I found that my Judgment began to prevail upon me to fix my Delight upon nobler Objects than I had formerly done; and the very beginning of this brought some just Reflections upon me, relating to things past, and to the former Manner of my living; and tho' there was not the least Hint in all this, from what may be call'd Religion or Conscience, and far from any-thing of Repentance, or any-thing that was a-kin to it, especially at first; yet the Sence of things, and the Knowledge I had of the World, and the vast Variety of Scenes that I had acted my Part in, began to work upon my Sences, and it came so very strong upon my Mind one Morning, when I had been lying awake some time in my Bed, as if somebody had ask'd me the Question, *What was I a Whore for now?* It occurr'd naturally upon this Enquiry, that at first I yielded to the Importunity of my Circumstances, the Misery of which, the Devil dismally aggravated, to draw me to comply; for I confess, I had strong Natural Aversions to the Crime at first, partly owing to a virtuous Education, and partly to a Sence of Religion; but the Devil, and that greater Devil of Poverty, prevail'd; and the Person who laid Siege to me, did it in such an obliging, and I may almost say, irresistible Manner, all still manag'd by the Evil Spirit; for I must be allow'd to believe, that he has a Share in all such things, if not the whole Management of them: But, I say, it was carried on by that Person, in such an irresistible Manner, that, (as I said when I related the Fact) there was no withstanding it: These Circumstances, I say, the Devil manag'd, not only to bring me to comply, but he continued them as Arguments to fortifie my Mind against all Reflection, and to keep me in that horrid Course I had engag'd in, as if it were honest and lawful.

But not to dwell upon that now; this was a Pretence, and here was something to be said, tho' I acknowledge, it ought not to have been sufficient to me at all; but, I say, to leave that, all this was out of Doors; the Devil himself cou'd not form one Argument, or put one Reason into my Head *now*, that cou'd serve for an Answer, no, not so much as a pretended Answer to this Question, *Why I shou'd be a Whore now?*

... and so ... the Question remain'd still unanswer'd, *Why am I a Whore now?* Nor indeed, had I any-thing to say for myself, *even to myself*; I cou'd not without blushing, as wicked as I was, answer, that I lov'd it for the sake of the Vice, and that I delighted in being a Whore, *as such*; I say, I cou'd not say this, even to myself, *and all alone*, nor indeed, wou'd it have been true; I was never able in Justice, and with Truth, to say I was so wicked as that; but as Necessity first debauch'd me, and Poverty made me a Whore at the Beginning; so excess of Avarice for getting Money, and excess of Vanity, continued me in the Crime, not being able to resist the Flatteries of Great Persons; being call'd the finest Woman in *France*; being caress'd by a Prince; and afterwards I had Pride enough to expect, and Folly enough to believe, tho' indeed, without ground, by a great Monarch. These were my Baits, these the Chains by which the Devil held me bound; and by which I was indeed, too fast held for any Reasoning that I was then Mistress of, to deliver me from. (200-02)

* * *

... When I saw I had gain'd my Point, I seem'd to hang back a little; my Dear, *says I*, don't hinder an Hour's Business for me; I can
put it off for a Week or two, rather than you shall do yourself any
Prejudice: *No, no, says he,* you shall not put it off an Hour for me,
for I can do my Business by Proxy with any-body, *but my* WIFE;
and then he took me in his Arms and kiss'd me: How did my Blood
flush up into my Face! when I reflected how sincerely, how affec-
tionately this good-humour'd Gentleman embrac'd the most
cursed Piece of Hypocrisie that ever came into the Arms of an
honest Man? His was all Tenderness, all Kindness, and the utmost
Sincerity; Mine all Grimace and Deceit; a Piece of meer Manage,
and fram'd Conduct, to conceal a pass'd Life of Wickedness, and
prevent his discovering, that he had in his Arms a She-Devil,
whose whole Conversation for twenty and five Years had been
black as Hell, a Complication of Crime; and for which, had he
been let into it, he must have abhorr'd me, and the very mention
of my Name: But there was no help for me in it; all I had to satisfie myself was, that it was my Business to be what I was, and conceal what I had been; that all the Satisfaction I could make him,
was to live virtuously for the Time to come, not being able to
retrieve what had been in Time past; and this I resolv'd upon, tho'
had the great Temptation offer'd, as it did afterwards, I had reason
to question my Stability: *But of that hereafter.* (300-01)

6. From *A Tour thro' the Whole Island of Great Britain*, 3 vols. (London, 1724-27)

VOLUME II, Letter 3

[Bath]

My Description of this City would be very short, and indeed
it would have been a very small City, (if at all a City) were it not
for the *Hot Baths* here, which give both Name and Fame to the
Place.

The Antiquity of this Place, and of the *Baths* here, is doubtless
very great, tho' I cannot come in to the Inscription under the Figure, said to be of a British King, placed in that call'd the King's
Bath.[1]

---

1 King Bladud (referred to below by Defoe), legendary ninth-century
British king, the (unclear) inscription proclaiming him the founder of
Bath.

There remains little to add, but what relates to the Modern Customs, the Gallantry and Diversions of that Place, in which I shall be very short; the best Part being but a Barren Subject, and the worst Part meriting rather a Satyr,[1] than a Description....

The whole Time indeed is a Round of the utmost Diversion. In the Morning you (supposing you to be a young Lady) are fetch'd in a close Chair,[2] dress'd in your Bathing Cloths, that is, stript to the Smock, to the *Cross-Bath*. There the Musick plays you into the Bath, and the Women that tend you, present you with a little floating Wooden Dish, like a Bason; in which the Lady puts a Handkerchief, and a Nosegay, of late the Snuff-Box is added, and some Patches; tho' the Bath occasioning a little Perspiration, the Patches do not stick so kindly as they should.

Here the Ladies and the Gentlemen pretend to keep some distance, and each to their proper Side, but frequently mingle here too, as in the King and Queens Bath, tho' not so often; and the Place being but narrow, they converse freely, and talk, rally, make Vows, and sometimes Love; and having thus amus'd themselves an Hour, or Two, they call their Chairs and return to their Lodgings.

The rest of the Diversion here, is at the Walks in the great Church, and at the Raffling Shops, which are kept (like the Cloyster at *Bartholomew* Fair,[3]) in the Churchyard, and Ground adjoyning. In the Afternoon there is generally a Play, tho' the Decorations are mean, and the Performances accordingly; but it answers for the Company here (not the Actors) make the Play to say no more. In the Evening there is a Ball, and Dancing at least twice a week, which is commonly in the great Town Hall, over the Market-House; where there never fails in the Season to be a great deal of very good Company.

There is one thing very observable here, which tho' it brings abundance of Company to the Bath, more than ever us'd to be there before; yet it seems to have quite inverted the Use and Virtue of the Waters, (*viz.*) that whereas for Seventeen Hundred or Two Thousand Years, if you believe King *Bladud*, the Medicinal Virtue of these Waters had been useful to the diseased People by Bathing in them, now they are found to be useful also, taken into the Body; and there are many more come to drink the Waters, than to bathe in them; nor are the Cures they perform this way, less valuable

1 See above, p. 290, n. 2.
2 See above, p. 240, n. 2.
3 See above, p. 232, nn. 1-3.

than the outward Application; especially in Colicks, ill Digestion, and Scorbutick[1] Distempers.

[Bristol]

Following the Course of the River *Avon*, which runs thro' *Bath*, we come in Ten Miles to the City of *Bristol*, the greatest, the richest, and the best Port of Trade in *Great Britain*, *London* only excepted.

The Merchants of this City not only have the greatest Trade, but they Trade with a more entire Independency upon *London*, than any other Town in *Britain*. And 'tis evident in this particular, (*viz.*) That whatsoever Exportations they make to any part of the World, they are able to bring the full returns back to their own Port, and can dispose of it there.

This is not the Case in any other Port in *England*. But they are often oblig'd either to ship part of the Effects in the Ports abroad, on the Ships bound to *London*; or to consign their own Ships to *London*, in order both to get Freight, as also to dispose of their own Cargoes.

But the *Bristol* Merchants as they have a very great Trade abroad, so they have always Buyers at Home, for their Returns, and that such Buyers that no Cargo is too big for them....

The greatest Inconveniences of *Bristol*, are, its Situation, and the tenacious Folly of its Inhabitants; who by the general Infatuation, the Pretence of Freedoms and Priviledges, that Corporation-Tyranny, which prevents the Flourishing and Encrease of many a good Town in *England*, continue obstinately to forbid any, who are not Subjects of their City Soveraignty, (that is to say, Freemen,) to Trade within the Chain of their own Liberties; were it not for this, the City of *Bristol*, would before now, have swell'd and encreas'd in Buildings and Inhabitants, perhaps to double the Magnitude it was formerly of.

VOLUME II, Letter 4

[Liverpool]

... This Town is now become so great, so populous, and so rich, that it may be call'd the *Bristol* of this Part of *England*: It had formerly but *one Church*, but upon the Encrease of Inhabitants, and

---

1 Of or pertaining to scurvy.

of New Buildings in so extraordinary a manner, they have built *another* very fine Church[1] in the *North Part* of the Town; and they talk of erecting two more....

This Part of the Town may indeed be call'd *New Leverpool*, for that, they have built more than another *Leverpool* that way, in new Streets, and fine large Houses for their Merchants: Besides this, they have made a great *Wet Dock*,[2] for laying up their Ships, and which they greatly wanted; for tho' the *Mersey* is a Noble Harbour, and is able to ride a Thousand Sail of Ships at once, yet those Ships that are to be laid up, or lye by the Walls all the Winter, or longer, as sometimes may be the Case; must ride there, as in an open Road, or (as the Seamen call it,) be haled a Shore; neither of which wou'd be practicable in a Town of so much Trade: And in the time of the late great Storm, they suffer'd very much on that Account.

[Chester]

As I am now at *Chester*, 'tis proper to say something of it, being a City well worth describing: *Chester* has four things very remarkable in it. 1. It's Walls, which are very firm, beautiful, and in good Repair. 2. The Castle, which is also kept up, and has a Garrison always in it. 3. The Cathedral. 4. The River *Dee*, and 5. the Bridge over it.

It is a very Antient City, and to this Day, the Buildings are very old; nor do the Rows as they call them, add any thing, in my Opinion, to the Beauty of the City; but just the contrary, they serve to make the City look both old and ugly: These Rows are certain long Galleries, up one pair of Stairs, which run along the side of the Streets, before all the Houses, tho' joined to them, and as is pretended, they are to keep the People dry in walking along. This they do indeed effectually, but then they take away all the view of the Houses from the Street, nor can a Stranger, that was to ride thro' *Chester*, see any Shops in the City; besides, they make the Shops themselves dark, and the way in them is dark, dirty, and uneven.

The best Ornament of the City is, that the Streets are very broad and fair, and run through the whole City in strait Lines, crossing in the Middle of the City, as at *Chichester*. The Walls as I

---

1 St. Peter's, consecrated in 1703.
2 Operative since 1715.

have said, are in very good Repair, and it is a very pleasant Walk round the City, upon the Walls, and within the Battlements, from whence you may see the Country round; and particularly on the side of the *Roodee*, which I mentioned before, which is a fine large low Green, on the Bank of the *Dee*....

VOLUME III, Letter 3

[Manchester]

From hence we came on to *Manchester*, one of the greatest, if not really the greatest meer Village in *England*. It is neither a wall'd Town, City, or Corporation; they send no Members to Parliament; and the highest Magistrate they have is a Constable or Headborough; and yet it has a Collegiate Church, several Parishes, takes up a large space of Ground, and, including the Suburb, or that part of the Town called ———[1] over the Bridge, it is said to contain above fifty thousand People;[2] and though some People may think this strange, and that I speak by guess, and without Judgment, I shall justify my Opinion so well, that I believe, it will convince you my Calculation is at least very probable, and much under what Fame tells us is true.

The *Manchester* Trade we all know; and all that are concerned in it know that it is, as all our other Manufactures are, very much encreased within these thirty or forty Years, especially beyond what it was before; and as the Manufacture is encreased, the People must be encreased of course. It is true, that the encrease of the Manufacture may be by its extending itself farther in the Country, and so more Hands may be employed in the County without any encrease in the Town. But I answer, that though this is possible, yet as the Town and Parish of *Manchester* is the Center of the Manufacture, the encrease of that Manufacture would certainly encrease there first, and then the People there not being sufficient, it might spread it self further.

But the encrease of Buildings at *Manchester* within these few Years, is a Confirmation of the encrease of People; for that within very few Years past, here, as at *Liverpoole*, and as at *Froom* in *Somersetshire*, the Town is extended in a surprising manner; abundance, not of new Houses only, but of new Streets of Houses, are

---

1 Salford (the name is omitted).
2 Despite Defoe's protests, a figure of 10,000 or so is more generally accepted by social historians.

added, a new Church also, and they talk of another, and a fine new Square is at this time building; so that the Town is almost double to what it was a few Years ago ...

7. From *Conjugal Lewdness; Or, Matrimonial Whoredom. A Treatise Concerning the Use and Abuse of the Marriage Bed* (London, 1727)

CHAPTER II

Of MATRIMONIAL CHASTITY, *what is to be understood by the Word; a Proof of its being required by the Laws of* GOD *and* Nature, *and that wrong Notions of it have possess'd the World. Dr.* Taylor's[1] *Authority quoted about it.*

If *Chastity* in general be so little understood, the *Chastity* I speak of is infinitely more out of the way of your ordinary thinking: *Matrimonial Chastity*! 'tis a new strange Term, said one of my critical Observers before I published this Work; you must be sure to tell us what you mean by it, or it will not be intelligible: What, *says he*, are you going to lay down Rules and Laws for the Marriage Bed! Are you going to enclose what Heaven has left free, and pretending to shew us the deficiency of GOD's Laws, supply that deficiency with some wiser Rules of your own? 'Tis against Nature, as well as against Heaven. But this Reproof is misplaced, and the Reprover mistaken. I am far from adding to the Restraints that Nature, and the God of Nature have laid upon us, but am for shewing you what Restraints they are; and particularly to let you see, there are some Restraints where you suggest, and perhaps believe, there are really none.

You acknowledge, that *Chastity* in general is a Virtue, and a Christian Duty; and I affirm there is a particular *Chastity*, that is to say, a limited Liberty, which is to be observed and strictly submitted to in the conjugal State; This I call *Matrimonial Chastity*, and the Breach of this I call, as in my Title, matrimonial Whoredom; let others call it what they will, I can give it no other Name than what I think it deserves.

---

1 Jeremy Taylor (1613-67), chaplain to Archbishop Laud and Charles I, was a devotional writer who did much to shape the Church of England. Among his other works, *A Discourse on the Liberty of Prophesying* (1647) is an argument for toleration.

CHAPTER VI

Of being Over-rul'd by Perswasion, Interest, Influence of Friends, Force, and the like, to take the Person they have no Love for, and forsake the Person they really lov'd.

As Matrimony should be the Effect of a free and previous Choice in the Persons marrying, so the breaking in by Violence upon the Choice and Affection of the Parties, I take to be the worst kind of *Rape*; whether the Violence be the Violence of Perswasion or of Authority; I mean, such as that of Paternal Authority, or otherwise; for as to legal Authority, there is nothing of that can interpose in it; the Laws leave it where it ought to be left, and the Laws of Matrimony, in particular, leave it all upon the Choice of the Person, and in the Power of their Will ...

Hence I might enter into a long Discourse of the Justice of young People on either Side, resisting the Perswasions, nay, indeed the Commands of those who otherwise they ought to obey, in a Case of this moment. I should be very loth to say any thing here to encourage Breach of Duty in Children to Parents; but as in this Case the Command seems exorbitant, so the Obedience seems to be more limited than in any other, and therefore I may go farther here than I would do in any of the Points of Subordination in other Cases.

It is a Maxim in Law as well as in Reason, there is no Duty in Obeying where there is no Authority to Command; or, if you will, thus: There is no Obligation to Obey where there is no Right to Command; the Parent has, no question, a right to Command, nay, to govern and over-rule the Child in all lawful Things: But if the Parent commands the Child to do an unlawful Action, the Child may decline it; for a Thing cannot be lawful and unlawful at the same time.

It is evident in the Case before me, if the Parent commands his Child to marry such or such a Person, and the Child either cannot love the Person, or at the same time declares he or she is engaged in Affection to another, the Command of the Parent cannot be lawfully obeyed, because it is unlawful for the Child to marry any Person he or she cannot love; nay, the very doing it is destructive of Matrimony, and they must either lie one way or other, or else they cannot obey it, for they cannot be married ...

CHAPTER VII

Of Marrying one Person, and at the same time owning themselves to be in Love with another.

TO Love and not to Marry, is Nature's Aversion; to Marry and not to Love, is Nature's Corruption; the first is Hateful, the last is really Criminal; and, as has been said in its Place, it is, in some Respects, both Murther and Robbery; it makes a Man *Felo de Se,*[1] with respect to all the Comforts of his Life; and it makes him a Robber to his Wife, if she be a Woman that has the misfortune to Love him....

But to marry one Woman and love another, to marry one Man and be in love with another, this is yet worse, tenfold worse, if that be possible! 'tis, in its kind, a meer Piece of Witchcraft; it is a kind of civil, legal *Adultery,* nay, it makes the Man or Woman be committing Adultery in their Hearts every Day of their lives; and can I be wrong therefore to say, that it may be very well called a Matrimonial Whoredom? if I may judge, it is one of the worst Kinds of it too.

CHAPTER X

Of marrying with Inequality of Blood.

INEQUALITY *of Blood:* This is an Article in Matrimony which they, who would be thought to expect any Felicity in a married Life, ought very carefully to avoid, especially if it relates to Families also. How scandalously have I known a Lady treated in a Family, though her Fortune has been the very raising, or at least, restoring the Circumstances of the Person who has taken her, only because she has been beneath them in Degree? That she has not been of noble Blood, or of what they call an antient Family; that she has not been what they call a Gentlewoman, and yet they have not found any Defect either in her Education or Behaviour? How has she been scorned by the Relations, and the Title been hardly granted her, which the Lord of Necessity gives her? And all because of what they call Mechanick Original.[2] Again, Sir G——— W——— has married a Lady out of a noble Family. Sir G——— is

---

1 A self-murderer ("felon of himself").
2 See above, p. 342, n. 1.

Master of a vast Fortune, has about seven thousand Pounds a Year Estate, and Cash enough in ready Money to purchase as much more. But, alas! he is of no Family; his Father was a Citizen, and purchased a Coat of Arms with his Money, but hardly can tell who his Grandfather was; and the Lady is taught to despise him at that rate, that it is hardly reconcileable to her Sense, that she should ever entertain him in the Quality of a Husband. It is true, that she had but a mean Fortune, *viz.* five thousand Pounds. What then? she had much rather have married a *Scotch* Nobleman, as she could have done, the Earl of —————, though he had not above a thousand Pounds a Year. But then she had had a Man of Quality, and she had had a Coronet upon her Coach; she had match'd like her self, and mingled with noble Blood, as she ought to have done. But now she is Debased and Dishonoured, she is levelled with the Canail; the old Countess, her Lady-Mother, considered nothing but the Money; and d—— it, she had rather have been King *Ch*——'s[1] Whore, and then she might have been a Duchess, and her Children had been Dukes of course, and had had noble Blood in their Veins by the lowest degree, and royal Blood on the other Side; whereas now, in short, she looks upon her self to be little better than Prostituted, and that meerly for an Estate.

CHAPTER XI

Of going to Bed under solemn Promises of MARRIAGE, *and although those Promises are afterwards performed; and of the Scandal of a Man's making a Whore of his own Wife.*

... I have now before me a very particular Case, in which Marriage is made a healing or protection to a scandalous Crime. Promise of Marriage is Marriage in the Abstract, say our Advocates for Lewdness; and therefore for the Parties to lie together is no Sin, provided they sincerely intend to marry afterwards, and faithfully perform it.

This is, in short, a scandalous Defence of a scandalous Offence; 'tis the weakest Way of arguing that any Point of such Moment was ever supported by. It is so far from covering the Offence against GOD, that it does not recompence the Personal Injury done to Man. I have hinted at it already in the Chapter; and given you there the Opinion of the best of Men, and particularly the Cen-

---

1   During his reign, Charles II bestowed titles on many of his mistresses.

sure of the Protestant Churches upon it, in which, as I said, they are more strict, and punish with more Severity, than in Cases of simple Fornication.

It may be true, that Promise of Marriage is Marriage, but it is not marrying; it may be called Marriage, or rather a Species of Marriage; and therefore our Law will oblige such Persons to marry afterwards, as well in Cases where they have not consummated the Agreement, as where they have; and will give Damages, and that very considerable, in proportion to the Circumstances of the Parties, where these Promises are broken; especially where the Person makes the Breach, by marrying another purely in Contravention of those Promises. And this is all the Remedy the injured Person can obtain.

Also such a Promise, especially if made before Witness, will be, and frequently is admitted as a lawful Obstacle or Impediment, why a Person under such an Obligation should not be allowed to marry any other; nay farther, the Person claiming by Virtue of such a Promise, may forbid *the Bans*, as we call it; or may stand forth, and shew it as a Cause, even at the very Book, why the two Persons coming to the Book may not be lawfully joined together; and the Minister cannot proceed, if such a Cause is declared, till the Matter is decided before the proper Judges of such Cases.

But all this does not reach the Case propos'd at all; for were Promises of Marriage thus allowed, and lying together upon such Promises lawful, you would have no more Occasion of a fair and formal Espousal, and we should have very little open Marrying among us. And what Confusion would this make in the World? How would the sacred Obligations of Marriage be enforced, Claim of Inheritances secur'd, Legitimacy of Children clear'd up, and Obligation of Maintenance be preserv'd? How and where would these Promises be recorded, when denied and revoked? How would they be brought into Evidence, and the Offender against them be convicted? In a word, what Confusion would such loose coming together make in Families, and in Successions, in dividing the Patrimonies and Effects of Intestate Parents; and on many other Occasions.

CHAPTER XIV

Of Clandestine, Forcible and Treacherous MARRIAGES.

IT is with a great deal of Reason and Justice, that our Laws have made stealing of Ladies criminal; I mean a Capital Criminal. It seemed a little hard, that a Gentleman might have the satisfaction of hanging a Thief that stole an old Horse from him, but could have no Justice against a Rogue for stealing his Daughter.

The Arts and Tricks made use of to Trapan,[1] and, as it were, Kidnap young Women away into the Hands of Brutes and Sharpers, were very scandalous, and it became almost dangerous for any one to leave a Fortune to the disposal of the Person that was to enjoy it, and where it was so left, the young Lady went always in Danger of her Life, she was watch'd, laid in wait for, and, as it were, besieged by a continual Gang of Rogues, Cheats, Gamesters, and such like starving Crew, so that she was obliged to confine her self like a Prisoner to her Chamber, be lock'd, and barr'd, and bolted in, and have her Eyes every Moment upon the Door, as if she was afraid of Bayliffs and Officers to arrest her; or else she was snatch'd up, seized upon, hurry'd up into a Coach and six, a Fellow dress'd up in a Clergyman's Habit to perform the Ceremony, and a Pistol clapt to her Breast to make her consent to be marry'd: And thus the Work was done. She was then carry'd to the private Lodging, put to Bed under the same awe of Swords and Pistols; a Fellow that she never saw in her Life, and knows nothing of, comes to Bed to her, deflowers her, or, as may be well said, ravishes her, and the next Day she is called a Wife, and the Fortune seized upon in the Name of the Husband; and perhaps, in a few Days more, play'd all away at the Box and the Dice,[2] and the Lady sent home again naked, and a Beggar.

This was the Case within the Times of our Memory, till the Parliament thought fit to make it Felony, and that without Benefit of Clergy,[3] and till some of these Fortune Ravishers have since that paid for their Success at the Gallows. And now, indeed, the Ladies are a little safer, and must be attempted with a little more Art, not taken by Storm, Sword in hand, as Men take fortified Towns; but they must be brought to give a formal Assent by the cunning of Female Agents, wheedling and deluding them, and playing the Game another Way, till they are decoy'd into Wedlock; the Man pretending himself Quality, and a Person equal in Estate; by which Craft a certain *Kentish* Lady of Fortune, was most exquisitely drawn in at once to marry a City Chimney-sweeper; and was forc'd to stand by it too, after she came to an understanding of the Bargain she had made; and another West Country Lady, a Highwayman, and the like.

---

1 See above, p. 358, n. 1.
2 See above, p. 263, n. 2.
3 See Appendix B.1.

These Matches, however, come within the reach of our Complaint, and are but with too much Justice branded with the Charge of Matrimonial Whoredom. It is true, in these Cases it is the Money more then the Sensuality, the Fortune more than the Woman; and so it might be called Matrimonial Avarice. But as the knowing of the Woman is the essential finishing Part of the Work, and the Title or Claim to the Estate is fix'd upon a full Possession, which they call a Consummation of the Marriage; the Word Whoredom is not foreign to the Charge, at least on the Man's Side, because he lies with the Woman, not as a wedded Wife, according to GOD's holy Ordinance, but meerly to entitle him to her Estate, which, in short, is perfecting the End of Matrimony; and no Man can say, it is a legal Marriage in the Sight of Him whose appointment only can make Matrimony lawful.

8. From *An Essay on the History and Reality of Apparitions* (London, 1727)

CHAPTER VIII

The reality of apparition further asserted; and what spirits they are that do really appear.

The affirming, as in the foregoing chapters, that the unembodied souls of men do not appear again, or concern themselves in the affairs of life; that the good would not if they could, and the bad could not if they would; does not at all destroy the reality of the thing called apparition, or do I pretend to argue from thence that there is no such thing as any apparition at all: on the contrary, I insist it is reasonable to believe (notwithstanding all that has been said) that there are such things as the apparition of spirits; and this I think I have already proved past the power of any scruple or cavil, as also that there have been such things in all ages of the world.

The doctrine of the existence of spirits is established in nature; where those spirits reside, is matter of difficulty, and our speculations are various about them; but to argue that therefore there are none, that they exist not, that there are no such beings, is absurd, and contrary to the nature of the thing; we may as well argue against the existence of the sun when it is clouded and eclipsed, though we see its light, only because we cannot see its beams, or the globe of its body; but let us go back to the principle.

Spirit, as it is to be considered here, is to be reduced to four general heads.

First, The author of all spirit, the fountain of all being, the original cause of life, and the creator both of spirit and of all the subsequents of it. This we justly adore, as the Infinite Eternal Spirit: *God is a spirit.*

Secondly, Angels or good spirits; which are real spirits; we have demonstration of it, and they have and do appear daily, as the great Author of all spirits directs, for the service of mankind, for they are *ministering spirits.*

Thirdly, Devils or evil spirits; these are really spirit too, of a spirituous nature; 'tis true they are deprived of their beauty, their original glory, because deprived of their innocence; they are deformed as well as defiled by crime, but they are not deprived of their nature; they are spirits still, though cast down and cast out, and are called *wicked spirits.*

Fourthly, Souls of men, whether good or bad; their condition may be as you please to speak of it, happy or unhappy; the case is the same, it does no way alter their nature, but still they are spirits. *The spirits of just men made perfect;* there's the happy spirits: *the spirits in prison,* and there's the unhappy; but both are spirits, and are to be discoursed of as such in this place.

Now let us bring all this down to our present purpose. I have asserted their being, let me inquire into their state, as it respects our subject; how far they may or may not, can or cannot appear among men, in their present circumstances....

CHAPTER XI

The Devil, subtle in his contrivance, as well as vigilant in application of circumstances, knows a man to be in perplexed circumstances, distressed for want of money, a perishing family, a craving necessity; he comes in his sleep and presents him with a little child dressed up with jewels of a great value, and a purse of gold in its hand, and all this as happening in a place perfectly opportune for the purpose, the nurse having negligently left the child out of her sight.

As he presents the temptation, he stands at the person's elbow; prompts him; says, Take away that chain or string of pearl, and the purse, the child is alone, it can tell no tales, take it quickly; are not you in distress, and do you not want it at this time to an extremity, and can any one ever discover it? the child's friends are rich, it will do them no hurt; if they valued such things, they would never have put them about a little child, it is no great matter to them; besides it is due to their vanity and ostentation, which was the only reason of dressing up a little child in such a manner. Come, come, take it up quickly, it may save you from ruin, and as soon as you are able, you may make them satisfaction again, and so discharge your conscience. The man, unable to resist the snare, consents, strips the innocent child of its ornaments, and goes away unseen; but in a moment or two wakes with the surprise, sees it is a cheat, and looks back on it with a double regret. 1st, That he is disappointed of the prize which he wanted, and fancied himself relieved by. 2ndly, That the Devil triumphs over him, and he is both deluded into the crime, and deceived in the expectation of its reward.

I could give this in the form of a relation of fact, and give evidence of the truth of it; for I had the account of it from the person's own lips, who was attacked in sleep, and (as he said with a sincere affliction) yielded to the temptation; and I committed the barbarous robbery, said he, with the utmost resentment; I plundered and stripped the poor smiling infant, who innocently played with me when I took off its ornaments, gave me the purse of gold out of its little pocket, and bid me keep it for her to play with....

What was this but an apparition of the Devil, a real, visible apparition; visible to the mind, though not to the body? and that in a double capacity too, the Devil without in the temptation, and the Devil within yielding to it....

I could give an account of another person whom the Devil haunted frequently, and that for many years together, with lewd apparitions; tempting him in his sleep with the company of beautiful women, sometimes naked, sometimes even in bed with him, and at other times in conversation prompting him to wickedness; and that sometimes he was prevailed upon to consent, but always happily prevented by waking in time: but the case has, on two or three occasions, been mentioned by other hands, and the person is too much known to allow the further description of it without his consent.

I cannot doubt but these things are stated formal apparitions of the Devil; and though the person may be asleep, and not thoroughly sensible either of what he is doing, or of what is doing with him, yet that the evil spirit is actually present with him in apparition I think will not admit of any question.

9. From *Street-Robberies, Consider'd: The Reason of Their Being So Frequent, with Probable Means to Prevent 'Em* (London, [1728])[1]

AS I have declared my self in the Title to be a converted Thief, I think it will nor be amiss, first to give a short Account of my own Life; and then proceed to what I have undertaken. I shall use freedom in what I am about to write, being I am not afraid I shall be call'd to an Account for any of my past Pranks: Every one knows there is more than one Act of Grace[2] within this twenty Years; and for the rest of my Gang, they are as cold as *Julius Cæsar*, or the great *Scanderbeg*;[3] I might have said as Rotten too, for some of them were not over Sound, when alive, but the Gallows and the Sea have made an End of 'em all. That is, some were Hang'd, and some Transported.

WELL then! a Cheat I stand confess'd on Record, (though now I deal plainly) therefore shall conceal my Name, that my Neighbours may not find me out; for as Thievish as I have been, I have borne all Offices in the Parish where I dwell, even Church-warden, without cheating the Poor, and am at present, and have been these twenty Years, accounted one of the honestest Men in it. Therefore I have spoil'd one Proverb, *Once a Thief, and always a Thief.* But to proceed.

I THINK I have read in History, for now I Study Books as I formerly did Men, that *Alexander* the Great claim'd *Jupiter* for his Father; and I have also read that many other Great Men have had a great many Fathers; or rather, that a great many Great Men in History, could never tell their own Fathers, which is indeed my one Case: For even my good Mother could not inform me truly. But thus much I know of my Progenitors, my poor Mother going into a *Goldsmith's* Shop to purchase a Ring, by an odd Sort of a Mistake, I don't know how, but it seems she walk'd off with a whole String of them: But the ill-natur'd Fellow had her pursu'd, took her up, and in short was very troublesome; for notwithstanding my Mother stood stiff in her Innocence, yet the malicious Wretch forc'd her to take up a new Lodging in *Newgate*, pretend-

---

1 There is some uncertainty concerning Defoe's authorship of this work. See, for example, Paula R. Backscheider, *Daniel Defoe: His Life* (Baltimore: Johns Hopkins UP, 1989) 518-19.
2 Probably a reference to pardons obtainable only from the monarch.
3 Scanderbeg (c.1404-68), an Albanian national hero, resisted the Ottomans under Sultan Muhammad II.

ing this was not her first Offence; and not having her Health there, she was obliged to take the Air an Hour or two at the *Old-Baily*, and tho' she declared her Aversion for her new Lodging, yet they forc'd her there again, though with this Promise, that she should very shortly take a farther Tour for a little good Air; and because it would be difficult for a weak Person to walk up *Holbourn Hill*,[1] she should be carry'd, with a suitable Attendance to her Quality. She told them her Inclinations would rather carry her some other Road. But *Willi nilli*, she was inform'd she should go that Way and no other....

WHEN my Mother found there was no good to be done with them, she e'en resolved to cast about to get out of their Clutches, not by breaking Prison, for Thieves thirty or forty Years ago were not so clever at that as *Shepherd*,[2] of immortal Memory. She had at that Juncture the Misfortune of being a Maid, that is, I mean, not with Child, yet she had Money enough to Bribe a Jury of Matrons,[3] that out of a good Conscience to prolong Life, swore she was Quick;[4] but with this Caution, if she was not, to get one should use his honest Endeavours to save their Honour, for they found there was good Ground to work upon.

MY Mother at first practiced with the Ordinary, giving him to know, she had no Occasion for his Assistance in shoving her out of the World, but beg'd his Help to bring one into the World. But the good Man, either out of Conscience, or Dislike, utterly refus'd; telling her how heinous the Crime was she wou'd commit....

BUT some Pirates happening to stop at *Newgate*, in their Way to *Wapping*,[5] took pity of my poor Mother, and being People of great Humanity, strove all they could to oblige her, and among them her Job was done ...

MY Mother now growing pretty near her Time, by the Prison Reckoning, tho' she was two Months behind hand in her own Account, made so many Friends to the *Goldsmith's* Wife, that out of Compassion, she good Woman got my Mother her Pardon. And in short, my Mother forsook her Tenement, though she paid nothing for her Lodging, for the Keepers were very willing to be rid of

---

1 That is, the route to Tyburn and her execution.
2 See above, p. 352, n. 1.
3 See Appendix B.1.
4 Pregnant.
5 A place of execution, east of the City along the River Thames, for those who had committed high crimes at sea.

her, for fear she shou'd lay the Child to some of them, as she often threaten'd in her Passion ...

BUT be it as it will, my Mother took a great Care of me, especially in my Education, only she did not let me Read or Write, for as she often told me, Learning was only to make People vain....

BY that Time I had arriv'd at my tenth Year, I had made some Progress in the Nimming[1] Art, and those that had the Care of my Education, told my Mother, there was no fear but I should make as good a Figure in the Business as the best of them.

I WAS full fourteen before I attempted any thing noble in the Science, as they Term it, and had a narrow Escape into the Bargain. A Fruit-Woman who had a Leathern Purse at her Side, and a great Basket of Fruit on her Head, set me a Longing, more at the Purse than the Fruit. I follow'd her through several Streets and Lanes without accomplishing my Intentions. At last, she put her Basket upon a Bulk, and Knock'd at a great House in *Crowtched Fryars*. Now, thought I, is my Time. When she had done with the People of the House, the Door was shut, and she going to put the Basket on her Head, I drew near, and offer'd her my Assistance. But she cry'd no I thank you, Child, I can help my self. While both her Hands were employ'd, I with my Knife, nimbly cut off her Pocket, and as nimbly ran off....

I must own tho' Young, a qualm of Conscience came over me for my Tricks, and the first Thing I repented off, was, the Robbing the poor Fruit Woman; therefore I resolved with my self to make it my Business to find her out, and make her Restitution.

MY first Days search was to no purpose, but the second Day I met with her in *Mark Lane*, at an *Apothecary's*, selling some Fruit: I bargain'd with her for a Basket of Strawberries, and order'd her to follow me; coming into the *Navy-Office*, I found the Coast clear, and proper for my Purpose. Good Woman said I, was not you Rob'd some time since, of such a Sum of Money, yes Sir, said the Woman, which has almost broke my Heart.

THE Person that Rob'd you, said I, was my own Brother, and therefore I am come to make you Satisfaction, here is a couple of Gu[i]neas for you, take it, and be more watchfull for the Future.

THE poor Woman was mightily overjoy'd, and gave me as many Blessings, as no doubt she had formerly Curses....

IN a few Days after this Affair, I hir'd a Chariot and Six, with several of my Accomplices for Servants, and took upon me the

---

1 Thieving.

Title of *John* —— Esq; In my Journey, I compos'd a short Cant-ing Vocabulary, for I hated Idleness: This Language is spoke gen-erally among Gentlemen Collectors of the Highway, and in most Branches of those Persons born under *Mercury*.[1] ...

IN the same Inn was a Chariot, that had a Portmantua behind it, which my Attendance observing, thought it would look as well behind mine; and one of my Brother Rogues being formerly a Horse-Courser,[2] I imagin'd it wou'd be too great a Luggage for the Gentleman's Horses; for he was bound to *London*, out of Humanity eas'd 'em of the Load.

WHEN they had finish'd the Affair, I was inform'd of their Adventure, therefore I thought it highly necessary to make but a short Stay there. So, while the other Company was at Dinner, we set on our Journey, and arriv'd at *Bath* in two Hours.

I ORDER'D the Portmantua into my Bed-Chamber, where my Impatience wou'd not rest till I had examin'd the Contents, there-fore was forc'd to commit Burglary on the Locks. I thought the Booty was but indifferent, and hardly worth the Carriage, when I found nothing but one Suit of Cloaths, half a Dozen Shirts, and a couple of Rings: But examining the Fobs[3] of the Breeches, I found a Bank Note of six hundred and thirty Pounds. I did not let my Company into that Affair, only told 'em of the other Things, which I gave among 'em, on Condition Care should be taken they were not expos'd in *Bath*, which Direction was follow'd, and a Bonfire made of the Portmantua in my Room, for fear it might be a means of a Discovery by some Accident....

Street Robberies Consider'd.

I SHALL Consider consisely in the ensuing Pages, what Methods in my Judgment, and Experience in the Facts themselves; how to prevent this present Pest of *Street-Robbers*, in the Capital of the Kingdom: At present a Man is not safe in going about his neces-sary Affairs, even in the Day Time, for several Robberies have been Committed in the face of the Sun; and tho' Numbers have been taken off every Sessions, yet these Mercurial Gentlemen rather Increase than Diminish....

---

1 Mercury, among other things, was the god of thievery.
2 A jobbing dealer in horses.
3 The chains attached to watches carried in small pockets (or fobs) of breeches.

Appendix B: Related Works by Other Writers

[Accounts of all kinds, usually purporting to be "true and authentic," tumbled from the presses during the early decades of the eighteenth century in order to satisfy society's seemingly insatiable appetite for counter-culture literature.]

1. **From *Hell Upon Earth; Or, the Most Pleasant and Delectable History of Whittington's Colledge, Otherwise (Vulgarly) Called Newgate* (London, 1703)[1]**

Now you must know, that this ancient Gaol [Newgate prison] is divided into three Parts; to wit, the *Press-yard*, *Master-side*, and *Common-side*; as for the Manner of the *Press-yard* Building, tho' there are glaz'd Windows to the several Chambers thereof, yet are they well fortified inwardly, by *Vulcan's* Craft, for fear any of the Students therein shou'd, when they get drunk and mad, tumble out at the Casements; for those Sinners who lie there, having well lin'd their Pockets by their several Vices and Irregularities committed in contempt of the *Law* are pretty often elevated with outlandish Liquors, taking more delight by half to spend their Time in Tipling, than spare an Hour in a Day to pray for their Deliverance from the Burden of Affliction....

Now, as concerning the Humours of the *Master-side*, when a Scholar in Iniquity comes to *Newgate*, by Virtue of a *Mittimus*,[2] which word sounds as terrible in his Ears, as *God-damn-me* in the hearing of a good *Christian*, he is deliver'd up to the Paws of the Wolves, lurking continually in the *Lodge* for a Prey; where, as soon as a *Scribler* records him for a Villain, he's adorn'd with a pair of Iron Boots, and from thence conducted (provided he has *Gilt*[3]) over the way to Hell; for really, no Place has a nearer Resemblance of that Eternal Receptacle of Punishment than the *Master-side*, for the *Cellar* (where poor relentless Sinners are guzling in the midst of Debauchery and new invented *Oaths*, which rumble like Thun-

---

1   This pamphlet has been attributed to John Hall (d.1707), whose biography was written by Paul Lorrain, Ordinary of Newgate prison.
2   A writ instructing a jailer to hold a prisoner.
3   Money, gold.

der through their filthy Throats) is a lamentable Den of Horror and Darkness; there being no Light. In this *Boozing Ken*[1] (where more than *Cimmerian* Darkness dissipates its horrible Gloom) the Students, instead of holding Disputes in *Philosophy* or *Mathematicks*, run altogether upon *Law*; For such as are committed for House-breaking, swear stoutly they can't be cast for *Burglary*, because the Fact was done in the Day-time; Such as are committed for stealing a Horse-Cloath or Coachman's Cloak, swear they can't be cast[2] for *Felony* and *Robbery*, because the Coach was standing still, not stop'd; And such as steal before a Man's Face, swear they value not their Adversary, because they are out of the reach of the new Act against *Private-Stealing*. Thus with an unparallel'd Impudence, every brazen'd Face Rascal is harden'd in his Sin, because the *Law* can't touch his Life....

But now passing by that part of the *Master-side*, into which Prisoners are brought upon real suspicion of Debt, I shall proceed to the Humours of the *Common-side*: Those Scholars that come here, have nothing to depend on but the Charity of the Foundation, in which side very exact Rules are observ'd; for as soon as a Prisoner comes into the Turnkey's Hands, three knocks are given at the Stair Foot, as a signal a *Collegian* is coming up, which Harmony makes those *Convicts* that stand for the *Garnish*,[3] as joyful as one knock, the signal of the Baker's coming every Morning, does those poor Prisoners, who for want of Friends, have nothing else to subsist on but Bread and Water: And no sooner are the Three stroaks given, but out jump Four Trunchion Officers (who only hate Religion because it condemns their Vices) from their Hovel, and with a sort of ill mannerly Reverence receive him at the Grate; then taking him into their Apartment, a couple of the good natur'd Sparks hold him, whilst the other two pick his Pockets, claiming Six pence a piece as a priviledge belonging to their Office; then they turn him out to the Convicts, who hover about him (like so many Crows about a piece of Carrion) for *Garnish*, which is Six Shillings and Eight pence, which they, from an old Custom, claim by Prescription, Time out of Mind, for entering into the *Society*, otherwise they strip the poor Wretch, if he has not wherewithal to pay it....

When the Prisoners are disposed to recreate themselves with

---

1 Drinking place.
2 Found guilty, convicted.
3 Money extorted from a new prisoner as a jailer's fee, or as drink-money from other prisoners.

walking, they go up into a spacious Room call'd the *High-Hall*; where when you see them taking a Turn together, it would puzzle one to know which is the Gentleman, which the *Mechanick*,[1] and which the *Beggar*, for they are all suited in the same Form of a kind of nasty Poverty, which is a Spectacle of more Pity than Executions; only to be out at the Elbows is in Fashion here, and a great indecorum not to be threadbare. On the North-side, is a small Room call'd the *Buggering Hold*; but from whence it takes its Name I cannot well tell, unless it is a Fate attending this Place, that some confin'd there, may have been addicted to *Sodomy*; here the *Fines*[2] lie, and perhaps, as he behaves himself, an outlaw'd Person may creep in among them: But what Degree of Latitude this Chamber is situated in, I cannot positively demonstrate, unless it lies Ninety Degrees beyond the *Artick-Pole*; for instead of being dark here but half a Year, it is dark all the Year round. The Company, one with another there, is but a vying of Complaints, and the Causes they have, to rail on the ill success of Petitions, and in this they reckon there is a great deal of Good Fellowship: There they huddle up their Life as a thing of no use, and wear it out like an old Suit, the faster, the better, and he that deceives the Time at Cards, or Dice, thinks that he deceives it best, and best spends it....

But the place which is most diverting to our *Collegians* (who sin to better their understanding) is in the *Cellar*, whose *Newgate* Fashion of having all Tables publick, all the Alehouses about Town now imitate, where we sit in the pleasant Prospect of a Range of *Butts*[3] and *Barrels*; and the only grievance herein, is the paying for *Pipes* and *Candles*, which are placed in square Pyramidal Candlesticks made of Clay....

Now if there should be any great Tumult or Uproar among the Prisoners, whose deepest Endearment is a communication of Mischief, then a Bell, which hangs over the *High-Hall* Stairs (to call the Turnkey, when out of the way, by single ringing, to let People in and out) is rung double; and at the Alarm, several Officers belonging to the Gaol, come running up to quell the Mutiny, which being appeased, the Ringleaders thereof (who are such high spirited Fellows, that would sooner accept the Gallows than a mean Trade) are conducted to a low Dungeon, as dark as the inside of the *Devils Arse in the Peak*, and hung all over with spider

---

1   Manual labourer.
2   Those subject to pecuniary penalty.
3   Large casks.

Texture, and there Shear'd, or put into *Bilboes*,[1] and *Handcuffed*; but in case the Place of Punishment should be first taken up by any Fractious Woman, that's given to Penknife, then are they punish'd in the *Press-Room*, where Men that stand mute at their Tryal, are Pres'd to Death, by having their Hands and Feet extended out to Four Iron Rings fix'd to the ground, and a great heavy Press of Wood made like a Hog-Trough, having a square Post at each end, reaching up to the Ceiling, let up and down full of Weights, by Ropes them upon, in which Torment he lies Three or Four Days, or less time, according as favour'd; having no Food or Drink, but Black Bread, or the Channel Water which runs under the Gaol, if his fainting Pains should make him crave to Eat or Drink.

But now I am arrived to the Women Felons Apartment, in the *Common-side*; where I view'd a Troop of *Hell-Cats*, lying Head and Tail together, in a dismal nasty, dark Room: Having no Place to divert themselves; but at the Grate, adjoyning to the Foot Passage under *Newgate*, where Passengers[2] may with admiration and pity hear them swear *extempory*, being so shamefully vers'd in that most odious Prophanation of Heaven, that Vollies of Oaths are discharg'd through their detestable Throats, whilst asleep. And if any of their riotous Acquaintance gives them *L'argent*, then they jump into their *Cellar*, to melt it; which is scarce so large as *Covent-Garden* Cage, and the Stock therein not much exceeding those pedling *Victuallers*, who fetch their Drink in Tubs, every brewing Day; as for the *Sutler*[3] there, I have no more to say of her, than that her Purity consists in the whiteness of her Linnen; and that the Licentiousness of the Women on this side is so detestable, that it is an unpardonable Crime to describe their Lewdness; which Sex, when bad, exceeds the prophaneness of Man....

But when the Time's approach'd, that a Gaol Delivery is made, then the Prisoners are betimes in the morning conducted down to the *Sessions-House* in the *Old Baily*,[4] making as they go along a jingling with their Fetters, like so many *Morrice-Dancers* in the *Christmas* Holy-Days; and such *Malefactors* as will not give Half a Crown to be in the *Bail-Dock*, where Criminals both Male and Female are secur'd, go into the Hold, where they resemble so many Sheep penn'd up in *Smithfield*[5] on a Market Day: There the eldest Pris-

---

1 Shackles.
2 Passers-by.
3 Proprietress, barmaid, etc.
4 See above, p. 45, n. 1.
5 Smithfield market in London, largely for the sale of livestock.

oners claim Twelve pence a piece of the youngest for *Hold Money*, with which Collection they make shift to get some of 'em Drunk before they go up to the *Bar*, to be arraign'd, or try'd; the same odious Custom is likewise observ'd by the Women in their *Hold*. And if it shou'd be a Prisoners good luck to be acquitted, he kneels on his Knees, and crys, *God bless the Queen, and all the honourable Court*, then joyfully returning to his Comrades, they make him spend his *quit*[1] *Shilling*, for his happy Deliverance. But after they are all try'd, the Judge proceeds to pass Sentence on the several Offenders, then those cast for *single Felony* are brought up; but such as never broke their Friends for Learning, not venturing a *non legit*,[2] throw themselves on the Mercy of the Court, and escape marking with an ignominious *T*,[3] by entering themselves in Her Majesty's service; and such as can read and claim the *Benefit of the Clergy*, a favour only design'd at first for Scholars, but now through long Custom, claim'd by the illiterate, are forc'd (upon the account of clearing the Land of Villains) to save their Bacon by Listing[4] too. But profligate Women (having not this Advantage) are Glim'd[5] for that Villainy, for which, rather than leave it, they could freely die Martyrs. Next, Sentence of Death is past on Malefactors; but upon this Point, the Women have a great Advantage over the Men by pleading their Bellies, who are then search'd by a Jury of Matrons, impanell'd for that Purpose, but either for favour or profit some are brought often in quick with Child (when they are not gone an Hour) to the great abuse of the honourable Court, not but that they deserv'd for it, but as the saying is, *No grass grows on the Highway*. Those cast for *Petit-Larceny*, shove the Tumbler, *i.e.* are whipt at the Cart's Tail.

The *Court* being broke up, and by an *O yes*, appointed to begin again at another certain Time, the Prisoners not cast for their Lives[6] return from whence they came, the *Thieftakers*[7] ogling them as earnestly as they trudge along (to know their shameless Faces another time) as a Gypsie does ignorant Country Wenches Hands, to tell their Fortune: But those condemn'd, go to the Condemn'd *Hold*,[8] there being two, one for Males, another for

---

1 Acquittal.
2 "He doesn't read" (Latin).
3 Branding on the left cheek with a large "T," proclaiming a thief.
4 Enlisting.
5 Burnt in the hand. See above, p. 113, n. 5.
6 That is, those not sentenced to be hanged.
7 See above, p. 320, n. 3.
8 See Appendix B.5.

Females: Who being relentless Wretches, unmindful of a future
State, make their dark dismal Den the rendezvous of Spittle,
where they Dialogue (as in Tobacco-shops) with their Noses, and
their Communication is Smoak....

Next *Sunday* following their fatal Doom, they go to Chapel to
hear Mr. *Ordinary* preach the Condemnation Sermon; which is
full of strangers, to see more miserable Wretches sit round the
condemn'd Table than to hear what is piously deliver'd from the
Pulpet: The other Prisoners being separated from the Congrega-
tion by such wooden Grates ... and the *Dead-Warrant*[1] sign'd, and
sent to the *Sheriffs*, and the Day appointed for their dying, a *Bell
Man*, at dead of Night rings his Bell under *Newgate*, and then with
a dismal Voice calls the condemn'd Persons to hear the following
Speech.

> *All you that in the condemn'd Holds do lie,*
> *Prepare you, for to Morrow you shall die;*
> *Watch all and pray, the Hour's drawing near,*
> *That you before th' Almighty must appear:*
> *Examine well your selves, in time repent,*
> *That you may not t'eternal Flames be sent;*
> *And when St. Pulcher's Bell, to morrow, tolls,*
> *The Lord above have Mercy on your Souls.*

On the morning they die, they are brought from their dark Den
(a lively Type of the Grave) to Chapel, where such as are disposed
receive the blessed *Sacrament*; then brought into the *Stone-Hall*
(where formerly Charity has been begg'd in old Shoes, hanging
out at the Grates) their Irons are knock'd off, and the Yeoman of
the Halter, there adorns them with a hempen Garment, which is
to espouse them to a better World, according as their Contrition is
sincere in this: Which solemn Ceremony performed, they are conducted down Stairs to the Cart, in which being seated and ty'd, a
Subaltern,[2] with a white Wand, and Guard of *Serjeants* conveys
them to the *World's end*; but in their final Voyage, they stop near the
West-end of St. *Pulcher's* Church, where a fellow leans over the
Wall, tingling a small Bell, and makes a short *Harangue*, putting
them in mind of their latter end; which ended, they proceed
onwards again, the Bell tolling at St. *Andrew's* Church, as they

---

1 See above, p. 287, n. 1.
2 An army officer of junior rank.

ride backwards up the Hill, the same solemnity being likewise observed at Saint *Giles* Church; where by the *Pound* they may perhaps make another stop at the *Crown*,[1] to enliven their drooping Hearts with a Glass of *Canary*;[2] then away they ride again, sometimes looking on the Mob, among whom they may chance to espy some of their ill Consorts following them to pick Pockets at *Tyburn*; other times casting up their Eyes (if endu'd with so much Grace) towards that Sacred Place, against which they have too often offended; next, with great earnestness throwing up their Hands (which are commonly deck'd with White gloves, book in one, and Nosegay or Orange[3] in t'other) in commiseration of the untimely end they've brought on themselves, and Disgrace to their Friends; then being arriv'd to the *Triple-Tree*,[4] consecrated by the Romish Church, for several of their *Martyrs* dying thereon, they declare their perplexed minds to Mr. *Ordinary*, and make a short speech to the People, whilst Mr. *Catch*[5] ogles their Habit, and gives instructions to his Man, who waits upon him with a Bag, in which he crams the Hats, Perukes,[6] Neckcloths, and rest of the Cloaths of the executed Persons; but penitential Psalm being sung, and Night-cap pull'd over the Eyes, the Cart's drawn away, and with Dismal Screeches they bid the World adieu.

After swinging an Hour between Heaven and Earth, as unworthy of either, they are cut down, stript, and tumbled into a *Highway-grave* together, against *Hyde-Park* Gate, unless their Friends buy them for interment or *Chyrurgeons* beg their Carcasses for Anatomizing Operations. This is all the Description I can give of this Place, whose Horror I hope may so much work on irregular Persons for the future, as to make them forsake wicked Courses; and it is my Wish that honest People will be more wary of giving Opportunities to graceless Wretches, who value not the Misery of this Mansion, where Villains Breathe their Discontents against *Magistracy* more securely, and have their Tongues at more liberty than abroad; and to conclude, this is a School which teaches much Wisdom, but too late, and with Danger; and it is better be a Fool than come here to learn it.

---

1 A tavern en route.
2 A light, sweet wine from the Canary Islands.
3 That is, to combat the stench of the condemned in the wagon.
4 See above, p. 275, n. 1.
5 Jack Ketch, public executioner in the 1680s, was well-known for his savagery and incompetence. The name "Catch" soon afterwards became an allusion to official hangmen.
6 Wigs.

2. Paul Lorrain, *The Ordinary of Newgate his Account of the Behaviour, Confession, and Last Speech of George Skelthorpe, that was Executed at Tyburn, on Wednesday the 23d of March, 1709* (London, 1709)[1]

At the Sessions held at *Justice-Hall* in the *Old-Baily*,[2] on Wednesday the 2d, and *Thursday* the 3d, and then adjourn'd to *Thursday* the 10th day of *March* 1708-9, Seven Persons being found Guilty of Death, received Sentence accordingly. Of these 7, One only is order'd for Execution, and the other Six have obtain'd a gracious Reprieve; which I hope they will take care to improve into further Mercy.

As soon as they were cast for their Lives,[3] I constantly attended them every day: And upon each of the following Solemn Days, *viz.*

1. *Sunday* the 6th.
2. *Tuesday*, the Anniversary of *Her Majesty's* Accession to the Throne, being the 8th. of this instant *March*,
3. *Ashwednesday* the 9th.
4. *Sunday* the 13th.
5. *Sunday* the 20th.

I preach'd to them and others then present, both in the Morning and Afternoons, upon these several Texts.
1. Upon *Job* 14.14. *If a man die, shall he live again? All the days of my appointed time will I wait till my change come.*
2. Upon *Psal.* 40.16. *Let all those that seek Thee, rejoice and be glad in Thee: Let such as love Thy Salvation, say continually, The Lord be magnify'd.*
3. Upon *Isai.* 55, 6 & 7. *Seek ye the Lord while He may be found. Call ye upon Him while He is near. Let the wicked forsake his way, and the unrighteous man his thoughts, and let him return unto the Lord, and He will have mercy upon him; and to our God, for He will abundantly pardon.*

---

1 This one-page broadsheet was one of many accounts of condemned criminals written and published by Paul Lorrain, Ordinary of Newgate prison from 1698 to 1719. They sold for between 3d. and 6d. and generally appeared the morning after the execution in order to gain the greatest sales. See Appendix B.6.

2 See above, p. 45, n. 1.

3 Sentenced to be hanged.

4. Upon *Luke* 24.46 & 47. (Part of the 2d Morning -Lesson). *And (Jesus) said unto them, Thus it is written, and this it beloved Christ to suffer, and to rise from the Dead the third Day: And that Repentance and Remission of Sins should be preached in his Name amongst all Nations, beginning at Jerusalem.*
5. Upon *Prov.* 28.13. *He that covers his Sins shall not prosper: But whoso confesses and forsakes them, shall have Mercy.*

I shall not here (as I usually do in the like Cases) set down the Heads of those Sermons: That would make this Paper of a larger Extent than I intend it. This only I shall observe, That I concluded every one of those ten Set Discourses with such an Extempore Exhortation and Application, as I thought most suitable to the Condemned; whom I visited and pray'd with in the Chapel twice every day, and had sometimes under private Examination. And then it was that I received from *George Skelthorp* his Confession, as hereafter follows.

This *George Skelthorp,* the only Person that is now to suffer, was try'd upon two Indictments, and found guilty of both. The first was for assaulting *William Hills,* upon the QUEEN's High-way (that is in the Streets from the *Strand* through the New Buildings to *Covent-garden*) and taking from him 4s. 6d. on the 18th of *February* last. The other Indictment was for his assaulting *James Booker* on the 27th of the said Month of *February,* and taking from him a Gold-Ring, a Muslin[1] Neck-Cloth, and 10s. in Money, in or about the same place, where he had committed the former Robbery. The Account that he gave me, First, of himself; and then of what has a relation to those Facts of which he was accus'd, and for which he was condemn'd, was this:

First, As to himself; He said, he was about 25 years of age, born at St. *Edmunds Bury,* in the County of *Suffolk,* That he had been for a time a Domestick Servant in the Families of some Gentlemen, both in the Country and here in Town, and for above these Seven years last past, in the QUEEN's Service, first in *Ireland,* in the Regiment of Colonel *Granfield,* in Captain *North's* Company; and then in *Flenders* in the same Regiment, and afterwards here in HER MAJESTY's First Regiment of Foot-Guards, in Brigadier *Totton's* Company: That as he had not had much Education in Matters of Religion, and knew very little of that which is a great Help thereto (*viz.* Reading) but what he had of himself pickt up of late; so he

---

1 Finely woven cotton fabric.

was easily induced to a Loose Life of Drinking, Whoring, and Breaking the Sabbath-day, and totally neglecting the Service of God. All which heinous and crying Sins were now very grievous to him, and lay very heavy upon his Conscience.

Secondly, As to what concern'd the Facts for which he was to die; he deny'd his being guilty of them, or of any Crime that should have brought him before any Justice; but this only, That he knowing the time when, and the places where some Sodomites were resorting about *Covent-Garden*,[1] he went to stand in their Way, and when any of them would (as they often did) carry him to a By-place thereabouts to commit their foul Acts with him, he went with them; and then he taking hold of them, threaten'd them, that he would presently bring them before a Justice, unles they gave him Satisfaction. By which means (he said) he got a great deal of Money at several times, of such Persons; who rather than suffer themselves to be exposed (some of them being Men of good appearance) gave him either Money, Rings, or Watches, or what else they had then about them. Which he would fain perswade me was the only thing that had brought this Prosecution upon him; acknowledging at the same time, that it was just with God thus to punish him, for having concealed and conniv'd at those foul Acts, which he easily might have discover'd and brought to Justice, as he ought to have done. But the Love of filthy Lucre had kept him from it; though it had not as yet (but he could not tell whether if he had gone on in that Trade, it would not at last have) brought him to yield to their lewd and foul Practices. This is the Substance of what he said; adding only as to this Matter, That there was a certain publick House about *Covent-Garden*, where he knew those Sodomites us'd frequently to meet, and had seen some of them there several times, And it now repented him, that he had not made a Discovery of them, as he often had fair opportunities for it.

He seem'd all along, from the time of his Trial to that of his Death, to be very willing both to learn and practice those Religious Duties, which (by his own Confession) he had too much neglected before. He desired both my Instructions and Prayers, which he had, and I hope were not bestow'd in vain. But God knows the Heart of Man. He was very attentive to the Word of God, when read and expounded to him; and I could not observe

---

1 The Strand and Covent Garden, as well as all the lanes which crossed them, were known places of sexual resort.

any thing in his Behaviour, but what was becoming a Man under his sad Circumstances. He pray'd very earnestly to God for the Pardon of his Sins; and declar'd, that he forgave all his Enemies, and dy'd in Charity with all Men.

When he was carry'd this Day from *Newgate* in a Cart to the Place of Execution,[1] I met him there, and discharged, for the last time, my Ministerial Office to him. I exhorted him more and more to repent and clear his conscience before he dy'd. To which he return'd this answer, That *he repented with all his heart of all the Sins that he ever had committed, and trusted in God for Mercy, through the Merits of* Jesus Christ. And here he further declar'd, That *what he had told me before was true; and, That his Guilt was no other than he had then confess'd to me.*

After this I pray'd and sung some Penitential Psalms with him: I made him rehearse the Articles of our Christian Faith: And then he said, That *by the Grace of God he would die in that Faith, and hop'd for Eternal Life and Salvation.*

Then he spoke to the People to this effect, *That he had serv'd the* QUEEN *seven Years, and been in five Campaigns; That he had been a wild Young-man, and would be rambling abroad instead of going to Church: That tho' he was not guilty of those Robberies for which he was now to suffer, (that is to say, just in the manner as they were sworn against him) yet as he had greatly offended God, so God had justly brought him to this his Shameful and Untimely End.* This he acknowledg'd. Now there being (it seems) one of the Witnesses that had sworn against him, close by the Cart, he was entring upon a Discourse with him in his own Justification of the Facts he was charg'd withal; but upon my telling him, That this was not a proper Time and Place to reflect upon any body but himself; and, That he should consider the few minutes he had now to live in this World, and think on that Great GOD, before whose Tribunal he [was] just going to appear, &c. he presently return'd to his Prayers, That *God would be pleas'd to forgive him a great Sinner.* He desir'd all Young Men, and others, to take Warning by him, and avoid his Sins, that they might not come to the like Condemnation. Sometimes he would express some uneasiness for his no[t] having had the same Mercy shewn him as the other six Persons that receiv'd Sentence with him: But being made sensible, that his Crimes appear'd greater than theirs, he seeme'd to be more satisfied, and acquiesce in the Justice of his Condemnation. He

---

1 That is, Tyburn.

solemnly (and that more than twice) declar'd here, That *he died in Charity with all the World, and freely forgave all those that had done him any Injury, as he desir'd to have Forgiveness at God's Hand.*

This being done, I retir'd; and after some further time allow'd him for his private Devotions, the Cart drew away, and he was turn'd off; all the while calling upon God in these and the like Ejaculations, *Lord JESUS have mercy upon me! Lord receive my Soul,* &c.

This is all the Account here to be given of this Dying Person, by

PAUL LORRAIN, *Ordinary of* Newgate.
March 23. 1708/9

London Printed, and are to be Sold by *Benj. Bragg,* at the *Raven* in *Pater-noster-Row.*

3. From *A Discourse and View of Virginia* [London, 1712]

Into the Bay of *Virginia,* formerly called *Chesapeack* Bay, runs six eminent Rivers, none twenty miles distant from another; three of which exceed the *Thames,* both in extent and progression of the Tides; these cause and continue the admir'd fertility of the Countrey, and by their greatness and contiguity temper those heats, which the dryer places of *Africa* are subject to, in the same degree of latitude.

Up these Rivers Ships of three hundred tuns sail near two hundred miles, and anchor in the fresh waters; and by this means are not troubled with those Worms which endamage ships, both in the Western Islands of *America,* and in the *Mediterranean Sea.* And to avoid a larger discourse of it, I will here note it, that our ships once past the Lands end,[1] are in no danger of Pirats, Rocks or Lee-shores, till they come to their Port, and fewer ships miscarry going to *Virginia,* then to any Port at that distance in the world.

Now for those things which are naturally in it, they are these, Iron, Lead, Pitch, Tar, Masts, Timber for Ships of the greatest magnitude, and Wood for Pot-ashes.

Those other Commodities, which are produced by industry, are Flax, Hemp, Silk, Wheat, Barley, Oats, Rice, Cotton, all sorts

---

1 Land's End, the southwestern tip of England.

of Pulse[1] and Fruits, the last of which in that perfection, that if the taste were the onely judge, we would not think they were of the same *species* with those from which they are derived to us from *England*. The vicious ruinous plant of Tobacco I would not name, but that it brings more money to the Crown, then all the Islands in *America* besides.

Now this is ascertained and contested, that such staple commodities, as Iron, Silk, Flax, Hemp, and Pot-ashes, may be easily raised in *Virginia*, an high imputation will lye upon us, why we have not all this time endeavoured to evidence the truth and certainty of it, to our own and the publick advantage.

4. **From Alexander Smith, *The History of the Lives, of the Most Noted Highway-Men, Foot-Pads, House-Breakers, Shop-Lifts, and Cheats, of Both Sexes, in and About London, and Other Places of Great Britain, for Above Fifty Years Last Past*, 2nd ed., 2 vols. (London, 1714)[2]**

VOLUME I

[Moll Hawkins, a Shoplifter]

This unfortunate Creature permitting her inclination to introduce her very early into all sorts of Vanity and to give Sense the Preheminence above Reason, her Wits were always put on the Rack of Invention to support her in Actions which ever tended to meer Debauchery; for the greatest Darkness that ever muffled up our Hemisphere in Obscurity, could not exceed the Blackness of her Soul, which had been dead and rotten in Trespasses and Sin, long before she made her *Exit* on the Triple-Tree.[3] Adultery and Fornication were her common Recreations, as well as Shop-lifting, for which last Crime, altho' she had seen many of her Acquaintance Monthly made Examples, yet would she not forebear nor desist from such Irregular and Life-destroying Courses, till it had brought her to the like miserable Catastrophe. But before *Moll Hawkins* projected Shop-lifting, she went upon the *Question-Lay*, which is putting herself into a good handsome Dress, like some Exchange Girl,[4] then she takes an empty Band-box in her Hand,

---

1 The edible seeds of leguminous plants, such as peas, beans and lentils.
2 "Alexander Smith" is probably a pseudonym.
3 See above, p. 275, n. 1.
4 Shop attendant in an Exchange arcade.

and passing for a Milliner's or Sempstress's 'Prentice, she goes early to a Person of Quality's House, and knocking at the Door, she asks the Servant if the Lady is stirring yet; for if she was,[1] she had brought home, according to order, the Suit of Knots,[1] (or what else the Devil puts in her Head) which Her Ladyship had bespoke over Night; then the Servant going up Stairs to acquaint the Lady of this Message, she in the mean time robs the House, and goes away without an Answer. Thus she one Day serv'd the Lady *Arabella Holland,* living in *Soho-Square,* when the Maid going up Stairs to acquaint her Ladyship that a Gentlewoman waited below with some Gloves and Fans, *Moll Hawkins* then took the Opportunity of carrying away above fifty Pounds worth of Plate, which stood on a Side-Board in the Parlor, to be clean'd against[2] Dinner-time.

Moll Hawkins, otherwise call'd *Fudge,* from her living with a Fellow of that Name, who was a most notorious Pick-pocket, was Condemn'd on the 3d of *March,* 1702 for privately stealing Goods out of the Shop of Mrs. *Hobday* in *Pater-noster-row.* She having been repriev'd for nine Months, upon the account of her being then found to be quick with Child, tho' she was not, she was now call'd down to her former Judgment. When she came to the Place of Execution at *Tyburn,* on *Wednesday* the 22d of *December* 1703, She said she was about twenty-six Years of Age, born in the Parish of St. *Giles's* in the Fields; that she serv'd three Years Apprentice-ship to a Button-Maker in *Maiden-Lane,* by *Covent-Garden,* and follow'd that Employment for some Years after; but withal gave way to those ill Practices which she now finds to be the Cause of her shameful Death.

[Anne Holland, a Pickpocket]

This was her right Name, tho' she went by the Names of *Andrews, Charlton, Edwards, Goddard,* and *Jackson,* which is very usual for Thieves to change them, because falling often-times into the Hands of Justice, and as often convicted of some Crimes, yet thereby it appears sometimes that when they are arraign'd at the Bar again, that is the first Time that they have been taken, and the first Crime whereof they have ever been accus'd; moreover, if they should happen to be cast,[3] People, by not knowing their right Names, cannot

---

1 A suit adorned with knotted lace or ribbons.
2 Before.
3 Found guilty, convicted.

say, the Son or Daughter of such a Man or Woman is to be whip'd, burnt,[1] or hang'd on such a Day of the Month, in such a Year; from whence would proceed more Sorrow to them that suffer'd, as well as Disgrace to their Parents. For this Reason, many such Persons are indicted with an *alias* prefix'd to several Names.... But as concerning *Anne Holland*, her usual Way of Thieving, was the *Service-Lay*, which was hiring herself for a Servant in any good Family, and then, as Opportunity serv'd, robb'd them: Thus, living once with a Master Taylor in *York-Buildings* in the *Strand*, her Mistress was but just gone out to a Christening as her Master came Home booted and spurr'd out of the Country,[2] and going up into his Chamber where she was making his Bed, he had a great Mind to try his Manhood with his Maid, and accordingly threw her on her Back; but she made a great Resistance, and would not grant him his Desire without he pull'd off his Boots; whereupon she first pluck'd one off, and whilst she was pulling off the other, one knocking at the Door, she ran down Stairs taking a Silver Tankard off the Window which would hold two Quarts, saying, she must draw some Beer, for she was very dry: However, she returning not presently, poor *Stitch*[3] was swearing, and staring, and bawling for his Maid *Nan*, to pull off his t'other Boot, which was half on and half off, but being extraordinary tight, could neither get his Leg farther in nor out: And there he might remain 'till Dooms-day for *Nan*, for she was gone far enough off with the *Wedge*, that's to say, Plate, which she had converted into another Shape and Fashion in a short time.

And once *Nan*, having been at a Fair in the Country, and coming up to London, she lay at *Uxbridge*, where being a good Pair of *Holland* Sheets to the Bed, she was so industrious as to sit up most part of the Night, to make her a couple of good Smocks[4] out of one of 'em; so in the Morning, putting the other Sheet double towards the Head of the Bed, she came down Stairs to Breakfast. In the Interim, the Mistress sent up her maid to see if the Sheets were there, who turning the single Sheet a little down as it lay folded, she came and whisper'd in her Mistress's Ear, that the Sheets were both there; so *Nan* discharging her Reckoning, she brought more Shifts to Town than she carry'd out with her; and truly she had a pretty many, or else she could not have liv'd as she did for some Years.

---

1 See above, p. 395, n. 5.
2 That is, he has been horseback riding in the countryside.
3 A slang term for one who lies with a woman (usually a verb).
4 Undergarments (similar to "shifts," below).

This unfortunate Creature, at her first launching out into the Region of Vice, was a very personable young Woman, being clear-skinn'd, well shap'd, having a sharp piercing Eye, a proportionable Face, and exceeding small hand; which natural Gifts serv'd rather to make her miserable, than happy; for several lewd Fellows flocking about her, like so many Ravens about a Piece of Carrion, to enter her under *Cupid's* Banners, and obtaining their Ends, she soon commenc'd and took Degrees in all manner of Debauchery; for if once a Woman passes the Bounds of Modesty, she seldom stops, 'till she hath arriv'd to the very Height of Impudence....

Nan Holland being thus oblig'd to shift among the Wicked for a Livelihood, for though but young, yet could she cant[1] tolerably well, wheedle most cunningly, lie confoundedly, swear desperately, pick a Pocket dexterously, dissemble undiscernably, drink and smoak everlastingly, whore insatiately, and brazen out all her Actions impudently. A little after this Disaster, she was marry'd to one *James Wilson*, an eminent Highway-Man, very expert in his Occupation....

VOLUME II

[Mary Carleton, a Cheat, Thief and Jilt]

She went to a Mercer's Shop in *Cheapside* with her pretended Maid, where agreeing for as much Silk as came to 6 *l.*, she pull'd out a Purse to pay him, but having nothing but Gold in it, which she was loth to part with, she desir'd the Mercer to let his Servant ride along with her in the Coach which was at the Door to her House, and she would pay him in Silver. The Mercer, willing to accommodate his Customer, order'd his Servant to attend her, whereupon being all coach'd, as they were riding along, she order'd the Coachman to set her down at the *Royal Exchange*[2] to buy her some Knots[3] suitable to the Colour of her Silk. Being arriv'd there ... she said to the Mercer's Man, *Friend, you may sit here in the Coach, while I and my Maid go up, and buy a few odd Things, and we will instantly return.* The young Man thought it good Manners to obey her Ladyship, and therefore sat still, permitting her Woman to take the Silk to match with Ribbons, as they said, so they tript it up Stairs, leaving the young Novice to take a Nap

---

1 Speak the jargon of criminals. See Appendix A.9.
2 See above, p. 356, n. 1.
3 Decorative bows of ribbon, etc.

in the Coach; but it might have bin a long one, had he stay'd till
their Return, for he ne'er saw 'em again.

5. From *The History of the Press-Yard: Or, a Brief Account of the Customs and Occurences that Are Put in Practice in that Ancient Repository of Living Bodies Called Newgate*, &c. (London, 1717)[1]

The Condemn'd-Hold,[2] falsly suppos'd to be a noisome Vault
under-ground, lies between the Top and Bottom of the Arch under
Newgate, from whence there darts in some Glimmerings of Light,
tho' very imperfect, by which you may know that you are in a dark,
Opace, wild Room. By the Help of a Candle, which you must pay
through the Nose for, before it will be handed to you over the
Hatch, your Eyes will lead you to boarded Places, like those that are
raised in Barracks, wherein you may repose your self if your Nose
will suffer you to rest, from the Stench that diffuses its noisome Par-
ticles of bad Air from every Corner. If you look up, you see the
Order of Nature inverted, by having the Common-side Cellar over
you, or if you cast your Eyes downward, all Things are equally surprising and unnatural: Here lie Chains affix'd to Hooks, and there
Iron Staples are driven into the Ground to bring those to a due
Submission that are Stubborn and Unruly. The Walls and the Floor
are all of Stone, and bear a Resemblance to the Hearts of those that
place you there, so that I may aptly be suppos'd to be seiz'd with a
Pannick Dread at the Survey of this my new Tenement, and to be
very willing to change it for another, almost upon any Terms.

6. Jonathan Swift, *The Last Speech and Dying Words of Ebenezor Elliston, who was Executed the Second Day of May, 1722* (London, 1722)[3]

Published at his Desire, for the Common Good.

I AM now going to suffer the just Punishment for my Crimes
prescribed by the Law of God and my Country. I know it is the

---

1 An anonymous work, sometimes ascribed to Defoe.
2 Those sentenced to die at Newgate spent their last days in the condemned hold (or hole). See Appendix B.1.
3 *The Prose Works of Jonathan Swift*, ed. Herbert Davis, vol. 9 (Oxford:
   Basil Blackwell, 1968) 37-41. Fraudently declared to be written by the
   condemned man himself, Swift's ironical pamphlet dramatizes the ritu-
   als of the public confession. See Appendix B.2.

constant Custom, that those who come to this Place should have Speeches made for them, and cryed about in their own Hearing, as they are carried to Execution; and truly they are such Speeches that although our Fraternity be an ignorant illiterate People, they would make a Man ashamed to have such Nonsense and false *English* charged upon him even when he is going to the Gallows: They contain a pretended Account of our Birth and Family; of the Fact for which we are to die; of our sincere Repentance; and a Declaration of our Religion. I cannot expect to avoid the same Treatment with my Predecessors. However, having had an Education one or two Degrees better than those of my Rank and Profession; I have been considering ever since my Commitment, what it might be proper for me to deliver upon this Occasion.

AND First, I cannot say from the Bottom of my Heart, that I am truly sorry for the Offence I have given to God and the World; but I am very much so, for the bad Success of my Villanies in bringing me to this untimely End. For it is plainly evident, that after having some time ago obtained a Pardon from the Crown, I again took up my old Trade; my evil Habits were so rooted in me, and I was grown so unfit for any other kind of Employment. And therefore although in Compliance with my Friends, I resolve to go to the Gallows after the usual Manner, Kneeling, with a Book in my Hand, and my eyes lift up; yet I shall feel no more Devotion in my Heart than I have observed in some of my Comrades, who have been drunk among common Whores the very Night before their Execution. I can say further from my own Knowledge, that two of my Fraternity after they had been hanged, and wonderfully came to Life, and made their Escapes, as it sometimes happens; proved afterwards the wickedest Rogues I ever knew, and so continued until they were hanged again for good and all; and yet they had the Impudence at both Times they went to the Gallows, to smite their Breasts, and lift up their Eyes to Heaven all the Way.

SECONDLY, From the Knowledge I have of my own wicked Dispositions and that of my Comrades, I give it as my Opinion, that nothing can be more unfortunate to the Publick, than the Mercy of the Government in ever pardoning or transporting us; unless when we betray one another, as we never fail to do, if we are sure to be well paid; and then a Pardon may do good; by the same Rule, *That it is better to have but one Fox in a Farm than three or four.* But we generally make a Shift to return after being transported, and are ten times greater Rogues than before, and much more cunning. Besides, I know it by Experience, that some Hopes we have of finding Mercy, when we are tryed, or after we are condemned, is always a great Encouragement to us.

THIRDLY, Nothing is more dangerous to idle young Fellows than the Company of those odious common Whores we frequent, and of which this Town is full: These Wretches put us upon all Mischief to feed their Lusts and Extravagancies: They are ten times more bloody and cruel than Men; their Advice is always not to spare if we are pursued; they get drunk with us, and are common to us all; and yet, if they can get any Thing by it, are sure to be our Betrayers.

NOW, as I am a dying Man, something I have done which may be of good Use to the Publick. I have left with an honest Man (and indeed the only honest Man I was ever acquainted with) the Names of all my wicked Brethren, the present Places of their Abode, with a short Account of the chief Crimes they have committed; in many of which I have been their Accomplice, and heard the rest from their own Mouths: I have likewise set down the Names of those we call our Setters,[1] of the wicked Houses we frequent, and of those who receive and buy our stolen Goods. I have solemnly charged this honest Man, and have received his Promise upon Oath, that whenever he hears of any Rogue to be tryed for Robbing, or House-breaking, he will look into his List, and if he finds the Name there of the Thief concerned, to send the whole Paper to the Government. Of this I here give my Companions fair and publick Warning, and hope they will take it.

IN the Paper abovementioned, which I left with my Friend, I have also set down the Names of several Gentlemen who have been robbed in *Dublin* Streets for three Years past: I have told the Circumstances of those Robberies; and shewn plainly that nothing but the Want of common Courage was the Cause of their Misfortunes. I have therefore desired my Friend, that whenever any Gentleman happens to be robbed in the Streets, he will get that Relation printed and published with the first Letters of those Gentlemens Names, who by their own Want of Bravery are likely to be the Cause of all the Mischief of that Kind, which may happen for the future.

I CANNOT leave the World without a short Description of that Kind of Life, which I have led for some Years past; and is exactly the same with the rest of our wicked Brethren.

ALTHOUGH we are generally so corrupted from our Childhood,

---

1 Decoys.

as to have no Sense of Goodness; yet something heavy always hangs about us, I know not what it is, that we are never easy till we are half drunk among our Whores and Companions; nor sleep sound, unless we drink longer than we can stand. If we go abroad in the Day, a wise Man would easily find us to be Rogues by our Faces; we have such a suspicious, fearful, and constrained Countenance; often turning back, and slinking through narrow Lanes and Allies.[1] I have never failed of knowing a Brother Thief by his Looks, though I never saw him before. Every Man among us keeps his particular Whore, who is however common to us all, when we have a mind to change. When we have got a Booty, if it be in Money, we divide it equally among our Companions, and soon squander it away on our Vices in those Houses that receive us; for the Master and Mistress, and the very Tapster, go Snacks;[2] and besides make us pay treble Reckonings. If our Plunder be Plate, Watches, Rings, Snuff-Boxes, and the like; we have Customers in all Quarters of the Town to take them off. I have seen a Tankard worth Fifteen Pounds sold to a Fellow in ———— Street for Twenty Shillings; and a Gold Watch for Thirty. I have set down his Name, and that of several others in the Paper already mentioned. We have Setters watching in Corners, and by dead Walls,[3] to give us Notice when a Gentleman goes by; especially if he be any thing in Drink. I believe in my Conscience, that if an Account were made of a Thousand Pounds in stolen Goods; considering the low Rates we sell them at, the Bribes we must give for Concealment, the Extortions of Ale-house Reckonings, and other necessary Charges, there would not remain Fifty Pounds clear to be divided among the Robbers. And out of this we must find Cloaths for our Whores, besides treating them from Morning to Night; who, in Requital, reward us with nothing but Treachery and the Pox. For when our Money is gone, they are every Moment threatening to inform against us, if we will not go out to look for more. If any Thing in this World be like Hell, as I have heard it described by our Clergy; the truest Picture of it must be in the Back-Room of one of our Ale-houses at Midnight; where a Crew of Robbers and their Whores are met together after a Booty, and are beginning to grow drunk; from which Time, until they are past their Senses, is such a continued horrible Noise of Cursing, Blasphemy, Lewdness, Scurrility, and brutish Behaviour; such Roaring and Confu-

1 Alleys.
2 That is, divide the profits.
3 Walls unrelieved by breaks or interruptions.

sion, such a Clatter of Mugs and Pots at each other's Heads; that *Bedlam*,[1] in Comparison, is a sober and orderly Place: At last they all tumble from their Stools and Benches, and sleep away the rest of the Night; and generally the Landlord or his Wife, or some other Whore who has a stronger Head than the rest, picks their Pockets before they wake. The Misfortune is, that we can never be easy till we are drunk; and our Drunkenness constantly exposes us to be more easily betrayed and taken.

THIS is a short Picture of the Life I have led; which is more miserable than that of the poorest Labourer who works for four Pence a Day; and yet Custom is so strong, that I am confident, if I could make my Escape at the Foot of the Gallows, I should be following the same Course this very Evening. So that upon the whole, we ought to be looked upon as the common Enemies of Mankind; whose Interest is to root us out like Wolves, and other mischievous Vermin, against which no fair Play is required.

IF I have done Service to Men in what I have said, I shall hope I have done Service to God; and that will be better than a silly Speech made for me full of Whining and Canting, which I utterly despise, and have never been used to; yet such a one I expect to have my Ears tormented with, as I am passing along the Streets.

GOOD People fare ye well; bad as I am, I leave many worse behind me. I hope you shall see me die like a Man, the Death of a Dog.

E.E.

N. B. *About the Time that this Speech was written, the Town was much pestered with* Street-Robbers; *who, in a barbarous Manner would seize on Gentlemen, and take them into remote Corners, and after they had robbed them, would leave them bound and gagged. It is remarkable, that this Speech had so good an Effect, that there have been very few Robberies of that kind committed since* [Defoe's note].

7. From *An Essay in Praise of Knavery*, 3rd ed. (London, 1723)

A *Highway-Man* is a generous Robber: He comes Arm'd, and like an open Enemy bids ye stand and Deliver. His Pistol gives Authority to his Word of Command; and to this, many Charged Blunderbusses[2] yield Obedience. They are some of them a sort of

---

1 See above, p. 286, n. 2.
2 A short musket of wide bore and flaring muzzle, used to scatter shot at close range.

Genteel Beggars, but (like Potentates in Treaties of Peace) insist upon Preliminaries Sword in Hand. They ask, and you must Grant; or Fire and Smoak, will certainly Ensue. And it is merry to see a whole Company of Armed Men, rather than they face the terrible Pistol, Deliver to a single Robber their Baggs of Money, Watches, Swords, and other Accoutrements; for the Noise of a Pistol is so very Dreadful in the Ears of some Travellers, that whether they are Wounded or not it has its Effect, and down they Drop like those that are Slain....

Of all the Set of little Villains, the *Pick-pocket* is the Chief. His Head is always Working to find out some Stratagem, to Dive into the Pockets of all sorts of Persons: And sometimes he is oblig'd to lie Siege for a Fortnight together, for a Watch or a Snuff-Box; and perhaps at last, be forc'd to Cut down the Breeches, and Expose the Posteriors, of a Rich old Miser, before his Hand can obtain Admittance. He has under him a large train of Pupils, from the sturdy Thief, that deals in Watches and Jewels, to the young tender Thiefling who stoops for Handkerchiefs. He is a Master of Arts in his Profession; and better skill'd in legerdemain, and Slight of Hand, than the famous *C—mpb—l*,[1] or any other Conjurers; and has a greater Knowledge in the Mystery of Iniquity, to Entitle him to his Degree, than the most Learn'd and Diligent Priest, in Theological Studies, who has made it his Business for many Years standing to make himself Master of Puns and Conundrums.

8. From T. Read, *The Life and Actions of Moll Flanders*, abr. ed. (London, [c.1723])[2]

[Her Last Will and Testament]

Thus I past my latter Days in a total Resignation of myself to the Will and Pleasure of my heavenly Father, till he was pleas'd to visit me with a *Dropsie* and *Asthma*, or Shortness of Breath, whereby finding Nature daily to decay more and more, and that I was not a Woman for this World long, I began to set my House hold in Order, and made my last Will and Testament as follow:

---

1 See *The History of the Life and Adventures of Duncan Campbell* (London, 1720), sometimes attributed to Defoe.
2 Read's conclusion, dealing with Moll's death and burial, was the one generally followed in chapbooks, though her burial was sometimes placed in Virginia rather than Ireland.

I *Elizabeth Atkins*,[1] of the City of *Galway*, in the County of *Galway*, (being at this Time in good and perfect Memory, thro' the Mercy of God, but weak and sickly in Body) do make this my last Will and Testament, in manner following; that is to say, I give to my deceased Husband's Brother, *Charles Carrol*, all my real Estate, lying about Athlone, in the Counties of *Roscommon*, and *West-Meath*, and to his Heirs and Assigns for ever.

Item, I give to my Gardiner, *Henry Kelly*, the sum of 50 Pounds of current Money of *England*.

Item, To *Jane Burke*, my Chamber-maid, I give the Sum of 40 Pounds.

Item, To *Catherine O-Neal*, my Cook-Maid, I give the Sum of 30 Pounds.

Item, To *Dorothy Macknamarra*, my House-maid, I give the Sum of 20 Pounds.

Item, To my deceas'd Husband's Brother, *William Carrol*, I give all the rest of my Goods, and Chattels, and personal Estate whatsoever; but out of the same to be decently interr'd, and all Funeral Charges to be paid, by the said *William Carrol*.

Lastly, I make and constitute my abovesaid Brother-in-law, *Charles Carrol*, Executor of this my last Will and Testament, written with my own Hand this 30th Day of *March*, in the Year of our Lord Christ, according to the *English* Computation, 1722.

Eliz. Atkins

Seal'd, publish'd, and declar'd
by the said Elizabeth Atkins,
for and as her last Will and
Testament, in the Presence of
Patrick Magey, James Mullens,
and John Hara.

[Her Death and Elegy]

In the time of her Sickness, which held for about nine Months, she was very penitent, and most zealously fervent in her Devotion, not in the least minding the Affairs of this World, but entirely prepar'd herself for a future State. She was constantly attended by some eminent Divines, but particularly one Mr. *Price*,[2] Master of the

---

1 Some later abridgements and adaptations used "Laetitia Atkins" as Moll's name.

2 The Reverend John Price (d.1729) was elected master of Galway Grammar School from October 1700.

Free-School in Galway. In this Godly Disposition for her latter End she continu'd till the 10th of *April* following the Date of her last will and Testament, when she departed this mortal Life, in the 75th Year of her Age, to the no small Grief and Sorrow of the Poor, to whom she had been very charitable whilst alive; for she allow'd 25 old Men 40 shillings a-piece yearly; to 20 old Women she allow'd 30 shillings a-piece yearly; and forty Pounds a Year for putting out poor Children to be Apprentices.

No sooner was the Death of Moll Flanders nois'd over the Kingdom of *Ireland*, but the prime Wits of Trinity College in *Dublin* compos'd on her the following Elegy:

> Alas! what News doth now our Ears invade?
> What Havock has grim Death among us made?
> With the impetuous Fury of the Dart,
> *Moll Flanders* he has wounded thro' the Heart:
> *Moll Flanders*, once the Wonder of the Age,
> Whilst she remain'd on this terrestial Stage,
> Is gone to take a Nap for many Years,
> For which ye ought to shed as many Tears.
> We mean her chiefest Mourners ought to be
> The chief Proficients in all Villainy,
> Such Persons who go on the sneaking Budge,[1]
> And will for Mops and Pails thro' *Dublin* trudge;
> House-breakers, Doxies who can file a Cly,[2]
> And those who out of Shops steal privately.
> But you that can't cry, yet would seem to weep,
> Your Handkerchiefs in Juice of Onions steep,
> Then rail upon the cruel Hand of Fate,
> Which would not grant *Moll's* Reign a longer Date.
> A longer Date, said we? Indeed too long
> She liv'd to do some honest People wrong;
> Such Wrong, that had she her deserved Due,
> She had been whipt, and glimm'd,[3] and hanged too;
> But all the Paths of Vice so much she trac'd,
> That hanging her had any Tree disgrac'd.
> Howe'er take care below, among the Dead,
> For tho' the mortal Life of *Moll* is fled,
> She may perhaps as now ye cannot feel,

---

1 That is, those who rob alone, chiefly dealing in petty larcenies.
2 Prostitutes who pick a pocket.
3 See above, p. 395, n. 5.

Your Shrouds, and Coffins, else your Bodies steal,
As Grave-diggers in *England* do, to be
Mangled to pieces in Anatomy.
But hold, deceased *Moll* we must not blame
Too much, for tho' she glory'd in her Shame,
Of being dextrous Thief, and arrant Whore,
Yet we some Pity for her must implore,
And give her deathless Memory some Praise,
In that she ended well her latter Days,
For of her num'rous Sins she did repent,
And dy'd a very hearty Penitent.

9. From *An Accurate Description of Newgate. With the Rights, Privileges, Allowances, Fees, Dues, and Customs thereof*, by B. L. of Twickenham (London, 1724)

"Of Transportation"

Having given a Description of the several Parts of *Newgate* ... I shall now proceed to speak a Word or two in relation to the Transportation of Criminals.

The limitted Time for Transportation, is generally in proportion to the Offence, *viz.* if for Felony, Seven Years; and for those who are under Sentence of Death, or such who buy Stoln Goods (knowing the same to [be] Stoln) Fourteen Years; and for such Criminals whose Actions appear to be very enormously Wicked, and are reprieved after Condemnation, they are generally Transported for Term of Life.

The Commencing of the Time of Transportation, is accounted from the Day the Keeper of *Newgate* delivers the Criminals out of his Gaol, to the Captain who Transports them to the Places assigned.

At the Captain's receiving of them out of *Newgate*, they (being Hand-cuff'd two and two together) are directed to the Transport Ship; between the Decks of which is a Prison or Gaol, wherein they are strongly secured, till such time as they arrive at the intended Port, being allow'd each Day such Subsistance as is requisite for them.

The Person who at present Transports those unhappy Creatures is known by the Name of Captain *Forward*, who twice a Year, or oftner, is imployed in this kind of Traffick, which he disposes of by way of Sale to the Plantations, *&c.* at *Annapolis, Boston* in *New England, Saffron River* between *Maryland* and *New England,* and *James River* in *Virginia*, in the following Manner.

First, At their coming into the Bay, the Captain sends his Boat ashore, to his Factor or Correspondent, who comes on Board, to whom the Captain delivers the List he received at *Newgate*, of the several Persons delivered to him, and upon View of the same, an Examination is made of what Number (if any) died in their Passage, what are remaining Alive, and in what Condition they are; which Inspection being made (and a Receipt or Discharge being given from the Merchant or Factor to the Captain for the same) Notice is immediately given to all the Planters, and other Inhabitants of the Islands, who thereupon come on Board, and take a View of every Person to be disposed of; and after having chosen such as they think for their Purpose, an Agreement is made for them, and the Money paid, which for each Person, is from 20 *s.* to 10 *l.* the Price being always in proportion to the Health, Age, and Trade of the Person.

And altho' these unhappy Persons are thus Transported from their Native Country, and sold (as Beasts are in *Smithfield*[1]) from one Man to another as Slaves, yet if they live to go through the first Four Years, and behave themselves well, their Slavery is then over, and they are generally rewarded with a Plantation of their own, of Tobacco, Sugar, Ginger, *&c.*

And provided that they are not inclinable to be the Proprietors of such Plantation, for the residue of the Time they are Transported for, be it either for Seven, Fourteen Years, or Life, they are at Liberty to spend the same as Servants, or in any other manner they please; but not to depart from thence before their assigned time of Transportation, on the Peril of Death.

10. From *The Matchless Rogue: Or, an Account of the Contrivances, Cheats, Stratagems and Amours of Tom Merryman, Commonly Called, Newgate Tom* (London, 1725)

Thomas Merriman was born in that matchless Place called *Newgate*: He was the Son of *Joan Merriman*, but may justly be called *Filius Populi*;[2] for his Mother, tho' beautiful and young, was so vicious[3] in her Inclinations, that she became a common Prostitute; and no-body was more notorious for Theft and Robbery. Being tried at the *Sessions* for Shop-lifting, she was found guilty, but

1 See above, p. 394, n. 5.
2 "Son of the people" (Latin).
3 Depraved, profligate.

pleaded her Belly, by which means she bilked *Tyburn* for a small Time. After the Expiration of Three Months, she was called down to her former Sentence, and executed with other Criminals. Her Penitence at the Place of Execution was remarkable, and she died with all the Marks of Sorrow and Contrition, very much pitied by all that saw her. The *Ordinary* declared, that he never attended any Person, who shewed more sincere Marks of Repentance, and so heartily bewailed her mis-spent Life. Much Intercession had been made to obtain a Pardon, and though Persons of great Rank and Quality interested themselves therein, yet their Sollicitation proved ineffectual, she being an incorrigible Offender, always abusing the Princely Favours which had been shewn her.

The Parish took care of *Tom*, and, when he attained to his Eighth Year, gave him such Education as their School could afford. As he had a sprightly Genius, he soon became a good Proficient in Reading, Writing, and Accompts, which so gained the Good-will, Love, and Friendship of those who were Overseers of the Charity-School, that they resolved to put him to a very beneficial Trade, and waited only an Opportunity of finding out an ingenious and honest Master....

Appendix C: *Defoe and* Moll Flanders: *Eighteenth-Century Views*[1]

[In his own day, Defoe was largely known as a controversialist. Yet *Robinson Crusoe* was a definite commercial success and *Moll Flanders* ran through several editions and reprints within a year and was serialized in *The London Post* between 14 May 1722 and 20 May 1723. Most of the existing references to him and his works in the 1720s take the form of personal attack, in part by Pope and the Scriblerian party. Then relative silence follows for almost half a century, his name kept alive through a small handful of works, including *Robinson Crusoe, The Family Instructor, The Complete English Tradesman* and *A Tour thro' the Whole Island of Great Britain*. Only in the final quarter of the century are there definite signs of interest in and appreciation of his writings, as reflected in literary journals, reprints of his works and George Chalmers' biography (1786).]

1. From *The True-Born Hugonot, &c. A Satyr* (1703)

Hymns let him write, when he should Mercy pray,
And Satyrize the State, *The Shortest Way*;
Invectives against Monarchy indite,
To make his Impudence surpass his Spight.
In Publick View he shall again appear,
Nor shall his City *Friends* protect him here ...
A true Malignant, Arrogant and Sour,
And ever Snarling at Establish'd Power ...
That *others* Lands has for his *own* Convey'd,
And *Bought* and *Sold* Estates, for which he never paid.

2. From Jonathan Swift, *A Letter Concerning the Sacramental Test* (1709)

One of these Authors (the Fellow [Defoe] that was *pilloryed*, I have forgot his Name) is indeed so grave, sententious, dogmatical a Rogue, that there is no enduring him.[2]

---

1 For a fuller account, see *Defoe: The Critical Heritage*, ed. Pat Rogers (London: Routledge, 1972). I am indebted to this work for various references here.

2 Both here and in the extract below Swift is comparing Defoe's *Review* with the rival *Observator* newspaper.

3. From Jonathan Swift, the *Examiner* (16 November 1710)

... two stupid illiterate Scribblers, both of them *Fanaticks* by Profession: I mean the *Review* and *Observator*.... The mock authoritative Manner of the one [Defoe], and the insipid Mirth of the other [John Tutchin], however insupportable to reasonable Ears, being of a Levil with great Numbers among the lowest Part of Mankind ...

4. From John Gay, *The Present State of Wit* (1711)

As to our Weekly Papers, the poor REVIEW is quite exhausted, and grown so very contemptible, that tho' he [Defoe] has provoked all his Brothers of the Quill round, none of them will enter into a Controversy with him. This Fellow, who had excellent Parts, but wanted a small Foundation of Learning, is a lively instance of those Wits, who, as an Ingenious Author says, will endure but one Skimming.

5. From Joseph Addison, *The Late Trial and Conviction of Count Tariff* (1713)

When the Count[1] had finished his speech, he desired leave to call in his witnesses, which was granted: when immediately there came to the bar a man with a hat drawn over his eyes in such a manner that it was impossible to see his face. He spoke in the spirit, nay, in the very language, of the Count, repeated his arguments, and confirmed his assertions. Being asked his name, he said the world called him Mercator: but as for his true name, his age, his lineage, his religion, his place of abode, they were particulars, which, for certain reasons, he was obliged to conceal. The court found him such a false, shuffling, prevaricating rascal, that they set him aside as a person unqualified to give his testimony in a court of justice; advising him at the same time, as he tendered his ears,[2] to forbear uttering such notorious falsehoods as he had then published. The witness, however, persisted in his contumacy, telling them he was

---

1 At the peace of Utrecht (1713-14), a series of agreements was drawn up, including the Treaty of Commerce. In a mock trial Addison satirizes this treaty, or tariff, which was supported by Defoe in the *Mercator; or Commerce Retrieved* (May 1713-July 1714).

2 Pope makes a similar reference in the *Dunciad* (II.147). See Appendix C.10.

very sorry to find, that notwithstanding what he had said, they were resolved to be as arrant fools as all their forefathers had been for a hundred years before them.

6. From Charles Gildon, Preface to *The Life and Strange Surprizing Adventures of Mr. D.... De F....* , *of London, Hosier* (1719)

If ever the Story of any private Man's Adventures in the World were worth making publick, and were acceptable when publish'd, the Editor of this Account thinks this will be so.

The Wonders of this Man's [Defoe's] Life exceed all that (he thinks) is to be found Extant; the Life of one Man being scarce capable of greater Variety.

The Story is told with greater Modesty than perhaps some Men may think necessary to the Subject, the Hero of our Dialogue not being very conspicuous for that Virtue, a more than common Assurance carrying him thro' all those various Shapes and Changes which he has pass'd without the least Blush. The Fabulous *Proteus* of the Ancient Mythologist was but a very faint Type of our Hero, whose Changes are much more numerous, and he far more difficult to be constrain'd to his own Shape. If his Works should happen to live to the next Age, there would in all probability be a greater Strife among the several Parties, whose he really was, than among the seven *Graecian* Cities, to which of them *Homer* belong'd: The *Dissenters* first would claim him as theirs, the *Whigs* in general as theirs, the *Tories* as theirs, the *Non-jurors* as theirs, the *Papists* as theirs, the *Atheists* as theirs, and so on to what Sub-divisions there may be among us; so that it cannot be expected that I should give you in this short Dialogue his Picture at length for the rest of his Life, I may perhaps give a farther Account hereafter.

7. From Giles Jacob, *The Poetical Register: or the Lives and Characters of all the English Poets. With an Account of their Writings* (1723)

This Author was formerly a Hosier,[1] but since he has been one of the most enterprizing Pamphleteers this Age has produc'd; some Parts of his Life his Inclinations have led him to Poetry, which has

---

1 A maker of or dealer in hose (stockings and socks) and knitted under-clothing.

thrown into the World two Pieces very much admir'd by some Persons, *viz.*

I. *The True-Born Englishman.* This is a biting Satire, and sold many Impressions; but his Descriptions are generally very low.

II. *Jure Divino,* a Poem of considerable Bulk in Folio.[1]

8. From the Preface to *An Essay in Praise of Knavery*, 3rd ed. (1723)

PREFACES to Writings are become as Essential to all manner of Performances, as a Hat or Peruke to a Man's Dress, Painting to a fine Woman, Sauce is to Meat, or Sparkling to Liquor; In short, no Work is Inviting without them, from the Learned Labours of the great Critick D——s[2] down to the renowned Author of Robinson Cruiso.

9. From *The Flying Post; or Weekly Medley* (1 March 1729)

Down in the Kitchen, honest Dick and Doll
Are Studying Col. Jack and Flanders Moll.[3]

10. From Alexander Pope, *The Dunciad Variorum* (1729)

BOOK I

Much to the mindful Queen the feast recalls,
What City-Swans once sung within the walls;
Much she revolves their arts, their ancient praise,
And sure succession[4] down from Heywood's days.
She saw with joy the line immortal run,
Each sire imprest and glaring in his son ...
She saw old Pryn in restless Daniel shine,
And Eusden eke out Blackmore's endless line;
She saw slow Philips creep like Tate's poor page,
And all the Mighty Mad in Dennis rage.

---

1 A volume of the largest size, formed of sheets of paper folded once.
2 John Dennis (1657-1734), poet and dramatist, but best known for such critical works as *The Advancement and Reformation of Modern Poetry* (1701).
3 A controversial couplet among Defoe scholars, suggesting to some that the readership of his criminal lives was of the lower classes.
4 Defoe is placed here in a tradition of writers generally viewed as dunces. Both Defoe and William Prynne had been sentenced to the pillory.

BOOK II

With that she gave him ...
A shaggy Tap'stry, worthy to be spread
On Codrus' old, or Dunton's modern bed;
Instructive work! whose wry-mouth'd portraiture
Display'd the fates her confessors endure.
Earless on high, stood unabash'd Defoe,[1]
And Tutchin flagrant from the scourge, below:
There Ridpath, Roper cudgell'd might ye view;
The very worsted still look'd black and blue.[2]

11. From Richard Savage (?), *An Author to be Lett* (1729)

I am very deeply read in all Pieces of Scandal, Obscenity, and Pro-
faneness, particularly in the Writings of Mrs. *Haywood, Henley, W-
lst-d, Morley, Br-v-l, Foxton, Cooke, D'Foe, Norton, Woolston, Dennis,*
and the Author of the *Rival Modes.*[3]

12. From the *Grub-street Journal* (29 April 1731)

On Monday in the evening died, at his lodgings in Rope-makers
alley, in Moorfields, the famous Mr. DANIEL DE FOE, in a very
advanced age. COURANT.[4]—It is no small comfort to me, that my
brother died in a (good) old age, in a place made famous by the
decease of several of our members; having kept himself out of the
dangerous *alleys* of those high-flying *rope-makers*, who would fain
have sent him long ago, to his *long* home, by *the shortest way with
the Dissenters.*[5] ...
    The members [of the Grub Street society] were so much
afflicted at the news of the death of that ancient ornament of our
Society, Mr. DANIEL DE FOE, that they were incapable of attending to the Papers which were read to them. Upon which our Pres-

---

1 For a similar reference by Addison, see Appendix C.5.
2 The line of dunces (above) continues, again deliberately aligning Defoe's
   name. The last two were fellow journalists.
3 A further list of recognized dunces, including Defoe's son Benjamin
   Norton Defoe. *The Rival Modes* (1727) was a play by James Moore
   Smythe, and the incomplete names are those of Leonard Welsted and
   John Durant Breval.
4 The *Daily Courant*, 1702-35.
5 An elaborate pun, involving Defoe's final lodgings, one of his most
   famous pamphlets, and his escape from the gallows over many years.

ident adjourned the consideration of them till the next meeting....
[Quotes an epigram] imagined to be the last work of the great
Author deceased, and evidence of his perseverance in his princi-
ples to the last.

13. From *Read's Weekly Journal* (1 May 1731)

A few Days ago dy'd Mr. Defoe, Sen.[1] a Person well known for his
numerous and various Writings. He had a great natural Genius;
and understood well the Trade and Interest of this Kingdom. His
Knowledge of Men, especially those in High Life, (with whom he
was formerly very conversant) had weakened his attachement to
any party; but in the main, he was in the Interest of Civil and Religious Liberty, in behalf of which he appeared on several remarkable Occasions.

14. From a Conversation with Alexander Pope, as report-
ed. by Joseph Spence, *Observations, Anecdotes, and
Characters of Books and Men* (1742)[2]

The first part of *Robinson Crusoe*, good. DeFoe wrote many things,
and none bad, though none excellent. There's something good in
all he has writ.

15. From Theophilus Cibber, *The Lives of the Poets* (1753)

[Defoe wrote] many other poetical pieces, and political, and
polemical tracts, the greatest part of which are written with great
force of thought, though in an unpolished irregular stile. The natural abilities of the author (for he was no scholar) seem to have
been high. He had a great knowledge of men and things, particularly what related to the government, and trade of these kingdoms.
He wrote many pamphlets on both, which were generally well
received, though his name was never prefixed. His imagination
was fertile, strong, and lively, as may be collected from his many
works of fancy, particularly his *Robinson Crusoe*, which was written
in so natural a manner, and with so many probable incidents, that,
for some time after its publication, it was judged by most people
to be a true story.... Nor was he less remarkable in his writings of

---

1 Senior.
2 Joseph Spence, *Observations, Anecdotes and Characters of Books and Men*,
  ed. J.M. Osborn, vol. 1 (Oxford: Clarendon P, 1966) 213.

a serious and religious turn, witness his *Religious Courtship*, and his *Family Instructor*; both of which strongly inculcate the worship of God, the relative duties of husbands, wives, parents, and children, not in a dry dogmatic mannner, but in a kind of dramatic way, which excites curiosity, keeps the attention awake, and is extremely interesting, and pathetic.

We have already seen, that in his political capacity he was a declared enemy to popery, and a bold defender of revolution principles. He was held in much esteem by many great men, and though he never enjoyed any regular post under the government, yet he was frequently employed in matters of trust and confidence, particularly in Scotland, where he several times was sent on affairs of great importance, especially those relative to the union of the kingdoms, of which he was one of the negotiators.

16. From the *Monthly Review* (March 1775)

Few novels are better known than the story of the Lewd Roxana; which, we see, is ascribed to the famous De Foe. It is not improbable that this is really one of Daniel's productions; for he wrote books of all kinds, *romantic* as well as *religious*; moral as well as immoral. History, politics, poetry; in short, all subjects were alike to Daniel.—The versatility of this man's genius procured him the admiration of the age in which he lived; but the breed of De Foes has so much increased, of late years, that hundreds of them are to be found in the garrets of Grubstreet, where they *draw nutrition, propagate* [novels and pamphlets] *and rot*: and nobody minds them.

17. From James Boswell, *The Life of Samuel Johnson* (1778)

He [Johnson] told us, that he had given Mrs. Montagu[1] a catalogue of all Daniel Defoe's works of imagination; most, if not all of which, as well as of his other works, he now enumerated, allowing a considerable share of merit to a man, who, bred a tradesman, had written so variously and so well. Indeed, his *Robinson Crusoe* is enough of itself to establish his reputation.

---

1 Elizabeth Montagu (1720-1800), a leading member of the "bluestocking" circle.

18. From George Chalmers, *The Life of Defoe* (1786)[1]

Of fictitious biography it is equally true, that by matchless art it may be made more instructive than a real life. Few of our writers have excelled De Foe in this kind of biographical narration, the great qualities of which are, to attract by the diversity of circumstances, and to instruct by the usefulness of examples.... The fortunes and misfortunes of *Moll Flanders* were made to gratify the world in 1721. De Foe was aware, that in relating a vicious life, it was necessary to make the best use of a bad story; and he artfully endeavours, that the reader shall be more pleased with the moral than the fable; with the application than the relation; with the end of the writer than the adventures of the person....

19. From the *Monthly Review* (December 1787)

He [Defoe] passed through a great variety of fortune, and met with difficulties and ill-treatment not only from the party which he opposed, but also from that which he espoused. This, indeed, was really honourable to him: a sincere friend as he appears to have been to the cause of liberty, civil and religious, he could not always concur in the measures and principles of those who professed at least to prosecuting the same design. By this means, like many other worthy persons, he often fell under the censures of those with whom he appeared to be united.... He is chiefly known as an author: his *Robinson Crusoe*, which has passed through seventeen editions, and been translated into other languages, will still preserve his memory: but his distinguished sphere, or that to which he principally applied himself, appears to have been policy[2] and trade.... The work [*History of the Union*] appears, to us, to be not only of the instructive, but even of the entertaining kind: the style is different from that of the present time, but by no means unpleasant. To those readers who wish for information concerning memorable events relative to their own country, this volume will doubtless be acceptable, as contributing both to their amusement and improvement.

---

1 Written in 1785, the *Life* was later appended to editions of *The History of the Union of Great Britain* (1786) and *Robinson Crusoe* (1790). Included in its second publication is "A List of De Foe's Works Arranged Chronologically," which was the first serious attempt to draw up a full list of the author's writings.

2 Politics.

20. From the *Monthly Review* (December 1790)

It would be a curious subject of investigation for any acute observer ... to inquire why it should be the cruel fate of most of those whose pens have been employed in the service of the public, to have justice studiously withheld from their characters, till they are beyond receiving any benefit from it; and when the men have sunk under anxieties, neglect, and injurious treatment, perhaps their memory, some time or other, receives the full payment of applause, with all the interest due on it! Three-score years after the death of the ingenious and well-informed Daniel De Foe, a gentleman "during a period of convalescence," amuses himself in writing his life; and has taken laudable, and we think successful pains, to rescue his memory from undeserved obloquoy. All this is so far well; and Mr. Chalmers, we doubt not, enjoys the conscious pleasure peculiar to good minds, in performing a generous act: but living merit can derive very little comfort from the instance.

De Foe, with great abilities, extensive knowledge, and a ready pen, living in troublesome times, became a busy controversial writer: he steadily supported the Whig interest, but could not (and what considerate honest man can?) go all lengths with his party: therefore, while he provoked the hatred of the Tories, he could not gain the entire love of the Whigs; and between both, his character has been transmitted to us under various misrepresentations. Mr. Chalmers has, with industrious and commendable zeal, traced every circumstance, as well as the distance of time would permit, to set his character and conduct in a true light; which ... he has happily effected; and, in particular, has satisfactorily vindicated his *Robinson Crusoe* from being a piracy of Alexander Selkirk's papers.[1]

---

1 From the first appearance of *Robinson Crusoe* in 1719, Defoe was accused of having plagiarized his work from the Scottish seaman Alexander Selkirk.

Select Bibliography

Bibliographies

Furbank, P.N., and W.R. Owens. *Critical Bibliography of Daniel Defoe.* London: Pickering and Chatto, 1998.

Hahn, H. George, and Carl Behn, III. *The Eighteenth-Century British Novel and Its Background: An Annotated Bibliography and Guide to Topics.* Metuchen, NJ: Scarecrow P, 1985.

Moore, John Robert. *A Checklist of the Writings of Daniel Defoe.* 2nd ed. Hamden, CT: Archon, 1971.

Novak, Maximillian E. "Daniel Defoe." *The New Cambridge Bibliography of English Literature, 1660-1800.* Rev. ed. Vol. 2. Ed. George Watson. Cambridge: Cambridge UP, 1971. 882-918.

Peterson, Spiro. *Daniel Defoe: A Reference Guide, 1731-1924.* Boston: G.K. Hall, 1987.

Stoler, John A. *Daniel Defoe: An Annotated Bibliography of Modern Criticism, 1900-1980.* 2nd ed. New York: Garland, 1984.

Biographies

Backscheider, Paula R. *Daniel Defoe: His Life.* Baltimore: Johns Hopkins UP, 1989.

Bastian, Frank. *The Early Life of Daniel Defoe.* London: Macmillan, 1981.

Moore, John Robert. *Daniel Defoe: Citizen of the Modern World.* 1958. Chicago: U of Chicago P, 1966.

Novak, Maximillian E. *Daniel Defoe: Master of Fictions.* Oxford: Oxford UP, 2001.

Sutherland, James R. *Daniel Defoe.* 2nd ed. London: Methuen, 1950.

Trent, W.P. *Daniel Defoe: How to Know Him.* Indianapolis: Bobbs-Merrill, 1916.

West, Richard. *Daniel Defoe: The Life and Strange, Surprising Adventures.* New York: Carroll and Graf, 1998.

Wright, Thomas. *The Life of Daniel Defoe.* 1894. London: C.J. Farncombe, 1931.

General Studies

Alkon, Paul K. *Defoe and Fictional Time*. Athens: U of Georgia P, 1979.

Andersen, Hans H. "The Paradox of Trade and Morality in Defoe." *Modern Philology* 39 (1941): 23-46.

Armstrong, Katherine A. *Defoe: Writer as Agent*. Victoria, BC: U of Victoria, 1996.

Backscheider, Paula R. *Daniel Defoe: Ambition and Innovation*. Lexington: UP of Kentucky, 1986.

———. "Defoe's Prodigal Sons." *Studies in the Literary Imagination* 15 (1982): 3-18.

———. "Defoe's Women: Snares and Prey." *Studies in Eighteenth-Century Culture* 5 (1976): 103-20.

Baine, Rodney M. *Daniel Defoe and the Supernatural*. Athens: U of Georgia P, 1968.

Ballaster, Ros. *Seductive Forms: Women's Amatory Fiction from 1684-1740*. Oxford: Clarendon P, 1992.

Bell, Ian A. *Defoe's Fiction*. Totowa, NJ: Barnes & Noble, 1985.

———. *Literature and Crime in Augustan England*. London: Routledge, 1991.

———. "Narrators and Narrative in Defoe." *Novel* 18 (1985): 154-72.

Birdsall, Virginia Ogden. *Defoe's Perpetual Seekers: A Study of the Major Fiction*. Lewisburg, PA: Bucknell UP, 1985.

Bishop, Jonathan. "Knowledge, Action, and Interpretation in Defoe's Novels." *Journal of the History of Ideas* 13 (1952): 3-16.

Blewett, David. *Defoe's Art of Fiction*: Robinson Crusoe, Moll Flanders, Colonel Jack *and* Roxana. Toronto: U of Toronto P, 1979.

Boardman, Michael M. *Defoe and the Uses of Narrative*. New Brunswick, NJ: Rutgers UP, 1983.

Booth, Wayne C. *The Rhetoric of Fiction*. 2nd ed. Chicago: U of Chicago P, 1983.

Boyce, Benjamin. "The Question of Emotion in Defoe." *Studies in Philology* 50 (1953): 45-58.

Brown, Homer O. "The Displaced Self in the Novels of Daniel Defoe." *Journal of English Literary History* 38 (1971): 562-90.

Burch, Charles Eaton. "The Moral Elements in Defoe's Fiction." *London Quarterly and Holborn Review* (April 1937): 207-13.

Byrd, Max, ed. *Daniel Defoe: A Collection of Critical Essays*. Englewood Cliffs, NJ: Prentice-Hall, 1976.

Chandler, Frank Wadleigh. *The Literature of Roguery.* 2 vols. New York: Houghton Mifflin, 1907.

Dobrée, Bonamy. "The Writings of Daniel Defoe." *Royal Society of Arts Journal* 108 (1960): 729-42.

Erickson, Robert A. *Mother Midnight: Birth, Sex, and Fate in Eighteenth-Century Fiction.* New York: AMS, 1986.

Faller, Lincoln B. *Crime and Defoe: A New Kind of Writing.* Cambridge: Cambridge UP, 1993.

Fitzgerald, Brian. *Defoe: A Study in Conflict.* Chicago: Regnery, 1954.

Furbank, P.N., and W.R. Owens. *The Canonisation of Daniel Defoe.* New Haven: Yale UP, 1988.

Harlan, Virginia. "Defoe's Narrative Style." *Journal of English and Germanic Philology* 30 (1931): 55-73.

Hunter, J. Paul. *Before Novels: The Cultural Contexts of Eighteenth-Century English Fiction.* New York: Norton, 1990.

——. "Novels and 'the Novel': The Poetics of Embarrassment." *Modern Philology* 85 (1988): 480-98.

Jackson, Selwyn. "Distance and the Communication Model." *Journal of Narrative Technique* 17 (1987): 225-36.

Jardine, Alice A. *Gynesis: Configurations of Woman and Modernity.* Ithaca: Cornell UP, 1985.

Kahn, Madeleine. *Narrative Transvestism: Rhetoric and Gender in the Eighteenth-Century English Novel.* Ithaca: Cornell UP, 1991.

McKeon, Michael. *The Origins of the English Novel, 1600-1740.* Baltimore: Johns Hopkins UP, 1987.

Mckillop, Alan Dugald. *The Early Masters of English Fiction: Defoe to Conrad.* 1925. Lawrence: U of Kansas P, 1962.

Novak, Maximillian E. *Defoe and the Nature of Man.* London: Oxford UP, 1963.

——. "The Defoe Canon: Attribution and Re-Attribution." *Huntington Library Quarterly* 59 (1997): 189-207.

——. "Defoe's Theory of Fiction." *Studies in Philology* 61 (1964): 650-68.

——. *Economics and the Fiction of Daniel Defoe.* Berkeley: U of California P, 1962.

——, ed. *English Literature in the Age of Disguise.* Berkeley: U of California P, 1977.

——. *Realism, Myth, and History in Defoe's Fiction.* Lincoln: U of Nebraska P, 1983.

Peters, Joan Douglas. *Feminist Metafiction and the Evolution of the British Novel.* Gainesville: UP of Florida, 2002.

Preston, John. *The Created Self: The Reader's Role in Eighteenth-Century Fiction*. London: Heinemann, 1970.

Price, Martin. *To the Palace of Wisdom: Studies in Order and Energy from Dryden to Blake*. Garden City, NY: Doubleday, 1964.

Richetti, John J. *Daniel Defoe*. Boston: G.K. Hall, 1987.

———. *Defoe's Narratives: Situations and Structures*. Oxford: Clarendon P, 1975.

———. *Popular Fiction Before Richardson: Narrative Patterns, 1700-1739*. Oxford: Clarendon P, 1969.

Rogers, Katharine. "The Feminism of Daniel Defoe." *Woman in the 18th Century and Other Essays*. Ed. Paul Fritz and Richard Morton. Toronto: Hakkert, 1976. 3-24.

Rogers, Pat, ed. *Defoe: The Critical Heritage*. London: Routledge & Kegan Paul, 1972.

———. *Literature and Popular Culture in Eighteenth-Century England*. Totowa, NJ: Barnes & Noble, 1985.

Sacks, Sheldon. *Fiction and the Shape of Belief*. Berkeley: U of California P, 1964.

Scheuermann, Mona. "Women and Money in Eighteenth-Century Fiction." *Studies in the Novel* 19 (1987): 311-22.

Schorer, Mark. "A Study in Defoe: Moral Vision and Structural Form." *Thought* 25 (1950): 275-87.

Secord, Arthur. *Studies in the Narrative Method of Defoe*. New York: Russell & Russell, 1963.

Sen, Sri C. *Daniel Defoe: His Mind and Art*. Calcutta: U of Calcutta, 1948.

Sherbo, Arthur. *Studies in the Eighteenth Century English Novel*. East Lansing: Michigan State UP, 1969.

Shinagel, Michael. *Daniel Defoe and Middle-Class Gentility*. Cambridge: Harvard UP, 1968.

Sill, Geoffrey M. *Defoe and the Idea of Fiction, 1713-1719*. Newark: U of Delaware P, 1983.

Stamm, Rudolf G. "Daniel Defoe: An Artist in the Puritan Tradition." *Philological Quarterly* 15 (1936): 225-46.

Starr, G.A. *Defoe and Casuistry*. Princeton: Princeton UP, 1971.

———. *Defoe and Spiritual Autobiography*. Princeton: Princeton UP, 1965.

———. "Defoe's Prose Style: 1. The Language of Interpretation." *Modern Philology* 71 (1974): 277-94.

Stephen, Leslie. *English Literature and Society in the Eighteenth Century*. London: Duckworth, 1904.

Sutherland, James. *Daniel Defoe: A Critical Study*. Cambridge: Harvard UP, 1971.

Swallow, Alan. "Defoe and the Art of Fiction." *Western Humanities Review* 4 (1950): 129-36.

Tinkler, John. "'A Strange Original Notion ... of My Being a Gentleman': The Gentility of Defoe's Rogues." *English Studies in Canada* 8 (1982): 282-95.

Uphaus, Robert W., ed. *The Idea of the Novel in the Eighteenth Century*. East Lansing, MI: Colleagues, 1988.

Watson, Francis. *Daniel Defoe*. London: Longmans, Green, 1952.

Watt, Ian. "Defoe as Novelist." *The Pelican Guide to English Literature*. Ed. Boris Ford. Vol. 4. Baltimore: Penguin, 1965. 203-16.

——. *The Rise of the Novel: Studies in Defoe, Richardson and Fielding*. Berkeley: U of California P, 1967.

Weinstein, Arnold. *Fictions of the Self, 1550-1800*. Princeton: Princeton UP, 1981.

West, Alick. *The Mountain in the Sunlight: Studies in Conflict and Unity*. London: Lawrence & Wishart, 1958.

Zimmerman, Everett. *Defoe and the Novel*. Berkeley: U of California P, 1975.

Zomchick, John P. "'A Penetration Which Nothing Can Deceive': Gender and Juridical Discourse in Some Eighteenth-Century Narratives." *Studies in English Literature, 1500-1900* 29 (1989): 535-61.

Studies on *Moll Flanders*

Alter, Robert. "A Bourgeois Picaroon." *Rogue's Progress: Studies in the Picaresque Novel*. Cambridge: Harvard UP, 1964. 35-57.

Backscheider, Paula R. *Moll Flanders: The Making of a Criminal Mind*. Boston: Twayne, 1990.

Bell, Robert H. "Moll's Grace Abounding." *Genre* 8 (1975): 267-82.

Bishop, John Peale. "Moll Flanders' Way." *Collected Essays*. Ed. Edmund Wilson. New York: Scribner's, 1948. 46-55.

Bjornson, Richard. "The Ambiguous Success of the Picaresque Hero in Defoe's *Moll Flanders*," *The Picaresque Hero in European Fiction*. Madison: U of Wisconsin P, 1977.

Blewett, David. "Changing Attitudes toward Marriage in the Time of Defoe: The Case of Moll Flanders." *Huntington Library Quarterly* 44 (1981): 77-88.

———. "Moll Flanders in Chichester." *Notes and Queries* 36 (1989): 51-52.

Bloom, Harold, ed. *Daniel Defoe's* Moll Flanders. New York: Chelsea, 1987.

Borck, Jim Springer. "One Woman's Prospects: Defoe's Moll Flanders and the Ironies in Restoration Self-Image." *Forum* 17 (1979): 10-16.

Brooks, Douglas. "*Moll Flanders* Again." *Essays in Criticism* 20 (1970): 115-18.

———. "*Moll Flanders*: An Interpretation." *Essays in Criticism* 19 (1969): 46-59.

Butler, Mary. "'Onomaphobia' and Personal Identity in *Moll Flanders*." *Studies in the Novel* 22 (1990): 377-91.

Caton, Lou. "Doing the Right Thing with Moll Flanders: A 'Reasonable' Difference between the Picara and the Penitent." *CLA Journal* 40 (1997): 508-16.

Chaber, Lois A. "Matriarchal Mirror: Women and Capital in *Moll Flanders*." *PMLA* 97 (1982): 212-26.

Columbus, Robert R. "Conscious Artistry in *Moll Flanders*." *Studies in English Literature, 1500-1900* 3 (1963): 415-32.

Connor, Rebecca E. "'Can you Apply Arithmetick to Every Thing?': Moll Flanders, William Petty, and Social Accounting." *Studies in Eighteenth-Century Culture* 27 (1998) 169-94.

Dollerup, Cay. "Does the Chronology of *Moll Flanders* Tell Us Something About Defoe's Method of Writing?" *English Studies* 53 (1972): 234-35.

Donoghue, Denis. "The Values of *Moll Flanders*." *Sewanee Review* 71 (1963): 287-303.

Donovan, Robert Alan. "The Two Heroines of *Moll Flanders*." *The Shaping Vision: Imagination in the English Novel from Defoe to Dickens*. Ithaca: Cornell UP, 1966. 21-46.

Elliott, Robert C., ed. *Twentieth Century Interpretations of* Moll Flanders: *A Collection of Critical Essays*. Englewood Cliffs, NJ: Prentice-Hall, 1970.

Erickson, Robert A. "Moll's Fate: 'Mother Midnight' and *Moll Flanders*." *Studies in Philology* 76 (1979): 75-100.

Gifford, George E. "Daniel Defoe and Maryland." *Maryland Historical Magazine* 52 (1957): 307-15.

Goldberg, M. A. "*Moll Flanders*: Christian Allegory in a Hobbesian Mode." *The University Review* 33 (1967): 267-78.

Hammond, Brean S. "Repentance: Solution to the Clash of Moralities in *Moll Flanders*." *English Studies* 61 (1980): 329-37.

Hartog, Curt H. "Aggression, Femininity, and Irony in *Moll Flanders*." *Literature and Psychology* 22 (1972): 121-38.

Higdon, David Leon. "The Chronology of *Moll Flanders*." *English Studies* 56 (1975): 316-19.

Howson, Gerald. "The Fortunes of Moll Flanders." *Thief-Taker General: The Rise and Fall of Jonathan Wild*. New York: St. Martin's P, 1970. 156-70. Rev. rept. of "Who Was Moll Flanders?" *The Times Literary Supplement* 18 Jan. 1968: 63-64.

Johnson, C.A. "Two Mistakes in *Moll Flanders*." *Notes and Queries* 207 (1962): 455.

Karl, Frederick R. "Moll's Many-Colored Coat: Veil and Disguise in the Fiction of Defoe." *Studies in the Novel* 5 (1973): 86-97.

Kettle, Arnold. "In Defence of *Moll Flanders*." *Of Books and Humankind: Essays and Poems Presented to Bonamy Dobrée*. Ed. John Butt. London: Routledge & Kegan Paul, 1964. 55-67.

Kibbie, Ann Louise. "Monstrous Generation: The Birth of Capital in Defoe's *Moll Flanders* and *Roxana*." *PMLA* 110 (1995): 1023-34.

Kietzman, M.J. "Defoe Masters the Serial Subject (Criminal Biography, *Moll Flanders*)." *Journal of English Literary History* 66 (1999): 677-705.

Koonce, Howard L. "Moll's Muddle: Defoe's Use of Irony in *Moll Flanders*." *Journal of English Literary History* 30 (1963): 377-94.

Krier, William J. "A Courtesy Which Grants Integrity: A Literal Reading of *Moll Flanders*." *Journal of English Literary History* 38 (1971): 397-410.

Kuhlisch, Tina. "The Ambivalent Rogue: Moll Flanders as Modern Picara." *Rogues and Early Modern English Culture*. Ed. Craig Dionne and Steve Mentz. Ann Arbor: U of Michigan P, 2004. 337-60.

Langford, Larry L. "Retelling Moll's Story: The Editor's Preface to *Moll Flanders*." *The Journal of Narrative Technique* 22 (1992): 164-79.

Leranbaum, Miriam. "Moll Flanders: 'A Woman on Her Own Account.'" *The Authority of Experience: Essays in Feminist Criticism*. Ed. Arlyn Diamond and Lee R. Edwards. Amherst: U of Massachusetts P, 1977. 101-17.

Lovitt, Carl R. "Defoe's 'Almost Invisible Hand': Narrative Logic as a Structuring Principle in *Moll Flanders*." *Eighteenth-Century Fiction* 6 (1993): 1-28.

Macey, Samuel L. "The Time Scheme in *Moll Flanders*." *Notes and Queries* 214 (1969): 336-37.

Martin, Terence. "The Unity of *Moll Flanders*." *Modern Language Quarterly* 22 (1961): 115-24.

McClung, M.G. "A Source for Moll Flander's Husband." *Notes and Queries* 18 (1971): 329-30.

McInelly, Brett C. "Exile or Opportunity? The Plight of the Transported Felon in Daniel Defoe's *Moll Flanders* and *Colonel Jack*." *Genre* 22 (2001): 210-17.

McMaster, Juliet. "The Equation of Love and Money in *Moll Flanders*." *Studies in the Novel* 2 (1970): 131-44.

Michael, Steven C. "Thinking Parables: What *Moll Flanders* Does Not Say." *Journal of English Literary History* 63 (1996): 367-95.

Miller, Henry Knight. "Some Reflections on Defoe's *Moll Flanders* and the Romance Tradition." *Greene Centennial Studies*. Ed. Paul J. Korshin and Robert R. Allen. Charlottesville: UP of Virginia, 1984. 72-92.

Novak, Maximillian E. "Conscious Irony in *Moll Flanders*: Facts and Problems." *College English* 26 (1964): 198-204.

———. "Defoe's 'Indifferent Monitor': The Complexity of *Moll Flanders*." *Eighteenth-Century Studies* 3 (1970): 351-65.

———. "Moll Flanders' First Love." *Papers of the Michigan Academy of Science, Arts, and Letters* 46 (1961): 635-43.

Olsen, Thomas Grant. "Reading and Righting *Moll Flanders*." *Studies in English Literature, 1500-1900* 41 (2001): 467-81.

Piper, William Bowman. "*Moll Flanders* as a Structure of Topics." *Studies in English Literature, 1500-1900* 9 (1969): 489-502.

Pollak, Ellen. "*Moll Flanders*, Incest, and the Structure of Exchange." *Incest and the English Novel, 1684-1814*. Baltimore: Johns Hopkins UP, 2003. 110-28.

Richetti, John. "The Family, Sex, and Marriage in Defoe's *Moll Flanders* and *Roxana*." *Studies in the Literary Imagination* 15 (1982): 19-35.

Rietz, John. "Criminal MS-Representation: *Moll Flanders* and Female Criminal Biography." *Studies in the Novel* 23 (1991): 183-97.

Rodway, A.E. "*Moll Flanders* and *Manon Lescaut*." *Essays in Criticism* 3 (1953): 303-20.

Rogal, Samuel J. "The Profit and Loss of *Moll Flanders*." *Studies in the Novel* 5 (1973): 98-103.

Rogers, Henry N., III. "The Two Faces of Moll." *Journal of Narrative Technique* 9 (1979): 117-25.

Rogers, Pat. "Moll's Memory." *English* 24 (1975): 67-72.

Scheuermann, Mona. "An Income of One's Own: Women and Money in *Moll Flanders* and *Roxana*." *Durham University Journal* 80 (1988): 225-39.

Shinagel, Michael. "The Maternal Theme in *Moll Flanders*: Craft and Character." *Cornell Library Journal* 7 (1969): 3-23.

Singleton, Robert R. "Defoe, Moll Flanders, and the Ordinary of Newgate." *Harvard Library Bulletin* 24 (1976): 407-13.

Sohier, Jacques. "Moll Flanders and the Rise of the Complete Gentlewoman-Tradeswoman." *Eighteenth-Century Novel* 2 (2002): 1-21.

Swaminathan, Srividhya. "Defoe's Alternative Conduct Manual: Survival Strategies and Female Networks in *Moll Flanders*." *Eighteenth-Century Fiction* 15 (2003): 185-206.

Swan, Beth. "Moll Flanders: The Felon as Lawyer." *Eighteenth-Century Fiction* 11 (1998) 33-48.

Van Ghent, Dorothy. "On *Moll Flanders*." *The English Novel: Form and Function*. New York: Rinehart, 1953. 33-43.

Watson, Tommy G. "Defoe's Attitude Toward Marriage and the Position of Women as Revealed in *Moll Flanders*." *Southern Quarterly* 3 (1964): 1-8.

Watt, Ian. "The Recent Critical Fortunes of *Moll Flanders*." *Eighteenth-Century Studies* 1 (1967): 109-26.

Yahav-Brown, Amit. "At Home in England, or Projecting Liberal Citizenship in *Moll Flanders*." *Novel* 35 (2001): 24-45.

From the Publisher

A name never says it all, but the word "Broadview" expresses a good deal of the philosophy behind our company. We are open to a broad range of academic approaches and political viewpoints. We pay attention to the broad impact book publishing and book printing has in the wider world; for some years now we have used 100% recycled paper for most titles. Our publishing program is internationally oriented and broad-ranging. Our individual titles often appeal to a broad readership too; many are of interest as much to general readers as to academics and students.

Founded in 1985, Broadview remains a fully independent company owned by its shareholders—not an imprint or subsidiary of a larger multinational.

For the most accurate information on our books (including information on pricing, editions, and formats) please visit our website at www.broadviewpress.com. Our print books and ebooks are also available for sale on our site.

broadview press
www.broadviewpress.com

This book is made of paper from well-managed FSC® - certified forests, recycled materials, and other controlled sources.

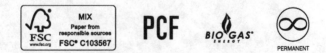